BEAUTY
IN THE
DARK

BELLA BEESTON

BEAUTY
IN THE
DARK

WHITE MOUNTAIN

Designed and typeset by Megan Sheer

Printed in Great Britain by CPI UK, 141-143 Shoreditch High Street, London, E1 6JE
Typeset in Monotype Arcadian Bembo

Although based on the author's experiences, it should be noted that this book
is a work of fiction presented entirely for entertainment purposes. The author
and publisher are not offering professional service advice. The stories and their
characters and entities are fictional. Any likeness to actual persons, whether in
terms of character profiles or names, either living or dead, is strictly coincidental.

To my aunts, those two centurions
who lived always with joy in their hearts and beauty in their eyes.

AUTHOR'S NOTE

'Beauty is in the eye of the beholder'; I have often mused on that proverb. It is in fact the proverb that inspired this book – but not in the sense that most people may interpret.

Sight has always been associated with beauty, and vice versa. One never hears of people remarking how the wind *sounds* beautiful, or the touch of silk *feels* beautiful, or the scent of cut grass in summer *smells* beautiful. And therein lies the title of this book. So often people neglect to consider the beauty of the other senses. Love, in every sense of the world, is not reliant on a physical projection of a person or thing before our eyes. It is always constant, in flux yes, but constant – even when the subject or object of that love is *unseen*.

It is that which drives the premise of my debut novel. I was so curious why I had never read a contemporary novel where characters without sight play such an important role.

And when I have come across such characters – mostly in classic books, fables, and religious texts – the narrative is always driven by a sense of pity or fantasy. Often the characters who are blind will be blessed with the gift of foresight, as if to compensate the 'victim' for their ill fortune.

With *Beauty in the Dark*, I wanted to write a novel where blindness isn't treated as a weakness, or something that requires a crutch to support it through life. Yes, of course, in the novel we have characters who do abuse the trust of the six wonderful women whose blindness affects their lives, but that is no different to people with perfect sight suffering the same mistreatment. Bettina, the great heroine of the novel, is strong and wise and content. But more importantly, her blindness doesn't define her in a negative way, but instead is embraced as if it is a gift. For Bettina, lacking the sense of sight has heightened her knowledge of, and relationship with, her other senses. When she smells the trees, or feels the wind or hears the song of the nightingale, she does so with infinitely more joy than anyone with sight can ever imagine. What's more, her mind is sharp, and its vision clear and vivid. I recall speaking to a blind lady who said that when I think of something, it is like looking through a window that hasn't been cleaned in years, into a vista cloaked in mist. 'Your sight blurs and distorts it,' she said. 'Whereas when in darkness, free of the sorcery of sight, your mind becomes a masterpiece, as if Rembrandt himself is painting every vision. You see every stroke of every thought in all of its brilliance.'

When I heard this, it prompted a revolution in my life. I became utterly intoxicated with this idea of 'discovering my lost senses.' They were blunt knives and frayed brushes; they were poetry without words and opera without notes. So, I sought to recover them. I would walk in the woods at night after dusk, and stay there until the stars wheeled overhead, and the only light was that of the moon turning the leaves silver. Even then I would close my eyes – sometimes even blindfold myself – and what happened was miraculous. At first I felt hindered. My mind was aching for my sight to help me navigate the woods, or give identity to the sounds. It needed my sight to handhold me, as if I was a child that couldn't be without its mother. But then, when I settled into the forest and breathed deeply, my senses sharpened. The sounds of the owls hooting from the boughs, of the foxes rustling in the grass, of the crickets and the whistling wind and the falling leaves, all became like a symphony. Not only that, but as I stepped nimbly between the great trunks and over the arcing roots, the touch of their bark on my fingertips was nerve tingling. I felt every blade of grass stroke my calves with the dew of the moon; I felt every raindrop that fell on the back of my neck, the silk of every spider web that clung to my groping hands. And yet somehow, I never slipped, or tripped, or walked into anything. I weaved in between those trees with the ease and grace of a ballerina. There was no concrete reason for why I could do this, only that beyond the sense of touch and taste and smell, I could *feel* the presence of everything, as if my mind was wise to the mass of everything. I seemed to be able to sense the heavy atoms of the trees and the much thinner atoms of the whispery air. I felt like a soldier with night vision goggles.

When I returned home later that night, I stayed up until dawn reflecting on this experience. And by the time the last star wheeled out of the sky and the world was visible once more, the story of Bettina, Cristina, Odile, Elfrida, Laura and Zu-Ting emerged. It wasn't until a few days later that Glenn figured in my plan. But, to form a bridge in the novel, and to have a protagonist who would have his senses revealed to him the way I had mine revealed to me, I wanted a romantic lead, someone who would see the beauty in the dark.

So, when the time came to write the story I wanted, I began to recall memories that had stuck with me from my travels writing throughout Europe and the Middle East. Statistically, I am still shocked at the number of people in the world – from businessmen to beggars, noblemen to nurses – who lead lives with impaired vision. I recalled the Bedouins I met whilst in the Gulf. When I approached them to talk, they would gaze over my shoulder and into the ether as they replied, as if I was an apparition and nothing more. Many members of these wandering tribes were blind. In that land of endless deserts and scorching suns, long days of being exposed to such elements had literally burnt away their vision like a feather in an inferno. And yet, they were all still so joyously happy. In fact, I couldn't ever recall having met a miserable blind person. At first, I thought I would have to address in the novel the despair that must naturally attach itself to a person who cannot gaze at a beautiful blue sky; over a vista of snow-capped mountains; or into the eyes of their lover. But the spirits I met were undimmed. More than that, they were often vibrant, cordial conversationalists who led fuller, more independent lives than many idle people in the West who possess perfect sight.

It was this that made me think that I wanted the six blind women that Glenn comes to know in the book, to have become strong and happy, despite their earlier sorrow. I think I have achieved that, and I hope the reader enjoys this journey into the beautiful darkness.

Finally, I would like to thank my editorial team for their invaluable help in assisting me with the completion of this book.

CHAPTER ONE

Breakfast at Ronda Round Manor House was always a bizarre affair, Glenn thought, as he made his way down the grand staircase towards the dining hall. Every morning, Glenn would walk down to breakfast to find his wife Eleanora sat alone at a table made for at least eighteen people. It was a strange daily tradition they had: to sit at opposing ends of the table and dine like royalty. But Eleanora had always liked it that way. After all, she had not known anything different. Ronda Round Manor had been in the family for centuries, and Eleanora, the daughter of Lesley Margaret and Harold John Beaumont, had grown up there.

Glenn, a mere Tebbhurst from an American family, could never understand the need for so much space, but accepted the house as his wife's family home. It was where they had built their life together after all. The Georgian house, which was as empty as the dining hall, had space for great numbers of people. The first floor on which he slept with his wife had eight bedrooms, all lavishly laden with four-poster beds and silk cushions. Tapestries dating as far back as the sixteenth and seventeenth centuries hung in every room, to remind guest and visitors of just how long the Beaumonts had resided in Ronda Round Manor. On the second floor above there were three more bedrooms, allowing space for any children and additional guests visiting who could not sleep on the first floor.

Everyone who stayed at the manor always had an experience they would never forget, Eleanora made sure of that. The place was peppered with furniture from the reigns of Queen Anne, King George II and III, often labelled with clear details of the date and name of the member of the Beaumont family who had procured or inherited it. As such, Glenn and Eleanora's home had always had the feel of a fabulously preserved museum.

That morning, readying himself for his working day in the City of London, Glenn followed the elegant wood panelling of the staircase all the way down to the entrance hall. Axminster carpets paved the way, fantastic embroidery weaving along the wide, clean hallways. But just as he was about to turn towards the dining hall for breakfast, away from the hallway which led to the drawing room and his office, Glenn noticed that the door to the ballroom had been left ajar.

Surprised to see the door open, for it was rarely used those days, Glenn followed his curiosity and pushed the door wide open. The ballroom, however, was quite empty, as tranquil as it had ever been. At one hundred and thirty metres long it was huge, Glenn thought, as though he had forgotten such a huge room existed in his house. Lingering for a moment in that vast, empty space, Glenn looked around. Polished dark wood panels lined the great expanse of space and light, reflecting the twinkles of the sunlit chandeliers. Early morning sunlight poured into the hall that summer morning, reminding Glenn of the former glory of his youth. He could recall the debutant ball at which he had met his wife as though it had been just yesterday. This was perhaps because the manor house itself, an enormous building which sat on the estate owned by his wife's family, had not changed at all since then. It had not lost any of its grace and elegance. It was a family heirloom, Eleanora was never shy to remind him, and as such, it remained preserved and pristine.

'Dance with me, honey?' he had whispered to Eleanora, the prettiest girl in the hall on that night so many years ago. He gave her his cheekiest grin – the one that always won over the ladies – but she had said no at first. He had made a joke, something about Brooklyn and the beef they had eaten, but she had not been amused. This New York boy would have to do better to impress this English Rose, he remembered thinking to himself that night. So he pulled out all the stops and charmed her into loving him. In the end she agreed. Glenn closed his eyes and recalled the music of that night, the laughter and the dancing; his wife had gleamed brighter than the moon as she twirled around the dance floor.

Breaking away from his reverie and wondering who had been in the room, Glenn left, closing the door gently behind him. His echoing footsteps kept him company in the high-ceilinged hallway as he made his way through the reception room towards breakfast. Panels of the past gazed down at him, great tapestries and bookcases of tomes long forgotten but dusted vigorously all the same. They made an elegant route towards the dining hall, where Glenn could already spot his wife, seated at her end of the table, dressed in a lilac three-piece suit.

Eleanora did not look up when her husband entered the room. She instead continued to gaze over her beloved horsing magazine, tutting intermittently when she did not like what she saw. At thirty-eight, she was still an attractive woman. The suit she wore complimented her thin, bony angles, giving them elegance and poise. Even at the other end of the hall Glenn could see how her pale blue, sharp eyes shot from line to line, scanning and analysing the text with fierce intelligence.

'Morning, honey,' he said to his wife. She raised her eyes at him in irritation, acknowledging him, before turning back to her magazine.

Used to the absence of any sort of pleasantry, Glenn settled himself down opposite his wife, which, due to the length of the table, was at least ten metres away from her. Reaching for a cup of coffee, Glenn prepared himself for their daily routine of silence at breakfast, and yet the memory of the debutant ball still stirred in his mind. He wondered if his wife remembered that night too. He even wondered if it had indeed been she who had been in the ballroom that night, so different was the woman sat before him.

'It looks mighty fine in the ballroom today, darling,' he said as gently as he could whilst also trying to be heard over the distance.

'The ballroom?' she muttered, not looking up from her page. 'What on earth were you doing in the ballroom at this time of day?'

'The door was open,' said Glenn. 'I wondered...' he began, but stopped. It was clear that his wife had not been in there that morning. 'Do you remember our first dance?' he asked instead.

'Ha!' Eleanora gave a loud snort, not unlike the horses in her magazine. 'I do. I remember it very well. God, I miss my youth.'

'You were the prettiest girl at that ball,' said Glenn, smiling at his wife, despite her derision. 'You know that, don't you?'

'Ha,' Eleanora snorted again. 'You say that now, but I know what you were up to at that ball. Those girls were all over you. There were plenty of pretty little things flapping around.'

'I was the American,' Glenn laughed. 'I was exotic to them. To you too, I think.'

'They were all wearing such tight-fitting, vulgar things,' sighed Eleanora. 'I'm surprised their mothers let them leave the house. Good God, do you remember? What a lark! They had no idea of matching colours; everyone seemed to have been swimming in a sea of pink: garish, stinking pink. What a bore.'

'I had fun,' shrugged Glenn, helping himself to the kippers on his plate, before adding with a whisper a comment that his wife barely heard: 'I fell in love, baby!'

Glenn tucked into his kippers with relish. They were salty and crispy, just how he liked them. He had always enjoyed traditional English breakfasts, despite his roots in the United States. Sometimes he missed his mom's pancakes, drenched in maple syrup and stacked high on a plate, but years of schooling at Eton had drilled into him the importance of kippers and eggs for breakfast. Eating them on a golden plate, however, was an experience he had only discovered in marriage. Eleanora insisted they only dine on gold-plated crockery. He still found it slightly absurd.

'Of course you found it fun,' laughed Eleanora, raising an eyebrow in her husband's direction. 'Because of all the girls! You had all those girls to look at, frolicking around, swooning over you. It was a bloody bore, if I recall correctly.'

Glenn tried to ignore the bitter, dull jealousy in his wife's voice by making a joke.

'Honey, you're still jealous,' he laughed, a loud, infectious laugh that echoed in the large hall.

'Rubbish,' scoffed his wife.

Glenn remembered the evening with a half-smile, for it was true that he had been quite a heart-throb amongst the ladies of the ball. At thirty-eight, his looks were not quite what they were in his youth, but when he looked in the mirror Glenn liked to think he could still recognise himself as the cavalier young man Eleanora fell in love with.

'Still got it,' he would whisper to himself in the mirror with a wink.

'It's also where I met you,' he said to his wife. 'That counts for something, surely? You were the best dressed, honey. That's true.'

'I was the only one with a title,' his wife shrugged, as if to say this was of far greater importance. 'I was the only baronetess at that ball. Imagine, the only titled girl.'

Glenn was never exactly sure of what to say in these moments. He knew his wife took great pride in her baronetcy. She insisted that for her it was a matter of pride, not snobbishness; the Beaumonts had been barons and baronets for centuries, as the tapestries on the oak-panelled walls depicted. Their nobility was as important to them as their health: it needed to survive, even in a world that moved further and further away from aristocratic values. Eleanora herself traced her ancestry back to a time when England was more French than English, when the Norman William the Conqueror had seized power at the Battle of Hastings, as far back as 1066, and further still.

'The only woman with a title,' Eleanora continued, gazing out of the window with great disdain, as if she were looking out over the crowd of girls she remembered. 'And the only girl with good breeding,' she added. 'I am a direct descendent of—'

'Louis XIII, yes,' Glenn interrupted. 'I know you are, honey.' Eleanora's husband would need more than two hands to count the amount of times he had heard his wife say that.

'Well then,' she replied, pursing her lips. 'It was no wonder you picked me out among all that riff raff. You were a good dancer. That's why I said yes in the end.'

Glenn said nothing, for indeed there was nothing he could say. He could neither dispute nor deny his wife's claim to be a descendent of the lost line of French kings. Glenn could only be happy that his wife considered him to be a good dancer, and if his memory served him correctly, it was an observation that many of the girls at the dance had shared. Still got it, he thought to himself.

Sighing and tutting in irritation, Eleanora turned back to her breakfast, a delicious plateful of toasts and preserves. She looked down at the plate and smiled with great satisfaction, but did not take a single bite. Glenn's wife was obsessed with keeping as thin as possible, and subsequently ate as little as possible, which made their daily breakfast routine at that grand table even more ridiculous. The fresh butter, cheese and sticky jams made on the estate were laid out lavishly, tempting to the eye and delectable to the taste buds, but often went completely untouched. However, this did not deter Eleanora from boasting to Glenn about where exactly everything had come from.

'Try the butter, dear,' she said, gesturing at the yellow slab presented on a gold tray at Glenn's end of the table. 'Do try,' she insisted. 'It was churned this week by the Thomases, you know, that rather shabby family on the bottom of the estate. The husband is a farmer. A smelly man, with terrible manners, but he does keep the herd in check. He is producing some of the finest milk, butter and cheese in England, mark my words. The estate will thrive from it.'

Glenn nodded and helped himself to the butter tray with a knife. To please his wife he scraped it onto his wholemeal toast and smiled as he ate it.

'Delicious, darling,' he said, elaborating on the fairly standard-tasting butter. 'Better than New England's finest, and that's saying something. They have big cows there.'

'I know it is,' she responded irritably, before sighing. 'I had best stop dawdling here. I need to get to the gym; I feel like I've gained three pounds just looking at that damn butter. Yes, I'll go to the gym and then head to the stables. I need to ride, God knows I do. It's a fine day to be with the horses.'

Glenn nodded politely as he listened to the little details of his wife's day to come. When she paused to pour herself another cup of tea from the silver teapot Glenn took the opportunity to share a few details of his coming day too.

'I should make my way to the office too,' he said, smiling cheerfully. 'God, it's always a schlep to get there!'

'A schlep?' said Eleanora, as if Glenn had sad something deeply distasteful.

'Sorry honey, you can take a guy out of New York, but you can't take New York out of a guy! A schlep's like a trek, a journey that'll take a while.'

Eleanora simply frowned at him.

'I wish you would speak *English*,' she muttered.

'It is English, honey!' he laughed. 'Man, the Tube will be busy and everyone will be angry the weekend is over. What's more, it's going to be a heavy day at the office. I have five charities coming to see me. Five! But it feels good. Finally I feel like I'm in a position to use my education. All those years studying international relations, they've meant nothing until these past few years. But now, now the foundation trusts me enough to let me put our money to good use. This is a real turning point, I know it, I just hope I'm ready.'

Glenn stopped speaking as his voice was drowned out by the loud rapping of Eleanora's spoon against her tea cup. Her face looked angry.

'I knew this wasn't bone china!' she hissed. 'One can't buy anything of worth these days. From a damned supermarket, I'm sure. That swine, Marcus, one of the tenants, offered to buy china for me. I asked him to buy me china from Harrods but he's swindled me, I'm sure of it. It must be tat from a supermarket. I should never have trusted him.'

'Were you listening to anything I just said?' Glenn asked, hurt by his wife's distraction and apparent indifference.

'Hmm?' she asked, distractedly, inspecting the teacup with her sharp gaze. Glenn shook his head and turned back to his breakfast. He thought that eating might sweeten the sourness he felt towards his wife. Silence stagnated and only the clink of silver on china, or silver on gold, serenaded the couple. Glenn's mind began to drift towards the day ahead. In his mind's eye he had already started his daily commute to his office in London's Cheapside, the traditional banking district close to St Pauls. He imagined the stops the train would make as it travelled from Virginia Water, their little commuter town in Surrey. It was just over an hour into the city every day, and Glenn could make the journey blindfolded. But somehow, in that moment, he could not leave his irritability behind. He stared at his wife.

'You're never interested,' he said to her, putting down his napkin to show that he was finished. 'For all you know, I could be working anywhere.'

'Oh please,' scoffed Eleanora. 'You work somewhere, I know that at least. And how many times have I told you not to talk to me about work? Why bother me with these trivial details? It's vulgar.'

'How is it vulgar?' Glenn asked indignantly. 'It's my job! It's work, honey. I'm a working man.'

'Well I don't want to know about it,' Eleanora retorted. Glenn felt a familiar tension rising between them. It stirred in his stomach and made him feel uncomfortable. His wife was not familiar with the world of work, and it was an inherited attitude. Her mother, Lesley Margaret Beaumont, had never worked a day of her life, despite her expensive habit of dressing herself in the finest fashions from Sloane Street and Harrods. Eleanora's father, Harold John, simply lived off the rents of his tenants, which he collected religiously, and various stock investments and dividends from bonds. Harold John Beaumont shared his wife's expensive tastes and refused to talk about the financial markets with Glenn. Like his daughter, he considered this to be extremely vulgar, despite it being Glenn's profession.

'My work pays for your lifestyle, honey,' Glenn said gently to his wife. 'You've never worked. Maybe you should try getting a job. You could do anything, I've always said that. You have good people skills, great experience. Why not try consulting? You might like it. I'm sure I could help you find a position in the financial sector.'

'Don't insult me,' snapped Eleanora, drawing herself up into her most elegant and proud posture. 'I did not attend St George's School or my finishing school in Ascot to bandy around with common brokers. Nor do I hold degrees from Oxford and Durham to chit-chat about exchange rates.'

'The financial world is not just full of brokers, honey,' Glenn replied, stung by his wife's reproach. But she would not hear of it.

'You and the City of London and your finances,' Eleanora sighed crossly, growing more impatient by the second. 'I think it's dirty. Making money from stocks and shares and gambling. In your world, anyone with a few pennies can be rich. All this "new money", it's foul. The only way to make money is from the land. That is what I believe and what my family believe. It has served us well so far.'

'But how long can you really make money from the estate, baby?' Glenn asked. 'Do you really think that's viable?'

'Viable?' laughed Eleanora. 'Glenn, my dear, it is not about making money. The land is the lifeblood of this estate, of this family. Our tenants will pay rent and the farmers will keep working the land. This has been the case for centuries. What could possibly change that now? God knows we make the best butter and cheese in England. The only place you'll get it better is France. We have a herd of five hundred cows and they milk beautifully every day.'

'Yes, but if you read around this subject, Eleanora, you'll discover that your market is being flooded,' said Glenn, sighing deeply. He did not know if he had the heart to explain to his wife that the dairy industry in general was dying for small farmers.

'What do you mean?' she asked him.

'There's an excess,' Glenn explained. 'Cheese and milk products from Holland, France and Germany are much cheaper and so easy to transport. They have an excess, even, and that excess is taken on by the markets here in the UK.'

'Markets? Don't you talk to me about markets, Glenn Tebbhurst. Do you really think I care about that?' Eleanora demanded. 'And do you really mean to insult me in every possible way this morning?'

'I'm not trying to insult you, honey,' Glenn began.

'Then why do you compare my products with that cheap, disgusting muck from the continent?' his wife hissed. 'Thank God the neighbours can't hear you, Glenn. I am ashamed of you.'

'But it's business,' Glenn protested, almost laughing at his wife's reaction. 'You have competition, don't you?'

'Not for our products,' said Eleanora stuffily. 'We serve only the best cheese and butter and you will not find them in the same supermarkets as this continental crudeness you speak of. We have a unique selling point. Our products are of a quality that can only be produced by the finest English traditional methods. They are only in the best food halls of London. Good God, Glenn, sometimes I think you do not understand an ounce of what I am trying to do here on the estate.'

Glenn turned to look out of the window as his wife continued to berate him for not understanding the working of the farm. As he looked out over the lawns, he saw one of the farmers carrying pails of milk in the distance. The farmer looked tired and dishevelled, and was no doubt forced to work for the estate and submit his produce under the Beaumont family's Ronda Round Manor brand. Sometimes Glenn felt that the Beaumont estate was clinging to feudalistic ideals that no longer had a place in 2011.

'Well, I don't see you trying to understand my line of work either,' Glenn replied tartly. 'Are you ever interested in the work we do with charities in Africa? We change people's lives, lady. We give people who never had a reason to believe their lives could change the hope that they can.'

'Africa? Where's that?' sighed Eleanora lazily, deliberately trying to irritate him. 'No one goes there, Glenn,' she said in her bored voice. 'No one cares about Africa anymore.'

Glenn could not quite believe what he was hearing. His morning had started so hopefully, as he glimpsed the ballroom and remembered the moment when he had fallen in love with his wife. Now, as he stood up to leave, he could barely recognise her, or himself.

'Forget about it. I have to get my train,' he said, shaking his head and looking away from her.

'Don't look me up later,' said Eleanora coldly. 'I'll be at bridge club.'

'Right,' said Glenn, and turned to leave. Sweeping from the dining hall, Glenn picked up his briefcase and headed to the front door. Portraits of previous Beaumont barons and baronets glared down coldly at him as he passed, their faces forever fixed in oil and gilded frames. The morning air was slightly chilled, a cool relief to him as he headed towards his usual commute.

There was something comforting about the regularity of that daily journey, Glenn thought, after the discomfort of breakfast with his wife. Walking briskly towards Virginia Water station, Glenn checked his watch. It was two minutes past seven, which reassured him; this meant he had five minutes to spare before his eight-minutes-past-seven train into London. Nevertheless, he walked quickly as he entered the station and flicked his travel pass through the ticket barriers.

The platform was crowded with the usual crowd of commuters heading into the city. After so many years of doing the same commute, Glenn immediately recognised his fellow commuters. There was a tall, thin and increasingly balding man around his age who always bought a newspaper from the platform coffee shop and immersed himself in it all the way to London. The coffee shop owner himself had not changed for years, a jolly man with Jamaican roots, who made interesting smelling breakfast treats for the commuters. Another regular on the train was a thin, spindly businesswoman, who was constantly checking her watch and sighing, even when the train was perfectly on time. These were the characters of Glenn's daily journey, and Glenn was glad to see them that morning.

Stepping onto the train, Glenn wondered if the others ever recognised him. The thing about Virginia Water was that everyone lived in their own manor house, hidden away, jealously guarding their privacy and quiet after the hustle and bustle of London. No one really wanted to talk to each other on that morning commute, and would only do so when forced to by a delayed train or a terrorist attack. Such was the way of life in that part of suburbia, and Glenn had grown used to being one of the hundreds of people commuting from Windsor to the City of London.

The train sped quickly towards the capital, and Glenn looked at his watch. He had at least forty minutes until his train pulled in to Vauxhall at seven fifty-two and he could catch the underground to Bank, which was just a few minutes' walk from his office close to Threadneedle Street in Cheapside. He decided to review the five charities he would be discussing that morning. Their bold mission statements jumped out at him and he was inspired for a while, reading through their work and visions for the future. As he shuffled through their portfolios, his mind wandered back to the moment he had started working in corporate fundraising.

'You're the man for the job,' his boss in New York had told him in a heavy Brooklyn accent. 'You talk the languages, you have the passion and, hell, you have some European style, fella. You speak, what, three languages?'

Glenn's boss had been referring to the fact that, though American by nationality, Glenn had been educated at Eton, the most British school of all, and had a lot of contacts in Europe. His New York charity wanted to expand their presence in London, England, and Glenn was excited to hear that they thought he was the man for the job.

'That's my home territory,' Glenn had replied.

'Then this is an opportunity for you, my man!' his boss had clapped him on the back. Glenn remembered the moment well. He had been young, a graduate, barely two years out of college. His charity had immediately set him to work in their public affairs and international relations departments, and before long, the position in London had made sense to everyone. Life was strange, thought Glenn, remembering his transatlantic journey. Shortly after he had arrived in London he had met Eleanora, and the rest, as they say, was history.

'The train will shortly be arriving at Vauxhall,' came the polite voice on the train tannoy, breaking through Glenn's nostalgic musing. 'Next stop: Vauxhall.'

Packing the portfolios back into his briefcase, Glenn made his way off the train into the thick, busy bustle of Vauxhall station. The commuter station was full of crowds of people making their way out onto the street or down into the underground. Glenn allowed himself to be pulled along by the tide of people, ensuring he was heading firmly towards the Victoria Line. He needed a northbound train to Oxford Circus. Arriving at a platform heavy with people, Glenn blended into a crowd of countless suited men and women living life on the broker belt, checking watches and dreaming of the coffee machines waiting in their offices. Glenn was pleased to see a train already arriving. He trundled into the packed carriage and was rattled towards Oxford Circus, where he changed onto an eastbound train on the Central Line.

Glenn relaxed, gripping onto the handrail, and allowed himself to be buffeted by the commuters around him, every man and woman wrapped up in their own world of entertainment or problems. What a schlep, he thought to himself. When the tannoy voice announced that they were arriving at Bank Station, Glenn checked his watch. It was eight-seventeen. He had arrived slightly earlier than usual due to the excellently timed connection from Vauxhall, and relished the thought of walking slowly through Cheapside towards his office before the working day began: a rare treat.

Emerging into the street, Glenn was met by throngs of people in business suits walking briskly towards their offices, checking their watches and frowning at the volume of people traffic on the pavements.

'Oi! Watch it!' a cyclist shouted to a taxi driver as he was pushed dangerously close to the curb.

'Get yourself a helmet, you plonker!' the taxi driver called back, waving a middle finger at the cyclist.

Glenn smiled. After the vast space of Ronda Round Manor, the emptiness of the dining hall, and the peaceful stillness of Virginia Water, Glenn was relieved to be in the midst of movement. London was waking up and the sounds, smells and scuffles of feet reminded Glenn of that with every step he took. As an American in England, the sounds of London were as fascinating to him as ever.

'Flowers!' cried a street-side florist, beckoning to Glenn to come and look at his selection. 'Flowers for your girlfriend, flowers for your wife, flowers for your mother, flowers for life!'

Glenn imagined the scowl on his wife's face if he brought her flowers from a street-side florist. She would say she could *smell* the dirt on them. He politely shook his head at the flower seller.

'Read all about it, read all about it!' cried a young woman selling a newspaper which showed pictures of various celebrities in hats at horse races and politicians doing things they shouldn't. Letting the sounds of the city wash over him, and watching London awaken around him, Glenn walked steadily towards his office. A new day at the Diversified Charities Foundation was about to begin.

CHAPTER TWO

Arriving at the office, Glenn looked up at the familiar tall stone columns in front of the building, happy to step into the quiet, organised interior, where more marble columns reached up to the high ceilings of the eighteenth-century building. As he stepped through the doors, he glanced at the smart brass name plate on the building, presenting a bold impression of the DCF: Diversified Charities Foundation. Thinking of the numerous charities he had to discuss that day, Glenn could not help but feel like the name of his foundation had never been more fit for its purpose.

'Morning, Molly,' he smiled at the receptionist. The young woman looked up from her morning work to smile back at Glenn.

'Good morning, Mr. Tebbhurst,' she said in her usually cheerful way. Glenn walked confidently towards the elevator which would take him to his office on the third floor. Stepping inside, he was met by his reflection as the elevator doors slid shut. He stared at the man looking at him, an older, rougher version of the young man he had remembered earlier that morning in the ballroom. He was wearing his grey suit, as usual. There were only two suits he wore to work and those were the solidly professional colours of navy and grey, combined with high-collared shirts tailor made for him in Jermyn Street.

Glenn wondered at his appearance for a moment. If he had spotted the man looking back at him in the mirror on the street, he would surely have taken himself for a banker. Indeed, he was dressed like a banker, or a broker, but his work was in fact with endowments managed by the DCF. He worked with philanthropists from all over the world, and those philanthropists, though keen to invest their money in charitable causes and the good of the planet, secretly enjoyed the level of class the DCF exuded. Glenn suspected they found great comfort in the foundation's eighteenth-century offices in Cheapside as they sat on the other side of the green leather and mahogany of his partner desk.

Certainly it was Glenn's job to make those people feel as comfortable as possible when donating large sums of money to good causes. It was a skill he never would have guessed he possessed: an uncanny ability to charm vast sums of money out of people. His clients were rich families, wealthy individuals in the city, the landed gentry of England, Wales, Scotland and Northern Ireland. They were often retired with lots of money to spare, or had inherited lots of money from relatives. Glenn sometimes felt like he spent the majority of his time working with people who had never in fact worked a day in their life.

And yet he was very good at working with these people for these were the people his wife liked: like her they did not believe in trade or manual labour. These were the people Eleanora would invite to their summer lawn parties and their soirees at Ronda Round Manor House. They were also the kind of people who would invite Eleanora, and, by default, Glenn, to their parties. She adored the atmosphere of these evenings, soaking up the same conversations, the same small talk and gossip, the same food that flavoured every event. Glenn on the other hand would endure the events, if only to make his wife happy and make the most of the networking opportunity for the DCF.

From the foundation's point of view, these events that drew in the moneyed crowds were excellent; Glenn would take any and every opportunity to mention the DCF's objectives. He would explain how he was working in a foundation which had a section for investment and his personal work was with the management of funds, specifically endowments. He would always drop big charities like Children's Education Subsidy into conversation, and any charities tackling the advance of global warming, which by 2011 was no secret. Impoverished children and melting icebergs were surefire ways of attracting support from the rich and famous. He also mentioned charities to do with saving independent farms, or developing farms that were more into bio-plantation as compared to chemical fertilisers. To his advantage, Glenn believed that all farming methods should be natural, which was a sentiment Eleanora and many of her landed friends shared. Crowds would listen with interest, no doubt glad of a break in the monotony of gossip that often circulated at such parties. In one conversation Glenn could turn potential donations of hundreds of pounds into the hundreds of thousands. Such was the extent of both his skills and the disposable wealth of Eleanora's friends.

At first Eleanora did not like this tendency of Glenn's to mix business with pleasure at her favourite parties. But she was so proud of her aristocratic roots and her vast network of wealthy contacts that she soon saw it as a personal achievement to show Glenn and his colleagues at the DCF just how many wealthy people she knew for whom a donation of a few hundred thousand pounds was nothing. Her busy social schedule at bridge clubs and women's clubs, where she rubbed shoulders with other aristocrats from Europe, meant she often came home to tell her husband that she had found new donors who wanted to contribute to him.

The elevator pinged to announce his arrival at the third floor, and Glenn stepped out to head towards his office. There were around eighty employees working in the DCF office, and though most of the office were English, his work with international philanthropists meant that his office was located next to the International Department. This department had the foundation's foreign language interpreters who provided the office with a range of languages needed for their international interactions. There were Arabic, Chinese and Russian speakers alongside a range of European linguists. Passing through the department Glenn noticed three of his colleagues busy working on preparations for the meetings Glenn would be attending that day. Natasha, who was a master of Russian, was sitting with Tuni-Tung, the Chinese liaison officer, and Kikka, the German charity treasurer.

'Good morning, girls,' Glenn called across happily. 'I hope you're ready for today. It's a big day for us.'

'Good morning, Glenn,' said Kikka, swinging around in her seat to grin at her colleague.

'Morning, sir!' called Tuni-Tung as she stirred her noodle soup.

'See you in the board room, Glenn,' said Natasha, glancing up from her notes for a brief second before looking back to focus on them once more.

Glenn raised a hand in passing and said hello to everyone he crossed as he headed quickly towards his office.

'Good morning, DCF!' he called out in his usual high spirits.

'Morning, Glenn,' people called back, raising their heads and smiling. Everyone knew Glenn by his American accent, the charming twinge of Brooklyn catching their ears and hearts every time.

If Glenn was lucky he would meet Amelia, the tea lady, before she moved to the next floor. A pleasant, rounded woman with a lovely smile, Amelia could be found pushing her tea caddy around the office every morning. Glenn had a fond affection for her, and did not consider his day complete without at least one cup of tea from her trolley. Rounding the corner towards his door, he spotted Amelia just past the entrance.

'Ah, Amelia,' he said, catching up with her. 'I've found you. One cup of tea, please.'

'The usual, my dear?' asked Amelia, smiling up at Glenn.

'You know me too well,' laughed Glenn. 'Milk, no sugar. Lord knows I'm sweet enough. And whatever Sonia is having.'

Glenn popped his head around the door into his secretary's office.

'Cup of tea, Sonia?' he asked the secretary, a smartly dressed, petite woman, with curly black hair. 'Good morning, by the way. You're looking spectacular today, Madam Secretary!'

'Good morning, Mr. Tebbhurst,' said Sonia, smiling and standing up as her boss hung up his coat on the stand in the corner of her office. 'Not for me, thank you, sir.'

'Just a cuppa for me then, please, Amelia,' said Glenn, popping his head back around the office door to speak to the tea lady.

'Right you are, my dear,' said Amelia, raising a rattling cup of tea on its saucer and handing it to Glenn.

'Thank you, sweetie,' smiled Glenn. 'You have a good day, won't you now?'

'Bless you, my dear,' said Amelia warmly. 'You too.'

Glenn stepped back into his office and quickly took a sip of the hot beverage, gasping for a bit of refreshment after the hustle and bustle of his commute.

'Messages and mail are on your desk, sir,' said Sonia, as she did every morning. Glenn marvelled at his secretary, who came in early every day to ensure her boss had everything he needed when he arrived.

'Thank you, Sonia,' sighed Glenn. 'I'd best head straight to my desk then. I have a meeting at nine a.m. with investors from Shanghai.'

'I hope they will be more than friends, sir,' smiled Sonia, following her boss into his private office and laying a few more documents on his desk.

'I hope so too,' laughed Glenn, sitting down behind his desk for a quick review of the investors. Sonia's joke was referring to the system he had devised for the DCF regarding the level of charitable support investors were willing to offer. Often the contributors liked to feel like participants in the work they wanted to support, so over his ten years of work in the foundation Glenn had created the titles of friend, fellow, patron and trustee. A friend was the term used for those who offered the lowest contributions, lower than £1,000. A fellow offered £1,000 pounds or over. A patron offered £10,000 pounds or more and a trustee offered over £100,000 pounds. He had developed these through his interactions with various contributors, notable English lords and chairmen of large companies; the dukes, barons and bankers who had supported the DCF for years.

Glenn had barely finished reading a report from a charity working in Nigeria before Sonia called through to tell him that Tuni-Tung was with the Chinese contributors in a conference room nearby. Glenn hastened to join the meeting, and when he got there was happy to see that pleasant discussions were already underway as Tuni-Tung spoke in Mandarin with their guests from Shanghai. When Tuni-Tung saw Glenn enter the room, she smiled and stopped what she was saying abruptly. This often happened when Glenn entered a board room; people knew Glenn was the only one who had the charisma to clinch a deal with investors. He could already see the relief in Tuni-Tung's eyes. Speaking rapidly in Mandarin to the three men opposite her, she then translated for Glenn.

'Good morning, Mr. Tebbhurst,' she said excitedly. 'I was just introducing the project these men are interested in supporting in Southeast Asia and now I have introduced you.'

'Thank you, Tuni,' said Glenn, smiling warmly at his interpreter. 'And welcome to you all,' he said, looking over at the men who were nodding and bowing excitedly across from him. 'May I take this opportunity to say how honoured we are to welcome you here, and how excited we feel about our cooperation here today. We are going to do great things together, gentlemen. I can feel it.'

One of the men spoke in very enthusiastic Mandarin to Glenn, who nodded politely before turning to Tuni-Tung for translation.

'Mr. Wao-Ching says he is so honoured to meet the great Mr. Tebbhurst, who is making so many children happy all over the world with his charity work,' said Tuni-Tung. Glenn nodded and turned back to the man who had spoken.

'And with your help, we can continue that good work,' he said, bowing slightly as a sign of respect. 'As I said, I have a great feeling about the collaboration. Our two great organisations can truly come together to bring about positive change.'

Tuni-Tung translated quickly and the Chinese men opposite her looked more excited than ever, nodding more frequently, and bowing back at Glenn. Settling himself down at the table, Glenn began to talk about the work the contributors would be supporting, using a spiel so familiar it flowed like honey from his lips.

'Every year we aim to save as many children as possible from civil conflict, no matter who they are or where they come from,' Glenn began. 'To date, it is estimated that the Diversified Charities Foundation has protected the lives of over five thousand children. We hope to support one thousand more children at least this year from global conflict and natural disasters. We cannot underestimate the threats posed to children across the world today.

'Even in the United States of America, which, as you know, is where I am from, children are at risk from elemental threats such as hurricanes and tornados. In your own beautiful and vast country of China, you have floods, earthquakes and of course threats which your contribution is heavily highlighting: coal mine disasters. Every year children lose their fathers to industrial disasters and due to no fault of their own they are subsequently condemned to abandonment and poverty. The DCF works to arrange and support foster parents throughout Southeast Asia, allowing those children to have a new chance and a better shot at life. We give these foster parents money every year to enable the essential nurturing, nutrition and education a child needs to survive. My job, as you're all aware, is to control that spending. In my department we control exactly how every single cent, penny and pound is spent.'

Glenn waited for a moment until Tuni-Tung had finished interpreting everything he had said into Mandarin before finishing.

'It's great that you all want to be involved,' he said, nodding again in appreciation at the Chinese men. The discussion that followed was brief, with a few details regarding the outreach of the DCF in the region. Glenn answered any questions the contributors had before looking down at his watch. An hour and a half had already passed and he needed to get to a new meeting. Glenn turned to Tuni-Tung and spoke directly to her.

'Tuni, look, I'll let you handle the meeting from here on in as I have some German visitors here that are very interested in The Children's Education Subsidy's work in the refugee camps in the Middle East, especially in Turkey. I need to introduce myself.'

'Sure, no problem, sir,' smiled Tuni-Tung. 'Kikka told me all about it this morning. I'll finalise everything here and send all the paperwork to Sonia.'

'Great,' said Glenn, winking at Tuni-Tung to show he had full confidence in her abilities.

'Oh, and Glenn?' said Tuni.

'Yes?' said Glenn.

'Great pitch, as always,' she smiled at him.

'All in a day's work,' he grinned.

Standing up to leave, Glenn was surprised when the three Chinese men leapt from their chairs to bow deeply as he left. In return he raised his hand in goodbye before leaving the room.

Glenn did not have to go far to find Kikka, who was already discussing the support of refugee camps in Turkey with two German industrialists. Kikka and the two Germans looked up as Glenn entered the room.

'Ah, Herr Tebbhurst,' said Kikka, beaming up at Glenn as she introduced him to the guests. Glenn smiled and nodded at the Germans, reaching out to shake both of their hands. He then turned back to Kikka and shook her hand too as a courtesy.

'Gentlemen, my name is Glenn Tebbhurst, I am here to help us build something remarkable today,' he said, turning back to the men. 'Whatever doubts you have, or questions, we're here to put your minds at rest. The future is in our hands today, gentlemen.'

The men nodded serenely at Glenn as Kikka translated.

'Now, please, just continue as you were, Kikka,' said Glenn, indicating with a gesture of his hand that she should carry on with whatever she was saying in German.

'Ja, okay,' said Kikka, nodding. 'I am just explaining the context in Turkey, sir, and how the sudden influx of refugees is a strain on the infrastructure of the country.'

'Great,' nodded Glenn, adding under his breath: 'Also, make sure The Children's Education Subsidy's role is clear and put an emphasis on education.'

Kikka spoke for a few more minutes to the industrialists, who were all quite typically German in their straight-backed aloofness. They were quite the opposite of the Chinese businessmen Glenn had encountered in the previous meeting. Their facial expressions barely changed as Kikka outlined the awful conditions of displaced people in informal refugee camps in Turkey. She said something and both industrialists turned to look at Glenn, who waited for Kikka's instruction.

'I was just explaining the role of the DCF in supporting The Children's Education Subsidy, Glenn,' said Kikka. 'I said you would be the best person to explain that.'

'Yes,' said Glenn, clearing his throat. 'Thank you, Kikka.'

Glenn turned to the Germans and began to explain the role he would play in their support.

'My point of control is making funds available,' he said. 'Kikka has probably explained what she aims to support in this project, and I can reiterate that we want to address the desperate need for education in these refugee camps, where children are simply abandoned and left to fend for themselves. We want to pay for teachers in camps so that the children can be stimulated, offering them the best chance of a future once they grow up.'

Kikka translated this into German, before adding something to Glenn.

'I just informed them also that we want to make sure the teachers get paid salaries, and that this money does not get abused or misdirected in the camps.'

'Perfect,' said Glenn. 'I can't stress enough how important this system of trust is in our execution of this project funding. We need you to trust us and can offer every assurance your funds will not go astray. It is my responsibility and honour to offer this assurance, gentlemen, I hope you will trust me in this.'

The two men nodded, clearly assured by Glenn's frankness. Confident that the deal was clinched, Glenn glanced down at his watch. He was already late for his next appointment.

'Well, I think everything is under control here, Kikka,' he said. 'If you don't mind, I might leave you to it?'

'Of course, no problem,' said Kikka. She quickly explained to the Germans that Glenn had to leave. The Germans nodded, without emotion, and reached forward to shake Glenn's hand once more.

'I look forward to working together,' Glenn said confidently, keeping eye contact with both men as they shook his hand.

Heading to the next conference room, Glenn felt infused with purpose. Every day he relied on his confidence and ease with words to convince the rich to help the poor. Would he ever get sick of this, he wondered? Glenn opened another door to find Natasha, his Russian interpreter, discussing something at length with two Russian businessmen. When he entered, Natasha quickly introduced him, or at least Glenn thought she did. He heard his named being uttered in a stream of unfamiliar Russian words. It was such a beautiful language, he thought to himself. Both men stood up to offer Glenn a bone-crushing hand shake. One of the Russians looked up at Glenn with wide, grey eyes, nodding quickly. He muttered something urgently to the other man, who nodded back and quickly ducked beneath the desk to take something. He emerged with a bottle of vodka and four shot glasses. The man with steely grey eyes said something loudly to Glenn, which Natasha quickly translated.

'Mr. Voloschnofk says he will toast your meeting with a drink, as is the custom in Russia,' she said, turning to Glenn with a slightly bewildered face.

'Oh,' said Glenn, surprised. 'Oh, I'm sorry, I don't drink!' he said with a smile. Natasha translated. The Russian pouring the vodka did not understand and looked to his companion for further instruction. The wide-eyed man said something in Russian and the other man began to pour vodka into four glasses. Natasha looked up at Glenn and smiled apologetically.

'He says you are just saying that because English men are too polite and you do not want to drink in front of your secretary,' said Natasha, adding: 'I think he means me.'

Glenn did not know what to say, but before he could say anything, Natasha had stood up.

'Can I speak to you outside for a moment?' she asked in hushed tones.

'Yes, of course,' said Glenn, happy for an excuse to leave the potent vodka fumes behind. Natasha quickly apologised in Russian, excusing them for a moment, before leaving the room with Glenn. When the door was firmly shut, she looked at Glenn with a dubious expression.

'What's up?' Glenn asked.

'Glenn, I'm not sure about these two,' she said, shaking her head worriedly. 'They want to give us hundreds of thousands.'

'Excellent!' said Glenn. 'They're trustee material then. What's the problem with that?'

'Well, they are Russian oligarchs and we don't know much about their history,' said Natasha. 'I'm worried that this might be a money laundering stint, or perhaps they are looking for assets. I mean, how did they make their money in the first place?'

Glenn sighed and nodded. He could understand Natasha's mistrust of the Russians. Years ago, at her age, he would have had the same doubts. But his experience of working with international philanthropists was not to judge a book by its cover and to do background research wherever necessary.

'These are honest men, not politicians, Natasha,' said Glenn, trying to reassure her. 'I trust them. They made their money in trade and bartering goods and oil products, and they don't even live in Russia anymore. They live between Monaco, Geneva and London.'

'Okay,' said Natasha, nodding. 'If you trust them, that's all I need to hear.'

Flattered by Natasha's faith in him, Glenn smiled.

'I do,' he said sheepishly. 'But I really don't want to drink that vodka.'

'Leave it to me,' laughed Natasha. They returned into the room, where four shot glasses of vodka had been laid out for drinking. Natasha said something quickly in Russian, gesturing at Glenn's body, causing the two Russians to look at him in alarm. Glenn had no idea what was being said but it seemed to do the trick: the Russians nodded and took back the vodka glasses.

'Excellent,' said Glenn. 'Now, shall we begin? I have been inspired by the charitable work with orphans that you support in Russia. Could you tell me more?'

The Russians spoke at length about the work they supported, leaving Natasha to translate.

'They are very involved with charities working to reduce poverty and encourage the adoption of orphans,' Natasha translated. 'They have so many orphans in Russia, children left parentless because of poverty or war. These gentlemen are explaining how hard it is to deal with adoption agencies in Russia, they say.'

'Is that true?' Glenn asked Natasha. 'I remember reading something in the newspaper about adoptions scandals over there.'

'Yes, sir, it's a very difficult system in Russia,' she said. 'Some say it is beyond anyone's control. These men are trying to improve the situation and options for orphans.'

'Well,' said Glenn, turning to the Russians. 'I don't know anything about this system. The workings of adoption agencies are beyond my power: my role is simply to manage the funds correctly. We spend the money on transport and agency fees and from there we cross our fingers and hope that things work out. I believe there are many things you need to clarify and discuss with Natasha today. Unfortunately I have two more meetings to attend, and must leave you to sort out the details. Please excuse me; I will leave you in Natasha's most capable hands, and believe me when I say I have great faith in this cooperation. Together we can achieve wonderful things.'

Natasha translated what Glenn had said into Russian. The two oligarchs stood and solemnly placed their hands on their chests before reaching out to shake Glenn's hand once more.

Glenn left the room and headed back to his office with a spring in his step. Thank God the meetings are going well, he thought to himself, throwing Sonia a smile as he entered his office.

'A productive morning then, sir?' Sonia asked him as she shuffled a few things on her desk.

'Very productive, Sonia,' Glenn grinned. 'I think we have gained some significant financial support with these new clients. With progress like this we can really help our charities do the work they want to do where they want to do it. Three continents covered in one morning! Not bad, huh?'

'Excellent, sir,' smiled Sonia. 'And look, you're in luck. Amelia is back!'

Glenn turned around when he heard the rattling sound of tea cups and teapots approaching. Sure enough, Amelia was passing by with the tea caddy.

'Same again, my dear?' Amelia asked him, dealing him one of her full smiles.

'Yes please, Amelia!' laughed Glenn, overjoyed at this marvellous Monday morning. Taking the tea from Amelia, Glenn headed into his office to start on the admin he knew was waiting for him. He had barely reached the second page of a funding proposal when his phone rang.

'Mr. Tebbhurst, your mother Iris is on the line,' said Sonia.

'My mother?' exclaimed Glenn in surprise. His mother, who lived in New York with his father, never called him. He called her once a week, without fail, but he could not remember the last time she had taken the initiative to call him. 'Huh? I usually call her. What's going on, Sonia?'

'Shall I put you through, sir?' asked his secretary.

'Yes, please do,' said Glenn. The phone clicked and a new line could be heard.

'Glenn?' came his mother's voice.

'Mom?' he said.

'Glenn, honey,' came his mother's voice. 'I miss you.'

'Mom,' said Glenn, laughing sadly. 'I miss you too.'

'You don't come often enough to New York, honey,' said said. 'You're always stuck with that wife of yours in England. How do you stand it? Last time I saw her she only spoke about herself and her bridge club. I hope she's cooking for you.'

'Mom,' said Glenn firmly, knowing his mother had not called to berate him about his choice of wife. 'Why are you calling? I call you, you don't call me. It's been a year since you called me first.'

Glenn heard silence on the line for a moment, before his mother let out a deep sigh and then a small, soft sob.

'I have some bad news, honey,' she said.

'Bad news?' yelped Glenn, his heart sinking in his chest. 'Is everything okay? Are you okay?'

'It's Dad,' she said, her voice small and croaky. 'As you know, your Dad has type 2 diabetes. He deals with it, he always has done. He takes everything the doctor recommends, and he has been managing well. You know how he suffers though, with low sensitivity on his feet, but that's all been getting better with his massages and his runs in the park. But, honey, the bad news is the doctor started warning him about the quality of his eyesight. We didn't think anything of it at the time but now, well, everything's changed.'

Glenn's mother began to weep and Glenn felt panic rising in him like a flood.

'Mom, what's happened?' he asked, not entirely sure he wanted to hear the answer.

'Your father woke up this morning and could not see anymore,' sobbed Iris.

'Couldn't see?' repeated Glenn. 'What do you mean he couldn't see?'

'He just couldn't see,' Iris went on. 'I was really shocked. He bumped into the cupboard, into the wall, he couldn't see anything. He tried to run his eyes under the taps in the bathroom but nothing happened. There was just nothing doing. So I waited then I took him to an emergency appointment at the hospital.'

'What did they say?' Glenn asked anxiously.

'Well, I don't know what we were expecting... But, dear Glenn, your father is blind.'

The words froze in Glenn's ears, sending an icy jolt to his heart. He could not believe what he was being told. His father, Bertie, was blind. Glenn tried to listen as his mother continued, but he found it hard to concentrate.

'I'm sorry to say he is now fifty-eight years old,' she said, with a note of despair in her voice. 'I have to live with a blind man. He has to have a cane, honey. But don't worry, I will walk around the park with him and keep him company.'

At this Iris broke down into sobs. She cried and Glenn wished more than anything that he could reach through the transatlantic phone call to hug her.

'He may have to have a dog,' Iris went on.

'But surely the doctors can try something?' asked Glenn. 'Surely they won't just accept that Dad has gone blind, when the day before he could see perfectly well?'

'Oh, I have seen two doctors, honey, and there's nothing to be done. That's what they have said. They concluded he is blind forever.'

'Mom, don't cry,' said Glenn as he listened to the gentle sobs on the other end of the line. 'I'm coming.'

'What?' sobbed Iris. 'Really?'

'I have to get on the next plane,' said Glenn urgently. 'I have to see him.'

* * * *

Travelling back to Virginia Water felt like an impossibly long journey for Glenn. The commute he took with great regularity suddenly seemed alienating to him. He needed to get home and pack his bags. Sonia had booked him onto the next flight to New York that evening, and he had not had a moment to call Eleanora to explain things.

Arriving home, Glenn walked through the entrance hall, straight through into the drawing room, where he hoped he would catch his wife before she headed out to her bridge club. Luckily he found her reclining elegantly over a fine chaise longue, flicking through a copy of a magazine with a bored look on her face. When he entered the room she glanced up at him.

'You're home early,' she said, looking up at the time on the great brass face of the grandfather clock.

Glenn said nothing as he threw his hat onto the hanger and threw himself down into an armchair.

'Why the long face?' Eleanora asked him, sitting up to examine Glenn's pallid complexion. 'Rough day at the office? I don't know how that's possible, I must say. How could you have a rough day when you work for a charity?'

'I had a rough day in the North Atlantic,' sighed Glenn, running a hand anxiously through his hair. 'Would you mind giving me an orange juice, honey?'

Sensing the seriousness of the conversation, Eleanora rose quickly to her feet and went to fetch Glenn an orange juice. She passed it to him and sat down in the chair beside him.

'Thanks,' said Glenn in a quiet voice.

'Tell me about it,' said Eleanora, looking into her husband's face. Looking up into her steely grey eyes, Glenn caught a glimpse of the sweet, loving wife he had fallen in love with. It was a rare sight these days but Glenn was glad that in this moment, Eleanora was there. 'I've never seen you looking so upset,' she added. 'You've turned all yellow and grey.'

'It's my father,' Glenn began, shaking his head in dismay. 'He's gone blind.'

'Blind?' gasped Eleanora. 'But how?'

Glenn shrugged.

'From the diabetes,' he suggested. 'From the stress, the New York pollution, you name it. It could be his nerves. For whatever reason, he's blind and there's nothing anyone is doing about it.'

Eleanora was quiet for a moment as she contemplated the situation. 'What will you do?' she asked.

'I received the news from my mother, she called me today at work,' said Glenn. Eleanora's expression hardened at the mention of Glenn's mother. Eleanora and Iris had never seen eye to eye, and their mutual animosity had only grown over the years. Eleanora looked away and sniffed miserably.

'I should go,' Glenn sighed. 'She needs support.'

'Well, obviously,' snapped Eleanora. Glenn could see her discomfort at the thought of him leaving. 'So just like that, you're going to leave me? And not just me. Your charities, the foundation?'

'The DCF understand, I've told them I'm going away,' said Glenn. 'Besides, that man raised me,' he added sternly. 'He is my father, and he is the wisest man I've ever known. He's my hero, my guru. How can I not go to him now, when this has happened to him?'

'You do whatever you want, I'm sure nothing I say is of any importance,' Eleanora replied sharply.

'Of course it is, darling,' sighed Glenn. 'Yes, I will go, but I'm not giving up on you, I'm not leaving you. I just have to support him. I have to support my mother too.'

'When will you go?' his wife asked him, sighing and turning to him with reluctant acceptance in her eyes.

'Tonight,' said Glenn. 'I need to work this out. I need to find out how the hell he went blind.'

CHAPTER THREE

Glenn awoke to the plane bumping down onto the runway in New York. His anxious heart had beaten itself into exhaustion as soon as he had settled down into his seat eight hours earlier, sending him into a deep but troubled sleep. Glenn looked down to check his watch and saw that it was three a.m., but looking out of the window he saw that there was still a bit of colour in the late evening sky. Disorientated, he wondered for a moment at air travel. He had flown out of London Heathrow at seven p.m., but the five hour time difference meant that his eight hour flight had landed in New York at dusk.

Glenn knew this journey well. When he had first started working for the DCF he had travelled back and forth between London and New York frequently, to visit his parents and his friends. The jet lag was bearable and well worth the feeling of excitement every time he inhaled the familiar smells of both cities again. But as he arrived this time, Glenn felt a great sense of discomfort as he took the familiar paths through the airport towards the baggage claim. Things were different now, he thought, imagining his father lying in bed with his blindness.

Heading towards the taxi rank, Glenn felt a small sense of relief when he spotted the yellow and black taxis queued up outside the airport, waiting to take people home. He waited in line until one stopped for him, and told the cheerful driver with his Brooklyn accent where he wanted to go.

'East Side,' said Glenn, momentarily enjoying the familiarity of the word on his tongue. 'Sutton Place.'

'Heading east then?' grinned the driver.

'Heading east,' nodded Glenn with a sigh before adding: 'heading home.'

The drive to the East Side was usually full of nostalgia for Glenn as he took in the sights of the familiar haunts. But that night he could only stare out of the window in a daze, growing increasingly worried about what state his father would be in when he arrived at their home. He knew this was where he had to be, but suddenly he felt afraid of what lay ahead. His father would surely be depressed and wretched; his mother would be full of despair. But before Glenn could predict what lay in store further, the beautiful brown stones of Sutton Place appeared. He spotted the United Nations building in the distance, lit up in all its glory. Glenn directed the driver to his front door before paying him, adding a large tip as he did so.

When the taxi pulled away, Glenn stood quite motionless outside his parents' villa. It was a front door he knew so well, recognisable by the beautiful hanging baskets full of flowers on either side, but somehow now it seemed different: everything seemed strange. Summoning up his courage, Glenn walked to the door and rang the doorbell. It was late and he felt bad for keeping his mother awake, but he could not have stayed in England an hour longer knowing the state his father was in.

The door opened, and there stood Iris, Glenn's mother, wrapped in a woollen cardigan, despite the warm summer evening. Her eyes were swollen from crying and her hair, usually so neat and tidy, was dishevelled from restless pacing.

'Oh, honey,' she said softly when she saw her son standing there. Her blue eyes filled with tears and Glenn allowed himself to be pulled into a tight embrace.

He held his mother tightly, whispering, 'It's okay, Mom, I'm here now.'

'Look at all your bags!' she said in surprise, looking down at the luggage Glenn had carried up with him from the taxi. 'How long are you staying for? A month?'

'For as long as it takes to get to the bottom of this,' sighed Glenn.

'And how does Mrs. Beaumont-Tebbhurst feel about that?' asked Iris, raising a coy eyebrow. Glenn smiled wearily at his mother.

'She'll manage,' he said.

'Well come on in, honey. I can't help you with your cases, and Lord knows your Dad can't. But at least we're on the ground floor. No elevators, no stairs, and I'm well connected here. I can walk along the

East River to the park and the hospital when I need to. Lord knows I'll need to visit more now, now that he... well, now that he is...'

'Mom, don't,' said Glenn, taking his mother in his arms once more, as if his arms could catch her tears. 'Don't cry. Please.'

'You're right,' sighed Iris, wiping her eyes and leading Glenn through to the kitchen. Walking straight to the drinks cabinet, she drew out a bottle of scotch whiskey and began to unscrew the lid.

'Mom, no,' said Glenn, gently going to her and taking the bottle away. Iris looked up at him with red, swollen eyes, and Glenn could see it was not the first drink she had taken that night. 'Don't drink.'

'What else am I supposed to do?' Iris asked, her voice breaking again.

'Take up Pilates, go for a walk, read a book,' suggested Glenn. 'But forget the drink. That could make you go blind too, Ma.'

'What else do I have here?' Iris asked reproachfully, a frown forming on her forehead. 'Your dad is blind, and Lord knows I will be looking after him.'

'That's what love is all about, surely?' said Glenn, gently.

'Oh, so that's your new philosophy from the old country, huh?' his mother demanded. She looked at him angrily and Glenn let out a deep, exhausted sigh.

'Don't be like this, Mom.'

Something in Glenn's weariness, or perhaps the pleading in his voice, made Iris hang her head in shame.

'If you want positive thinking, then go to him,' she said. 'He's convinced it is destiny. You know your father.'

'Is he still awake?' Glenn asked hopefully, keen to see him.

'He stayed up,' sighed Iris. 'Lord knows he doesn't know the difference between night and day anymore.'

Iris led her son towards their bedroom, where Bertie Tebbhurst sat snoozing lightly in a chair. Iris went to him and gently touched his shoulder. His eyes started to open and then he stared directly at Glenn, who stood in front of him, unsure of what to do or say. For a moment he thought his father could see him, that the blindness had gone away; that the nightmare was over. But his hope died as quickly as it had come.

'Is he here, Iris?' came his father's croaky voice. 'Has Glenn arrived?'

Glenn's heart sank. His father was staring right at him, frowning slightly as he took in the darkness before him. Glenn did not know if he had the voice to say anything. He was afraid if he spoke, his voice might break and his father would hear how devastated he was. Iris looked up at Glenn and nodded at him, indicating that he should speak.

'I'm here, Dad,' said Glenn. He walked over towards his father, who raised his arms up towards the sound of Glenn's voice.

'Glenn? Is that you?' said Bertie, tears forming in his eyes. 'Oh my boy, come here and kiss me. I'd get up but I'm not sure if I'd be able to find my seat again!'

'Oh baby,' murmured Iris, rubbing her husband's shoulders. 'Don't say that.'

Glenn went straight to his father and hugged him gently before kissing his forehead with the deepest affection.

'I flew as soon as Mom told me,' said Glenn. 'How are you feeling, Dad?'

'She shouldn't have told you, son,' Bertie tutted. 'Nothing to see here. Just an old man with type 2.'

'Oh don't, Bertie,' wailed Iris, shaking her head in dismay. 'You talk too much about your diabetes.'

'What, honey?' Bertie asked, his blank eyes staring out at nothing. 'It is! It happens to almost everyone here in the States. Around nine percent of the population has type 2 and I'm not the first diabetic to go blind. No, sir. Nor the last.'

'Dad,' said Glenn weakly. 'I didn't know things were so bad.'

'Bad?' laughed Bertie. 'It's not all bad, son. I have to walk with a cane that will guide me, sure, but I would have had to have one of those sooner or later anyway. I'm not getting any younger, and neither is your mother, though she'd be the last to admit it!' He laughed heartily then. 'I just have to know how to use this cane, I have to check, even when I'm with your mother. I can feel any impediments, including those on the sidewalk. You won't see me tripping up. It's not all bad. In fact, blindness is a good excuse.'

'A good excuse?' blinked Glenn. 'A good excuse for what?'

'Well, to ignore people you don't like!' cried Bertie, roaring with laughter. 'No, I'm just kidding, boy. First of all, people sympathise. They all feel bad and try to make life as easy as possible for you. Then I get priority on transport, especially on airplanes. They'll take me first to the plane, and I get help onto trains, buses and all sorts.'

Glenn beamed down at his father, who was genuinely smiling. He had forgotten just how positive his father could be in the face of adversity. His mother, however, could not stand it any longer. She left the room, masking her tears. But Glenn was still glowing from his father's brightness.

'You're my guru, Dad,' he said proudly, shaking his father's shoulder. 'You're the eternal optimist, I get it from you. When Mom told me, when I heard, I thought you would be a broken man. I thought Mom would be the optimist, but you are.'

'Your mother?' laughed Bertie. 'Fat chance. She's just scared of being seen with a cripple like me for the rest of her life.'

'I was worried about her when I got the call,' said Glenn. 'She seemed so heartbroken. I'm also sad, Dad. I honestly feel so sad about this. I need to find out why this has happened to you.'

'Son, what're you gonna find out?' asked Bertie. 'I'm blind. Do you think being blind is the end of the world? I can still imagine. Hell, I can imagine whatever I want. When I was in hospital I listened to all those nurses all around me, chatting away, and I imagined they were all the most beautiful girls I'd ever seen. When a girl comes along sounding pretty, with a lovely-sounding voice, I can imagine she's Marilyn Monroe or Grace Kelly! I can find the good things in people now. I see all the good and not the bad.'

For a moment Glenn did not know what to say. He was stunned by his father's confidence.

'Dad, you're such an optimist,' was all he could repeat. His father simply smiled and shrugged.

'For good reason, dear boy,' said Bertie. 'I can retire much earlier now, too. I was going to retire in a couple of years anyway.'

Bertie Tebbhurst had long worked as a consultant to the New York museums and to McKenzie.

'It's all going to be much easier from now on,' he said, snorting with laughter. 'I don't need to write anymore, I can just talk! And dictate. I can read things through voice or audio. I can read emails through audio now. The world has changed, son, what's the use in good sight anymore? Technology sees for us! My doctor even told me there's a phone that exists on which you can feel the letters. I don't even need to learn Braille! Cheer up, Glenn, everything's gonna be just fine.'

Glenn did not know how to respond to this. He decided instead to focus on the medical diagnosis.

'And this doctor,' he asked. 'Who is he? Has he tried to find out what's wrong with you?'

'Now, Glenn, don't go stirring up trouble,' his father warned him. 'Look, the doctor told us it could be anything! Diabetes messing up my retinas, something to do with circulation, nerve instruction from the brain, or even something purely physical, a faulty mechanism of the eye; it could have been anything.'

'Look, I've come here to get to the bottom of this,' said Glenn, feeling suddenly angry at the thought of these doctors who did not know what had happened to his father's sight. For no matter how optimistic Bertie was, the fact remained that he had gone blind from one day to the next.

'I'm still here, Glenn,' his father said, gently. 'I'm still here for you and your Mom.'

'Oh, Dad, I know that,' said Glenn, emotion swelling his heart beyond belief. 'But the first thing I'm going to do tomorrow is head up to the Columbia University Medical Centre to see what they have to say. Then, if they don't have answers, I'm going elsewhere.'

'Don't expect me to trail around all of these with you, son,' chuckled Bertie. 'I'll slow you down.'

'Of course I won't drag you around, Dad,' said Glenn sadly. 'I will do this research on my own.'

'Well, if you do go to Columbia, you'll meet my doctor,' said Bertie.

'What's his name?' Glenn asked, taking out a pen and paper from his pocket.

'Her name is Dr. Bokher,' said Bertie. 'And be nice to her. She's a good doctor.'

Glenn jotted down the name of the doctor, glad to have a starting point on his search for answers. Exhausted, he put his pen and paper away and knelt down in front of his father. 'I will find out what happened to you, Dad,' he said, trying to sound more confident than he felt.

'You sound tired, son,' said Bertie. 'They overwork you in that foundation in London?'

'No, Dad, all's fine back home,' said Glenn. 'I'm just worried about you, that's all.'

'What good did worrying ever do anyone?' his father smiled. 'Go to bed, Glenn, you need a good night's sleep.'

'Goodnight, Dad,' said Glenn, heeding his father's words. Kissing his father on the forehead once more, Glenn watched as Bertie closed his eyes and settled back into his chair. He went back to the kitchen to find his mother, who was sitting at the dining table, peeling an orange. She looked up when Glenn came in; Glenn saw she had been crying again.

'Shall I help you put Dad to bed?' Glenn asked, laying a hand on his mother's shoulder.

'Don't bother yourself,' Iris said, smiling and shaking her head.

'It's no bother, Mom,' said Glenn. 'That's why I'm here: to help with this. I can fix this.'

Iris nodded, reaching out her hand to take his in hers for a moment.

'I'm glad you're here, Glenn,' she said. 'You bring hope with you. You've always been like that.'

'I'm glad I'm here too,' said Glenn, and he meant it. 'There's gotta be a way.'

Mother and son went back to the bedroom and changed Bertie into his pyjamas, helping him find the right holes for his arms and legs. There was something tender about the process, so tender in fact that Glenn felt tears in his eyes. When Bertie was ready, they helped him into bed, where he slumped softly into his pillows and quickly fell asleep.

'Goodnight, Mom,' said Glenn, kissing his mother on the cheek.

'Goodnight, darling,' she said. 'Your room's made up. I'll make you pancakes in the morning, okay?'

'Okay,' smiled Glenn, despite the heaviness he felt inside. Barely mustering the energy to change into his own pyjamas, Glenn fell onto his bed and into a deep sleep.

Iris' pancakes had their usual effect on her son the next day. They were light, fluffy, and covered with fresh strawberries and maple syrup. Though he could see how his father's diabetes had developed after a lifetime of breakfasts like these, Glenn was happy to be full of energy. He chatted for a while with his father over coffee and then stepped out into the street to hail a taxi.

'Columbia University Medical Centre, Fort Washington Avenue,' said Glenn. The taxi driver nodded and sped across New York City to the hospital. When he arrived he went straight to reception, where a handsome young man looked at him with kind eyes.

'Can I help you, sir?' he asked.

'Yes, I'm looking for Dr. Bokher?' said Glenn. 'She treated my father recently.'

'Do you have an appointment, sir?' asked the receptionist.

'No, but it's urgent,' said Glenn. 'Please, if you could let her know I'm here?'

'Sir, Dr. Bokher is a very busy physician, if you could let me know some dates that work for you I would be more than happy to make an appointment?'

'Listen, I've travelled from London to see my father who has apparently turned blind overnight,' said Glenn, losing his patience. 'Are you really telling me I have to wait to see Dr. Bokher? I don't have time to make an appointment. I've left my job, my wife, everything behind to be here.'

The receptionist looked stunned for a moment before reaching for his phone. He quickly began to dial a number.

'Dr. Bokher?' he said after a brief delay. 'There's a man here who would like to see you. It seems quite urgent. Yes, I have told him he needs to make an appointment. No, he is still here. Okay, I will ask. Sir, please, what's your name?'

'Glenn Tebbhurst,' said Glenn. 'Bertie's son.'

The receptionist nodded once or twice before putting down the phone.

'Alright, Mr. Tebbhurst, Dr. Bokher can see you in thirty minutes,' he said. 'Just make yourself comfortable in the waiting room and she will be with you shortly.'

'Thanks,' said Glenn, nodding his head gratefully towards the young man.

'Please take a seat,' the receptionist said, smiling kindly.

Glenn sat down in the waiting room and looked at the various posters on the wall all advocating healthy diets, regular exercise and vaccinations. His mind wandered off towards his father the night before, how positive he had been and how distraught his mother was. How had this all come to pass, he wondered? Could Type 2 diabetes really make a man go blind?

'Mr. Tebbhurst?' came a voice from above, shaking Glenn from his thoughts. He looked up to see an attractive, young doctor of South Asian origin. 'Hello, Glenn, my name is Dr. Bokher. I am your father's ophthalmologist. I understand you wanted to see me?'

Glenn followed Dr. Bokher to her office, where she welcomed him in and closed the door behind them.

'Please, take a seat,' she said. Glenn sat down opposite her at the desk, feeling slightly odd to be sat on the other side of a desk for once. He was usually the one contributors and clients consulted, not the other way around. 'You must have lots of questions for me, Mr. Tebbhurst,' Dr. Bokher began.

'Yes,' said Glenn. 'This news has come as quite a shock to us, Bertie's family. We can't understand how this has happened. How can a man turn blind from one day to the next?'

'I understand this is a difficult situation for you all, Mr. Tebbhurst,' said Dr. Bokher. 'Especially for your father. Ophthalmology is a complex field of medicine, even for those of us who work in it, so I want to make this as simple for you as possible. I want to start by showing you the machine we used to identify your father's blindness. Come with me.'

Dr. Bokher led Glenn through to a room nearby, where a small white machine was waiting for them. Glenn vaguely recognised the machine. It looked like the tool opticians used to measure one's eyesight.

'This is an OCT machine, which stands for Optical Coherence Tomography,' said Dr. Bokher. 'This machine is a non-intrusive method of viewing the retina, and scans its different layers. Do you understand the function of the retina, Mr. Tebbhurst?'

'I'm not sure,' said Glenn, thinking back to his school biology lessons, which seemed so long ago.

'No problem,' smiled Dr. Bokher. 'I like to describe the retina as a bit like the film used in an old camera. In fact, the Latin root of the word comes from "net". Neat, huh? The retina is a light-sensitive layer of tissue, found in the inner coat of the eye. Light, which enters the retina through the cornea and lens, causes multiple chemical and electrical reactions which then trigger nerve impulses. These impulses are then sent to various parts of the brain via the optic nerve. Does that make sense?'

'I think so,' said Glenn.

'Good, okay, so the OCT machine allows me to map and measure any sickness found in the retina. These measurements then help me diagnose any glaucoma or retinal diseases, most commonly macular degeneration caused by ageing and other diseases caused by diabetes. I guess you're wondering why I'm showing you this. Well, this is the machine I have been using to monitor your father's eyesight for the past few months. It's usual for diabetics to come and see me for regular retinal scans. When your father was brought in two days ago, I was not only able to see the retinal damage, but confirm that your father can now be considered legally blind.'

'Legally blind?' asked Glenn. 'What does that mean?'

Glenn was finding the whole conversation difficult to deal with. He was usually the one in control, the man who knew what to say and when to say it. Now he was being faced with facts and figures he knew nothing about and could do nothing about.

'Well, it means that your father has visual acuity of less than six/sixty,' said Dr. Bokher. 'This means that your father would have to stand six metres from something to see it, with the help of lenses, whereas a person with normal sight could see it from sixty metres. When someone reaches this stage, or below, they are considered legally blind and can benefit from any and all disability support available to them.'

'But,' stammered Glenn, struggling to believe what he was hearing. 'How can this be? He always managed his diabetes so well.'

'Let's head back to my office so I can show you some of the photographs I have taken of your father's retinas,' said Dr. Bokher. They walked back to her office and Glenn waited as she retrieved the pictures from her filing cabinet. A file was brought out, labelled "Mr. Bertie Tebbhurst".

The images Dr. Bokher showed him were strange and alien, unlike any part of the human body Glenn had ever seen. It was a large, pale pink circle, with red blood vessels running through the centre of it. Dr. Bokher began to point out the different sections of the picture. She used words Glenn had never heard of before, like vitreous gel and macula, which were all essential to understanding of Bertie's blindness.

'How can diabetes cause blindness?' asked Glenn, staring down at the pictures.

'In my experience, diabetes can affect many parts of the eye, not just the retina, but the macula, lens and the optic nerve,' said Dr. Bokher. 'All of these affectations have the potential to severely damage the eyesight or blind people. Cataracts affect the lens and glaucoma affects the optic nerve, but in your father's case, I think we are looking at damage to the retina. That leaves us with two diagnoses: the first is diabetic retinopathy, which affects the blood vessels in the retina. The second is diabetic macula edema, or DME, which swells the macula, a small area of the retina.'

'And which do you think my father has?' Glenn asked.

'I believe your father has experienced diabetic retinopathy, at a severe late stage.'

'Is there a cure?' Glenn dared himself to ask. Dr. Bokher shook her head.

'At this stage?' she asked. 'No, and I would not recommend surgery in this case. But look, I have a consultation now. I'm going to recommend you visit a colleague of mine at the Memorial Sloane Kettering Cancer Centre,' said Dr. Bokher. 'He is an excellent ophthalmologist, his name is Dr. Luka, and I think he can tell you more about this condition. Here's his number, make an appointment, okay?'

'Thank you for your time, Dr. Bokher,' said Glenn.

'Take these with you,' said Dr. Bokher, handing Glenn copies of the retinal photographs. 'I hope you find the answers you're looking for. Say hi to your father for me.'

Glenn thanked Dr. Bokher again and left her office, feeling heavier than he had done all day. When he arrived home to Sutton Place he went straight to his father's office to call through to Dr. Luka, whose receptionist gave him an appointment that week.

That evening and the rest of the week he spent with his father and mother, helping them with the new experience of blindness. They took gentle walks with Bertie's new cane, and Glenn tried his best to remain cheerful. His father, who had been optimistic just days earlier, was becoming subdued and depressed. Glenn wished he knew how to comfort him or help him in some way.

When the time came for his appointment with Dr. Luka, Glenn was ready to know more. Arriving at the Memorial Sloane Kettering Cancer Centre, Glenn was amazed by the impressive architecture of the building. He wandered towards Dr. Luka's office after seeking directions from reception. He knocked and entered to find the doctor reviewing files on his desk.

'Ah, Mr. Tebbhurst, come in,' he said, smiling warmly. Glenn strode forward and shook the doctor's hand before settling down into the seat opposite his desk. Taking out the copies of the retinal scans Dr. Bokher had given him, Glenn put them down on the desk in front of Dr. Luka.

'Yes,' murmured the doctor, reviewing the pictures. 'Yes, Dr. Bokher explained the case to me. Very interesting, very interesting indeed.'

Glenn was not sure if interesting was the word he would have used to describe his father's situation. The word devastating seemed more appropriate.

'In your opinion, Dr. Luka,' Glenn asked. 'What has caused my father's blindness?'

'I would say that this is a case of proliferative diabetic retinopathy, or what we in medicine call PDR,' said Dr. Luka. 'I am sure Dr. Bokher explained to you how diabetics often suffer from diabetic retinopathy? The high levels of blood sugar associated with diabetes damage the blood vessels in the retina. You see the blood vessels here, in the picture? When diabetic retinopathy takes place, the blood vessels begin to haemorrhage, leaking fluid which then blurs the vision. The retina is the part of the eye that detects light, so as you can imagine, if these bloody leaks start appearing all over it, the transmission of light into signals sent via the optic nerve to the brain becomes faulty. Imagine how this looks at a much later stage. Do you see these white marks and scars in the picture? As the retinopathy develops, these new, abnormal blood vessels can multiply and destroy the cells in the retina.'

'But how could this all happen so quickly?' Glenn asked.

'It's a great question,' said the doctor. 'Retinopathy usually advances in stages. The first stage is what we might call a mild stage, a non-proliferative stage, where microaneurysms begin to grow in the retina's blood vessels. They can leak fluid into the retina. This can then progress to a more moderate stage; the blood vessels in the retina may change shape. They may enlarge and grow distorted, sometimes losing their ability to carry blood, which is the objective of a blood vessel. At the next stage, those blocked blood vessels begin to deprive the retina of blood so the retina starts to secrete growth factors.'

'Growth factors?' asked Glenn.

'These signal the retina to grown new blood vessels,' Dr. Luka explained. 'Then, at an extremely advanced stage, the stage your father has reached, we see a proliferative effect. The growth factors have signalled the retina to grow new blood cells, so the retina does. But these new blood cells are fragile. They grow along the inside surface of the retina and scar tissue caused by broken blood vessels can then cause retinal detachment. The retina can start to pull away from the underlying tissue. In severe cases, retinal detachment leaves people blind, permanently. I'm afraid to say that this is what I can conclude has happened to your father.'

'And can anything be done? Is there a cure or a treatment?' Glenn asked.

The doctor shook his head.

'At this stage? No,' he said.

'But why did no one see this happening?' Glenn demanded. 'How did his condition progress to this severe stage? I need answers, doc. I can't walk away without an answer!'

'Here's the sad truth for you, Mr. Tebbhurst,' sighed Dr. Luka. 'Around forty-five percent of Americans who have been diagnosed as diabetics, Type 1 or Type 2, have diabetic retinopathy. But maybe fifty percent know about it. Your father, I'm sorry to say, was not in the informed fifty percent.'

Glenn left Dr. Luka's office with a low, desperate sense of failure. He was determined to find more concrete answers to his questions and refused to accept that his father's eyesight was beyond medical help. But after ten more days of back and forth between specialists, bouncing from Dr. Luka's office to Dr. Naif at Bensinai, to Dr. Noelle, to Dr. Malik, to Dr. Mahone, Glenn gave up on finding satisfactory answers in New York. He decided it was time to head back to London and seek advice there.

Packing up his copies of the retinal photographs, Glenn gathered his things together.

'Will you come back and visit again soon?' Iris asked hopefully, sitting on his bed as he squeezed the last few things into his suitcase.

'Leave the boy alone, Iris,' chided Bertie from his armchair by the window. 'He has a life to lead, remember?'

Glenn smiled sadly at his mother and pulled her into a hug.

'Of course I will, Mom,' he said. 'I just wish I had found out what I needed to know here in New York. Perhaps the doctors on Harley Street will have something else to say.'

'We love you, son,' said Bertie, staring into the distance. 'Lord knows we love you.'

Glenn enjoyed one final evening with his parents before flying back to London. His mother cooked a delicious meal, and both Iris and Bertie seemed in lighter spirits.

'To your safe return,' said Bertie, raising a wobbly toast to his son and staring in the wrong direction.

'Thanks, Dad,' Glenn smiled sadly, raising his glass in return.

Leaving his parents behind was hard, especially as they seemed so vulnerable, but Glenn had to get back to London. After the long flight back, he arrived home at Ronda Round Manor in the early afternoon. He had called Eleanora when he landed to let her know when he would be home, and to his surprise, found a feast waiting for him. She had decked out their long dining table with all sorts of freshly cooked dishes.

Glenn set down his suitcases and waited for her clacking footsteps to reach him. Eleanora appeared, dressed in a smart green suit, and kissed him affectionately on the lips.

'Darling,' she said tenderly. 'Welcome home. Are you hungry?'

Glenn pulled his wife into a hug before looking down at the colourful spread of food. The smell was tantalising, but Glenn did not have time to stop and eat.

'But you only just arrived,' Eleanora exclaimed angrily when Glenn told her he would be leaving again shortly.

'I know, honey, but the specialist on Harley Street could only do today,' he said. 'It's today or next month. I'll be back tonight and we can see each other then?'

Eleanora stormed off, muttering to herself, but Glenn did not have time to pursue her with apologies. Heading straight back into London, Glenn arrived at Harley Street just in time for his appointment with Dr. Molner, one of London's finest ophthalmologists.

Within the warm, comfortable walls of Dr. Molner's consulting office, Glenn told the doctor all he had discovered, showing him the photographs of his father's retinas and listing the suspected diagnoses. When he had explained everything, and recounted his various meetings with doctors and ophthalmologists in New York, Dr. Molner nodded curtly.

'It seems you have done some fairly extensive research already, Mr. Tebbhurst,' he said, looking mildly impressed.

'I'm desperate,' said Glenn, honestly. 'I've been looking up doctors everywhere, research conferences, even seminars. There must be someone who can tell me more. Can you help me, doctor?'

The doctor leant back into his chair and turned away from Glenn for a moment. When he turned back to Glenn he had an expression of great sympathy on his face.

'Would you permit me to give you some advice, Mr. Tebbhurst?' he asked politely.

'Of course,' said Glenn.

'It seems to me that your research into the causes of your father's blindness is not bringing you any peace,' the doctor began. 'From the retinal photographs you have shown me, your father's eyesight is beyond repair. I am sorry to confirm the conclusions of the doctors you have previously seen. Preventative measures could have been taken, but at an earlier stage of development. Your father is blind, Mr. Tebbhurst and this is something you will have to accept. My advice to you, if you choose to take it, is to focus more on how your father can live with his blindness. If you are so desperate to continue researching, I propose you attend seminars directed towards living with blindness. There is one coming up next month in fact, in Aachen, Germany. It is run by the International Charity for the Blind, the ICB, and it is called "Beauty in the Dark". I'm afraid that is all I can suggest at this stage, and I do recommend the conference for you, sir, truly. That is my professional medical opinion on the matter.'

Glenn left Harley Street unsure of how he felt. One the one hand, he felt relieved that the past few weeks of constant searching could come to an end, but on the other hand, he felt like he had failed his father. That night he arrived home to an empty house for Eleanora had gone off to play bridge, perhaps to spite him for his hasty departure earlier that day. He went straight to his office and looked up the conference Dr. Molner had mentioned. He found it easily. The International Charity for the Blind had a website which excitedly announced their upcoming conference, 'Beauty in the Dark', which would take place over three days, including interactive workshops and various speakers. Glenn went to bed that night thinking of the conference before he fell into a deep and exhausted sleep.

As his first week back at work passed and he went from meeting to meeting at the DCF, Glenn's mind drifted back to the conference in Aachen. Used to investigating charities for the Foundation, Glenn researched the International Charity for the Blind and was impressed by their work across the globe. Perhaps the doctor was right, he thought. Perhaps he should stop searching for causes and cures and focus on addressing the problem at hand. Millions of people across the world had to live with blindness, his father was no different.

'Would you like to come?' Glenn asked Eleanora one evening after work, though he already knew what the answer would be. She seemed bored already by the time he had finished describing the charity, before he had even started to describe the conference.

'Aachen?' she said, raising her eyebrows in unison. 'God, who wants to go there? It's northern, it's cold, and they're still naming it wrong after all these years.'

'What do you mean?' asked Glenn, unable to keep the exasperation from his voice.

'Everyone knows it should be Aix-la-Chappelle,' said Eleanora. 'It belongs to France really.'

Glenn ignored his wife's snobbishness and her obsession with French history and set his mind to convincing her to let him go.

'It's only three days, honey,' he said. 'I think I should go. In fact, I need to go. For my father.'

'Must you always play the hero, Glenn?' his wife asked wearily.

'I can't help it,' Glenn said, smiling sadly. 'You wouldn't love me any other way, would you?'

Drawing close to his wife, Glenn took her in his arms. She would not look at him, choosing to stare at his chest instead.

'I suppose you had better go then,' she said stiffly.

'And you're sure you don't want to come?' asked Glenn. 'Sure you won't miss me too much?'

'Quite sure,' his wife sighed, smiling at last, unable to resist her husband's cheeky grin.

CHAPTER FOUR

Aachen was entering autumn, which gave the city more colour than it usually had, Glenn thought as his taxi pulled away from the airport. Glenn looked down at his watch to see how he was doing for time. The evening introduction to the conference was in thirty minutes, and he hoped he would not be late. He had been hoping he might be able to head to his hotel first, to put down his light travel case and relax after the flight, but time was pressing. He would go straight to the conference. In that taxi from the airport to the conference centre, Glenn looked around at the city, which he knew had once been the seat of the great King Charlemagne, and the crowning place of all German kings, and felt a little disappointed. It was in fact a grey and fairly unimpressive town.

Arriving at the conference centre, Glenn spotted a huge banner sporting the words: *'Beauty in the Dark': Living with Blindness*. It was, Glenn had learnt, the International Charity for Blindness' seventh annual speaking event. A strange, curious excitement rose in Glenn as he saw a small crowd of people making their way into the reception. He felt nervous, wondering if people might consider it strange that he was there on behalf of his father. He worried too that perhaps only doctors and professors would be attending, or perhaps only blind people. But as he stepped out of the taxi and glanced out around the crowd of people, Glenn saw to his relief that everyone looked like him, curiously making their way into the hall.

'*Danke*,' said Glenn, handing over the fare to the taxi driver, a robust, moustachioed German with red cheeks.

'*Bitte*,' the driver said back gruffly before pulling away. Glenn wheeled his suitcase into the reception, where he was happy to see a cloakroom full of other travel bags. Clearly he was not the only one who had travelled from afar. Spotting friendly faces, Glenn headed straight to the registration desk, where two young people were marking down people's names. He approached one of them, a thin and enthusiastic young woman, who quickly searched for his name on the list.

'*Ja*, Glenn Tebbhurst, we have you right here,' the girl said formally. 'Here is your welcome pack and your name badge. Is this your first time at an ICB event?'

'It is,' said Glenn, smiled confidently. 'I'm a bit of a newbie. Should I be nervous, miss?'

'No, sir,' laughed the girl.

'Well then, I'll take your word for it,' he grinned at her.

'*Willkommen*, Mr. Tebbhurst,' the girl smiled, blushing slightly. 'Now, please make your way into the hall. In your own time, sir.'

Glenn looked over at the small queue forming by the doorway into the conference hall. A tall, well-built man with a head of blonde hair was welcoming people into the hall with handshakes, speaking English and various other languages with a broad German accent. Perhaps due to his smartly fitting grey designer suit, and his chiselled jawline, the man reminded Glenn of an action hero. He had that same distinguished quality about him.

'*Hallo*, welcome,' he said to the guests, welcoming them one by one. A huge poster caught Glenn's eye, where the same man was presented in a portrait photograph next to the ICB's logo. His face looked even more angular in the photograph, Glenn thought. The man had bright blue eyes, set off by pink lips and a rather charismatic smile. The poster looked more like a political campaign poster than a poster for a charity fundraising event. Glenn turned back to the man shaking hands and prepared to meet him. Perhaps he would be the answer to all the problems he was having with Bertie, Glenn thought.

'*Das ist Herbert Farrand*,' said the girl at the reception desk, who had noticed him watching the man. Glenn turned around to look at the woman addressing him, delighted for a chance to practice his German. But after a few sentences, no doubt noticing his bewilderment, the girl behind reception chuckled and began to speak English.

'It's okay, you can speak English,' she said. 'This is an international conference after all.'

'And there was me thinking I was being polite!' Glenn chuckled, winking at the young woman. 'You can't blame a fella for trying, but I can see around here I've got competition. What's his name?'

'Herbert Farrand,' the girl nodded. 'He is the President of the ICB, and fortunately speaks English very well.'

Glenn looked over at Herbert Farrand, taking in the lines of his suit and the easy joviality he seemed to be creating around him. He was speaking fluent Italian now and charming a group of men in suits.

'He has quite an interesting story,' said the girl. 'He studied commerce at the technical institute in Leipzig. That's where I'm from, so I know. Then, if I recall correctly, he opened up an Italian restaurant that failed and then went on to get a job as a clerk in a trading company. It's funny how people's lives change.'

Glenn wondered why the girl was telling him all of this, but listened curiously all the same. It seemed odd that a man with no background in charity work could now be running the ICB. And yet, looking at Herbert Farrand, Glenn saw a man who seemed totally at home in his role.

'How did he start working with the blind?' Glenn asked.

'He started working for a laboratory later in his life,' she said. 'That laboratory did testing for lenses, cutting lenses for glasses,' said the woman. 'From that he had an introduction to the world of blindness and the visually impaired. Part of the job was to send a lot of these lenses to charities. That's where he hooked onto some worldwide charity as a clerk, and had the idea of establishing a charity for the blind.'

'Quite a story,' said Glenn, impressed, before thanking the girl and joining the queue. When it was his turn to reach Herbert Farrand, Glenn was glad to know a bit more about the handsome man's story.

'*Hallo*, welcome,' said the President, pulling Glenn into an unsurprisingly strong handshake. Glenn looked into the blue eyes he had seen on the poster and found them twinkling and curious.

'It's great to be here,' said Glenn, grinning at his host. 'Looks like you've got one hell of a show in store for us, Mr. Farrand.'

'Ah, an American!' smiled Herbert, his eyebrows jumping up in appreciation. He flashed a smile, revealing two rows of perfectly pearly teeth. 'You are most welcome, sir.'

'Thanks,' said Glenn, touched by the warm welcome. 'I'm Glenn, Glenn Tebbhurst. You'll know my name by the end of the weekend!'

'Will I?' laughed Herbert. 'Well, Glenn, Glenn Tebbhurst, you are most welcome,' he said before turning to the next guest. '*Hallo*, welcome,' he said, leaving Glenn to go and find his seat.

Glenn looked around at the large conference room and saw that he had arrived just in time. There were hundreds of attendees, many of whom had clearly arrived early to find good seats. Glenn walked quickly towards an empty chair he saw not too far from the podium, and settled down. Glancing around at his neighbours, he noted that the conference had drawn a variety of people, some of whom were blind. Glenn recognised them immediately by the long white canes propped up against their chairs and knees. His mind flashed back momentarily to his father, whose vacant gaze had disturbed Glenn immensely first of all. Now, seeing the elderly woman next to him stare happily into the middle distance, and a young man three seats away looking contentedly into the void in front of him, Glenn felt a relieving sense of ease.

Before he could study his neighbours more closely, the crowd erupted into applause. Looking to the podium, Glenn saw Herbert Farrand make his way to the stand, welcomed by an older looking man who stood at the podium momentarily speaking into the microphone. He looked taller than he did up close, Glenn noted, watching as the President nodded in thanks. The room slowly began to hush.

'Ladies and gentlemen, ladies and gentlemen, thank you,' he said in his Germanic accent, smiling and waving at the crowd. 'Thank you for this warm applause and thank you all for being here. I would like to launch this weekend's conference with a small introduction. As some of you know, and some do not, my name is Herbert Farrand. I am the Founder and President of the International Charity for the Blind. It is my great pleasure to welcome you all today to the ICB's 2011 conference, poetically titled: "Beauty in the Dark: Living with Blindness". We have a fantastic line up of seminars and workshops awaiting you over the next few days, and we hope you can walk away from us here in Aachen with more knowledge and understanding than you have now of living with blindness. For there are many different ways to go blind, but the end result is always the same: you can't see.'

Some people in the crowd laughed at this, but Glenn was not sure if it had been meant as a joke or not. Herbert Farrand seemed to have a constant smile on his face. Glenn wondered if he ever stopped smiling.

'Science,' Farrand continued, 'over all these years, has never found a cure for total blindness. Of course, failing eyesight can be improved, and there are stages where further deterioration can be avoided. There are injections, processes that can partially restore the retina, laser treatments, but so often such methods fail and in the end, people find themselves in darkness: in total blindness.

'Do people live with blindness? Can they thrive? And how?' he went on. 'Some people go on for thirty years after that fatal diagnosis. Some go on for one hundred years. Indeed, some are born blind and have known nothing else. Some of those who suffer from blindness become depressed and fed up with their situation. There are suicides, oh yes, many, and many attempts. Others simply don't know how to live with it and become dependent on their loved ones, on social security systems. Oh yes, they become truly handicapped. They lose their initiative. But, ladies and gentlemen, yes, some people live with blindness, and not only live with blindness, but thrive in their lives despite being blind.

'That is why we are here today,' he said, raising his arms in welcome. 'We are here today to learn, simply, how to live with blindness. Now, I will turn you over to our most famous professor, from the University of Berlin, Professor Emeritus, no less, who has been a visiting professor in Oxford and the Karolinska Institute in Stockholm. He is the ultimate doctor-turned-professor, an ophthalmologist who is widely admired for his specialisation in the psychology that leads to the optimism that allows every blind person to live happily ever after. Ladies and gentlemen, it is my great pleasure and honour to introduce Professor Steinmetzer.'

The audience erupted into applause once more as Herbert Farrand stood down to welcome a thin man with high cheekbones and brilliantly bright eyes to the podium. The new speaker walked slowly and confidently.

'Thank you, ladies and gentlemen, thank you, and thank you, Herbert,' said Professor Steinmetzer in an elderly German accent. Glenn noticed that the professor twitched slightly as he spoke, perhaps from nerves or perhaps out of habit. He also noticed that a great hush had fallen over the conference room as a reverence for the speaker became apparent in the air.

'It is my great pleasure and honour to be here today,' Professor Steinmetzer began. 'I have always supported and admired the great work of the ICB. Now, what year is it?' he asked the audience. People began to laugh. Steinmetzer laughed too, his elderly face crinkling into a hundred wrinkles.

'It's important for my speech!' he cried, laughing heartily. 'Alright, alright, I know. It's 2011. I have some figures from the World Health Organization here. Ladies and gentlemen, did you know that across the globe, an estimated 285 million people are visually impaired, with thirty-nine million of those fully blind? Did you also know that eight percent of all visual impairment can be prevented or cured? Considering that you are all here today to learn about living with blindness, I suspect your interests are in the twenty percent that can't. As Mr. Farrand just told us, there are many ways in which people go blind. I can tell you that around eighty percent of the world's blind population is over fifty. Ageing is a sure culprit. But how many children are hit with blindness in childhood because of malnutrition and mistreatment? Some people contract diseases that lead to blindness, some are hit by environmental factors: they go blind just because the sun burnt their eyes in the desert. I could list a hundred scientific conditions and causes of blindness to you today, ladies and gentlemen, but that is not why we are here.

'I have family members who are blind,' said the professor. 'I am sure some of you here today are in the same position as me, wondering what we can do to ease their suffering or help them live as normal a life as possible.'

Glenn shifted uncomfortably in his seat, thinking of his father. His father did not even know he was there, sat in a conference, learning about blindness for his sake. Glenn wondered what Bertie would say if he could see him there, but Professor Steinmetzer exuded a confidence that he found reassuring. With every passing moment, he knew the conference was where he was meant to be.

'Well, I have transitioned from a normal doctor, a specialist in ophthalmology as Mr. Farrand told you, into the field of blindness-related psychology. Why, you may ask? Well, I have realised that psychology for a blind person, who is beyond treatment and cures, is more important than science. Once you are blind you are blind, but the rest of your body has to live.'

At this the crowd broke into a fresh round of applause, celebrating this powerful statement. The woman next to Glenn rapped her walking cane against her chair in approval. Glenn himself was hanging on the professor's every word, deeply impressed by the man's authority on a subject now so dear to his heart.

'I am here to tell you my approach to living with blindness, developed over years of research and personal experience with the blind,' the professor continued. 'I believe everyone must accept destiny, whether that's to be rich and live with wealth; poor and live with poverty; or to even live under an oppressive regime, with no freedom of expression, and accept the rule of a dictator who tortures people for speaking their mind. Do you know that barely ten percent of the world's population lives in a true democracy? Can I be so bold as to make a controversial statement here, ladies and gentlemen? People who have lack of liberty and food are much worse off than people who lack sight.'

The crowd burst into applause again at this statement. The blind woman next to Glenn began to whoop with appreciation. She was calling something in an Eastern European language, perhaps Hungarian.

'That, ladies and gentlemen, is my first principle,' said Professor Steinmetzer. 'Live with your destiny.'

Something stirred in Glenn's mind at this. He remembered what his mother had said about his father. *You know your father. He thinks it's destiny.*

'The next principle I want to impress upon you all,' Professor Steinmetzer continued, 'is that sight is one of five senses, meaning that someone living with blindness still lives with four other senses. Remember what I said earlier: once you are blind you are blind, but the rest of your body has to live. Blindness should be accepted as a physical impediment, just like someone living without a right arm. Does he not still have a left arm? And can someone who has an allergy to almonds or peanuts not go on to live a healthy, normal life? Those things are also permanent physical impediments.

'Ladies and gentlemen, there are some here today who live with blindness,' the professor continued. 'I have seen many cases in which a body suffering from loss of sight compensates in some other force. As a doctor, as a friend and as a researcher, I have seen cases of this: where the body starts compensating for the physical impediment of blindness. I'm going to tell you a story. I once met a little boy, aged twelve years old, who could multiply eight numbers by seven numbers. To make that clear, that's trillions by billions! He was a real jock in maths, and I was convinced it was his brain's way of compensating for his blindness. I also met a man in Pakistan who had memorised the Quran, despite his blindness. I met a woman who could recount thirty pages of poetry, and remembered every line and rhyme perfectly. She could not read as we who see can read, but her capacity to memorise words was exceptional. I have a theory also that if a person is blind, maybe he or she is compensated in other ways: with greater fitness, a better heart and better circulation. There's a study group here to talk about that this weekend.

'There's also a study group here run by one of the remarkable women we will introduce soon. Bettina from Germany, from this great country where we are today, will explain to you how the blind can live as if they have full eyesight. She will take you into her world and teach you how to make a cup of tea: how to boil the kettle, pour the water into a cup, add your milk, sugar, lemon, and not spill a drop of it on yourself. She will teach you how to dictate like a scribe and read like she's reading one hundred and fifty words a minute. Under Bettina's instruction, you could even take shorthand. She will teach you miracles! I hope you are all as excited as I am.'

For the first time the crowd began to mutter, breaking the reverent silence that had existed before. There was an excited flow of whispers making its way around the room at the mention of this workshop. Glenn too was excited. This Bettina, whoever she was, clearly knew how to live with blindness, and then some. He could not wait to share what he learnt that weekend with his father, and felt, with a pang of guilt, that his father should have been there with him.

'Of course, I will tell you also to come to my workshop!' Professor Steinmetzer continued. The crowd laughed at this, as the professor had opened his arms in mock welcome. 'And I'll tell you tried and tested ways to handle the psychological strain of blindness, from the time you get up, put on your makeup, and get dressed without anyone else. I'm not saying you'll be able to drive, ladies and gentlemen, but I am saying you can wake up and face the day like any other human being, without the fear of accidents or vulnerability. That's what I am here to teach you in my workshops over the next three days. I hope to see you there, though I understand I have stiff competition. Without further ado, let me turn you over to the main personalities of this conference, these icons of teaching and gurus of guidance for living a different kind of life. They will be your champions for the next three days. Back to you, Herbert.'

The crowd erupted into applause once more, and Glenn looked around curiously, as excited as everyone else to hear from the woman named Bettina. He watched as Professor Steinmetzer went back to his seat, and Herbert Farrand came back to the podium.

'Thank you, Professor Steinmetzer, as ever, for your rousing words of support and courage for the blind,' he began, raising his arms for another round of applause. The crowd clapped and clapped for the professor, who smiled and waved from his chair. 'And now I have the honour of introducing the stars of our conference, the leading lights for blind people across the world. May I please introduce Bettina Hartmann.'

Glenn waited with everyone else for Bettina to appear. A hush fell over them as, slowly, a tall, curvaceous woman in her late twenties stood up on the stage, close to Professor Steinmetzer. Her hair was a delicate shade of blonde and she gazed ahead with great elegance. Even from that distance, far away across the room, Glenn could see that she was an exceptionally beautiful woman. He could just make out the pale, pretty blue of her eyes. She had been sat in a row with five other women beside Herbert, who now stood up and went to the podium. The women sat around her were also incredibly beautiful. Glenn wished he was closer so he could see them better, but before he could attempt to move, Herbert had started to speak once more.

'This beautiful woman was educated in Würzburg, one of the best universities in Germany,' said Farrand. 'She was born blind and has lived all her life with blindness. She grew up with parents who had no trace of hereditary blindness. This is not uncommon in the blind community: many blind people are alienated from the rest of their family by their condition. Bettina, for example, has a brother with full eyesight. Bettina is an example to us all, and the team leader of this group of fantastic women who will be collectively guiding the workshops this weekend.'

Herbert began to clap and the rest of the room followed suit. Bettina, who gazed placidly ahead, nodded slightly in thanks and sat down. Glenn watched as she gracefully rearranged her long skirt and tucked a stray lock of blonde hair behind her ear.

'Next, I would like to introduce Laura Jones from Chesham, in Buckinghamshire, England,' said Herbert. A girl with long red hair and bright green eyes stood up, dressed in a smart black suit. She looked around the same age as Bettina and had an incredible figure. When she smiled, Glenn found it hard to look away. What a dazzling beauty, he thought, admiring her from afar.

'She too was born blind. Abandoned by her parents, she has lived through many ups and downs,' said Herbert. 'Fostered by families with no experience of the blind, she suffered great discomfort during her youth, and she can tell you all about it. She can also tell you about her development as a person and how she overcame the difficulties of her youth. In fact, you will love speaking with her as every story she tells seems to be packed full of drama! And, I must not forget to mention, she is also an exceptional businesswoman.'

'Oh Herbert!' squeaked Laura, frowning in mock dismay at the President before sitting down once more. Herbert laughed at this and shook his head at the audience.

'I was told to give accurate introductions!' he squeaked, his smile wider than ever. Glenn was surprised to see that every one of the women sat in the line sat next to Bettina and Laura was blind. They all seemed so accomplished, especially Bettina Hartman. He was happy that the seminars would be led by people who had truly experienced blindness and could speak from first-hand experience.

'Next, all the way from New Orleans, please welcome Odile Brown,' said Herbert. A woman who looked much older than the other women in the line stood up. Though older, she had a timeless cuteness about her, especially in her face, which was cupped by a perfectly blonde bob. She was slim, quite shapely, and very pale. 'Odile is here to talk to anyone who is interested about living with blindness whilst raising a family. Odile knows what it means to be a blind housewife raising her children and has been through great difficulties in her life. She has Type 1 diabetes, which she was born with, and subsequently no longer has her sight. Odile can address the question of raising a family whilst coping with the challenges of blindness and cyclical moods.'

Odile smiled into the distance before sitting down slowly as a loud round of applause serenaded her. Herbert cleared his throat and went quickly onto his next introduction.

'Elfrida Diaz-Cruz is a Spanish teacher from Mexico,' he began. A short young woman with big, bright eyes and thick black hair stood up proudly. Even from afar Glenn could appreciate the woman's classic Hispanic beauty. 'Elfrida was a late developer in blindness. She lived with both the normal teenage experience of sight and the later loss in her twenties. We who can see can only imagine what that must have been like. To see the world and then to lose that ability must have been heartbreaking, but Elfrida put her sorrow aside and entered the world of teaching. She found solace and dignity in her profession. She is here to talk to us this weekend about how to live with blindness through good education.'

The crowd applauded Elfrida rapturously and waited for the next introduction. Herbert began to introduce a young Burmese-Chinese woman called Zu-Ting. She was small and fragile-looking with a short black haircut. Dressed up in an exquisite traditional costume, she, like the four other women, was beautiful. She nodded her head shyly as she stood up.

'Zu-Ting's story is one we might find hard to imagine here in Europe,' said Herbert. 'Her blindness developed after years of work as a child. It is no secret that child labour is a huge problem in the developing world, and Zu-Ting's story should serve as a terrible example of that. Forced to work long hours in difficult conditions, Zu-Ting lost her childhood and her sight. This is a case of tragedy and strength, one we can all learn from and be inspired by.'

Glenn was stunned by the variety of life experiences they were being introduced to. He was impressed by the vast outreach of the International Charity of the Blind: truly an international effort.

'And last, but not least of course, we have Christina Binder,' said Herbert, when the applause for Zu-Ting died down and the young Asian woman sat back in her seat. Christina, a young, blonde woman with clear Germanic roots stood up and raised a hand shyly to the crowd. She was thin, with an impressive height that added to her striking appearance.

'Christina has lived the life of a character in a dramatic novel, in the way that reality often surpasses fiction,' said Herbert. 'Her blindness also came at a later date in life. It was contracted in a jungle whilst she was on mission in the Central African Republic. She went there as a missionary, having dedicated her life to God as a nun, but her experience did not go to plan. I will leave her to tell her own story in her workshop this weekend, and encourage you to learn from her experience, for it is truly remarkable.'

The applause for Christina was hesitant at first due to the tragic nature of her story, but it eventually increased. After all, the young woman had not stopped smiling throughout Herbert's introduction.

'Now I have introduced you to the pillars of the seminar,' Herbert went on, when the applause for Christina came to an end. 'I can only say welcome once more, and how happy I am to see so many people gathered here to learn about blindness. The workshops begin tomorrow and I look forward to seeing you all there. If anyone cares to join us to toast to the occasion, we will be serving drinks in the Charlemagne Room now, next to reception. Otherwise: until tomorrow!'

Herbert Farrand's final address was met by rapturous applause from the audience. Glenn clapped along, still waiting for all the information he had received that evening to sink in. Without noticing, he yawned, and caught the eye of someone sitting nearby who tutted disapprovingly. Glenn felt extremely rude for he did not want to appear bored. In truth he had not felt this stimulated since he had found out about his father's blindness. He felt like he had been walking around in a dull, grey cloud since his trip to New York, but now, finally it seemed like relief was at hand.

However, even Glenn had to admit he was exhausted.

Following the crowd out of the conference hall, Glenn decided to skip the drinks in the Charlemagne Room. Instead, he headed to his hotel, just a short walk from the conference centre, where he knew a large, soft bed would be waiting for him. He called through to Eleanora before he went to bed but there was no answer. He assumed she was at bridge club and decided to try again in the morning. Dialling through to another number, Glenn waited for the connection to click into place.

'Hello?' came his mother's voice.

'Mom,' said Glenn, happy to hear her voice. 'How are you doing? It's Glenn.'

'Hello, honey,' said Iris, sounding deflated but happy to hear him. 'We're doing okay.'

Glenn heard the exhausted strain in his mother's voice and did not believe her.

'Mom, how are you really doing?' he asked. There was a pause on the line, followed by a deep sigh.

'Well, honey, it's not easy,' was all she said. 'But let's not talk about me. How're things on that side of the pond? How's that wife of yours?'

'Okay,' said Glenn. 'I'm in Aachen, in Germany.'

'Germany?' yelped Iris. 'What are you doing there? You on a business trip, honey?'

'No, I'm at a conference,' he said. 'Listen, Mom, is Dad there? I'd love to chat with him for a minute.'

'Of course, honey,' she said. 'He's been playing dominos with himself by feeling the shapes of the holes with his fingers. I think it's keeping him occupied. Hold on, I'll get him.'

Glenn waited as he heard his mother's feet wander across the wooden floors of their Sutton Place home, searching for his father.

'Glenn!' came his father's bright but slightly croaky voice. 'What are you doing calling an old man like me? Shouldn't you be out saving the world?'

'Hi Bertie,' said Glenn, smiling into the phone. 'I just wanted to call and see how you're doing.'

'I'm doing just fine, son,' said his father. 'All the better for hearing from you. Your mother tells me you're in Germany? Is that true? Eating sauerkraut or apple strudel, huh? You always liked that as a boy.'

'I'm here for a conference, Dad,' Glenn told his father. 'It's being given by a charity called the International Charity for the Blind about living with blindness. There are some amazing speakers here, who really thrive living with blindness. I just wanted to find out more,' he added, embarrassed. 'To help you, and advise you, when things start changing.'

'Oh, things have already started changing, Glenn,' sighed Bertie. 'But thank you. You're a good boy.'

'I'll let you know what I find out over the weekend. There is hope here, I can feel it. The energy these people have is like nothing I never expected. I wish you could experience it,' said Glenn. 'And, Dad?'

'Yes, son,' said Bertie, whose voice was breaking slightly.

'I love you,' said Glenn. 'Don't lose hope, okay?'

'Never,' croaked Bertie. 'Goodbye, Glenn.'

Glenn knew his father could not speak anymore. He did the same thing when emotion threatened to overwhelm him. He did not like anyone to see or hear him cry, not even his wife; especially not his wife.

'Glenn?' came his mother's voice.

'Mom, hi,' said Glenn.

'Your father's tired,' said Iris gently. 'He needs to rest now. Thanks for calling, honey. Will you be safe over there?'

'Mom, I'm in Germany, not Central Africa!' laughed Glenn, thinking of the story of Christina, who had lost her sight in the jungle.

'Alright,' chuckled Iris. 'You take care now, honey.'

'You too, Mom,' said Glenn, before hanging up the phone.

As he lay back on his pillows, Glenn's mind reeled with everything he had learnt that day. The words of Herbert Farrand and Professor Steinmetzer echoed in his head, reassuring him that everything was going to be okay in a way that his father could no longer do. Tiredness washed over him and just before he fell asleep, a face stirred in his memory, a face encircled by luminous blonde hair, and a pair of bright blue eyes.

CHAPTER FIVE

When Glenn reached the conference centre that morning, he could hardly contain his excitement. The list of workshops in his welcome pack was tantalising. He had already earmarked the workshops he would go to, starting with 'The Philosophy of Blindness,' an introductory workshop given by Bettina Hartman. Entering through the reception, Glenn saw people milling around, clutching their schedules and chattering excitedly to one another. Some of the blind attendees of the conference moved and tapped their white canes, walking gracefully through the crowds. Glenn wondered if his father would ever walk smartly through a crowd like that, but after the previous day's introductory speech, for the first time, he cradled hope in his heart.

Walking deeper into the conference centre, Glenn soon found what he was looking for. A small sign notified guests that 'The Philosophy of Blindness' seminar would commence at 10 a.m. He popped his head around the door to see who was attending the seminar. The room was not yet full, with plenty of empty spaces. At the front of the room, sorting through a pile of papers with small, gentle movements, sat Bettina Hartman.

Glenn took a small intake of breath; this was the first time he had seen her up close. The beautiful features he had seen from far away yesterday now came into focus. Her nose was delicate and her blue eyes were framed by pale, sandy eyebrows, shaped into perfect arches. The entrancing glow of her blonde hair was intriguing to him for it seemed natural and effervescent all at once. Pausing to watch her for a moment, Glenn then walked in quickly, happy for the chance to greet Bettina at her rostrum. Slowing down as he neared her, he realised he did not know how to approach a blind person without seeming intrusive or rude. He suddenly had the same uncomfortable feeling he had had when he had first stood in front of his blind father. Glenn noticed how Bettina wore conservative cottons, a dark blue coat and a pair of grey silk trousers which shone in the light of the conference room. Her beautiful, misty, pale-blue eyes gazed ahead of her as she glided her hands through the air, as if orchestrating the movements of her body. For a moment, Glenn did not know if she could see him or not, but before he said anything, she smiled.

'Hello,' she said, still staring ahead. 'Are you here for the seminar?'

It was the first time Glenn had heard Bettina speak, and she had a light, strong voice, with barely a hint of a German accent in her English.

'I am,' smiled Glenn. 'I wanted to introduce myself before you began. I'm Glenn Tebbhurst.'

'Have you come all the way from America to our little workshop, Mr. Tebbhurst?' Bettina asked, her face barely moving as she expressed surprise.

'No, I've come from London,' said Glenn. 'I am American, but I live and work in England now—'

For some reason, Glenn hesitated before adding: 'with my wife.'

Somehow, something wanted him to keep that secret. He felt strange.

'You are very welcome here, Mr. Tebbhurst,' said Bettina, smiling warmly once more.

'Please, call me Glenn.'

'You are very welcome here, Glenn,' Bettina said again, laughing lightly. 'Welcome to our seminar.'

'Oh, I feel welcome!' smiled Glenn, flashing her his most friendly smile before realising she couldn't see it.

Not wanting to distract Bettina further, especially as the workshop would begin soon, Glenn gave his thanks and went to find a seat. He saw a couple of people chatting in one row and went to join them. They all introduced themselves. Margarita and Francine were two Italian women who cared for the blind in Rome, and Samuel, who sat next to them, was a Catholic priest who took care of blind people in his local community centre in Brandenburg. Glenn was happy to tell them all that he was there for his father.

'I just want to help him through this,' he explained. 'He's a great guy but he's going to struggle. I've spent my life helping others and now my Dad needs help and I'm totally stuck.'

'Your Dad's a lucky man,' said one of the Italian women, tears brimming in her eyes.

'I think I'm the lucky one, being here to meet all you fine folks,' he said, smiling at everyone. He thought he heard the Italian ladies sigh slightly, and somehow, out of the corner of his eye, Glenn could have sworn he saw Bettina watching him, if it was possible for a blind person to watch with their ears.

When the room was almost full, Bettina stood and glided over to the main door quite effortlessly and closed it, indicating that her workshop was about to begin.

'Welcome, ladies and gentlemen, to my study group entitled 'The Philosophy of Blindness,' she said.

The room clapped in appreciation. All eyes were fixed on Bettina as she navigated the aisles gracefully, back to her rostrum. Glenn was surprised to see that she did not use her white cane to do this, and wondered how blind people might sharpen their memories as a result, and if this was why she did not require it, for Bettina seemed to know her way around the podium as if it were her home. Once at the rostrum, she cleared her throat lightly, raised her long porcelain-white arms with the elegance of a ballet dancer, and began to speak.

'During my time here, I have already been listening to some of you chatting and socialising,' she said simply, smiling as she gazed into the distance. 'I want to tell you how I am going to approach the seminar before I begin. I want to divide this session into stages, so to speak. First, I want to address the psychology of living with blindness, the first and certainly the highest and hardest hurdle we and our loved ones face. And then I'd like to talk about acceptance, because I would like to discuss with you all the concept of accepting blindness as destiny. Then I will move onto the more physical and philosophical augmentation of the senses relative to blindness. This may sound strange to you all – especially those of you who have studied conventional philosophy – that this acceptance that other senses will be heightened is a philosophical acceptance. But I will lay down my experience, inform you all, and then, allow you to judge for yourselves.'

Bettina continued to talk until she directed everyone in the room to pick up the blindfold in front of them and cover their eyes. Everyone did so obediently, smiling with mixtures of nerves and excitement.

'Now, this is just a taster today,' she said. 'Tomorrow we will launch the *Blindness in the Dark* exercise, whereby two volunteers will experience what it feels like to live a whole day as a blind person. For today, however, I just want to show you what happens to your senses when you lose your sight. So for all of you who have not yet put on your blindfold, please do so now.'

Glenn pulled the thick blindfold over his eyes and settled himself in his seat. It felt very strange to be suddenly in the dark in a room full of strangers.

'How are you feeling?' Bettina asked them all. 'Are you ready for a few experiments?'

The crowd laughed nervously, but Glenn doubted that anyone in that room was truly worried. Bettina had a curiously effortless way of making them all feel safe.

'Who can tell me where the window is?' she asked the room. 'Anyone? Just raise your hands and point. Mm hmm. Alright, anyone else?'

The room was full of the rustling sound of people raising their arms and pointing at the window. Glenn made a guess but in truth was not entirely sure. Bettina neither confirmed nor denied anyone's answers. She said nothing, but Glenn heard her footsteps walking towards the window. They were particularly loud and Glenn felt his ears tingling at the sound. His hearing seemed already twice as strong. With a smooth whoosh, the sound of the window opening filled the room. Suddenly the outside world could be heard: the birds singing, the cars driving, the wind rustling gently through the trees. Glenn felt the cool breeze tickle his neck and almost shivered. He felt the breeze on his ears too, and on his cheeks. He felt it brush against the back of his hands.

'Now, who can tell me where the window is?' Bettina asked them. Again, the rustling sound of arms rising filled the room. Glenn paid attention to his body. He felt the breeze tickling the left side of his neck, and the birds were twittering louder in his left ear. The window would have to be to the left of him somewhere. He raised his arm and pointed.

'Okay,' laughed Bettina. 'Take off your blindfolds.'

Glenn took off his blindfold along with everyone else and was happy to see that he was pointing in the direction of the open window. Bettina walked over and closed the window once more.

'Well done,' she said, making her way back to the podium. 'Who can tell me if the window was in the same place on their first guess or on their second guess?' she asked.

'Neither!' laughed one burly looking man who spoke with a Scots accent.

'No problem, sir,' said Bettina, smiling warmly. 'Anyone else?'

'I guessed right the second time,' said Glenn.

'Thank you, Glenn,' said Bettina, and Glenn was surprised that she remembered him. His face went a little pink and he was glad she could not see it. 'And could you tell us the difference in the first and second time? What informed your decision to choose the correct direction?'

'When you opened the window I could feel things,' said Glenn, quite pleased to be the one to be asked. 'I could smell… the freshly cut grass outside. The birds were singing and the air coming in through the window was cool against my skin.'

'Excellent,' smiled Bettina. 'How would you describe your senses in that moment? Normal, or heightened?'

'Heightened, without a doubt,' said Glenn. 'It doesn't get more heightened than that! I just wonder what it would be like to do this in London or in New York.'

'Thanks, Glenn,' said Bettina, raising her long arms to start speaking once more. 'Living without sight, whether born blind or losing it at a later date, means that one naturally evolves to hear better, smell better, feel better and, some would argue, even think better. Various scientists have proven that people who live with blindness have a more accurate memory. They say also that they will be able to understand mathematics better, and calculate figures better. I have long held the belief that the blind have a far greater capacity to associate events. The associations I want to talk about are the moments we experience in our infancy, say, two years old. The feelings and instincts, the sounds and smells we experience in those moments can be evoked anew at age eight, twenty-eight, eighty-eight, whatever. And this happens because at that age we are less reliant on only our sight. We delight in all of our senses. We are discovering the world and so we swim and dance and sing in our senses!' Bettina was triumphant, eyes closed, arms raised, a beautiful smile stretched across her face. 'It is one of my favourite theories,' she continued, lowering her graceful arms back down by her side, 'and an advantage we – the blind – have over people who can see. There is a heavy correlation between events in our memories. Now,' said Bettina, drawing her hands together. 'Does anyone here today have any questions for me?'

For a moment the room was silent as people processed the philosophies Bettina had shared with them. Then a tall man with greying hair who sat beside a woman whose vacant gaze could only indicate blindness raised his hand.

'Please, go ahead,' said Bettina, who seemed to sense the man's movement before he had even cleared his throat to announce himself.

'I was just wondering, Miss Hartman,' the man began in a soft French accent. 'When did you accept your own blindness?'

'Well, I was born blind,' said Bettina. 'I never knew what it was like to see. My parents were good people. They were kind and supportive, and my mother especially tried her best to make me feel normal as I grew up. She knew that there were other children around me who were cycling and playing with balls and watching amazing things on television sets, so she taught me how to make the most of the rest of my body. She's my hero actually. Are there any other questions? Who else has something to ask?'

'You seem very well read for a blind person,' said a woman in the audience. 'Have you studied Braille? How did you have access to so many ideas?'

'Do you have a Kindle?' Bettina asked the woman.

'Uh, yes, I do,' said the woman.

'So do I,' smiled Bettina. 'I'm an avid reader, if I can use that word, because in fact somebody else reads the books to me. Yes, I have studied Braille, and that was how I learnt to read. But these days I am using audio books to educate myself. I have a whole library on my Kindle, and the list is only getting longer.'

The room chuckled warmly at this. Glenn watched the young woman speaking to them with such admiration. Bettina was proving to them that her blindness was no impediment to her dreams. But there was one question Glenn was burning to ask, and it came from a fear he had for his father. He worried that now his father was blind, he would no longer be able to lead a normal social life. Bertie Tebbhurst had so many friends and was such a man about town. Glenn wondered how many of his friends would stick around when he gazed eerily into space and thought every woman that approached their table was beautiful.

'Is it difficult to socialise with people who have full sight?' Glenn asked Bettina, unable to keep the question inside any longer. 'Or do you find yourself mostly making friends with the blind?'

A man in the row in front of him looked around and glared at Glenn as if he had asked something extremely rude.

'What kind of question is that?' said the man in a sharp Polish accent.

'It's a question!' laughed Glenn. 'Come on! Can't a guy ask a simple question?'

'I recognise your voice, Glenn,' said Bettina, smiling. 'That's a tough question.'

'I'm sorry,' said Glenn quickly, shaking his head. 'Listen, forget I said anything.'

'Certainly not,' laughed Bettina. 'I asked for questions, did I not? Now, to answer yours, I have many friends with 20/20 vision. In fact, most of my friends are full-sighted. I like to challenge them. We often play hide and seek in big groups and most of the time I find whatever is hidden before they do. I cannot rely on my sight, so I rely on senses that are so much more heightened than theirs. Every Easter we play, and I love it. We play based on clues. Last year I won against ten other people, all with good eyesight. I do not judge anyone by their ability to see or not see.'

Glenn was heartened by Bettina's answer. It gave him hope that Bertie's friends in New York would not abandon him. Winning at hide and seek despite being blind was exactly the kind of thing his father would be great at. Glenn grinned at the thought. He was grinning throughout the last few questions and answers.

'Okay, ladies and gentlemen, thank you very much for your time and participation this morning. Now we have a choice of options for you to choose from,' she said. 'You can go to the lovely Laura's workshop entitled *Travelling with Blindness*. Odile will be delivering another, that one is called *Blindness at Home*. Then there is a workshop called *Sports and Blindness*, for this please follow Elfrida to her conference room. Zu-Ting will also be holding a seminar on *Politics and Blindness*. And for anyone interested in religion, Christina will be talking about *Divinity and Blindness*. I wish you all an informative and educational few days here during the conference.'

As chairs scraped and people made their way to the exit, Glenn went straight to Bettina.

'Jeez, I'm just speechless. That was a wonderful introduction to your philosophies, Miss Hartman,' he said, hoping she knew he was there in front of her. 'You are clearly a remarkable woman.'

'And you were a wonderful student, Glenn,' said Bettina, staring just past him with her pale, blue eyes. 'I'll look forward to meeting you again over the next few days. We'll need volunteers for the special practical workshop tomorrow, you know. Don't be shy to sign up.'

'The day in the dark event?' asked Glenn.

'Exactly,' said Bettina. 'It's a bit more than a day in the dark though.'

'Thanks for reminding me,' said Glenn. 'I'm *definitely* interested. I'm your man! Where do I sign up?'

'Come and find me at lunchtime, we'll sign you up then,' said Bettina, smiling broadly. Her face seemed brighter and happier than it had done earlier that day.

'I will,' said Glenn. 'Until then.'

He said goodbye and walked towards the next workshop he had highlighted on his list. It was Laura's *Travel and Blindness* workshop.

Glenn wandered through the corridors of the conference centre until he found what he was looking for. Laura had decorated the door for the conference with flags from lots of different countries, as well as old airline ticket stubs. The effect was colourful and inviting, and Glenn felt very happy to step through the doors. He recognised Laura immediately by her long red hair and sharp green eyes. She was already chatting away to the people seated in her seminar.

'Ah, one more!' she cried when she heard Glenn shuffling into the room. 'Come on, all aboard.'

'Sorry I'm late!' he called out. 'I'm Glenn, Glenn Tebbhurst.'

'Sit yourself down, Glenn, there's a good man,' said Laura. She had a lovely British accent and Glenn was happy to have a small reminder of home. She was dressed in a fashionable green shirt with smart blue jeans and seemed very at ease with herself. Like Bettina, up close Laura was more beautiful than he had imagined. Her face was softly freckled and she had a gracefully long neck. Glenn could hardly believe both Laura and Bettina were in their twenties; they seemed so confident and content in their lives. Most of the twenty-somethings Glenn encountered at the DCF were nervous, shaky interns who could barely look him in the eye. To be fair, neither Bettina nor Laura could look Glenn in the eye either, but they certainly showed no qualms about standing in front of hundreds of people, speaking about something so personal to their lives.

When it appeared no one else would walk through the colourful doorway, Laura walked over and closed it. Like Bettina, she did not even use a white cane, though Glenn saw one propped up in the corner of the room.

'Welcome, *willkommen, bienvenue*, friends!' cried Laura. 'I'm here to talk to you about travelling with blindness today. Thank you all for coming along and choosing to learn a bit about this vitally important aspect of living with blindness.'

As Laura spoke, Glenn felt very pleased he had come to this. His father and mother both loved travelling, and though Bertie was convinced that travelling as a blind person had a lot of perks, Glenn knew that his mother would worry about their mobility. Iris and Bertie had taken trips Glenn could only dream of, though some he could remember from his early childhood. Now, with Bertie's blindness, their passports seemed doomed to sit gathering dust in a drawer.

'I know some of you here today might be wondering why a blind woman is giving a seminar about travel,' Laura began. 'After all, isn't the point of travel to *see* new places? I don't see them, it's true, but I feel them. I touch them, hear them, smell them and breathe them, like any other travelling nomad.'

Laura spoke with great eloquence, thought Glenn, admiring the young woman's style.

'It might shock some of you to know that travelling with blindness can in fact be quite easy,' she said, captivating everyone, including Glenn. 'It may not seem so, but we are privileged as blind people. In the developed world, and increasingly in the developing world, we are helped across streets, helped in museums, and, most importantly, helped in the transport world. In my experience, it has not been an impediment to travel as a blind person: humanity helps the blind.

'However, I do not want you to think that people who live with blindness are completely dependent on others. No, you may have seen how many people travel with a white cane. Can anyone tell me what the white cane symbolises?'

Glenn looked around the room, though why he did he wasn't sure, for no one raising a hand would be seen, instead people would just have to shout.

'I do,' a man said loudly.

'Great, please share with the group,' said Laura in her cheerful way.

'Which type of cane though?' he asked.

'Good question,' laughed Laura. 'Perhaps you could explain that too.'

'Alright,' said the man, a serious-looking German. 'The cane most people know about is the long cane. This is traditionally white and some people call it the Hoover cane.'

'Very good,' said Laura. 'It was named after Dr. Richard Hoover. Go on, please.'

'The long cane is used to help the blind get around,' the man continued. 'It can detect obstacles around the person walking with it and helps that person navigate a safe path.'

'How long's a long cane?' asked one woman with a Texan accent. A few people laughed at her question, including Laura, her pearly white teeth flashing at them all.

'As long as necessary,' she said. 'The length of cane depends on the length of the human! The taller the person the longer the cane.

Traditionally, the cane should reach from the floor to someone's sternum, but it varies more these days. Some organisations insist on giving everyone much longer canes, to gain a better idea of the space around them.'

'There's also a guide cane, which is shorter,' said the man who knew about the canes. 'That cane is shorter to detect closer objects, perhaps steps or obstacles in the near vicinity.'

'How short is the shorter one?' the Texan woman piped up, making people laugh again.

'Well, it should only reach the waist of the person using it,' said Laura. 'But the cane I want to talk to you about today, and is most useful for travel, is the Symbol Cane. This is white, light and easy to carry around, and serves as an identifier. It does not have any protective use, only as a way of showing others that the holder is blind and should be given assistance if needed.'

Walking over to the corner of the room, Laura picked up her own Symbol Cane. She had to unfold it first.

'It's lightweight but strong, made of aluminium, and tells anyone who needs to know that I need special assistance,' said Laura, showing them all. 'When they see this at an airport, a wheelchair arrives within seconds!' she laughed. 'But of course it is not essential for travelling with blindness. Many people travel without waving their white cane at anyone who will look at it.'

Laura went on to talk about the many travels she had taken, with all the little stories, jokes, misunderstandings and joys she had found along the way. Glenn listened with fascination, following her from England to Brazil, to India and Kenya, to the Philippines and back to inter-railing across Europe. Again, he could hardly believe she was only in her late twenties.

'Blindness should not and must not be an impediment to our hopes and dreams,' she said. 'These days I like to travel a bit closer to home. I love rowing along the river from my hometown to surrounding villages. I go with a group and we row from one village to the next, stopping at traditional English pubs and having picnics in the summer. It's beautiful and I do not let my blindness stop me doing that. Anything is possible, even rowing boats and putting ourselves in vulnerable situations. There is no mountain you cannot climb. But look, I don't want to talk too much about this now as my colleague Elfrida is running a whole workshop to do with sport. I don't want to steal her thunder. Thank you all for coming and listening to me, you have been a wonderful group.'

'You've been a wonderful teacher!' Glenn called out, much to the appreciation of everyone in the room. They all cheered for Laura.

Glenn left Laura's workshop with such a glow on his face. He was truly inspired by her reluctance to let blindness define her life choices. She loved travelling and refused to let the loss of her sight impact that. Looking down at his list, he looked at what was next. Odile's name was marked, so Glenn headed towards her seminar room, which he had passed en route to Laura. Glenn arrived just in time for the introductions.

'What's your name, fella?' Odile asked Glenn in her New Orleans accent as he settled himself into a seat.

'Glenn,' he said confidently.

'Oh, Glenn!' she said with surprise. 'Hello there, Bettina has told me about you.'

'She did?' said Glenn, surprised by the little leap of his heart. He felt suddenly warm and happy inside, amazed that he had made a personal impression on Bettina Hartmann.

'She did,' said Odile, nodding warmly.

'All good I hope!' Glenn laughed, making the rest of the class laugh.

'All good,' Odile smiled before turning to the rest of the class. 'Right, all of you, now we're all here and introduced, I'd like you all to take some deep breaths. I want you to breathe very deeply, as deeply as you can. Breathe in and hold that breath, okay?'

They all began to breathe in, looking slightly confused.

'Hold that breath and hold it, and when you're ready, breathe out again,' said Odile. 'That's very good. Now, I am sure some of you are wondering why we are breathing in and out at a seminar about blindness at home. But let me assure you that good respiration is one of the most important keys to happiness as a blind person. Breathing deeply does a series of things to your body and mind. Your mind begins to focus on the air you take in and release from your body. As you focus on your breathing you stop focusing on any discomfort, frustration or anxiety you are feeling. The air enters your body and your diaphragm rises; oxygen fills your body and carbon dioxide starts to flow out.

'Now, we have focused on breathing, let's listen to some music,' said Odile. Glenn relaxed as he was played various tracks from different musicians such as Strauss, Bach and Mozart; and then the two most famous blind musicians, Stevie Wonder and Ray Charles, for thirty minutes. Each time they were asked to identify the composers or singers. Music, said Odile, who now lived in New Orleans, was very much part of life for the blind. She spoke about the many different aspects of life within the home relating to blindness, including cooking. Glenn listened carefully. His father had never been much of a chef in the kitchen, that had always been Iris' strong suit, but hearing from Odile that it was possible to cook as a blind person was fascinating to him. She talked them through the kitchen, the safety procedures and her favourite methods of identifying vegetables and herbs. After a thorough question and answer session, Odile began to wrap things up, just in time for lunch.

'If you really want to learn about blindness in the kitchen,' said Odile, 'I advise you to sign up for the practical *Beauty in the Dark* full-day workshop tomorrow. Then you will learn how to cook a whole meal in the dark. But for today, that's it from me, folks. You'll all be happy to know that a few things I made earlier are now ready for you to try in the welcome room. Have a great lunch break, and I'll see you all again over the weekend.'

Glenn was glad it was time for lunch. All that talk of cooking had left him famished. He followed the stream of hungry conference attendees out towards the food stands. Delicious aromas were filling the corridors of the conference centre. Odile was French by origin so her food was typically French in design and taste. Pastries, cheese and dried meats were laid out on huge platters and Glenn could not wait to taste them. Glenn filled a plate and headed outside for a bit of sunshine and fresh air in the conference centre's garden. He thought he would be joined by others but found himself quite alone, which was a relief after the busy crowds of the conference. Or at least he thought he was alone.

Sitting by a fountain by a small row of flowers, Bettina Hartmann was apparently basking in the sun. Glenn started to walk towards her, and then stopped, afraid she might want to be alone. She had been talking all morning and probably wanted a break. But before he could turn around, she turned towards him.

'Glenn?' she said.

'Yes, it is,' he said, unable to suppress a smile. 'Am I disturbing you?'

'Not at all,' said Bettina. 'I'm just soaking up some sun. Autumn is my favourite season. The trees seem to release this incredibly sweet smell, as if they know that soon they will lose their leaves when winter comes.'

'Going out in a blaze of glory,' smiled Glenn, taking a deep inhalation. 'Hold on, I've been practicing this...' Glenn took some deep, long breaths. Bettina listened to the sound of air filling his lungs and laughed.

'I can tell you've been in Odile's workshop,' she chuckled. Glenn laughed too and sighed. The smell was indeed lovely.

'It's a strange smell, quite fresh and smoky,' he said, exhaling deeply. 'It's new to me. You know, my folks live in New York and at this time of year they head up towards Boston to see the autumn leaves there. It looks like the whole landscape is on fire; the trees are that bright and orange. If they go this year, it'll be the first time my Dad will go as a blind man. Thanks for letting me know how he can enjoy it.'

'The power of smell,' said Bettina, gazing gently into the distance, a small smile on her lips. 'It's beyond imagination, Glenn.'

Glenn offered Bettina some of his food and she happily shared his cheese and pastries.

'Man, the food is good here!' he said, tucking into a slice of smoked cheese. 'It was worth coming just for the buffet.'

Bettina laughed and Glenn glowed inside to hear it. He tried not to stare but he was fascinated by how normal Bettina seemed to be, despite being blind since birth. She held out her hand and took food from the plate as if she could see. Her movements were slower, Glenn noticed, but she needed no guide.

'Right, back to business,' said Bettina, after her third *vol-au-vent*. 'We should get back to the conference, Glenn. Thanks for the lunch. And hey, have you thought about the workshop tomorrow?'

'I have, and I'd like to sign up,' said Glenn. 'I think I'll do you proud, Miss Hartmann.'

'Great,' said Bettina, smiling. 'Thank you, Glenn.'

'Don't thank me yet,' he laughed. 'I might be a total disaster. Are you ready for that?'

'I am,' she laughed. 'Thanks again though. It takes guts to put yourself up for something.'

'From where I'm standing, it's you ladies who have that guts this weekend,' he said, sharing one of his most charismatic smiles which was again lost on Bettina.

'Have a good day, Glenn,' she said.

'Thanks for the company,' said Glenn. They walked together back into the hall before heading their separate ways. Glenn watched her leave. Then he glanced down at his sheet and saw that his next session was with Elfrida. He was particularly excited about this workshop because it involved learning how the blind could exercise without assistance. Bertie was a sporty man and would want to stay in shape, especially with Iris breathing down his neck.

'Many people are surprised to know that blind people work out as much as anyone else,' said Elfrida as Glenn arrived slightly late to her workshop. Elfrida was an attractive young woman with strikingly dark eyes. She spoke with a strong Spanish accent which escaped from beautiful, full lips. Her skin was a lovely olive colour, much darker than the other ladies giving seminars. Elfrida was warm and welcoming and her teaching experience shone through in the seminar.

'But that's just not true, *amigos*!' she continued. 'Today I'm going to show you just how they do.'

Glenn noticed that the room was a mixture of blind people and those who could see, but the number of blind people was far higher this time. Some of the blind people in the group were dressed in sports clothes.

'Now, there are lots of ways to exercise,' said Elfrida. 'Why don't you share with me how you like to work out?'

The group was shy at first, but slowly people began to raise their hands.

'I like to swim,' said one man, a tall, Swedish-looking fellow.

'I run and sometimes hike,' said a woman to his left.

'I hit the gym twice a week,' said someone else.

'I'm a rower,' said Glenn, thinking back to his rowing days at Eton.

From cycling to boxing, everyone in the room had their own approach to staying fit and healthy.

'Whether a sport is done outside or inside, on a trail or in the gym, can have a huge effect on the blind,' said Elfrida. 'Many parks, trails and pools have no Braille on their signs, and it is rare to come across any gym or fitness centre with audio-guides or Braille facilities. But for both inside and outside sports, the blind need a strong community of inclusion to provide them with the safety they need. For example, walking paths can be given strong boundaries and curbs for white canes to detect. Benches need to be built to provide frequent rest stops for those in need of them. You may have noticed how, in the conference centre here, the garden is full of benches, and the path has a strong curb. That is because it was built by an inclusive community.

'What I want to focus on today is indoor sporting activities,' said Elfrida. 'You will see that the room has been equipped with machines for a demonstration. May my volunteers please step forward?'

The group of people dressed in sports gear stepped forward, some wielding the white canes Glenn had been introduced to in Laura's seminar.

'Now,' said Elfrida. 'When big companies design machines for people, they do not think of the blind. But some advances have been made lately. For example, these stationary cardiovascular workout machines have all been equipped with Braille instructions and voice-activated consoles. Let's see how they work.'

Glenn watched with a few of the other conference attendees as those dressed in sports wear activated treadmills, spinning bikes, elliptical trainers and stepping machines with their voices.

'This is incredible,' one man said to Glenn, raising his eyebrows and shaking his head in disbelief. Glenn recognised the man as a professor from a Spanish university. The professor was in awe. 'They can work out like everyone else!'

'Gosh, they're so brave,' the woman next to Glenn whispered in his ear. 'They're blind but still they have the confidence to demonstrate to us folks how life works for them.'

Glenn nodded, smiling at the woman.

'I'm in awe,' he said. 'They put us all to shame.'

When each of the machines had been used, Elfrida thanked the volunteers and asked them to come and form a group in front of her.

'Not everyone likes to use machines to exercise,' she said. 'Some people prefer dance classes, aerobics or yoga. Hell, maybe they even like kickboxing! But how many of you here today think your yoga teachers or aerobics teachers have knowledge of how to make their classes appropriate for the blind? Most instructors rely on vision to teach: they say, "follow my lead" or "copy this movement". But a blind person cannot do this. This is why we advocate for physical guidance in sports lessons.'

Glenn watched as Elfrida placed the hands of each of the volunteers on her body as she explained the movements she wanted them to make.

'Alongside detailed instructions, the instructor can show her blind students the movements physically,' she said. 'If the group is large, the instructor can also pair the blind student with a student who has sight. That student can then assist the blind person if the routine is particularly difficult.'

Elfrida then took a new volunteer from the watching crowd, the Spanish professor Glenn had met earlier, and asked him to assist a blind volunteer. Glenn watched in awe as the whole group performed an aerobics exercise routine.

'Fascinating,' croaked the professor, who was marvelling at the volunteer he had assisted.

The whole group left Elfrida's workshop feeling elated. Glenn could not wait to tell his father what he had seen and to find out which gyms in New York gave access to such blindness-friendly machines. His mind was blossoming with ideas as he made his way to the next workshop on his list: Zu-Ting's workshop on *Blindness and Politics*.

When he arrived, he saw that Zu-Ting was dressed in a gown made of silky, flowery material. She was twirling and dancing slowly, her eyes closed, apparently preparing for her workshop. She had fine, delicate features, and exquisitely-shaped eyes. She could have stepped right out of an ancient Chinese painting, Glenn thought, the favourite wife of an Emperor or a glorious courtesan. Where had all these beautiful women come from, he wondered, thinking back to the four other women he had already met that day? He settled himself down in a seat just before she began.

'Welcome, my friends,' she said, almost singing the words. 'You know, as a blind woman, you could still be a ballet dancer. You could be a teacher, a doctor, a singer, a mother; but I am different. I am going to run as a politician. After all, being blind does not mean you cannot have democracy.'

The crowd laughed at this, Glenn included. He remembered the words from Professor Steinmetzer's speech, about how worse off people were without democracy than without sight. Here was Zu-Ting, hoping to combat both of those inequalities.

'Being blind does not mean I cannot run for the city council as a councillor, then MP, then cabinet minister,' Zu-Ting continued, standing tall and speaking as though she was giving a speech into a megaphone. 'I have lived a hard life, harder than many, and I am determined to change things. I would like to be the Minister of the Interior, so I can run the police, the strong arm of the government, and the border patrols. If they do not give me the Minister of the Interior, I want to be the Minister of Education, to ensure that children are given every opportunity to enjoy their right to education: a right I was denied. If they deny me that, well then, I will run for Minister of Sports and Tourism.'

Again, the crowd laughed and Zu-Ting smiled.

'I will be a politician, that is my bottom line,' she continued. 'Even if I get attacked, imprisoned, have to fight in demonstrations, I know there is nothing they can do to me that is harder than the challenge of living this life with blindness. I have a brain to consult the people; I have a body to do the manual work of the people; I have hands to shake hands, arms to carry babies, and lips to kiss the foreheads of my followers. What's more, I have a good tongue to give good speeches, and more importantly, I have goods ears to be able to listen to the people.'

Zu-Ting went on to outline her political ambitions, and revealed to them all how she, like Bettina, had learnt so much through audio books. She had learnt all she needed to know about economics, history, diplomacy and conflict resolution through the vast array of material made accessible for the blind through audio devices. Her workshop ended with her solemn vow to save the world through democracy and peaceful dialogue.

'I'd vote for you!' Glenn could not help but call out to her. Zu-Ting squealed with delight.

'Me too!' called someone else.

'Who said that?' she called out.

'Glenn,' he laughed.

'Well, I'll be sending you a ballot paper, Glenn,' she called out to him.

'I'll be waiting!' he called back, heading through the door.

Glenn made his way to one last workshop, feeling moved by Zu-Ting's passion but also weary after so much listening. Luckily for him, Christina's seminar on *Blindness and Religion* had a peaceful, sombre feel to it. It was held in the conference centre's chapel room and Christina stood like an angel before them. She had a graceful beauty, a soft, gentle elegance that Glenn had never seen before. Her height combined with her fine cheek bones left a truly striking impression. Christina gave a gentle introduction to the many characters in religious stories who suffered from blindness, detailing many of the blind Catholic saints and drawing parallels in her own life between sight and religious enlightenment. She concluded by saying that all blind people have been awarded absolution by God, the Pope and Saint Peter, for having suffered and accepted their destiny.

'May God be with you,' she said in parting. 'May he be your eyes when you cannot see.'

As Glenn left Christina's seminar and followed the crowds heading off towards dinners and hotels, he felt emotion overwhelming him. As soon as he was away from the crowds he began to cry. *I don't know if I'm dead or alive*, he said to himself, *but I swear I could be dead and sitting in heaven with all these women.* They were beautiful, smart, strong and inspiring: flying onto the horizons of their lives with their wings of happiness and cheer. Such great optimists could have been sent by God, he thought, laughing through his tears. Christina's piety had clearly rubbed off on him, but this exceptional group certainly seemed like God's gift to Aachen.

As Glenn finally reached his hotel, feeling the weariness of the long day, he knew he had found great teachers in these women. He knew he was going to find a way to make his father live like them: a happy person, enjoying a fulfilled life, despite his blindness.

CHAPTER SIX

Glenn awoke the next day, happier than ever to get out of bed. He was excited for what lay ahead of him. Bettina had signed him up for the practical day of experiencing life without sight. In truth, he had no idea what it would be like. He was clueless, as he explained to Eleanora on the phone that morning.

'Blindness in the dark?' she exclaimed, sounding deeply unimpressed. 'But what for?'

'To experience what it feels like,' said Glenn. He had caught her just before her Sunday morning horse riding session near Henley, and Glenn could tell she was itching to get out into the open air.

'But why?' she asked in her lazy voice. 'Why do you need to do that, darling?'

'So I can relate to my father more,' he said. 'So I know what it feels like to live with his condition, to experience the sensations he will be experiencing. I think if I do this, it will be a great comfort to him as well as to me. I gotta try, right?'

Eleanora sighed.

'Just sounds like a lot of silly girls running around playing pin-the-tail-on-the-donkey to me, with people like you!' Eleanora laughed down the line. 'My mother thinks you're stark raving mad, Glenn Tebbhurst.'

Glenn did not care what Eleanora's mother thought of his trip to Aachen, nor did he tell his wife what his mother thought of her. Iris Tebbhurst thought Eleanora the maddest of the mad, and that was a nice way of putting it.

'Besides,' Eleanora drawled on. 'Wouldn't it just be better to get your father a guide dog and let the dog do the seeing for him?'

'I'd best get going,' said Glenn, feeling hurt by his wife's ridicule and ignoring her insincere suggestions. 'I don't want to be late. Bye, honey! Have a great ride!'

'Alright, well I'll see you soon, darling,' said Eleanora, before hanging up the phone.

Walking to the conference centre from his hotel, Glenn wished he had not called his wife that morning. He thought that checking in with her after breakfast would lift him; instead it had left him feeling drained of the positive energy he had felt when he woke. His thoughts were suddenly damp and sceptical and he approached his day of blindness with heavy feet. Perhaps she was right, he thought, maybe it was all nonsense. After all, how could he ever *truly* know what his father was going through? Still, he had promised Bettina he would volunteer, and he did not want to let her down.

When he arrived at the seminar room where the exercise was to be held, he saw her there, standing in front of an enormous wooden structure. It looked like a theatre set. The pretty frontage of a grand house stood facing them, with windows, cladding, a door, even drainpipes. Bettina was alone, except for a few technicians arranging things nearby. She seemed to be standing very still, in quiet contemplation.

'Wow, what's this?' Glenn asked, breaking the silence and gazing up at the wooden panels above them. 'Did I just walk into Disneyland?'

'Good morning, Glenn,' she said, her bright blue eyes gazing slightly past him. As ever, Glenn wondered how she knew where he was, down to the inch, without being able to see him. There was something almost mystical about it. 'I'm so glad you've decided to volunteer. This is the set for our experiment today.'

She turned and gestured lightly at the props behind her.

'A house?' said Glenn, looking up at the potted plants sat on the windowsills.

'Yes, a house,' smiled Bettina. She was still for a moment, and though her eyes did not move, Glenn felt as though she was studying him: his movements and his breathing. 'Is everything alright, Glenn?' she asked.

'Yes, fine,' said Glenn, though he realised he had said it too quickly to sound truly convincing. 'I'm super, absolutely great. Man, I can't tell you how excited I am to get involved with this. What an honour! What a privilege.'

'Are you sure?' she asked, still giving the impression that she was feeling every atom of the air around him, their weight, their freedom, and with it, the subtle tension that enveloped him like a bubble. Glenn watched Bettina's kind, accepting face for a moment, wondering why it was he had a heartrending desire to open up and share his troubles with this strange woman. His lips parted, and he took a step forward, hands held out. But before he could say anything, the door opened behind him, and in walked five beautiful women. They were the other blind women he had met: Laura, Odile, Elfrida, Zu-Ting and Christina. They glided in as if on wings of air. Trailing them, disrupting the grace of the entrance, was a tall, bespectacled man.

'We have our second volunteer!' Laura called excitedly. The man they had with them appeared reluctant. He smiled nervously, towering above them all, and looked at Glenn.

'This is William Houston,' announced Elfrida.

'Er, call me Bill,' the man smiled, raising a hand hello to Glenn. Glenn nodded back. Then Bettina stepped forward, holding out a hand to the new volunteer.

'Thanks for volunteering, Bill,' she said. 'Well, that's settled. We have two volunteers and the set is ready. You two are in for quite an adventure.'

Bill smiled and nodded, glancing nervously at Glenn again, who smiled reassuringly. Glenn recognised Bill from some of the workshops the day before. If he recalled correctly, Bill had been the one asking innocent but fairly ridiculous questions to the speakers.

'We shouldn't be disturbed, Bettina,' said Odile in her New Orleans drawl. 'Everyone else is attending workshops given by other speakers. We're all set.'

'Fantastic,' said Bettina. 'Well, if everyone's ready, shall we begin?'

Glenn and Bill followed Bettina into the fake doorway of the house and the five other women followed. As they stepped over the threshold, Glenn noticed that everything inside was cloaked in thick, unnerving darkness. The windows on the outside had been painted on, and did not in fact allow any light to enter into the constructed set. The light that entered through the doorway grew dimmer and dimmer until finally, it was swallowed up by the darkness. As the door closed behind them with a soft click, Glenn felt a piece of material being placed over his eyes. It was wrapped tightly, ensuring that absolutely no light could enter.

'Whoa,' Bill chuckled nervously once his blindfold was attached. 'We gonna be in the dark all day?'

'No, Bill,' came Bettina's voice. 'You're going to live as a blind person all day. Yes, you will be in total blackness. But try not to think of it as darkness – that will limit you, it will inhibit your other senses, which are equally as joyous and wondrous as sight. By the end, you will have an amazing sense of gratitude for your other faculties through which your body perceives the stimulus of the world. You will be more whole, more complete.'

Glenn felt the hairs on the back of his neck prickle at the effect of Bettina's speech. He almost felt tears well up into his eyes. Meanwhile, although he could see nothing, he could hear the breathing of the six women, and Bill, around him. He felt the warmth emanating from their bodies. He felt their presence, their spirits.

Just as Bettina had taught them the day before, Glenn felt his other senses heightening as his eyes lost their power. His ears pricked at every sound and his nose could smell the sweat rising from his body. He jumped slightly as he felt an arm take his.

'Sorry,' came Bettina's voice again, close to him. She laced her thin arm inside his. 'I didn't mean to scare you. I just want to guide you at first, so that you avoid any accidents. It can be very strange at first. Your balance relies on vision. You need to train your body to balance by feeling, instead of seeing. That will take time.'

'Thanks,' he said. 'I feel safer with you here.'

'Are you always this charming in new, strange places?' she asked him.

'Always,' he grinned.

Glenn was not sure how he felt about the experience at hand. He felt extremely vulnerable placing one foot in front of the other as Bettina walked him forward. She possessed no sight herself, but her stride was confident as she led him into the house. They walked for what seemed like a long time before being asked to sit down.

'Go on, don't be scared,' said Elfrida, who was guiding Bill. 'There's a settee behind you. Go on, down you go. There, see?'

Glenn also sunk downwards, fighting against his body's defensive instincts, which feared there would be nothing beneath to catch him. He felt the weight of the soft settee take his weight, and his body loosened, shaking off the tension that had stiffened his body.

'There,' came Bettina's voice. 'We are in the drawing room of the house now. You are sat on the settee, and can you tell me what you feel beneath you? Can you tell me about the texture of the material you are sat on? That is how your memory will locate this settee for you when you need to find it again. These settees are made of a rough weave of tapestry, can you tell?'

'No!' laughed Glenn nervously. 'I can't tell anything.'

'Why is that, Glenn?' Bettina asked calmly.

'Because I can't see!' laughed Glenn.

'Well, I can feel there must be some colour in here,' said Bill, chuckling lightly. Glenn felt the tall man's hands rubbing the sofa around him.

'What?' Glenn exclaimed, laughing again. 'How can you perceive colour when you can't see?'

'Bill is probably feeling all of the actual weaving that goes into these beautiful tapestries on the settee,' said Bettina. 'You should learn from that. He could be feeling beige, or in his mind's eye, looking at some sort of zebra in a savannah, black and white against the wide-spreading gold. Maybe he is looking at some sort of beautiful tiger with bright orange, white and black on her face? Do you think he can feel that?'

'I don't know what Bill feels,' said Glenn, unable to keep the cynicism from his voice. 'But surely it is impossible to *feel* colour. That's nuts!'

'I can feel the zebra skin,' said Bill in a quiet, awed voice. Glenn took advantage of the darkness and rolled his eyes.

'Alright, boys, who wants a cup of tea?' Laura asked in her adorably British accent. 'I'm gasping!'

'You would ask that,' laughed Bettina. 'But yes, who fancies a nice cup of English tea?'

'That would be wonderful,' said Bill, the perfect student compared to Glenn. 'Count me in.'

'Yes, I would like one too,' agreed Glenn.

'Very well,' said Bettina brightly. 'We will show you how to make it then.'

'What?' Bill stammered. 'We're going to make a cup of tea... without sight... with hot water... that can scald?'

Glenn laughed, a booming laugh that told Bill that Glenn thought he was ridiculous.

'You can laugh, Glenn,' said Bettina. 'But you will be using big knives and a gas stove today. You will be cooking a stew with a whole variety of vegetables, meats and spices. You will have to select those spices using everything but your sight.'

'Ha! Good luck, Bill. Sounds tasty,' said Glenn. 'What is the dish?'

'Hungarian goulash,' said Odile. 'And you will be cooking too, Glenn.'

'Why not *enchiladas*?' Elfrida asked angrily.

'Or chicken *chow mein*?' asked Zu-Ting.

'Because I chose goulash!' laughed Bettina. 'And this is not a cookery competition, girls. This is going to be hard for Bill and Glenn. They are going to be preparing food without the faculty of sight for the first time in their lives. It'll be like they are children again.'

'Let's at least start with a cup of tea though,' said Laura, a plea in her voice. They all laughed at this. It seemed like Laura would die of thirst if she did not have a cup of tea with milk as soon as was possible. It was her English blood.

'Alright, to the kitchen!' said Bettina enthusiastically. Glenn allowed himself to be led to the kitchen, which was not too far away. He was enjoying listening to all the different voices of the girls as they accompanied him and Bill on their journey. It was confusing and disorientating at first to hear so many voices and not see who they belonged to, but he was quickly getting used to the feeling, and what was more, he was appreciating the sound of a person's voice like never before: its richness, its texture, and its timbre. It was as if the voice had a whole new quality of substance. As if it was physically present in the air, just like an arm groping in the dark. Remembering their characters and traits from the day before, he was slowly starting to put voices to names.

The process of making the tea consisted of making a physical assessment of a typical modern gas stove. The gas knobs had small marks on them to indicate which hob they controlled and which heat they were turned onto. The fire needed to light the gas was provided by an electric spark, administered through a small button.

'The modern Prometheus. Click, and hey presto!' laughed Elfrida. 'We have fire!'

Both Glenn and Bill jumped at this. The thought of an open flame and no one to see if it was under control was highly unnerving. It was Bill's job to fill the kettle, and to Glenn's amusement, the subsequent splashing and clattering sounds indicated that he was not finding it very easy. When the tea was finally brewing in the cups, and they had all settled down at the table to drink it, Glenn could not fathom how long it would take them to cook an actual meal, considering it had taken at least half an hour to simply boil some water for tea.

'Now, who knows what goes in Hungarian goulash?' Bettina asked the group as they sipped their hard-earned beverages. It was a peculiar feeling, thought Glenn, to sit around a table in the dark, talking with strangers. But for Bettina and the five other blind women he knew this was everyday life. Soon the clangs of teaspoons on china, stirring and plopping and sipping and laughing added colour to the darkness and Glenn began to feel at ease. He could now recognise the women from their various accents and styles of speaking.

'Well, I know the greasy part of the meat needs to be cooked for at least four hours,' said Elfrida. 'You know, the white part.'

'Alright, what else do we know?' Bettina asked the group.

'We need beef,' said Odile, who had already proven her knowledge of cooking in her workshop. 'We need onions, chopped finely; garlic, crushed; carrots, sliced and diced; parsnips, cut into small, delicate pieces; celery, chopped up; two large tomatoes, fresh, juicy and peeled;

two green peppers, fresh and crunchy; three potatoes, scrubbed and sliced; two tablespoons of Hungarian paprika—'

'Two tablespoons?' squeaked Christina. 'May the Lord God forgive you for trying to kill us, Odile! We will be consumed in a fiery, paprika-fuelled inferno!'

'Alright, fine, one tablespoon of Hungarian paprika,' Odile continued, sighing. 'And one tablespoon of ground caraway seed; one bay leaf; ground pepper, salt and water. That, my friends, will make you the best Hungarian goulash you've ever tasted.'

'Thanks, Odile,' said Bettina. 'Are you boys ready to start work?'

'But how will we know where to find all of this, or what everything looks like?' asked Bill, sounding worried. Glenn had the distinct impression that Bill did not know his way around the kitchen with or without his sight.

'We'll help you,' said Bettina. 'Just remember, you have four senses that still function perfectly well without your fifth: smell, touch, taste and hearing.'

'Should we really be handling knives?' Bill asked uneasily.

'I'm sure they're a pretty colour,' said Glenn, teasing his companion. 'Come on, Bill, be a man, my friend! What's there to lose?'

'Our fingers?' Bill whispered to Glenn, but of course it was dark and his whisper had actually fallen on Bettina's ears. She laughed.

'No one is losing any fingers today, I can assure you of that, Mr. Houston,' she said. 'Right, let's get started.'

'I'm ready!' cried Glenn with as much enthusiasm as he could muster.

Without further ado, they set to their tasks of identifying vegetables, knives, chopping boards and spice jars. Pots and pans were taken from the cupboards and clanged onto surfaces as the two men tried to prepare the meal in total darkness. Glenn's job was to identify the spices needed for the goulash, which proved a trying task. He sniffed a variety of herbs and spices that caused him to sneeze, including dried parsley and chilli flakes.

'Here,' said Bettina, coming close to him and guiding his hands. 'You don't need to inhale the spices to smell them. Remember, your remaining senses are working harder now, they do not need to be suffocated. Hold the herbs a bit further away to avoid intoxication.'

Glenn soon learnt how to tell dried mint from oregano, and whole pepper corns from mustard seeds. He felt proud of himself for making so much progress, and when he was stuck, or help was needed, assistance was always at hand as the girls hovered nearby.

'Smells like sage to me,' Odile would say.

'No way, that's tarragon!' Laura would jump in, sniffing deeply.

'Surely it's thyme?' suggested Zu-Ting.

Meanwhile, Bill bumbled around and seemed to trip up a few times, even though his job was simply to remove the gristle and white fat from the beef. The two men were struggling, feeling their way around the kitchen, trying not to endanger themselves or the women by setting the house on fire or cutting off fingers and thumbs.

'How do you feel the difference between a conventional pan and a non-stick pan?' Glenn heard Bill ask.

'By feeling it, see?' said Laura.

'Oh yeah!' he exclaimed.

Bill continued to ask ridiculous questions while Glenn took out the middle of the huge buffalo tomatoes, removing the seeds and squelchy pulp with his bare hands. All around them the six blind women seemed to take courageous steps, without white canes, effortlessly at ease moving around their inky environments. Glenn wondered how they could do this every day, using only the senses of smell, touch, hearing and taste to navigate the world around them.

After hours of preparation and chatter, the Hungarian goulash was bubbling away on the stove. It was set to cook for another hour or so.

'Right, time for another cup of tea?' said Laura. 'Bill, you're an expert with the stove now. Put the kettle on, won't you?'

'Am I?' asked Bill in a small, nervous voice. Everyone laughed.

'Glenn, I'd like you to come with me while Bill makes tea,' Bettina's voice came to Glenn's right side.

'Sure,' he said. 'I'm your man.'

'Come on,' she said. 'I'll guide you.'

Bettina led Glenn out of the kitchen and along what felt like a long hallway. Glenn could sense the space around him, lifting his arms gently to feel how far the walls were from his body.

'I can give you a tour,' she said. She led Glenn into a wide, open space and took his hand. She guided it to touch something in front of them. His fingers brushed against what felt like marble, cold and hard.

'This room is full of statues, recreated for this exercise,' said Bettina. 'There are replicas of Roman, Greek and even modern classics. Feel it for yourself.'

Glenn trailed his fingers over the smooth shape of a statue, following the curve of a strong, muscular shoulder. He traced the shoulder down along the arm and over a pair of magnificently shaped hands.

'It's beautiful,' he whispered. 'It must be Greek The pectoral muscles are portrayed in a specific way in Greek corporeal sculpture.'

'A cultured man,' sad Bettina.

'Who?' asked Glenn, his hand still on the sculpture. 'Him or me?'

Bettina let out a loud laugh.

'And a joker!' she cried. 'My, what a wit I have here.'

'At your service,' Glenn grinned. He wished he could see Bettina's smile but all he saw was the darkness. Bettina led him along a row of statues, each time asking him to reach out and feel the textures, shapes and patterns he found with his fingers.

'There are paintings here too,' she said. 'We have portraits and landscapes from various art movements that have been replicated and given extra texture, allowing the blind to feel the shape of the artist's brush. There are buttons on the wall that will begin an audio description of the painting. It can tell you exactly what the painting is, who it is by, and what it depicts. There are also buttons around to increase or decrease humidity and temperature, to keep everything safe and protected here.'

Glenn heard a noise behind him, and recognised it quickly as Bill's heavy breathing as he stumbled into the room.

'Do you have Mr. Houston there?' Bettina asked.

'Yes,' came Odile's voice.

'Good,' said Bettina. 'We have a little test for you both. You are both familiar with the art world, I assume?'

'Oh yes,' said Bill confidently. 'Show me a Picasso and I can give you the date of its creation, where it's been exhibited, and hell, I can even tell you who's in it!'

'I'm happy to hear it,' said Bettina. 'You should have no trouble in our little task then.'

Glenn felt Bettina's hand on his arm again as she led them both across the room. He felt extremely safe with her, he noticed.

'Okay,' she said. 'Now, you are both standing in front of a painting. I'd like you to feel it, analyse its textures, and tell me under whose brushstrokes this painting has been composed.'

Feeling self-conscious, even though he knew no one could see them, Glenn extended his hand to the painting, and felt Bill beside him doing the same. He felt the different lumps and bumps of the impasto style, trying to distinguish shapes as he did so. Nothing came to his mind.

'It feels like a rendering of Hell, or purgatory,' Bill murmured. 'There are horns and lashes of fire and dark rock, I can feel them, yes... Wait! No, ignore that... Hmm, yes... Now I feel it. I am tracing the outlines of flowers and vegetables; of a wicker basket being held by a woman. There are carpets too, I think, and chickens, and there are people,' before finally he added with triumph: 'It is a marketplace!'

The subsequent silent pause was deafening.

'Er, actually, this is a painting of a ship in a storm,' said Bettina. Glenn tried his best to suppress a snort of laughter. 'Feel, Bill. Try to feel the shapes of the scene, of the story being told.'

The two men put their hands back on the painting and began to explore it once more. Sure enough, after a while, Glenn felt the crests of the sea, the sails of the ship, and the wildness of the stormy sky. The textures were all clear.

'This,' breathed Bettina in a low, awed whisper, 'is Rembrandt's *The Storm on the Sea of Galilee*, painted in 1633.'

'The Golden Age painter himself,' sighed Glenn in return. Bettina smiled.

'Yes,' she whispered. Together they felt a connection somehow in that moment, a moment that was soon pierced.

'Well, of course,' said Bill, laughing confidently. 'Rembrandt, hell of a painter, probably the best of the masters from Germany.'

'He was Dutch,' said Bettina. Odile had to laugh, as did Glenn.

'It's amazing,' said Glenn. 'I never knew I could feel art.'

'It's normal for us,' said Bettina. Glenn heard the pride in her voice.

'All of this was made for this workshop?' Glenn asked her, utterly amazed by the effort and attention to detail that had gone into the exercise.

'Of course,' said Bettina. 'We want to show people how the blind can experience all aspects of life, from food, to sports and to culture. I bet you never knew blind people could tell a Picasso from a Matisse? Don't worry, no one does.'

'I must confess, I didn't,' said Glenn humbly. 'I can be a bit ignorant sometimes. I think I know something about everything, and usually I do. But this, well... this is different.'

'Come on, let's head back to the others,' said Bettina. 'We have a quick sports workshop with Elfrida before tea.'

They wandered back in silence and Glenn thought about just how much he liked to listen to Bettina's voice. Away from the hustle and bustle of the group in the kitchen, and away from his sight, his ears had taken great pleasure in listening to her.

Arriving in the gym of the house, Glenn felt the machines he had seen the blind volunteers use the day before with his hands. They were cold and large under his touch, and he knew he would have to activate them with his voice.

'Just talk to the machine,' said Elfrida. 'Say "activate" and listen to what it says.'

'Activate,' said Glenn, loudly and clearly. The machine whirred and burst into life, welcoming him and asking him for his height, weight and fitness level. As soon as the treadmill was activated, he was able to command it to do as he liked. Slowly, he began to jog at a light pace. Glenn could barely believe it. He was running in total darkness and felt very comfortable doing so. He heard Bill grunting and wheezing on a spinning bike to his left. It was commanding him to work harder.

'Excellent work, boys!' Elfrida called to them. Glenn was so used to the dark now that even the new sounds buzzing in his ears, the whirring and clicking of the machines, the women's laughter, did not distract him. Somehow the sounds and noises began to colour the room around him, in a way he could not really describe, not even to himself.

'Okay,' Glenn heard Bettina's voice once more. 'It's time for our board meeting. Bill has kindly made us tea for the occasion.'

The two men were led from the house gym towards another large room. The room had a spacious feel to it. Glenn marvelled at how he was beginning to sense the space in a room with no clue at all as to what it looked like. There was something about the lightness and heaviness of the air, and the movement of air within the room, that seemed relevant to its size.

'Now, as Herbert is not here, I will be heading this meeting for the ICB today,' said Bettina.

'Where is Herbert?' Glenn heard Laura ask.

'He's raising funds, as usual,' said Odile. Glenn pictured the lithe figure of Herbert Farrand circulating the conference, collecting donations from attendees, smiling as he did so. Somehow the ICB's President did not seem nearly as impressive as the women he represented, especially Bettina. But before Glenn could ponder the matter further, his attention was snapped back to the meeting.

'Listen carefully everyone, you ladies included,' Bettina continued. 'I'm giving you all notepads and pens now. Pass them around, that's right, one each, please. You are all going to write down the minutes of this meeting.'

'But how can we write if we can't see?' asked Bill, sounding baffled.

'Let's try and see, shall we?' said Bettina. 'Christina, will you please serve us all some tea?'

'Of course, Bettina,' said Christina. Glenn heard the soft sound of hot liquid being poured from a teapot into china cups. Cups were passed around to each of them. Glenn heard Bill hiss and yelp as he picked up his too quickly.

'Careful, dear, it's hot,' said Christina.

When everyone had their tea, Bettina began the meeting. She welcomed them all individually before getting to the matter at hand. It involved various issues, starting with a medical agenda; proposals about psychology for the blind and natural remedies for the blind. The meeting then moved into social security for the blind, and finally, one miracle treatment being discussed currently by the ICB: removing and replacing the optic nerve altogether, with two new reports of successful operations.

As fascinating as the subject at hand was, Glenn doubted whether many of the people there in that room were truly focused on what Bettina was saying. He certainly was focusing far more on keeping his pen on his notepad and imagining what letters he needed to write down in his head. His hand kept veering off the pad and he knew his was not the only one. Not far from him, he heard Bill sighing with effort, spilling tea and dropping his pen, and even the blind women around the table seemed to struggle. Bettina however, spoke, sipped tea, and scribbled loudly on her notepad as she headed the meeting.

'It sounds to me as if some of you have failed the test of being good board members today,' she said with a smile in her voice. 'Perhaps we should try a slightly easier exercise.'

Glenn heard a rustling sound as Bettina arranged something in front of her.

'I would like each of you to take the box I am giving you. Inside you will find the pieces of a Russian *matryoshka* doll, and I would like you each to put your *matryoshka* back together. This is a test for you, my friends. I will time each one of you on this talking watch.'

Glenn received his box along with everyone else, and started to feel the pieces inside. He thought at first that the task would be simple, but it took him nearly an hour to piece the doll back together. His hands and mind were working in unison, feeling the texture of each layer, trying to differentiate between the smooth painted edges of the outer shells and the rougher wooden edges of the inner shells.

'Finished!' said Odile, before everyone else.

'Excellent work, Odile,' said Bettina. 'Could you please go and check on the goulash?'

'With pleasure,' she replied, and shuffled off towards the kitchen.

'I give up,' sighed Laura. 'This is boring.'

Glenn heard Laura abandon her pieces back into the box with a big huff. Bettina too was working hard on the task, and to Glenn's surprise he finished not long after her. Bill was flailing, however, and repetitively dropped his pieces under the table. They bounced and clacked across the floor.

'You can do it if you set your mind to the task, Laura,' said Bettina. 'Okay, let's try a new task. Lego! This task is especially for our guests from the States'.

'Something for the Americans, huh?' laughed Glenn. A new rattling sound filled the air as Bettina passed Lego blocks around the table.

'The challenge is to assemble a version of the White House as quickly as possible. You'll notice that the pieces have additional markings on them. This is to tell us which colours they are. The ones with two clear indentations on the side are white. Find them and construct your own White House. Okay, we are ready. Go, Bill! Go, Glenn!'

Glenn felt his fingers fumble over countless pieces of Lego, struggling to construct the columned façade he remembered of the White House. Across the table, he heard Bill sighing with exasperation. Glenn knew he was winning the race.

'Goddamit!' Bill cried at last. 'I'm terrible at this. I'm terrible at everything.'

'Don't be so hard on yourself, Bill,' said Laura kindly. 'This is difficult stuff.'

Zu-Ting was the first to finish. Glenn and Bill could not see of course, but it was perfect. Zu-Ting was precocious, she could complete a Rubik's cube in seconds, and her skill with this task was equally impressive.

Half an hour later and Glenn had completed his White House.

'Great job, Glenn,' said Bettina. 'You're a natural.'

'Thanks,' said Glenn, grinning into the darkness and tracing the shape of his White House. 'What can I say? I know my American politics!'

'I know my limits,' said Bill miserably. 'God, it will take me a thousand years to complete this task.'

'I think you're wonderful in the kitchen. Odile!' Bettina summoned. A few moments later footsteps could be heard coming back from the kitchen.

'You called, Bettina?' said Odile. A delicious smell had followed her from the kitchen.

'Yes, why don't you take Bill into the kitchen to help?' said Bettina, a meaningful tone in her voice.

'Of course,' said Odile. 'We need to prepare a salad. Come on, Bill, I need your chopping skills.'

Glenn heard their footsteps fade away as Bill wandered off with her towards the kitchen.

'Alright, that's enough,' said Bettina not too long after. 'I believe it's time for dinner. Who's ready for goulash?'

The room filled with hungry cheers. They made their way into the dining room, where they now had to learn to lay the table. Cutlery and crockery were presented and Bill and Glenn set to work.

'Odile has taught me so much,' said Bill happily as he ran his hands over plates and bowls, searching for the right pieces of crockery for the table. 'She taught me to cut lettuce, endives, peppers, cucumbers, beetroots, and then how to mix a sauce of mustard and vinegar. It tastes delicious, Glenn, just you wait and see! I mean, not see, wait and taste!'

Glenn was happy to hear Bill enjoying himself so much. He personally was having a hard time folding handkerchiefs. When he finally found the way to make them fold in the right way, they all sat down at the table to eat. Serving the goulash, and using the knives and forks in the dark, proved tricky, but they made it through somehow. All the while Glenn wondered at how bizarre it felt to eat in total darkness, especially as everyone around him seemed to be tucking in with great gusto. The six blind women were eating happily, complimenting the food, discussing the day and drinking deeply from their glasses. Glenn felt he could have been at one of his wife's dinner parties, minus the aristocrats and overindulgent foods. The ambience was vibrant, warm and inviting. He felt utterly at ease and happy in the intimacy of the meal they were all sharing together. Only Bill seemed to have trouble; he managed to stick a piece of baguette in his eye.

After dinner, Bettina announced they would take the dishes back to the kitchen and play card games. Glenn had given up protesting by now, knowing that Bettina would have a way to show them how this was possible without sight. Sure enough, they were presented with a pack of heavily embossed cards, on which the hearts, diamonds, spades and clubs could be felt easily. They played an extremely entertaining round of poker, laughing and teasing each other until eventually it began to feel like a family evening.

Elfrida challenged Bill to a game of chess in the dark, which ended almost as it began. In just five moves.

'This is ridiculous,' huffed Bill, clearly not used to losing. 'And you're only winning because you're a sportswoman.'

'What?' laughed Glenn, overhearing their conversation. 'What do sports have to do with chess?'

'Strategy,' said Bill sulkily. 'Who cares anyway. I'm a Houston champion in checkers, that's how I'll get my revenge.'

Within fifteen minutes, Christina beat him at his preferred checkers in a landslide victory. Clearly deciding board games in the dark were not his strong suit, Bill joined the others in their poker game. But before the game had come to an end, a game in which Glenn had succeeded in bluffing long enough to knock Bettina out of a round, a buzzing sound announced that the workshop had finished. Some of the women around the table let out long sighs.

'Okay, it looks like we've finished for the day, team,' said Bettina. Glenn could tell she was trying to sound bright and cheerful but he heard the sadness in her voice. 'It's time to turn the lights on.'

She stood up and went to the wall nearby, where she flicked a switch. Through the corners of his blindfold, Glenn saw a rim of bright, white light. One of the women came up behind him and untied his blindfold whilst another did the same for Bill.

'My, oh my,' he heard Bill breathe, as light poured into his eyes once more. Glenn blinked uncomfortably as the world burst into brilliance. He found himself sat in a large, well-presented drawing room. It was totally unlike what he had pictured in his mind's eye. In fact, the sudden arrival of light gave him the distinct feeling that the world had changed somehow.

'How long were we in the dark for?' he asked Bettina, watching her as she came into bright focus.

'Six and a half hours,' she said. Glenn noticed that she, like many of the blind women, had become quieter and looked slightly unsettled. He could tell the light was having an effect on them, even if it did not affect their vision.

'It's a whole new world,' said Bill, laughing stupidly.

'Yes,' said Bettina. 'But I hope you enjoyed being in our world, if only for a short while.'

'You bet,' chuckled Bill. 'Imagine my wife's face when I tell her I can cook goulash, and cook it blind.'

The women laughed at this, as did Glenn. They all made their way to the exit located at the edge of the room. Stepping out of the set, Glenn felt a little strange, a little sad. He looked back at the house. A part of him wished he could go back into the darkness. He had not seen a thing inside but he had felt so much, especially the warm camaraderie of the women, the sense of togetherness they had created in just six hours. Glenn could not remember the last time he had been made to feel so at home.

'See you all tomorrow,' said Bettina, picking up her coat and bag from a chair. 'I think we all deserve big congratulations for what we achieved today. Well done, Bill, and well done, Glenn.'

'What a day! Wow. Thank you,' said Glenn, but before he could say any more, Bettina had walked away. Like the other women, she must have been exhausted after such an intense day of teaching. Glenn made his way out of the conference centre, sharing a few words about the experience with Bill before setting off on his own.

Outside the sun was setting and the sky was full of glorious dusk pinks and yellows. He should have been relieved to be seeing again, to be soaking up the colours of such a sublime sunset, but when Glenn arrived back to his hotel room, his mind wandered back to the house he had spent the day inhabiting. In a stark moment of realisation, he knew that if he was truly honest with himself, he wished he was still there.

CHAPTER SEVEN

When Glenn awoke the next morning he thought for a short moment that he was still in the workshop. The room was dark and he could barely make out the shapes around him. But he quickly remembered that it was daytime, and his curtains were drawn. Stretching, Glenn wandered over and opened the thick fabric, letting light spill into the room. Outside, it was a dark autumnal morning, but bright sunlight was already filtering through the clouds. His memory drifted straight back to the previous evening, when the blindfolds had been removed and the lights had been turned on again. He focused on the moment when light had struck him the day before, attacking him with a thousand stars as his eyes adjusted to the change.

'Jeez,' he muttered, rubbing his eyes. It was strange, he thought, how invasive light felt sometimes.

Gathering his things, Glenn dressed and ate a quick breakfast at the hotel before heading over to the conference centre. When he arrived, he was surprised to see so many people milling around. The centre was heaving with new, excited crowds. It was Monday, Glenn realised, wondering if the start of the working week had attracted a new audience. Sure enough, in the main conference hall, a sort of fair had been erected. Countless information stands and podiums had been set-up for various groups and companies. Slogans jumped out at him from every angle and bright product advertisements dominated the room.

Taking a coffee from the coffee stand, Glenn began to weave his way around the hall.

He noticed that there were lots of groups involved in different subjects surrounding blindness. There were very technical workshops with machinery, explaining the design and function, with practical applications and tests available on site. There were some entrepreneurial groups trying to raise funds for their new initiatives. Glenn leaned in to see that they had developed applications for iPads and tablets, and various e-devices which could help the blind with audio and textual assistance. The hall had a distinctly international feel to it too. From every direction, different accents and languages could be heard buzzing through the crowd. From Hindi to Spanish, and Arabic to Russian, the whole world seemed to have arrived in Aachen.

Glenn soon spotted the charismatic Herbert Farrand surrounded by a group of Koreans and some smartly dressed businessmen from Hong Kong. The ICB President seemed to be in his element, smoothly chatting away, clearly happy to be entertaining.

Glenn too was used to crowds and impressing businessmen and yet that morning he did not feel so comfortable with the crowds. After a while he felt suffocated by the innovative scene and the endless talks being delivered by engineers and salesmen, and after seeing the price tag on some of the devices being promoted, his interest was neutralised completely. How could the struggling blind afford this sort of thing, he wondered? He tried to escape to the garden, moving slowly through the crowds, but before he could, three people approached him, one Indian woman and two Chinese men.

'Sir, sir, wait!' called the Indian woman. 'We have been waiting to talk to you!'

'Me?' said Glenn, surprised to hear this. The woman seemed almost breathless with excitement.

'Yes, sir, you are Glenn Tebbhurst, the man from London, no?' she said with bright eyes.

'The man with the money!' one of the Chinese men said, chuckling.

'We've heard about you,' said the other man, smiling as broadly as his colleagues. 'Sir, please, allow us to monopolise your time for a moment. We know you must have many good initiatives you would like to sponsor, but please, lend us your ear for two minutes!'

'Monopolise me, huh? Well, that's quite an ask gentlemen, and lady, but,' Glenn started to say, but the three of them were so excited to have found him, they never allowed him to finish.

'We have been developing a 3D touch screen for the blind,' the woman began, launching into her pitch without further ado. 'With this screen, and our guidance measures, blind people can operate everything through physical, descriptive touch. There will be apps for all sorts of things: travel, GPS, education! There will be physical 3D access to all kinds of apps for social media and entertainment. We'll even hook up with companies streaming television series and help them to create 3D media.'

Glenn could not understand how a 3D touchscreen like this could ever be created and wondered if the blind would truly appreciate access to such an innovation, but he did not want to engage with these tycoons.

'Listen,' he began, scanning the crowd for a way out. 'It sounds great, folks, but I'm not sure if I'm the right person to…'

But once again the woman jumped in.

'I know, I know, you are probably wondering how much this will cost, and how much you would have to donate,' she went on, the smile never leaving her face. 'Well, I have good news for you, Mr. Tebbhurst. We need only one million dollars.'

'Only a million dollars?' said Glenn, almost laughing. 'Well, that's a fine round figure you've got yourself there, Miss!'

'Only a million,' said one of the Chinese men, nodding his head enthusiastically.

'You've got the wrong man, excuse me,' said Glenn curtly, shaking his head in disbelief. Abandoning all politeness, he simply turned away and made a quick retreat into the crowd. As he did so, he found himself approached by more and more people who wanted to offer him investment opportunities. If they didn't want his money, they wanted gossip from the day before.

'Is it true they tie you to the chair so you don't fall off?' one girl asked him, a serious expression on her face. 'I heard how one poor fellow fell out of a window!'

'Did they make you put your hand in the fire on the stove to warn your body of danger?' asked another.

'I heard one of you fainted and they had to call an ambulance?' said another.

'What? No!' laughed Glenn. 'We spent a day in the dark, that's all. There were no dramas, no incidents. It was quite fun, actually. You should try it sometime, ladies. Now, if you'll excuse me...'

He turned to leave the group of girls, and as he did so, he almost walked straight into Bill, who was enjoying being interrogated by a similar gaggle of young women.

'I gotta say, I froze like a rabbit when the light came on,' Glenn heard him tell them. 'I couldn't tolerate the lights, they were blinding me. Get me back in the dark, that's what I told them! Ah, Glenn, hey there!'

'Hi, Bill,' said Glenn, feeling awkward to have stumbled across Bill's retelling of the previous day's events. He lingered for a moment as Bill went on, then turned to leave, hoping he could escape the crowds and get to the garden. He also hoped he might bump into one of the six blind women he had spent the day with, but could not see them anywhere. Despite the interrogations, his mind kept drifting back to the strong bonding experience they had all shared together.

Suddenly Glenn felt something warm and wet on his hand. He looked down and saw a handsome golden retriever licking his fingers. The dog wagged her tail enthusiastically as Glenn looked down at her.

'Sorry, sorry!' came a voice from behind. Glenn turned to see a squat young man trying to pull the dog back. Glenn knew from his glazed expression that the man was blind.

'That's alright,' said Glenn, reaching down to stroke the dog's beautiful coat. She panted happily as he did this, and turned to her owner with a wagging tail. 'Ain't you a beauty? What's your name, sweetie?'

'She's Sandy, and I'm sorry, she loves to lick, this one,' said the young man. 'We'd best get back to the workshop. Feel free to join, it's the Guide Dog Assistance workshop, first room as you leave the hall. See you!'

'See you!' Glenn called after him happily. Glenn watched as the friendly dog guided his master back out of the conference hall. Happy to find a clear path out of the hall, Glenn followed them, thinking of something his mother had said. When he had visited his father she had worried that he would become a man being pulled around Manhattan with a guide dog. Bertie had liked the idea, but Iris had been against it from the start.

'Imagine having a mangy mutt around the place, all day long!' she had protested. 'We'll be living like animals. No, sir, I don't want a dog in the house. And I don't want you being pulled around Central Park by one either.'

Lost in his thoughts, Glenn did not notice that he had almost bumped into someone.

'I'm sorry, please excuse me,' he said quickly, not looking up, before continuing on his way.

'Glenn?' a familiar voice called him back. He turned to see Bettina looking in his direction. She was looking at him as if she could see him standing there, as if she had twenty-twenty vision.

'Bettina!' he said, very happy to see her in the hall. 'I'm sorry, I was miles away. I completely missed you. How did you... how did you know it was me?'

'I smelled you as you walked by,' she said. 'I could smell you from quite a distance in fact.'

'Heightened senses,' said Glenn, grinning. 'It really is a thing!'

'So you listened in my workshop then,' said Bettina, grinning back. 'You're a good student, Glenn Tebbhurst.'

'You're a good teacher,' he said. 'The best. I was never this attentive in school!'

'I'm sure you were, Glenn! Well, I have an advantage. I smell everything, I feel everything,' said Bettina. 'Just as you can see me and I can't see you, I can smell you but you cannot smell me. We have different instincts, that's all.'

Glenn watched Bettina as she spoke, and though he agreed with her on all points, he did not share something with her that he felt in that moment. He could smell her. It was a flowery, subtle smell that seemed to surround her. The truth was Glenn liked Bettina's smell very much: that, he felt, was instinctive too. Surprised and warmed by this realisation, but not wanting to share his feelings, Glenn changed the subject.

'I just saw Bill,' he said, a small smile forming on his lips. 'He's saying that last night he preferred being in the dark than having all these neon lights above us. He's saying that all these spots of light can blind us and ruin our sight. What a damn fool he is!'

Bettina laughed at this, revealing her beautiful smile. Glenn felt a smile form on his own face at the sight of hers.

'Oh really?' she said. 'And you, Glenn, how did you feel?'

'How do I feel? Man, what a question! I want to tell the whole world about what I've seen here this weekend. I'll be talking to my father about the whole experience,' he said. 'Dad will be fascinated. This has been such a successful visit for me, to learn and appreciate the difficulties of living with blindness. I learnt so much yesterday. You know, one thing that surprises me though is that I thought every blind man would have a dog, but there is only one dog here, for the workshop.'

'Yes,' said Bettina. 'We have a study group now in Room Seven for the advantages of guide dogs and their abilities, but new technology has largely replaced dogs. Look around you at the evidence. Between the cane and the electronics, everyone can manage.'

'Okay, well if you have no need for a guide dog, how would you feel about a guide *man*?' asked Glenn, grinning. 'Would you like to walk with me? I was heading out to find some air. I might go to the garden, to where we sat yesterday?'

Bettina's eyes stared ahead, and as ever, her emotions were hard to read. But after a moment she smiled.

'Yes, Glenn, I will walk with you,' she said, smiling. 'I consent: you can be my guide.'

'Thank you kindly, ma'am,' he said, smiling back at her.

Glenn took her arm gently in his and led them out of the hall. When they reached the garden, Glenn felt very relieved to be out in the open air. The conference crowd had been stifling. They walked slowly and chatted lightly about Bertie in New York, and how Bettina felt the conference had gone. Though they walked side by side, when he could,

Glenn stole glances at his companion. He was concerned to see that Bettina, though hard to read, looked melancholic.

'Well, I'd best let you get back to the conference,' he said, once they had completed a tour of the garden. 'You must have lots to do. I don't want to keep you away from your responsibilities.'

'Yes, and I'll see you tonight anyway,' said Bettina.

'Tonight?' said Glenn, his heart performing a somersault. What was tonight, he wondered?

'Yes, at the dinner Herbert is holding,' said Bettina. 'You and Bill have both been invited as a thank you for participating in the Blindness in the Dark workshop yesterday. You don't have plans, do you?'

'No,' said Glenn quickly. 'No plans. I'll be there, with pleasure.'

'Your wife is invited too, if she can make it,' said Bettina. Glenn was surprised by this, as he did not recall telling her about Eleanora.

'She's still in London actually,' he said. 'I came alone. But I will be there, I promise. I can't wait!'

'Good, I'm glad,' said Bettina, and a small smile returned to her face.

'Me too,' said Glenn, and before he could help himself, the words escaped from him, flowing like honey: 'I like talking with you so much, Bettina. It's just terrific.'

'Until tonight then,' she said. Moving forward, she pulled Glenn gently into a hug. For a moment he felt her soft, warm body pressed against his. She kissed his cheek before pulling away. 'I'll see you tonight, Glenn.'

Glowing from the hug he had received, and the deepening connection he felt with this strong, enigmatic woman, Glenn wandered back into the conference. After a while he realised he was not interested in the gadgets and gizmos on offer and headed back to his hotel to rest for the afternoon. The prospect of seeing Bettina and the five other women at dinner was far more exciting than 3D tablets and business pitches. Lying down on his bed, he fell into a deep sleep.

At the dinner later on that evening, which was held at a traditionally German restaurant in Aachen, Glenn was seated next to Bettina. When he arrived, Herbert welcomed him like a VIP. The President was dressed in a smart black suit with a bow tie and looked more suave than ever.

'Ah, here he is!' the President cried, taking Glenn's hand warmly in his own. 'Our second guinea pig! Welcome, Glenn, you are most welcome. Bill is here, too, and yes, I think that is everyone now.'

'Hi, Herbert,' said Glenn, smiling at the warm welcome. 'You're looking like a man on top of the world!'

'I am, sir, I am!' laughed the handsome man. His blue eyes twinkled in the candlelight and Glenn was reminded of the huge poster he had seen on arrival.

'Come, we have seated you next to Bettina,' he said, ushering Glenn to the table. 'No Mrs. Tebbhurst this evening? I was rather hoping we might meet her.'

'No, not tonight,' said Glenn. 'She's not here; she's back at home, in England.'

'Well, not to worry, we will be your family for the night!' roared Herbert, clapping him on the back and smiling his charming smile. 'Come, you are between me and Bettina.'

Herbert Farrand had seated himself at the head of the table, with Odile to his left and Glenn to his right. Bill was seated further down, and was loudly chattering away to Elfrida about chess tactics.

'You took the mate out of checkmate,' Glenn heard him say.

'I think someone has sour grapes,' Glenn heard her say, laughing as Bill tried to justify his poor performance.

'Don't forget, Bill is the checkers champion,' said Laura, quipping across the table at them, her green eyes dancing playfully. 'That's why Christina beat him!'

'Thanks be to God,' said Christina, smiling. 'He was on my side that night.'

'Well, I call that an unfair advantage, having God on your side!' laughed Bill.

Glenn felt very happy to be back among the six blind women. The warm, communal feeling they had enjoyed over the Hungarian goulash had returned and he felt honoured to be a part of the group. There was something so lovely about every one of these women.

'Thank you so much for inviting me, Mr. Farrand,' said Glenn, nodding his head appreciatively at the President, who was stuffing his napkin into his shirt in preparation for the dinner to come.

'Not at all,' he said, waving his hand dismissively. 'Call me Herbert, please. And it's Bettina you should be thanking, in fact. She was the one who insisted you and Mr. Houston join us tonight.'

Glenn turned to look at Bettina, and saw how she was gazing ahead, smiling. He realised he had not yet said hello.

'Well, hi there,' he said, leaning forward slightly so that she might hear him. 'I believe you are to thank for us being here with you tonight. What an honour!'

'You're welcome,' she grinned. Despite her smile, there was something about her expression that still had a touch of melancholy, and Glenn was sad to see that. Bettina, for all her strength and support of others, seemed to be struggling with something, though what that was, Glenn had no idea. Perhaps one could only be cheerful with one's eyes open, he thought, but dismissed that idea immediately. Had not Bettina shared with them all her joy of treasure hunts, of playing hide and seek with her friends, and loving life, even with blindness? No, it was something else.

The first course arrived before Glenn could consider the matter any further.

'Oh, yes! How delicious!' Herbert exclaimed, tucking into his bowl of soup. '*Gemüsesuppe!*'

Glenn looked down at his own bowl. It looked like a thin broth, with large vegetables and small meatballs inside.

'It's a traditional German soup,' Bettina explained to him. 'Try it, I'm sure you'll like it.'

Lifting his spoon to his lips, Glenn tried the soup. It was indeed delicious.

'People have been making this in Aachen for many generations,' said Bettina, taking a taste herself. Glenn watched her, between mouthfuls of his own soup, and could not help but notice just how beautiful she was. She had such beautiful cheeks, a perfectly small nose, a rounded chin and the most luscious pair of lips he had ever seen. The incredibly bright blondeness of her hair, tied up in a smart bun, was a joy to behold. She started to make polite conversation across the table with Herbert, but as she turned in his direction her hand fell between Glenn's legs. The tips of her fingers brushed the inside of his thigh.

Glenn froze.

'I'm sorry,' she whispered quickly, taking her hand away and nodding politely as Herbert spoke back to her. Glenn waited for them to stop talking before he responded.

'Not at all,' he said at last, swallowing hard, his voice shaking. He waited a moment. 'Bettina, I,' he began to say.

'Glenn…' said Bettina quickly, as if to stop him. But he had already started and could not stop now.

'Bettina, I don't know how to interpret this,' he said in a low whisper. 'I can't help asking myself, should I stop thinking about how I like you so much?'

No sooner than the words had left his mouth than Bettina stood up. She rose from her chair and left the dinner. She did not look at Glenn once before she left, but he did not expect her to. After all, blind or not, he was the reason she was leaving. He felt puzzled and strange, and wondered if anyone else had noticed her swift departure. They had not, however, and were far more focused on enjoying their starters and chattering to each other.

Why did she leave, Glenn asked himself? She had not uttered a single word. He did not know Bettina, but he had gauged so far that she was not the type of person to cause a scene or create drama. He wondered if he should follow her, and how she would interpret that. He suddenly realised that they barely knew each other at all. It was she who had touched his leg, and yes, of course, it could have been an accident, but her sudden flight set his doubts aflame. Had he offended her, or did she think she had offended him? His mind reeled with the possibilities.

'Glenn?' a voice broke through his reverie. He looked up to see Herbert peering curiously at him. 'Are you still with us? I was asking you how you found the workshop on Sunday.'

'Sorry,' said Glenn, shaking his head quickly. 'It was good, yes, very good. I couldn't believe it. The set... the activities. It was an amazing experience.'

'Did you learn something?' Herbert asked, his slight accent making him sound like a kind teacher teasing an answer out of a pupil.

'Yes, lots,' said Glenn, and he began to talk lightly with Herbert about his day in the dark. He was happy to have the distraction. Herbert himself seemed completely oblivious to Bettina's departure. Perhaps she always left dinners early, Glenn thought.

'And I have heard your interest in blindness is personal,' said Herbert, 'not financial!' The young man began to laugh. 'Forgive me, Glenn, but so many people are looking for ways to make money from blindness.'

'My interest is personal, yes,' said Glenn quietly. 'My father...'

'Yes, yes, Bettina told me, your father has gone blind,' said Herbert, waving the fact away. 'That is good. It is good you came to us to learn something. Oh, where has she gone? Ah, anyway, where was I? Yes, yes, it is good you came to learn from us. You have clearly made an excellent impression on the girls here too.'

Before long, Herbert began to discuss various details of the conference, the forums he had attended, the successes and shortcomings of their fundraising initiatives and multiple problems. From a fundraising point of view, Glenn was curious as to how Herbert felt the conference had gone.

'This was a very successful time for us,' said Herbert. 'We rarely have such an opportunity to fundraise, but this weekend was rather special. In fact, I should announce this to the group.'

Turning away from Glenn and standing up, Herbert cleared his throat loudly and clinked a fork against his glass. He waited patiently for them all to stop talking.

'Ladies and gentlemen, ladies and gentlemen!' he called to the group. 'I would like to make an announcement. Please, put down your *Gemüsesuppe* for one moment, my friends.'

The others, who had been chattering away with each other, fell silent, some letting out small cheers for their President.

'It is my great pleasure to tell you that this weekend we raised enough money to fulfil our budget for the upcoming financial year!' Herbert announced. The news was met by gasps and whoops of approval from the five blind women.

'Truly?' yelped Odile.

'Bravo!' called Bill from the other end of the table.

'But that's several million dollars,' said Elfrida, astounded by the news. 'Are you sure?'

'Yes, I'm sure, Elfrida,' smiled Herbert. 'Why do you always doubt me?'

'That's incredible,' cried Laura. 'Well done, Herbie!'

'Great work, Herbert,' sighed Christina, her eyes filling with tears. 'This is the work of God. Thanks be to him, and praises!'

'I think it was more the hard work of all of us here on earth, Christina,' scowled Zu-Ting. 'Congratulations, Herbert!'

The women all rose from their seats and moved slowly towards their president, whom they hugged and patted affectionately. Herbert smiled and responded warmly to their attentions.

'You are all most welcome, and thanks to you all,' he said, shaking the hands of the five beautiful women. 'We could not have done it without you. Now, everyone sit down, I see the main course is arriving!'

Sure enough hot plates of veal *zurichois* were delivered to the table by a group of waiters. Glenn looked down at the dish and his mouth watered. The meat looked so deliciously tender; normally he would not be able to wait to start such a feast. But the absence of Bettina niggled at him and he could not muster up an appetite. He ate to be polite and continued to chat with Herbert all the way through to their dessert of apple strudel. When the dinner was finished and the plates had been cleared, Glenn waited until he could politely excuse himself before leaving.

'I'm usually the last to leave, but look at me, retiring already!' he laughed. 'Thank you and goodnight, folks. It's been a pleasure but my bed is calling me.'

The five women, Bill and Herbert protested, but when they saw he was serious they continued to order more drinks and bid him goodnight.

Glenn did not know if he was expecting to find Bettina outside, but when he left the restaurant and entered the cool night, he looked around for her. She was nowhere to be seen. He walked quickly back to his hotel and called his father. He knew he should also call Eleanora, but somehow it did not feel right, not after what had happened. Besides, Glenn had always found his father's voice comforting. That night was no exception.

'Son, what a pleasant surprise,' came Bertie's voice from the other side of the world. Glenn told his father about his day, about the various gadgets and the guide dog and the dinner, entertaining him all the while with talk of German customs in Aachen. He tried to sound as upbeat as possible, avoiding any mention of the strange feeling Bettina had left him with.

'These women sound quite incredible,' said Bertie. 'Don't tell your mother, son, but I'm jealous! I bet they're all beautiful.'

'They are,' said Glenn, thinking of Bettina's pink lips and her soft, rounded cheeks. Her image was frozen in his mind and hard to shake away. 'Jeez, Dad, you can't even begin to imagine how beautiful they are.'

'Is everything alright, Glenn?' his father asked after a while.

'Yes, of course,' Glenn lied. 'Why do you ask?'

'You just sound a little down, that's all,' said Bertie. 'I'm your Dad. I notice these things.'

'I'm just tired, Bertie,' said Glenn, letting out a fake yawn. 'It's late here. I should probably try and get some sleep now.'

'Right you are, son,' said Bertie. 'Thanks for calling. Your mother sends her love.'

'Be sure to send mine back,' said Glenn. 'Goodnight, Dad. Take care of yourself, OK?'

'Goodnight, Glenn,' his father said. 'You'll feel better after a good night's sleep.'

Hanging up the phone, Glenn sunk back onto his pillows. What a day, he thought. Glancing across the room he saw his suitcase there, half-packed, ready to be carried onto his flight back to London the next day. It felt strange to be leaving so soon after such an intense and life-changing experience. Where had Bettina gone, he wondered, and what was she thinking now? Was she lying awake too, somewhere in Aachen, thinking about what Glenn had told her? And why had he told her, he wondered? Glenn closed his eyes and saw her face in his mind, and though he tried, he hardly slept the whole night long.

CHAPTER EIGHT

Glenn walked to the goodbye breakfast the following morning with a heavy feeling in his stomach. He was tired and wished he had slept more. He also couldn't stop thinking about Bettina, and wondered if she would be there at the conference centre. His steps felt clumsy as he walked. Bettina's sudden departure the night before had not only left him doubting his feelings about her, but about everything – his marriage, his very life.

As he walked, he thought hard. Glenn was under no illusion that his relationship with his wife was in a good place. He and Eleanora had always had their differences and that had never been a problem, but it had never been a good thing, either. He knew that the differences between some couples complimented each other; his own parents were a great example of that. Iris was a worrier and Bertie was too carefree. But somehow their differences grounded them and gave them the incentive they needed to change for the better. Eleanora did not have a grounding effect on him, however. In fact, she often made him feel like he wanted to run away.

Such were his thoughts as Glenn entered the conference room, where breakfast was being served and many people were arriving. The crowds of the previous day had dispersed slightly, as many of the conference attendees had already gone home. Nevertheless, Glenn could not remain pensive for long, because the room was alive with animated discussion. Everywhere he looked he saw conference members milling around, tucking into plates stacked high with all sorts of German delicacies.

Glenn was quite amazed by the variety of food available. He wondered how it was possible to have five types of muesli, each variation loaded with different nuts, seeds and dried fruits. He stepped towards them for a closer inspection, fascinated by the different combinations and feeling his stomach rumbling with hunger. One type was packed full of hazelnuts but had very few raisins; another was loaded with sunflower seeds; another featured clusters of toasted almonds coated in honey.

'Glenn!' a familiar voice called through the din of the breakfast. Glenn turned away from the muesli to see Herbert Farrand striding towards him. The handsome man was bursting with energy; he wore a pale suit with a mellow navy tie. This outfit seemed to say a sad goodbye rather than his previous outfits, which had said a charming hello.

'Good morning, Herbert,' said Glenn. 'It's a sad day! Everyone here is walking away with a heavy heart, I'm sure of it.'

'Oh, thank you, Glenn, and welcome, welcome, welcome to our little German breakfast!' laughed the ICB President. Herbert surveyed the stands around with a wide smile on his face, not unlike a baseball coach admiring his team before a match.

'It's quite a spread you have put on for us,' said Glenn. 'Man, you could feed an army with this! I can't wait to get stuck in, I'm starving.'

'*Natürlich*,' Herbert replied in German, his smile as constant and charming as ever. 'We would not want our guests to go away with empty stomachs, now, would we? No, no, that is not how we do things at the ICB. Besides, it is a chance for you all to see how our blind cooks are working.'

'Blind cooks?' said Glenn, puzzled by the expression.

'Yes, all of the breakfast provided today was made by chefs who are blind,' said Herbert. Then, drawing closer to Glenn, he whispered: 'It's my job to give the blind as many opportunities for growth as possible. This is a great business opportunity for them.'

Glenn nodded politely, both impressed and slightly disturbed by Herbert's ability to transform situations into opportunities to make money.

'I can see that!' he said.

'Go, see for yourself!' said Herbert, patting Glenn on the back. 'Gerta over there is showcasing the twenty different cheeses she produces on her family farm in Bavaria. They are smelly, let me warn you, but very delicious.'

Herbert gestured to a woman arranging cheeses of all colours, shapes and sizes on a stand nearby.

'Lana, in pink, with the unfortunate haircut, cures meats and sausage in Dusseldorf,' he went on, pointing to the next stand along. 'This is something very special; with a bit of bread and butter, it will melt your heart.'

Herbert began to give Glenn a little tour of all the breakfast on display, pointing out different stands as if they were tourist attractions to visit.

'Gilette from Marseilles is the lady in the white uniform,' he continued. 'Look, she is showing us her smoked fish today. They look as appetising as English kippers. Her and her husband smoke it all themselves, so you can only imagine how they smell! Ha! That is a joke, Glenn, just a joke.'

Glenn recognised the woman at the last stand. Odile was standing there, looking as composed as she had done the night before at the dinner. If he remembered correctly, she was an excellent chef. That morning she presided over a feast of her own making.

'And last but not least we even have our own little baker, Odile,' said Herbert. 'She has created five different breads, all with a different kind of seed! Of course, don't forget to visit Alice's jam stand after you have been to Odile. She has around seven different jams, all made in Poland, from the fruits that grow locally there.'

Glenn had enjoyed following Herbert's hand as he pointed to each of the chefs and their various produce. It all looked absolutely delicious. An artisanal food fair, full of delights, ready to be tasted by everyone at the breakfast. It was a feast for the eyes and stirred a ravenous hunger in Glenn's stomach.

'This is amazing,' he said. 'What a great concept. It looks like a very German spread but in fact it's very international. And totally prepared by the blind? That's fantastic. No one back home would believe this.'

'You must understand, Glenn,' said Herbert. 'This is the role the ICB plays in international society. We make the unbelievable believable and the impossible possible.'

With that Herbert looked away, like the man in the poster, his chiselled face locked in a serious, sincere expression. Glenn was impressed; he had the distinct impression that the President could talk about the ICB's qualities for hours on end.

Luckily for Glenn, his stomach made a loud grumbling noise.

'Oh, listen to me, talking away when you are starving in front of me!' Herbert exclaimed. 'Come, let me introduce you to the ladies who are making these treats.'

'That's alright,' Glenn said quickly. 'I don't want to hold you up, Herbert. You must have so much to do. I'll just go and get stuck into some muesli.'

'Very well, as you wish,' said Herbert, smiling before marching off to talk to some others.

Glenn walked over to the food tables, scanning the room for Bettina. He could not see her anywhere. Most people were sat at long tables, tucking into plates of cheeses and dried meat, laughing and exchanging email addresses before they went their separate ways. Glenn saw Bill sat at the end of one table alone and quickly turned away, hoping he had not seen him. He had nothing against the Texan, but he didn't want to make small talk with him all morning. Helping himself to muesli, Glenn was pleasantly surprised to see Odile overseeing her baked bread stand not far from him. She looked as pretty as ever, now dressed in a smart apron and wearing a stylish hairnet.

'Hello Odile,' he said. 'What a fantastic display you've put on for us!'

'Is that Glenn?' she asked. 'Or Bill?'

'It's Glenn,' he said, forgetting that not everyone was like Bettina. Not everyone could smell him from metres away. 'Do I really sound like Bill? Oh dear, I guess it's true what they say about loud Americans: we're all the same!'

'Oh no, I'm sorry, Glenn! I'm glad it's you,' Odile whispered, grinning broadly. 'I was afraid you might be Bill coming for a new cookery lesson. I don't think I can teach that man anymore.'

'Why?' asked Glenn, smiling to hear Odile speak so honestly.

'Because he is truly a lost cause,' she said.

Glenn laughed at this, remembering the calamity and clattering of pots and pans in the workshop kitchen. The Texan had truly caused some havoc.

'Have you come to try some of the bread, Glenn?' Odile asked him. 'It is made using traditions from my French family. I learnt a lot from them when we visited France when I was growing up. In the States, people go crazy for my bread, just crazy.'

'May I try?' Glenn asked. 'Please, I'm dying of hunger here!'

'Help yourself,' smiled Odile. Taking her at her word, Glenn tucked into a delicious loaf covered in poppy seeds. There were multiple breads to choose from: all sprinkled and baked with different things. The poppy seed bread sat next to almond bread, which sat next to loaves covered in pine nuts, and more loaves sprinkled with sunflower seeds.

'My favourite is this one,' said Odile, reaching forward slowly to a pile of loaves baked with sesame seeds. 'I love sesame. Bettina loves this one too. I always make it for her, when we're in the same place.'

'You must all miss each other, when you're not at these conferences,' said Glenn, hearing the tone of sadness in her voice. 'All you fantastic ladies, in every different corner of the globe. Do you see each other often?'

'We try to,' sighed Odile. 'But yes, we're an international group, spread all over the world. We just try to make the most of the time we can have together, like this weekend in Aachen.'

'It was so lovely to meet you all,' said Glenn. 'Boy, I've had a swell time here.'

'We think so too,' smiled Odile. 'I'm so glad Bettina invited you along last night to the restaurant.'

'Is Bettina here?' Glenn asked tentatively. He wondered if Odile had noticed her sudden departure the night before, but she seemed unfazed by the question.

'Not that I know of,' she answered. 'I'm sure she's around somewhere though. It's not like her to leave without saying goodbye.'

Glenn felt his spirits lighten immediately. He knew then that he would get a chance to say goodbye after all, and to broach the rather awkward events of the previous evening. Relieved, he tucked into a piece of poppy seed bread.

'Gosh, that's delicious!' he exclaimed. The bread was wonderfully baked, with a thick consistency and a unique taste with the poppy seed topping.

'*Merci beaucoup*,' Odile said, smiling into the distance. 'I advise you taste some of the jam on offer too. It's delicious. *Bon appétit*, Glenn.'

'Thanks, Odile,' said Glenn. Wandering along the food tables, Glenn helped himself to a feast fit for a king, chatting to all the ladies as he did so. He sampled beef sausages, cured meats, a variety of smoked fish and some truly delectable cheeses. Every woman had a story to tell about how she had made her food stuffs and the difficulties she had faced with her blindness. Glenn was in awe of them all, and had to laugh with the jam maker about his choice of jam, protesting that because they were all so delicious, he didn't know which to choose to spread on his bread. There was apricot, pear, apple, strawberry and raspberry jams, all packaged in little glass jars with tweed coverings.

'Try them all!' cried the woman in good cheer. 'Taste every single one and then choose your favourite.'

'That's just it,' laughed Glenn. 'I don't know if I'll ever be able to decide!'

When Glenn had eaten his fill, he glided over to a group of women he recognised. Laura, Elfrida and Christina were playing a game with Zu-Ting.

'What's the game, ladies?' he asked, hoping they didn't mind him intruding on them. He felt immediately happy again to be in their company.

'Glenn!' cried Zu-Ting, standing up to shake his hand in welcome. 'Good, a fair judge, you can help us.'

'Help with what?' he asked.

'We need an adjudicator,' said Christina. 'Elfrida is cheating at cards and we know it.'

'I don't want to cause any trouble,' said Glenn, chuckling, hands raised, 'or make any enemies.'

'Ever the diplomat,' laughed Zu-Ting. 'Fine, then Elfrida gets away with it. Where's Bettina when we need her? She can always smell a rat when there's one around.'

'Who are you calling a rat?' Elfrida laughed. 'Don't blame me if you have sour grapes. You're starting to sound like Bill.'

'Let's just be grateful that he's not here!' laughed Zu-Ting.

'Thank God!' chuckled Christina. They all laughed then. The camaraderie among the women was so special, Glenn thought, laughing with them as they teased each other.

'Speaking of Bettina, where is she?' asked Laura. 'Glenn, have you seen her?'

'No,' said Glenn. 'I was going to ask you the same question. She left so suddenly last night…'

'She does that sometimes,' sighed Christina.

'You look away for a second and: poof! She's gone,' said Zu-Ting, dealing out a fresh round of cards. 'Come on, Glenn, sit and play with us.'

Glad of the invitation, Glenn settled himself down among the women and checked his hand. It was good. He was happy to feel the Braille on the cards once more. The embossed texture was pleasant to the touch. He enjoyed a few successful games with the women before Herbert Farrand appeared once more, this time with Odile at his side.

'My, this looks cosy!' exclaimed the President, winking at Glenn. 'Will you girls let Mr. Tebbhurst go this afternoon, or will you keep him here forever? He has a wife, you know.'

'He is free to leave whenever he likes,' said Laura. 'The only foul play here is Elfrida's cheating. Odile, come and control this woman.'

'I am not cheating!' cried Elfrida, hitting Laura lightly with her cards. Odile laughed at this.

'People are starting to leave,' she said, clearly listening hard to sounds of scraping chairs and retreating footsteps.

'All good things come to an end,' Herbert sighed. 'Further to last night's announcement, we've made a fine sum, ladies, I can tell you that.'

'So next time we get better hotels, right?' said Laura, raising an expectant eyebrow at the president.

The five women laughed and Glenn laughed too. He looked down at his watch. He would have to join the departing crowds soon too. He had only a couple of hours left before his flight left for London, and he still had to collect his luggage from the hotel.

Looking around the room once more, he searched for Bettina, but couldn't see her anywhere. Perhaps he would see her outside, he hoped.

He had already looked in the garden and she wasn't there. If the five other women hadn't seen her, he didn't fancy his chances.

'I'm sorry, ladies,' he said, smiling sadly. 'But I think I will have to split soon.'

'Already?' exclaimed Zu-Ting, her eyebrows forming a frown on her delicate forehead.

'Split?' said Laura. 'You're leaving us?' said Christina.

'My flight leaves soon,' he said. 'Otherwise I would have happily played with you ladies all afternoon. It has been such a pleasure to meet you all. Truly. I want to say something, actually...' The women all watched expectantly as Glenn paused to take a deep breath. 'Every one of you has such an inspiring story to tell,' he said warmly, 'and I have been as inspired as everyone else over these past few days. You're all amazing. Thank you.'

'Ah, Glenn, you're too kind!' squeaked Laura. 'That's so sweet.'

'I mean it, from the bottom of my heart,' said Glenn. 'Your kindness this weekend has been overwhelming. You've helped so many people, I'm sure of it. Really, I mean every word.'

'I'm sure you do,' said Christina, reaching out and placing her hand on his for a moment. 'You have been a great listener, Glenn. We are so grateful for that.'

'And a great talker,' said Laura, smiling at him. 'We're grateful for that too.'

'Don't forget you can vote for me, Glenn,' said Zu-Ting, 'but only if you become a Chinese citizen.'

'Where's the immigration office?' Glenn asked with mock urgency. 'Sign me up!'

The group laughed. Everyone had put down their cards. It was strange, Glenn thought; in the same situation but with full-sighted people, everyone would be looking at him. Instead, the group had just stopped whatever they were doing and were focusing, in that moment, on the sounds and the feelings of the moment. Each of them stared ahead with small smiles on their faces.

'Take care, Glenn,' said Odile. 'You're a special man. I'll send you some of my recipes. Do you have email?'

'I do,' said Glenn. Taking out a pen and paper, he jotted down each of their email addresses in turn.

'Do write, Glenn,' said Laura, smiling as she gazed ahead.

'I will,' he nodded.

'And we'll write back,' laughed Zu-Ting. 'Good luck with your father, Glenn.'

'Give him our best,' said Christina. 'I will pray for him.'

'Thank you,' said Glenn. 'Thank you all so much.'

He stood up and looked around the room once more, hoping Bettina might walk through a doorway at any second, or start speaking from a podium. But she was nowhere to be seen.

'Will you say goodbye to Bettina for me?' he asked the group.

'We will,' said Odile, nodding at him with a warm smile.

'Tell her,' he began, but faltered, not sure what he wanted to say. 'Tell her I enjoyed our chats,' he said at last. 'Goodbye, ladies.'

'I'll see you out,' said Herbert, placing a hand on Glenn's shoulder.

The two men walked away from the group of women who continued to play cards. When they were out of earshot, Herbert leant close to Glenn's ear and spoke softly.

'They're quite a fantastic group, aren't they?' he said, almost whispering to Glenn.

'They're all extraordinary women,' Glenn replied, shaking his head sadly, sheepishly.

'Yes, and they all love you,' said Herbert. 'They love me, naturally, but it means something when they warm to someone new.'

'What can I say?' laughed Glenn. 'I have a way with women.'

'You're right, you're right,' said Herbert, nodding his head quickly. 'You are a naturally charismatic man. Anyone can see that.'

'Thanks, Herbert,' said Glenn, grateful if a little bemused by the praise.

'A man like you looks like he can take on the whole world before breakfast,' said Herbert appreciatively. Glenn was surprised to hear this, for he thought exactly the same of Herbert Farrand.

'Well, if there's ever anything I can do to help,' said Glenn.

'You know, I think you could help us with some fundraising,' said Herbert, nodding at the thought.

'I thought you had fulfilled your budget for the coming year?' said Glenn, remembering Farrand's announcement of the night before.

'Yes, yes,' said Herbert, waving his arm as if to wave the millions of dollars away. 'But there are more years to come. More projects, more people suffering with blindness, more changes to implement. And I know you would like to help these women, Glenn. I know you care about them and what we are trying to do here. I can see you have a good heart.'

Glenn thought about that for a moment. Yes, he thought: he did want to help them.

'Just think about it,' offered Herbert. 'There's no rush. We will come and see you in London. We'll get so much done, I can assure you of that.'

They left it at that. Shaking Herbert's hand, Glenn took his leave from the conference. Later on, as the plane stood on the runway, ready for boarding, Glenn realised he was leaving Germany and all he had learned behind. He felt a pang of sadness touch his heart and felt less like he was going home and more like he was going away. But amongst that, a nagging discomfort remained. He had not said goodbye to Bettina, and he wondered if he would ever see her again.

CHAPTER NINE

Winter in London was a sombre affair, thought Glenn, looking out of his office window one afternoon. The light autumnal skies turned a steely grey, threatening to rain down on the city at any moment. Glenn's routine of work at the charity and commuting through the busy throngs of the capital had taken him a while to settle back into. Almost three months had passed now since his trip to Aachen and the conference, and Glenn couldn't get memories of the experience out of his head. At home and at work, his mind drifted back to the workshops, to those six incredible women, and to the moment when Bettina's hand had brushed against his knee. Though he had taken down some of their email addresses, Glenn hadn't made any contact with any of the women yet. But he had spent a lot of his time on the phone to his mother and father, discussing that trip and the hope and promise it offered to help ease Bertie's condition.

Presently, checking his watch, he saw that it was a good time to call them in New York. Dialling through, his heart warmed to hear his mother answer, though threaded through her voice were myriad subtle tones of melancholy.

'The doctors at the hospital say that he's blind and that's that,' Iris told him miserably, choking back her tears. 'They say his insurance won't pay for any of the more experimental operations. You know, the one to replace the optic nerve?'

'The hospital at Columbia University have said that?' Glenn asked, surprised. 'I can't believe it, Ma. Who is running these joints? Are they sure?'

'Yes,' his mother sighed. 'They say he doesn't qualify and anyway, at his age, it's too risky.'

'But I've read about successful operations in Japan,' countered Glenn. 'Those patients were even older than Bertie! Am I the only one doing research here? Jeez!'

'Mm, well, they won't try it here,' said Iris. Glenn couldn't stand to hear the despondency in his mother's voice. His parents had been coming to terms with his Bertie's blindness for months now, but they seemed to be going backwards in their vigour for tackling the condition, or at least accepting it positively. And this was all despite Glenn's enthusiasm; his retellings of all he had learnt at the conference in Aachen.

'So they won't try anything?' Glenn asked. 'They're not going to risk anything, right? Typical, just typical.'

'No, they say there's an accumulation of protein behind the eye that is refusing to let sight occur,' she answered. 'It's that damn diabetes. It's always the way with Type 2. It's all setting in now.'

'Look,' said Glenn, suffering at hearing his mother so upset. 'I can't listen to this anymore. I wanna do things my way. I think I might be able to help. How is your schedule looking?'

'Honey, we don't have a schedule!' said Iris, and Glenn was happy to hear her laugh for the first time in a long time, even it was a laugh of despair.

'I'm going to call you back tomorrow, OK?' said Glenn. 'Speak to you soon, Mom.'

Hanging up, Glenn set his mind to the task ahead. Exhausted and wishing he could avoid the hustle of returning to Virginia Water via central London, Glenn made his way home quickly. When he reached Ronda Round Manor, he felt a knot of anxiety twisted tight in his stomach. He knew the conversation ahead of him would not be easy.

In the dark grey light, the graceful Georgian curves of the building appeared oppressive and alien somehow after the modern offices of the charity where he spent most of the day. He'd felt the same thing when he returned from Aachen after the conference centre. Somehow the antiquity of the manor house felt outdated and fading compared to the evolving world around it. Glenn travelled a lot for his work and was no stranger to coming and going to different places. But returning home to Eleanora after Aachen had been a difficult and strange transition. He felt different to the man who had been there before the trip to Aachen, and before he father's blindness – he could just feel it in his bones.

Stepping through the front door, Glenn hung his hat and coat on the stand before heading through to the drawing room. It was early evening so there was a fifty-fifty chance of Eleanora being at home, or at her bridge club. As he shuffled through the entrance hall he spotted a light on, and with it, a commingling sensation of excitement and disappointment. A part of him wanted to be alone to contemplate all he'd learnt that weekend; another part craved for company.

'Nora?' he called, walking into the drawing room. His wife was reclining on an elegant *chaise longue*, sipping a cup of camomile tea and poring over a newspaper. She looked up as he walked in, scowling.

'I have told you not to call me that,' she said.

'Sorry, honey,' said Glenn, smiling as he bent down to kiss her. 'Come on, honey, let me know you love me?'

She raised her arms and held them around his shoulders for a moment.

'Hello, dear,' she said, a subtle smile spreading across her face.

'Hello, darling,' he replied. He settled himself down into his favourite armchair opposite. 'I've been thinking about something, something important. Can I talk with you for a moment?'

'Mm hmm?' murmured Eleanora, her eyes turned back down to the newspaper.

'Are you gonna keep reading that?' he asked her. 'If so, I'll go and talk to the statues. I'll get more respect from them.'

'What is it?' she asked in surprise, raising her eyebrows at his tone.

'I'd like to invite my parents over, for a few weeks, to give them a break from their routine,' he said. 'I could even arrange some meetings with doctors in London. The London Eye Hospital on Harley Street might be worth a visit. The doctor there still seems unsure of the diagnosis.'

Eleanora let out a deep sigh and put down her newspaper.

'How long exactly would you like them to stay for?' she asked.

'I'm not sure,' said Glenn, shrugging. 'Does it matter? I can ask them how long they would like to stay. A week, perhaps. Maybe two.'

'Well, that's all very well, Glenn, but don't expect me to drop everything and look after them,' said Eleanora. 'I have a very busy schedule this January.'

Glenn said nothing, standing up to pour himself a cup of tea from the silver pot standing on the table.

'Of course, of course,' he said diplomatically. 'I can keep flexible hours at work and spend time with them. You would not need to trouble yourself beyond the norm.'

Eleanora eyed her husband suspiciously.

'I know you, Glenn Tebbhurst,' she said. 'There will be some kind of famine or refugee crisis in Yemen or Timbuktu and you'll be at the office all day. I'll be stuck with them, I'm sure of it.'

'They are my parents,' said Glenn, feeling himself growing impatient with his wife. 'They have suffered quite a blow to their lives recently. I'm their only son and I want to do this for them. Can't you understand that?'

'Oh, darling, I know that,' said Eleanora. 'I do, and I sympathise. I'm not a monster. But one does wonder, you know… one does not want to be lumbered for months on end with, well, your disabled father and your mother. Let's not forget how your mother feels about me. She'll be as loath as I am to spend any time together.'

'Listen, I'll do my best to make sure no one gets *lumbered* with anyone,' said Glenn, sounding out the word his wife had used with distaste. 'They're my parents and I'd like them to come over. End of story. '

'Suit yourself,' sighed Eleanora. 'I'll warn my parents of their visit.'

Leaning back in his chair after a long sip of tea, Glenn took this prickly announcement as a sign that his wife had reluctantly agreed to the visit. No, he thought, she would not be happy with them there, and nor would her parents, but Glenn wanted to see his father. He had family too. Reclining, he looked up at the paintings lining the walls: the faces of the Beaumont ancestors peered down at him miserably. He had never liked how almost every wall in their house had a bewigged, grumpy face looking down at him, reminding him that he was not a Beaumont, merely someone who had married into their family. He remembered the workshop and the fantastic scene they had traced with their fingers and felt a pang of nostalgia. He closed his eyes and remembered the surrealism of that moment, being totally cloaked in darkness and utterly absorbed in one's senses. Bettina was next to him, telling him about her incredible world of touch and sound. All he had to do was listen.

When Glenn called his mother to invite them over to London the next day, she sounded happy to hear the news.

'Your father will be thrilled,' she said excitedly. 'I'll tell him at lunch time.'

'I'm going to ask my secretary to call you to arrange flights, alright?' said Glenn, winking at Sonia, who nodded enthusiastically behind her desk in the adjacent room. He chatted with his mother for a few more minutes before hanging up and briefing Sonia.

'They need to be comfortable and well-attended,' he told his secretary, unable to keep the anxiety from his voice. 'Perhaps we should call ahead to the airport in New York, someone could meet him, you know, with a wheelchair or something?'

'I'm sure we can arrange that, sir,' said Sonia, smiling kindly at her boss. 'Leave it with me. I'll make sure they have a safe and comfortable journey.'

'Thanks, Sonia,' said Glenn, placing a grateful hand on her shoulder for a moment.

'You seem nervous,' she said. 'Is everything alright? You're never nervous, sir.'

'Yes,' said Glenn. 'I just... well, its Dad's first time flying with his condition. I don't want him to feel afraid. He's always loved flying and, well, things will be different now.'

'Didn't you say you attended one of those workshops in Aachen about travelling with blindness?' Sonia asked. 'I remember you mentioning it.'

The memory jogged in Glenn's brain and Laura's face popped into his mind. The red-haired British girl had indeed spoken at length about the ease with which blind people travelled these days.

'Yes, that was Laura,' Glenn smiled at Sonia. 'You're right!'

'Well, I'm sure when I call to book the tickets I can discuss your father's situation with the airline and they will do everything within their power to make his journey as easy as possible,' said the secretary.

'You're a gem, Sonia!' he cried. 'I'll leave it in your capable hands.'

He had total faith in Sonia's ability to ensure the airline took care of his father, but that did not stop him feeling nervous as he stood waiting in the arrivals hall at Heathrow Airport. He'd seen on the boards that their plane had landed and watched anxiously as the door opened and closed, letting people through. Glenn felt a mixture of relief, happiness and sadness when he saw his father being wheeled through, his white cane clutched stiffly in his hands, Iris strolling slowly beside them with her suitcase. It was the first time Glenn really noticed that his parents were getting old. His mother wore an elegant blue cashmere cardigan and his father had worn a thick blue blazer to match. He was wearing dark glasses and seemed to be chattering very happily with the man pushing his wheelchair.

'Say, where's that accent from?' Glenn heard him asking as the wheelchair rolled forward. 'My son's here somewhere and he's from London. He doesn't sound like a Londoner, sadly. I would have liked him to pick up a bit of cockney accent.'

Glenn raised a hand to his mother and the assistant. The bearded man smiled at Glenn.

'You must be the son? I've heard a lot about you,' he said.

'Oh really?' said Glenn in his best cockney accent. 'All good I hope?'

The man laughed at this, waved a goodbye to Glenn and bid the couple a nice trip.

'What a kind man,' said Iris, regarding the airport attendant fondly as he wandered back through to the terminals.

'What a champion, pushing me all along here!' chuckled Bertie. 'What did he look like, Glenn? Was he a strapping kinda fella? Or was I just imagining it?'

'You,' scowled Iris, shaking her head at her husband. 'You think everyone is either beautiful or handsome now you've lost your sight.'

'What can I say? It's a gift!' he cried.

'He did look strong, Dad,' laughed Glenn, leaning down to take his father in his arms. 'But not as strong as your son! Come here, you. Give your boy a bear hug.'

They embraced tightly and Bertie kissed his son softly on the cheek. When they parted, Bertie raised his hands and began to trace the shape of Glenn's face. Glenn felt self-conscious at first, there, in the middle of the airport, but after a while he enjoyed watching his father's smile as he cupped the shape of his son's chin, nose, and jaw.

'Good to be here, son, good to be here,' said Bertie, choking back the emotion which threatened to drop tears down his face. 'Your mother's so happy to see you. I don't need eyes to see that.'

Glenn looked down and saw his mother beaming up at him as he drew her close for an embrace. They held each other tightly and Glenn felt his mother fighting back the tears too.

'You are both so welcome here,' he said loudly, smiling warmly down at both of them. 'Welcome to London, folks! Eleanora's looking forward to seeing you both.'

Bertie scoffed. 'I bet she is!' he laughed.

Glenn and his mother exchanged nervous glances. It was no secret that the Tebbhursts did not get on well with Glenn's wife. Nor did they get on well with her parents.

'Are Mummy and Daddy still running the estate?' asked Iris.

'Now, now, none of that please, Mom,' he chuckled. 'I need harmony in my household. But, as you've asked, yes, sort of,' he said, taking his mother's suitcases and loading them onto a trolley with Bertie's bags. 'Eleanora does a lot of the work too now.'

'Oh, she's decided she likes work now?' asked Iris, raising an eyebrow.

'Mom,' Glenn warned his mother with a knowing smile. 'Be nice, okay?'

'Me?' cried Iris. 'Always!'

They spent the journey home catching up in the taxi. Glenn sat in the front and every now and again caught side of his father's face in the rear-view mirror. There was a new sadness there which Glenn could only assume came from the fact of being in England but not being able to see it. Bertie too had worked in London for a period. Glenn knew how much his father loved the green countryside around the capital city. The heaviness of his father's condition settled on him for a moment before he banished it from his mind, refusing to let it pervade their happy reunion.

'It looks beautiful, Dad!' he cried. 'I promise you!'

Pulling into Ronda Round Manor, Glenn was happy to hear Iris draw a deep, excited breath.

'It's as beautiful as ever,' she said. 'Even in winter.'

'In snow it's really a sight to behold,' said Glenn. 'I feel like a king of the manor in winter! Come, let's get inside and put you two by the fire. I'm sure Eleanora's started one in the drawing room.'

'I'm sure,' said Iris confidently. 'She's probably burning peasants on it as we speak.'

'*Mom,*' Glenn warned.

'It was a joke!' she protested. 'Look, even your father's laughing!'

The sight of Bertie bursting into laughter was enough to banish any thoughts of admonishment from Glenn's mind. He helped his father out of the car, and watched with surprise as his father swept his white cane from side to side, guiding himself with some skill towards the front door. Carrying the suitcases up into the house, Glenn called out for his wife, who appeared a few moments later, dressed in a classic navy blue suit. She looked very beautiful, Glenn thought, and had no doubt wanted to show off her timeless figure to her mother-in-law, who scowled behind her smile.

'Iris!' cried Eleanora with masked hostility.

'Eleanora,' said Iris. 'You're looking beautiful, sweetheart.'

'And you look tired, my dear,' said Eleanora, frowning slightly. 'Come on in. Where is the injured soldier? Do we need a stretcher?'

'Hullo, Eleanora,' said Bertie in his deep Brooklyn accent. Eleanora bent down and gave Bertie a kiss, and gasped as he raised his hands to feel her face as he had done with Glenn. She glared over at Glenn, her eyes wide with shock. Glenn nodded back at her reassuringly.

'Oh, how strange,' she said awkwardly, clearing her throat and attempting to move away.

'Sorry if I made you feel uncomfortable,' said Bertie, chuckling slightly as he gazed into the distance. 'I can only see with my hands now.'

'I see,' said Eleanora stiffly.

'You're as beautiful as ever, Eleanora,' said Bertie, grinning into space. Eleanora glanced at Glenn, not knowing where to look or what to say.

'My parents are here too,' she said quickly. 'They're just through in the drawing room. I thought we could all have dinner together, now that we're all here.'

'What a lovely idea, sweetheart!' said Iris. 'You know how much we love to see the lord and lady of the manor!'

'Well, technically that's us,' said Eleanora, raising an eyebrow and gesturing to Glenn and herself. 'But yes, I suppose they are still attached to the estate.'

Glenn groaned inside at the thought of the dinner to come. The two sets of parents were incredibly different and no doubt there would be tensions.

'We have fresh duck, only killed this morning,' said Eleanora. 'It's going to be delicious! Now, Glenn, would you be so kind as to take your parents to their room. I believe your father will need some assistance?'

'Of course, darling, that all sounds marvellous,' said Glenn. 'We'll be down shortly.'

'Awaiting you all in the drawing room then,' she said, with a short, sharp smile. 'The wine is cooling.'

Glenn led his parents to a small room they had made up on the ground floor of the house. It was not one of the guestrooms but Glenn had had it converted into a bedroom for his father's visit. It did not make sense for his father to sleep upstairs in one of the guestrooms there. The staircase was far too steep and they did not have a carer to help Bertie get around. When they had set their things down and relaxed for a moment, Glenn led them back through to the drawing room, where Eleanora was chattering animatedly to her parents.

'Ah! Glenn! Bertie!' cried Eleanora's father, Harold John Beaumont. Short and rather rounded, Harold was a jolly but snobby fellow. 'You old devils! Come and give old Harry a shake!'

Harold plunged his hand towards Bertie, grabbing his free hand and shaking hard.

'Ellie's told us you've had quite the trauma, sir, oh yes, quite the trauma,' said Harold, so loudly that Glenn wondered if Eleanora's father thought blind people were hard of hearing too. 'Terrible news, just terrible. My heart goes out to you, sir, it really does. Great stuff your lad here has brought you over to Blighty for some good old-fashioned English medicine! I'm sure our doctors in Harley Street will have something to say. Those American doctors always seem so terribly dim on the television, but I must say, I'm probably biased, oh yes, a proud Englishman I am – and a Beaumont to boot!'

'Iris, oh how wonderful to see you!' Eleanora's mother had cooed from the other side of the drawing room. Lesley Margaret Beaumont was as fond of Iris Tebbhurst as she was of instant coffee; both left bitter tastes in her mouth. The feeling was mutual and the two women made high-pitched, irritable small talk for a while before Eleanora announced it was dinner time. Glenn stayed by his father's side as he used his cane to make his way through the house.

'My goodness!' Lesley hissed underneath her breath. 'What if he breaks the china? Or one of our legs?'

'Your legs will be quite safe, Lesley,' Glenn said loudly to show he had heard. Eleanora hushed her mother and Glenn thought he saw a small smile appear on his father's lips. Even Glenn had to admit that the Beaumonts' apparent understanding of blindness as a form of deafness was quite amusing.

The *canard à l'orange* was deliciously prepared as ever by the cook Eleanora hired for special occasions. Eleanora's parents were fascinated by Bertie's blindness and transformed him into some sort of martyred saint.

'It is so good that you are still socialising, still staying busy,' Lesley drawled in her clear-cut English in between mouthfuls of tender duck. 'I think if I went blind, I'd just stay in bed all day!'

'Not me,' chuckled Harold. 'Oh no, I'd be out there, strapped onto a horse and I'd go for a hero's suicide.'

'Daddy,' squeaked Eleanora. 'Don't talk about things like that.'

'Sorry, darling, I forgot you were such a sensitive little soul,' Harold smiled affectionately at his daughter. 'You could never stand us talking about death, even if it was just shooting foxes and rabbits on the estate.'

'I hope you're not implying that blind people should be shot, Harold?' smiled Iris, raising an eyebrow.

'Oh Gods no!' squawked Harold, his face falling and his mouth dropping. He looked quickly at Bertie who was clearly amused by the conversation. Glenn was happy to see a smile on his lips. He caught his mother's eye and she smiled too. He had the impression that they were enjoying being in the company of others, even if it was people as mad as the Beaumonts.

By the time they'd finished their thick and creamy slices of tiramisu for dessert, Bertie was yawning and Glenn knew it was time to bring the evening's entertainment to a close. He'd forgotten how tired his parents must have been after their long journey. With that, wishing the others goodnight, Glenn led his parents to the fireplace in the drawing room, where he suggested they rest until they wanted to sleep.

'Goodnight, honey,' said Iris, smiling sadly up at her son. 'We're happy to be here with you.'

'And I'm happy you're both here,' said Glenn. 'Home feels more like home with you two around. Now go! Sleep and have sweet English dreams!'

Over the next few days, Glenn allowed his parents to settle in before taking his father to Harley Street to see a specialist there. It had been years since he had travelled with his father on the underground, but this would be a different experience. Everything took twice, if not three times, as long. Glenn was just glad his father could not see the pointed looks people gave him. Even on the tube, where people generally kept to their own business, people stared.

As they approached the London Eye Hospital, Glenn was not entirely sure why they were going. His father was adamant that there were at least five different ways of recovering eyesight. He had been telling Glenn all about them since the day he arrived. His initial stoicism had given way to hope that he might find a cure. He was dreaming of them, but Glenn, though he nodded supportively, was not dreaming. He secretly hoped that the meeting with the doctor would allow his father to see sense and accept his condition. When they finally reached the doctor, Glenn let Bertie do the talking.

'I know it's too late for me to undertake optic nerve surgery,' said Bertie. 'But, Doc, I know there are other ways out there.'

'Yes, Mr. Tebbhurst, having looked at your notes I can confirm that you would not be eligible for the optic nerve experimental treatment,' sighed the doctor, a young man who seemed sympathetic towards Bertie's position. Glenn wondered how many blind people this doctor saw every day, each one hopeful, each one praying for a cure.

'What about stem cell injections?' his father asked.

'This has been used in the case of macular degeneration, yes,' said the doctor. Turning to Glenn, he began to explain. 'Macular degeneration occurs when the cells supplying blood to the retina break down. They begin to deteriorate and eventually lead to the dysfunction of the retina. When that happens, I'm afraid that's usually it, really, one's vision is almost completely lost. But this is a treatment with some hope.'

'How does the treatment work?' Glenn asked.

'Perhaps your father can tell us,' smiled the doctor.

'Well, I've heard that they call the stem cells the "grandfather cells" because they can grow into any cell type,' said Bertie excitedly.

'Exactly,' said he doctor. 'Stem cells can replenish a type of cell called retinal pigment epithelial, the cell which carries nutrients to the retina. Because, as your father says, stem cells have this malleable quality, they can be moulded into these retinal pigment epithelial cells. It's quite ingenious. Those cells can then replenish nutrients in the retina. They are created using IVF embryos in the lab and then injected into the eye.'

'It's like planting new crops,' chuckled Bertie, gazing into the distance.

Glenn listened intently to all that was said with fascination.

'Would this treatment work for my father?' he asked, daring to hope. 'Could you bring his eyes back, doctor?'

But the doctor was already looking grave.

'I'm afraid the damage to your father's retina is quite severe,' he sighed. 'Even with injections, the chances of replenishing it are very slim. You used the analogy of planting new crops, Mr. Tebbhurst. Well, in some cases, the ground is so badly worn, nothing will grow there anymore. I fear this treatment would be expensive and ultimately disappointing for you.'

'What about gene therapy?' asked Bertie. 'Surely that's worth a try?'

'Gene therapy?' said Glenn. The doctor was shaking his head once more.

'I'm afraid gene therapy only works with patients with a genetic mutation that plays havoc with the photoreceptors in their eyes,' he explained. 'It is a new and exciting treatment, similar to the stem cell therapy, injecting genes that produce a protein necessary for the photoreceptors to work into the eye. But your father is not eligible for this.'

They discussed their options for a while longer, during which time Glenn began to wish that they had never visited in the first place. One by one, all of Bertie's dreams of recovery were dashed down by scientific impossibility. Even the most advanced technologies in Japan could not help him. When they finally left, Glenn put an arm around his father.

'I fear we've hit a dead end,' he said gently. 'Dad, I want this to work out, I want things to get better, but perhaps we should be realistic...'

'Never!' cried Bertie amiably, shaking his head. 'I won't give up, Glenn. There's gotta be a cure.'

As the weeks went on, Bertie would not stop talking about the multitude of experimental therapies out there in the world. Using cameras, stretching the lens, pupil surgery: Glenn's father dreamt of them all. But Glenn was not dreaming. He tried as hard as he could to relay all he had learnt at the conference in Aachen, about acceptance and the advantages of being blind. But Bertie was fixated on cures, encouraged by Iris, who was finding it harder than anyone to adjust.

'They're as mad as each other,' Eleanora whispered to him one evening as the two elderly Tebbhursts sat in the drawing room, discussing articles Iris had found. 'They won't give up!'

'I don't know how to help him,' said Glenn, feeling a great sadness fall upon him. 'He's going back to New York tomorrow and I feel like I've just made things worse.'

'Well, I think it's for the best they go back now,' said Eleanora, stiffly. 'If they hang around here any longer we'll have Japanese surgeons performing miracles in our very own drawing room.'

Glenn knew his wife did not like having Iris and Bertie in the house. She had made that quite clear from the start and lately had been spending more time at the stables and at bridge club.

'They'll be gone soon enough,' said Glenn, feeling put out by Eleanora's cold approach to care. 'In the mean time I want to make sure they have everything they need.'

The journey to the airport was a solemn one. Glenn tried to be cheerful, pointing out various castles and points of interest en route, but inside he felt increasingly guilty. He felt like he was abandoning his parents, sending them back to their misery in the States. They were both quiet, and Glenn knew the hope his father was harbouring for a miracle cure was fading. He just wished he could convince him that there was life after blindness. Then a strange pang jolted him. It was a feeling like homesickness, for in that moment Glenn wished Bettina was there with them. She was such a strong figure whose zeal for life despite her blindness could set an example for Bertie and make everything better.

'You'll call, honey?' Iris asked her son as he hugged her tight at the security gate.

'Of course, Mom,' he said. 'What a question. I'll call you as soon as you arrive back at Sutton Place. How does that sound?'

'My champion,' she smiled at him, raising a hand to his face for a moment, her blue eyes filling with tears. 'Goodbye, sweetie.'

'Speak to you then as well, Dad,' said Glenn, taking his frail father gently in his arms. The once so animated man stared placidly into the distance, nodding his goodbye and forcing a smile.

'Speak soon, son,' he said, raising his shaking hands to feel and grasp Glenn's shoulders.

With that, the family went their separate ways. Glenn drove back towards Virginia Water, feeling as though he didn't want to go home. The idea of returning to Ronda Round Manor did not appeal to him at all. Instead, he turned towards Richmond, driving into West London, then leading north. In the winter light, the parks looked beautifully bare. Glenn knew where he wanted to go.

Parking near South End Green, he strolled up to Hampstead Heath, glad to be in the open air and wide skies after the cramped, busy interior of the airport. The grassy wilds of the heath, separated by the dense woodland, drew Glenn up Parliament Hill to the viewpoint looking out over London. A breeze moved across his face and he closed his eyes for a moment. The darkness was a strange kind of bliss. He remembered the six and a half hours he had spent totally in the dark with Bettina, Laura, Odile, Elfrida, Christina and Zu-Ting. Smiling to himself, he remembered the chaos Bill had caused in the kitchen. Glenn still wondered how only three days could have had an all-transforming effect on him. With a pang of guilt he realised he had not contacted any of the six blind women who had made him feel so at home.

Glenn glanced around to check he was alone. Then, struck with a sudden idea, he took the scarf from around his neck and felt it in his hands. It was soft cashmere and as black as coal; how perfect, he thought. Wandering into a large area of woodland nearby, he took the scarf and wrapped it around his eyes like a blindfold. The pale winter light vanished and all that was left was heavy darkness. Glenn marvelled at the familiar feeling of his senses heightening: the birds singing in the trees; the ruffling of the breeze. He felt the coldness on the skin around the blindfold, and his neck, now exposed to the cold, felt refreshingly tingled. Remembering what Bettina had taught him in their day in the dark, Glenn moved slowly from tree to tree, inhaling all the smells of the forest and listening to every crunch of leaves and twigs beneath his feet.

'This is living,' he cried to himself, no longer caring who heard or saw him there. 'This is life! This is what it is to be alive!'

If only his mother could experience this, he thought, stepping carefully through the undergrowth. Surely then she would see that her husband's blindness was not the end of the world.

After an hour of wandering in the dark, Glenn took off his blindfold, experiencing that same reality check he had felt after the workshop in Aachen. Light flooded back into his life, and for a moment, he wished it would go away. Sighing, he headed back down the hill towards the car, vowing that as soon as he could, he would write to the six blind women who had revealed life to him with a whole new clarity.

CHAPTER TEN

Sitting back at his desk at the Diversified Charities Foundation office, Glenn took a break from the pile of papers surrounding him. It was mid-morning and he was already feeling slightly overwhelmed by the amount of work he had to do. Feeling the need for a distraction, he decided to seek out his colleagues for a coffee break. When he opened the door to his secretary's office, Sonia was typing away and looked up with a smile.

'Can I get you anything, sir?' she asked him.

'No, thanks, Sonia,' Glenn smiled back. 'Have you seen Amelia anywhere? I'm gasping for a coffee.'

'She'll be on the next floor now, I'm afraid, sir,' said Sonia. 'Shall I call her down?'

'Oh no, that's fine,' said Glenn, thinking how he could do with a walk. 'I'll probably bump into her somewhere. I'm just going to chat to the girls in the International Department for a moment.'

'I'll keep all messages here for you then, sir, for when you get back,' said his secretary.

'Thanks, Sonia,' said Glenn, marvelling, as ever, at her efficiency.

Life in the Cheapside office was busy as various reports needed to be written up for sponsors, and meetings had to be set up with charities to monitor their progress. Striding casually from department to department, Glenn enjoyed the respect he received from everyone around him. They all looked up and nodded hello when they saw him, some running over to ask for his opinion or advice. He helped where possible, happy to offer his experience to his colleagues. All the while, Glenn was thinking about what Herbert Farrand had said: maybe there was something he, Glenn, could do for the International Charity of the Blind.

'Ah, here's Glenn,' he heard a familiar voice as he walked through the doors of the International Department. Glenn saw Kikka the German interpreter looking up at him.

'Hi,' he said, strolling over to join her. 'Are the others here?'

'Tuni is coming,' said Kikka. 'She's just at reprographics. Natasha is at her desk. She's mid-report so very "in the zone". Best not disturbed, if you know what I mean.'

Glenn looked over and saw the young Natasha scanning through a document with her usual Eastern European fastidiousness.

'Keep it up, Nat!' he called over to her with a grin. She lifted her eyes for one second to nod her bashful thanks.

'What brings you to us, Glenn?' Kikka asked. 'Do you need some translation?'

'Oh no,' said Glenn, shaking his head. 'I just had a few things on my mind and wanted to think clearly. Walking always gives me a clear head. I was hoping to find Amelia and her tea trolley somewhere but I'm afraid I've missed her.'

'How is your father?' Kikka asked him, a concerned frown forming over her face. Glenn glanced up at Natasha, who had stopped what she was doing and was watching her boss carefully.

'He's well, physically,' said Glenn. 'But mentally, well, it's a bit of a struggle. I'm a bit lost with it all, to be honest. I just feel so ready to help but so helpless… ah, forget about it. '

'My uncle went blind,' said Natasha, who had stood up and was wandering over to join them. 'It took him such a long time to adjust to his disability. Even now he's so bitter. He thinks there will be a cure and will not hear anything else about it.'

'That's it exactly,' said Glenn. 'My father is the same! He needs time, I know, but his refusal to accept even the basic diagnosis worries me. He's a dreamer, he always has been, but I'm afraid he's focusing on the wrong dreams.'

'In what way?' asked Kikka.

Speaking freely for the first time in a long time, Glenn felt a heaviness lifting from him as he talked through his father's visit. He spoke about those weeks in a way he had not been able to do before, not even with his wife. Back home, Eleanora seemed overjoyed that she had Ronda Round Manor back to herself again. As soon as Bertie and Iris had left, her spirits had lifted and she was back to her normal self instead of hiding away in different corners of the house.

'I think we should stop all visits for a while,' she had said firmly. 'God knows we need some peace and quiet around here, Glenn.'

No, Glenn had not felt able to talk to Eleanora about anything that had come to pass with his father. She seemed determined to keep Bertie and his blindness at a healthy distance and Glenn felt that was for the best. If she herself could not accept his blindness, how could she help Bertie accept this change to his life?

'I'm sorry your father is struggling, Glenn,' said Natasha. 'It can't be easy for you.'

'I just wish I could help,' said Glenn, rubbing his forehead with a frustrated fist. 'When I went to that conference in Aachen, I really felt like I understood and even appreciated blindness. I know I'm not the one who has to live with it, but I thought if I could share what I learnt with my father, he could find some peace. These women, the six blind women I met there, were so amazing.'

'These women are becoming famous,' laughed Kikka. 'You always talk about them, and it's not like you to talk like that about people from conferences. You go to so many, and not to mention it's usually people talking about you in that way!'

'I'm quite a star, huh?' he laughed.

'Everyone raves about you, Glenn,' said Kikka. 'You hold the DCF together!'

'That's just business! These women were different; they were real. You would not believe the stories they told,' said Glenn, shaking his head and smiling fondly at the memories. 'One of the women, Laura, is so bold and funny. She has travelled all over the world with her blindness and would be the last to complain about it. Then there's Christina, who survived a terrible mission into Africa as a nun, blinded but alive, and now dedicates her time to helping others who suffer. Zu-Ting is one to watch: she wants to go into politics! She won't let anything stand in her way, especially not her blindness. And best of all was Bettina. She was… she was…'

'What was she?' asked Natasha. Glenn looked up to see both of his colleagues hanging on his every word.

'Bettina was so special,' said Glenn. 'I've never met a woman with so much strength.'

'Perhaps your father should talk directly to these women?' suggested Natasha. 'They sound so incredible.'

'I don't think my Dad should be left alone with beautiful women!' laughed Glenn.

'If he's anything like you, I'm sure he's the perfect gentleman,' smiled Kikka.

At that moment Tuni-Tung returned with an armful of documents, all neatly labelled and ready for reading.

'Hello!' she called over to them. 'Why do I always miss the fun? What are you all talking about?'

She listened carefully as Kikka quickly filled her in on the conversation.

'Well, you could always write about them?' Tuni-Tung suggested. 'You could propose that we support the International Charity for the Blind as a charity in the next financial year?'

'Set up a case?' asked Glenn. 'Would it qualify?'

'Why not?' said Tuni-Tung. 'It's all you talk about these days, Glenn. Maybe by supporting them this way, you can help your father learn more?'

'Where do I start?' he asked, liking the sound of this plan. 'I'm more of an action kind of guy. I usually let you guys do the planning.'

'Well, with research first,' said Kikka. 'I know you have been assisting your father with his condition for a while now, but you will need to really find out what support is out there for the blind before you start advocating the ICB's mantra of acceptance – and fundraising for it.'

'I can do that,' said Glenn confidently. 'I can definitely do that! Listen, I have an idea: I was thinking I could perhaps write case studies of the six women I met, telling their stories and using their journeys to illustrate the role of the ICB in facilitating healthy mental and emotional recovery, if not physical recovery. What do you think?'

'I think you've found a new project, Glenn,' smiled Kikka.

'Thanks, Kikka,' said Glenn. 'I feel like I'm on a roll! Thanks to all of you.'

With that, Glenn wandered back to his office, his mind ticking through the next steps of his plan. He had not found coffee, but he had found something even better: a new way forward. Writing case studies about each of the six women he had met meant seeing them again and that was something Glenn wanted very much. He knew that in order to make a case for supporting the ICB he would have to do some initial ground work. He would have to find out for himself why the charity's work was so needed in order to justify Diversified Charities' support.

'Sonia, I'm going to be spending the next few days out of the office,' Glenn told his secretary as he arrived back at his office.

'Certainly, sir,' said Sonia. 'I'll take messages and brief you with a call every morning if there is any urgency.'

The next few days were a whirlwind of learning. Glenn decided to start his research by going back to the doctor who had seen his father at the London Eye Hospital. He knew that the meeting had not been a success, but perhaps the young man would have recommendations for him regarding where to look for further information.

When he entered the consulting room the doctor recognised Glenn immediately.

'Mr. Tebbhurst, welcome back,' he said warmly. 'Please, take a seat.'

'Thanks,' said Glenn. 'You're probably wondering why I'm here.'

'It's not unusual for the loved ones of patients to return with questions,' said the doctor, shrugging kindly. 'Sometimes they find a disability harder to manage than those who suffer from it.'

'Well, that would certainly be the case for my mother,' sighed Glenn. 'She has never felt comfortable with my father's blindness.'

'And you?' asked the doctor. 'How has the deterioration of your father's condition affected you?'

'In ways I had not foreseen,' Glenn told the doctor honestly. 'I have spent some time trying to understand how people come to terms with their blindness. In fact, I think I am one of the anomalies: I am dealing with my father's condition better than he is.'

Glenn went on to tell the doctor about all he had learnt in Aachen, about his day in the dark and the six incredible women he had met there. The doctor laughed when Glenn told him about making the goulash and Bill losing at chess and was beaming by the time Glenn had finished.

'What a fantastic organisation,' said the doctor. 'What was the name again?'

'The International Charity for the Blind,' said Glenn.

'I will be recommending this to my patients,' said the doctor, making a note.

'It was a doctor who recommended I go,' said Glenn. 'He told me I should stop wasting my time looking for a cure and find out how to show Bertie how to live with his blindness.'

'That's good advice,' said the doctor, letting out a deep sigh. 'In your father's case, I'm afraid that is the best solution we can ask for.'

'I would like to start looking into how the blind are rehabilitated after diagnosis,' said Glenn. 'I was wondering if you could tell me where to start looking?'

'Of course,' said the doctor. Picking up his pen and paper once more he began to scribble down an address. 'Here, go first to my colleague upstairs, who can talk you through our rehabilitation programme. Then I suggest you go to the Wellcome Institute Library to do a bit of research there about how people have been dealing with blindness throughout history. It could be a great insight for you. If nothing else it can be humbling to see how far we have come, and enlightening to know how people dealt with blindness in the past.'

'Thanks, doc!' he called out. Taking the doctor's advice, Glenn went first to visit the colleague who worked just two floors above in the hospital. A woman with a firm expression but kind eyes opened the door to Glenn and nodded her head when he explained he had been sent to see her.

'I'm sorry for the short notice,' said Glenn. 'You must be very busy.'

'Not at all,' she said, waving his apology away. 'It's my job. I help people to understand what is happening to them when they lose their sight, and try to explain to them how losing their sight does not mean they will lose their lives.'

'I appreciate it,' said Glenn, nodding in thanks.

'Let me talk you through the programme,' she began. 'We call it vision rehabilitation and though we do not provide it here at the medical, ophthalmology level, we do recommend it for patients when they leave.'

'So who provides this, if not the ophthalmologist?' Glenn asked.

'It is the responsibility of the patient to find this care, and we do everything we can to help them find it,' the physician explained. 'There are things that the blind need to recover and restore in order to live fully independent lives again.'

'Such as?' Glenn asked, taking out his notepad to make notes.

'Well, most people focus first on the physical rehabilitation,' said the doctor. 'But we suggest focusing first on communication skills. After all, these are the skills one needs to interact with the people and the world around us. We encourage the adoption of reading Braille and learning to use new assistive technology with computers.'

'And after communication, what next?' asked Glenn, jotting down as much information as he could.

'Then we propose that the emotional issues are addressed with counselling, not only for the patient, but for the family around them,' the doctor continued. 'This is to help friends, family, spouses and dependents address and come to terms with the blindness. It can be very hard for them, as I am sure you have noticed yourself.'

Glenn thought of his father's scepticism of talking therapies. He doubted if Bertie would ever agree to sit and discuss his feelings with a counsellor. Glenn himself would be reluctant to do so.

'Two of the most important skills the blind will need to learn are those of independent living and personal management,' the doctor continued. 'For example, they will need to know how to perform simple acts of self-care once more: washing, eating, preparing themselves for bed. They will need to know how to modify and repair their home, take care of their social lives, use the telephone and manage their finances. These are all huge tasks to take on with a disability, and cannot be addressed here at the hospital.'

'What about travel?' asked Glenn, remembering how his father had arrived at Heathrow in a wheelchair. Was it possible, he wondered, for the blind to be fully independent when travelling? Laura from the conference had said so, but he still doubted it.

'That too will need to be addressed,' said the doctor. 'The independent movement of a blind person involves many risks, outside and inside. He or she must be taught how to navigate their homes and the transport systems available with their new disability. This can be a great challenge for some. Here there must be discussion of the white cane or alternative means of evaluating the immediate environment. This evaluation is often a constant process.'

'Beyond that,' said Glenn. 'Beyond the home and getting from A to B, how are the blind rehabilitated back into work? Can they work again?'

'That involves a whole process of vocational re-evaluation,' said the doctor. 'It can lead to job loss or job modification, in some cases simply new job training for the blind and the colleagues of the blind. There are also possibilities for job placements, whenever the person feels ready to start work once more. Many abandon work though, preferring the benefits provided by the state than the struggle or reintegrating into a system that does not suit their disability. This, as you can imagine, often leads to poverty.'

Glenn could not imagine how much strength and determination it would take to go back to a job once blind. Thanking the doctor for her time, Glenn set his notes in order and left the hospital. He tried to imagine for a moment how he would function in the busy, bustling streets of Cheapside, just getting to work, let alone managing all the cases and meetings he was responsible for in the office. The thought made him shiver. He was only glad his father was past the point of working now, and could retire in peace, blind but not tormented by the pressures of his consultancy work.

That night, Glenn could not sleep. Eleanora snored gently beside him but his mind raced with everything he had learnt that day. He could not wait to get to the Wellcome Institute Library the next day, as the doctor had recommended, and take up his research there.

When dawn came, he rose early, leaving his wife in bed, and headed straight into central London. It was so early that he avoided the crushing crowds of the commuters at Virginia Water. When he arrived at the Wellcome Institute in Euston, the city had already woken up, and he had to wait half an hour for the library to open.

'Can I help you, sir?' asked the young woman on the desk when the doors finally opened and Glenn wandered in. She looked surprised to see someone entering the library as early as her.

'Yes, I wonder if you can,' said Glenn. He explained that he was looking to learn a bit more how blindness had been dealt with throughout history. The girl nodded as he spoke, listening carefully. When he had finished, she invited him to take a seat and she would look up some titles for him.

Wandering into the library, Glenn was happy to be in the Wellcome Institute. It was a fantastic building, positioned just next to the University College London. A few early bird students could be seen perusing the aisles for volumes, carefully searching through the names of authors and titles throughout history. Glenn knew that the library hosted up to 750,000 volumes and had been exploring the connections between health, science and art since 1936. The collection was magnificent to behold.

'Here we are, search for these,' said the librarian, handing Glenn a piece of paper with lots of codes written down upon it.

'Thanks a million,' said Glenn. 'You've done a swell job, honey.'

'Don't mention it,' grinned the girl. 'Good luck.'

Glenn would need luck, he thought, looking down at the list. There were at least thirty numbers written there: thirty books for him to pore over and extract important nuggets from. Glad to have set a couple of days aside for his research, Glenn started to gain an idea of how blindness had been interpreted throughout known history.

He read first about the struggles of historians to grasp any kind of documentation of what living with blindness was like before the nineteenth century. In ancient history, the blind are often only known by their depictions in literary or religious texts, as the beggars of the world, or those blessed or cursed by moral or religious interference. Blindness could be a punishment for social wrongs, or a blessing to a saint, blinded by enlightenment. There were doubtless many blind people who suffered at the mercy of the sighted around them, living their lives as beggars or dependents of those who would support them, but they went unreported in the annals of history.

'Tiresias is a good examples of interpretations of blindness in ancient Greek history,' the librarian told him the following day, bringing more books over to his table.

'How so?' asked Glenn. 'I'm not big on the Classics so I might need some education here!'

'Tiresias was blinded by Athena,' she said, 'but Athena then gave him other gifts to compensate for his blindness.'

'Which gifts?' asked Glenn.

'She gave him the power to utter prophesies,' said the librarian. 'She also allowed him to speak with and understand birds and live a very long life.'

Though this was simply a Greek myth, Glenn could not help but think of Bettina, who had convinced them all so sweetly of their heightened senses in her seminar. Had she not opened the window and let in the bird song, so beautifully loudened by their lack of sight? For a moment, Glenn wished he could tell her that; he wished he could tell her the story of Tiresias' blindness and how it had made him think of her.

Glenn found it increasingly hard to find any historical evidence or accounts of how blindness was accepted. The history of the blind seemed more concerned with blind celebrities, famous for their poems or music. Homer, John Milton, Turlough O'Carolan had all spun their yarns from a position of blindness, but none wrote more than a sentence about the woes of being blind or how the world treated them.

'To be blind is not miserable; not to be able to bear blindness, that is miserable,' wrote John Milton. The words settled in Glenn's heart like a stone. John Milton had borne blindness until his dying day and in a world that had little to offer in way of help or rehabilitation. Bertie Tebbhurst, however, had a chance at happiness again.

'There was a blind poet from Syria called Al-Ma'arri, a great philosopher born in Aleppo,' Glenn told Eleanora after his second day of research. 'He contracted a disease as a child which made him blind. I read that he was great, though in his day he suffered criticism that his pessimism showed a lack of vision that could only be matched by his physical lack of sight.'

'Mm,' said his wife disinterestedly. 'That's interesting.'

Glenn knew he could not force his wife to care about his father's situation and he did not blame her for it. But he could not stop talking about all he had discovered. It filled him with a new sense of discovery and purpose.

'Even these men like Milton and Al-Ma'arri were writing and doing things with their blindness,' he said. 'They were shaping texts and the worlds around them. Blindness doesn't have to be debilitating. Dad could do anything! Don't you see? This is not an end, it's a beginning!'

'Well, not to be pessimistic myself, dear, but don't put too many ideas in his head, will you?' she said.

'What do you mean?' Glenn asked, stung by the question.

'Well, these men all sound quite miserable,' said Eleanora. 'Do you really want your father to turn into a sulking writer, penning poems about his dark view of the world?'

'Is it so much to ask to get some positive feedback from you, honey?' he said.

'Don't blame me, will you?' she said. 'I prefer to give constructive criticism.'

Feeling hurt by her words, Glenn decided not to discuss his father's condition any more with his wife. She clearly had no interest and saw his research as futile. Instead, he looked forward to discussing his findings with the librarian he had befriended at the Wellcome Institute.

'He was a great scholar, Al Ma'arri,' she said, nodding her head. 'I saw you had been reading about him. He studied in Aleppo, Tripoli and

Antioch, I believe, and when he hid himself away in hermitage, students from across Syria would go to study with him there. I'm glad you're reading about blindness depicted in the East as well as the West. It might be interesting for you to look at examples of the blind in the Qur'an, if you're already looking further east to Arab writers,' she suggested when he shared what he had read the next day.

'With pleasure,' said Glenn. 'Man, you're really helping me out here. I'm learning so much!'

But as in all the religious texts, blindness in the Qur'an was simply used as a lack of spiritual belonging. Beyond the religious texts, Glenn was sad to discover that blindness in history meant misery and second-class citizenship. It was only as history progressed and the age of Enlightenment dawned that blindness was truly considered.

'This is crazy,' Glenn confided in the librarian, whom he now knew by name. Hannah was a smart young woman and was always keen to hear how Glenn was getting on.

'What is?' she asked.

'It says here that philosophers in the eighteenth century argued over how the world was interpreted – through sight or through touch. Those who argued that it was interpreted through sight also questioned the point of educating the blind. Such philosophers questioned the value of learning to read and write if the people learning would never be able to see.'

'That's preposterous!' Hannah whispered loudly.

'There's more,' said Glenn. 'The debate raged between philosophers Locke and Berkeley. Berkeley at least believed that the essence of things was understood inside, not on the outside. I mean, at least the blind are included in religious discussions at this stage, but some of the things they argue over are mad.'

'Philosophy is ever rational,' said Hannah, smiling at Glenn's outrage. 'But don't worry, Glenn. Just look at the case of Nicholas Saunderson in the eighteenth century.'

After some digging around in the multitude of texts he had been given, Glenn finally came across the story of one Nicholas Saunderson.

Though he lost his sight at a young age, he went on to tutor students at Cambridge on the subjects of mathematics and Newtonian physics. Despite the philosophical doubting going on around them, even Newton himself said that Saunderson, blind from birth, was one of few men who had truly understood his ideas. Those ideas would go on to shape physics as Glenn knew it today.

Glenn read on: as schools opened across Europe to start educating the blind. Before the invention of Braille, various calligraphers, scholars and educators started to develop different methods of teaching the blind to read and write. The Frenchman, Denis Diderot, had ideas that Glenn saw reflected in Bettina: the view that things that can be seen can be felt too. Such ideas influenced his thought on a tactile form of writing, which spread from Paris to Vienna to London, Bristol and Edinburgh, all the way over to the Americas. Though much of the discussion about how to educate the blind was developed by those with sight, Glenn read, the new era of schools and institutes for the blind created a platform on which the blind could meet and discuss new ways of living and dealing with their blindness.

Discovering Braille was a delight Glenn wished he could have shared with someone else. He read how Louis Braille, a student at Paris' Royal Institute for the Blind, had developed a system of raised dots in 1821. It was a system that would change the way blind people learnt and lived forever. The book Glenn read had samples of the Roman alphabet, and shorthand symbols used for faster reading. He closed his eyes and let his fingers trace over the raised letters, marvelling at how a system once created for military communication by Charles Barbier, a French officer, had been adapted into a system of communication. Of course it all felt alien to him, but Glenn could sense the importance of this form of communication just by touching it. Whereas the blind might feel alienated by a world dominated by the seeing, the seeing might feel alienated by a form of communication they struggled to understand.

'I just can't believe people were resistant to it at first,' Glenn told Hannah as he gathered his things to leave the library. 'They felt threatened by Braille's new system of reading and learning. Why were people so afraid of progress?'

'Of course,' said Hannah. 'It meant the seeing could no longer control how the blind learnt and grew.'

'This has been such a fascinating few days of reading,' said Glenn, shaking the hand the librarian offered him. 'It's really opened my eyes, so to speak!'

'For me too,' she smiled. 'I hope everything goes well with your report and for your father, Glenn. He has a wonderful son, that's clear.'

'Thanks,' said Glenn, and with that he headed back to his office. As he wandered from the streets of Euston towards the underground stop, he could not help but think of all the stories of different lives he had read. The saints, the victims, the poets and the philosophers, all had played a part in the history of the blind. Those stories carried through centuries, if not millennia, because they were special. The stories he had heard in Aachen were not of heroes and struggle in the epic sense, they were more about daily challenges. Those were the challenges blind people had faced since the beginning of time, but surely they would never make it into the history books. Bertie Tebbhurst's story would never be told, nor would Bettina Hartmann's, thought Glenn, though both of those people had suffered. Who would write their stories, Glenn asked himself?

Arriving back at the office, Glenn picked up his messages from Sonia and sat down behind the leather and mahogany of his desk. He wondered when to start tackling the work he needed to catch up on. But somehow his mind was fixed on the notes he wanted to write up about the ICB, their relevance and importance today, and the six women who shared their life experiences with those who needed it. It was time, he thought: it was time to take action.

Searching through his address book, Glenn found the page he had shared with Laura, Odile, Elfrida, Christina and Zu-Ting in Aachen, on the day he left to fly home. Their email addresses were all there. He spotted Laura's and remembered that she lived in the UK. Deciding to start with her, he turned on his computer and opened up his email. Clicking on the tab for a new message, Glenn began to type.

Subject: Meeting?

Dear Laura,

Glenn here, we met in Aachen at the ICB conference. I have such fond memories of the workshops you and your colleagues gave there.

I remembered that you were based in the UK and was wondering if you might be interested in meeting me. I have started a new project that I could use your help with.

If that sounds good, just let me know when and where.

Awaiting your answer, with best wishes,
Glenn

Pressing send, Glenn knew that all he had to do now was wait. Until then, he would prepare himself to listen to the inspiring stories of courage and determination the world needed to hear. And once he had listened, he would try to write them down, as best he could.

CHAPTER ELEVEN

To his surprise, Glenn did not have to wait long for Laura's reply to his email. Within days she had responded. He was sat in his office one afternoon, with a cup of tea freshly served to him by Amelia, avoiding a pile of work that had been delivered to him by Sonia. Glenn excitedly clicked on the mouse and opened the message.

Subject: RE: Meeting?

Hi Glenn!

It's wonderful to hear from you. Yes, I would be very happy to meet you and help if I can. Perhaps you could come to my end of town?

I live in Bayswater. If you like, we could meet at the Lancaster Gate Hotel for tea on Saturday?

Looking forward to it,
Laura

Eleanora was as disinterested as ever in Glenn's endeavours to understand better the means by which people lived with blindness. When he told her he would be going into London to meet one of the six blind women he had met at the conference, she simply shrugged and asked to accompany him into the city.

'I'd like to go to Harrods,' she said. 'I need to look into new dinner set options.'

'Honey, come on! We have a perfectly good dinner set,' said Glenn, puzzled by his wife's need for excessive goods in the house.

'That's what you think, darling, but some of us weren't blessed with taste and some of us were,' she said, raising an arched eyebrow. 'Besides, I'm bored. The manor stinks of farm ever since the Thomsons started shifting manure across the courtyard. God knows it's made the whole place stink to the high heavens!'

'I can't smell a thing, sweetie, but you're more than welcome to come into town with me,' he said.

'You're a darling, aren't you?' she smiled at him.

'I am, aren't I?' he laughed.

Glenn shook his head, smiling at his wife's exasperation at the farm she loved so much. Life at Ronda Round Manor had returned to a steady normality since his parents had left. The farm work continued from a distance and his wife complained about it all from the comfort of their drawing room. Glancing over at her as they stepped out towards the station together, Glenn admired his wife's smart, closely cut outfit. She was a very attractive woman, he thought, with her sense of style and classically beautiful face. Once upon a time he had thought she was the most beautiful woman he had ever known; his heart had melted at her every sigh and smile. But now something was shifting inside of him. As they made their way to Virginia Water station, towards Central London, Eleanora read her copy of *Horse and Hound* and Glenn thought about the last words he had spoken to Bettina at the dinner in Aachen.

As the train sped along the tracks, Glenn tried to put such thoughts from his mind. He pulled his wife's hand into his and looked at her beautiful face. She did not look at him so he watched suburban London pass him by. Once they arrived in Knightsbridge, Glenn and his wife strode to Harrods.

'When shall I pick you up?' he asked as she swooped back to give him a kiss on his cheek. 'Give me the time and the place, ma'am, and I'll be there!'

'Don't bother darling, I'll catch the train back myself,' she said. 'God knows you'll be hours, talking with these blind people! Have fun now.'

With that Eleanora turned around and set off to the famous department store. Glenn watched from the curb as she walked away, then set off towards Bayswater. Walking quickly up Brompton Road, he decided to turn off at Hyde Park Corner and walk the remaining half a mile across Hyde Park to the Lancaster Gate Hotel. As he strolled into the wintery park, Glenn marvelled at the brilliance of the snaking Serpentine. That large body of water had been impressing people since its construction centuries ago. He closed his eyes and imagined for a moment how he would experience the Serpentine if he had no eyesight. He imagined those eighteenth-century philosophers driving themselves mad with their endless debates on whether or not the blind could truly experience the world around them. Meanwhile, he thought with a smile, a blind man or woman would be nearby and basking in their other senses, feeling the sounds, smells and vibrations of the park around them in a uniquely brilliant way.

Glenn was lost in thought when he finally arrived at the Lancaster Hotel. It was not a spectacular hotel by any standards, and looked as though it had only just scraped its four stars. But through the windows Glenn could already see a log fire burning away, and after the cold winter air, such warmth looked very inviting. He quickly climbed the stairs to enter the softly lit lobby, and there he asked for the tea room.

'Just through there, sir,' said the receptionist with a polite smile. 'You can't miss it.'

Glenn followed the direction the young man had pointed in and spotted Laura immediately. Her flaming red hair gave her away, flowing out over a smart green coat. For a moment, Glenn raised his arm to wave, before he remembered that Laura was blind and would not be able to see him. So instead of waving, he walked over to her table and cleared his throat loudly.

'Laura!' he said. 'It's me! It's Glenn!'

'Glenn!' she cried in response, her face lighting up as she heard his voice. She did not look at him, but raised a hand gently towards him and found his arm. She squeezed it gently. 'Oh, hello! What a lovely idea it was to meet up. Come and sit down, I've already ordered a pot of tea. Do you mind Earl Grey?'

'It's my favourite,' said Glenn, watching with a mixture of curiosity and admiration as Laura picked up the hot pot of tea and began to pour out two cups for them. 'Ever since I was Anglicised by you Brits I've been drinking Earl Grey every morning, noon and night!'

'It's freezing out there, isn't it?' said Laura in her lively, expressive way. 'Oliver and I almost froze to death walking over. We only live five minutes away but it was bracing!'

'Excuse me?' said Glenn with surprise. 'Is someone else joining us?'

'Oh!' she laughed. 'Sorry, dear. I forgot to introduce him. Oliver, won't you come and say hello?'

Glenn waited in anticipation for this man Oliver to arrive. He looked around at the neighbouring tables, over towards the door and over his shoulder. But when he turned back, he saw Laura rummaging around in her big, green leather bag for something. Suddenly she pulled out a large, fluffy cat. It let out a grumpy meow and scowled at Glenn for a moment.

'Here he is, Oliver Twist himself,' said Laura, gently stroking her feline friend.

'Oh, Oliver Twist!' laughed Glenn, admiring the cat's magnificent coat. 'I was expecting someone more, well, human.'

'Hush now, Glenn. Don't offend him!' said Laura with a mock-hushing gesture. 'He is a real man. Have you ever seen such a fine tomcat?'

'No I don't think I have,' chuckled Glenn. 'Hello, Oliver. You are very fine, aren't you? How do you do? Will you take a cup of Earl Grey with us too?'

'I'm afraid I'm the only one who talks in our relationship,' said Laura, smiling her brilliant smile. 'He has the eyes, I have the voice.'

'Why Oliver Twist?' Glenn asked, smiling at the name.

'Because of his twisting, curly hair,' said Laura. 'His coat gets very tangled sometimes. So he's a real live Oliver Twist.'

The cat named Oliver Twist began to purr loudly as his mistress stroked him gently.

'How old is he?' Glenn asked, reaching out to stoke him with a steady hand. The cat purred even louder as Glenn's hand smoothed down his fluffy fur.

'He must be three or four now,' said Laura. 'We moved to Bayswater together. I live in an apartment not far from here.'

'Do you always take him out to tea with you?' Glenn asked, still recovering from the surprise of the cat in the bag.

'Not always, but we take walks in the park sometimes,' she said. 'We were walking just now.'

'Cat walking?' laughed Glenn. 'Is that a thing?'

'Of course it is!' she protested. 'Of course, you can imagine what the locals say: "Shouldn't you have a guide dog, not a guide cat?"'

'Well, shouldn't you?' laughed Glenn.

'Guide dogs are overrated,' said Laura. 'Besides, I'm a cat person. Can you really imagine a cat person living with a dog, twenty-four-seven? It goes against nature. No, it's just me and Oliver these days. I saved him from a rescue shelter a few years back, you know. He was in a right state, poor thing. He had been abandoned by a family in East London. We're survivors, both of us.'

Glenn watched her fondly for a moment as she stroked her beloved cat. Both pet and owner seemed delighted with each other's company.

'It's nice to see you again, Laura,' said Glenn, sensing the note of sadness in Laura's voice. He remembered what Herbert Farrand had said about her at the conference. She had been passed from foster home to foster home, constantly abandoned by people who could not handle her blindness. But there she sat, a strikingly attractive woman, full of positive energy and an inspiration to so many people.

'You too, Glenn,' she said. 'I was so happy to see your email. I knew you lived in London but I didn't think we'd ever see each other again. It's always a bit like that at ICB events. We meet fantastic people and spend a few days with them and then it's all over. It's a bit sad really, if I think about it.'

'That's what I thought,' said Glenn quickly, happy to hear he wasn't the only one missing the people from the conference. 'It was such a fantastic weekend. I've been thinking… well, I haven't stopped thinking about it actually.'

'I'm not surprised,' laughed Laura. 'You were one of the best volunteers we've ever had. Everyone says so.'

'Really?' said Glenn, surprised to hear this. For a moment he wondered if Bettina had thought that too. He blushed suddenly at the thought and was glad Laura could not see his reddening cheeks.

'Well, you and Bill,' said Laura. They both burst into laughter at that. For a while they chattered about Bill's funniest moments at the conference, reminiscing about his bizarre and rather pompous behaviour.

'He was entertaining, that's for certain,' said Glenn. 'But jeez, I hate to be on a par with that man. I was better, surely?'

'He was American,' said Laura, shaking her head and smiling fondly.

'I'm American!' laughed Glenn.

'I know, I know, but we'll never forget Mr. Bill Houston from Texas,' she chuckled. 'Nor Glenn Tebbhurst from New York.'

'We New Yorkers are very memorable you know,' Glenn said, grinning his cheekiest grin.

When they had exchanged Christmas stories and their newly vowed resolutions for the New Year, Laura's face took on a more curious expression.

'So, Glenn,' she began, setting down her empty cup of Earl Grey so he could refill it. 'You mentioned in your email that you had something to discuss with me.'

'Yes,' said Glenn, wondering how to broach the subject. He poured the tea slowly to buy himself some time. In his office, at his desk, it had all sounded so wonderful: a pamphlet of case studies, championing the six blind women of the conference. But now that he sat there in front of one of them he felt shy. He suddenly realised how intrusive it might seem to ask someone to be a case study in a public document that would be read by many people. Talking to people in a seminar was one thing; being portrayed in writing was something else. Besides, what if she thought the idea ridiculous? After all, she had every right to. Who was he, a seeing man, to write about the blind?

'Glenn,' whispered Laura, 'is something the matter?'

'No,' he said quickly. 'Well, no, not exactly. I'm just not sure where to start.'

'I often find the best place to start is at the start,' quipped Laura, grinning as she gazed into the distance beyond Glenn. For a moment he wished he could just close his eyes and not see her. It would be much easier. Then a reassuring realisation dawned on him: he could. Closing his eyes, he tried for a moment. Laura said nothing of course; she could not see him. As the darkness replaced the bright hotel tea room, Glenn felt his confidence and comfort returning.

'Alright, Laura, I'll start from the start,' he said, taking a deep breath. 'I've had an idea.'

The more he spoke, the easier it became to articulate his ideas about the case studies and the pamphlet. It was easy to express his gratitude and appreciation of Laura and her comrades from the conference. He even heard himself openly praising Bettina in the highest terms.

'So you see, I think it would be wonderful to write about you – about you all,' he finished. 'I know your stories will move people to change the way they think about blindness. You've changed me, and I hope you will change my father.'

Glenn stopped there and held his breath for a moment, waiting for Laura's response.

She nodded, taking a shuddering breath in and swallowing hard.

'It's been a long time since someone has asked me to talk about my past,' she said. 'I try to avoid it. I even lie sometimes, so that people don't ask questions.'

'But why?' asked Glenn.

'I feel ashamed,' said Laura.

'Of being blind?' asked Glenn, horrified for a moment that she might feel that way.

'No,' said Laura, smiling sadly and shaking her head. 'I feel ashamed of being abandoned.'

Glenn felt his heart twinge for a moment as her words sunk in. Looking at Laura, one would never know she carried such troubles within her. Like most people, she buried them deep inside, hoping no one would ever disturb them.

'We didn't have much time to really talk in Aachen,' said Glenn gently. 'I met a beautiful woman, a talented woman, but I don't know you at all, Laura, and I would like to. No one should feel ashamed of being abandoned.'

'Where would you like me to start?' she replied, smiling faintly.

'Well, to quote a wise woman, often the best place to start is the start,' said Glenn, and to his great relief, Laura's smile widened.

'Well, I've answered my own question then, haven't I?' she said. For a moment her gaze seemed to wander into her memories, though Glenn was not sure if this was the case for the blind. Perhaps in the mind of a blind person, the internal gaze could wander through memories in a different way, he thought. Laura's memories would be made up of sounds, tastes, touches and feelings.

'Whenever you feel ready,' said Glenn, reaching down to take a pen and paper from his bag. He wanted to record as many details as he could in their meeting in order to write powerful and informative case studies.

'The start,' said Laura, reaching out to stroke Oliver, who had clambered onto her knee. 'Well, I suppose that would have to be in Chesham. Do you know it, Glenn?'

'The small town in the Chilterns?' asked Glenn, vaguely remembering driving past the town on the way to a horse riding event with Eleanora.

'That's the one,' said Laura. 'It's a small town with not much going on. I don't remember it too well to be honest. My mother was from there, born and bred, for generations. Her family has never strayed far from Chesham. My dad was from the north, though, and he never let us forget it.'

'How do you mean?' asked Glenn.

'He was a very proud man,' said Laura, gazing into the distance behind Glenn's shoulder, which for her was an eternity of darkness. Her eyebrows frowned slightly as she recalled the memory. 'He drank too much. If he wasn't drinking at home he was drinking at the pub. He would come home late and start arguments with my mother. He was always quite sweet to me, though at the time, I didn't like it. All I could smell was the whiskey on his breath, or the cigarette smoke in his clothes. I was afraid of him, I think. His voice was like thunder.'

'And your mother?' Glenn asked, writing down a few notes as quietly as he could so as not to disturb Laura's thoughts.

'She never liked me much,' sighed Laura. 'I think it was because of the blindness. She didn't know how to deal with it all. She tried, I think, but with Dad always away, often drunk or angry at her, she couldn't cope.

I tried not to cry or ask for too much. But when she fell pregnant for the second time, and my Dad's drinking got worse, she couldn't do it anymore. She put me into care.'

'She sent you to a foster home?' Glenn asked, trying to hide the dismay in his voice. 'I can't believe that!'

For a moment he envisioned the young Laura, quiet and obedient, dropped off at a state foster home, not knowing where she was or what she should do. She must have been so confused. The very thought made his heart sink.

'She thought it was for the best,' said Laura, shrugging; a strangely cold indifference crept into her voice. 'She couldn't cope. She wanted me to be with people who could look after me.'

'And did they?' Glenn asked. 'Did they look after you in the home?'

'At the first one, yes,' said Laura. 'They could see I was an invalid and would need special treatment. The other children were not interested in me, which was fine.'

'You said the first one,' said Glenn, after a pause. 'Did you stay in more than one home?'

'Oh yes,' said Laura, smiling bitterly now. 'Yes, the first one filled up quickly and I had to be moved on. I was passed from home to home for months because nowhere had the right facilities to support a disabled person like me. I had accidents, falls, there was bullying; those months were hell. It took almost a year before they finally found a family to foster me. No one wanted a blind girl, you see. I was very sad, Glenn, in those months in care.'

'Of course,' said Glenn gently. 'It sounds like quite an ordeal.'

'Well, it was nothing compared to what came next,' said Laura. Glenn listened with quiet trepidation as Laura told her story, wondering what could be worse than the neglect she had experienced in care.

'Laura, don't feel like you have to...' he began, wanting her to feel comfortable.

'It's fine, Glenn, don't worry,' she said, smiling warmly at him. 'The only people they found to adopt me was a farming family in Wales. They were called the Joneses.'

Glenn watched a dark expression fall across Laura's face as she mentioned their name.

'The Joneses lived on a farm deep in Snowdonia,' she continued. 'It was in the middle of nowhere, and as such, I met almost no one. It turned out that they were looking for more of a farm-hand than an adopted daughter. When I arrived, and they saw how useless I would be for the cows and the sheep and the milking, I think they were a bit angry at the foster home for misleading them. Nevertheless, they trained me all the same. They gave me chores and taught me how to milk the cows; how to shear the sheep and feed the chickens.'

'All without sight?' Glenn asked in amazement.

'Of course,' said Laura. 'The couple had two other daughters who were quite useless on the farm too. They were older and younger than me.'

'Were they friends to you?' asked Glenn.

'Friends would be a very generous term,' sighed Laura. 'They were intrigued by me. The farm was a very lonely place for a little girl. I grew very depressed, and at school things were hardly better.'

'Did you go to a local school?' asked Glenn.

'Yes, well, the local special school,' said Laura. 'It was a depressing place, a school for special children they called it. But special could mean a number of things: they simply grouped the deaf, blind, disabled and dyslexic children together and called it a school. The teaching standards were terrible.'

'But you are so educated,' said Glenn, puzzled by this news. 'You strike me as a remarkably intelligent young woman.'

'I am,' said Laura, smiling suddenly. In a flash, the confident, bright Laura was back with him. Glenn was so happy to see her smile return, if only briefly. It was like a ray of sunshine passing through the darkest of clouds.

'I listened to the radio as much as I could,' she continued. 'It was like gold to me, my radio. I listened every night, away from the family, after I had completed whichever chores I had such as feeding the chickens and cats, cleaning the floors and collecting pails of milk from the cow-milking sheds.'

Glenn was happy for this momentary relief in the darkness of Laura's time in Wales. He imagined her nestled into an armchair, wrapped in a blanket against the cold, Welsh winter, listening to her favourite radio shows.

'I listened to everything,' she said, a smile fixed on her face. 'I learnt so much through the radio.'

'I can see that,' said Glenn, smiling. He listened as she listed her favourite radio programs and presenters, laughing at some memories and appearing wistfully nostalgic at others.

'But the school was bad,' she went on, her features darkening once more. 'We were miserable, and the other girls were so nasty to me. They were jealous of my grades and the things I knew. They were abusive by the end.'

'Physically abusive?' said Glenn.

'Physically, mentally, emotionally,' said Laura. A sudden, deep sadness had settled on her face and she looked strained for a moment. 'It was a hard time, Glenn, a hard time. All I can remember is the misery and loneliness. And the hunger, of course.'

'Did they not feed you?' Glenn asked.

'My foster mother's favourite dish was a fatty pork soup that tasted like dirty dish water,' said Laura, shaking her head with a bitter frown. 'Lumps of white fat would be floating in a watery broth. I hated it and refused to eat it by the end. This made jolly Mrs. Jones very angry, I can tell you. "Ungrateful wretch!" she would yell at me. "We take you in, put a roof over your head, and this is how you repay us!" If I refused her soup I would not know a minute's peace for a whole night. Sometimes she would just grab me by the ear and push my face into the bowl.'

'The bowl of hot soup?' Glenn asked, horrified by what he was hearing. Laura nodded. Glenn felt his insides tighten as he listened to this young woman's heartbreaking tales of abuse. He imagined the blossoming teenager growing up in such misery, longing for escape, for something more than her lonely existence.

'And your mother,' he said, 'did she never send for you? Did she never want you to come home?'

Laura shook her head. Tears were forming in her eyes.

'No,' she said. 'My mother did not want to see me. I wrote to her, many times. I asked if I could come and visit her and my baby sister. I wanted to go home, to live with her again. She never answered my letters.'

'Have you ever met your little sister?' Glenn asked quietly.

'No,' said Laura. 'Not even once. I know they lived together though, her and my mother. I guess my mother could handle a normal child. She was probably easier to deal with. A blind child is quite a hindrance.'

'And you haven't tried to make contact more recently?' Glenn asked.

'What would be the point?' said Laura, laughing slightly. 'Do you really think I can go back to them now, after all these years? I would be ashamed to even try.'

'And your father?' asked Glenn. 'Surely he tried to get in contact?'

'No,' said Laura, a single tear rolling down her cheek now. Glenn wished he could reach forward and wipe it from her face. Instead he passed her a handkerchief, pushing it gently into her hands. She took it and raised it to her face, softly brushing away the wetness beneath her eyes.

'But he knew?' said Glenn. 'He knew you were in foster care?'

'Who knows,' Laura shrugged. 'I do not know what happened to him. I suspect he left my mother. He was always drinking himself silly. Perhaps he drank himself to death.'

Glenn said nothing as a silence grew between them.

'In all cases,' Laura said at last. 'I broke free.'

'How?' asked Glenn.

'I finished my exams at sixteen,' said Laura. 'I was smart, smarter than most of my fellow students. I received my qualifications and I left home.'

'Where did you go?' Glenn asked. But a small smile had formed over Laura's lips.

'Can I tell you next time?' she said. 'All this talking, all these memories… I think I need a bit of time to process.'

'Of course, Laura, of course,' said Glenn, quickly putting down his pen and closing his notepad.

'Thanks, Glenn,' she said. 'I hope I've been an interesting case study so far.'

'Of course,' said Glenn, suddenly worried that he had tired her out. 'Jeez, we've been talking for hours. What's the time?'

Glenn searched around for the grandfather clock he had passed on his way into the tea room. It was indeed already early evening. They had talked for three hours solid and the pot of tea in front of them was stone cold.

'Later than we thought,' laughed Laura. 'Funny how reminiscing about the past makes you totally forget the present, isn't it?'

'And the future,' said Glenn, suddenly worrying that he would arrive home to Ronda Round Manor quite late. Sensing his worry, Laura smiled at him.

'How is your wife, Glenn?' she asked him. 'She's a very lucky woman to have a husband like you.'

'Is she?' asked Glenn, laughing. 'Yes, I suppose she is!'

He wondered if Eleanora ever thought herself lucky to be married to him.

'Someone who cares and listens,' said Laura, setting her mouth in a way that meant approval. 'That's rarer than you think in this world.'

'Listen, this has been great! Your story is incredible so far, Laura. It's so moving, and so powerful. When can we meet again?' Glenn asked her as they both stood up to take their coats. As ever, Glenn wondered if he should offer to help Laura as she rose slowly to her feet, but as ever, he remembered how independent she was. The story she had told today was a testament to that.

'Same time next week?' Laura suggested.

'Perfect,' said Glenn.

'We can take Oliver for a walk in the park if you like,' she said, reaching down to stroke the ginger tomcat nestled in her bag.

'With pleasure,' laughed Glenn. He was already looking forward to watching Laura walking her cat. He did not know such a thing existed.

'Brilliant,' she said. 'Then next weekend I'll tell you all about the great escape.'

'Thanks, Laura, for meeting me and for sharing your story with me,' said Glenn. He hesitated for a moment, wanting to say more, to express something deeper, but Laura seemed to understand. The blind had that uncanny ability, he thought: that sixth sense of empathetic understanding.

'Thank you, Glenn,' she said, and with that turned to leave, taking out her white cane to navigate back to her home. Glenn watched her for a moment, feeling a strange mixture of pride and protectiveness after the terrible story she had told. He wanted to follow her and make sure no one harmed her. But at the same time, he knew they had reached the turning point in Laura's story. He knew that what came next was good; whatever happened next took her away from that cold, miserable farm in Wales, towards the future Glenn had met her in. The next part of the story would take Laura to the ICB and to travel and hope and acceptance of her blindness. Strolling back towards the nearest underground station, Glenn smiled at the thought. He could not wait to hear part two of Laura's story.

CHAPTER TWELVE

In the week following Glenn's meeting with Laura, thoughts about the young woman's upbringing troubled him greatly. As wonderful as it had been to see her again, and share in her warmth and bright spirit, the stories she had told were nothing short of painful. He wondered how she could be the person she was today after enduring so much hardship. It was truly a miracle. Glenn had always thought there were laws and measures in place to protect the vulnerable in his country, but he now realised how naïve he had been; the abandoned and vulnerable always slipped through the cracks even in a civilised society.

Though Glenn did not find any interest in his wife, who had little time for sob stories and even less time for depressed young women, he did find good listening ears in his colleagues at Diversified Charities. They had been supportive of Glenn's proposal to gather case studies from the start, and were intrigued to hear how the first meeting had gone. They listened intently as Glenn told the tale of the meeting in the Lancaster. They were as intrigued and horrified by Laura's story as he had been.

'It's going to be quite a story to tell,' said Glenn. 'I'm determined to do her justice.'

'You're the perfect person to write it, Glenn,' said Kikka. 'You have such a wonderful way with words.'

'I've got to be,' said Glenn. 'This is my chance to tell this woman's story to the world.'

'It'll make a great case study,' said Tuni-Tung, nodding her head appreciatively as Glenn finished. 'Laura's story really appeals on a human level. It'll be a tear-jerker: the donors will love it.'

'You're too business-minded sometimes, Tuni,' said Natasha, frowning at her friend in the International Department. 'I think it's really sad. This poor girl. What a crying shame that such exploitation goes on under our very noses.'

'This Laura has suffered so much,' said Kikka, shaking her head in her Germanic way.

'Well that's just it,' said Glenn, confiding in the women around him. 'I think there's so much more to Laura's story than this early suffering. The next stage is going to be really interesting, I can tell. Something must have happened to change things for her, to bring her into the life she's living today. If you met her, you'd never know she has suffered so much.'

'That's a credit to her then,' said Natasha.

'Looking forward to the next instalment,' said Kikka, smiling enthusiastically. 'Let's hope things get better.'

'Things often have to get worse before they get better though,' said Tuni-Tung cynically.

'That's true,' said Natasha.

'Let's just wait and see what she says,' said Glenn, hoping that the next instalment of Laura's life would be more hopeful than the last.

Wandering back to his desk, he sat down to review the notes he had made about Laura so far. They had been scribbled down quickly in the Lancaster as they spoke, and reviewed only slightly on his train ride back to Virginia Water. Looking down at the sentences, Glenn thought about the intimacy of such a document: it contained the details of someone's deepest, darkest sorrows. Laura was the first of the women he had interviewed and he could not help but wonder what stories the others would have to tell. He knew Zu-Ting had worked as a child labourer for years in China. What would her story be like, he wondered? Most of all he wondered about the story of Bettina and the history that lay behind that melancholic look.

Those melancholic looks occupied Glenn's thoughts until the weekend, when he took the train once more into London and headed towards Kensington Gardens, where Laura had suggested they meet. It was not far from the Lancaster so he knew she would not have to walk far. He spotted her straight away, sitting on a bench by the Round Pond, her figure recognisable a hundred metres away. As he drew closer, he saw that she was wearing a scarlet trench coat and her hair looked incredibly bright against the soft, ironed material.

'Laura!' he called out to her as he approached the bench.

'Glenn,' she said warmly, raising a hand to touch his arm. 'It's wonderful to hear your voice again.'

Glenn looked at Laura for a moment. She had tied her long red hair up into a loose bun and delicate strands fell around her face, making her look more fairy-like than ever. Her bright eyes glittered in the sun and she looked stunning, he thought. How, he wondered, had someone so beautiful fallen upon such hardship? How could her abusers have looked into those pretty eyes and hurt her?

'It's a lovely spot here,' he said, gazing at Laura, who was staring blankly ahead, a small smile on her face. 'Man, I'm discovering London with you, Laura!'

'Yes, it's one of my favourites,' she replied. 'I love the Round Pond. Though I don't suppose I need to tell you it's not exactly round.'

'How do you know that?' asked Glenn, glancing back towards the pond before them. It was true, he thought, scanning the edges. The pond took on more of a rectangular shape.

'I've walked around it enough times to know,' said Laura. 'And I read it somewhere. It was built in 1730 by George II. I suppose the joke was on him. But we love it all the same, don't we Oliver?'

Glenn looked around, searching for the ginger tom cat he knew would be joining them on their walk today. But the cat was nowhere to be seen.

'Where is Oliver?' asked Glenn.

'Oh, he's fooling himself that there are fish he can catch in the pond,' she said. 'Don't worry, he'll soon give up and come to say hello.'

Glenn smiled at the thought of Laura's independent cat marching around the not so round pond, vainly searching for a fishy feast.

On the water, fathers were launching model yachts with their sons, pushing the dainty little ships into the water and watching them sail. There was a peaceful air about the place, there on that Saturday afternoon. The bustling streets of London were just hundreds of metres away, but there in Kensington Gardens, one could forget that there was a city nearby. A little girl nearby started to beg her mother for a piggy back. Laura laughed as she heard this.

'Do you have children, Glenn?' she asked.

'No,' said Glenn. 'No, we haven't started a family. I'm not sure if we ever will!'

'That's a shame,' Laura replied. 'I think you would make a great Dad.'

'Do you, huh?' he laughed. 'Well, I'd make a mean baseball partner if I had a boy. I'd probably make a good hockey player for a girl too!'

Glenn glowed inwardly at this compliment. Children were something he and his wife rarely discussed, let alone contemplated. Somehow they had not been on the cards for the couple from Ronda Round Manor. Both sets of parents asked when they might be allowed to expect grandchildren, but neither Glenn nor Eleanora had ever been able to give them an answer.

'How has your week been?' Laura asked, perhaps sensing the sensitivity of the subject of children and wanting to move the conversation along.

'Busy,' sighed Glenn. 'We have a lot of work now at Diversified Charities, the foundation I am working with.'

'Ah yes, the foundation you are writing the case studies for?' she asked.

'Exactly,' said Glenn. 'I wish I could spend more time on this project, but the whole world seems to be jostling for my attention. I'm drowning in funding proposals and charity briefs.'

'That sounds like a day in the office at the ICB,' said Laura, laughing her sweet, expressive laugh.

'Does it?' asked Glenn, thinking of Bettina and Laura juggling thousands of files and funding proposals. 'Is that where you're working now?'

'No, not full time,' said Laura. 'I work with the ICB on a voluntary basis at different times of the year. My work is nearby, in fact, near Edgware Road. It's a fantastic walk there in the mornings, especially in summer. I work full-time for an organisation called the Sussex Gardens Institute for the Blind.'

Glenn nodded, wondering when would be a good time to take out his notepad and start making notes. It was so easy and relaxed with Laura, he sometimes forgot he was there for the purpose of writing up a case study on her.

'Shall we pick up where we left off last week?' he suggested. 'I've only heard half of your story so far.'

'The worse half,' said Laura, smiling bitterly. 'Sure, let's continue. Whatever you feel is best. But shall we walk and talk?'

'Yes, of course. Whenever you're ready,' he said. Laura stood up slowly and began to call for Oliver, who soon appeared, scuttling towards them at lightning pace. Leaning down, Laura attached a leash to the leather collar on his neck. He purred as she fastened it against his fur. Glenn noticed her long, elegant fingers, perfectly pale as they tickled Oliver's neck.

'Doesn't he mind being on a leash?' Glenn asked, amazed to see a cat so meekly accept bondage.

'Does he seem bothered?' Laura asked, a note of anxiety in her voice.

'No, not at all,' laughed Glenn. 'That's why I'm so surprised. Cats are generally such independent creatures.'

They began to walk with Oliver trotting along beside them, his whiskers bouncing up and down.

'So, where were we,' Laura began, setting off on a circuit around the park. 'The last time we spoke I told you I left home at sixteen, didn't I?'

'Yes,' said Glenn. 'I believe you called it "the great escape". Is that what it felt like?'

'It did,' sighed Laura. 'That summer, when school ended, I packed my things up and jumped on a train to London. I didn't have much money, but what I did have was stored away in my bedroom. I took it with me and when I arrived in London I used people's sympathy to help me find my feet. That's the one advantage of being blind. People feel so sorry for me, and so guilty that they can see and I cannot, that they will do anything to help. As soon as I stepped off the train, a man asked me, "Can I help you, love?" I must have looked very lost and afraid; I was sixteen, alone and in a big new city.

'The noise at first was so overwhelming: the trains arriving, the hundreds of footsteps marching up and down the platforms, the talking people, and the constant announcements on the Tannoy. So I told him I had just arrived from Wales and needed to find somewhere to stay for the night. He worked at the station I believe, at London Paddington, and took me to his office. There he made some calls and consulted with two of his colleagues. They even offered me a cup of tea. "Listen," he said after a while. "We've found you somewhere to go to. I get off in about an hour, my shift's ending, so if you wait here I'll take you when I'm finished. How does that sound?" Well, I thought it sounded wonderful. He was so kind. And they say Londoners were rude and cold! What a lovely man. Back at the farm on Wales they would never have believed it.'

'Where did he take you?' Glenn asked, glad to hear someone had helped the sixteen year old Laura as she arrived in the metropolis. London was a dangerous place to be for vulnerable teenagers.

'Well, Barry, that was his name, took me to Sussex Gardens, where I work now,' said Laura.

'The same place?' asked Glenn.

'Yes,' she said. 'He walked me through the streets outside the station and I was so afraid at first, of all the people, all the strange smells and sounds. But eventually we reached a quiet, peaceful building, and a receptionist met us there. I remember her voice, as clear as day. She welcomed me to the Sussex Gardens Institute for the Blind. She then asked me if I had travelled to London alone and if I had a place to stay. I told her I was there alone and could not go back to where I had come from. I told her my story, the story I told you last week, and she took pity on me. I don't know if I believe in God, Glenn, or fate, but I do believe that on that day, I was blessed with the greatest luck. The woman behind the reception was called Sandra, and she offered me a job, right then and there, on the spot. She said they needed a helping hand in the office and I was perfectly qualified for the work.'

'Just like that?' asked Glenn, amazed by this remarkable twist of fate.

'Just like that,' smiled Laura. 'She took me to a hostel that night, where I spent a few days, and then she found a house for me to live in. I was sharing with three other women. It was a sort of halfway house, a refuge, I suppose. From there I could walk easily to my job in Sussex Gardens.'

'What kind of work were you doing?' Glenn asked.

'Oh, all sorts,' said Laura. 'I was welcoming people, filing, arranging documents. I had always been good in school, and the documents used at the Institute were often in Braille. This made my life easier than it had ever been. Most of all I was learning things I had never been taught, like how to use my white cane properly. Come on, shall we go there?'

'Where?' asked Glenn.

'To the institute,' said Laura. 'I want to show you this amazing organisation.'

'With pleasure,' said Glenn, and slowly they headed out of the park towards Sussex Gardens, Oliver the cat in tow. They wandered in silence for a while, Glenn contemplating all he had heard, and Laura lost in her memories. After a while she spoke fondly of her early memories of London, after the shock of the big city had worn off. Walking through the streets, Glenn could imagine Laura there, a young woman coming into her own after years of misery.

When they finally arrived at the Sussex Gardens Institute for the Blind, Glenn was impressed by a modern, attractive entrance to the building. It looked like an inspiring and welcoming place to work. Laura introduced the Institute with such pride in her voice that Glenn worried for a moment that she might burst into tears.

'So you've worked here since you were sixteen?' asked Glenn. 'How old are you now?'

'I'm twenty-four,' said Laura. 'But no, I have not worked here since I was sixteen. I worked here for two years after that first appointment. They were wonderful years, full of learning and challenges, and I took every opportunity I could to develop my skills, with people and with administration. When I turned eighteen, it was time to leave. I felt such a great urge to get out and see the world. Many of the people who came to the reception at the Institute were from all over the world, or just very well-travelled. I was inspired by every tale of Africa, Asia and the Americas I heard. By then I had saved up enough money to take a big trip, so I informed the management and they gave me their blessing. They were worried, of course, but they were starting to understand who I was too. They knew that whatever they said, I would follow my own path, and it was thanks to them that I had the confidence to do so.'

Wandering over to a bench near the Institute, the companions sat down, and Glenn saw this as an opportunity to take out his pen and notepad for note-making.

'Your speech on travelling with blindness in Aachen was spectacularly memorable,' said Glenn, smiling as he recalled her many anecdotes. 'I must admit, I was amazed that someone without sight could travel so independently.'

Laura laughed at this.

'I know,' she said. 'I think I amazed myself. But the thing is, Glenn, blind people have been portrayed as useless and vulnerable since the beginning of time. They are perceived as the victims of a great injustice, and the only remedy is care and molly-coddling, but I cannot live like that. I need to feel like I can get up in the morning and do whatever my heart desires, without help, just me, myself and I. I knew travelling alone was going to be hard, and I was afraid, I can't deny it. But I had already taken a great leap of faith when I left that dreadful farm in Wales. I was ready. I think I was born ready.'

'Where did you go?' Glenn asked.

'Well, I started off with a tour of Europe,' said Laura. 'I packed my bags and took the Eurostar from London St. Pancras to Paris. I spent a few weeks in Paris, exploring the city and staying with a friend in her commune on the seventeenth arrondissement. She took me everywhere, to the galleries, the parks, the nightclubs, we had so much fun. Then I took off for Toulouse and the south of France, heading to Nice, and then along the coast down to Spain. I think I spent about three months in Barcelona. I was really getting the hang of Spanish, and eventually moved on to find some work at an orange grove in Seville. I picked oranges for about a month over the summer, can you imagine? It was wonderful work. The owner of the farm taught me how to distinguish between good and bad oranges by feeling and smelling them. His son was reluctant to employ me at first, naturally of course, because he worried I would not be able to see the oranges well enough to tell the good from the bad! It was the father who scolded his son and said appearances can be deceptive, or something like that in Spanish. Anyway, the son, Juan-Pablo, fell in love with me and we had a little romance. Nothing too special, mind you, I was not planning on settling in Spain.'

'So you left him?' Glenn asked.

'Yes, I did,' said Laura, laughing for a moment. 'Poor boy.'

'Poor boy indeed!' he said. 'You're quite a catch, Laura.'

'Yes, but I was leaving anyway,' she said. 'When the orange season was over, I jumped on a bus and went all the way to Porto in Portugal. I made some terrific friends there, especially a group of artists who took me in and cared for me like a stray cat! They were so kind and loving. We went on many trips together, to ancient castles, little fishing ports and some incredible little mountains. I was sad to leave that time, but my itchy feet were feeling ready to move again.'

'Where did you go next?' Glenn asked.

'Next I went south, down to Gibraltar, to see the monkeys, and took a boat from there to the port of Livorno in Italy. It was a very long crossing, but I loved the idea of crossing the Mediterranean by boat. I was tired of buses, cars and trains. From there I embarked on quite a journey, backpacking down to Rome and then up to Venice. From Venice I went up through Slovenia to Vienna and from Vienna to Munich. In fact, that's where I met Bettina.'

Glenn's heart jumped at the sound of the name.

'You met Bettina in Munich?' he asked.

'Yes, in Munich,' said Laura. 'And I suppose it was at that point, when I met Bettina, that things really started to change for me.'

'How so?' asked Glenn, curious to learn how this remarkable woman had had an effect on young, adventurous Laura.

'Well, in a multitude of ways,' she said. 'When I arrived in Munich I stayed in a hostel on the edge of the city. After travelling for so many months I was quite tired. I wanted to rest and perhaps explore the city for a while. I had heard many beautiful things about Munich, and was curious about its history and food. After the chaotic spirit of Spain, Portugal, Italy and Slovenia, Germany seemed so organised and peaceful. It seemed like the perfect place to unwind for a few days. The owner of the hostel I stayed at had heard that there was a conference for the blind underway in the city, run by the International Charity for the Blind. She was a very kind woman, quite reserved, and curious about blindness herself, so she drove me to the conference and we went in together. That's where I heard Bettina speak for the first time. Do you remember how you felt when you heard Bettina speak for the first time, Glenn?'

For a moment, Glenn started, afraid that his secret interest in Bettina was plain for all to see.

'What do you mean?' he asked quickly.

'When you heard her speak in Aachen,' said Laura, clearly unfazed by Glenn's reaction. She stared straight ahead as always, gazing into the middle distance.

'Oh,' said Glenn, unsure of what to say. 'I was impressed, I suppose. I thought she spoke very well, and in English too.'

In truth, Glenn had been enraptured by Bettina from the very start. From the moment she had welcomed him into her seminar, and talked his group through their heightened senses, he had been awestruck.

'Well, I was amazed,' said Laura, laughing slightly. 'Imagine: I was eighteen years old, almost nineteen, and in front of me stood a woman who had lived with blindness her whole life long: a successful psychologist and co-founder of an international charity. If I wasn't impressed enough by her speech, I was even more impressed when she came up to me after the conference and spoke to me, so kindly and with such warmth. When I told her I was just visiting Munich, she asked me if I wanted to have lunch with her some time. We spoke and I shared with her my travel stories and a bit about my life, and before we said goodbye, she invited me to her home town of Winterhausen on my way north to Berlin. She said she was visiting her parents there, and it was a beautiful part of Germany to see if I had time.'

'And you went?' Glenn asked. 'To Winterhausen?'

'Yes,' said Laura. 'It was close to Wurzburg. Such a beautiful, charming little German town. Bettina picked me up from the train station and drove me to her home. Her parents were so sweet. They did not speak too much English, but I could feel in their gestures and in the way they fed me just how welcoming they were. I think Bettina had the kind of upbringing every blind child dreams of, in fact, every foster child dreams of. Her parents had accepted their daughter's disability and had done everything they could to make her life as comfortable as possible. I attributed that to her success and told her as much. Do you know what she said to me then?'

'What did she say?' asked Glenn. His notepad lay abandoned now. He was simply listening, enraptured by this story of Bettina's home and background. He could imagine it all so clearly, even though he had never set foot in Winterhausen. He knew nothing about Bettina but somehow he could picture her in his mind as clear as day.

'She said that confidence and drive are not qualities we are born with,' Laura remembered, a small smile forming on her lips as she recalled the words. 'They are qualities we nurture in ourselves with hard work and experience. She said I had far more experience than her of the difficulties of life, and if I harnessed that experience, and put it to good use, I could do anything.'

'Wise words,' said Glenn.

'They were,' said Laura.

'And you can do anything, Laura, believe me,' he said.

'Thanks, Glenn,' she smiled. 'You're a very convincing man when you want to be.'

'That's my job!' he laughed. 'I convince people to make good choices.'

'That sounds like Bettina,' grinned Laura. 'When she heard that I had not attended university, or even college, she asked me what I wanted to study if I had the chance. Well, all I knew was that I wanted to help organisations like the Sussex Place Institute for the Blind grow. I also wanted to be able to help others make good things happen, make little ideas grow into big changes that involved people.'

'So what did she suggest?' Glenn asked.

'I thought she would propose a degree in international relations or something to do with the charity sector, but she didn't,' said Laura. 'Bettina proposed that I apply for a degree in business, to give me the essential skills I could then offer the kind of charities and organisations I wanted to support. When we said goodbye, she emailed me the outline of a course at the London Business School. I was in Berlin at the time and looked into it. It looked fantastic but there was no way I could fund myself through the university program for three, potentially four years if I went to masters level. I had barely saved enough for my travels, and my money was running out quickly. So I wrote to Bettina to thank her for the suggestion but it would not be financially possible. I didn't think I would ever earn enough to study.'

'What did she say?' asked Glenn.

'She said I didn't need to worry about the finances,' said Laura. 'I was amazed by her response. She said she would find sponsorship for me through the ICB.'

'And did she?' asked Glenn.

'She did,' said Laura. 'The ICB agreed to fully sponsor my studies and Bettina vowed to make me a part of the ICB voluntary staff when I had graduated.'

'What a generous offer,' said Glenn, deeply impressed by Bettina's generosity and kindness towards Laura. She was clearly a woman who saw potential and did everything she could to nurture it.

'It changed my life,' said Laura. 'With Bettina's help I made a strong application and was accepted for study the following September. When I returned to London it was as a student; for the next four years I made some of the best friends of my life. I learnt French, German, and specialised in marketing and personal relations. Finally I felt like I belonged somewhere, and it wasn't because of the university, or the career I was building for myself. It was because at last I felt like I was in control of my own life: I was going somewhere.'

'And you graduated recently then?' Glenn asked.

'Yes, with flying colours no less!' she said. 'And imagine my joy when I received my final results and a letter came from the Sussex Place Institute, offering me a brand new position in personal relations. They wanted me to be the new face of the Institute, welcoming people and assessing them for access to our services.'

'Congratulations, Laura,' said Glenn warmly. 'That is fantastic news. How does your job work now then?'

'My role is to direct people towards what they need in the Institute,' said Laura, becoming quite business-like as she spoke. 'I work as a personal consultant to our clients. I measure their degree of blindness and then measure our response. For example, some clients might need help getting hold of a white cane, or an introduction to life with a guide dog. Some are at varying states of blindness and might need to be referred to a hospital or recommended for operation. I personally deliver four-month training programmes in how to walk in the streets without danger and have helped to develop other programmes we offer here at the Institute. We identify new risks, new dangers, threats from mugging, theft, exploitation, and also day-to-day conveniences such as shopping and accounting. I also talk people through the new instruments we have on offer to assist the blind and visually impaired: the talking watches, talking clocks, magnifying classes et cetera. We try to keep as up to date with new market arrivals as possible.'

'That sounds like an incredible job,' said Glenn. 'It must feel very different from your first job on reception.'

'Yes,' laughed Laura. 'But I never stay too long away from reception. I have my own office, it's very grand, and yet I feel more at home on reception, meeting people when they come in. it feels more human to me somehow.'

Glenn thought about his own office, hidden away in the depths of the Diversified Charities Foundation. The people he helped were thousands of miles away, in war zones or deserts he would never see. He rarely met the beneficiaries the DCF helped and supported through difficult times. Laura was right on the front line.

'And you said your work for the ICB was voluntary?' Glenn asked, wondering how Laura found time to do work for the ICB on top of her busy schedule.

'Indeed,' she said. 'As Bettina puts it, I became an asset for the ICB. I speak three European languages and had a business education from one of the finest business schools in the world. Since graduating I have become a part of their mission. I am so proud of the work we do.'

'What would you consider to be the major contributors to the happiness you feel today?' Glenn asked, scribbling down a few notes as he spoke.

'Oliver,' said Laura, grinning. Glenn looked around to see the tom cat rubbing himself against his mistress's leg. 'He keeps me sane. We found each other when I had just started at university and we've been together since.'

'And besides Oliver?' said Glenn. 'Does your work bring you happiness?'

'More than I can say,' said Laura. 'But in terms of the major contributors to my success and the happiness I feel in my life now, there is only one. And that is Bettina.'

'Because of everything she has done for you?' asked Glenn. Laura nodded.

'She is our team leader, in every sense of the word,' said Laura. 'She gave me hope when I could not imagine a future.'

Glenn smiled at Laura's words. She had clearly found a mentor in Bettina: someone to look up to when life had let her down.

'Thank you, Laura, for sharing this wonderful story with me,' he said. 'I am touched. Truly.'

'Is there anything else you would like to know, Glenn?' she asked him.

'No, I think that's great,' he said. 'I have a lot to write about you, Laura. I feel confident I can bring your story to life.'

'I trust you, Glenn,' she said. 'I've put my story in your hands.'

'It's safe with me,' he said.

The street lights around them suddenly blinked on and Glenn realised that night was falling. Though she could not see, Laura too seemed to sense that the hour was late.

'I think I'd best take Oliver home for some supper,' she said. 'Once again we have talked ourselves into the evening. But it was such a pleasure to meet with you, Glenn.'

'The pleasure was all mine,' said Glenn, reaching out to squeeze Laura's hand. 'Thanks to you and Oliver for your time.'

'Will you be in touch with the others now?' Laura asked. 'I'm sure they'd all be happy to talk to you.'

'Yes, I'll have to consult my list and see who's next,' said Glenn, already wondering which of the five other blind women he should reach out to for an interview.

'Well, good luck and don't be a stranger, eh?' said Laura.

'I won't be,' said Glenn. 'You can count on that! Goodnight, Laura, and goodnight to you too, Oliver.'

'Goodnight, Glenn,' she said, and turned to wander back towards Bayswater, her cat at her heels. A passing couple looked disapprovingly at the sight of a cat on a lead, making Glenn grin as he walked back towards Edgware Road where he could start taking trains back to Virginia Water. After the story he had heard that day, somehow Glenn had the feeling that women like Laura would never care what other people thought. She would always go her own way, he thought, and what a way that was.

CHAPTER THIRTEEN

Back in the office, Glenn was counting down the days before his next trip back to New York. After spending those days with Laura, he was keener than ever to see his father and share Laura's story with him. The whole narrative occupied his thoughts, like a secret he needed to share. He would fly the following weekend for a week so had lots to sort out in the office. He knew Diversified Charities were very flexible with his hours and time off, but he had already started probing funding streams for the ICB and it would be foolish to leave without securing a few meetings for his return.

With the help of his colleagues, things were looking positive on the donor front. Natasha and Tuni-Tung were sure that with the support of Glenn's case study pamphlet, donors would be keen to support the fantastic work that Bettina and the five blind women were doing across the globe.

A knock rapped upon his door, taking his mind away from the daunting pile of paperwork for a moment.

'Come in,' he called, putting down his pen.

The door opened and his secretary, Sonia, walked in, cradling more files for him to review. He groaned at the sight of the fresh material.

'Oh, Sonia!' he cried. 'Does it ever end?'

'I won't take that personally,' said Sonia with a sheepish smile, putting them down on his desk.

'Don't,' murmured Glenn, sighing deeply. 'It's the work you're bringing me I'm afraid of, not you, Sonia. You're a brilliant secretary. You do know that, don't you?'

'I do,' she smiled. 'And you're brilliant at what you do, sir. That's why you're so in demand!'

'How will I ever get through all of this before I fly to the States?' he groaned.

'Well, Amelia has left you a cup of tea,' said Sonia. 'That should cheer you up. And a biscuit.'

'Really?' asked Glenn, feeling his spirits lift at the thought of a quick sugar boost. Sure enough the cup and saucer delivered by Amelia had a big digestive biscuit balanced near the teaspoon. Glenn took the cup of tea thankfully in his hands and bit into the biscuit, savouring the sweet and salty taste for a moment.

'I'll leave you to it, sir,' said Sonia. 'It looks like you have a lot to finish before you fly out.'

'Thanks, Sonia,' said Glenn. 'Take care of yourself while I'm away, alright?'

'Will Eleanora be going out with you?' his secretary enquired after his wife before closing the door.

'Not this time,' said Glenn. 'Thanks, Sonia. I'd best get on.'

'Right you are, sir,' she smiled. 'You know where I am if you need me.'

Sonia closed the office door behind her, leaving Glenn alone once more. No, his wife would not be joining him on his trip to New York. He thought about their conversation again for a moment. Their discussion had been quite brief. Eleanora insisted her responsibilities were with the farm and that the tenants couldn't possibly be without her for a week.

'It'll be lambing season before we know it, and the Thompsons will make a mess of it, as they do every year,' she complained when he had broached the subject. 'I'll be the one who loses profit, dear, mark my words. It's always the same story.'

'But it's just a week,' said Glenn, gently protesting. 'Surely a few days won't make a difference? You know you'll miss me, honey!'

'A week!' she yelped. 'A week can make the difference between a good year and a bad year.'

'A week can also make a difference between a happy husband and a sad husband,' he protested, but with a smile.

'You'll do just fine,' she said, giving him a quick kiss on the lips.

Glenn did not even attempt to ask when his wife had become so concerned with the farm's daily needs and activities. He knew deep down that Eleanora did not want to spend a week with his blind father and his anxious mother. There was nothing he could do to persuade her and if he was really honest with himself, a part of him did not really care. Bertie and Iris were his parents after all, and he rarely enjoyed spending time with them and Eleanora together. There was a constant tension between them all that made him feel deeply uncomfortable. When the time came to fly, Glenn was happy to wave his wife goodbye on the doorstep of Ronda Round Manor and drive to London Heathrow. After all, there was another reason he was so excited to cross the Atlantic this time.

Glenn had managed to make contact with another of the six blind women from Aachen, one he knew he would not find so easily in Europe. Odile had lived in New Orleans since her early twenties and Glenn had decided to write her an email, along the same lines as the one he had written to Laura. He wanted her to be his next case study in the pamphlet, and had told her as much.

Subject: Meeting up?

Dear Odile,

I hope this finds you well. It was a pleasure to meet you at the conference in Aachen. I am just getting in touch because I will be flying over to New York to visit my father this weekend. If there was a possibility to meet you in New Orleans, I would welcome the chance. It would be great to see you again and I have a small project I could use your help on.

Let me know if this could work for you, and we can discuss dates.

Best wishes,
Glenn

Odile had still not replied by the time Glenn reached his parents' house in Sutton Place, but Glenn had not yet given up hope. If there was any chance to meet another of the six blind women whilst he was over in

America, he would not let it go lightly. He mused on the project until he greeted his parents and became lost in the joy of their reunion.

'How have things been then?' Glenn asked his father as they settled down to drink coffee. It was Saturday morning and the house smelled like the mornings Glenn remembered as a child. His mother had just cooked bacon and pancakes, leaving deliciously smoky smells in the kitchen. The aroma of freshly roasted coffee beans filled his nostrils and Glenn felt at home immediately. Little had changed in their routines since those years ago, except now, of course, Bertie no longer made his famous coffee. His blindness did not permit that yet. Nor was he allowed to eat the bacon and pancakes, due to strict restrictions on his diet following the developments of his diabetes. However, it was the coffee-making he missed most.

'Oh, he tries,' said Iris, shaking her head in woe. 'But the result is not good. Don't tell him I said that!'

'He's blind, not deaf, Mom!' laughed Glenn. 'Jeez, did you get the wrong memo?'

'Your mother's just jealous, son,' said Bertie. 'I've always been the better coffee-maker in this household. This blindness is a blessing to her. Now she can make it and no one complains.'

Glenn was glad to hear his father joking and making light of his vision loss. He had been afraid when the couple had come to London that they were losing all hope in finding normality in their lives again, choosing to chase impossible miracle cures instead. For a while they chatted through the last few months since their visit to London, telling Glenn about the visitors who had been and gone, the walks they had done and the things they had been eating.

'I don't see why I need to bother with a fancy diet anymore,' sighed Bertie. 'My eyes are gone. The diabetes has done its worst. Why do I still need to eat so much salad?'

'Because the rest of your body needs to live too, Bertie Tebbhurst!' his wife scolded him. 'Now Glenn, honey, why don't you tell us what's happening in London? How is your work? And Eleanora, is she doing fine?'

Glenn launched into an account of life in England, discussing his work with Diversified Charities, the house, the farm, and Eleanora's bridge victories. As soon as he could he began to tell them about his meeting with Laura.

'And she's a friend of yours?' Iris asked.

'Yes,' said Glenn. 'We met at the conference I told you about. Do you remember? The one in Aachen? With the workshops for the blind?'

'How could we forget?' laughed Bertie. 'You never stop talking about it!'

'That's true, Dad,' Glenn grinned at his father. 'For good reason. It was so eye-opening for me.'

'Funny turn of phrase for a conference on blindness!' yelled Bertie before bursting into raucous laughter.

'That is such a "dad" joke,' frowned Glenn, though in truth he was happier than ever to hear his father making jokes as he used to before. 'But seriously, Bertie, it helped me to understand so much more about the benefits of accepting blindness rather than fighting it. I've started a new project, interviewing the six blind women I met there. So far I have only interviewed Laura. But my, what a story she had to tell.'

Slowly Glenn began to tell Laura's story, from her abandonment as a child to her fostering nightmare in Wales.

'Poor baby,' said Iris, her eyes brimming with tears. Glenn's mother had always been quick to cry. 'It's just unthinkable – abandoning a blind child.'

'Setting one to work on a farm is even worse,' said Bertie. 'God, those Brits are backwards, aren't they? How do you survive over there, Glenn?'

'I remember I'm a New Yorker, born and bred, Pops! Sadly I don't think Laura's case was uncommon,' he explained to his parents. 'It was tragic and unfortunate, and a sign that people slip through the cracks of our ever-so-carefully-constructed social welfare systems. But after the tragedy, her story was unique. What happened next was what made it truly remarkable for me.'

'What happened?' Iris asked, mesmerised by this tale of misery.

Glenn launched into Laura's story of escape and recovery. When he told them about her travels, both parents were spell-bound.

'But how?' asked Iris. 'The poor girl was blind!'

'That didn't stop her,' said Glenn, hearing the pride in his voice now. 'She said as soon as she had broken free that first time, she knew she had nothing to be afraid of. Laura is a testament to the argument that blindness does not, and should not, be an impediment in life.'

There was silence for a while as everyone reflected on Laura's story. They sipped their coffee quietly, and it was Bertie who spoke first.

'You know, Glenn, it's admirable you're writing down these girls' stories,' he said. 'But why are you doing this?'

'To raise awareness of the work they do,' said Glenn, hesitating for a moment before going on. 'And, to help you, Dad. I can't stand idly by while you think your life is over. These women can give you hope. They have given me hope!'

'But son, this Laura was blind from birth,' said Bertie. 'I'm an old man who turned blind in his sixties. This girl has had twenty-four long years to learn how to live with her blindness. I don't know if I'm ever gonna be able to live like her.'

It was true, thought Glenn: Bertie had not been born blind like Laura. Which was why, more than ever, Glenn hoped Odile would reply to his email about a visit to New Orleans. He remembered what Herbert Farrand had said when he had introduced her at the conference in Aachen: that she too had been diagnosed with Type 2 diabetes, and had lost her sight in her mid-twenties. Her story was more like his fathers and would resonate more, Glenn thought. He was desperate to talk to her and learn more about a story so close to his father's: a story that he knew had a happy ending, just like Laura's.

'Don't worry, Dad,' he said. 'Leave it to me, OK? You'll know what I'm talking about soon enough.'

Luckily for Glenn he did not have to wait long for Odile's reply. She replied that Sunday evening, proposing Glenn call her the following morning to discuss his trip down to New Orleans.

'Glenn!' she cried down the line in her heavy New Orleans accent. 'I'm so happy to hear from you. It's go great you're coming down country. You can see my centre, and meet some of the blind people there. How are you?'

'Odile!' Glenn cried back. 'God it's good to hear your voice! I'm well, thanks. Thanks very much for your email. I'm so glad we can meet. It's swell!'

'Swell, huh?' she laughed. 'Someone's back in the States, I can tell!'

'I never feel more American than when I'm in America, baby!' he laughed.

'How's your Dad?' she asked.

'He's well,' said Glenn. 'Better than before.'

'Great, is he coming too?' she asked. 'We have plenty of support staff at the centre. He can check it out, get a feel of the work we do.'

'I wish,' said Glenn. 'He'd love New Orleans, I'm sure. But they had a bit of a heavy time of it on their last trip. I think they'd just like to stay home for a while. It will just be me. Will that be OK?'

Glenn knew his father would not want to travel anymore. The trip to London had been exhausting, and though neither Iris nor Bertie would admit it, the prospect of travel did not excite them as it had before the blindness. Glenn had the feeling it frightened them.

'Just you is perfect,' said Odile. 'There's a Holiday Inn not far from the centre, you can book in there. Do you have a pen there? I'll give you the address.'

Glenn noted down the address and arranged the details of his trip with Odile. It would be a three hour flight down from New York, which he could take that Friday afternoon. His return flight to London was flexible so he would simply extend it to the Sunday, and fly back from New Orleans that morning. It would be a lot of travelling, but somehow Glenn could not miss this chance to meet Odile again and capture her story on paper.

When the time came to fly, Glenn was reluctant to leave his parents. As ever, they had created such a warm and loving environment for his visit. He held his mother close as she kissed him goodbye, and promised to call her, as he had always done, once a week.

'You take care of yourself down south, son,' said Bertie, grinning. 'There's jazz and trouble in Louisiana!'

'Wish you could come with me, Dad,' said Glenn quietly. 'You'd love Odile. She's so sweet.'

'What, and make your mother jealous? No, sir!' cried Bertie.

'Jealous, my eye!' scolded Iris. 'Go on, Glenn, or you'll be late for your flight.'

'New York isn't the same without you, son!' his father called after him.

'Of course it isn't!' laughed Glenn.

Waving them both goodbye, he headed back to La Guardia airport to take his flight to New Orleans. When he finally walked onto the plane he was full of an excitement he had not felt since he travelled to Aachen. He felt like he was going on holiday for the first time in years. The plane was full of people heading down south for the New Orleans music scene, and Glenn was happy to be with them.

He caught his first glimpse of the majestic Mississippi River as the plane descended. Many times he had heard songs sung about the Mississippi and there it was below him, as clear as day. He watched as the great body of water snaked through green, fertile land. Bumping down into Louisiana, Glenn had a great feeling about his trip ahead.

Finding the Holiday Inn Odile had recommended was easy enough. Following her clear instructions, Glenn took a taxi to the centre of the city. His driver was a friendly local called Jim.

'Where you from, friend?' he asked Glenn.

'London,' said Glenn. 'Though I'm from New York originally.'

'A Yankee down south!' cried the driver.

'That's me,' grinned Glenn.

'What brings you to New Orleans?' the driver asked Glenn, turning down the rhythmic music playing on his radio and grinning at his passenger.

'I'm here to visit a friend,' Glenn replied. 'She works here in New Orleans as a therapist for the blind.'

'The blind?' exclaimed the driver. 'Man, there's one blind man in my life. Ray Charles. You know Ray, son?'

'I do,' smiled Glenn, remembering the blind singer who had died a few years before, back in 2003. Blindness had not held him back from making wonderful music and an international career.

'They called him the jewel of Georgia,' said Jim. 'But I say that man was from New Orleans! That's where he left his soul, man.'

The rest of the journey was serenaded by Ray Charles CDs and multiple renditions of 'Hit the Road Jack'. By the time Glenn arrived at the Holiday Inn, a small, blue and white house built in the old French colonial style of the city with a pretty garden on a quiet street, he was humming to himself. He carried his suitcase up the bright white steps to find a smiling, friendly receptionist there to welcome him.

'Good evening, sir, welcome to New Orleans!' said the young man. His skin was the colour of rich coffee and his eyes were bright with youth.

'Well hi there!' said Glenn brightly. 'What a lovely hotel this is.'

'One of the best in town,' said the receptionist. 'But I would say that. I work here! Don't take my word for it, sir, see for yourself.'

With a flash of his dazzling smile, the young man took Glenn up to his room. It was bright and airy, with a fantastic view out onto a small square.

'Will this do for you, sir?' the man asked.

'This will do just perfectly,' said Glenn.

'If there's anything you need, sir, just call,' he said. 'We are here to make your stay as comfortable as possible. If there's nothing else, then all that's left to say is you have a nice day now.'

Glenn smiled inwardly at this fantastic customer service, unique to the United States. Only in America would one be told to have a nice day so many times in one trip.

'Is there somewhere nearby I can grab a bite to eat?' he asked. 'Something traditional, local to the city perhaps?'

'Of course, sir!' laughed the receptionist. 'Just down the street, there's a great creole restaurant, called "Mama's Cafe", down on Canal Street. They'll feed you well, I promise.'

'Thanks,' said Glenn. When he was alone, he sat down on the bed for a moment, registering where he was. He felt like a version of himself he had not been in a while; an adventurous soul. Pulling on a lighter jacket, for it was much warmer down south, Glenn headed out into New Orleans in search of dinner.

When he arrived at "Mama's" he was met by friendly staff and colourful décor. He settled himself down at a table and ate the waiter's recommendations, a delicious selection of crab, fresh salad leaves and fried potatoes. A few women dining nearby kept glancing over at him and he threw them a smile. Still got it, he thought.

Feeling full to the brim, Glenn wandered back to the hotel. The streets were coming to life now. It was a Friday night and the city's reputation as musical heaven and jazz Valhalla was now clear to see. Piano keys and thumbed bass guitar strings filled the air, alongside the excited chatter of visitors and locals. Glenn, however, was done for the day: exhaustion crept through his body, and when he finally reached his bed he collapsed into a very deep sleep.

Feeling groggy the next morning after the flight, Glenn drank lots of coffee before heading over to the address Odile had given him. Her centre for the blind was not far from the hotel, just a few streets along from the charismatic canal street. It was a modern building with an impressive sign written stylishly in Latin letters and Braille: The International Charity for the Blind (ICB) New Orleans.

Glenn felt a strange sense of pride welling in his chest when he read the letters, thinking of Bettina, and Laura, and all he had learnt about the charity since the conference in Aachen. There in the bright light of the Louisiana sun, Glenn saw the ICB building as a beacon of hope for the people of New Orleans.

Heading through the double doors, a small beep announced his arrival to the reception. Glenn was met by a friendly receptionist. The young woman, who had curly black hair, was clearly blind. She gazed blankly ahead, a smile fixed on her lips.

'Welcome to the International Charity for the Blind, New Orleans Branch,' she said warmly. 'Can I take your name and email, please?'

Glenn gave his name, address and email.

'And what can we do for you today, Mr. Tebbhurst?' she asked him, when his details had been logged into the system.

'I'm here to see Odile Brown,' said Glenn. 'Is she in the office?'

'She's always in the office,' said the receptionist with a smile. Picking up her phone, the receptionist called through to Odile. After a few moments, Odile arrived. Glenn felt his smile grow as she approached him for she was as beautiful as ever. She had a petite face with cute features, surrounded by thick, blonde hair. Her eyes were dark and searching and her skin looked browner than it had in Aachen, a gift from the American weather. Other than her apparent tan, Odile looked exactly the same as when he had first met her.

'Glenn?' she cried as she walked through the door towards him. She could not see him so she extended her hands to feel his shoulders and his arms. 'Is that you?'

'It is!' he replied, just as excitedly. 'It's fantastic to be in New Orleans, Odile. And to see you.'

'You are most welcome,' she replied. 'Has Alicia welcomed you well?'

Glenn turned back to the receptionist called Alicia and grinned. She smiled ahead, not seeing him, but sensing his smile.

'She has,' said Glenn. 'What a fantastic receptionist you have here. Can I steal her?'

'No chance!' laughed Odile. 'Besides, she'd never survive in the English weather.'

'No, ma'am!' the receptionist chuckled.

'Come on in,' said Odile. 'I have so much to show you.'

'Lead on!' cried Glenn. His excitement at seeing Odile again was bubbling inside of him.

As they wandered up through the building towards Odile's office, they chatted about the months since Aachen and Glenn felt the same sense of warmth he had encountered in Odile ever since he met her. They entered a suave, peaceful office, decorated with incredible wall carvings. For a moment Glenn remembered his day in the dark, feeling the impasto textures of the paintings created for the blind.

'Great office!' he exclaimed. 'So this is your hot seat! I like it.'

'I don't spend much time here to be honest,' said Odile. 'I prefer to be out and about, seeing how everyone's doing. I just use this spot for interviews with journalists or new members of the centre. It's my talking room.'

Glenn had the feeling that the whole centre was about talking, in some way, shape or form. It had a relaxing effect on him as soon as he walked through the door.

'What kind of questions do people ask when they come here?' he asked.

'All sorts,' said Odile. 'People often want to know if it is possible to live independently, without carers or guide dogs. They want us to walk them through the impediments of blindness, so they know for certain if they can make it on their own. This is considered the therapeutic centre for the blind in New Orleans. I was trained by Bettina, who sent me to a course at the local university. I have three years of instruction in counselling and six years' experience of counselling now. I'm the voice people hear when they're struggling.'

'And Bettina trained you herself?' Glenn asked.

'She facilitated my training,' said Odile. 'She was young at the time, barely graduated. But she took a chance on me and helped me help others to live with blindness.'

Glenn wanted to hear more about Bettina. The story sounded similar to Laura's, but before he could ask more, Odile was pushing papers into his hands.

'We have plenty of information available here,' she said, 'multiple documents that provide basic information for living with blindness. Here, take a look.'

Reaching into her desk, Odile brought out several pamphlets with various titles. They were presented in Braille and Latin script.

'Let me give you a tour,' said Odile. Following closely behind, Glenn paid attention as he was led through labs where there were machines made for enlarging script and surface area, for touch-related technology, for the latest audio assistance.

'This is amazing,' he breathed. 'I can't believe this is all available to the public.'

'This room here is for training we give to the fully blind,' said Odile. 'We guide them through the practicalities of daily life, but especially how to walk in the streets and how to avoid running into walls. Our trainers come from both the blind and the seeing communities. You'd be amazed by the complexities of travelling from A to B with blindness, Glenn. I could never have imagined such things when I was seeing.'

At this, Glenn remembered why he had wanted to see Odile so much. Her story was not so different from his father's. She too had lost her sight after living with it for such a long time.

'Just things like how to search for green lights, or red lights, or deal with buzzers,' she continued. 'How to use new modern machines to help make healthy lifestyle choices, all of these things – they take some getting used to.'

'It sounds like you're doing a great job here, Odile,' said Glenn. 'You deserve a medal! Should I arrange the ceremony now or later?'

'I do my best,' said Odile. 'I know what it is to struggle with blindness, Glenn. I wouldn't wish it on anyone.'

'Of course,' he said, suddenly regretting his brashness.

'I'm here to serve the people,' she said.

'And the ICB funds this centre entirely?' Glenn asked.

'Yes,' said Odile. 'I am given a small subsidy, enough to make an honest living, and the centre is fully run by ICB. Herbert Farrand himself sent over the machines that you saw in the laboratory. He bought them on a visit to the centre two years ago. He said they were a gift to us for all the great work we are doing over here.'

'How kind of him,' said Glenn, nodding appreciatively. Herbert Farrand had struck him as the charismatic, persuasive face of the ICB at the conference, but hearing how he had done this, Glenn could see that there was more to him than smart suits and a handsome face.

'Let me take you out to lunch, Glenn,' said Odile. 'My treat. I want to show you the best place for *muffulettas*.'

'*Muffulettas*?' said Glenn, who had never heard the word before.

'Oh boy, you're in for a surprise!' laughed Odile.

With the expert ease of a local, Odile led Glenn down the vibrant, colourful street towards her favourite lunch spot. There they were served delicious glasses of freshly made lemonade and eventually, the famous *muffulettas*.

'I'm only eating this because it's an occasion,' said Odile. 'Usually I'd avoid the carb-loading.'

Glenn watched with a growing appetite as the delicious round sandwich was brought over to their table.

'The *muffuletta* was brought over by the Italians,' Odile told him. 'This round bread is from Sicily, and it's lighter than focaccia, thank God. It's more like the French bread I ate as a child.'

'So you grew up in France?' Glenn asked before taking his first bite of the enormous sandwich packed full of cheese, meats, and pickles. He groaned with delight as he tasted the different flavours between the crispy circles of bread.

'I did,' said Odile. 'So as you can imagine, it really means something for me to say the *muffuletta* is special. Back in France we have the finest patisseries and best breads in the world. But luckily for me, New Orleans was built on immigration, like most of this country. And most of those countries brought the best things over with them!'

Glancing around at the restaurant clientele, Glenn saw people from all backgrounds and walks of life. New Orleans was certainly a melting pot of races, cultures and flavours. Glenn wondered why Odile had left France and remembered the task he had set himself.

'Odile, I wanted to ask you something,' he said.

'Fire away,' she said, tucking into her own *muffuletta*.

Glenn launched into a small description of the pamphlet he was planning, incorporating case studies of the six women's lives.

'And you want to write about me?' Odile asked. She seemed surprised.

'Of course,' said Glenn. 'I've made it my mission to write about all of you. It's become a calling for me! Your story is not only inspiring, but unique. It's your story that will speak to those who have suffered the loss of vision at a later stage. People like my father.'

'He's still struggling, huh?' said Odile. Glenn nodded.

'He's living life as if he's going to see again one day,' he said. 'No matter what I say, he can't accept the truth.'

'If you can't convince him, Glenn, that's saying something. You have such a great way with words. It's hard to accept though,' sighed Odile. 'God knows it's hard to accept.'

'I need your help,' said Glenn. 'I know that in your story there will be nuggets of wisdom to help him through.'

'You know, my son says he's proud of me now,' said Odile, her face taking on a pensive expression. 'He's fourteen years old. He's so happy with what I've become, after all those years of darkness. I'm happy too. But it was hard, Glenn. I nearly lost everything. I did lose everything, before I found it all again. I often wonder how things could have been so different, if I had just taken control of my diabetes; if I had just taken control of my life.'

'When I hear my father talk about what it felt like at the end, when his vision went, I can't handle it,' said Glenn. 'It sounded so frightening. I hate to think my Dad went through that. Is it as scary as he described it to be?'

'It is,' said Odile. 'At least it was for me. Frightening is the word, Glenn. There is no other way to explain it. The psychological effects of going blind are deep and complex. I wish I had more time to go into this now, Glenn, but I'm going to have to get back to work.'

'Of course,' said Glenn, forgetting his friend had a centre to run.

'I've booked us a table at my favourite restaurant tonight, though,' she said. 'You're going to love it. We can talk some more then and you can tell me about this fascinating project of yours.'

'That sounds perfect,' grinned Glenn. 'I'm looking forward to it.'

'It's so great you came down to visit, Glenn,' said Odile, smiling into the distance. 'It really means a lot to me. I hope I can help you, in whatever way I can.'

'I'm sure you can, Odile,' he said. 'Until tonight?'

'Until tonight,' she nodded brightly.

'Has anyone ever told you that you're the spitting image of Mireille Darc, the French actress?' he suddenly asked her. 'It's amazing. You could be her double.'

To his surprise, a shadow passed over Odile's face.

'I haven't always looked this way, Glenn,' she said quietly. 'But I guess that's all part of the story. See you later, OK?'

They stood up to leave and Glenn wondered what Odile had meant by this. He also wondered if he should ask Odile if she would find her way back to the office okay but he stopped himself immediately. Of course she knew her way back: she was blind but anyone could see she knew exactly where she was going. Saying goodbye and heading back to his hotel, Glenn wondered if that had always been the case. She had mentioned dark days and a period of struggle. He would soon find out, he thought, readying himself to hear a new story of courage in the face of blindness that evening.

CHAPTER FOURTEEN

Glenn waited for Odile at the table she had reserved for them at the restaurant in the French Quarter. It had been a short ten-minute walk from his hotel and he had been glad to wander through the city a little. As he sat waiting, he listened with delight when various jazz musicians started playing in neighbouring cafes and bars. He felt his feet tapping away as the music throbbed through him, remembering what Odile had said just hours earlier. Music resounded in someone, it didn't need to be seen or visualized. He let the plinking piano keys tickle his bones and the cymbals sing in his ears.

By the time Odile arrived, Glenn was so lost in the music he almost didn't see her. But he caught sight of her just in time. She looked stunning, as ever. He thought of Mireille Darc once more. Odile's thick hair brushed across her face and she was dressed in a bright red dress which seemed, he thought, to match her personality perfectly.

'Odile!' he called to her, waving even though he knew she could not see. She smiled and turned in his direction. He stood up to meet her halfway.

'I hope you don't mind, I've taken us a table outside. It's a beautiful night,' he said. 'The waiter recommended it.'

'I would have done the same, Glenn,' she grinned. 'The music is great here, isn't it?'

'Fantastic,' he smiled. 'The street feels like it has a soul. I thought New York had soul but New Orleans is something else!'

'Oh it does,' she laughed. 'You'll see.'

They made their way back to the table, where Glenn had already taken his pen and paper out, ready to record their conversation. He had also brought a dictaphone with him this time, to make sure he captured everything. He had regretted not doing so with Laura, for her testimony was truly remarkable. Something about the way Odile talked about the past made him suspect hers would be too and he did not want to risk missing anything.

Before they started talking seriously, however, Odile ordered their drinks and food. Glenn let her take the lead for she seemed to be an expert in New Orleans cuisine, and he knew as a rule that locals would know the food better than he ever would.

'So, where do you want to start?' she asked when they had finished bowls of delicious crab chowder. 'Do you have a plan for this case study?'

'Well, I was thinking you could start with your early life, before the blindness,' said Glenn. 'You said you grew up in France. I'd like to hear more about that, if you don't mind. Let's "start from the start" so to speak.'

'That's right,' said Odile, taking a deep breath. 'I grew up in France. It was my home, though honestly, Glenn, it seems like a lifetime ago.'

The thirty-six-year-old started to tell her story: the tale of a bored teenager stuck in a small town in the northern region of Normandy.

'There was nothing to do,' she said. 'I could finish school and then work in a bakery, like my mother, or a factory, like my father's family. The boys there were not interesting. They were farmer's sons who drank cider and drove tractors. They didn't speak proper French, only the rural patois. It was too much for me, and too little at the same time. That was not the place for me so I tried to find a new way of life by going to university in Rouen. I thought it would be great. It was the birthplace of Joan of Arc, after all. But I was disappointed, and left halfway through my first year.'

'You left university?' asked Glenn. 'But why?'

'I felt the people on my course were phoneys,' she said, shrugging. 'We were studying political science and all they cared about was drinking in bars after class. They listened to terrible music. The music they wanted to go and see had no soul. I felt like I was still at home with the farmers and the fields; it was small town thinking in a big city. So I left.'

'Where did you go?' asked Glenn.

'First I went back to see my parents, to tell them I was leaving,' said Odile. 'As you can imagine, they were not happy. But I was not happy. I was so young and full of energy, but I felt my country was restricting me. I felt that France was not right for me; it did not share my spirit. So I worked for one summer in a terrible bar in my town until the day I had enough money to buy a one-way flight to New Orleans.'

'Why New Orleans?' asked Glenn, puzzled by this seemingly random choice.

'Do you need to ask?' Odile answered, grinning at him and looking around at the street. Glenn too looked out at the street, watching the people smiling and dancing to the bursts of jazz emanating out of cafes. It was a remarkable place. He waited for Odile to keep talking, jotting down a few notes on his notepad.

'I was young and had fed my soul with Ella Fitzgerald, Louis Armstrong and Dr. John,' she continued. 'At nineteen years old I followed my dream and it led me here. There's a bit of history here for the French too, and I liked that. I picked up a job working as a waitress in a street not far from here. I met a man called Phil King. He sang the blues and had the sweetest smile. He ran a kitchen over in Algiers. I was waiting tables there and he asked me out one time. He took me for a picnic along the Mississippi and told me the stories of his grandmothers and grandfathers, singing the blues in their swamps and plantations. That man had a soul and it sung to my soul. We were married within a year.'

'Are you still married?' Glenn asked.

'Oh no,' laughed Odile with a note of bitterness. 'That's a different story.'

'Okay,' said Glenn. 'So you left France, came to New Orleans, worked and married. What next?'

'Next the challenges came,' she sighed.

'With your husband?' Glenn asked.

'Yes, no,' Odile shook her head. 'I was the challenge, and some men can't handle a challenge. That's what life became, you see. We had our first son, Benjamin, not long past our wedding day, and then our little girl, Sasha, came one year later.'

Digging around in her bag, Odile brought out a picture of two beautiful children, with coffee coloured skin and bright smiles. They were very clearly her children: her character shone in their eyes.

'Lovely kids,' smiled Glenn. 'You're a lucky Mom.'

'They are,' she said.

'And you were happy then, at first?' Glenn asked.

'Very happy,' she said. 'But life was tough, bringing up two kids with not a lot of money coming in. By my early twenties I was trying to feed two hungry mouths. Phil was working flat out and I was picking up waitressing work when I could. Life was hard. Food was expensive so we were not eating well. New Orleans is a great place to eat for a day or two, or a week or two, but for years? Oh no, it makes you heavy. I ate fried this and fried that more and more when the kids came along. I didn't have time to cook properly. I ate when I could and that was often bad. If I could count the fries I ate during that period, you'd be disgusted, Glenn. But my priority was feeding the kids and putting money in the bank. When I turned twenty-seven, I was as round as a house; I weighed over a hundred kilos. Can you imagine?'

Glenn shook his head. Indeed, to look at Odile, a slim, perfectly-proportioned woman, one would never think she had been so heavy.

'That's what I meant about Mireille Darc,' she said. 'When I was that big, I looked as far from her as was possible.'

'I think you'd look like her at any size,' said Glenn. 'You're a very beautiful woman, Odile.'

'Well, I was not in good shape,' she said. 'That was when the diabetes came. It took over my body and took my eyes with it.'

'Type 2?' said Glenn, scribbling down notes as she spoke.

'Exactly,' said Odile. 'Like your Dad.'

'I hate that disease! Did it come suddenly?' Glenn asked. 'Or gradually, over time?'

'I knew my eyes were getting bad,' she said. 'But I didn't have the time or money to do anything about it. I barely had a moment to notice. I knew something was up, though. I finally went to the doctor when I was struggling to see the next car when driving. He did some tests and told me.'

'Was there anything that could be done?' Glenn asked.

'Yes, at first,' said Odile. 'The doctor set me a strict diet which was impossible to follow. I tried to lose the weight, to shed those pounds, but it was so hard. I did my best but it made life at home so hard. I was struggling to see and did not have enough energy to get through the day.'

'You were already exhausted and the diet exacerbated that?' Glenn asked, thinking of how his father too detested the diet his doctor's recommended. Odile nodded and then hung her head for a moment.

'I was exhausted, yes, but it was more than that,' she said. 'People don't tell you what happens to your personality when you go blind. They tell you what happens to your retinas, your optic nerve, your brain, your nerves, but they don't bother to tell you how it will change everything about the way you relate to people around you.'

'And your husband, how did he handle everything?' Glenn asked tentatively, aware that this might be a sensitive subject.

'Badly,' said Odile, and he could hear the bitterness in her voice once more. 'We had fights, every night, into the early hours of the morning. The kids would wake up and he would be late for work. I stopped working and he took on more work. He resented me for that I think. He told me it was my fault: he said I was unfit to be a mother, unfit to look after our children. I hated him for saying that. I think he made me believe it because soon I was so low, I couldn't bring myself to care for them anymore. I was disorientated, hungry and angry. He went to the courts and took action against me, disqualifying me from raising the children.'

'What a jerk! How old were the children at the time?' asked Glenn, disturbed by what he was hearing.

'Eight and nine,' said Odile. 'Our boy was nine and his little sister was eight. They were little champions, but they suffered. I suffered. We were separated and I couldn't handle that. I was so depressed, Glenn, that darkness was worse than the blindness that followed. I stopped getting up in the mornings. I stayed in bed until it hurt to stay in bed any longer. Every week I swung in and out of depressions, taking so many pills I barely knew my name anymore. That's when Phil decided it was time to take me to a special home for the blind. Lord knows I couldn't see a damn thing.'

'He put you in a home?' Glenn asked. 'That dog put you in a home?' Odile nodded sadly.

'He said it was for the best,' she said. 'And perhaps it was. They diagnosed me with schizophrenia. But since then I've really thought about it and I'm not so sure I was schizophrenic. I was crazy, angry and confused, that's for sure, but I had just been declared clinically blind; what did they expect?'

'How did you see your children?' Glenn asked. 'Did they visit you? You had rights, you know. You were well within your rights to see your children.'

'My husband said he would visit often with the kids,' she replied. 'They were only allowed to visit me with him there. It was always so strange when they came there. I couldn't see so I would cry a lot, you know, when they came. My husband said they would find this distressing and did his best to avoid coming too often. The visits became rarer and rarer, until the point where I'd see them once a month. I say see, but even that was not possible. I felt them, I smelled their hair, I listened to them talk. But I couldn't see my babies anymore. I lost it then. I was so lonely.'

'I can't even begin to imagine what that felt like,' said Glenn. 'What about your family in France? Did they come to see you?'

'Of course,' said Odile. 'And of course I couldn't see them anymore. This person who smelled like my mother and sounded like her no longer had a face. I couldn't see my father's eyes. It was very distressing. I knew I would never see my parents again. This was a terrible period of my life, Glenn. They demanded that I come back with them to France, so they could care for me.'

'And did you go?' asked Glenn.

'Of course not,' said Odile proudly. 'How could I? My children were in New Orleans. My life was here; it had just been taken away from me. I knew if I went back to France with my parents I would become a vegetable, living in their house, in that town I hated, and I would never see my children again.'

'So you stayed?' asked Glenn.

'For three years,' said Odile. 'I was kept under great supervision for my weight and given medicines for my depression. My life had gone from something so full and happy to nothing: an emptiness full of sadness. I never imagined I would go blind in my lifetime. I wasn't prepared. No one around me knew what to do or say.'

Glenn thought of his father and shook his head; that was exactly how he and Iris had felt. They saw what Bertie had lost and could not handle it.

'I began to feel very angry,' she went. 'A deep rage grew in me, like a volcano waiting to burst.'

'Towards whom?' Glenn asked.

'Towards myself,' she said. 'I knew the diabetes was my own fault. I hadn't taken care of myself. But more than myself I hated my husband. He had the sole custody of my children and he no longer cared for me. He did not touch me when he came to visit. He said as little as possible. Oh, that hurt so much, and I hated him for it. You cannot imagine what it means to a person, to lose their sight and then lose any kind of loving touch. Those words he used to say, the way he used to stroke my hair; it was all gone, Glenn. I lost my husband in that time. I hated him so much for abandoning me and staying away.'

'It was a terrible thing to do,' said Glenn. 'You're surely better off without a man like that? He didn't deserve you. Men like that... they're spineless.'

'Well, he certainly thought he was better off without a woman like me,' she said. 'I soon heard he married someone else, someone younger and prettier, though I've never seen her, you understand. I would never see her. But I heard from Phil's mother that she was an easy type, a young lady with a love for his food, like I had been, once upon a time.'

'So your marriage ended because of the blindness?' Glenn asked.

'In divorce, yes,' she said. 'It ended for many reasons. It could have been anything, I think. Marriages are supposed to endure hardship, to survive the bad times. That's what we said at the altar, "in sickness and in health, for richer and for poorer". Some marriage that turned out to be.'

Odile was quiet for a while. A new song had started playing across the street and Glenn could tell by the way she cocked her head that she was listening to it. He thought about his own marriage to Eleanora and wondered if it would survive the devastation of blindness. Her reaction to his father's vision loss was astoundingly tactless. He did not imagine she would be much kinder to him. She was so rarely kind to him. Glenn had called her only once on the whole trip but she did not seem to mind.

A distance was growing between them but neither of them seemed to care. They had spoken only minimally while he had been away, to check in.

'Have things become easier between you?' Glenn asked quietly. Odile shook her head.

'I would say we don't see each other anymore, but that would be a lie,' she said. 'He sees me when he drops off the children. I don't see him, of course.'

'So you see the children again now?' Glenn asked.

'Yes,' sighed Odile, smiling at last. 'All thanks to Bettina.'

'Bettina?' said Glenn, surprised to hear that Bettina was associated with such an intimate part of Odile's life.

'Yes, she came to the institute,' said Odile. 'She had been travelling around, touring the various blind foundations in the United States. She was visiting rare cases, or so she said.'

Glenn sensed that Odile was distracted by the music so he decided it was better to take a break for a while and enjoy the ambience. The rhythmic jazz passed through the café and serenaded them as they tucked into fresh lobster served with buttered, yellow corn. When they had chatted about lighter things, Odile herself brought the conversation back to her story.

'You know what they say about jazz, Glenn?' she asked.

'What's that?' he said.

'If you have to ask what jazz is, you'll never know,' said Odile, smiling. 'That's what I told Little Miss Bettina Hartmann when I first met her. I think Louis Armstrong said it, many years ago.'

'So that's when you met her?' Glenn asked. 'When you were staying at the institute?'

'Yes, in the Institute for the Blind, where I was staying,' said Odile. 'I was a wretch, miserable and lonely, sitting one day in my room listening to Ella Fitzgerald. That was my only comfort: listening to jazz. A song came on, the one about seeing the light. Do you know it, Glenn?' she asked.

'Of course,' he grinned.

'Really? Do you remember how it goes?' she asked.

'I do!' he laughed, then sang a few lines for her.

'Beautiful!' she laughed. 'That was beautiful, Glenn. Now tell me: are there many people in your life who remind you of the song that was playing when they first walked into the room?' Odile asked him.

'Not that I can recall,' said Glenn, smiling at the thought.

'Well, I remember Bettina that way,' said Odile. 'I heard a voice humming along to the song, out in the garden. I asked who was there and this German accent came out! "Bettina," she said. "My name is Bettina Hartmann." I asked her why she was humming jazz so badly. "I'm new in town," she said. "Go easy on me, won't you? What's jazz anyway?" "Where are you from?" I asked her. "If you have to ask what jazz is you'll never know!" "I'm from Germany," she said. And I said: "That explains it then!"'

Glenn laughed at this.

'You said that?' he yelped.

'I did!' laughed Odile.

'She told me she was working for the International Charity for the Blind,' Odile went on. 'She was their special envoy. She said they were touring blind centres in the States in the hope of opening up new branches of their charity offices. She said they were visiting rare cases, people who grew up in vibrant multicultural metropolises, or had heavy family lives. The American south had its own problems, you know, between black and white, so they were interested in that too. "My boss, Herbert sent me here," she said. "How about you?" Just like that she asked for my story, just like you're doing now, Glenn. I told her my story and she listened. I felt her come and sit down on my bed and take my hand. The tears were falling by then and I wept by the end. All the time she listened as I told her about my wretched life, my loss, my children, and my depression. She said "I understand" and I had to ask, "How can you? You're young and smart with your whole life ahead of you. How old are you?" She said: "I'm twenty-one. And I can understand your pain, Odile, because I have lived my whole life with that pain." "What do you mean?" I asked her. And she told me. She had been born blind. I couldn't believe it. This young woman who was travelling around the world as a special envoy for a charity was as blind as I was. "How do you live?" I asked. "I can't imagine living my life beyond this institute." "You will," she said, with such determination and belief that I just had to believe her. And that was the first time anyone had told me everything was going to be okay again. No one else in my life had said that to me: they had all seen my blindness as a dead end.'

'How did she help you?' Glenn asked, almost beside himself with curiosity and admiration for Bettina, who had helped Odile years before she had even met Laura in Munich.

'Well, she said I was the kind of person they were looking to help,' she said. 'I had bridged two continents, spoke French and had a family life. We spoke French together, she and I. That's when I really started to trust her and believe someone was going to help me.'

'What did she do then?' Glenn asked, scribbling notes down on his pad as Odile spoke, curious to hear more about Bettina. Though she was not there, Glenn felt like her presence shone through in Odile's story. He could almost feel her in the room.

'First she led me through a personal rehabilitation program that she was demonstrating to the staff of the institute,' said Odile. 'She allowed me to attend alongside the nursing staff. She said the more people she trained in ICB methodology, the better. I think I did very well because she said I should be involved in the training of other inmates at the institute. Then she helped me return to sheltered housing before I felt well enough to live on my own, independently. She went to the lawyers and called for a correction to the custody law that kept me from seeing my children, arguing that I was now fit and well. When they said I would only be eligible when I was in at least part-time employment, she said I had work. This was news to me!'

'She lied?' asked Glenn, surprised to hear this.

'No,' laughed Odile. 'She just hadn't told me that she'd hired me.'

'Hired you? Where?' asked Glenn.

'At the new branch of the ICB she planned to open in New Orleans,' said Odile proudly. Suddenly the story all clicked into place. Bettina was the reason Odile was running the ICB centre for the blind in the city.

'She paid my expenses and a retainer,' Odile went on. 'And sent me to the university to learn how to counsel the blind. That's where I learnt all the skills I use today. We formed a great relationship, Bettina and I. I run the North American branch of the ICB and represent the charity at all national events, and there are many here in the United States.'

'When my father was diagnosed with blindness from diabetes, I was shocked to hear how many people in the US lose their eyesight this way,' said Glenn.

'It's horrendous,' said Odile, shaking her head. 'I'm just ashamed to admit I'm one of them. It was too late for me, but it's not too late for some. It's just that healthcare here in the US is so expensive, Glenn. Most folks can't afford it. They just hope their ailments and sickness will go away. And as for healthy eating, that's just not possible sometimes, especially not in a city like New Orleans.'

'Is the diet so bad here?' Glenn asked, savouring the delicious flavours he had tasted that evening. 'I feel like I've eaten like a king!'

'Have you not had a good enough taste of it?' asked Odile, laughing. 'If they're not frying chicken they're covering it in creamy sauces, mayonnaise, fried potatoes, even fried eggs. A salad here in America is covered in grease. They'd fry cucumbers if they could, and lettuce leaves! Here fizzy drinks are more popular than water. Children are being abused by the food they eat, it's no joke, and they'll suffer for it later in life.'

'And you help people to live with these challenges?' Glenn asked.

'Of course,' said Odile. 'One of the main things Bettina taught me to teach others is how to live with blindness. I adjust that to how to live with blindness caused by diabetes by advocating a healthy lifestyle as much as possible. That's not always easy, Glenn. Imagine if you lose your eyes, how can you cut up vegetables for a salad or prepare healthy meals? It's much easier to jump into a fast food restaurant and order a hamburger. Do you see how those behavioural patterns are entrenched in our everyday lives?'

'I do,' said Glenn, thinking how the same could be said for food culture in the United Kingdom. 'People get into vicious cycles that they can't get out of. My wife hates all the junk people eat, but then most people can't afford to eat her organic produce. It's a tricky dilemma because bad food is cheaper.'

'You sound like you have quite a bit of experience in this,' said Odile.

'I live with it, literally!' he laughed.

'That workshop you were part of in Aachen, when we made that goulash, do you remember that?' she asked him.

'Of course I do,' said Glenn, smiling at the memory. 'I remember how much difficulty Bill had making the salad too.'

'Oh God, Bill!' laughed Odile. 'He had such a hard time!'

'Bill was terrible!' cried Glenn.

'And that's exactly my point, Glenn,' said Odile. 'His struggle is what I'm talking about. Preparing food that's healthy and nutritious is difficult for the seeing. Imagine how difficult it is for the blind. It's not easy. It takes time and patience beyond the norm. The people who come to my centre experience what you experienced but with the knowledge that it would be every day, not just a day in the dark. We train people over weeks, sometimes months, until they feel confident in their new skills and abilities.'

'How do they respond?' asked Glenn. 'Are the workshops successful?'

'Of course they are,' smiled Odile. 'I give them.'

Glenn beamed at this proud, confident woman, so different to the woman she had been after her diagnosis. He felt very happy to see that inner light shine through, gleaming in her perfectly dark eyes.

'I think that's one of the main reasons Bettina hired me,' she went on.

'Because of your experience in the kitchen?' asked Glenn, remembering Odile's excellent instruction in the house in Aachen.

'Sure, and because I've fed kids,' she said. 'And that's a challenge in itself. Managing a family with blindness is impossible to most people. But we have developed a methodology. It's one of the ICB's greatest accomplishments.'

Odile discussed this approach further, all the way through to dessert, when she insisted Glenn try a selection of New Orleans finest sweets to finish.

'I want to, I really do! But man, all this talk of healthy eating,' he said warily. 'I'm not sure about this, Odile…'

'Relax, you're here one night only!' she said. 'You deserve a treat, Glenn, and I can tell you're a man who looks after himself.'

'Can you?' he said, flashing her a smile she could not see. 'You can sense a lot without your eyes, I can tell. You're right though! I'm fit as hell so I guess I could handle a dessert.'

'I think so,' smiled Odile.

'Alright,' he grinned, allowing her to order him a tableside flambé of bananas, ablaze, soaked in flaming Caribbean rum, brown sugar and banana liqueur; a plate of pecan pie, served with vanilla bean ice cream; and a slice of heavenly lemon meringue pie. They enjoyed the sweet treats together before taking a coffee and listening to the music. The jazz around them was tooting and honking through the streets, much to Glenn's delight. He had not had this much fun in a long time, he realised.

When the evening finally came to an end, he walked Odile back to her house. It was not far from the centre she worked at, so like Laura in London, she did not have a troubling commute.

'Thank you so much for your time and help,' he said, taking her hand in his to say goodbye. 'You must feel so proud of what you've achieved here, Odile.'

'I do,' she said. 'But it's when my boy tells me he's proud, that's when it really means something. I hope your father will find his way, Glenn. I think with you helping him, he'll have no trouble.'

'If I could just help him to accept his condition,' said Glenn, but stopped before he went too far. He did not want to ruin their wonderful evening with negativity. 'I'm sure it will be fine.'

'Never give up, Glenn,' said Odile, sensing his doubt and worry. 'That's what Bettina taught me. Be confident!'

'She really saved you, huh?' he said.

'She really did,' said Odile, nodding happily. 'By learning to accept my blindness I was given a second chance. It changed my life and helped me to rebuild my family. There is no gratitude in this world greater than the thanks I have for Bettina.'

'She's quite a woman,' said Glenn, before he could stop himself. 'You all are,' he added quickly. 'I'm so stunned by your collective beauty and determination.'

'Goodnight, Glenn,' laughed Odile. 'Safe travels. I know we'll meet again one day.'

'I'm reassured by your faith,' said Glenn, laughing. 'Until the next time then, Odile. If you're ever in London, call me! I'll be your guide and your host. Don't forget it, OK?'

'I'll look you up,' she said, grinning.

'Goodnight, Odile,' he said. She waved one last time and headed into her house.

Turning back into the night, Glenn wandered back to his hotel, in no rush to reach his empty bed. He walked slowly past the jazz bars, poking his head into a few that sounded particularly exciting and listening for a while. New Orleans serenaded him as he drank fresh juice at bar after bar. He would have to go back to London the next day, he thought, but a part of him wanted to stay away; he wanted this journey of discovery to continue. It would though, he knew, when he returned to his life in England. There were four more of the women from Aachen to interview after all. He drank deep and soaked up the music, closing his eyes so his ears worked double-time. All the while, thoughts of Bettina swam in his mind, mixing with his heightened senses, pulling him further into a world where she touched lives so softly but so deeply.

CHAPTER FIFTEEN

Glenn's return to England was a sombre one. He returned from the bright lights of New Orleans to the daily grind of London. The skies were grey and his commute was as dull as ever. He took the same trains, with the same commuters, from Virginia Water into Cheapside. The dullness of the journey was better than the emptiness he found at Ronda Round Manor, however. Eleanora seemed to barely notice he had returned, and sniffed at his gifts from Louisiana.

'You're gonna love it,' Glenn cried enthusiastically, taking his wife in his arms and attempting to dance with her. 'It's come from the birth place of jazz! Get ready for your head to spin and your heart to go wild, honey!'

'I'm sure I can find a place for this,' she smiled falsely, taking the CDs of live jazz performances he had brought her from the street market and putting them on a shelf in the drawing room.

'Don't you wanna listen?' he asked her.

'I'll put them somewhere I can pick them up later,' she said.

Glenn knew that the 'place' she would find for them would be the bin, or at best, the attic.

'At least give me a kiss?' he grinned cheekily at her.

'Oh alright then,' she laughed and fell into his arms.

After the interviews with Laura and Odile, Glenn was not sure who or when he would next be able to interview. His workload was piling up at Diversified Charities and he had responsibilities to fulfil. He spent many hours mulling over the stories both women had told him and working out how to present them in the pamphlet. He felt both had very different angles. Laura, who had grown up blind, had been failed by the systems set up to protect the vulnerable, on many different levels, but had risen above her misfortune. She had proven not only to herself but to Bettina that her strength came from her ability to break away from the restrictions life had put on her. Odile, on the other hand, had faced a devastating life change when she lost her sight: she lost her marriage, her independence, and for a while, her children too. But Bettina saw in her the skills she needed to share with others in an already impoverished region of the United States.

However, the next interviewee soon became apparent when he was assigned a business trip to Mexico, to meet potential funding partners. His bosses had been open to the idea of supporting the International Charity for the Blind, but told Glenn that if he wanted to push for this initiative, he would have to prove that there were funds available to support it. They set up meetings with three of the major banks in Mexico City, banks the DCF had dealt with in the past, and Sonia arranged his travel.

'How far is it to drive from Mexico City to Acapulco, Sonia?' he asked her, when she presented him with three different flight options.

'Do you have meetings in Acapulco too, sir?' Sonia asked with a frown, looking down at her notes.

'No,' grinned Glenn. 'But there's someone I'd like to visit there.'

Elfrida Merguez lived in Acapulco, Glenn knew that for sure. He could not miss this opportunity to write another case study. He also wanted to meet her again. Her workshop on sports activities for the blind in Aachen had been truly enlightening. Though he could not remember the finer details of her story, Glenn was sure Elfrida had a history worth hearing. He made contact that day, sending an email to the address she had given him when they said goodbye.

Subject: Meeting up?

Dear Elfrida,

I hope this finds you well. It was a pleasure to meet you at the conference in Aachen.

I will be visiting Mexico City for work in coming weeks and was wondering if it was possible to meet you. I can easily travel over to Acapulco.

I remember from the conference that you run a school for the blind. It would be great to see it. I am working on a project and I believe you might be able to help me with it.

Do let me know if this could work.

Best wishes,
Glenn

Unlike Odile, Elfrida replied instantly, inviting Glenn to visit her at her school in Acapulco. He made a note of the address, and a note too to make arrangements for a driver when he arrived in Mexico City.

Eleanora was fairly unimpressed when she heard Glenn would be going away once more. Not because he would be leaving her for a week, but because she had heard unsavoury things about Mexico City.

'Do you know how unsanitary it is there?' she asked stiffly the evening before he left, as he carried his packed suitcase down to the drawing room. She was lounging in an armchair, flicking through a copy of *Horse and Hound*. 'They have diseases on every street corner. Why on earth they would send you to Mexico to raise funds, I dare to think. That country hasn't a penny to its name.'

'I believe they use pesos there,' he said through gritted teeth. 'Besides, honey, you don't have to worry about me. I know how to look after myself.'

'That's irrelevant,' she sighed. 'I don't know why they are risking your health and comfort for a few *pesos*.'

'Darling, Mexico City is one of the wealthiest cities in the Americas!' Glenn protested, frustrated by his wife's snobbery.

'Don't be angry,' she scolded him. 'I'm just worried about you, that's all.'

'It will be fine,' he said, softening his tone. He went over to her and planted a tender kiss on her forehead. 'You don't need to worry, honey. Just trust me, OK?'

'Do they even wash in Mexico?' she asked lazily. 'I mean, don't expect them to wash your food if they can't wash themselves, darling. Avoid salads.'

Glenn glanced over at her. When he saw the blue of her eyes and the strong, attractive shape of her shoulders, he still felt desire. She still had that power over him. But when he heard her speak, he heard only the dripping disdain and his desire faded fast. It vanished as quickly as it had come. He thought about Odile's marriage, which had faced a terrible trauma, and failed. Her husband had left her when she needed him most, and who knows, thought Glenn, perhaps most marriages would fail at the hurdle of blindness. Eleanora, who had never known hardship in her life, and did not approve of hard work, would surely leave him if he ever suffered the fate of his father.

When he kissed her goodbye, these were the thoughts running around his head. He tried to act normally, but something was changing deep inside. Glenn no longer found comfort in the arms of his wife.

'I'll take care of the farm, don't worry,' she said, frowning and patting his face. She clearly mistook his sadness for concern about the farm.

'Er, thanks,' he said, turning to leave. 'Bye, honey! I know you'll miss me!'

'The lambs will be fine!' she called out after her. 'The Thompsons will do a wonderful job, I'm sure.'

Glenn was relieved when the flight took off from London Heathrow to Mexico City. Up in the air he felt free of the things that restricted him on earth: his job, his wife, his father and his worries. He simply embraced the limbo, above the clouds, where nothing could touch him; no emails, no calls, no conversations. Closing his eyes, he fell into a deep sleep, and as ever, before he lost consciousness, the last thing on his mind was Bettina Hartmann. He wondered what role she had played in Elfrida's story.

Before he met Elfrida, thought, Glenn had to represent Diversified Charities in New Mexico. As the plane swept down over the Gulf of Mexico, past fertile green mountain ranges, Glenn was surprised to see the sprawling, grey mass of the capital. Before they reached the airport, they passed over miles of slums. He knew Mexico City had extremely impoverished areas, but was not expecting it to be so large.

When the plane landed he headed straight to his hotel in a taxi driven by a sweet driver called Pablo.

'How long you staying in Mexico for, *señor?*' he asked Glenn as he unloaded his suitcases at the hotel.

'Just a week,' he said.

'Ah, not long enough,' grinned Pablo. 'Otherwise I would introduce you to my *amigos* and we would enjoy some time together, eh?'

'Alas, next time,' smiled Glenn. The driver bid him goodnight, leaving him to check into his hotel, The Alpha, and fall into a deep sleep.

By the time it came to make his journey across the coast to Acapulco, Glenn was glad to be getting out of the hot, busy capital of Mexico City. His meetings had been largely unsuccessful due to the lack of funding available in Mexico and everywhere he looked Glenn saw the poverty that hit the city's poorest the hardest. Every day had been a heaving, grinding mess of human activity, and Glenn longed for the cooler climate of the coast. He hired a driver and headed out of the city in a comfortable, air-conditioned Mercedes.

Driving into the coastal city of Acapulco, Glenn did not know much about where he was staying in Acapulco. He had simply asked Sonia to book him somewhere near the sea. When they arrived at the address he had given, Glenn was surprised to see a bright white hotel, with a perfectly neat garden outside, and Mexican bell-boys rushing out to take his luggage.

'Hold on, fellas! It's okay,' he said to them. 'I can take them...'

But the boys did not understand English, it seemed. They simply bowed and nodded, taking the bags from the car and rushing them up the steps. Glenn followed, and was taken to a beautiful room looking out over the ocean. The whole hotel had a distinctly colonial feel to it. When he had taken a quick shower to cool down, he picked up the phone and called the number Elfrida had left for him.

'Glenn?' she said, when she heard his voice. '*Hola, buenos dias!* Welcome to Mexico, my friend!'

'*Hola!*' said Glenn, excited to hear her voice. 'I'm in Mexico, baby! Yeah!'

'When are you coming to me?' she asked. 'I'm at the school tomorrow, wanna come visit?'

'That would be great,' said Glenn. 'I'll follow the instructions you gave me. Don't worry about me, I'm good in a new city. I always find my way!'

'You do that, Glenn, and if you get lost just ask for the ICB, everyone knows it,' she said.

The next day Glenn woke early to take a walk on the beach. It was a beautiful stretch of sand and coast, looking out over the ocean, and back over the city. It was very hot so he did not stay there long before jumping into a taxi and reading the driver the address. The driver hesitated when he heard it.

'Are you sure, *señor*?' he asked.

'Yes,' said Glenn. 'Why? Is there a problem?'

'No problem, *señor*,' said the driver. The driver's hesitation became apparent as they drove out of the city centre, towards more destitute neighbourhoods. With every kilometre they drove, the paint grew thinner on the walls of houses, until the houses disappeared altogether, replaced by shacks and caravans. When they finally reached the end of one particularly impoverished street, the driver pointed to a white building in the distance.

'Sorry, *señor*, I cannot drive any further,' he said. 'The road is not good.'

Glenn looked down and saw the road was indeed full of potholes.

'That's fine, I'll walk! I need the exercise,' he said, handing he driver the fare.

'*Señor*,' said the driver, his face looking worried. 'This is not a good place for a foreigner to walk alone. Many thieves live here. These people do not have so much.'

'I can see that,' sighed Glenn. 'Don't worry about me, I can take care of myself! I'm the guy no one wants to mess with, believe me, fella! Besides, I'm already late. Someone is expecting me.'

Glenn made his way down the street towards a large set of buildings in the distance. They were hard to miss for they seemed to be the only buildings on the street made of concrete. The others were all made of board, tarp and corrugated metal. Avoiding the various deposits of animal excrement and litter on the ground, Glenn found himself outside what was clearly a school building, looking up at a brilliantly polished sign. It read:

The ICB School for the Blind, Acapulco.
Headmistress: Elfrida Merguez.

Glenn's heart swelled with pride and anticipation when he saw Elfrida's name, despite the poverty he saw in the neighbourhood. Children were arriving at the same time as him and seemed to pay no notice to him. He tried waving awkwardly at them before he realised, of course, that they were blind. Some of them seemed to sense him though, as they began to shout things to him in Spanish.

'*Hola, hola!*' Glenn called back, making them giggle.

Soon a loud voice shouted back at the children, calling for an end to their cries. Glenn turned to see Elfrida marching towards them, looking angry. The children quietened as soon as they heard her, and made their way inside. Dressed in a simple blue dress, and a knitted cardigan, Elfrida looked very different from the way she had looked at the conference in Aachen. One thing hadn't changed though: she was still incredibly beautiful. Her dark hair was plaited and swung over her shoulder, shining in the bright Mexican sunlight.

'Glenn,' she said. 'I know you are here because the children are shouting "*gringo*!" at you.'

'Elfrida!' said Glenn, beaming at her, and taking her outstretched hand in his own. 'It's great to see you! What does it mean?'

'*Gringo*?' she said. 'It means American.'

'Is that Spanish?' he asked.

'No,' she said. 'They say it is what the Mexican people cried at the Americans when they invaded Mexico. They wore green uniforms, so the Mexicans shouted: "green go home!" That's the legend anyway.'

'Is it true?' Glenn asked.

'Who knows,' smiled Elfrida. 'But it is not a bad word, believe me. They could have called you something else, and then there would be trouble.'

Glenn laughed at this. Elfrida was clearly a headmistress who knew how to control her pupils. There was something very attractive about that too, he thought, admiring her.

'Come on, Glenn,' she said. 'Let me show you around. Class is about to start.'

'I can't wait,' said Glenn. 'I'm done with stuffy business meetings in banks. I want to see some real work happening!'

They chatted as they walked, Elfrida using a white cane to guide her through the doors.

'I used to teach four students here,' said Elfrida. 'That's how everything started. There were four blind children in the neighbourhood, so I taught them four to five subjects, in different forms, in one hour. Now we have over one hundred and twenty pupils, Glenn, from across Acapulco, even from villages near the city. And fourteen teachers.'

'That's amazing,' said Glenn.

'A miracle in this neighbourhood, I'm telling you,' she said. They wandered around the school and Glenn saw how the children ranging from the age of ten to fifteen learnt biology, chemistry, mathematics, Spanish, English and French.

'The most important lessons we run now, I believe, are the social studies classes,' Elfrida explained.

'What happens in social studies class?' asked Glenn.

'We've tailored the class to the needs of our blind students here at the school,' said Elfrida. 'So we are starting to teach something a bit more practical than in the average middle school. We try to teach general services, how to manage and make a living as a blind person in industry, familiarising the children with nuts and bolts, cutting grass, setting the table for dinner, simple carpentry, cooking, walking, and sports.'

'I remember your sports workshop well in Aachen,' said Glenn. 'They were so fantastic! I never knew I could run on a treadmill without sight.'

'Do you remember, really?' she beamed.

'Of course, Elfrida,' laughed Glenn. 'You're hard to forget.'

'I'm glad to hear that,' she said, laughing too. 'I can't tell you how glad, Glenn, because this is something I have developed myself: a methodology of practicality.'

Glenn was enormously impressed by Elfrida. She had not only developed her own methodology, but taught three different levels every day, from the third grade to the fifth grade.

'I teach between ages six and seven in the mornings,' she said. 'Then I teach ages eight to nine in the afternoon. We split the classes between the fourteen teachers. We try and tailor our curriculum more generally to blind learners, with Braille, and audio assistance.'

'And the ICB funds this?' Glenn asked, taking in the smart infrastructure of the building.

'Yes, all the teachers are paid the same wage as they would be at a government school,' said Elfrida. She led him on a tour around the school all morning, introducing every teacher and classroom there was to see. Eventually they ended up in her office, where hot cups of Mexican coffee were being served.

'So tell me, Glenn, you said in your email that you needed help with something,' she said, taking a sip of her coffee. 'How can I help you?'

'Well, it's more how I can help you,' said Glenn. 'What can I do to help? That's what I'm here for, after all!'

'That's a question I don't hear so often,' smiled Elfrida. 'What can you do, Glenn? Well, you could go to the Ministry of Education and Minister of Finance. You can ask them to pay twenty percent of our expenses. They put all their money into expanding Mexico City, not Acapulco. All they think about is Mexico City, but education is so limited for everyone in Acapulco. No one dreams of getting out of this town.'

'What do you mean?' asked Glenn. 'How can that be? I look around me and see a school full of blind kids getting an education. The future is theirs for the taking.'

'Here the only jobs are for tourism,' she said. 'Look around you, Glenn. We were brought up to serve the tourist. As long as the government sees Acapulco as a tourist goldmine, they're not going to bother investing money in making it better.'

'So what do you want, Elfrida?' Glenn asked her. 'Tell me, please. I want to help.'

'I want to make this school into a proper high school, where kids can get the qualifications they need to go places.'

'Do you think you have the capacity here for that?' Glenn asked.

'I think so,' said Elfrida. 'We need the money to expand, sure, but I know what's missing from this place, and that's a future. We don't give these kids what they need for the world out there.'

'Hmm, interesting. I like your ambition. It will be hard though,' said Glenn, taking a sip of his coffee and looking up at the ceiling and walls around him. 'High school is complicated. You'll need to be able to deal with children beyond the ages of fifteen, probably between fifteen and eighteen. That's when things will get tough.'

'Tell me about it,' sighed Elfrida. 'My sister has boys, sixteen and seventeen. They're a nightmare.'

'High school is the age of teenagers and trouble-makers,' grinned Glenn. 'It's when kids really start growing up! This is the time for the jock, the prom queen, teen doubts and big dreams!'

'Yes, but we're talking about the blind growing up,' said Elfrida. 'That's different, I can tell you.'

'Wouldn't there be deeper levels of rebellion?' said Glenn, imagining the levels of frustration running through their minds. 'I mean, what was it like for you?'

'For me?' asked Elfrida.

'Yes, growing up blind,' said Glenn. 'What were the challenges you faced? How did you overcome them?'

'Well actually, I did a lot of my growing up with full sight,' she said.

'Ah, I didn't know,' said Glenn, and suddenly he remembered why he was there. 'Actually, Elfrida, that's something I've wanted to talk to you about.'

'What's that?' she asked.

'About growing up,' he said, and launched into his planned initiative to write case studies about Laura, Odile, her and the three other blind women he had met at the conference in Aachen. When he had finished, Elfrida was nodding with interest.

'And you would like me to tell you my story?' she asked.

'Yes,' said Glenn. 'I want to write it. I think it could really help.'

'And you think that this could help us build the high school?' she asked.

'Well let's see,' said Glenn, taking out his notepad and pen and making a few quick notes. 'How much did it take to build what you have here?'

'1.5 million dollars,' she said.

'And you'll need to hire high-school level teachers for this,' said Glenn. 'Several,' she said.

'I think you're going to need around ten million dollars,' said Glenn.

'Is it possible to raise that amount of money?' she asked.

'Not in Mexico,' he sighed, remembering his unsuccessful meetings in the capital. 'But perhaps from another source. It's definitely something I can work on. Building a school in Acapulco is something concrete for donors to support. They will see real, physical results and reports on the progress. If I could tell your story too, it would convince them that the management is under control. That's often a fear donors have when they support a project. They need to know that the people on the ground are going to do the best job they can.'

'Wow, Glenn. You speak with so much experience,' she said, clearly impressed.

'It's my job!' he laughed. 'I'm the man who makes things happen!'

'And you think I'll convince them?' she asked.

'After what I've seen today?' asked Glenn, laughing. 'Without a doubt.'

'So what do you want to know about me, Glenn?' she asked. 'For your case study?'

'Everything,' he said. 'From where you were to where you are now. Let's start from the beginning.'

* * * *

When Glenn woke the next day, he had an immediate feeling of anticipation. Today was the day he would hear Elfrida's story. She had arranged to pick him up from his hotel at ten as it was Saturday, and the school was closed. Taking a quick coffee in the hotel restaurant downstairs, Glenn decided to take a walk on the beach, as he had done the previous morning. This time he walked beyond the section of the beach reserved solely for his hotel, further along, for about a mile.

As he walked he noticed how the landscape had changed around him. The clean white sand he had dug his toes into just half an hour before was dirty, even black in places, and bits of litter lay washed up on the shore. It was clear to him that nobody took care of this part of the beach. The illusion of a pristine, white beach was clearly for tourists alone. The people on that part of the beach were different too. Young men in dirty clothing played football, or sat around in small groups. A couple of policeman could be seen leaning against a tree further on, eyeing the young men suspiciously. Beyond the confines of his hotel beach, Glenn realised, the reality of Acapulco came into the light, and it was not pretty.

Remembering what Elfrida had told him about the majority of children in Acapulco being brought up to serve tourists, Glenn had started noticing that the entire staff inside his hotel were Mexicans beneath the age of twenty. They looked too young to be working in hotels, he thought, but perhaps they would work there their whole lives long. He sat down, gazed out at the sun rising over the bay and let out a deep sigh. There were so many imbalances in the world, he thought, and so little way of rectifying them. Like in Mexico City, the rich seemed to be super rich and the poor seemed to be extremely poor.

And yet life continued as normal for some, he thought, noticing a beautiful young couple reclining on the beach in front of him. The woman was clearly South American, with the curvaceous, firm body so typical of the continent. She was wearing a yellow bikini and kept tossing her immaculately black hair over her shoulder. Her husband was reading a paper and sipping a glass of champagne, apparently immune to his young wife's charms. Glenn wondered how people could live like this when nearby there were such clear signs of poverty.

'So this is what you get up to on your work trips?' Glenn heard a familiar voice behind him. Confused, he spun around to see Eleanora, clad in a light linen suit, standing just metres away from him on the beach. She was beautifully dressed, as ever, and had tied her blonde hair back to keep herself cool. Beneath a straw hat and designer sunglasses, Glenn could already sense his wife's displeasure.

'Nora!' he cried. 'What are you doing here?'

'I've told you not to call me that!' she scolded him angrily. 'More importantly, what are *you* doing here?' she demanded, tearing off her sunglasses and gesturing at the beautiful, bikini-clad woman just metres away. Glenn spun around again to see what she was pointing at. The girl was gazing over at them with big black eyes, looking highly unimpressed.

'What?' yelped Glenn. 'Oh! No, no, I'm not here with them.'

'I can see that,' Eleanora raised an eyebrow. 'But you're making a point to stop and stare. Sexy, curvy and busty; I didn't know that was your type, darling.'

'What? Honey!' Glenn cried. 'It's not like that! I was just passing by. I was taking a walk before my meeting.'

'Meeting?' laughed his wife, smiling. 'You look a bit overdressed for a meeting here, darling.'

'Look, hold on,' he said. 'Baby, this is crazy. When did you arrive? What are you doing here?'

He went to her and pulled her into his arms, feeling the familiar softness of her body against his. Stepping back, he looked into her face.

'Hello, darling,' she said brightly. 'I thought I'd take a little trip out to see you.'

'Yeah,' laughed Glenn. 'I can see that. This is a first, honey.'

'Are you glad to see me?' she laughed.

'Of course I am!' he smiled. 'Welcome to Acapulco, sweetheart. I'm just surprised, that's all. It's unlike you to take an interest in my work.'

'Is it?' she asked. 'Oh, well, I suppose I wanted to see what all your raving was about. I wanted to help you. I thought you might need an assistant, you know. Someone to give you a hand.'

'Honey,' said Glenn, unable to believe what he was hearing. 'This is just amazing news. I'm stunned.'

'Don't be!' she said, grinning. 'I'll be your assistant. Can't a wife help her husband sometimes?'

Glenn was speechless. He pulled his wife into his arms, trying to steady his racing mind. This was so unusual, and so unlike Eleanora, and yet she was there, and from her own lips she had said she wanted to help him.

'Well then, I guess I'd better introduce you to Elfrida,' he said.

'Elfrida?' she said, bristling slightly. 'A woman?'

'Yeah, of course!' laughed Glenn. 'Haven't you been listening to me these last few months? The interviews? The six women I met in Aachen?'

'Of course,' she smiled. 'Of course, darling. Ready when you are. I've checked into the hotel, all is sorted. I told the boys at the desk I was your wife.'

'Right on!' he cried. 'You're gonna love Elfrida. She's swell!'

'Oh Gods, I can tell you're in the Americas when you start using your Americanisms again, darling,' sighed Eleanora.

'Come on, you,' laughed Glenn. 'Let's get to work.'

Leading her up the beach, Glenn scanned the hotel entrance for signs of Elfrida, keen to hear the rest of her story and introduce her to his new assistant.

CHAPTER SIXTEEN

Returning to the hotel, Glenn held his wife's hand, and recognised Elfrida standing by a small car. She was leaning against it, apparently waiting.

'Elfrida!' he called over. 'Sorry I'm late,' he said, walking over to her. 'I was just on the beach, I'm a sucker for the ocean! And look who I found!'

'Darling, she can't see!' his wife whispered loudly.

'Oh, right!' laughed Glenn. 'Elfrida, this is my wife, Eleanora. She just flew over from England to help me with my work.'

'Mrs. Tebbhurst!' exclaimed Elfrida. 'It is such a pleasure to meet you. Welcome to Acapulco!'

'A pleasure to meet you too,' said Eleanora, bowing slightly, clearly unsure how to greet a blind person. Glenn smiled at this. 'Though I didn't expect you to be quite as young,' she added. 'Nor as beautiful.'

'Thank you, Mrs. Tebbhurst, that is a very nice compliment!' smiled Elfrida. 'Will you be joining us today?'

'Where are we going?' Eleanora asked brightly.

'I'm taking Glenn to see where I grew up,' she said.

'Oh, how delightful!' exclaimed Eleanora. 'Is it a villa? I saw some spectacular villas on the way in from the airport.'

'Not exactly,' laughed Elfrida. 'Are you ready?'

'I am,' said Glenn. 'Would you like to have a coffee in the hotel before we go, Elfrida? Or something cooler perhaps? A lemonade? Let me treat you, please.'

'No, thanks,' she said, shaking her head.

'It's a great hotel,' he said. 'I've never experienced anything quite like it. I feel like royalty! Honey, you're gonna love it. Elfrida, it's great inside!'

'I know,' she said. 'I know of it, but I've never dared go inside.'

'Dared?' said Glenn. 'What do you mean? What's there to dare, Elfrida?'

'Hotels like this don't like people like me hanging around,' she said, smiling sadly. 'I don't need eyes to see that.'

'Oh,' said Eleanora, looking Elfrida up and down with a frown on her face.

Glenn turned to look up at the pretty façade of the building, which was approached by a set of white stairs from the road. On both sides of the door there were security men, scanning the road, not unlike the policemen further along the beach. They saw Glenn watching and turned their eyes to Elfrida. The two men looked at each other and did not seem impressed.

'What the heck! I thought security was a bit high,' he said. 'Do they always watch people like that? Hey, you! What are you looking at?'

'Glenn, really!' scolded Eleanora.

'They only watch Mexicans like that,' shrugged Elfrida. 'And security is high for a good reason. There's a lot of crime here in Acapulco. But don't worry, today you're with me, and you'll always be safe with me. Come on. Let's take the car to my neighbourhood.'

'Yeah, let's get out of here. That kind of behaviour makes me mad,' muttered Glenn. 'Let's head over to your home, Elfrida. I can't wait to see where you grew up!'

'Calm down, Glenn,' she said kindly. 'Home is a big word. I want to show you where I'm from, that's all. So you can understand.'

Glenn wondered what he had to understand, but it soon became apparent as they made their way from the hotel back towards the slum district of Acapulco. The brightness of the modern city was replaced by the darkness of the impoverished suburbs. Eleanora drew closer to Glenn as she watched the city transform around her. He knew she had not spent much time in the developing world; it must have all have come as quite a shock.

'Are you OK, honey?' he whispered to her.

'Fine! Oh, just fine!' she said in a high-pitched squeak.

'We're nearly there,' Elfrida told them from the front passenger seat.

'How has this part of city been so underdeveloped?' Glenn asked her, taking in the tarp and corrugated metal lining people's homes. 'I look around and see so much poverty, so close to such decadence. I don't get it.'

Children dashed out into the street as the car passed, laughing and running after the wheels. Their mothers, exhausted, shouted at them from doorways and windows.

'It's always the way with industry and development,' said Elfrida. 'This city was developed by a lot of Americans and rich Brazilians. All they think about is their little pockets of the city. For all they care, there could be cholera outbreaks in my neighbourhood, but it doesn't touch them. Their walls are high and their security guards are tough. It's always been that way. Mexico will always be a slave to money. This government will do anything for a bit more investment from their rich friends abroad. Am I not right, Juan Pablo?'

Elfrida began to talk rapidly in Spanish to her driver. The driver, a small Mexican called Juan Pablo, was silent and seemed by his manner to be a loyal friend of Elfrida.

'Do you use Juan Pablo for all your journeys?' Glenn asked her.

'Yes,' she said with a smile. 'He's my driver, appointed by Bettina herself.'

'Bettina appointed you a driver?' said Glenn, wondering when Bettina would come up in Elfrida's story.

'Who's Bettina?' Eleanora asked them.

'She's the reason we're all here,' said Elfrida, pride clear in her voice.

'Bettina is one of the six women,' Glenn explained to his wife, feeling slightly strange to be discussing her. 'She's very hands on in setting up the ICB's centres around the world.'

'ICB?' said Eleanora.

'International Charity of the Blind,' said Glenn. 'Honey, are you sure you've been listening to me this past year?'

'Go easy on her, Glenn!' laughed Elfrida. 'Not everyone's as crazy about the ICB as you are!'

'True,' smiled Glenn. 'So Bettina set up your driver. That's kind of her.'

'It's also just practical,' said Elfrida. 'If I'm the headmistress of the school, I have to be able to visit the families of the students if there is a problem, meet suppliers, handle the ICB's responsibilities here. I cannot drive anymore so I need Juan Pablo's eyes, and his car.'

They drove deeper and deeper into the slum Glenn had discovered the previous day, past the ICB School, through rows and rows of badly constructed homes. Elfrida said nothing until they reached one street. There was little to mark the street from others, except perhaps a tall street lamp, which bordered the street and an empty highway. The car could go no further, for the street was not fit for a vehicle to pass through. Elfrida said something to Juan Pablo and he stopped the car.

'Here we are,' she said to Glenn. 'This is where I grew up.'

Glenn looked out at the desolate wasteland of abandoned houses and makeshift constructions. Plants grew over much of the concrete, making the place look slightly like a jungle. He saw Eleanora gaze around in horror.

'It's, er, nice,' he said, swallowing hard.

'You don't have to lie, Glenn,' Elfrida smiled kindly at him.

Stepping out of the car, Glenn followed Elfrida, but Eleanora grabbed his arm.

'Glenn!' she whispered. 'Is it safe? Are you sure it's safe?'

'Honey,' he whispered back. 'I'm sure it is, but if you'd like to stay in the car, that's also OK?'

Eleanora glanced around the slightly dirty car and then out of the windows, clearly wondering what her next move should be. Gathering her bag, she scrambled out of the car after Glenn, following him as Elfrida led them to a concrete structure with a rusting, metal roof. The young Mexican stood outside and said nothing for a moment. The house seemed abandoned. Stepping forward, she pushed the door open.

'This is where we lived,' she said, walking over the threshold. Her voice was not emotional, but slightly colder in tone than it had been before.

'How many of you lived here?' Glenn asked, ignoring his wife's anxious hand-wringing beside him.

'Just me, Mama and Papa,' she said.

'In one room?' asked Glenn, taking in the measure of the house. There were four walls and a small area behind a curtain, where he assumed they had used a toilet. It was hardly enough for one person, let alone three.

'In one room,' Elfrida nodded. 'It's been a while since I came back here. It's easier to forget and to stay away.'

Glenn said nothing and continued to look around

'But you remember the way perfectly?' he asked. 'Even without your sight?'

'The smells on this street I will never forget,' she said. 'Nor the journeys I made when I lost my sight. Every day, the same walk for years.'

Slowly, Elfrida walked around the room, raising her hands to trace the four walls of the house. Glenn thought she looked beautiful there, in the darkness, the curvaceous outline of her body against the peeling paint. Her long black hair swayed slightly with the breeze coming in through the open door.

'Strange,' she said. 'As a child it always seemed so small, because I could see. Now it feels bigger. Blindness is funny that way.'

'Where are your parents now?' Glenn asked, wondering what had happened to this abandoned, empty home.

'My father died,' she said. 'I never really had much of a relationship with him, but he died when I was eighteen. My mother is dead, too.'

'I'm sorry for your loss,' Glenn said, seeing the sadness that haunted her face. It was mixed with pain. He looked around at Eleanora. She seemed unmoved by the story; she was too busy glancing over her shoulder for thieves.

'It's better that way,' she said. 'This was no way to live. They were not good to me, you know, Glenn. My parents were never good to me.'

'Poverty brings out the worst in people,' said Glenn. 'Even the best intentions get lost in hunger and desperation. I've seen that a lot in my line of work.'

'Perhaps,' she sighed. 'So much loss and nothing to gain from revisiting it.'

'I'm sorry you have come back here for me,' Glenn said quickly. 'If this is too much, or you don't want revisit the past, Elfrida, there is no obligation. I just want to be clear on that.'

'Yes,' said Eleanora quickly. 'We can leave. We should leave.'

But Elfrida was shaking her head.

'No, Glenn, you misunderstand me,' she said. 'You asked me to tell you my story. Well, it starts here. Beneath this roof. This is where the story starts.'

Feeling around with her hands, Elfrida took the remaining wooden chair – Glenn and Eleanora were already seated – and lowered herself down to sit on it. Like that she began to tell her story.

'I was the only child of Jose Merguez and Christina Velasquez,' she began. 'My father and mother both worked as cleaners in the city. They took on jobs together, but often my father went to drink instead. He was a drinker, oh yes. He loved to watch bullfighting at the farms just outside of Acapulco. He would gamble, place bets, and lose all our money. My mother cleaned the rooms alone. Do you know how much work that is for one person?'

Glenn shook his head.

'Imagine cleaning a whole floor of a hotel in an afternoon, alone,' said Elfrida. 'That was my Mama's job. So when my father couldn't help, she took me along with her. Not to double the money, I was a kid – I didn't get paid. She took me along to do my Papa's share of the work.'

'But what was your father doing all day?' Glenn asked, horrified by this story.

'Sleeping late, drinking,' she shrugged. 'It was his way. But if my Mama didn't clean those rooms good, she knew she'd be fired. People would complain, all those good, rich white folks, who came from clean houses and clean neighbourhoods. That's why she took me along. We needed to clean those rooms and bring the money home.'

'That's terrible!' said Glenn, remembering with a pang of guilt what Eleanora had said before he left. He looked over at his wife, who gazed at him with utter horror and disgust. He knew what she was thinking: he knew she could not wait to get back to that safe, smart hotel, where everything was clean and far from the realities of life in Acapulco. He knew in his heart that she would have been one of those complaining white women that had made Elfrida's mother's life so hard.

'That was life,' she said.

'A child working in a hotel,' Eleanora shook her head. 'How terrible! What an awful thing to allow.'

'And the hotels didn't say anything when they saw you there?' he asked.

'Of course not,' she said. 'They just wanted the job done. So when my Mama took me along they knew it was gonna be quicker. So they said nothing. I said, "Mama, please, let me go to school!" and all she said was "What are you gonna learn in school that you can't learn with me here with this mop and bucket?" That was that; that was my life. I helped my Mama get paid close to ten cents an hour, a few pesos.'

'So you didn't go to school?' Glenn asked, taking out his notepad and starting to take notes in the dark.

'I did,' she said. 'After a while I told my Mama I would only work on weekends. So I went to school in the week and straight afterwards, I went to help my Mama clean. Every weekend I helped her clean. We were always working. But when we got back, no matter how late, I tried to study. It was impossible in the house. We were three people living in the same room. My Papa got mad when he saw me turning on a gas lamp, and my Mama needed her sleep. But I found a way.'

Stepping out of the house into the bright daylight, Elfrida began to walk further down the street, towards the highway and the old streetlamp. Glenn followed her, despite Eleanora's anxious tugging on his arm.

'Glenn!' she whispered. 'Are you sure about this? Do you know where we are? Should people like us be here? Will we not be targets?'

'We're guests, honey,' he said to his wife. 'Let's be respectful, OK?'

When Elfrida reached the light, she touched it and smiled.

'This is where I spent most of the nights of my childhood,' she said, stroking the streetlamp slightly. 'I brought my books here and read by the light. It was not perfect, and sometimes the light flickered, but it was good enough for me. I think this lamp is what helped me pass all of my exams. I learnt English under this lamp, Glenn!'

Glenn looked up at the lamp and guessed that it probably did not work anymore. He thought of the powerful symbolism behind this one lamp, built for one purpose, but used by one determined and underprivileged child for another.

'So you went to high school?' Glenn asked.

'I did,' she nodded. 'The other kids bullied me, of course. I was poor as they come, and that was saying something. Most people at the state schools are poor; otherwise they'd be in the private schools. But I was the poorest of all, and I was miserable. I did not have a very loving start to my life.'

'But you had your sight,' said Glenn. 'You did not go blind as a child?'

'No, not until I was seventeen,' she said. 'I saw the world for what it was for seventeen years and then God took my eyes from me. Perhaps he knew I didn't like what I saw. The blindness came out of the blue. I didn't expect it, no one did.'

'How did it happen?' Glenn asked. 'An accident?'

'No,' she said. 'Well, maybe. I don't know what made me go blind, Glenn, or at least no one told me. The doctor's told me nothing. My mother begged them for answers but they did not say. Now that I'm older and have spoken to more people, I believe I experienced some kind of chlorine poisoning.'

'Really?' asked Glenn. Elfrida nodded.

'Ingestion has been known to cause blindness,' she said. 'And around that time they were testing new methods of water treatment in the city.'

'What?' cried Eleanora. 'Is the water not safe to drink here? Oh Gods, what horror!'

'But that's crazy,' exclaimed Glenn. 'And totally illegal! Elfrida, this is so awful!'

'Plenty of things are illegal in Acapulco, Glenn,' she shrugged. 'They were sanitising the sewage, I knew that much.'

'And you ingested a large amount?' he asked, thinking of the effects of chlorine on the body. He knew that it could cause blindness if not treated quickly.

'I must have done,' she said. 'I felt awful. I was sick, my stomach hurt very badly, but my mother could not take me to the doctor. We could not afford one. So eventually, when she thought I was dying, she rushed me to the hospital. The doctors never told me what had happened. They just asked my mother why she had not brought me sooner. Mama was very angry with me, asking me where I had been playing, what I had been doing; all these things. But I couldn't see her. I closed my eyes against the pain, feeling it everywhere in my body, and when I eventually opened them again, I saw nothing. Only darkness.'

'You were blind?' said Glenn quietly.

'I was blind,' she replied, in a small voice.

'Did you try and see more doctors?' he asked. 'Did you try to recover your sight?'

'This is Mexico, not England, Glenn,' sighed Elfrida. 'I had no money, no qualifications, and no family to help me. My Mama was just angry I couldn't clean with her anymore. My Papa too. He was angry with me at first, and then he just didn't care. They put me in the corner of the house and told me to sleep.'

Glenn could not look at Elfrida as she told her terrible story. He could not believe fortune could be so cruel, and parents could be so heartless.

'My Papa got angry with my Mama too,' she said. 'When the money stopped coming in, he started beating her. He couldn't afford to drink so he beat my Mama. I was glad then that I was blind, so I could not watch that. But maybe it was worse to hear it all. Every sound, every cry, every slam against the wall, I heard it ten times louder.'

'I can't listen to this!' Eleanora hissed in her husband's ears. 'What horror!'

'And you had to stay in the house?' Glenn asked, ignoring his wife. 'They did not send you back to school?'

'How could they?' she answered. 'They had no money, no way to get me there. My Mama went out to work and came back so exhausted. Papa went out all day looking for friends who might offer him a drink, or a ride to the bullfights. I was left alone, and there was no way I was giving up on me.'

'What did you do?' Glenn asked.

'I did what I could to get by,' she said. 'I needed to get my education, but I had no money for books, and anyway, I couldn't read books anymore. I wanted audio books and a CD player. So I begged.'

'On the street?' Glenn asked. She nodded.

'At first, yes,' she said. 'I walked away from my neighbourhood, and followed the houses with my hand, until I heard cars and people passing by. Every day, when my parents left the house I left. I would sit there with a cup and wait for people to pass, sometimes saying, "I am blind, please help me." I think people felt sorry for me, you know, because of my age. Maybe they saw their daughter or sister on the street, so they would throw in a few pesos. At the end of the day I would count them, feeling the shapes of the coins to know how much I had made.'

'Did you do well?' Glenn asked, admiring Elfrida's courage.

'I did,' she laughed. 'Sometimes I made around six dollars a day. Six! More than my mother made in a day, working until her back broke in those hotels. I saved up my money, and when I could, I bought a CD Walkman, and CDs, about everything I would have been learning at school. Oh, I had so many CDs! I think by the end, I looked crazy. My parents thought I was crazy.'

'It's terribly hot, oh!' Eleanora exclaimed suddenly, looking at Elfrida in alarm. 'I'll go and sit in the car, darling. Would that be alright? Terribly sorry, Frida.'

'It's Elfrida,' smiled the Mexican. 'That's fine, Mrs Tebbhurst. Juan Pablo will go with you.'

'Oh!' she exclaimed. 'Really? How, er, lovely.'

'He'll keep you safe, honey, OK?' Glenn whispered to his wife. He watched as a disturbed-looking Eleanora was escorted back to the car by the little Mexican man before turning back to Elfrida.

'Sorry about that,' he said. 'Eleanora is somewhat new to the struggles of others.'

'No problem, Glenn,' smiled Elfrida. 'It's brave of her to come out here.'

'So, did they mind you begging?' Glenn asked.

'They never knew,' she shrugged. 'I hid everything from them. My father died not long after I went blind. He was thirty-seven.'

'That's so young,' said Glenn.

'Perhaps, but in Mexico, it's not so young,' she said. 'I was eighteen then. I should have been graduating. Instead, I told my mother I would beg for us. She was happy to take a break. For a while, it really kept us going, you know. I begged from the highway by our street all the way up to the hotels you are staying near now. They probably recognise me! Or maybe not; many years have passed.'

'So what changed?' Glenn asked. 'I can't make the connection between you begging through the streets of Acapulco, and you becoming the headmistress of the ICB School.'

'Everything changed one day,' said Elfrida. 'I was begging as usual, making money for the audio books I wanted to buy. I heard a voice call down to me, asking my name in Spanish. She had a strange accent, not from around here. She asked me why I was begging, so I told her: for my education. She asked me to tell her more, so I told her what I was studying, what I hoped to do. She asked me if I felt blindness was an impediment to my hopes and dreams and I made a joke. I said it might slow things down. She laughed, and told me her name.'

'Bettina?' Glenn guessed, feeling a small thrill as he spoke her name.

'Exactly!' cried Elfrida. 'How did you know?'

'A gut feeling,' said Glenn, smiling. Inside he was beaming. 'I knew it would be Bettina, coming to the rescue! She has a habit of doing that, I've noticed.'

'Well, yes, Bettina introduced herself, and told me she was travelling for the International Charity for the Blind, researching different institutes in Mexico,' said Elfrida.

'So Bettina was already looking for projects to sponsor in Acapulco?' Glenn asked.

'No,' laughed Elfrida. 'She was on holiday!'

'Really?' laughed Glenn, happy to hear that Bettina took holidays sometimes too. Saving the world must have been tiring without a break every now and again.

'Yes, she was taking a small vacation after visiting Mexico City for work,' said Elfrida. 'She had been told by Herbert to go to the United States, Canada and Mexico, on a fundraising mission. She was sent to various institutions in New York, in Houston –'

'In New Orleans,' said Glenn.

'Yes, exactly,' smiled Elfrida. 'How did you know?'

'I saw Odile earlier this year,' he said. 'In her home city. I told you, I want to capture all of your stories!'

'Of course, you'll stop at nothing, I'm sure of that, Glenn!' laughed Elfrida. 'Well, after visiting New Orleans, Bettina made her way down to New Mexico. She liked to visit "new" places, it seems! Eventually she reached Mexico City. She visited institutions recommended by Herbert Farrand but found them uninspiring. She said they were not clean and lacked any kind of enthusiasm to change for the better. People were there to hide in a corner, she said, away from the world. She told me she was sent to Mexico for the high sun levels in the country, based on research that indicated some correlation between high levels of sunshine and blindness. But she could not stay long; she found the city so dirty and noisy. There were too many drunks, she said, and bullfights! However, I think it was more the poverty and high degree of social inequality that she couldn't stand. It's strange, the way you experience poverty as a blind person. It's not visual; it's in the way people talk, the way they smell. There's crowdedness and emptiness in poverty, all at the same time.'

'I can second that,' sighed Glenn. 'It's devastating to see how the rich are so rich and the poor are so poor. I can't bear to see it everywhere, it breaks my heart.'

'Welcome to Mexico,' Elfrida shook her head unhappily. 'Anyway, Bettina took a few days out in Acapulco. She heard from people in New Mexico that it was a place she could come to for relaxation. She took a hotel on the beach front, not unlike you, Glenn, and on her second day there, she started talking to me.'

'But how did you go from talking in the street to being a teacher in a school?' Glenn asked.

'Well, Bettina asked me what my dream was, so I told her,' said Elfrida. 'I wanted to educate myself, and then educate others. That afternoon, I took her home to meet my mother. She could sense that I lived in a poor neighbourhood, and asked me where the school was. I told her there was not one. The next day, she came back to my house, in the morning, before I'd woken up, with an idea. She asked me if I would like to build a school in the neighbourhood. I thought she was joking at first, so I laughed, but she was serious. She said she could set aside enough money for the initial construction. Nothing too complicated, she said, but solid rooms, big enough to teach the blind from that area. She asked if I would be willing to take classes in Braille, in order to teach children to read it.'

'Were you?' Glenn asked, though of course he already knew the answer.

'It was the greatest skill I ever learned,' she said. 'Finally, I could read again! Bettina left me a small amount of money so I no longer had to beg, and enrolled me in a class. When she returned in six months' time, she set me a test. I was quick and she was impressed. She told me that with six months more training, I would be ready to start teaching. On that trip, we also went to find a site for the school. The area where the school is now was a wasteland before, where people dumped trash or left things they no longer wanted in their homes.'

'She built the school there?' Glenn asked.

'She took advice from a construction company in the city, asking if the place would be appropriate,' Elfrida explained. 'They said there was no reason why the land could not be bought and built on. Work started immediately. The final result was a small, walled schoolyard, and two rooms. One classroom and one office. Bettina and I went into the community, searching for blind children in need of education. Some parents wanted us to teach all of their children, the seeing and the blind, because most of them were not going to school. But Bettina said we had to be strict and take only the blind, who were often kept like vegetables in the corner of their houses. We took on eight students and that was how it all began.'

'Were they boys or girls?' Glenn asked.

'A perfect balance,' smiled Elfrida. 'There were four boys and four girls. They respected me a lot because I helped them. I could recognise every one of those kids from the way they sounded, the way they smelled. Bettina helped me with that. She taught me how to recognise people without seeing them.'

Glenn remembered how amazed he had been when he had walked past Bettina and she had recognised him straight away. He was fascinated to hear that she had helped Elfrida discover this skill also.

'Oh, I knew all of them,' Elfrida laughed at the memory. 'I even guessed what they were wearing. I'd say, "Paulo, are you wearing your green polo shirt? What happened to the black one?" The kids loved it.'

'What did you teach them?' Glenn asked.

'Well, all sorts of things,' she said. 'I combined all the subjects; I loved to plan my lessons so they had a bit of geography, some history mixed with maths, and languages of course. Bettina really liked this approach when she came back to visit, so this is how I taught, until we could hire teachers to teach formal subjects.'

'How old were the children?' asked Glenn, quickly jotting down notes.

'They were between ages eight and eleven,' she said. 'They're all teenagers now. It's amazing to see how they have developed and grown. So many lives have been transformed by that chance meeting I had with Bettina on the street that day. I used to wonder why she chose to help me, out of all the beggars she passed in the streets of Acapulco. There were so many to help. So I asked her.'

'What did she say?' Glenn asked.

'She said that she had never met someone begging for education,' said Elfrida. 'She had met many beggars asking for money for food, for shelter, for their families, and that though these causes were great, she had never met someone who needed money for audio books! She could see I was longing for the education I had lost. She told me that she knew if she didn't help me then, she would never be able to look at a street lamp in the same way. It would always remind her of the little girl reading there, because she had no lights at home, until the day she lost her eyes, then even the streetlamp couldn't help her learn.'

'That's beautiful,' said Glenn.

'That's Bettina,' smiled Elfrida. She then said something in Spanish that Glenn could not understand, though he assumed it was a prayer, or a blessing.

'And your mother,' said Glenn. 'Did she ever get to see the school? Or see you teaching?'

'No,' said Elfrida, and she made the sign of the cross. 'Her heart gave out not long after I met Bettina. The irony of life, I guess. When I finally had money to make her life easier, she died on me.'

'I'm sorry,' said Glenn.

'She is at peace now,' said Elfrida. 'I would rather she be with God in heaven than cleaning the rooms in your hotel.'

Glenn felt guilty for a moment, recognising the terrible inequalities the hotel he was staying in perpetuated. His guilt turned into anger.

'That's it,' he said, shaking his head. 'We're going back to my hotel.'

'What?' said Elfrida.

'I'm taking you back to my hotel for lunch,' he said.

'No, Glenn, I can't,' she started to object.

'I refuse to take no for an answer,' he said. 'You'll be the finest damn guest they have ever served, believe me. You're my guest and I want you to sit and eat in the hotels your mother worked her whole life cleaning. I cannot bear to think I am sleeping in a hotel you are too afraid to enter.'

They walked back to the car, where Eleanora was fanning herself on the back seat, scanning the horizon for vagabonds.

'Juan Pablo, please take us back to the hotel!' cried Glenn. 'We're going for lunch. All of us!'

Elfrida's driver looked from Glenn to his boss, who looked stunned.

'Glenn, I don't know…' said Elfrida. For a moment Glenn caught a glimpse of the teenager she had once been, vulnerable and poor, afraid to be shooed away by racist hotel guards.

'Please,' he said gently. 'I really must insist. Do this for me, Elfrida. Please. Do it for yourself, too. You are so welcome there, as my guest, as my guide.

'Darling, I'm not sure…' Eleanora began.

'No, honey, it's fine,' he said firmly, stepping into the car. 'I won't take no for an answer.'

On their way back to the hotel, Eleanora whispered in his ear.

'Darling, are you sure you want to upset the owners?' she asked. 'I mean, is it safe to upset the status quo in a place like this? God knows I'd hate to see the poor girl thrown out of…'

'No one is getting thrown out of anywhere,' said Glenn. 'I'll make sure of that.'

However, when they reached the hotel, Eleanora put a hand to her head.

'Oh dear, I do feel faint,' she murmured. 'Darling, perhaps it would be best if I skipped dinner? I don't want to spoil it for you.'

'OK, honey,' said Glenn, knowing his wife well enough to know that her sudden illness was more to do with her fear of embarrassment than anything else. 'I'll see you upstairs.'

'Such a pleasure,' his wife smiled sweetly at Elfrida.

'Great to meet you, Mrs. Tebbhurst,' smiled the young woman. 'Enjoy your night in Acapulco.'

Forgetting to say goodbye to Juan Pablo, Eleanora walked quickly towards the elevator, fanning herself as she went. 'Ready?' Glenn asked his new friends.

'I guess so!' smiled Elfrida.

And so Elfrida allowed herself to be taken to the hotels she had once begged outside. She put her arm on Glenn's arm and let herself be led into the luxurious dining room, where a delicious lunch buffet was being served. Juan Pablo came too and Glenn announced to them both that he had never sat in finer company. The discomfort he saw on their faces only strengthened his resolve. He refused to let them feel ashamed. His heart thumped terribly at the thought of a wonderful human being like Elfrida feeling shame in a hotel that had shamed her and her city.

'How do you feel?' he asked her quietly, when their dessert plates were taken away.

'Strange,' she said. 'I remember coming here with my mother. It still smells the same.'

'Let's take coffees! Waiter, coffee please! Listen, you honour me by eating with me here today,' he said. 'Thank you for sharing your story with me, Elfrida. I think it's exactly what I needed to help donors understand just how much you are doing with ICB support.'

'Thank you, Glenn, for being who you are,' she said.

His heart grew to bursting point at this and finally, after a long period of doubting, he remembered why he loved working in the charity sector so much.

'It's people like you who make me do what I do,' he said, raising his glass in a toast to her.

Glenn was so glad he had seen Elfrida again, and travelled to Acapulco. In Elfrida he had found hope in a desperate situation. Together, they drank coffees and eventually began to laugh, toasting to Elfrida, the wonderful work of the ICB, and of course to Bettina, a person who in blindness saw so clearly what the seeing could not.

When they had said their goodbyes, Glenn went upstairs to find his wife gently snoozing.

'Thanks for coming today, honey,' he said. 'I know it was hard for you.'

'Who'd have thought we'd ever be together in Mexico,' she grinned.

'I know,' he smiled. 'You see? My work does have some perks.'

'I've missed you,' she said, raising a hand to stroke his hair. 'I've missed my husband.'

'Of course you have,' he grinned at her.

'I'm serious!' she scowled, slapping him lightly on his shoulder. He laughed at her frown.

'Come here then, wife,' he said, lying down beside her and feeling a need for her that he had not felt for a long time. As the sun set over Acapulco, husband and wife made love, and the distance Glenn had felt for so long was closed.

CHAPTER SEVENTEEN

Letting the cold breeze rush in from the window onto his bare chest, Glenn let out a great sigh of satisfaction. Looking down, he saw his wife's naked shoulder resting on his stomach. He reached out a hand to stroke the blonde hair and marvelled at the touch: how long had it been since they had enjoyed so much intimacy, he wondered. Glenn could not recall the last time he had reached out to touch Eleanora's hair with such ease and love. As his memories stirred, so his wife stirred beneath him, opening her eyes to the afternoon sun filtering in through the window.

'What's the time?' she murmured, nuzzling her cheek against her husband's hard chest.

'Time for us to stop lazing around in bed, baby,' he grinned down at her. Rising up slightly, he leant down to kiss her head. The scent of her body gripped him with fresh desire and he ran his hands down the length of her naked form.

'There's nothing else to do in Acapulco,' she groaned, smiling at the pleasure his fingertips aroused on her bare skin. 'Only the beach and the bar.'

'I can think of a few things,' Glenn whispered, pulling her gently but firmly into his arms to show her his intent. She giggled like a bride on her wedding night as he lifted her on top of him.

'Oh, I'm sure you can, Mr. Tebbhurst,' she said, allowing him to wrap her arms tight around her waist. 'I think I can too.'

The arrival of Eleanora in Acapulco breathed a miraculous air of revival into their relationship, and their bedroom. Like the *tehuano*, the ancient wind which blows across southern Mexico, from the Isthmus of Tehuantepec all the way over to the Gulf of Tehuantepec, Glenn felt the musty dryness of the past decade of their marriage blown away by a new, revitalising force. Whatever had brought his wife to Mexico –

curiosity, jealousy, something inexplicable – Glenn was glad of it. He knew the trials of the day in Acapulco's darkest slum and the hard nature of Elfrida's story had left his wife longing for the comfort of his arms. He had been more than glad to hold her and kiss her gently, long after their lovemaking had reached its exhausted conclusion. The following days were a blur of sunshine on the beach, quiet dinners in the restaurant, and pleasure-filled nights in their hotel room. Between the latter, Glenn had time to think about all he had learnt from Elfrida and the ever-impressive work of Bettina and the ICB.

When one evening, he had satisfied his wife, Glenn went and leant by the window to take in the glowering red sunset.

'It's amazing how the rich can live here,' he said at last. 'Elfrida's struggle is not uncommon and yet it is the last thing the Brazilians and Yankee tourists will see when they visit.'

'*Elfrida, Elfrida, Elfrida,*' sighed Eleanora, struggling to hide the bitterness in her voice. 'What must I do to get that woman off your mind? Am I not enough for you, darling?'

'Honey, don't be like that,' he said, turning back to her and slinking back to the bed. 'Don't you know how much I love you?'

His wife smiled at this and raised one coy eyebrow.

'Why don't you show me?' she said in a silky voice.

'You're insatiable,' he murmured, leaning in to kiss her. 'I'm sorry, honey. I get so distracted by these stories. We can only imagine how difficult life was for women like Elfrida. Their lives have been so terrible. Just the other night she was telling me a bit about one of the other women I met in Aachen, a girl from Hong Kong. She lost her sight in a sweat shop, where she worked as a child.'

'Good God, how many of these women are there?' Eleanora exclaimed, alarmed by his husband's endless supply of horror stories.

'I told you!' he laughed at her reaction. 'Six. The Six Women of Aachen. It sounds like an epic, doesn't it?'

'Or a tragedy,' his wife offered.

'True,' sighed Glenn. 'But tragedy or not, I have to record their stories, and I think this little lady in Asia is my next trip.'

'You're going to go to Hong Kong?' asked Eleanora, and Glenn could see a mixture of curiosity and suspicion cloud her expression.

'I'll have to at some point,' he sighed, leaning back against the soft pillows once more. 'I need to. This girl is gonna have the story that really touches people. She'll be very important in the context of both the ICB and the DCF's support for them. But I don't have to go immediately, it won't be for a while, sweetie. We'll have time to get back to Ronda and have some time together there.'

'Back to Ronda?' said Eleanora, a small smile appearing on her face. 'But that's in the wrong direction.'

'Huh?' said Glenn, not catching her meaning.

'I mean, Hong Kong is that way,' she said, pointing out to the ocean, which washed from the Acapulco shoreline out west into the Pacific. Glenn stared at her for a moment, wondering if she was being serious. The small, mischievous smile stayed on her lips.

'You wanna go to Hong Kong?' he asked her. 'Now?'

'Why not?' she smiled.

Glenn searched his mind for a moment, pondering her question. Why not, indeed.

'Are you sure, honey?' he asked. 'It will be a business trip, and, well, it will be Hong Kong.'

'Once a jewel of the Empire!' cried Eleanora. 'I wouldn't miss it for the world. Besides, someone has to keep an eye on you, with all these beautiful blind women about. What sort of wife would let her husband out of her sight in Asia? Only a blind fool!'

'I don't know, honey…' Glenn hesitated. He was not sure how Eleanora would fare in the bustling, wild streets of Hong Kong. They would not be tucked away by the ocean as they were in Acapulco. They would be in the thick of the city, one of the largest, craziest cities in the world. But his wife had moved in front of him. She had slowly shrugged her camisole off her shoulder to reveal a length of creamy, pale skin.

'Are you sure you want to leave me behind?' she whispered, her blue eyes glittering as they looked playfully up at him. Doubt fled from Glenn's mind as his body responded to his wife's nakedness.

'How could I?' he asked helplessly, turning to her with fierce passion.

Hours later, when they had sated their desires once more, Glenn went down to the hotel travel desk to book flights to Hong Kong.

'Not London, *señor?*' the young man behind the desk asked, clearly alarmed to be booking such a huge departure from the original journey.

'No,' grinned Glenn. 'Not London this time.'

'Where would you like to change, *señor?*' the young man asked. 'We can put you on a flight from Mexico City to Los Angeles, and then from Los Angeles directly to Hong Kong. Or you can fly via New York or Madrid?'

'I like the sound of LA,' said Glenn, thinking about how he needed to buy a new suit. 'Book it up and we'll leave in the morning.'

'Yes, sir,' nodded the young man, clearly impressed by Glenn's decisiveness. But who would not be decisive, thought Glenn, when he followed the orders of the goddess waiting for him in their bedroom? With the flights booked, Glenn pulled out his smart phone and began to type out an email.

Dear Zu-Ting,

I hope this finds you well and that you will recall my name when you read this. This is Glenn Tebbhurst, from Aachen.

I am writing to you from Acapulco, where I have just had the pleasure of meeting your friend and colleague, Elfrida. She showed me the wonderful work she is doing here in Mexico and advised me to visit you if I wished to see more of the excellent achievements of the ICB at work in the world.

My wife and I have subsequently booked ourselves onto a flight to Hong Kong! We leave tomorrow and I hope to be able to visit you there.

With my best wishes,
Glenn

The smartphone made a whooshing sound as the email sped away to Hong Kong, leaving Glenn satisfied that the necessary contact had been made. He tucked his phone away and leapt up the stairs, back towards his room, where he knew Eleanora would be dressing for dinner.

'So?' she called from the bathroom when he entered the room.

'We'll be in Los Angeles tomorrow afternoon!' Glenn called back, rushing to his wife to kiss the back of her neck as she applied perfume. 'Mm, you smell great.'

'And I would like to keep it that way!' she squealed, shrugging him away from her. 'No more of this sweaty bedroom! Making love in the tropics is never advisable.'

'You do know how humid it will be in Hong Kong, honey?'

'Oh darling, don't fret!' she laughed. 'God knows there's always air-con!'

Glenn and Eleanora enjoyed one last night dining by the Mexican ocean before retiring for an early sleep. They were so exhausted from doing nothing they both slept heavily in the night and then again on the drive to the airport. But by the time the plane had landed in Los Angeles, Eleanora was already halfway through her second glass of champagne and desperate to start shopping in the glamorous Beverly Hills boulevards.

'We have twelve hours until we need to be back on the plane, honey,' Glenn called to his wife as she dashed towards a taxi outside of the airport terminal.

'Yes, darling, that's just enough time!' she called back. Glenn followed her into the taxi and then around Los Angeles, remarking at every possible moment how different it felt to go shopping with his wife on the sunny West Coast streets than back home in London.

'You know, I think life could've been quite different if you had left your farm and come to live with me in New York,' Glenn grinned at his wife as they tucked into dinner in Beverly Hills looking out over the Hollywood sign emblazoned on the hillside. Eleanora had up until that moment been too busy scouting for celebrities to listen to her husband, but when he mentioned their early life, she turned her blue eyes towards him.

'Is that so?' she said, reaching to take a sip of her gin and tonic. The candlelight flashed in the clinking ice in her drink and her eyes.

'I think you would've made a wonderful expat, throwing parties, buying ranches, teaching a few Yankees some real manners,' he chuckled. 'We would have had a blast!'

'God, me? In America?' she scoffed. 'I hardly think so, darling. I'd have spent my life correcting your bad grammar and longing for the other side of the pond.'

Suddenly the magic of the last few days faded slightly as Glenn heard the familiar tones of his wife's disdain fill his ears. Masked under a layer of sexiness and spontaneity, Eleanora's acid tongue had lain dormant. Hearing it again made her husband wince slightly. She watched him for a moment and seemed to sense his discomfort for she leaned over and took his hand.

'Oh don't be a bore, darling,' she said quickly, a slight plea in her voice. 'You know I love to visit the States. I'm just a Beaumont –'

'Born and bred, I know,' Glenn sighed.

'Well, exactly,' she smiled sweetly at him. 'I'd have made a rotten American wife, I assure you. Besides, you've done so well in London! The City has really made you into something.'

'I was something before I came to London,' Glenn shrugged.

'Well, I of all people should know that, shouldn't I?' said his wife, raising an eyebrow.

'What do you mean?' Glenn asked her.

'I mean I was the one who saw you on that dancefloor,' she said, her hand sliding beneath the table to stroke his leg. He jumped at the sensation, remembering another hand touching his leg, almost a year ago now, in Aachen. An image of Bettina floated into his mind, but he pushed it away immediately, focusing on the blue eyes resting on his face. Eleanora looked up at him, still as beautiful as the girl he had begged to dance with him at the Ronda Round Manor Ball.

'You said yes,' Glenn grinned at her.

'For my sins, yes,' she laughed. 'Yes, I did.'

The overnight plane to Hong Kong left just as both Eleanora and Glenn were ready to sleep. They slept the whole way, waking just in time to look out of the window and see the stunning city of skyscrapers rising from the coast below.

'Good God, what's all this!' she exclaimed as the smog from the city clouded the windows.

'Welcome to Asia,' Glenn smiled grimly.

The madness of the city did not wait long to introduce itself to the couple from London. They had barely collected their luggage from the carousel when ten to fifteen taxi drivers hounded them with broken English and unrecognisable Chinese cries. Eleanora looked at them in horror as they smiled at her, pleading with her to come to their taxi.

'Best price, best price!' they cried.

'Good car for good lady! Beautiful lady!' others cried.

'Come on, honey,' said Glenn, gritting his teeth and steering them through the crowd towards a suitable driver. He was no stranger to touts and overenthusiastic taxi drivers. His travels had taken him to countless airports. Luckily he saw a smart-looking limousine waiting not far from the terminal exit. A driver stood in a crisp, clean uniform at the door, waiting for a customer.

'Can you take us to The Hong Kong Palace?' Glenn asked the driver. 'We have reservations there.'

'Of course, of course,' said the driver, nodding quickly and bowing slightly as he went to take their luggage. Once he had placed their luggage in the trunk of the limousine, he quickly opened the doors, allowing Glenn to slide into the comfortable red seats. Eleanora slid in after him.

'This is stylish,' she said approvingly.

'Anything to get away from those drivers!' Glenn laughed. His wife glanced back at the sea of touts anxiously.

'They won't try and get in, will they?' she asked.

'No, honey,' laughed Glenn.

'I must say, I expected a bit better from an airport on ex-British soil, didn't you?' she said, settling herself into her seat.

'Ex-British?' said Glenn. 'Baby, it's been quite a while since the British had any say in Hong Kong.'

'It shows,' she said coldly.

Glenn chuckled to himself. He wondered how much Eleanora still considered the United States to be 'ex-British'. Exhausted from the travel, the couple watched as the urban sprawl of Hong Kong spread out before them, impressed by the height of the buildings on that foggy morning. When the limousine stopped, Glenn looked up to see a hotel, though it was not the hotel he was expecting.

'Excuse me?' he said, calling to the driver who had already started to unload the suitcases. 'Fella, I think you've taken us to the wrong spot.'

'No, no, Bo Sung bring you to perfect hotel for Hong Kong,' said the driver, continuing to unload the bags. 'Only $300 a night! Perfect, and cheaper than Hong Kong Palace.'

Glenn stepped out to take a look at the hotel. He glimpsed velvet walls through the windows in the rooms above, and mirrors on the ceiling. Before he could stop her, Eleanora had stepped out and started up the steps.

'This looks promising,' she drawled. Glenn followed her up the steps.

'Honey, I don't think…' he began, but Eleanora was already greeting the lady at the reception.

'Well, hello, how do you do!' Eleanora spoke in loud, slow English.

The woman at the desk must have been in her fifties, for her hair was grey and pulled back behind her ears. She was a stout character, who eyed Eleanora up, before ringing a little bell. A moment later a slim, attractive young man came out, dressed in very little clothing. She shouted something at him and smiled at Eleanora, waiting for her approval.

'English! English!' the driver who had called himself Bo Sung shouted to the woman.

'Ohhhh!' laughed the little old woman, looking at Eleanora. 'Boy good? Good for you?' she asked Glenn's wife.

'What on earth is she talking about?' Eleanora demanded.

'I think she's asking if he will do,' said Glenn, hiding a smile.

'*Do* for what?' she asked, a confused frown forming on her face. Meanwhile, the little old woman had rung her bell once more. This time a young woman came out, dressed in traditional clothing but revealing a healthy stretch of bosom.

'For you!' she cried at Glenn.

'Oh God!' screeched Eleanora, finally understanding the situation. 'He's brought us to a brothel!'

Glenn turned quickly to the driver and paid him $20 before stepping out into the road to hail another cab. One stopped quickly and Glenn repeated his hotel name once more.

'Let's get out of here!' Eleanora hissed, dragging her designer suitcase as far away from the seedy hotel entrance as possible. 'What if we're seen? What if we get arrested?'

'I think this is all pretty legal here, honey,' said Glenn. 'But yes, let's get going.'

'Pretty wife needs good man!' the old lady called to Glenn, looking annoyed to have lost custom.

'Was that a gigolo?' Eleanora asked in disbelief as they drove away. 'Was he for… for *me*?'

'Yes,' laughed Glenn. 'Why? Have you changed your mind? Should we go back?'

'Glenn!' she scolded him, looking desperately angry. 'What sort of place breeds taxi drivers who will take decent, well-to-do people like us to brothels? I'm not sure if this was a good idea. Hong Kong is *not* growing on me at all!'

Fortunately The Hong Kong Palace was only ten minutes away and the couple were quickly welcomed and ushered into a fine suite overlooking the city. Fatigue drew the couple into quick showers and the cool sheets of their bed. The sixteen hours of plane journeys, broken up by the busy shopping jaunt in Los Angeles, sent them straight to sleep.

Glenn was woken later that afternoon by the sound of Eleanora dressing beside him.

'Up already?' he murmured.

'I'm desperate to see the city!' she said excitedly. 'Come on, darling. Let's get out.'

Surprised to hear his wife so animated after the morning's debacle, Glenn quickly made himself ready, pulling on the new tailored suit he had bought in America. Eleanora blushed slightly when she saw how handsome he looked in it, and proudly slipped her arm though his.

'My man in Hong Kong,' she grinned at him.

'My lady,' he nodded.

Laughing, they headed out into Hong Kong. Glenn soon understood why Eleanora was so keen to get out into the city. Remnants of a colonial past haunted its every corner, or rather, embellished it, depending on one's viewpoint, reminding anyone who visited that the British had built their Empire on the trade they oversaw in Hong Kong. The port city gave them access to the world, and the world paid them handsomely. Even then, decades since the British relinquished their hold on the city, expats from across the world flocked to the freedom, the tax havens and the warm climate. The richest of the commonwealth brought their trade there, settling for the high quality of life and investment potential.

Still, the Chinese domination was becoming increasingly apparent in the city. Chinese millionaires and billionaires had based their businesses there, and their pleasure industries. To Glenn the whole city seemed like a hodgepodge of financial strongholds, tax evasion, sex tourism, business and gastronomy. Binding and blurring it all together was the humidity.

'Oh, the humidity!' yelped Eleanora, wiping sweat from her brow and wishing she had worn something lighter. 'How long is it until we get there?'

Glenn took out his phone and looked at the email Zu-Ting had sent him. She had given him an address which he had found on a map application. The walking route suggested half an hour if they passed through a market street. He led them towards a massive bazaar, a space that could rival the slums of Kolkata and Mumbai for its diversity of rich and poor states of being.

'Look how free they are to trade!' Eleanora exclaimed. 'They sell their wares and make their money, with no small thanks to the British.'

'How so?' Glenn asked his wife.

'Well, the British brought commerce to this city,' she said proudly. 'We brought trade and prosperity!'

Glenn highly doubted that the merchants they saw in the market that day were descended from men who had benefited from British rule. As far as he knew, the British ensured the lion's share of all profits went back to King and country. Moreover, the British influence his wife seemed so eager to point out seemed overshadowed now by a far greater power. It was no secret that Hong Kong, though on first glance it might look like a liberated colony, was no more than a satellite of China.

Nevertheless, the merchants sold their wares and tried to fleece them all the same. Men all around stood selling all sorts of things: imitation lighters, imitation cameras. It was all imitated, this and that, reshaped and manufactured in the cheapest possible way, but sporting the same renowned brand.

'How can these people survive on this?' Eleanora wondered aloud. 'Surely no one buys this trash?'

'It's the way of life,' shrugged Glenn, rather admiring the creativity that had gone into so much imitation. 'Someone must buy these things, otherwise why would they make them?'

Glenn was often predisposed to take the positive view, his wife the negative: a fine balance usually kept them both happy. More troubling to him than the trashy goods on sale were the dangerous looking youths eyeing up his wife's expensive bag.

'Just keep moving, OK?' he said in a low voice, placing a reassuring hand on her back. 'I'm not sure how safe we are here.'

'Ha!' cried Eleanora. 'These ruffians couldn't take us, even if they tried!'

Glenn was not so sure about that. There were many young people skirting the edges of stores selling silk scarves, 'Soney' tablets and 'iFones'. The imitation brands were quite hilarious. Big brands such as Samsung and Panasonic had been tweaked, though the products looked exactly the same.

'I thought Oxford Street was crowded,' Glenn had to laugh, weaving in and out of the busy shoppers and ducking beneath heavy, leather belts.

'Everything's in miniature though,' his wife appraised the ambience with a critical eye. 'It's like every little shop is a shelf in a department store. I must say, darling, this is all frightfully charming, but give me Harrods any day.'

Soon they arrived at a stretch of market that was far from the Harrods deli counter. A huge line of stalls sold all sorts of strange delicacies: fish, octopus, eels and heaps of dried, crispy meat. Behind the flashing piles of silver and tentacles, Eleanora shrieked as she saw a basket of snakes.

'Eugh!' she spat. 'They cannot eat snake, surely?'

'Snake good, snake nice with ketchup!' the old man behind the stall said enthusiastically. 'You want try, nice lady?'

'Certainly not,' Eleanora grimaced. 'But what about the little dogs? Won't the snakes attack them?'

'You want dog?' the man asked, surprised but eager to serve. 'He is for sale!'

'No thanks,' laughed Glenn.

'You want processed already?' the man asked, his grey whiskers perking up as he tested his salesmanship. 'We have them already processed, back in the fridge.'

'Processed?' asked Eleanora. 'What do you mean by *processed*?'

Glenn, however, knew the answer before it came.

'No head, no intestines,' said the man, blinking as he tried to understand Eleanora's ignorance.

'You eat dog?' she squeaked, her face paling.

'You prefer snake?' said the man, changing tack. 'I show you how we process. Very good, very clean: we take off the skin and then remove internal organs.'

'But a snake is full of venom!' she exclaimed. 'Full of poison.'

'No, no, that is just glands!' chuckled the old man. 'No problem!'

'Get me out of here,' Eleanora murmured to Glenn, holding a hand over her belly, clearly ready to throw up. Nodding, Glenn steered her quickly through the crowds, towards the end of the market street. Gasping, his wife shook her head.

'I hope this Zu-Ting has some good news for us, Hong Kong is really turning out to be the pits,' she said miserably.

'Come on, honey,' Glenn grinned at her. 'It's not all bad. Your hunky husband is with you, right?'

When they finally reached the end of the market street, Glenn saw on his smart phone that they had arrived at the location of Zu-Ting's factory.

'Strange,' he murmured, looking from his phone to the shop front they stood outside.

'What is, darling?' his wife asked.

'It's just that this is the address,' he said. 'But this doesn't look like a factory to me.'

They both looked into the fancy window of a boutique store. Necklaces and bracelets twinkled in their display cases. Glenn led Eleanora into the shop and glanced around. There were no signs of factory work anywhere.

'Welcome,' a voice called out. Glenn turned to see a small woman bowing to them. 'Can I help you, sir, or madam?'

'I'm sorry,' Glenn said quickly. 'I think we're in the wrong place. I'm looking for a factory or workshop of some kind, but that's clearly not here!'

'Clearly,' smiled the woman. 'Not here, at least. This is the salesroom and I am a saleswoman. But the factory you seek is here, sir.'

'But, this is a boutique,' stammered Glenn, glancing around once more to make sure he had not missed anything. 'Where? There's no room?'

The woman smiled at him.

'You are at the right address, sir,' she said calmly.

'You speak terribly good English for someone from, from... well, from here!' laughed Eleanora.

'I have an English father,' smiled the woman. 'My mother is Chinese. My name is Emmeline, by the way.'

'Hello, Emmeline,' Glenn smiled at her. 'Tell me, how does one squeeze a factory into five square metres?'

Emmeline laughed at this.

'With difficulty, I imagine!' she smiled. 'Tell me, have you come to see the factory?'

'Yes,' said Glenn.

'Do you have an appointment?' she asked.

'Yes,' Glenn nodded his head. 'We are here to see Zu-Ting.'

'Oh, you're here to see the boss!' she said in delight. 'I had best show you in then.'

Wondering where on earth 'in' could possibly be, Glenn and Eleanora watched as the saleswoman went to a nearby jewellery cabinet. Through the glass they could see emeralds, rubies and diamonds fixed delicately into gold and silver jewellery pieces. To their surprise, the cabinet began to move. Emmeline swung it open, revealing a large doorway leading into what looked like a fully functioning factory.

'How...?' Glenn breathed.

'Wow!' Eleanora cried.

It suddenly struck Glenn as they walked through that door that his wife had most likely never set foot in a factory before. She detested manual labour of any kind. But as they took in the scene in front of them, narrated by the whirrs and chatters of factory machinery, Glenn could see Eleanora was impressed. A huge table spread out along the back, seating at least one hundred people, fifty each side, each working away on a piece of jewellery. They all had small frames or gadgets in front of them, boxes of inventory and stones lying close by, jewellery waiting to be assembled. Glenn saw necklaces, bracelets, hanging pendants, rings and earrings to name but a few of the items being magnified and beautified on the table.

Glenn looked around, hoping to spot Zu-Ting, but he could not see her. Nor could Emmeline for she leant down and asked the first girl something in rapid Cantonese. The girl popped her head up from her task and pointed down the line, to the middle of the row.

'Ah,' smiled Emmeline. 'She is supervising! Come with me please.'

Glenn and Eleanora followed the saleswoman as she approached Zu-Ting, but before they had reached the boss, just metres away, Glenn saw her. He had forgotten just how beautiful the ICB's representative from Hong Kong was. Her long black hair was tied back elegantly in a bun and her skin looked as pale and soft as ever. Dressed in fashionable jeans and a smart blazer, Zu-Ting looked every inch the beautiful, young entrepreneur Glenn knew she was. Before Glenn or Emmeline could say anything, something remarkable happened.

Zu-Ting raised her head.

'Glenn?' she said. He couldn't hear her but he had read her lips. She was still staring straight ahead.

'I thought she was blind!' whispered Eleanora, surprised and perhaps slightly frightened by the girl's reaction.

'She is,' Glenn whispered back. 'But she recognises me. We met before, remember?'

'But…' Eleanora began. Glenn did not hear what his wife had to say next for he was already rushing to greet his friend.

'Zu-Ting!' he laughed. 'Thank you for letting us visit you in your factory. This is incredible!'

'You are most welcome, Glenn, and you are most welcome in Hong Kong!'

'My wife is here with me also,' Glenn replied.

'Welcome to our factory, Mrs. Tebbhurst.'

'Er, thank you,' said Eleanora awkwardly, not knowing where to look. 'It's just like a… well, a factory.'

'I couldn't have put it better myself!' laughed Zu-Ting. 'Come, we'll have to find some chairs. Yes, here. I have some chairs here in the back.'

Moving away from the buzz of the main work table, Glenn helped Zu-Ting to arrange a circle of three chairs. They settled into the seats and chatted for a while about their arrival, Zu-Ting's work, and first impressions of Hong Kong. After a while the talk turned to the factory and the work being done there.

'I can give you a tour if you like?' their host suggested.

'With pleasure,' smiled Glenn. 'How about that, honey?' he turned to his wife. 'A guided tour.'

'Marvellous, I'm sure,' Eleanora laughed nervously.

'Great,' laughed Zu-Ting. 'I'll introduce you to Ti-Pen, Sutang, and Moswang.'

Their host led them to each girl and they saw that each worker was doing something different. Glenn could not help but notice too that each of the girls was disabled in some way: one was blind, another could see but had been born disabled and lived in a wheelchair, and the third had polio. Nevertheless, they were assembling their pieces with exceptional speed and attention to detail, much to Eleanora's astonishment.

'But how!' she breathed. 'How can they assemble these tiny zircon diamonds into such minuscule frames? If they can't see, how do they know where to put everything?'

'This is the miracle of repetitive work,' said Zu-Ting proudly. 'But this is not a sweatshop, Mrs. Tebbhurst. We pay these women enough to be independent: we make sure they have enough money for rent, food, and comfort, and no one works more than eight hours a day. Their skill and prowess come from experience and discipline.'

'An exemplary employer,' Glenn nodded in approval.

'These are exemplary employees, Glenn,' Zu-Ting assured him, the passion ringing in her voice.

'I notice that many of these women have not had easy lives,' Glenn sighed, noticing the disabilities in the group.

'Indeed,' nodded Zu-Ting. 'Some are blind. Some are crippled. Even Emmeline, who you met on the front desk, suffered years ago from polio. This factory is a place for these women to receive equal opportunities and fair pay.'

'How admirable, giving them a chance!' Eleanora exclaimed loudly. Glenn winced; he knew how patronising her words might sound to Zu-Ting. But their host was eager to agree.

'Many women here have a story beyond their physical hardship,' she said proudly. 'I interviewed them all before I hired them. There are so many cases: some were orphans, others divorced with nowhere to go, some escaping an abusive relationship.' Zu-Ting paused and nodded. 'Yes, they are strong women, in need of support of course, but strong.'

'And you say they like the work?' Eleanora asked, more sceptical than Glenn.

'Look around you,' said Zu-Ting in a low, contented voice. 'Tell me what you see.'

'Mm, well,' Eleanora began, laughing awkwardly. Glenn gazed round too, taking in the cheerful, beaming faces; the high-spirited exchanges;

the efficiency of the work. He was no stranger to factories; in his line of work they were a common setting. Yet this was a factory with heart and soul bursting through it, and this nourished its production line, instead of intimidation and forced labour.

'Listen, there is still much to do here today,' said Zu-Ting. 'But by four o'clock, everyone goes home. I will leave here at four-thirty. If you like, can I invite you to dinner?'

'With pleasure!' said Glenn with a broad smile. 'Would seven-thirty work for you?'

'Yes, that is perfect,' grinned Zu-Ting. 'You said you were staying at The Hong Kong Palace? I'll make my way there.'

'Excellent,' said Glenn, allowing himself to be led off the factory floor by his gracious host. When they had said goodbye, and Eleanora had had one last look around the jewellery shop, they headed back out into the smog of the bustling city.

'You don't think she'll want to eat snake or dog, do you?' Glenn heard his wife ask him anxiously. He let out a belly-aching laugh.

'I have no idea,' he said, smiling, for in truth he did not.

CHAPTER EIGHTEEN

Relaxing in their hotel room that night, Glenn watched as Eleanora leant against the long stretch of glass at the window. The scene below was spectacular: The Hong Kong Palace commanded fantastic views across the large expanse of bay, and despite her misgivings about the city, Glenn's wife was becoming increasingly impressed by it. Hong Kong sprawled out before her eyes like an obedient, bowing servant. She took a sip of champagne and turned towards her husband. His eyes traced the lines of her body through her bathrobe.

'Do you feel refreshed?' Glenn asked her with a yawn. He was happy to be showered and relieved of the clinging sweat and pollution of the city.

'Exhausted more like,' she sighed. 'This place is full of misery.'

'It's how it is,' said Glenn, shrugging and feeling philosophical. 'It's a weird balance of yin and yang. I don't understand it either, this difference between the super-rich and super poor.'

'It's unpleasant,' said Eleanora.

'It's how it is, honey,' Glenn said once more, falling back into the crisp white sheets of the bed with a heavy sigh. 'Look, Hong Kong was home to two of the richest men in the world in the sixties and seventies. Pao built a fortune. He had twenty million tonnes of shipping load! It's not so uncommon here. Hong Kong has a tradition of super wealth, built through your British colonies. It's the fairy-tale fantasy location of big money, darling. Many dreams came true here.'

'Well I see a fairy-tale of poverty and misery,' she spat.

Glenn heard the disgust in her voice and wondered if Hong Kong was the right place for them to be continuing their renewed spring of marital bliss.

'Hey,' he said gently, gazing up from plump pillows. 'At least we're in the middle. Not super rich and certainly not super poor.'

'That's hardly something to celebrate,' she laughed dryly.

'Well, at least we're in love then,' he grinned. Eleanora turned from the window and, in turning, slipped out of her robe. Glenn's breath caught in his chest as he savoured the sight of his wife's body set against the stunning skyline beyond the window. In a few short steps Eleanora had reached the bed and climbed on, wrapping her legs around him.

'Let's make love then,' she whispered in his ear. 'Before we have to eat snakes or dogs or God knows what else.'

Glenn could barely breathe a word as his body succumbed to aching passion. The sun fell in the sky as the couple rediscovered the warm pleasures of each other's embrace, there in the cool of their air-conditioned suite.

* * * *

'Zu-Ting!' Glenn called out to his friend when he saw her waiting on a sofa in front of the reception desk. Glenn was not surprised to see her dressed so beautifully in fine scarlet and orange silks. Her dark hair tumbled down over her shoulders.

Glenn marvelled for a moment at Herbert Farrand's ability to attract the most beautiful women into his service, before turning to Eleanora, who followed him out of the lift. She too was a sight to behold. He held out an arm so his wife could take it, proud to be the man she chose to lean on. She had dressed up in a stunning midnight-blue dress, accompanied with a matching bag and fine stilettos.

The young Cantonese woman craned her neck and smiled when she heard Glenn's voice.

'Glenn, good evening. Good evening, Eleanora.' She stood up smoothly. 'I have a car waiting outside, forgive my presumption,' she grinned.

'Will we not be dining here?' Eleanora asked quickly, a hint of desperation in her voice. 'The restaurant is lovely! The chef is French – he is said to make exquisite food.'

BEAUTY IN THE DARK

'No, we are going to a surprise restaurant,' Zu-Ting smiled enthusiastically. 'I am your host after all. Let me show you Hong Kong.'

'Oh, are we dressed right for the occasion?' Eleanora asked awkwardly. There was a pause for a moment before she realised her mistake. 'Oh God! I am *so* sorry. Of course you can't see what we're wearing. I really can put my foot in it sometimes –'

'It's OK,' said Zu-Ting soothingly. 'You can wear anything you like.'

'Sounds great,' smiled Glenn. 'So, shall we?'

As they followed Zu-Ting through the hotel foyer, out towards the waiting car, Glenn felt his wife tugging on his sleeve.

'Yes?' he laughed, looking down at her.

'Do you really trust a blind girl's taste in restaurants?' she said in a hushed whisper.

'As a matter of fact, I do,' he grinned. 'This is fascinating, darling, do you know that a blind person's taste buds work ten times better than those of a person with sight? How incredible is that? Anyway, I think Zu-Ting's taste in restaurants is probably spot on, honey!'

As if sensing their concern, Zu-Ting turned and said, 'You do like Asian food, Mrs. Tebbhurst?' she called to Eleanora.

'Oh, er, well I'm partial to it once or twice I suppose?' Glenn's wife was blushing furiously. 'I mean, I've had Chinese once before, in Leicester Square. I didn't like it much…'

'Well, luckily for you we are not in China,' grinned Zu-Ting. 'Come, you'll love this place.'

They drove through the city at dusk, listening to Zu-Ting's titbits of tourist information. Glenn preferred to sit back and let the city wash over him than peer around at hotspots. After twenty minutes he noticed that they were drawing into the port of the city. Huge ships stood at bay, waiting to be loaded or shipped away.

'We're at the port,' he exclaimed.

'Yes,' smiled Zu-Ting. 'Can you smell the fresh, sea air? And the fish! Oh, the fish!'

'The port?' yelped Eleanora, who could indeed smell the fish, and found the stench unappealing.

'Yes,' Zu-Ting smiled at them once more. 'We're going to be dining on a boat.'

The car pulled up before an elegant, moored-up boat with a thousand twinkling lights and hanging flowers. They were whisked on deck and all around them smartly dressed *maître-d's* glided round, serving tables and welcoming new guests. Zu-Ting spoke to one of them in quick, polite Cantonese. The man nodded and led them quickly to a table overlooking the bay. Waves lapped gently at the side of the boat creating a very charming ambience.

Zu-Ting quickly launched into the history of the boat and her memories of the best meals she had eaten there. She began to list the names of the hundreds of dishes cooked in the kitchen, naming each for its own distinct taste. Glenn was soon distracted by something in the distance, however. Three waiters were touring the restaurant with a large fish tank set on a wheeled carriage. The carriage, stabilised with four wheels, was pushed by two men in the back, and led by another. The tank was at least two metres long, with perhaps two cubic metres of water gently sloshing against the glass sides. Within swam twenty to thirty fish of different shapes, colours and sizes.

'What's that?' Glenn asked Zu-Ting. 'Why are the waiters wheeling a fish tank around?'

'Why do you think?' she laughed. 'So we can choose a fish!'

With a sharp call in Cantonese, Zu-Ting beckoned the waiters to them. Hearing her signal, the men hurried along with their fishy carriage. Dressed in smart black suits, they quickly reassembled themselves into bows and stood attentively by the table.

'Good evening, honoured guests,' one said, bowing low. 'We bring you fish caught fresh today for your selection.'

'What's in there?' squeaked Eleanora, peeking into the tank warily.

'We have sea bass, sea bream, an exquisite John Dory, and a selection of red snappers,' another waiter answered in excellent English. 'Please tell us which fish you like and how you would like it to be cooked. We can cook it in four different sauces: *cajun*, a mixed spice or a *ciboulette* with spring onions. Alternatively we can simply fry the fish in oil and serve it with nothing more than fresh lemon and soy sauce?'

'Wow, look at that. It's quite the formality!' grinned Glenn, his mouth beginning to salivate at the list of fish and sauces available. 'Well, I'm damn hungry. I'll take the sea bass, though make it Western-style, will you? Just a bit of lemon is good for me.'

'Oh, Glenn, you should take the *ciboulette*,' Zu-Ting insisted. 'It will taste lovely, especially with the fresh spring onions.'

'That does sound good,' he considered. 'Alright. You heard the lady, fellas! Sea bass with *ciboulette* and a touch of soy for me.'

The waiters set to work immediately. The nearest waiter picked up a net and thrust it into the water to pull out a fresh sea bass. His aim was trained to be true and he caught the fish immediately. It flapped around in the net until the waiter passed it to his colleague, who drew what looked like a sword from his belt and took the fish in his hand. In one deft movement, he slashed the side of the fish and cut out a filet, tossing it straight from the fish into the frying pan. To Glenn's surprise, and Eleanora's horror, the waiter then tossed the fish straight back into the fish tank where it swam lethargically.

'My God!' Eleanora cried, letting out a sharp scream. 'But it's dead!'

Glenn watched as the fish writhed around, a stream of cloudy, red blood trailing it. Meanwhile one waiter began to cook the fillet in a hot pan, delicious aromas rising up as he worked.

'That's horrific!' his wife squeaked once more.

'When in Rome,' chuckled Glenn, who seemed to be more amused than horrified by the incident.

'You must be squeamish?' Zu-Ting laughed at Eleanora.

'He put that bloody fish right back in the tank!' whispered Eleanora. 'It's inhumane! It's unthinkable.'

'You must not know much about Chinese history, Mrs. Tebbhurst,' laughed the young woman, staring into space as if looking back in time. 'Do you really think a people who have died and killed in their millions in countless wars of independence feel touched by the bloody sight of a dead fish?'

'She's right, honey,' laughed Glenn. 'You won't find much sympathy here. But let's not get Zu-Ting started on politics. I recall swearing to her that I would become a citizen of Hong Kong just so I could vote for her if she ever ran for office!'

'I haven't forgotten, Glenn,' smiled Zu-Ting.

'Well, I don't think *that* is likely,' sighed Eleanora.

'Me running for office?' Zu-Ting asked, suddenly proud.

'No!' laughed Eleanora. 'Heavens, no! Glenn becoming a citizen of Hong Kong!'

However, when the fish was cooked and served to Glenn on a plate, adorned with fresh lemon and a delicious sauce, Eleanora's husband wondered whether he could get used to such a diet. Tasting a bit whilst the women ordered their fish confirmed the succulent freshness of the catch. It was delicious.

'So, are you going to tell me why you've come to Hong Kong now?' Zu-Ting asked between dainty mouthfuls of red snapper and rice. 'I'm very curious. You didn't say much in your email. Why were you visiting Elfrida in Acapulco?'

'That's a very good question,' Glenn smiled, setting down his fork before launching into his story. He told Zu-Ting all that had come to pass since they had met at the conference in Aachen: the deterioration of his father's optimism, his idea for the case studies, his visits to Laura, Odile, and Elfrida, and all he had learnt in those trips.

'He's made it his mission to visit you all,' Eleanora added with a small laugh. 'Imagine! He's trotting around the globe with his little notepad, writing down your stories as he goes. Look, here it is now!'

Glenn's wife had caught sight of the notepad and pen he had placed on the table. Glenn laughed.

'I'm becoming a fine reporter,' he chuckled. 'Nora's right, Zu-Ting. I'm writing down stories as I go, and so far they have been incredible. Every one of you six women I met in Aachen has led an extraordinary life. The world needs to know about it, and with your help, I would love to convince the board at the Diversified Charities Foundation to support you girls in your work. To do that I need to make a solid case.'

'Wow, Glenn,' Zu-Ting nodded, clearly impressed. 'You're a real hero, do you know that?'

'I just want to help,' he said, leaning back in his chair as if to lean away from the praise. 'I want my father to understand what it means to accept blindness and let light back into his life once more.'

'He's my hero,' cooed Eleanora, leaning over to stroke her husband's cheek. 'Isn't he perfect? And my, isn't this fish fresh? How deliciously fresh!'

All fears of bloodied waters were gone it seemed, for Eleanora was tucking into her meal with gusto. Glenn was glad to see her so content and was glad that he could share his fourth meeting with the six women from Aachen with his wife.

'So now you know why I'm here,' he said, looking Zu-Ting directly in the eye. 'Would you feel comfortable sharing your story with me, with us?'

Zu-Ting took a deep breath and turned away from Glenn for a moment. Though she was blind, Glenn sensed that she needed to look away. Her face seemed to cloud with memories from the past. Eleanora looked as though she was about to say something, but Glenn stopped her with a look. He knew their host was simply preparing, and soon enough she took a deep breath to announce the start of her story.

'I was enslaved for many years,' she began. 'I lived in a factory, making mobile telephones. It was eye-watering work. Every day we worked on the minuscule infrastructure with little to no light reaching us in the basement. For eighteen hours a day, from the age of eight onwards.'

'And your family?' Glenn asked. 'Did they approve of this work?'

'Yes,' Zu-Ting nodded. 'They had no choice really. We were very poor. There were five children, too many mouths to feed, no matter how hard my father worked.'

Glenn remembered Elfrida's story in Acapulco and was grateful at least that Zu-Ting's father had worked. Still, he could not imagine what level of poverty would drive a father to sell his daughter into near slavery.

'For years I worked in that basement,' she said bitterly. 'I prayed for delivery, for escape, but I was bound by duty and honour. Like all the others there, working away, I knew it was my fate to work day after day.'

'Were you blind from birth?' Glenn asked, scribbling down in his notepad as she spoke.

'No,' she said, shaking her head. 'They took my eyes. They took my freedom, my sunlight, my family, and then, like lights going out, they took my sight. A disease infected my eyes and there was no doctor. I was blind by the age of fifteen. That was when I knew things had to change; I knew if no one was coming to save me, I had to save myself.'

'What did you do?' Eleanora asked, gasping at various points in the young woman's story.

'I heard of factory girls like me receiving help from foreigners in the city,' she said. 'Hong Kong is very international, as you know. I knew many people were working here from countries where life was different. I had heard tales of human rights, of worker's rights, of fair wages and working hours. These stories were like myths to us, like the legends of old China. "Don't be a fool, Zu-Ting!" the other girls scolded me. "Those white people will not help you! They are too busy! They do not care for the likes of you!" they said. But I did not listen. When I went blind I became less capable so the factory owners reduced my hours and made me peel onions in the kitchen instead. This was good for me because I could slip away in the daytime and look for the people I knew could help me.'

'Which people?' Glenn asked, his pen poised and his curiosity piqued.

'I went to the embassies,' said Zu-Ting. 'I asked people to lead me there. They took pity on me, a poor blind girl, and helped me on my way. I went first to the British Embassy, then to the American, French and German embassies. I told them what I had lived through, what I had suffered, how I had lost my eyes and my childhood, and offered to work for them.'

'What did they say?' Glenn asked.

'They said no, of course,' she grimaced. 'But they offered me the addresses of charities to write to for help.'

'And you wrote to them?' Glenn asked.

'They wrote for me,' she grinned. 'They recorded my life story. I stood there until they had written every last bit down in a letter of some kind: every hardship, every painful detail. Every week I went back to ask if there was a response. The people in the embassies came to know me by name. Some were more welcoming than others. In the end, the American embassy asked me to stop returning there. But that did not stop me. I always returned. For many months there was nothing, until one day, I was at the German Embassy. A kind woman told me of a charity in Frankfurt that had taken some interest in my case.'

Glenn had a feeling he knew who was responsible for that.

'The ICB?' he asked.

'Exactly,' grinned Zu-Ting. 'They wanted to meet me. A representative flew over from Frankfurt and waited for me at the German Embassy. I think you know who it was, Glenn.'

'Bettina,' he nodded.

'Ah, this Bettina again,' said Eleanora, raising an eyebrow. 'She does pop up everywhere, doesn't she?'

'Yes, Bettina,' Zu-Ting smiled. 'Another hero, or heroine rather. Bettina arrived and asked to be shown the conditions in which I was working. I took her to the factory, by the back entrance, where no one would spot us, and gave her a sense of the place.'

'But she was blind,' said Glenn, confused by this part of the story.

'Yes, but one does not need eyes to feel the heavy weight of injustice, nor sense the bonds of indenture,' said Zu-Ting. 'Bettina understood the situation immediately, and that same day moved me into the safety of her hotel. I stayed with her for some weeks and she proposed that I help her create a new factory, where people living with blindness or other handicaps could earn a fair wage. This whole concept was to be funded by the ICB in Frankfurt.'

'How did you feel when Bettina proposed this?' Glenn asked her.

'I thanked every god I had ever heard of that Bettina Hartmann had come to Hong Kong,' Zu-Ting said, beaming at the memory. 'I agreed that day, and for the past eight years of my life I have been turning that vision into a reality.'

'Your factory is fully funded by the ICB?' Glenn asked Zu-Ting.

'Not any more,' she shook her head. 'Now we are producing good products at a good rate. We make profits that keep the factory going. Any proceeds beyond the wages and expenses of the business go into new expansion, new hiring, or otherwise back to the ICB.'

'A nice model,' said Glenn, thinking as a businessman and fundraiser for a moment. Creating a self-sustaining factory that honoured the initiatives of the ICB and also had the potential to bring in revenue was a smart and sophisticated strategy. Bettina was more of a businesswoman than he thought, Glenn smiled to himself. Perhaps Laura, with her business degree from the London Business School, had helped Bettina fine-tune the framework. But surely this was before Bettina found Laura in London, Glenn pondered. In which case the genius must have come from Bettina and Herbert Farrand.

'You seem thoughtful, Glenn,' Zu-Ting smiled at him.

'I am,' laughed Glenn. 'I can't stop thinking about how amazing you women are. And now my wife here can finally understand why I'm so crazy about your stories.'

'Oh, forgive my husband!' laughed Eleanora, clearly uncomfortable. 'He's terribly American about these things. Very emotional and over-zealous, that sort of thing.'

'Can't a guy express awe?' asked Glenn, shaking his head at his wife's stuffiness in the face of his compliment.

'I dare say you can express anything, darling,' Eleanora smiled sweetly at the man by her side.

'Well, anyway,' sighed Glenn. 'It's been an honour to hear your story, Zu-Ting. And great to hear about some honest, ethical business going on in this town.'

'You've noticed the problems we have here in the city then?' their host asked Glenn.

'The poverty and the wealth, side by side?' asked Glenn. 'It's hard not to notice.'

'It's appalling,' said Eleanora with great distaste. 'To think this was once British overseas territory!'

'Well, in many ways it is still British overseas territory,' Zu-Ting laughed darkly. 'In all but name.'

'What do you mean?' asked Eleanora, and Glenn could have sworn he saw a glimmer of hope in her eyes.

'Well, with all the British investment over here,' Zu-Ting answered. 'This is a tax haven. It's an easy place to run a capitalist company. Some of the biggest companies in the world started up here, and continue to benefit from Hong Kong's position in the world. So rest assured, Mrs. Tebbhurst, the British are still thriving in – and benefitting from – this unique city.'

'Yes, well,' sniffed Eleanora. 'It's not *quite* the same as calling it our own, is it?'

'Darling,' Glenn said in a gentle warning tone.

'What, darling?' Eleanora snapped back. 'Thatcher made a bloody fool of the whole country when she let Hong Kong go. The "Handover" was a silly mistake.'

'It's funny,' said Zu-Ting coolly. 'In China, they like to call it the "Return". Curious difference, no?'

'I'm a bit hazy on the details,' said Glenn. 'When exactly did Hong Kong come back to China?'

'Darling, you're usually so good at history!' exclaimed his wife.

'Sorry, honey!' he laughed. 'But come on, when have you ever missed a chance to educate me?'

'True,' she smiled. 'Well, whatever you want to call it, the British Empire took one last blow in 1997, when Hong Kong was ceded back to China. We ruled Hong Kong island from 1842, taking the Kowloon Peninsula in 1860 and a lease of New Territories in 1898.'

'The New Territories were only leased to the British for ninety-nine years, however,' said Zu-Ting. 'By the time that lease had come to an end, the New Territories had become inextricably part of what we now know as Hong Kong, with all the developments and infrastructure imaginable spreading across the territory. It would no longer be possible for the British to return the New Territories and keep their other territories as they were impossible to separate. Meanwhile, since

China had been discussing the sovereignty of Hong Kong for decades, pressure was growing from the international community. The People's Republic of China wanted it back, and took it!'

'And the British couldn't do anything about it,' Glenn nodded.

'Yes they damn well could have!' snapped Eleanora. 'Pathetic politicians were sent to do a hard job, and they failed.'

'China is a difficult force to withstand,' Zu-Ting said quietly. 'Many people here in Hong Kong will tell you that.'

'Pah, bloody shambles!' was all Eleanora could say. 'A lack of spine, that was all it was. Pure cowardice!'

'And yet the people of Hong Kong are glad that the British were here,' said Zu-Ting. 'Now we have learned the business language of the world, English, and we do not suffer the socialism of our neighbours in China.'

'Well, that's something at least,' Glenn's wife scoffed miserably. 'But ultimately it was a terribly regrettable loss.'

'Honey,' Glenn warned her once more.

'What, darling?' she snapped. 'Has the world turned so entirely upside down that one must hold one's tongue on any issue regarding ex-colonies?'

'I'd say it could be wise,' Zu-Ting said gently. 'You've seen how they kill fish now, Mrs. Tebbhurst. Here in the "ex-colonies" we have a terrible history of barbarianism, you know.'

Glenn laughed at this and shook his head.

'Excuse our Western ignorance, Zu-Ting,' he said. 'You have been the loveliest host in this great city.'

'You are very welcome here, Glenn,' she smiled. The conversation then turned to lighter topics, and business, as Zu-Ting enquired about Glenn's work in London. They both agreed that collaboration between the DCF and the ICB could only be beneficial for all.

'I'm surprised you haven't spoken to Bettina since Aachen,' said Zu-Ting. 'You two were very friendly if I recall correctly?'

Glenn smiled at the memory of his time with Bettina in Aachen.

'I'm sure she'll be next on his list of women to visit,' Eleanora sighed dismissively.

Glenn said nothing however. He knew he would have to approach Bettina eventually regarding the proposal, but for the time being, he was keen to learn more about her role supporting the other five women.

'Bettina is the glue who keeps is all together, really,' Zu-Ting smiled fondly at the thought of her friend. Glenn closed his notepad, satisfied that he had learnt all he needed to learn from Zu-Ting regarding her life story. After a few rounds of tea, Glenn assured his host that she would always be welcome in London.

'Come and visit us some time,' he grinned. 'If you can leave your factory for a break, that is.'

'Funny, isn't it,' Zu-Ting smiled. 'When I was enslaved, I dreamed of days off and time to travel and explore the world. Now that I am free to take holidays, I don't want to go! I love my workers too much.'

Eleanora laughed nervously at the concept of work being so central to a person's life.

'Charming,' she said. 'Well, do come over if you can get away.'

They left the restaurant and drove back to the hotel, where Zu-Ting bid the couple a warm farewell. Glenn let Eleanora excuse herself quickly and return to the room so he could have a moment with Zu-Ting.

'I'm sorry for my wife's comments,' he said quietly. 'She doesn't travel much.'

'It's OK,' laughed Zu-Ting. 'We're used to it here. Thanks for coming, Glenn. It means a lot to me. More than I can say.'

They shook hands and Glenn waved his friend off. When her taxi had rounded the corner, he breezed through the lobby and made for the lift. When he opened the door to the hotel room, he was surprised to find his wife already packing her bags.

'Ready to leave already?' he asked her.

'Well, darling, there will be a flight to London in the morning and there's no point delaying really, is there?' she said, folding a dress into the case.

'I'll be happy to get home,' Glenn admitted. 'All this travelling is exhausting.'

'Amongst other things,' his wife said, turning towards him, her blue eyes sparkling with mischief. 'I think I'll pack this away too,' she said, reaching up to the top of her back and unzipping her dress. In one graceful movement, the elegant dress fell away, leaving her naked body behind.

'I thought the fish executions tonight might have put you off!' Glenn laughed, allowing himself to be pulled onto the bed.

'Nonsense,' she whispered. 'I want you, Glenn. All these women thinking you're a hero, it's really rather a turn on.'

'Really?' Glenn smiled. He put his hand to her neck and swept her hair away. 'Kiss me, then.'

Eleanora kissed her husband and the force of her passion drew them deep into each other. As she lay sleeping in his arms hours later, sated and more exhausted than ever, Glenn smiled. No matter what Eleanora thought of Hong Kong, he mused, her attraction to him was getting stronger and stronger by the day.

CHAPTER NINETEEN

Arriving back at Ronda Round Manor was a relief for Glenn for the first time in years. Usually when he arrived back from a work trip it was to a lukewarm welcome from his wife, and snooty glances from the ancient portraits of the Beaumont ancestors staring down at him on the walls. But this time, with Eleanora tucked affectionately beneath his arm, he led them through the front door like a groom leading his bride over the threshold of their new home. This was the depth of renewal he felt in his heart, body and soul.

'Shall we have dinner?' Glenn suggested, wondering if he should quickly head down to the Thomases' to see if the estate tenants had any fresh eggs or cured meats available.

'I'd rather go straight to bed,' Eleanora grinned at her husband.

'Your wish is my command,' he laughed.

So, like teenagers, the two slipped back into their bed, long-abandoned due to years of disinterest, and made love at the manor once more. Unlike the wild, exotic nights they had spent in Mexico and Hong Kong, that night was tender and gentle, a return to the loving embraces of lovers who have known each other's bodies as long as they have known their own.

Returning to the office was suddenly an unpleasant prospect to Glenn, who usually looked forward to the routine and purpose his work gave him. But the routine and purpose of satisfying his wife was now far more appealing than the commute into Cheapside. Not only that, but he realised how the commuter crowds of London were bursting full of negative energy – something he had become blind to, and perhaps even part of those last few years – which left Glenn at that moment longing to be back in his wife's arms, kissing her neck and caressing her silky legs.

'Good morning, sir,' came Sonia's cheerful greeting as he walked into the office. It took him by surprise for he had been walking in a daze for the past half hour. 'Welcome back. I trust you enjoyed your trip?'

'Yes, very much,' he said, nodding at his secretary with a smile.

'And did your wife accompany you to Hong Kong, sir?' she asked him.

'My wife?' asked Glenn, wondering if Sonia could see their wild lovemaking across the globe sketched in his eyes.

'Yes, sir,' she said. 'She contacted me for your address in Acapulco?'

'Ah, yes, of course,' smiled Glenn. 'She did indeed. We had a pleasant trip.'

'Very good, sir,' she said, nodding happily. 'Now, I've left any post and paperwork on your desk, all dated and prioritised accordingly, and have cleared your schedule for this morning's meeting.'

'What meeting?' asked Glenn, unaware that he had arranged any meetings for his first day back. He had assumed he would be swimming through a sea of paperwork all day, attempting to catch up on all he had missed in the past fortnight.

'The board meeting,' said Sonia. 'I faxed the details to your home office on Friday?'

Glenn pictured his home office, abandoned since before his trip, and untouched since he had returned. His normal habit was to spend a few hours in the office once returning from a business trip, but this return had been different. He and Eleanora had barely left their bed all weekend.

'I must have missed it,' he said. 'But this is unusual. I met with the board only recently and we're not due to meet for another few weeks?'

'I know, sir,' said Sonia. 'But this is a special meeting with senior board members, called to discuss the work you have been doing for the ICB.'

'Really?' Glenn exclaimed, utterly taken aback to hear the news. He had expected it would be a long, hard slog to convince senior colleagues that the International Charity for the Blind would be worth supporting. Now they were instigating the meeting.

'*Really*,' smiled Sonia. 'You should probably head up now.'

As the elevator climbed the several floors up to the boardroom, Glenn was curious to know why the board had taken such premature interest in his project. As far as he knew, the only people who knew about his case studies were his colleagues in the International Department, and none of them had access to his precious notebook, where the stories were safely tucked away. Glenn felt for the notebook, which he kept in his breast pocket, and flicked it open in the elevator. Inside were countless scribblings collected from Laura, Odile, Elfrida and now Zu-Ting; traces of his time on the continents – smudges of ink, splashes of sauce, films of dust and drops of sweat – scattered the pages.

Glenn found the boardroom already headed by Florence Valon, the secretary of the board. A formidable woman, Florence had tied her mousy blonde hair back in a tight bun and wore a smart suit. She sat with her hands crossed, drinking a coffee and gazing out of the window across the Thames. When she heard Glenn enter the room, she spun her chair around to face him.

'Ah, Mr. Tebbhurst,' she intoned with a small smile. 'Glad you've come back to us. We've been waiting for your return.'

'Florence,' Glenn nodded, leaning over to shake her hand. As a board member, he had known Florence for almost a decade now, and yet no matter how hard he tried to engineer some small talk, still she remained stiffly professional. 'Forgive me, I only heard about the meeting this morning.'

'Well, we've wanted to speak to *you* for some time,' she smiled. 'Take a seat, the others will join us shortly.'

Glenn settled himself at the large table and looked out across the city. It was a far cry from Hong Kong, he thought, but knew that much of the wealth the British made in in the former dependency had funded the flourishing and expansion of the British capital. He did not have long to peruse such thoughts, however, as a stream of men filed into the room. Glenn recognised the first three figures: Derek Scott, a banker-turned-philanthropist; Nick Davis, an oil man, and Chris Hodges, a contemporary artist. The three familiar gentlemen, alongside Glenn, were present at any big decision making meetings at Diversified Charities, and all of them were coordinated by Florence. The man who followed them in, however, was unfamiliar to Glenn. The only thing he recognised about the man was the cane he carried: it was an aluminium white walking cane, used only by the blind.

'Glenn, you know Scott, Davis, and Hodges, so let's not waste time on introductions,' said Florence in her commanding tones. 'But you will not know Mr. James. I'll allow you to introduce yourselves.'

Glenn hovered awkwardly, not knowing whether or not to attempt to shake the man's hand. He decided against it, assuming the man would not see a hand to shake anyway. His face looked familiar somehow but Glenn could not place him.

'Glenn Tebbhurst,' he said. 'I am a board member and assist the allocation of funds to major international projects. Have we met before?'

'Probably,' said the man. 'Samuel James is my name, Mr. Tebbhurst. I work in operations.'

'On the third floor?' Glenn asked, a vague memory pushing into his mind. 'Samuel James from operations? Didn't you run the half-marathon for us two years ago?'

'I did,' the man grinned suddenly, making him look ten years younger. His distant stare did not waver.

'I thought I recognised you,' Glenn smiled kindly. The last time he had met Mr. James the man had been fully seeing. He had been athletic and alert. The man standing before him now was quite the opposite: he was fragile, thin and clearly nervous.

'Mr. James is attending the meeting today,' said Florence. 'Come, Mr. James, take a seat. Let us begin.'

Florence proceeded to run through the agenda of the meeting which would feature a discussion of the budget, a progress report from Glenn regarding his current projects, and an open discussion about future investments and operations. When they finally reached this final stage, Nick Davis turned to Glenn.

'We are all intrigued to hear more about the research you have been doing, Glenn,' said Davis, a charismatic man in his late forties. 'I am sure Mr. James here will be interested too.'

'Well, I've been following up on a charity I discovered for personal reasons over a year ago,' said Glenn, preparing to launch into his story. Choosing his words carefully, Glenn told the board about his father's blindness, conscious all the time that Samuel James sat opposite him and had presumably suffered the same fate: a sudden loss of sight. He told them about the conference in Aachen and his response to the Living with Blindness philosophy upheld by the organisation.

'It's this concept that struck me most,' he said, pausing for a moment to reflect on the ideas he had learnt in the workshops. 'The prospect of embracing and accepting blindness in order to live a happy and fulfilled life.'

'And since then you have been researching this charity?' Derek Scott asked him. The banker had a shrewd, calculating gaze which was often difficult to endure for too long. Glenn nodded.

'Yes, in a way,' he continued. 'I have been meeting with the six members who ran the workshops over there, visiting each of them in their local context. One was here in London, another in New Orleans, one more in Mexico and most recently another in Hong Kong. Each woman has led an extraordinary life and I have tried my best to capture the key elements of their stories.'

'They are all women?' Chris Hodges asked, a curious intellectual whose neat appearance contrasted with his creative mind.

'Yes,' smiled Glenn. 'Six incredible women. I have only been able to interview four so far, but the result has been powerful. Each one of these women has experienced great hardship through their disability, but given the chance, has dedicated her life now to improving the experiences of other blind people in their community. Acceptance and adaptability is the thread that binds them all together.'

Bettina too was a thread that bound them all together, thought Glenn, but he didn't mention it then. He took out his little notebook and began to read fragments of the girls' stories, leafing through the pages and pausing on particularly powerful anecdotes.

'Fascinating,' nodded Davis.

'Inspiring,' said Scott.

'And is there a medical branch of the ICB?' Florence asked him.

'In what sense?' asked Glenn.

'Do they provide corrective treatment?' she asked him.

'Well, no,' said Glenn. 'That's kind of the point. They encourage, facilitate and train people to live with blindness on a daily basis, without the need for surgery or change.'

'No treatments at all?' asked Davis.

'No,' Glenn shook his head.

'Ah,' said Florence, frowning slightly. Glenn saw Samuel James shifting uncomfortably in his seat.

'Is that a problem?' Glenn asked.

'Perhaps we should explain why Mr. James is attending the meeting today?' said Derek Scott. 'Get the ball rolling?'

'Certainly,' said Florence. 'Glenn, Mr. James has joined us today because earlier this year he had an accident. Perhaps you would like to share your story, Mr. James? I daresay it will be one more for Mr. Tebbhurst's notebook.'

Glenn watched as Samuel James nodded. He was a young man, in his late twenties perhaps, though his newfound disability made him look older.

'I'm a rugby player,' he said. 'I've played it since I was twelve years old. I'm a natural hooker, but play defence sometimes. Played, anyway. Earlier this year I took a huge shock to the head in a rugby scrum. I blacked out and was taken to hospital. When I woke up my vision was blurry, and at first I thought it was the drugs. But when things stayed foggy, I told the doctors. I hoped they would be able to do something. After a month there was no improvement. You see, my vision has gone from 20/20 to 12/20. I'm like a cripple now.'

Glenn watched Samuel James as he spoke and could clearly imagine the man he had been before his blindness. Sporty, fun and desperate to move around. This vision loss had clearly damaged his spirit. His use of the word 'cripple' spoke a thousand words.

'What did the doctors say?' Glenn asked him. 'Did they give you some indication of what had happened?'

'They said the trauma had damaged the optic nerve,' he said. 'They said I will probably never be able to see fully again.'

'But Mr. James does not want to accept that,' Florence cut in with a sweep of her hand. 'And as a DCF employee, we are happy to sponsor his recovery.'

'Which is why we have been in discussions with the Japanese regarding a treatment available to improve his vision,' said Scott.

'New treatment?' said Glenn. 'But the doctors told Mr. James the damage was irreparable?'

'According to *them*, Glenn,' said Hodges. '*We've* looked further afield.'

'This is a new treatment,' said Florence. 'If the operation is successful, we could look into ways of partnering with this International Charity for the Blind by offering to sponsor such operations.'

'But if it's unsuccessful…' Glenn began, not wanting to state the obvious.

'Mr. James himself has volunteered to undergo the operation,' said Davis. 'That shows some faith, huh?'

'How does the operation even work?' Glenn asked.

'I sense a sceptic!' laughed Scott. 'Well, they use a micro-camera to scrape protein from the area where protein is accumulated and has often caused loss of vision. It's a £20,000 operation and we are willing to pay.'

'We are happy to put forward the sponsorship money as an investment in not only Mr. James's life, so he can live normally once more and play rugby again, but also in future cases of blindness,' said Davis. 'This could be revolutionary, Glenn! The DCF could sponsor this treatment for many more people to come.'

'Where will the operation take place?' Glenn asked them all.

'There's an Anglo-American clinic specialising in ophthalmology here in the city,' said Samuel James.

'The American O Clinic,' said Scott. 'For the visually impaired.'

'And it's a good clinic?' Glenn asked. 'It's been investigated?'

'Naturally,' said Florence, putting her hands together, and looking impatiently at Glenn.

'It's world-class healthcare,' said Davis, nodding approvingly.

The board room was buzzing with excitement and Glenn could sense it, especially because he could did not feel it. The one man he had not heard much from was the man who would undergo this operation.

'Are you sure about this, Samuel?' Glenn asked tenderly. 'I'm sure there are others who would try. It could be risky.'

'No, I'd like to,' said Samuel James quickly. 'I don't want to live like this,' he said, gesturing at his white cane and his eyes with a pained expression. Glenn felt his heart contract for a moment as he remembered his father's expressions of unhappiness and longing for the sight he had lost. He knew he should advise caution, suggest coping mechanisms, tell inspiring stories about workshops in the dark, but somehow the young man's depleted youth caught in his heart.

'Alright,' said Glenn, nodding before turning to the rest of the board. 'It would seem you have unanimous support here. If all are agreed then we sponsor the operation.'

'I knew we could count on your support, Glenn!' laughed Scott. 'Then it's arranged, we are all in agreement. The operation will be performed in a private clinic on Harley Street.'

'Who is the doctor?' Glenn asked.

'Dr. Alicia Slaughter,' Samuel James answered.

'A rather unusual name for a surgeon,' Hodges raised an eyebrow.

'Indeed,' frowned Glenn.

'It's just a name,' Florence reassured them. 'Her qualifications are exceptional and she studied this specific operation first-hand in Tokyo, in three different hospitals over there.'

The meeting was drawn to a conclusion, and Glenn shook Samuel James's hand.

'Good luck,' he said. It crossed his mind to say more but he remembered that Samuel James was not his father. He was not asking for Glenn's optimism or advice about his blindness, only the financial support for the operation.

'Thank you, Mr. Tebbhurst,' said the young man, his pale face bright with happiness. 'This operation means the world to me. Who knows, hopefully I might finally be able to have my old life back.'

Bidding his fellow board members goodbye, Glenn headed back to his office to start his paperwork. He bumped into Natasha on the way, who greeted him with a smile.

'I heard they took an interest in your case studies up in the board room?' she said. 'That's great, Glenn!'

Glenn did not feel like telling his colleague that the board had taken very little interest in his case studies. The goal of the ICB, as a facilitator of blind rehabilitation, seemed totally lost on the board members who seemed entirely focused on cures and miracle technologies – perhaps because that's where the money was, he wondered with suspicion. Nevertheless, Glenn hoped for Samuel James's sake that the operation would be successful. After all, if it worked for him, perhaps it could work for his father.

* * * *

The operation was planned for the following week, and the prospect of it filled Glenn with hope. Though he had never really spoken to the man from operations, he now was starting to feel a great affinity with him. When the day for the operation came, he went to visit Samuel James in hospital before surgery. He was propped up in bed dressed in the customary white hospital gown, and surrounded by his friends and family. His girlfriend, a pretty young lady with shoulder-length blonde hair, looked nervous and excited. She introduced herself to Glenn and conveyed her optimism.

'We're so grateful to the DCF for funding this operation,' she said. 'Thank you, so much. We're cautiously optimistic, we really are.'

'Come off it – "cautiously" – our boy will be back out on the pitch in no time!' his Dad cried in a broad cockney accent. 'No more scrums for him perhaps, but he'll be playing again, I promise you that.'

'Not for a while, Dad. Anyway, let's not get ahead of ourselves,' chuckled the young man.

'How are you feeling?' Glenn asked him.

'OK, thanks,' Samuel replied. 'I just want it to be over with, to be honest. I want to have my sight back again. I want to be able see the faces of these amazing people around me.'

'And within a week that should be the case,' came a voice from the corner of the room.

They all turned to see a tall, thin woman wearing a white coat standing in the doorway. Her dark brown hair was tossed back into a ponytail and she was looking at them all with intelligent brown eyes.

'I am Dr. Slaughter,' she said, introducing herself to Samuel James's parents and to Glenn. 'Your son is the first person in the United Kingdom to undergo this surgery.'

'He's always been a brave lad,' Samuel James's father said proudly.

'You missed the description of the surgery earlier,' his girlfriend laughed. 'It's pretty gruesome. It involves a camera attached to a scraper which goes right inside the eye, under full anaesthesia, and scrapes proteins from behind the eye.'

After this, Glenn shook the doctor's hand and wished them all luck before turning to leave. The one person he noticed who was not smiling was Samuel's mother. She had the same anxious look of fear in her eyes as his own mother. Glenn dealt her a reassuring smile and headed out of the room, willing the operation to go off without a hitch.

Arriving home later that evening, Glenn found Eleanora curled up on the sofa, perusing a copy of her monthly *Horse and Hound*. Slipping down beside her, he kissed his wife and sighed.

'You're back late,' she murmured, stroking his hair. This was a new affectionate gesture she had adopted since their return from Hong Kong. Glenn savoured the sensation of her fingers brushing gently over his forehead.

'I wanted to see our guinea pig before his operation,' he said.

'And how was he?' she asked.

'Relieved,' he answered, remembering Samuel's excited eyes.

'And how do you feel?' she asked.

'Hopeful,' Glenn answered after some reflection. 'That's all. I don't know, something seems a little – Oh, it doesn't matter. Actually, you know, doing things like this, helping people, it really gives me a time to pause and be thankful. I'm not a doctor, but I can still make a difference, you know? A big difference in someone's life.'

'Oh, of course you do. That is what your job is all about. Now, are you going to stop talking about work and kiss me anytime soon?' she cooed in his ear. Glenn grinned.

'Come here then, you,' he chuckled, pulling Eleanora into his arms.

That night they made love and Glenn slept with the excitement of a child awaiting Christmas morning. He woke at sunrise and went out for a run, happy to feel endorphins pumping around his body. When he reached the office an hour later, Glenn was walking with a spring in his step. He decided he would track down Amelia for a chat by her tea trolley before she made her rounds on other floors, wondering if she might have any cake for him today.

'Morning, Sonia,' he called cheerfully through to his secretary, hanging up his coat and heading straight to his desk.

'Sir,' he heard Sonia's voice. Surprised to hear the tone, he turned to look at his secretary. Her face was pale and she held the phone in her hand.

'What is it?' he asked, looking from her to the receiver.

'Mr. Tebbhurst, it's the hospital,' she said.

'Dad?' Glenn breathed.

'No, it's Mr. James,' she said, shaking her head. 'The operation did not go well.'

Glenn's heart sank like a stone as he drove towards the clinic where the operation had taken place the night before. Sonia had been told very little, simply that the operation had been unsuccessful and that Samuel James was still recovering. When he arrived, he saw Samuel James surrounded by his family. His girlfriend, who had been so excited and perky the night before, now looked tired and drained. Her eyes were red from crying. Glenn felt awkward being there, not a family member, but concerned all the same. Turning away, he decided to go somewhere he could find answers.

Dr. Slaughter looked tired behind her desk.

'Come in,' she said when she saw who had knocked on her door. 'I suppose you're here to tell me I'm being sued?'

Glenn entered and closed the door behind him.

'What happened?' he asked, taking in the doctor's weary expression and nervous shaking. She shook her head.

'There were complications,' she sighed. 'The surgery has risks, as Mr. James knew. We scraped away the proteins but many blood vessels were broken in the process. The result was irreparable damage.'

'Irreparable?' asked Glenn. 'But this operation was supposed to rectify what was already considered irreparable damage.'

'I know that, Mr. Tebbhurst,' said the doctor, looking him squarely in the face. 'But the operation has failed to do that. Mr. James's sight has significantly deteriorated.'

'How significantly?' he asked.

'He will have only 4/20 vision now,' she sighed. 'If he's lucky.'

Glenn could not believe his ears.

'But you've done this operation before,' he said, struggling to maintain his panic. 'You have experience.'

'Yes, but every experience is different,' she said. 'We could not have foreseen this reaction. I am deeply sorry for Mr. James.'

'He will be heartbroken,' Glenn shook his head bitterly.

'You were sponsoring the operation, right?' the doctor asked him.

'Yes,' said Glenn.

'I won't be sending a bill,' she said in a weak voice.

With that, Glenn stood up and walked out of the room. He wanted to visit Samuel James, to see his family and tell them how sorry he was, but he couldn't do it. He could not face them. Sitting in the taxi, he realised he could not go back to work either. His driver dropped him off at the nearest underground station and he made his way back to Virginia Water in a daze. When he walked into the house, he heard footsteps.

'Oh,' exclaimed Eleanora, who looked dressed up to go out. 'You're home early, darling.'

Glenn looked at her and felt helpless. Before he could stop them, tears began to brim in his eyes. He fell to his knees and began to sob.

'Darling!' his wife called to him, rushing to his side. 'What is it? What's happened?'

Glenn could not speak for a long time, but allowed his wife to stroke his hair on the sofa. He felt broken and wracked with guilt, as if he himself had held the guilty scalpel that had cost Samuel James his vision. For hours they stayed like that until Glenn asked his wife if she had somewhere to be.

'No, no,' she said softly. 'It's not important. I'm here. That's what you need.'

Slowly, his voice breaking, Glenn told Eleanora what he had learnt that morning at the hospital. She listened as he recounted the way the family had looked; how he had seen their grief and anguish as their son, brother, boyfriend, friend lay sleeping in the hospital bed.

'You can't blame yourself,' Eleanora hushed him. 'All you did was provide the money for the operation.'

'But I should have known,' Glenn sighed. 'Jesus Christ, have I learnt nothing from all of these women? These heroines who have tried against all odds to help people live with blindness? They're content with an independent life; not once did they ever speak to me about corrective surgery or miracle treatments. What have I done?'

'It wasn't you, darling,' Eleanora soothed him.

'The board consulted me for me expertise,' he groaned. 'They waited to hear what I have discovered this past year. And what did I do? I stood back and let them take a terrible decision!'

'Darling,' Eleanora pleaded. 'Please, calm down! You can't blame yourself. You're just a man.'

'Well, *that* man's sight is on *my* conscience...'

'Nonsense,' snapped Eleanora. 'You're talking utter nonsense.'

Glenn felt her warm body slip from beneath him as she rose to her feet. She left the room to fetch something, leaving her husband alone with the portraits of her ancestors. Even the Beaumonts seemed to look down at him and say: what have you done? Glenn could not take it anymore. He closed his eyes, wishing the world would disappear and take his desperate guilt with it.

'Drink this,' said Eleanora, striding back into the room with a small bottle. Glenn did not recognise the label but his wife insisted it would help him relax. Taking it in his hands, he took a few swigs. The medicine coursed through his veins and he soon felt drowsy.

'Have you drugged me?' he asked, managing a small smile as he looked up into his wife's beautiful face.

'Something like that,' she smiled back. It was a small smile, a sad smile. 'It will help you sleep a dreamless sleep.'

'Thank you,' he croaked, tears welling in his eyes at this show of kindness from Eleanora. 'Baby...' he began to say, but darkness soon enveloped him. Thick waves of heavy sleep rolled over him as he sunk into blissful, dreamless sleep.

Glenn was woken by a shaft of sunlight sifting through the window. Blinking, he saw the sunrise creeping up over the woodland beyond the estate. He lifted his arm to look at his watch and saw that it was already eight o'clock. He must have slept for hours! *Damn it*, he thought: *I'll be late for work*. But as soon as he tried to rise, Glenn felt a soft hand on his shoulder.

'Shh, easy now,' came his wife's voice. Glenn turned to look up at her.

'Honey, why didn't you wake me?' he asked. 'I have to get to work.'

'I called Sonia and cancelled your appointments,' she said in a firm voice.

'What?' he said, staring at her, confusion blurring his mind.

'You need a break, Glenn,' she sighed. 'You've been trying to do two jobs: firstly, your work at the DCF, and secondly, all this interviewing with these women. It's too much. You're going to burn out, and then where will you be?'

'I have to go,' he struggled to lift himself up. It was difficult, he realised. His body felt heavy.

'Glenn!' Eleanora called, a sharp desperation in her voice. He turned to her when he heard it. 'Please!' she said.

Glenn stared into his wife's blue eyes for a moment and was surprised to see genuine concern and fear there. It had been so many years since he had seen such tenderness in her. Hesitating for a moment, he let out a deep sigh and slowly lowered himself back onto the pillows. He scanned down his body, from his thumping head, through his chest and down to his legs. It was true, he admitted to himself: he felt utterly exhausted.

'Maybe you're right, honey,' he sighed, shaking his head.

'Yesterday,' she said. 'You were a broken man.'

Slowly, the memories of the day before flooded back into Glenn's mind. Samuel James lying there in the hospital bed; Dr. Slaughter's fear of a lawsuit. His breakdown in front of Eleanora.

'You've taken on so much, darling,' his wife said soothingly. 'It's time you took a break. A real break.'

'I suppose a day off can't hurt,' he smiled.

'I've told them you'll take the week off,' she said.

'A week?' he yelped.

'I've also told them you are not to be contacted in that time,' Eleanora nodded.

Glenn's mind raced for a moment as he considered what his wife was saying. It had been a long time since he had taken a week away from the DCF or his mission to capture the blind women's stories. The concept, though disconcerting at first, was not bad. He did not want to burn out. He had seen too many colleagues go through that, putting their health, happiness and wellbeing aside to focus on work.

'A week off,' he said, sounding the words out to see how he felt about them.

'Isn't it exciting?' Eleanora giggled.

Glenn turned to his wife and looked into her eyes.

'Thank you, baby,' he said. 'For looking out for me.'

'Oh, kiss me, you silly man,' she laughed. Leaning over, she placed her face in front of his so he could kiss her passionately.

'A week, huh,' he smiled, slipping a hand beneath her shirt and stroking the warm skin on her back. 'That's a lot of time off. I wonder what we will get up to?'

'Oh, I can think of a few things, darling,' she smiled, her blue eyes twinkling mischievously. 'Can't you?'

CHAPTER TWENTY

Glenn was surprised by how quickly he came around to the idea of a week off work. Taking deep breaths, he sighed deeper than ever, as if trying to sigh away the stresses of the week. Perhaps the time off would help clear his mind a bit, he thought. He had barely been back in the office two weeks and his heart was already beating double the speed, his mind racing and his body exhausted. Working in the charity sector was taking its toll on him; he could feel it.

'Salmon or carnation?' Eleanora's voice cut through his reverie.

It was the fourth day of his week off and he lounged in bed, watching his wife dress. They had already attended the Henley Regatta boat race enjoying the sunshine and the ambience together. Eleanora thrived at these society events, dressing herself and Glenn up in smart suits and outfits so they made an appearance in the photo albums and newsletters of the well to do. She made countless trips to her favoured designers for days such as these, and today was no exception: it was a day for fashion. Glenn examined the two smart skirt suits his wife was flourishing over her body.

'What's the difference?' he laughed. 'They're both pink.'

'Men!' his wife scolded him. 'You're useless at fashion. What's a girl to do when her husband can't tell the difference between the mellowness of salmon and the pale, freshness of carnation pink?'

'Honey, you'll look great in both,' he smiled, taking in the fine curve of her lower back as she slipped into the salmon suit. 'What does it matter?'

'What does it matter?' she cried. 'Darling, we're going to Windsor! We could be *seen* by someone!'

By someone, Glenn knew his wife was referring to any members of the royal family they might cross in the grounds of Queen Elizabeth's home. He thought it highly unlikely that the aristocratic elite of the country would be mingling with the commoners exploring the grounds, however.

'Well then,' he said. 'Those *someone's* won't feel like *anyone* when they see you walking along the Thames in salmon, or carnation, whichever you choose. You look like a billion dollars, baby.'

'You're sweet, darling,' she cooed, her face full of uncertainty. 'But be serious now: salmon or carnation?'

When Eleanora had finally settled on the carnation suit and matching shoes, Glenn drove them over to Windsor, happy to be leaving the house. The trees were shaking off their leaves as autumn reached its end, depositing crunchy piles of brown and yellow on the small country roads. Within ten minutes, the turrets and parapets of the castle were in sight and Glenn felt his heart skip with excitement. He had always loved castles, even as a little boy. He sometimes wondered if his attraction to Eleanora hadn't first been piqued by the fact that she grew up on such an ancient estate.

Parking the car, they took the main path that led out to the grounds.

'I daresay the Montagues or the Fitzwilliamses will be around here somewhere,' his wife sighed. 'They're always receiving invitations to the castle.'

'I doubt it,' Glenn laughed.

'Oh, they're very well to do,' she said quickly. 'They're certainly on Her Majesty's favourite list. I shan't even attempt to guess why. What a sorry sort they are.'

'I invited you here with me,' said Glenn, pulling her hand gently into his own. 'Isn't that something to be happy about?'

'Of course, darling,' she smiled. 'Of course.'

They wandered through the grounds, taking in the majestic terraces and browning chestnut trees. In the distance, Eton could be made out and it reminded Glenn of his school days. As they walked, talk turned to the history of the castle, first built by William the Conqueror after the 1066 invasion.

'Of course, since then they have done remarkably well,' his wife said, happy to be discussing the king her family could trace their bloodline back to. 'The Plantagenets were utterly unbreakable. They had to destroy themselves to lose power. We Beaumonts were always loyal. When the call came, we strove to defend King and country. There are annals that detail our defence of this castle, you know. Thanks to us, it survived the Civil War, despite those dastardly Parliamentarians digging their heels in and making it their headquarters. What a cheek, to challenge and decapitate God's own anointed King!'

'It survived the wars of the twentieth century too,' said Glenn. 'That's perhaps even more impressive.'

'Perhaps,' his wife smiled. 'And I daresay their estate does much better than ours. Look at all these little farms and smallholdings. The Windsors must make a fortune.'

'We're not doing too badly at Ronda Round,' said Glenn. He was thinking about their tenants, the Thomases, and how hard they worked to bring in the dairy products Eleanora sold from the estate. Walking hand in hand, Glenn realised just how the years had flown by; it seemed so long ago that they were newlyweds, basking in the warmth of each other's bodies, and yet at the same time it could have been yesterday. He pulled his wife closer to him.

'What's this?' she asked, her blue eyes shining as she looked into his face. His long, strong arms were snaking around her, drawing her into a kiss.

'Just me,' he whispered.

'Well, just you, control yourself!' she giggled. 'We are in public, and what's more, we are on royal turf!'

'Come on,' laughed Glenn. 'You trying to tell me those princes don't kiss their princesses in the castle grounds? I wonder how many hearts have been broken here on this very spot.'

'It's hard to imagine, isn't it?' said Eleanora, laughing at her husband and raising a hand to stroke his face.

'What is?' he asked.

'Life as a royal,' she said. 'Hidden from view, desperate for privacy yet forced into the public light. I imagine it feels quite trapping.'

Glenn nodded, trying to imagine such a life.

'And yet they wanted for nothing,' he said, thinking of the women he had met in the past year: stricken by poverty and harassed by misfortune. 'Remember how Elfrida grew up? Her mother worked for almost nothing and she barely escaped death.'

'Terribly unfortunate,' his wife sighed.

'Laura too,' said Glenn, his mind swimming with the image of the poor, abandoned girl living on the Welsh farm, longing for escape. 'Now that's someone who felt trapped.'

'Mm,' Eleanora hummed in agreement.

'God, and let's not forget Zu-Ting's story,' Glenn sighed. 'She had the worst time of all. Imagine losing your sight to such hard working conditions. It beggars belief.'

'Oh God, how depressing!' Eleanora squealed, turning and spinning slightly on the spot as if she could shake the thoughts away from them. 'Let's not talk about this anymore, darling.'

Glenn's mind had moved to a dark place, however. The castle, with all its historical wealth and power, became oppressive to him: it symbolised everything that was unjust and unequal about the world. Like Hong Kong, it remained a bastion to an old order, an order in which the rich were rich, remained rich and grew richer, and the poor faded into the dirty, busy thoroughfare of historical anonymity.

'Thank God for the ICB,' he sighed, managing a small smile as he thought of the six women in Aachen. Glenn was so lost in his thoughts that he had not seen his wife watching him with concern. They walked in silence for a while before Eleanora gasped.

'That's it!' she exclaimed, taking Glenn by surprise.

'What is it?' he asked.

'*Swan Lake* is playing tonight, at the Royal Opera House!' she said, her face a mask of excitement. Glenn hesitated for a moment before reacting, for in truth, he was not a huge fan of opera.

'Oh, how wonderful, honey,' he smiled, for he knew she loved the opera. 'We haven't been in such a long time.'

They wandered for a while longer, Glenn taking in the turning leaves of autumn and Eleanora taking in the crowds who bustled around the grounds.

'God, it's the Duchess of Hampshire's daughter!' she hissed. 'What a terrible dress that is! Does she really need to insult us all with her lack of fashion sense? I would have thought Barbara would think twice before letting that girl leave the house like that. What's more…'

Eleanora's voice faded into the background as he walked beside her, broken only occasionally by a shriek of laughter. He sometimes wished his wife was more present; he wished she could be more aware of the environment around her. As the wind rustled in the nearby trees and the light glanced off the castle windows, Glenn thought of that moment a year before, when he had stood in the woods, blindfolded. Like a madman he had laughed to himself and cried out his pleasure to the silent trees. His wife, however, seemed more interested in the people tramping through the grounds, no doubt equally attentive to their fellow visitors.

After a cup of tea and a freshly baked scone laced with clotted cream and jam, the couple set off for Ronda Round Manor, where they made love before heading into the city for dinner. This is the life, Glenn thought to himself, smiling as the tube sped beneath London, taking them to the heart of the capital.

'I love you,' Glenn whispered in his wife's ear as they ordered dessert in their favourite French restaurant.

'This place is giving you funny ideas!' Eleanora laughed loudly, a little tipsy from the fine vintage she had ordered with her steak tartare. 'God, it's been years since we were here.'

'We used to come every weekend!' Glenn smiled at the memory. 'You wore that little green dress. The one with the silver pattern around the neck.'

'You remember that?' his wife looked at him, her eyes watching him with alert interest.

'Of course,' he said. 'I remember more than you think.'

'Like the time we…' she began, her mouth twitching into a grin. 'When we were the last ones here?'

Glenn nodded and then burst into laughter.

'And we hid in the cloak room to wait for the last waiter to go home before making love, in the candlelight,' he said. 'Yes, I remember, Nora. We watched the lights on the Thames afterwards.'

'For a while,' she laughed. 'You soon changed that.'

'If I recall correctly, it was your idea,' Glenn grinned.

'You couldn't take your eyes off of me throughout that whole dinner!' she protested. 'I believe it was a mutual decision.'

'Of course, Eleanora Beaumont was never one to break the rules,' Glenn laughed at his wife. 'But I still can't, you know.'

'Can't what?' she asked.

'I still can't take me eyes off of you,' he said, looking deeply into that startling, piercing gaze. She looked back and Glenn saw a softening there; a gentle, tender affection.

'Nor I,' she said.

'Why did you marry me?' Glenn asked her, suddenly struck by the thought.

'Excuse me?' she said, taken aback.

'Why did you choose to marry me in the end?' he asked again. 'I'm curious.'

Eleanora held his gaze for a moment and then looked away. Her eyes searched the horizon, taking in the shape of central London across the Thames. St. Paul's cathedral was set against a host of stars peeping through the smog. After a small moment, she began to speak.

'When I met you I was young,' she said. 'Young and privileged. My father was well off and my mother was a snob. I won't deny it.'

Glenn's mouth dropped open to hear his wife speaking so frankly. He had never heard his wife speak of her parents in that way.

'Oh, they had ideas about who I should marry,' she continued. 'They knew the sort of chap: rich, powerful, and successful. They wanted a prince, but without the title. Royalty is too pernickety, they said; it would be uncomfortable for me to integrate into the elite. Besides, my mother has always said the Beaumonts are more English than the Windsors. She would have considered it a muddying of the bloodline!'

'I certainly wasn't royalty, I'll admit that much,' Glenn laughed. He was curious to hear his wife speak in such depth about this moment, so said no more.

'You weren't,' she said drily, but looking back at him with a small, wry smile. 'You were, well: something else.'

The waiter brought their crème brûlée, a favourite dessert of theirs which they traditionally shared after dinner. The crisp top lay waiting for a spoon to crack it and Glenn offered his wife the honour. She smiled as she tapped and cracked open the creamy deliciousness beneath the surface.

'So,' he said, after a few spoonfuls, encouraging her to continue.

'So,' she said. 'Mummy and Daddy had an idea of the sort of suitor I required. They introduced me to Edwards and Phillips and Georges, but I was utterly unimpressed. These men were self-important, snobbish, and obsessed with their heritage. I was too obsessed enough with my own to be interested in anyone else.'

'So you married me because of my boring, Yankee background,' laughed Glenn. 'I gotta admit, I was no competition for a landed lady like you.'

'Of course not,' his wife laughed too. 'Actually, you were just you, Glenn.'

'Just me?' he said.

'Just you,' she smiled. 'Just Glenn. I overheard you when you entered the ballroom that night at Ronda Round. The footman asked you for your name and your title and you said. "It's Glenn. Just Glenn." Lucian, the footman, was totally confused!'

'I remember that!' laughed Glenn. 'He asked if I as someone's valet, or there to pick someone up.'

'Yes,' Eleanora giggled. 'And then you said no, but offered him a lift if he needed to go somewhere.'

'Poor Lucian,' smiled Glenn. 'He didn't know what to do.'

'Poor fellow, he was startled!' Eleanora smiled.

'Yes,' grinned Glenn. 'So I confused him even more. I said, "Look here, mister, I know I'm allowed to be here, but if you're really not sure, hand me a tray and I'll serve drinks, hand me a plate and I'll serve food".'

'Why did you say that?' Eleanora asked.

Glenn looked at his wife for a moment, taking in the smooth curve of her cheeks and the fine, creamy colour of her skin. She was still as beautiful as that day, he thought.

'Because I saw you,' he said. 'I thought: I will do anything to stay at this party if it means I get a chance to speak to *that* girl.'

Eleanora stared at him, looking for traces of exaggeration. But Glenn's face was as honest as his heart.

'But why didn't you dance with me when I asked you?' he said, remembering Eleanora's cold rebuff that night.

'Because you scared me,' she said.

'Scared you?' he laughed. 'I've been called many things, some not great, but scary is not one of them, honey!'

'It wasn't you,' she said. 'It was me. It was the feeling I felt inside when I saw you. I wanted at once to run away, out of the room, deep into the night, and at the same time, to never leave your arms.'

A memory spun into Glenn's mind for a moment, not of that night, but of another night, over a year before. He felt the pang of anxiety as he felt Bettina's hand brush his thigh, his whisper to her, then her immediate departure. She had stood up and walked away, never to be seen by Glenn again.

'The cheque, sir,' came the waiter's voice, breaking through his reverie.

'Ah, thank you,' he answered, taking the cheque. He looked back at his wife.

'So what made you choose my arms, when I asked you to dance the second time?' he asked her.

Eleanora sat back in her seat, her strong, sharp shoulders resting against the wood of her chair. She looked for a moment like a queen deciding whether or not to knight a trusted servant.

'Because I knew then I couldn't let you leave the room that night, because if I did, I knew I'd lose you forever,' she said.

'You wouldn't have,' Glenn grinned, a brave new confidence growing with every word he heard his wife speak. 'I would have done anything to see you again.'

Eleanora gazed at him, her eyes soft as she breathed in the words of her husband. Suddenly, her eyes grew wide and alert.

'Gosh, we'd best fly!' she cried, looking at her watch.

Glenn grabbed his coat and threw some money on the table before running to the theatre with his wife. It was not far, perhaps ten minutes at a fast walk.

Glenn had never been much of a fan of the ballet, but he sat obediently by his wife's side as *Swan Lake* flowed before him. The grace of the dancing was sublime and fully captured Eleanora's attention; she cooed and sighed as the limbs and tutus spun across the stage. When the event was over, she wanted to know what Glenn thought of it all.

'I thought it was wonderful,' he lied. 'I was thinking of something throughout, though: how can blind people appreciate dance and visual performances? In Aachen we did a workshop on paintings and sculptures, but one can feel those things.'

'Mmm,' Eleanora mumbled. 'Right.'

'I mean, one cannot feel a dancer,' he said. 'So how does that work?'

'You'd have to ask a blind person,' his wife said coolly.

'You're right, I'll make contact with one of the girls when I'm back,' he said excitedly. 'Which one though? Odile's into music, Laura's into cats, Elfrida's into teaching and Zu-Ting's into politics!'

'Oh, Glenn, can you drop it? Please?' Eleanora snapped suddenly.

'Huh?' said Glenn. 'Drop what?'

'All this talk of those blind girls!' she sighed. 'I'm sick of it. You're on holiday, for God's sake.'

'Honey, I...' he began.

'No, darling,' she hissed impatiently. 'You're obsessed. All you talk about is these women.'

'Baby, don't be jealous,' he began, but again she cut him off.

'Jealous?' she cried, her voice booming. 'How dare you?'

Glenn was stunned by the ferocity of her answer. He said nothing, glancing around to make sure the crowds were out of earshot. Some people had turned to look at them, raising eyebrows at their distasteful display of emotion. Damn the British, Glenn thought irritably. His wife, usually the one casting distasteful looks, was clearly enraged, enough so to speak out in public.

'Honey, maybe we should find somewhere quiet to talk about this?' Glenn suggested, taking her hand gently in this. 'I can see you're upset. I want to make it better.'

Staring into her eyes, Glenn saw the iciness creep into her gaze. He could not look, deciding instead to lead her gently towards a bench nearby. The crowds were clearing as they sat down. For what seemed like an age, neither spoke. The precious magic of the evening was broken and it pained them both.

'How can you think I'm jealous?' she asked him, breaking the silence at last. Eleanora spoke in a small but defiant voice.

'Baby, I just…' he started.

'You just assumed the only reason I wouldn't want you to talk about these women is because I think you're screwing them,' she said, raising her eyes, still cold, to meet his.

Glenn said nothing. He looked down at his feet, ashamed.

'It wasn't like that,' he said.

'Darling,' his wife laid a soft hand on his. 'You must understand that I'm worried about you. You must see that, surely? All these months, dealing with these traumas, these stories, these hopeless cases…'

'Hopeless?' said Glenn.

'Oh, you know what I mean!' she snapped. 'These unfortunates, these poor souls… it's taking its toll on you. You've lost weight, darling. You don't smile as much anymore. And when that poor boy lost his sight last week, well, I thought you had lost yourself along with it.'

Glenn listened to everything she said, nodding occasionally to show he understood.

'I didn't know you felt this way,' he said eventually. 'I didn't know things were so bad. I feel tired, it's true, exhausted even, but I am coping with the stress.'

'I know it's been difficult, with your father and his blindness, but I've enjoyed these moments so much recently,' she said. 'Moments together away from it all.'

'Me too, honey,' he said.

'Let's get away then,' she said suddenly.

'Where?' he said. 'We've only been back two weeks!'

'I've already decided,' she grinned. 'I've always wanted to go to the fjords of Norway, haven't you?'

Glenn blinked at his wife, totally surprised by her words.

'Sure, but honey, this is unlike you!' he laughed. 'What about London? The farm?'

'Oh, London be damned!' she giggled, suddenly happy again. 'Take me to the fjords, Glenn. Let's have another adventure.'

Glenn thought about his wife's proposition, weighing it up in his mind. A trip to Scandinavia shimmered in his mind's eye for a moment: the peace, quiet and vast stretches of nature. The prospect was deeply appealing.

'I'm a free agent,' he said, sighing happily. 'I'm ready to go when you are, baby.'

'Then it's settled!' Eleanora leapt to her feet. 'But I have one condition, darling. It's an important one.'

'What's that?' he asked.

'No talk of the six blind women, OK?' she said, an anxious tone in her voice. 'It's time you took a break from all of that. Don't you think so?'

Glenn considered her words for a moment.

'I do,' he said. 'OK, honey. You have my word.'

'Then let's go and pack!' she squealed. 'I'll arrange everything.'

Laughing, Glenn ran after his wife as she skipped towards the Leicester Square Underground station, desperate to get home.

* * * *

Leaving Ronda Round Manor in the Thomases' careful hands, Glenn and Eleanora caught an afternoon flight to Oslo.

'Why not a morning flight?' Glenn had asked her the night before as they scanned the flight times on his laptop.

'Because I don't want to get out of bed earlier than we have to,' she growled, pouncing on her husband and pushing the laptop aside.

The memory of that long night of sensual pleasure circulated Glenn's mind as they flew across the North Sea. He could not keep his eyes off of Eleanora, who, likewise, eyed him hungrily on the flight. On arrival at the airport, the couple were met by their driver, Jan.

'Welcome to Norway,' Jan boomed in a heavy accent. He was a blonde, bearded hulk of a man, almost twice as broad in the shoulders as Glenn. He towered above them and clapped them both on their arms. 'We are going to have a great time.'

Glenn was surprised by the words, for Jan seemed to express very little emotion at all, certainly not a sense of impending happiness. Looking around the airport, however, Glenn saw that very few people were smiling. The rows of people awaiting friends, relatives, and lovers to arrive looked distinctly unhappy. It must be the Norwegian style, he thought to himself.

Following Jan to a big four-wheel drive, which stood waiting to whisk them off to the fjords, Glenn turned to his wife with a smile.

'I'm impressed,' he said. 'You really have arranged everything.'

'Your secretary is not the only one who can arrange travel, darling,' she gave him a dry look. 'I rather love planning trips. At least to slightly more savoury destinations.'

The sun was already setting over Oslo as they drove past the city. Further north than London, Glenn could already feel the Scandinavian night drawing in. Jan was mostly silent for the drive, but responded in helpful grunts when his passengers had questions. When Eleanora had fallen asleep on his shoulder and Glenn turned his eyes towards a starry sky above the dark, mountainous horizon, the car pulled up at a small port town.

'Welcome to Bergen,' said Jan, in the same monotone he had used when he had welcomed them to Norway. Driving past rows of colourful houses, Glenn could see the lights of the town glittering on the sea. They had already reached the eastern coast.

The car pulled up outside a cosy-looking hotel, a traditional building with windows revealing a warm, welcoming atmosphere inside. Glenn woke Eleanora so they could check in and slip into a huge bed, decorated with countless plump pillows. Jan bid them goodnight and left the couple to the friendly receptionist, a local woman who had been born in the town.

'You will find people from all over the world in Bryggen,' she smiled at them, a big, toothy smile that made her guests feel welcome, before returning to a naturally staid expression similar to Jan's.

'I thought this town was called Bergen?' Eleanora exclaimed irritably, still sleepy from the travel.

'It is,' said their host. 'But in Norwegian, we call it Bryggen.'

Exhausted from the travels, Glenn and Eleanora decided to skip dinner and headed straight into each other's arms, where they slept deeply in their bed of many pillows.

Waking to a knock on the door, Glenn watched sleepily as the same woman as before entered the room with a tray full of breakfast.

'Thanks!' Glenn called, pulling on his dressing gown to inspect plates full of smoked salmon, eggs, and piles of pancakes topped with freshly made blueberry jam; coffee steamed in a pot, and a jug full of thick milk lay waiting for them.

'Don't forget to try the caviar with pickled herrings,' the woman said in an attempt at friendliness. 'It was the favourite of King Olav Kyrre, the man who founded this city in 1070.'

She indicated a grey pot of fish eggs and some large fish fillets.

'Er, thanks,' said Glenn, trying not to look at the pot.

'How frightfully disgusting!' Eleanora squealed when the woman left.

'Tell me about it,' laughed Glenn.

'To think, in 1070 my ancestor, King William of Normandy, was founding England, and over the sea this King was founding a town full of pickled fish!' Glenn's wife giggled at the thought.

The couple tucked into the breakfast before heading out into the town. They wrapped up warm and explored the beautiful harbour town. The colourful houses and air of seafaring gave it a beautiful quality. The medieval buildings reminded visitors that Bergen was once the first capital city of Norway.

'In the thirteenth century, the Germans were here,' one craftsman in the town told them. 'Their guild of merchants even opened an office here!'

'The Hansas?' asked Eleanora, surprising both Glenn and the craftsman.

'Exactly,' he said, puzzled.

'How charming!' Eleanora exclaimed. 'They only had four offices in the whole of Europe.'

'Darling, how did you know that?' Glenn asked as they walked away.

'You're not the only one interested in the world, darling,' his wife sighed exasperatedly. 'At finishing school, we were taught all sorts of useless rubbish. You can quiz me on European medieval trade routes and practices anytime.'

Glenn laughed at this and kissed his wife. How could they have lived together for so long, he wondered, and still know so little about one another?

Wandering to the train station, Glenn and Eleanora set off on the Bergen Railway to Voss. The train set off, transforming its passengers into a theatrical chorus of 'ooo' and 'ahh' as they passed fjord after fjord. Glenn could hardly believe they had made a railway that passed through such rugged terrain. When they reached Voss, they joined the other tourists on a bus to Gudvangen, the village which sat deepest in the Nærøyfjord, where a boat lay waiting for them.

'Oh, how charming!' Eleanora exclaimed. Information posts informed them that the Nærøyfjord was among the narrowest fjords in Europe.

'Wow, it's a UNESCO heritage site,' said Glenn, reading about the area. The bus had left them at the harbour, but a quick glance back revealed the small village, a quaint, beautiful settlement surrounded by steep mountains. Snow laced the peaks and had started to drift down into the valley. Gudvangen was nothing compared to the village they would reach by boat, however. After two hours of sailing down the Nærøyfjord, they reached Flåm, a village embraced by nature. Houses built in a style that reminded one of Viking settlements, the village was at the mercy of vast mountains and heavily-flowing waterfalls.

'I didn't expect to be here two days ago,' Glenn whispered in his wife's ear as they strolled, hand in hand around the village.

'It's fun sometimes to do something unexpected, no?' his wife whispered back mischievously. 'Let's sleep here tonight. I hope to the gods we see the lights!'

'The aurora borealis?' Glenn exclaimed. 'Will it be possible here?'

'Expect the unexpected,' Eleanora smiled.

'But baby, I've always wanted to see them!' he laughed. 'Hold on, our luggage is still in Bergen.'

'I've had it brought over,' Eleanora said, her smile widening.

Glenn followed as his wife led them to a small, intimate hotel, right at the fjord's edge. It was a cabin, with a log fire and a chef waiting to cook them a three-course meal. They dined on fresh fish and the best cuisine they had to offer.

'I don't think even King Olav was treated to such luxury,' Glenn murmured to his wife over their candlelit table. To his surprise, a crème brûlée was brought to them for dessert, before the chef bid them goodnight.

'For old times' sake,' Eleanora said softly, looking deep into her husband's eyes.

'Eleanora,' he said, feeling his heart melt under her intense, attractive gaze. 'This was such a good idea.'

'See?' she said, grinning. 'I do have good ideas sometimes, don't I?'

They took a few spoonfuls of crème brûlée, savouring the dessert before passion took them into their soft, cosy bed. Naked and struck by each other, the couple made love in a wild and frenzied manner. The wildness of the nature around them pounded in their hearts and minds, driving them towards satisfaction.

In the middle of the night, after sleeping for a while, Glenn woke with a start. A strange, curling light was passing over the wall. His heart beating in his chest, he rose from his bed and walked slowly over to the window. Pulling the curtain aside, he let out a soft, small cry. Blazing in the sky above, the aurora borealis danced in green and pink glory, casting eerie, magnificent colour onto the snowy peaks and the silent, glistening fjord.

'My God,' he heard Eleanora whisper behind him. Glenn turned to her standing there behind him, her eyes bright with wonder.

'It's breath-taking,' he said, turning back to watch the display. 'I can't believe my eyes.'

'Be grateful you have them then,' his wife said softly.

'What do you mean?' Glenn asked.

'I know how much you appreciate those blind women, darling,' said Eleanora, sighing, her hands soft against his waist. 'But you have to admit, sometimes, being able to see has its positive sides. Look at that sky.'

'It's a blessing,' he said, nodding his head. And with a guilty pang in his stomach, for he had sworn to his wife to forget them, at least while they were in Norway, Glenn thought of the six blind women. The next woman on his list would have something to say about this, he thought; he would welcome the chance to discuss with her the stirring spirituality he felt when he looked up at the aurora borealis in the sky. Yes, he would contact Christina as soon as he got back to London, Glenn thought, before putting the thought far from his mind.

Turning back to the sky, Glenn felt his wife's naked body pressed gently against his back. With her by his side, he suddenly imagined that they were Adam and Eve, after the fall, staring back into a heaven from which they were banished.

'I want to stay like this forever,' he whispered.

'Why don't we?' his wife whispered back.

Glenn said nothing, for he knew why he had to go back. He did not want to see another man lose his sight needlessly. He did not want his father to lose faith. The work he had started was far from being finished; he knew it had only just begun.

Turning back to his wife, he pulled her back towards the bed, and sweetly, gently, they made love beneath an exploding sky.

CHAPTER TWENTY-ONE

'I'll be with you in a moment,' Glenn smiled to his wife, kissing her on the cheek. He watched her walk sleepily upstairs to their bedroom, their luggage left abandoned at the bottom of the stairs. It seemed like only hours ago they had been nestled together in their Nordic cocoon, but stone-cold reality had brought them home again, to Ronda Round Manor, where life inevitably had to go on.

When Glenn knew his wife had reached the bedroom, he walked quickly to his office and switched on the light. The room, a stately space, looked sad and abandoned after weeks of neglect. Since the incident with Mr. James, Glenn had not dared enter or even contemplate the prospect of his case studies. But now, rejuvenated by the aurora borealis and his sense of purpose, Glenn sat down at his desk. Switching on his computer, he began to type out an email he had been itching to write for days:

Dear Christina,

I hope this email finds you well. My name is Glenn Tebbhurst and we met at the 'Living with Blindness' workshop held by the ICB in Aachen, Germany, last year.

I've been meaning to write for some time. Since attending the conference I have become increasingly interested in the work of the ICB, particularly that of your colleagues, Laura, Odile, Elfrida and Zu-Ting. I have visited them all in their home cities, and have learnt a lot about blindness.

My wish is to support the ICB by fundraising at Diversified Charities Foundation, my own charitable enterprise. I have been writing down the stories of those whom I have met to create case studies to be used for fundraising purposes. I feel my portfolio of stories would not be complete without your own, therefore I ask if it might be possible to meet you in Frankfurt in the near future.

Best wishes,
Glenn

Finishing the email, Glenn headed up to the bedroom, where his wife was already asleep, exhausted from the return flight from Oslo. Slipping into the bed beside her, Glenn too fell into a deep sleep, pushing the excitement around visiting Christina from his mind.

Arriving at his office the next morning, Sonia was thrilled to see him.

'Mr. Tebbhurst,' she said, a mixture of worry and relief on her face. 'Welcome back.'

'Thanks, Sonia,' Glenn smiled kindly. He hung up his coat on the stand and yawned.

'How are you feeling?' she asked.

'Like a billion dollars in the bank,' he said, chuckling. 'Things are much brighter now. It was good to take a break.'

'I heard about Mr James…' Sonia sighed. 'The poor fellow.'

Glenn's heart contracted at the sight of Sonia's melancholy.

'He should never have had that operation,' he shook his head sadly. 'Diversified Charities failed him.'

'No,' said Sonia, hanging her head. 'We did what we thought was right.'

'Yes, but *was* it right, Sonia?' Glenn said. 'Now that man is blind. Permanently.'

'DCF did not make Mr. James blind, sir,' his secretary said with brave conviction.

'Who did then?' he asked her.

'Well, medicine did,' she said. 'Operations are always loaded with risk, you know that. We need better treatments, yes, new methodologies and procedures.' She was quiet for a moment, eyes darting here and there, before she said, 'You know, it's ridiculous… If the Russians and the Americans can develop nuclear weapons, why can't they develop a cure for blindness? If we can put a man on the moon, why can't we give people their sight back?'

'That's just our problem, Sonia,' Glenn smiled a sad smile. 'We put too much stock in cures instead of focusing on acceptance. With acceptance comes greater understanding and happiness. I should have known that – I *did* know that. I should have said something.'

'Perhaps you're right,' said Sonia. 'In all cases, sir, we are glad to have you back among us.'

'I'm glad to be back,' he smiled, before retreating into his office.

Glenn sighed as he sat down at his desk. There was some truth in his answer: he was happy to be back in the thick of the work he loved. But another part of him, a deeper, more animal part of him, longed to be wrapped around Eleanora's body in the cold depths of Norway. He shivered with pleasure at the thought.

Shaking away those blissful memories, Glenn opened up his computer to find an email waiting for him. With a rush of excitement, he saw Christina's name waiting in his inbox:

Dear Glenn,

Blessings to you, and thank you for your email. I preach daily at 11.00 at St. Catherine's Church, just off the Hauptwache Plaza in Frankfurt, and on Sunday from 10.00–17.00. You are most welcome to attend!

Willkommen in Frankfurt.

Mit freundlichen Grüßen,
Christina

Spinning in his chair, Glenn strolled back to the door and swung it open.

'Sonia,' he said, smiling. 'Book me onto a flight to Frankfurt. I'm leaving again.'

* * * *

Spurred on by the importance of his mission, Glenn set off for Frankfurt that weekend, keen to catch Christina's Sunday sermon. Eleanora had not been happy with the news but her husband tried his best to console her.

'It's just a few days, honey,' he said. 'I'll be back before you know it.'

'I thought we'd seen the last of those women,' she sighed, looking away and tensing up at his touch. Her face was miserable and her usually soft, rosy cheeks were red with anger. 'New Orleans, Acapulco, Hong Kong and now Frankfurt! When will it end?'

'You can come with me if you like?' he said hopefully.

'To Frankfurt!' she exclaimed. 'What on earth would I do there? Eat sausages and make gingerbread houses?'

'Honey, it's a beautiful city,' Glenn began.

'Oh, what rot!' she snapped. 'No, darling. I won't go. You go and interview your millions of women, that's your choice. I have a farm to run.'

'There are only six!' Glenn laughed, refusing to let his wife's sour attitude infect him. 'Oh, honey, I'm sorry. I know this isn't easy. But really, Christina is the fifth, and then there's Bettina. That's just two women left to speak to.'

'Who is this woman?' Eleanora demanded. 'Who is this Christina?'

'Honey, she's a blind priest,' Glenn said flatly.

'But I'll miss you,' Eleanora pouted, her anger fading into sadness. 'Doesn't that mean something to you?'

'Of course it does!' Glenn grinned. 'Don't you think I'm gonna miss you too?'

Taking her in his arms, Glenn held his wife tight. He inhaled the flowery scent of her perfume and stroked the soft firmness of her lower back.

'Don't you think I'm gonna remember all those days we spent in Norway?' he asked her gently. 'All those nights? I go crazy just thinking about them. Don't you?'

'Yes,' she murmured, wrapping her arms around him. She began to cry.

The next morning, after making love with Eleanora all night, Glenn took a taxi to Heathrow. Two hours later he was shooting into the sky towards Frankfurt.

Once there, Glenn went straight to St. Catherine's Church from the airport. Frankfurt sprawled around him, a handsome, graceful city. Different to Aachen, Glenn marvelled at the spires and cobbled streets as they passed by outside his window. Arriving at St. Catherine's, Glenn was stunned to see the impressive Lutheran church, a surprisingly modern building. He could hear voices inside, and on entering through the arched doors, found a sea of children all sat calmly, surrounding the pulpit. He thought it must have been a local Sunday School. In the middle of the children stood a familiar figure dressed in a long white tunic and red sash.

Even in her robe, Christina's pale, ethereal beauty shone. Her white skin blended with the purity of the cloth, and her bright blonde hair shimmered in the soft church light. Glenn could not understand what the German priestess was saying, but he could feel the effect it was having on her young audience. They laughed and let out sighs of awe as she told a story, using a few soft toys and pictures as props. Around her was a basket, a fish, and a few fake loaves of bread; Christina was telling the story of Jesus feeding the multitude. He watched as she stared ahead, her eyes filled with biblical visions, and conveying them to the children in her deep, warm German.

Only at the end, when the children stood up to leave, did Glenn dare to venture a round of applause.

'Bravo!' he called out. 'Bravo, Christina!'

Christina's head rose.

'Glenn Tebbhurst?' she smiled. 'Are you in my church?'

Like Zu-Ting, Christina seemed to recognise him immediately and he still found the sensation astonishing, almost supernatural.

'How did you know?' he laughed. The rest of the congregation turned to stare at Glenn, surprised to hear the sudden smooth English tones of the priestess.

'I'd recognise your voice anywhere!' she said with a chuckle. 'Come – come and say hello, my friend.'

Glenn went to Christina and took her hand warmly in his.

'My dear Glenn,' she smiled. '*Willkommen*.'

Turning to the congregation, Christina began to introduce Glenn to them all in German. After a moment, they all repeated her words of welcome.

'*Danke*,' said Glenn.

'*Sprichst du Deutsch*?' she asked, her eyes suddenly wide with surprise.

'Just *danke*,' chuckled Glenn. 'And *bitte*.'

'Well, that's a good start,' she smiled. 'OK, Glenn. Let me change and say goodbye to my congregation. A shepherd must always ensure her flock is ready to leave.'

When she came back, she was dressed simply in jeans and a warm winter coat. She found Glenn, neck-craned, gazing up at the organ and the ceiling.

'What do you think of our church, Glenn?' she asked him.

'It's beautiful,' he said, turning to smile at her. 'It's much more modern than our musty old churches in England.'

'That's because it was rebuilt in 1950,' she said. 'The original church dated back to the fourteenth century, and was converted to a Lutheran building when the city of Frankfurt adopted the blessed religion in 1533. Goethe himself was baptised here, did you know that?'

'Wow,' Glenn smiled at the thought of the famous German writer as a baby.

'Yet in 1944, it was destroyed by the Allied bombings,' Christina continued. 'Like so many other beautiful buildings in this city. So what you see today, Glenn, is a church reborn, but as dedicated to St. Catherine in spirit and praise as ever.'

'Who was St. Catherine?' Glenn asked as they began to walk out of the church.

'Catherine was one of the earliest Christian saints, a woman martyred for her faith,' Christina said in her gentle, frank way. 'Now tell me, Glenn. Have you eaten?'

'Not yet,' he said, suddenly feeling the emptiness in his stomach.

'Then come, let's go to my house and eat,' she said.

'I should just drop my things at the hotel,' said Glenn, checking his watch.

'What hotel?' laughed Christina. 'You are staying with me, Glenn. It is the least I can do.'

'That's really too kind, Christina,' Glenn began to protest, but she held up a hand in front of her, as if to catch his words in the air.

'Is there ever such a thing as too much kindness, Glenn?' she asked. 'Ask yourself, and I think you will find the answer.'

The question left him speechless.

'I'll tell you about St. Catherine on the walk home,' Christina smiled, taking out her white cane. Slowly, they walked out of the church, down the steps, Glenn following her lead. 'Catherine was a learned woman, a scholar who lived in Alexandrian Egypt during the reign of Roman Emperor Maximian. Challenged to a debate by the emperor himself, Catherine convinced the wisest and most learned men in the land to convert to Christianity, and leave behind their cruel, pagan ways. Some of them agreed! The emperor tortured her to try and break her faith, and in failing offered his hand in marriage. She told him she had wed herself to Jesus Christ, so he decided to kill her on a breaking wheel. But he failed in this too: the wheel blasted apart! So eventually he beheaded her, and thus sealed her martyrdom.'

'A loyal wife of Jesus then,' Glenn remarked.

'Well, we don't all end up on the wheel thankfully! Most of us end up in the pulpit, and continue St. Catherine's great work of spreading the word of God.'

It was only a short walk to Christina's house. She lived in a wide, well-presented street with colourful flower boxes sitting in the windows. They entered a bright house, decorated simply but tastefully, and Christina asked Glenn to make himself feel at home.

'Will you help me cook, Glenn?' she asked him.

'With pleasure,' he said, eager for the chance to help his host. He felt comfortable in Christina's home; there was the same familiar warmth there that he had felt in the day in the dark workshop in Aachen. Whilst they sliced runner beans and diced onions, Christina chatted to Glenn like an old friend.

'It's wonderful you're working towards helping the ICB, Glenn,' she said. 'Your contribution could be invaluable.'

'It's nothing compared to the work you girls are doing,' Glenn smiled at her.

'Women, Glenn,' she corrected him.

'Right, sorry!' he laughed nervously. 'Women, of course.'

'Actually, I'm not spending much time on ICB work these days,' she said. 'I am spending ninety percent of the time on my Christian work and missions. It's Bettina who runs everything. She's working at the head office here in Frankfurt.'

Glenn reacted nervously at the sensation of his heart soaring as it heard news of Bettina.

'So, she's here in this city?' he asked quickly. 'I mean, do you see her often?'

'Bettina?' said Christina. 'Sometimes, but not often. I don't think I've seen her since the conference in Aachen.'

'Me neither,' said Glenn.

'You two were good friends, if I recall correctly,' Christina smiled at the memory. 'You laughed together. I remember that.'

'I just regret we didn't get a chance to say goodbye,' said Glenn, recalling that last day, searching for her in vain. In a flash, he felt Bettina's hand brush his leg, her sudden straightening up beside him, her standing, departing, vanishing: never to be seen again.

'She's a chronically busy woman,' said Christina gently. 'I've never met someone with so much energy. Never take it personally, Glenn.'

'That's OK,' said Glenn, shaking the memories away. 'It's not her I've come to see. It's you, Christina. There's something I would like to discuss with you.'

'The case studies,' said Christina, nodding her head. 'Elfrida wrote to me. I knew you would come to me, even before I received your email.'

'So you know why I'm here,' he said.

'To add me to your collection,' she smiled.

'Only if you want to,' Glenn said quickly. 'You're under no obligation to... well...'

'Tell my story?' she finished his sentence for him.

'Yes,' he said.

'I think you already know that my story was an unhappy one,' she said, pausing for a moment as she went to pour vegetable stock into the deliciously sizzling stew. Glenn knew what Christina was referring to. He remembered Herbert's introduction at the conference in Aachen; had he not told them all that Christina had contracted a tropical disease in Africa following the kidnapping of her Mother Superior?

'I only want you to share if it feels right,' Glenn said gently. 'It's your story, Christina. Only you can decide if it should be heard.'

'It should be,' she said. 'But over dinner. Let's cook, Glenn.'

The two chopped fresh parsley and seasoned the stew of sausages and potatoes until they were satisfied with the result. Just as they had done in Aachen, they laid the table and prepared themselves for a delicious, home-cooked meal.

'Thanks be to God for this meal, and for bringing Glenn safely to us in Frankfurt,' she said, closing her eyes to pray before they ate. Only after Christina had spoken to God to bless the food, and the two of them had broken fresh, crusty bread over their soup, did she finally begin to speak.

'I am not from Frankfurt,' she said, laying down her spoon to rest for a moment. 'I was born somewhere close to Hannover. I don't know where exactly. All I know is that I was abandoned as a baby. My mother, God rest her soul, left me on the doorstep of the Medingen Abbey, in the forest. There, I was brought up by the Lutheran abbesses who resided within its walls.'

'Abbesses?' said Glenn, pulling out his notebook to take notes. 'Is that a kind of nun?'

'Yes, in a way. They were Lutheran abbesses, women priests who had chosen a lifetime of solitude with Christ. I grew up among them, those gentle, kind women. They adopted me, and taught me to read and write. I learnt to play the organ too, to grow vegetables with the seasons, and to praise the Lord for his bountiful gifts of friendship and companionship at the abbey. I attended a local school, and when I reached the age of eighteen, my school friends in nearby Hannover wanted to go to university, to study to become doctors, lawyers, and teachers. But I wanted only to take my vows and become a Lutheran abbess.'

'And did you?' Glenn asked.

'I did,' she smiled, her vacant gaze settling upon something he could not see. 'How happy I was that day. I spent two happy years at the abbey. When I reached my twenty-first birthday, one of the sisters, an abbess called Hilda, returned from her work as a missionary in the Central African Republic. The tales she told, Glenn! Only God knew such wonders could exist, and such terrors. I was mesmerised by her. She was in her fifties perhaps, a matriarch to us all, and to me especially, a mother figure I think. I would have followed her to the ends of the earth.'

'And did you?' Glenn asked the same question as before. Christina laughed.

'I did,' she sighed. A small, pained smile rose to her lips. 'I travelled with her to the heart of Africa. Oh, how I can still hear the birds! I can still feel that burning sun on my skin, see that deep, rich red earth on my shoes. We worked there for one year, helping people, providing them with materials to build churches and salvation for their souls. We helped hundreds, maybe thousands, see the light and enter God's fold.'

'You converted people?' Glenn asked.

'No, no, it was not like that,' she said. 'We simply invited people to join our services. We taught them our songs. If they chose to believe, then we embraced them like brothers and sisters. If they chose to stay away, we loved them like dear friends. Hilda was the finest teacher of all. She became my great tutor and my best friend. When things started to become dangerous, people wrote to us from Medingen. They warned us, but we did not listen, for we knew we lived under the protection of God himself, and as such, no harm could befall us.'

'But it did,' said Glenn quietly.

'Yes,' said Christina, nodding slowly. 'One night, catastrophe fell around us. Local militias attacked our safe house, kidnapping Hilda. They took her away and we never saw her again. Some say she was eaten by cannibals, but I think that is just superstitious rubbish. I never met cannibals in Africa, not one. I think it is a myth espoused by white people to dehumanise their African brothers and sisters.'

'What did happen to her?' Glenn asked, his pen poised above his notebook. 'Did you find out?'

'No one knows,' said Christina. 'I tried to search for her, I travelled far and wide, asking people in their local languages if they had seen her. No one had. I grew weak and sick with worry and no longer had the strength to fight the disease which corrupted my frail body. I contracted a virus, on my travels, from dirty water or some rogue insect.'

'What was it?' Glenn asked.

'It is still unidentified by the greatest institutes of tropical medicine in Germany,' Christina shook her head. 'All I know is that I dropped down one day, in the middle of a village, and could not get up again. I later learnt that I fell into a coma and was rescued by the German embassy. I awoke here in Frankfurt, in the hospital's department for tropical medicine. When I opened my eyes, I could see only darkness.'

'You were blind?' Glenn asked. Christina nodded.

'I refused to believe it at first,' she said. 'I thought someone was playing a cruel trick on me. I thought someone had turned out all the lights. I did not even believe I was in Germany, though everyone around me spoke German. I was delirious, still recovering from the fever. I cried out to God for help but he did not answer me. Like Jesus on the cross, I asked him: "Father, why have you forsaken me?" But he did not answer. Nor did he come to me in my dreams as he had done before. I was in the dark. Totally alone.'

Glenn listened as Christina recounted the loss of her faith. He could barely begin to imagine how that must have felt. When her eyes no longer saw the world around her, her heart lost faith, and there was nothing she could do about it.

'I could not understand how God could have done this to me,' she shook her head.

'But I see you now, as devoted as ever,' said Glenn, wondering how she returned to her faith. 'You preach with the surety of faith; with the determination of one who has never stopped believing.'

'Yes,' she smiled. 'How grateful I am for that. I am also grateful to God for those dark months. For out of the darkness came light, Glenn: he showed me a new path.'

'How did you recover your faith?' Glenn asked her.

'I lived in the tropical institute for just under a year,' she said. 'They kept me there for observation. Abbesses came each week to see me, but I sent them away in anger, blaming them for no real reason. I wanted them to hurt as I was hurting. They came back every week, until I told the hospital to refuse them entry. Then they came no more. Doctors came and went, though; this I could not change. They spent long hours attending to me, testing me, assuring me that I would be rehabilitated to deal with my new disability. But only one doctor managed to truly break my misery. His name was Heiner.'

'And he was a doctor at the tropical institute?' Glenn asked.

'Yes. Heiner was a kind man, very gentle and soft. One day he came to me and told me he would like to introduce me to his sister. He knew I did not like the abbesses visiting me, so he assured me his sister was not religious. Heiner simply told me she would help me see the light. I don't know why, but I trusted him. His voice made me feel safe.'

'So you agreed to meet his sister?' Glenn asked.

'Yes. She was a remarkable woman. She came in as softly as a mouse, and introduced herself. She worked for a charity in Frankfurt and had dedicated her life to rehabilitating those who had been born blind or lost their sight over the course of their lifetime. She asked me why I thought my life was over. I told her to stop teasing me; I said, "See with your own eyes! I am blind!" I wept then and told her that I had lost my way. But she held my hand and told me my life was just beginning, if I could only try to see it that way. I asked her why she taunted me with fancy words and false promises, and she told me she spoke only the truth. The truth! I laughed at this. Had I not spent my whole life preaching the truth, God's truth, only to have it smashed by reality: by the loss of my great friend, the Abbess, and the loss of my eyes?'

'And what did she say?'

'She said, "I am the truth",' said Christina. 'She said, "I am also the reality. I am blind and my dear, Christina, how I see!"'

Goosebumps dotted the back of Glenn's neck.

'Who was she?' he asked. His heart yearned for one name.

'Bettina Hartmann,' Christina whispered. 'Bettina helped me to leave my sorrow behind and embrace the real world. I would never go back to the Abbey, but slowly I began to see that God had taught me a harsh lesson, one that I must learn from. I went out into the world, without eyes but with a heart full of purpose. I studied Divinity at the university here in Frankfurt, and proceeded to publish the university's first ever PhD thesis in Braille.'

'You have a PhD?' Glenn exclaimed.

'Yes, in Divinity,' she smiled, then blushing she added, 'You might be surprised to know that I am well known in academic circles, Glenn, even in London. I am one of the world's leading experts, though I balance research with preaching and voluntary work with the ICB.'

'So you volunteer for the ICB now?' Glenn asked, his hand passing side to side over the notebook, scribbling down notes.

'Yes, I spread the word of the ICB's work in Lutheran communities across the world,' she said. 'For me, the two are intimately linked.'

'Christianity and the ICB?' said Glenn. 'How so?'

'Life is full of disaster,' she said in her soft, commanding manner, as though she were once more in a pulpit, preaching to her flock. Her arms were held wide, her spine ramrod straight, her chin held high with grace. 'Floods, tornadoes, poverty, famine, sickness, loss, grief and blindness: all are part of life's pattern of disaster. How do we live with such uncertainty and, indeed, such certainty that all we hold dear can be taken away from us in an instant? Why does God force these things upon us? At the heart of every answer to these questions is one thing: acceptance. There is a deep contradiction between the earth's ability to destroy and the human will to survive. The only way we can weather such a storm is to accept and surrender ourselves to that which we cannot control. With acceptance comes gratitude for those things we have, and with gratitude comes happiness. There are two pillars of understanding that, if possessed, support true and nourishing happiness: acceptance of our destiny is one, and the other is gratitude.'

Christina's words hung in the air like a golden mist. Glenn wished his father was there to hear Christina speak. The feeling of rapture he had experienced at her seminar in Aachen returned to him. What wonders, what energy she could kindle in a man, Glenn thought. Such wonders could so deeply benefit his father; and his mother too.

'That seems very in line with what Bettina said at the conference,' Glenn said, closing his notepad. 'Thank you, Christina. For sharing your story and your insights with me. They were invaluable.'

'You are most welcome,' Christina smiled serenely. 'You know, Glenn, life is full of omens – signs that God wants us to interpret. Perhaps this is a sign for you... Tomorrow I meet Bettina. She has invited me to the office to collect some leaflets to distribute during my sermons. Why don't you come along?' she asked him.

'Me?'

'Yes, you,' Christina laughed. 'Oh, it would make a great surprise. Bettina would never expect you to come with me.'

Glenn considered the idea for a moment.

'It's strange,' he said, trusting the confidentiality he felt in the warm atmosphere of Christina's kitchen table. 'I feel like the last year I have heard so much about Bettina, so many wonderful stories of bravery, dedication and support in the face of difficult circumstances. I find it hard to believe I've only ever met her once.'

'You're nervous,' Christina said, smiling.

'A little,' Glenn admitted.

'Don't be.' Christina laid a reassuring hand on his. 'Bettina will be so happy to see you, and who better to tell her about the work you've been doing than you yourself?'

'I do need to hear her story, and talk to her about the way forward. You see, I'm keen to forge a link between the ICB and the DCF and the only way to do that is to see if she approves of my initiative.'

'Oh, she will,' smiled Christina. 'So that's settled. You'll come with me tomorrow?'

'Alright,' Glenn nodded. Christina, he was discovering, was a hard woman to say no to.

'Let's have some dessert to celebrate then!' she laughed. 'You still need to be presented with your crown.'

'My crown?' said Glenn, puzzled by the word.

'Your *Frankfurter Kranz*,' Christina laughed again. 'Wait here!'

Christina made her way slowly over to the fridge, where she took out a large metal tin. She brought it to the table and asked Glenn to fetch some plates. Glenn returned to the table to find a masterfully baked cake waiting for him.

'Christina, this looks amazing.'

'*This* is the Frankfurt Crown Cake, and we make it here in the city for guests,' she smiled. 'Come on, you have to cut the first slice.'

Glenn cut into the cake with relish, delighted to see layers of thick cherry jam oozing beneath the soft yellow sponge. The buttercream plastered on top looked fluffy and delicious.

'The nut brittle you see is a mixture of almond flakes,' she said. 'We call it *Krokant*.'

Glenn slipped a forkful of cake into his mouth and savoured the taste.

'It's fantastic!' he said, tucking in to the rest of his plate.

'*Willkommen in Frankfurt*, Glenn,' Christina laughed at his ferocious appetite. 'We can take Bettina a slice tomorrow.'

'Great idea,' he smiled, imagining the delight on Bettina's face.

As thoughts of the meeting the next day wandered through his mind, and the texture of the cake delighted his taste buds, Glenn fell into a fuzzy, warm reverie. So deep was his pleasure that all other thoughts slipped away from him, including those of Eleanora and the call he had promised to make to her that night.

CHAPTER TWENTY-TWO

The next morning Christina watered the beautiful orchids in her kitchen while Glenn finished his cup of coffee. He watched her, wondering how she experienced flowers if she could not see them.

'They have the faintest smell,' she said, smiling gently when he asked her. 'And the softest texture. I feel their presence in the room. They are God; an infinitesimal example of his marvellous creation.'

Glenn smiled, feeling the strange sense of awe he always felt after hearing a story from one of the six women from Aachen. Christina was a miracle of faith, someone who had truly been tested.

'There's beauty all around, Glenn,' she continued, smiling at her flowers. 'There's beauty in the dark.'

'I'm learning that,' he sighed. 'I'm learning so much from you all and I'm so grateful for that.'

'It takes a strong man to admit there are things he still has to learn,' she said, somehow knowing instinctively what Glenn was talking about. 'Your father will learn in time, and become a great student. His son gives me faith in that. Even Jesus, who learnt the trade of his father Joseph, that of carpentry, struggled at first. He was human too, just like your father.'

'Yes,' said Glenn, nodding but feeling guilty inside. He remembered Mr. James. Glenn was not sure he had the same confidence as Christina, and that made him feel bad.

'Are you ready?' she called to him as she pulled on a heavy winter coat.

'Yes,' he smiled. 'I've put the cake in the bag.'

Walking out into Frankfurt on that December morning, Glenn felt the air rush around him, crisp and icy. The city was clearly preparing for Christmas. Bright lights were being strung around shops and pretty festive scenes were displayed in windows. They wandered along, chatting about the different Christmas traditions in Germany, England and the United States.

'Don't you miss seeing your parents at Christmas?' Christina asked.

'Eleanora always likes to spend it at home,' he said. 'Our parents don't always get along so well. It's not always easy to find the balance with them.'

'But surely now, with your father's condition, it is better?' she asked.

'My in-laws are not exactly your average empathetic human beings, Christina,' he said with a rue smile. Glenn thought about Lesley and Harold, tiptoeing around his father, eyeing him as if he had a disease. In fact, he thought, but did not say to Christina, the Beaumonts were so far removed from the average human experience, that they were more dusty, aristocratic statues than humans.

'In the States we do a lot of things like you guys over here,' he said, returning to happier memories of his own parents. 'We have the candy canes, the gingerbread, the snowmen.'

'And do you have Jesus Christ?' Christina laughed. 'I believe that's also an important part of Christmas!'

'Honey, there is more Jesus Christ in America than diabetes, and that's saying something!' Glenn laughed.

'That's good to know,' she smiled. 'Ah, here we are. The ICB.'

Glenn looked up to see they were walking down a beautiful street which must have dated back to the 1800s. From the end of the road, Glenn could see the building ahead of them. The words 'International Charity for the Blind' were written below the German translation, marked in a striking blue against the white of the building.

To his surprise, when they reached the entrance, Glenn suddenly felt nervous. There on the doorstep, he had a strange and strong desire to run away, far away, and never come back. But before he could do or say anything, Christina took him by the arm.

'Let's go and find Bettina,' she said in the manner of an assertive preacher.

They rang the buzzer, and Christina announced her name.

'Christina!' came the voice in the machine, a voice Glenn recognised immediately as Bettina's. '*Willkommen!*'

Bettina rattled off a stream of affectionate German before buzzing Christina up.

'She'll never believe who I have with me!' Christina whispered as she led Glenn up the stairs. After a short climb, they reached an open plan office, with the ICB logos and a few posters sticking to the walls. As the ICB head office, Glenn was imagining something more grand, with a large staff and a busy, buzzing environment. It was in fact smaller than Odile's branch of the ICB in New Orleans, and the only person who appeared to be working there was Bettina.

Glenn caught a glimpse of her blonde hair tied back above her small, slim back through the open doorway to an office. She was wearing a black polo neck sweater and appeared to be finishing off something at the computer. She called through to Christina in German before appearing, dressed in a flowing blue skirt, decorated with small beads of lapis lazuli. Blue, Glenn thought. Bettina always wore blue. He said nothing, for he knew she could not see him.

However, as she walked slowly towards Christina to locate and embrace her, Bettina stopped in her tracks. She said something in German.

'Yes,' Christina answered in English, grinning widely. 'I have someone here with me. He is staying with me whilst he visits Frankfurt.'

Glenn felt stupid, standing there, saying nothing, but he could not find the words to speak. He knew that somewhere deep inside, a part of him longed for the recognition he wanted to feel, without sound, speech, sight or touch: he wanted to see if Bettina knew instinctively who he was.

'Glenn?' she said, the corners of her plump mouth curling into a smile. 'Is that really you?'

His heart flipped at her words and he beamed from ear to ear.

'Hello, Bettina,' he said.

'Hello,' she answered him. She was not looking at him, but Glenn had the distinct impression she was taking him in: the sense of him, the essence. Perhaps it was because he was doing the same. Without knowing why, and knowing that no one in the room would see him doing so, he closed his eyes, and tried to absorb more than what his eyes could see. The energy he felt vibrating in the room was full of warmth and welcome.

'I hope you don't mind me coming here, unannounced,' he said, opening his eyes after a moment. 'I was visiting Christina and she said you were meeting today.'

'Of course I don't mind,' she said gently. 'You are most welcome in Frankfurt, Glenn. And in our office.'

'*Danke*,' he said, his mouth dry.

'What's this!' Bettina laughed; a tinkling, delicate sound. 'He speaks German now?'

'*Ein bisschen*,' Christina laughed too. 'We need to teach him some more.'

'With pleasure,' Bettina smiled.

'We've brought cake,' said Glenn, glowing with the warmth of Bettina's reception. 'Want some?'

'You know the way to impress me, Glenn,' Bettina laughed again, running a hand through her hair, her face full of disbelief. 'Wow. Yes, I will have some. Thank you.'

Whilst the two women embraced, Glenn took out the cake and looked for some plates and cutlery in the small office kitchen. Meanwhile Christina and Bettina chatted away in German, preparing coffee at the machine nearby. When Glenn had arranged three large slices of cake on the plates, topped with buttercream and dripping with juicy jam, he placed them at a table in the centre of the office and waited for the women to arrive.

'The office is smaller than I imagined,' Glenn said, looking around at the sparse interior.

'We just do marketing here in Frankfurt, Glenn,' said Bettina. 'The formal headquarters are in Aachen, but I prefer to commute here from home.'

'Bettina lives in Wurzburg,' Christina explained. 'It's maybe one hour from here.'

'Ah,' said Glenn. A memory stirred in his mind of Laura meeting Bettina in Wurzburg.

'So Glenn,' said Bettina. 'I think you have had a busy year.'

'Christina told you?' he said. 'About the case studies?'

'Christina,' smiled Bettina. 'Laura, Odile, Elfrida, Zu-Ting. Name me one of my staff who has not told me about them.'

'So you know?' Glenn asked, relieved that his mission was not a secret and was, he hoped, appreciated.

'I know how beloved and respected you now are on three different continents,' she laughed. 'But if you were happy to share with me now, I would like to hear in your words what you are doing, and why.'

Glenn sat back in his seat and took a sip of his coffee, wondering where to begin. As ever, Bettina's presence created comfort and reassurance, not fear and nervousness. He felt he could be open and honest with her about everything. So he began, from the start, from Aachen to London, to New Orleans, to Acapulco, to Hong Kong and to the tragedy of Mr. James.

'I believe in the work of the ICB,' he said, after recounting his discoveries. 'I can't tell you how much courage and faith it has given me in recovery and rehabilitation, for my father and all others who have experienced vision loss. The women I have interviewed, your fantastic staff, have opened my eyes, Bettina.'

Glenn waited for her to speak, watching as she listened in her still, polite, and quietly analytical way.

'What do you think?' he asked her, slightly nervous.

'I think you still have one story missing from your inventory,' she said, a small smile on her face.

'Well, yeah,' Glenn said clumsily. 'But I understand if you don't...'

'Have confidence, Glenn,' Bettina said suddenly. Her voice and her expression were both firm. 'What you are doing is great. Your words have touched me more than I can say. I want to help you.'

'That's great,' Glenn sighed with relief. 'Thank you, really.'

'I think you will find my story quite different from all the others, though,' she said with a sad smile. 'Unlike Christina and the others, my journey through life was quite smooth.'

'It will complete the set,' said Glenn, taking his notebook out of his pocket. He flicked past the pages of notes he had made the night before about Christina, and paused, pen poised, at a blank page. 'Please,' he said. 'Tell me your story.'

'Well, I was born blind, that was my first and only misfortune in life,' she said. 'But my parents loved me so much. They were professors at the University of Wurzburg, and ensured I had everything I needed to grow up as easily as possible. They brought me up to *cope* with my disability, unlike so many others.'

Bettina paused for a moment to smile at the memory.

'You see, Glenn, mine is not a sad tale of suffering,' she said. 'I had a very happy childhood. I grew up in Wurzburg in a beautiful house with my parents and my younger brother, Heiner. We had a dog called Chevro and two cats called Magda and Luba. Every summer we would go hiking in Bavaria, or swimming in the lakes close to Berlin. My parents took us to all the greatest cities in Europe, and much further, to China, the Americas, Australia and Japan. We never suffered hardship: we were the lucky ones.'

Glenn listened to Bettina's story and images floated into his mind of happy family holidays, loving embraces and the deep friendship between Bettina and her doctor brother, Heiner. He wondered whether Heiner looked like Bettina; a male version of her blonde, voluptuous beauty was hard to imagine. He looked down at his notepad and began to make notes as she spoke.

'I went through high school like any other child and excelled in my exams,' she said. 'I went on to study psychology at the University of Wurzburg. My parents were convinced I would join them in the faculty! But I was not content with academic life. I wanted to be useful, so I started volunteering in Wurzburg, Frankfurt and Berlin. I worked with the blind who had never tried to adapt to their condition, who had been shunned, abandoned or stigmatised for their disability. I dealt with a lot of shame in those months of volunteering, shame beyond imagining, and I had learnt in my degree that the greatest antidote to shame was empathy. So I tried my best to empathise with those who suffered. That was when Herbert found me.'

'Herbert Farrand?' said Glenn, remembering the sharp, serious figure from the conference in Aachen.

'Yes, Mr. Farrand,' said Bettina. 'He came to one of the sessions I helped with in a local community centre in Berlin. He said he was looking for some help in setting up a charity for the blind. I was very impressed with his vision.'

'What was his vision?' Glenn asked.

'He wanted to look for pioneers in the blind world, women who could show that the blind can live fulfilling and normal lives, just like the seeing,' she said. 'So we worked together on a plan. He sent me around the world to search for women like me: women who could make a difference.'

'And so it began,' Glenn smiled.

'Yes, and so it did,' Bettina said. She was not smiling, however.

'Were you happy with your position?' Glenn asked. 'It was your first job out of university. You're still in it now so it must have been worth your while to stay with the ICB.'

'Oh, yes,' she said. 'I am so happy in my work.'

Glenn heard the words Bettina spoke, but could not quite connect them to the melancholy look on her face. It was a look he had seen before, at the conference in Aachen.

'Do you know how many lives you have touched?' Glenn asked her gently.

'They have touched mine too,' she said.

'I heard the word saviour, heroine and friend more times than I could count when I spoke with Laura, Odile, Elfrida, Zu-Ting, and even Christina here,' he said quietly. 'You've made so many people happy, Bettina.'

Bettina simply nodded her thanks, the melancholy look washing over her face once more. Glenn wondered about this look for it seemed to him that Bettina had led a blessed life and now lived her dream of helping the blind live normal lives. He could not understand her sadness. But before he could probe further, Christina suggested they look back at photos of every trip Bettina had taken out to the five women.

Glenn was astonished to discover photographs that Christina and Bettina could trace and recognise. They had been printed in a special way to create certain reliefs and textures the blind could feel with their fingers.

'This is amazing!' he cried, stunned by the miracles of technology. 'What a beautiful creation for the blind community.'

'Try and see as we see,' Bettina urged him, taking his hand in hers and drawing his fingers across the surface of the photograph. It was a photograph of Laura and Bettina in front of Big Ben in London. Both women looked younger, and the surface of their faces, their shoulders, and the façade of the British clock tower were all raised and slightly distorted. The detail was magnificent, Glenn marvelled, bending down to inspect the photograph closely.

'Here,' said Bettina, taking a photograph and pulling it quickly to her breast so Glenn could not see it. 'Close your eyes and tell me, who do you think this is?'

Glenn held out his hand and allowed Bettina to lead him down to the photograph. His fingers passed over the bubbly surface as he took in the topography of a face, a smile, a rush of hair.

'Is it Zu-Ting?' he asked, tracing the sharp cheekbones he thought he could feel there.

Bettina laughed.

'Let me see,' Christina said excitedly. She too felt the photograph beneath Glenn's fingers, and she too began to laugh.

'Oh dear,' she said, and Glenn opened his eyes to see a picture of Odile and her children.

'Not quite,' he laughed. 'I think I need to practice.'

'Try this one,' said Bettina.

Glenn took the whole photograph in his hands this time and concentrated hard. He allowed his whole hand to cross the surface of the painting before trailing his fingers above the contours, dips and mountains of the scene before him. He knew there was a figure in the photograph. He traced the curve of an arm before reaching the stiff column of a neck. When he reached what he knew to be the lips of this person, he knew who it was.

'It's you,' he grinned.

'Very good, Glenn,' Bettina said warmly.

Glenn did not take his fingers away from the photo. Nor did he open his eyes. He began to trace the rest of Bettina's body, from the firmness of her round cheeks, to the small, smooth bump of her belly. She was wearing something, a coat perhaps.

'This was taken in winter,' he said, his fingers moving onto what he thought might be the sharp branches of bare, leafless trees.

'Go on,' she said, intrigued by his progress.

'You are wearing wellington boots,' he laughed. 'Was it raining?'

'Snowing,' she said.

'That explains the woolly hat,' he laughed. 'It feels cosy.'

'It was,' Bettina said. 'It was made for me by one of the blind volunteers at the centre in Aachen. Christina has one too.'

'It's a wonderful hat,' Christina laughed. 'Made with love and butterflies!'

'There's someone else here,' said Glenn, tracing the outline of another pair of shoulders. 'They have the same cheeks as you!'

'My mother,' said Bettina, and Glenn could hear the smile in her voice.

'Behind you, in the distance, there is a building,' he said. 'A big house, maybe a farm.'

'My parent's house,' she said.

'Where you grew up?' Glenn asked.

'Yes, in Wurzburg,' she laughed. 'Glenn, have you opened your eyes?'

'No!' he cried indignantly. 'I'm playing by the rules here!'

'I'm impressed, Glenn,' he heard Christina say. 'You're a natural.'

'It looks, well, it feels, like a beautiful home,' said Glenn.

'It is,' she said in a quiet, happy voice.

'I wish I could see it,' he said, genuinely yearning to see the place where so many happy memories had been made.

'You can, Glenn,' Bettina chuckled in her warm, deep way. 'Just open your eyes.'

'Not yet,' he grinned. 'I'm having too much fun.'

Bettina let out a sigh of pleasure beside him, and Glenn beamed to hear it. It was such a soft, sweet sound, a sound that confirmed for him that she too was having fun. The thought filled him with happiness; the strangeness of that moment in Aachen seemed to have vanished between them.

A sudden rustling beside them told Glenn that Christina was searching for a new photograph, and indeed, after a few seconds, a new photograph had been placed in front of him.

'Tell us who this is, Glenn,' the young priestess said sweetly.

But before Glenn could even begin to analyse the photograph, a loud buzz filled the room.

'Oh,' said Bettina. Glenn's eyes opened instinctively. Someone was at the door.

'I wasn't expecting anyone,' said Bettina. She looked confused. 'Were you?'

'No,' said Christina, shaking her head.

Standing up, Bettina walked slowly to the receiver and pressed a button.

'Hallo?' she said.

'*Bettina!*' came a man's voice. He spoke in rapid, excited German, which Glenn of could not catch. The voice was familiar, though. Glenn had heard it before. Bettina too seemed to know the man, for she answered in a surprised but familiar way. She buzzed him in and then turned to Glenn and Christina.

'It's Herbert,' she said.

'Herbert?' Christina repeated, a note of unpleasant surprise in her voice.

'Yes, he's here to visit me,' she said. 'He has something he needs my help with.'

'But I thought he was out of the country?' Christina asked.

'*Ja*, but apparently he's back,' Bettina shrugged before turning to Glenn with an apologetic smile. 'I'm sorry, Glenn. It would seem our little reunion has been interrupted.'

'Not at all,' said Glenn, waving the apology aside. 'Business comes first!'

'I wonder why he's here?' Christina voiced aloud.

'We'll soon find out,' said Bettina.

The door to the office swung open and Herbert Farrand strode in, unsmiling, in his smouldering, charismatic way. When Glenn had first set eyes on the President of the ICB, he had been struck by the man's presence. He was a handsome man, dressed as impeccably as ever in loose, beige chinos and a pale blue shirt. At the conference in Aachen, Farrand had been wearing smart, shimmering grey suits and ties, but here he was, clearly dressed for life outside of the office. Behind him, a tall, slim woman walked in, dressed in a loose pink dress. She was extremely fit and, despite clear attempts to hide it, had clearly had some work done on her pouting lips and rock-hard bust.

'Bettina!' Herbert cried, throwing open his arms and pulling his colleague into a tight embrace before spotting the others. 'And, wait, what's this? Christina! And, who's this? Where do I know you from?'

Farrand took Christina's hand warmly in his, not taking his eyes off of Glenn.

'It's Glenn, Glenn Tebbhurst,' Glenn explained.

'You remember Glenn, from Aachen?' said Bettina.

'I do,' said Farrand, his blue eyes fixed on Glenn's face. He took Glenn's outstretched hand. 'You're the banker, from London.'

'Fundraiser,' Glenn corrected him.

'Right,' Farrand brushed the difference aside. 'You're the workshop man, if I recall correctly? You participated and made a good impression on everyone. And you were a bit smarter than that strange Texan. What was his name? Phil?'

'Bill!' laughed Christina. 'Oh dear. I had forgotten Bill.'

'Yes, you were Mr. Nice Guy,' Farrand smiled, appraising Glenn with icy, blue eyes.

'I guess I was,' Glenn smiled.

'Mr. Nice Guy has turned out to be even nicer since then,' said Bettina.

'Oh yeah?' said Farrand, still studying Glenn closely. 'How so?'

'I'll let him tell you,' said Bettina.

'*Ja, ja.* OK,' said Farrand. 'But first let *me* introduce *you* to someone. This is Ariane.'

The tall blonde woman who had followed him into the office raised a bored hand.

'Hallo,' she said.

'She was my fitness instructor, can you tell?' he winked at Glenn, presumably because Glenn was the only one who could see. 'But now she's my girlfriend. We've been travelling all over together. In fact, we just came over from our villa in the Bahamas.'

'The Bahamas?' cried Bettina, smiling. 'Wow. Europe must be cold in comparison?'

'I'm freezing,' Ariane said miserably. 'I want to go back, but he has business.'

'Business?' said Bettina.

'Yes, that's why I'm here,' he said. 'But come on, let's catch up a little first! Let's at least drink a coffee.'

The new arrivals came and sat around the table, sweeping the photographs aside and resting themselves after their journey.

'We've been racing across France for the last couple of days,' said Farrand. 'We were staying with friends in Bordeaux and I forgot how slow French roads were. I was so happy to reach the *Autobahn* after Alsace. My little machine only shows her true colours above one hundred and fifty.'

'How have you been travelling?' Glenn asked, wondering what the little machine could be.

'Come and check out my wheels,' Farrand answered, slapping Glenn on the back and drawing him over to the office window. Glenn followed him and looked down onto the street, where a sleek, black Porsche stood parked outside the office. 'Pretty, isn't she?' he grinned. 'She's a dream to drive.'

'Very nice,' said Glenn, who had never shown much interest in cars.

'You want to take a spin?' he asked Glenn.

'Thanks, but, I think I'll pass,' Glenn answered, smiling politely.

'You're more of a Mercedes man, I can tell,' said Farrand, winking at him. 'Good man. Mercedes is a fine German brand.'

Glenn said nothing, turning back to the table, where Christina looked slightly uncomfortable. Ariane was eyeing her up, clearly disconcerted by her blindness and the dog collar at her neck.

'Don't be shy, sweetheart,' Farrand called out to her. 'Make friends! These women make my world go around.'

Glenn watched as the uncomfortable Ariane cleared her throat.

'So,' she said to Christina. 'Do you work out?'

'I like walking,' the priestess said kindly.

'Nordic walking?' Ariane asked.

'No, just German walking,' Christina smiled serenely.

'Herbert,' said Bettina, walking over to where he and Glenn stood. 'Perhaps while Glenn is here he can tell you what he has been doing for us?'

'I'm listening,' said Farrand, sitting himself down and taking a sip of his espresso.

Glenn began to tell the President what he had set out to achieve by interviewing the six women he had met at the conference in Aachen. He briefly detailed the failure of Mr. James' operation and outlined his plans to approach the board to fundraise for the ICB. The more he spoke, the more Herbert seemed interested in what Glenn had to say. When Glenn had finished, the President nodded, raising an impressed eyebrow.

This sounds like the foundations of a great partnership, Mr. Tebbhurst,' he said. 'I share Bettina's enthusiasm.'

'If we can, I would love Diversified Charities to support these women in their work in the field,' said Glenn. 'Now I have their stories, I have the material I need to really push this forward at a senior level.'

'Funds are always welcome, Glenn,' said Farrand. 'Where would we be without our financial supporters? We will speak more about this.'

With that, Farrand turned to Bettina.

'Bettina, we need to discuss something,' he said.

'OK,' she said, looking down at her watch. 'I've got some time.'

'Now that you're working full-time here in Frankfurt, I have some duties to assign to you,' he said.

'Let me get my tablet,' she said helpfully.

When Bettina had fetched a tablet on which she could record Farrand's words easily, she nodded and agreed until the last request.

'Now, I have something of a little fundraiser I'll need you to attend this weekend,' he said. 'It's last minute, I know, but it will make all the difference if you are there.'

'I'm sorry, this weekend I can't,' said Bettina, putting down her tablet for a moment.

'I need you there, Bettina,' said Farrand sternly. 'You have a way with the guests. They like you. They like to look at you. Plus, it will be fun! Put on a pretty dress, drink some champagne, eat some delicious canapés and voila, we will have funds for new projects!'

'It's my brother's birthday,' said Bettina. 'I'm sorry, Herbert.'

'I thought the whole point of you being based in this office was to have someone available for these sorts of things!' Farrand snapped angrily. 'Isn't that what I pay you for?'

'With all due respect, Herbert,' Christina said quietly, 'Bettina works harder than anyone in the ICB. She would only say no to something if she really had to.'

'Thank you, Christina,' Bettina said calmly. 'I think Herbert is just frustrated.'

Farrand was silent for a moment, clearly chastised by the words of these two women. Glenn watched all with fascination.

'I'm sorry, Bettina,' Farrand said stiffly. 'If you can't make it, I'll just have to find someone else.'

'That's alright, Herbert,' she replied gracefully. 'Now, perhaps we should talk more about the upcoming quarter in my office?'

'*Ja, ja, genau,*' Farrand answered in German.

'Christina, Glenn,' Bettina raised a hand as if to reach her friends. 'This will all be very boring for you. Let me pass you the leaflets, as promised, and perhaps we should let you get on with your day?'

'As you wish, Bettina,' said Christina, clearly disappointed that their visit had been cut short. Bettina went to a nearby table and collected up a box of leaflets. She picked them up and passed them to Glenn.

'Are you OK to carry these, Glenn?' she asked him.

'Of course, Bettina,' he said, suddenly aware that he had to say goodbye to her.

'Well then, this is farewell for now,' she said, holding out a hand.

'I hope to meet again,' he said, balancing the box so he could take her hand in his. They squeezed each other's palms in goodbye and said no more.

'Can I leave too?' Ariane asked in her bored, disinterested voice.

345

'No, sweetie,' Farrand commanded. 'I won't be long and then we can get out of here.'

Saying their goodbyes, with promises from Farrand to call Glenn in the week to discuss fundraising, Christina and Glenn took their leave. Walking past the shining black car, Glenn could tell Christina was unhappy.

'He likes to turn up unannounced,' she said when they reached the end of the street.

'The President?' said Glenn.

'*Ja*,' sighed Christina. 'I'm sorry, Glenn. I think Bettina was so happy to have us surprise her there in the office.'

'That's OK,' said Glenn. 'She has a lot of work to do, I understand that.'

'That *man*,' Christina said bitterly. 'He just barges in like a storm whenever he likes, commanding her to do this, demanding that we all follow this, that and the other policies.'

'The charity sector often attracts those kinds of personalities at a management level,' said Glenn with a chuckle. 'Sometimes it's the storm that gets things moving.'

'It's *Bettina* that gets things moving,' Christina protested. 'Do you think the way he spoke to her was correct, Glenn?'

Glenn considered his answer for a moment.

'No,' he said. 'I think he treated Bettina unfairly.'

'He spoke to her like she was an object to be paraded at a fair,' said Christina. 'And when she was not available, he knew that he had lost an attractive, persuasive bargaining chip for his little fundraiser.'

'Is he really that sort of man?' Glenn asked.

'Did you not sense the perfume of that woman? God bless her heart, but I suspect you can confirm to me that she was a vain woman – very beautiful, lots of make up?' Christina asked.

Glenn laughed but made no comment about Farrand's taste in women.

'I just think Bettina has proved herself time and time again,' he said. 'I've never met anyone like her. She can handle men like Herbert. Jeez, she can handle anything.'

They walked in silence for a while, back towards the house, where Glenn's suitcase was already packed and ready to be taken to the airport. When Glenn was ready to go, and they had said their goodbyes, Christina put her hands on both his shoulders. She closed her eyes and he assumed she was saying a prayer. But when she opened them, her expression was strange. She had a knowing smile on her lips.

'You know, I've listened to a lot of confessions in my life, Glenn,' she said.

'Oh yeah?' he said, laughing. 'I'm not surprised. It comes with the job, right?'

'It does,' smiled the priest. 'I have seen thousands of people in church, wanting to confess, to share their thoughts, fear and feelings. I've listened to it all.'

Glenn said nothing, wondering where Christina was going with her words.

'I've seen men in love,' she said.

'Oh?' said Glenn, his heart shifting uncomfortably in his chest. He looked down at his friend's serene face.

'Herbert Farrand does not love this Ariane,' she said, laughing softly. 'He lusts for her body. But you, Glenn, you are different.'

'Me?' he said, surprised by her words.

'You are in love,' she said.

For a moment, Glenn did not know what to say.

'My wife and I,' he began. 'Eleanora and me. We have had our difficulties in the past, but...'

'I'm not talking about your wife, Glenn,' said Christina, smiling softly. 'But I think you know that, don't you?'

Whatever Glenn knew or did not know, Christina's words sowed a storm in his head. It raged as he checked in to his flight, boarded the plane back to London, and fastened his seat belt for the ride. Had those hours with Bettina not been delightful, he thought to himself, revisiting the memory of that morning? Had not the feelings he had felt in Aachen over one year ago, after knowing Bettina for the briefest of moments, returned that morning, filling him with the bright glow of hope, warmth and belonging? And, God, he thought: had she not been so damn beautiful? Carefully and decisively, Glenn tried to push such thoughts from his mind, for he knew who Christina had been talking about. But it was not Bettina who would be waiting for him at home, it was Eleanora.

CHAPTER TWENTY-THREE

Herbert Farrand's promise of a call within the week actually turned out to be a call the next year. It was April by the time Glenn heard from him, and the chilliness of that wintery meeting in Frankfurt was already beginning to fade as spring approached. Glenn had been glad of the interval, relishing the chance to write up the case studies of the previous year. With Bettina's story came the complete set of six, and he was finally moving closer towards having something solid and constructive to show the board.

The phone ringing snapped him out of his train of thought. Glenn picked it up in a daze.

'A call for you, sir,' came his secretary's cheerful voice. 'A Mr. Herbert Farrand, calling from Germany?'

'Ah,' said Glenn, looking up from his computer. 'Great. Thanks, Sonia. Put him through, will you?'

'Certainly, sir,' said Sonia. A small beep followed as the call was connected.

'Mr. Farrand,' said Glenn. 'This is a nice surprise.'

'Glenn, hallo,' came Farrand's voice, firm and steady. 'I'm finally calling you. Can you tell I've been busy?'

'Apparently so,' laughed Glenn. 'How are you, Mr. Farrand?'

'Oh, fine, fine,' he said. 'A bit tired. But such is life.'

'How is Ariane?' Glenn asked, remembering the tall, striking beauty who had accompanied Farrand to their meeting in Frankfurt. He recalled the sheen of the Porsche and the couple's journey from the villa in the Bahamas.

'Who?' came Herbert's answer.

'Your partner,' said Glenn. 'We met in Frankfurt? It was Ariane, wasn't it?'

'Oh, right,' said Farrand flatly. 'Actually, it was not working well, so…'

'Ah, I see,' said Glenn. 'I'm sorry, I didn't mean to intrude.'

'Don't be sorry, Glenn,' came Farrand's cold, business manner. 'I'm not.'

Glenn could tell from the way Farrand spoke that things with Ariane had not worked out in his favour.

'Right,' he said quickly, clearing his throat as if clearing his windpipe could clear away the awkwardness of that moment. 'So what can I do for you, Mr. Farrand?'

'I am calling regarding the matter we discussed in Frankfurt,' he said. 'Bettina is convinced that you are doing saintly work for us. Christina thinks so too. My question for you today is, how can you help us in a more, well, let us say, *practical* way?'

'You mean with fundraising?' Glenn asked, knowing instinctively what Farrand had called for.

'Exactly,' said Farrand. 'Let's be straight about it, Glenn. Hmm? I don't want to "beat around the bush" as you English people say.'

Frankness was a quality Glenn appreciated in his business dealings, so Farrand's approach was quite refreshing.

'Well, how about you start by telling me who your friends are,' said Glenn. 'Who is supporting you now? Where can I go to maximise donations and charitable giving?'

'We have many sources,' came Farrand's answer. 'I like to diversify our funding pool. For example, now we have donors in Germany, in the States, and in Switzerland.'

'OK, let's talk about Switzerland,' said Glenn, knowing from experience the wealth of funding potential in that rich country. 'Do you have some contacts I can reach out to in Geneva, Bern or Zurich?'

'Yes, yes, I have a man in Zurich,' said Farrand, sounding already bored by this discussion. 'His name is Kirschenbauer. He helps me a lot. You can approach him, no problem.'

Glenn froze. The name seared through his brain unpleasantly. Shaking his head, he wondered if he had misheard.

'I'm sorry, can you repeat that?' he asked Farrand. 'The line might be bad. I think I misheard.'

'Kirschenbauer,' he repeated, loudly this time. 'K-I-R-S-C-H-E-N-B-A-U-E-R. Franz Kirschenbauer.'

Glenn could not believe what he was hearing.

'And this is someone you work with for fundraising?' Glenn asked, speaking slowly and carefully. 'This is someone you would like me to contact?'

'*Ja*,' said Farrand. 'Take him out for lunch, that usually works. He likes *Rösti mit Speck*.'

'That sounds nice,' said Glenn, thinking quickly and choosing his words with care. 'Well, that seems like a good place to start, Mr. Farrand. Small steps, you know how it goes. I'll be in touch with him and see where we go from there. How does that sound?'

'*Ja*, OK,' said Farrand. 'I'll leave you to it then, Glenn. Be in touch when you have some news for me, OK?'

'Certainly,' said Glenn, forcing a cheerful tone into his voice. 'Great. Thanks for the call, Mr. Farrand.'

'Come on, Glenn,' said Farrand, chuckling lightly. 'You must know by now that you can call me Herbert.'

'Thanks for the call, Hebert,' said Glenn.

When he put the phone down, Glenn let out a long, deep sigh. *No way*, he thought to himself. Picking up the phone again, he called through to Natasha in the International Department. The phone rang a few times before she answered.

'Natasha, Russian Affairs. How can I help?' she introduced herself.

'Natasha, it's Glenn,' he said quickly. 'I have a question for you.'

'Fire away, Glenn,' Natasha replied.

'Where have you heard the name Kirschenbauer before?' he asked.

'Kirschenbauer? As in Franz Kirschenbauer? Zurich? Dodgy practices?' she said.

'Exactly,' sighed Glenn. 'Thanks, Nat. That was all.'

Glenn hung up the phone and felt a deep discomfort stirring in his heart. Natasha had just confirmed for him that Franz Kirschenbauer was indeed the man Glenn thought he was.

Unknown to many, Kirschenbauer had a reputation beyond the golden, untouchable borders or Switzerland. A mild way of putting it was that Kirschenbauer was a controversial banker. Deeper in the financial industry, however, Kirschenbauer was known to be one of the biggest money launderers in Europe. Any affiliation with him was bound up in shady dealings.

Reaching into his desk drawer, Glenn pulled out his notebook, where Bettina had scribbled down the number of the Frankfurt office. Deliberating for a moment, Glenn decided to put through the call.

'Hallo?' came Bettina's voice on the line.

'Hello, Bettina? It's Glenn.'

'Glenn!' she said in a joyful tone. 'What a nice surprise. How are you?'

'I'm well, thank you,' he said.

'And how is your wife?' she asked. 'Is it Eliana? Elena?'

Glenn's heart leapt uncomfortably for a moment at the thought of Bettina knowing his wife's name. He wondered why it had such an effect on him. After all, the two women had never met.

'Eleanora,' he said, clearing his throat. 'She is well, thank you. How are your parents? Your brother?'

'They are all fine thanks, Glenn,' she said. 'I wish you could have met them, but you were in Frankfurt for such a short time.'

'I received your Christmas card,' said Glenn, remembering the very sweet, handwritten card she had sent him on behalf of the ICB. 'Thank you, Bettina. It was lovely.'

'I'm glad it arrived OK,' she said. 'I saw the address for DCF on the internet. I thought it would find you there. My, it already feels like a long time since Christmas!'

'Yes, it feels like ages since I saw you last,' Glenn said, before he could stop himself. But, to his surprise, Bettina seemed to agree.

'Yes, it does,' she said, a small note of something more than agreement in her voice. Did she miss him, Glenn wondered? He would never ask her, of course. But he wondered. For a moment, Glenn had completely forgotten why he had called her. He felt tongue tied and did not know what to say.

'Glenn?' she said after a pause. 'Is there something wrong?'

'How can you tell?' he asked, laughing nervously, surprised by her words.

'I can hear it in your breathing,' she said. 'The heightened senses of the blind, remember?'

She chuckled down the line, and Glenn's heart soared to hear her laughing. Then, with a sinking feeling, he remembered why he had called her.

'Bettina, is Mr. Farrand there?' he asked her.

'Herbert?' she said. 'In Frankfurt?'

'Yes, is he in the office?' Glenn asked.

'No, he's not,' she said. 'I'm sorry, Glenn. I can ask him to call you from Aachen?'

'No, that's not necessary,' said Glenn, sighing with relief. 'It's you I need to speak to. It will be easier if he's not there.'

'Glenn?' she said. 'What is this about?'

'Have you ever heard the name Franz Kirschenbauer?' Glenn asked her.

'No,' she said. 'Never. Why do you ask?'

'I have some bad news,' he sighed, and without further hesitation, Glenn started to tell Bettina all he knew about Kirschenbauer's antics in Switzerland. The man was notorious for his facilitation of money laundering across the world, enabling large corporations to avoid paying taxes by funnelling funds into false charity schemes.

'Kirschenbauer *is* bad news,' Glenn concluded. 'And this could look really bad for the ICB.'

'What do you mean?' Bettina asked and Glenn could hear the anxiety in her voice. 'Glenn? What could look really bad for the ICB?'

'If Farrand is working with someone like Kirschenbauer, it means the ICB's whole financial set-up could be corrupt,' he said. 'If major donors and partners find out about it, they will sever ties with your charity immediately. What's more, Kirschenbauer is a mastermind in teaching big businesses how to reward people at the top. Farrand is probably benefitting from this relationship in a big way.'

'But Herbert,' came Bettina's small voice. 'Surely he can't be doing this?'

'I'm sorry, Bettina,' Glenn said gently. 'I don't want to believe it either. But this association with Kirschenbauer doesn't look good.'

'What can we do?' she asked quickly. 'God knows I've spent my whole life working to build up the ICB. If we go under there is so much to lose. We provide employment for hundreds of people. So many lives will be ruined.'

'We need to find out as much as we can, as quickly as we can,' said Glenn, seizing the moment. 'We need to speak to Kirschenbauer, to find out how he deals with the ICB.'

'But if Farrand is already dealing with him, how can we?' Bettina asked.

'Good point,' said Glenn, feeling stupid for even suggesting it. He thought fast, searching his mind before answers, and as he did so, a face surfaced in his memory.

'Listen,' he said quickly. 'I have a friend in Zurich, Martin Studehoffe. He constantly deals with cases like this and he will be able to tell me more.'

'Does he know Kirschenbauer?' Bettina asked.

'Yes, intimately,' Glenn said darkly.

'How can we trust him then?' she asked.

'Because he's one of the good guys,' said Glenn. 'He's an old friend.'

'Well, when can you speak to him?' Bettina asked him.

'I can see if he's available next week,' said Glenn. 'Or next month. He's not always easy to find.'

'Next week?' cried Bettina. 'Glenn, we need to get to the bottom of this immediately! The reputation of the ICB is at stake.'

Glenn heard the urgency in Bettina's voice and knew she was right.

'Alright, but he's a hard man to track down,' he said. 'I'll need to head over there to find him.'

'OK, I'll come with you,' Bettina said.

Glenn had not expected her to say this.

'Are you sure?' was all he could ask her. He had not even considered that she would want to come along.

'I want to know as much as possible, Glenn,' she said. 'We have so much to lose. If we can avoid a catastrophe, I'd like to know how.'

'I'll ask my secretary to book you a flight from Frankfurt to Zurich tomorrow,' he said.

'No, Glenn, I can book my own flight,' she protested.

'No, Bettina,' Glenn said firmly. 'None of this should be on your records, or the ICB's records. If this is as bad as it looks, any connection you have to Kirschenbauer and Zurich could look incriminating.'

'OK,' she said, and Glenn heard her swallowing hard.

'Come to the Baur au Lac Hotel when you arrive,' said Glenn, remembering the name of a comfortable hotel in Zurich. 'I'll be waiting for you there.'

'OK,' she said in a sad voice. 'My God, Glenn. What has he done? What is he doing to us?'

'Let's reserve judgement until we know more,' Glenn said calmly. 'I'll see you tomorrow, alright?'

'Tomorrow,' said Bettina firmly, and Glenn heard her spirits brightening. 'Well, that's something good at least.'

'What is?' Glenn asked, confused for a moment.

'That I will see you tomorrow,' she said. 'Goodbye Glenn.'

Glenn bid her farewell and hung up. He leant back in his seat for a moment, looking up at the ceiling. Before he did anything else, before he called through to Sonia to book the flights and the hotel, Glenn wanted to process what Bettina had just said. She was happy that she would see him tomorrow. *I will see Bettina tomorrow*, he thought, with a flip of his heart. And then he thought of something else.

'Oh God,' he groaned, for he realised that before he saw Bettina, he would have to tell Eleanora he was travelling again.

* * * *

Well, it could have gone worse, Glenn thought, unbuttoning his shirt that night and climbing into bed.

'I'd appreciate a bit more notice in the future,' his wife had said stuffily, punishing her husband with a hard glare.

Glenn had told her about his impending travel over a dinner of fresh lamb, plucked from the estate and slaughtered the previous weekend. The meat was bathed in a fresh mint sauce and made for a delectable impromptu farewell dinner.

'It was pretty sudden, honey,' he tried to explain. 'I only found out myself this morning.'

'What's the big deal anyway?' she asked, raising a cynical eyebrow. 'Aren't all charities funded by tax-avoiding multinational corporations? Or men who made millions in illicit industries and now give to charity as some sort of compensation?'

'Baby, no!' cried Glenn. 'Is that really what you think? Jeez, you always look on the dark side.'

'It's the only reason Daddy gives to charity,' she shrugged. 'The tax relief is huge.'

'Well, I don't want to see the ICB go down in flames because of one man's corrupt shenanigans,' said Glenn. 'I won't let that happen.'

'Always the hero,' his wife sighed. 'I'm sure the Six Sirens of Aachen will be delighted you're saving their skin. Can't these damsels in distress look after their own affairs? Surely they've read Butler and de Beauvoir? Or is feminism only available for those of us with eyes to read about it?'

Glenn refused to even engage with such a detrimental comment.

'One of them is coming with me,' he said instead.

'Oh? Which one?' Eleanora demanded.

'Bettina,' said Glenn.

'You've never mentioned her before,' she said. 'Zou-Tooty did, I think. She's the German one, isn't she? The ring leader?'

'Zu-Ting,' Glenn corrected her. 'No, well, I've never had a reason to mention her.'

Glenn looked away and pretended to be very interested in the fresh mint sauce Eleanora had served with the lamb so she could not read anything on his face. Nothing had ever happened with Bettina, he knew that; he had never been unfaithful to his wife. But Glenn still did not trust himself when her name was mentioned.

'I'll be back by the weekend,' he promised Eleanora, still avoiding her gaze. 'Will you be OK without me until then?'

'Ha!' she laughed. 'It's lambing season! I'll barely notice you're gone, darling.'

'Phew,' he smiled at her, happy to know she would have her hands full. 'Can we go to bed early then?' he asked her.

'I thought you'd never ask,' she said, raising an eyebrow once more.

The couple made passionate, sensual love into the early hours of the morning, happy to share the warm embrace of each other's bodies before their separation. Glenn promised to call his wife when he arrived, and set off early for his morning flight to Zurich.

He dozed on the plane and woke to see Lake Zurich stretched out below them as the plane descended. Glenn watched the snowy peaks of the Alps in the distance, shimmering in the morning sun, and remembered the spectacular fjords of Norway for a moment. He felt the same excitement, the same sense of adventure he had felt then, except of course Eleanora was not by his side. He missed her, he realised, looking sadly at the empty seat beside him. But Bettina was down there, in that majestic Swiss city, waiting for him to help her uncover the fraudulent dealings of the ICB President.

Arriving at The Baur au Lac Hotel, Glenn was pleased to find a warm reception. He was offered coffee and newspapers, which he accepted, before asking the receptionist if Bettina had arrived yet.

'Yes, sir,' said the smartly dressed young man. 'Would you like me to inform her of your arrival?'

'That would be excellent,' said Glenn, retiring to the hotel lounge. He sat himself in a comfortable chair in a corner, a considerable distance away from other people. Glenn knew he and Bettina had grave matters to discuss, and the clientele that frequented The Baur au Lac could very well know Kirschenbauer; they might even know Farrand. Switzerland was a small country so they would have to be careful. Such was the mood of his thoughts when Glenn heard a familiar voice beside him.

'Hi,' said Bettina, making him jump. She had walked over unaccompanied, much to the bemusement of the hotel staff, who had watched her walking with her cane. Perhaps they too, like Glenn, wondered how she could always find her way to him, unguided.

'Bettina,' he stood up, buttoning up his suit jacket. 'It's great to see you again.'

Bettina was dressed in a more businesslike manner than usual. A smart navy suit hugged her curvaceous figure tightly, and two small sapphires sparkled in her earlobes. Her face, usually glowing with health and warmth, was pinched with worry.

'You too,' she said, smiling sadly. 'If only it were under better circumstances.'

'Indeed,' Glenn sighed heavily. 'Come on. Let's have a coffee.'

Naturally, Bettina wanted to know all there was to know about Kirschenbauer and his antics in Switzerland. Glenn tried his best to explain.

'It's not just him,' he said finally. 'Switzerland is full of private banks, and if it's not in Zurich, shady deals are being made in many other places in Switzerland.'

'But why do they target charities?' she asked him.

'It's obvious, no?' he said, scanning her intelligent, attentive face. 'They are a prime target for money laundering. There are more people than I care to admit pretending to build hospitals in Afghanistan, schools in Sudan, and support reforestation programs in the not-so-Democratic Republic of the Congo. These charities are simply assets of big banks, using their status and position to smuggle money, diamonds, gold and precious minerals into the West. A charity is the perfect ruse.'

'That's awful,' Bettina shook her head. 'I've heard about these things. I've read about them, but I never thought they would ever touch my life. I work in a charity, for God's sake.'

'Therefore you work in one of the most lucrative sectors in the financial industry,' said Glenn, smiling bitterly. 'Have no illusions about that, Bettina.'

'Right,' she nodded sadly. 'So have you managed to track down your friend?'

'Studehoffe? I've been trying,' said Glenn, taking out his phone to check his email. There was nothing from him yet. 'I've left messages with his concierge, his wife and his secretary. Something should get through to him. I didn't mention anything about Kirschenbauer. It's a dangerous name to mention.'

Luckily for Glenn, Martin Studehoffe had received his message, and had sent a small missive to the hotel, which he found when he retired upstairs to change. It was enigmatic to the point of conspiracy, Glenn thought, laughing as he read the words:

Glenn,
Welcome to Zurich. Same time, same place?
Martin

Martin was referring to a time and place only he and Glenn could know. Glenn knew immediately where that was, and hastened downstairs to find Bettina.

'When Martin and I first met, at a conference in Davos, he invited me to visit him in Zurich,' Glenn explained to Bettina as they stepped out of the hotel to head into town. 'We had lots to talk about then, and now, whenever I travel back to the city for work, we always meet up in the same place, at the same time, for coffee.'

'Where are we going then?' Bettina asked.

'Three o'clock at The Odeon,' Glenn grinned at her.

'And he'll be there?' Bettina asked, intrigued by this system.

'Oh, he'll be there,' laughed Glenn.

Sure enough, in those bright halls of early nineteenth century splendour, Martin sat at a table, reading a newspaper through his thick spectacles. Glenn looked up at the interior, barely changed since its grand opening in 1911, and led Bettina over to the table.

'Old friend,' said Glenn, striding towards Martin's familiar, thin figure.

'Glenn!' Martin looked up, standing to embrace his friend. 'My, you haven't changed an inch! You're still a handsome fellow.'

'You too, fella! Thanks for meeting me,' said Glenn, smiling broadly at the sound of his friend's distinctive Swiss-German accent.

'Of course, dear man,' said Martin, returning to his seat. 'So, you're back in Zurich?'

'Just for a day,' said Glenn. 'Just today, in fact.'

'Ah,' nodded Martin, turning his eyes to Bettina. 'With your lovely wife? We've never had the pleasure of meeting, madam. My name is Martin Studehoffe.'

'Oh! She's not my...' Glenn began quickly.

'I'm not his...' Bettina said at the same time.

Both burst into nervous laughter.

'Martin,' said Glenn firmly, regaining his composure. 'May I introduce you to Bettina Hartmann? She works for the International Charity of the Blind in Frankfurt, Germany.'

'Ah, the ICB?' said Martin.

'You know of us?' Bettina asked, a small smile rising to her lips.

'I know of your great work,' he said. 'But I'd be intrigued to know more.'

Bettina then preceded to quickly introduce herself and say a few words in German. Martin, clearly happy to speak in his own language, albeit without the Swiss dialect, chattered away with her for some minutes. Glenn listened to all, happy for the opportunity to hear Bettina's silky, firm voice speaking in her mother tongue. He watched her as she commanded respect and interest from his friend. When she stopped, Martin nodded seriously.

'Then you are here in grave circumstances,' he said in English, raising his eyebrows and continuing to nod from Bettina to Glenn. He glanced around the café, to make sure the coast was clear. 'Well, well now. Kirschenbauer, eh? That is a sticky situation. He is a sticky man.'

'We need your help, Martin,' said Glenn.

They ordered coffees and pastries and began to talk.

'It's a tremendous culture of fraud that goes almost entirely undetected,' Martin told them. 'Money laundering in charities is done across the board. Whether it's done through paying salaries, external consultants or siphoned out through expenses, Kirschenbauer will be advising the wrong course of action at every turn.'

'He is a maverick in this field,' Glenn added. 'And the worst thing of all is that everyone knows it. He might as well open up his own walk-in money launderette!'

'The Kirschenbauer Clean Up?' said Martin, grinning at his friend. 'Or is that not elusive enough?'

'Elusive or not, the irony of it all is that everyone he touches is stained for life,' said Glenn.

'Sorry to burst your bubble, boys, but I'm not big on finance,' said Bettina in a small, shy voice. 'Can you please explain some of this to me?'

'Of course, Ms. Hartmann,' Studehoffe nodded with deference. 'What would you like me to explain?'

'Well, all of it,' she said, smiling helplessly. 'First of all, what *is* money laundering? I keep hearing this term, and if this is what Herbert is doing, I need to understand what it really means.'

'That's why we're here, Bettina,' Glenn said gently. 'So you can get the information you need. Don't be shy, OK? Martin's here to clarify things a bit for us.'

'The explanation of money laundering is in the title, Ms. Hartmann,' Martin explained kindly. 'When you launder something, you make it clean, no? Thus money laundering refers to a cleaning process, in which funds earned in an illegitimate way are converted into legitimate assets. Dirty money is washed into clean money. The clue is in the name.'

'So what does this mean for Herbert?' she asked. 'The ICB generates income, through the factory in Hong Kong, and through legitimate donors?'

'Of course it does, Bettina,' said Glenn, sighing sadly. 'The dirty money is not coming into the ICB. The money you receive does not need to be cleaned. It is clean. Herbert is most likely using Kirschenbauer to help him siphon off that money into his own accounts, under false pretences.'

'Glenn's right,' nodded Martin. 'That would be my guess too. He is legitimising illegal transfers of money into his own accounts.'

'But how can we prove any of this?' Bettina asked. 'Herbert has never allowed me to meet any of the bankers he deals with on the accounting side of things. I've never had a reason to meet them either. Only at fundraising events, but even then I'm more on the entertainment side of things.'

'You're the eye candy,' said Glenn darkly, remembering what Christina had said about Bettina's role at fundraising events.

'Yes, I suppose I am,' Bettina nodded angrily. 'And all this time, I never complained because I thought it was for the ICB. God knows I'd do anything for my charity. I've let those men flirt with me, thinking I'm their little perk for forking out a million or two.'

'I understand you're upset, Ms. Hartmann,' said Martin. 'But in answer to your question, there is a very easy way to prove Farrand's criminality.'

'How?' she asked.

'With a set of accounts,' said Studehoffe.

'But I've never seen our accounts,' she said. 'They're not in Braille. I don't think anyone has seen the accounts, except Herbert of course.'

'Most charity accounts are handled by an external fiduciary,' said Studehoffe. 'Whoever is looking at them, they will most likely be far from the prying eyes of staff and beneficiaries. My advice to you, Ms. Hartmann, is to endeavour to gain access to those accounts. Once you have them, your Mr. Farrand will not have a leg to stand on.'

'So we should go to the fiduciary?' said Glenn.

'Exactly,' Martin nodded, before looking down at his watch. With a gasp, he finished his cup of coffee in one fell swig. 'Now, I must be incredibly rude and tell you both that I have another appointment.'

'Still busy as hell, huh?' laughed Glenn, rising to his feet to clasp his old friend's hand.

'Some things never change, eh, Glenn?' he smiled, his dark eyes twinkling behind his spectacles.

'Thanks for this, Martin,' said Glenn. 'It's been very useful to talk to you.'

'Well done for finding me,' he replied with a wink. 'I wish you all the best in this.'

When Martin had left them, Bettina and Glenn walked slowly back to the hotel, both lost in their own thoughts. When they reached the lake, Bettina turned to lean on the railing for a moment. Glenn wished she could see the scene in front of her: the dazzling blue lake beneath the bright blue sky; the amphitheatre of mountains encircling them. But perhaps she saw in her own way, he thought. She too must have felt the softness of the air and heard the splashing of the birds on the water.

'Oh God,' she said suddenly, grasping the railing and shaking her head. She seemed neither angry nor sad. Simply frustrated. 'How am I ever going to get my hands on those accounts?'

'The only way is to convince Herbert to get us a copy,' he said, sighing deeply. 'There is a certain level of financial transparency required of all charities, so he has to be able to show something.'

'He'll know there's something fishy if I ask him,' said Bettina. 'He'll smell a rat straight away.'

Glenn thought hard for a moment and an idea came to him.

'What if I ask for them?' he asked.

'You?' said Bettina.

'Yes, me,' he said, turning away from her so he could think. 'If I am going to start fundraising for you, for Herbert, for the ICB, it would not be unusual for me to ask to look over the accounts. Farrand knows I'm in the financial business. He knows I'd never take on a project without exploring every nook and corner of the current incomings and outgoings.'

'Do you think he'll give you access?' Bettina asked incredulously.

'Sure, as long as I sign a confidentiality agreement,' said Glenn, thinking fast.

'But if you do that, how can you expose what you find?' Bettina asked.

'If we find what I fear we will find, exposure is going to be the least of Farrand's problems,' he said. 'Besides, we can cross that bridge when we come to it.'

'Glenn,' Bettina said in a small voice, her face pained slightly. 'You've been so kind. You are so kind. But are you sure you want to do this? These men, this Kirschenbauer; they sound like they could be dangerous.'

'Let me handle that,' said Glenn with a grin, hesitating for a moment before putting a reassuring hand on Bettina's shoulder. 'I want to help,

Bettina. I will not stand by and watch Farrand tear down all the good work you and the others have been doing just so he can line his pockets. I've seen too much of what you women do to let anyone jeopardise the future of the ICB.'

'So what next?' Bettina asked.

'A *rösti*?' said Glenn, suddenly feeling his hunger. Bettina laughed.

'Glenn, I'm serious,' she said. 'What's our next step?'

'So am I!' he laughed. 'We only have a few hours left in the city. We can't leave Zurich without having eaten at least one *rösti*. Tell me I'm wrong?'

'I suppose that's true,' said Bettina, the smallest of smiles radiating from her face. Glenn watched with interest as her usual melancholy, the dark cloud of something sad that hovered around her, seemed to lift slightly.

'Let's eat then,' said Glenn. 'And, to answer your question about what comes next: leave it with me. Go back to Germany and don't speak about this with anyone. Act normal, with everyone, but especially around Herbert. I'll speak to him and find a way to speak to the fiduciary company that regulates his accounts.'

'Do you think he'll buy it?' she asked.

'He will, because he is greedy enough to want the extra funds that I will promise him. I'll have one condition: I'll need to write a placement memo for fundraising that will have an appendix showing the honesty of their accounts through a full audit. I will ask for a full audit to get him more money and therefore he must give me access to the accounts. He'll eat up the proposal like a piece of cake.'

'It's genius,' smiled Bettina. 'Genius!'

'Well, I *am* a genius,' Glenn laughed. But to his horror, Bettina did not laugh. She simply looked away, her face falling. Glenn felt like a total fool and wished he had not said that. The last thing he wanted was for Bettina to think that he was an arrogant idiot like Farrand or those pompous donors she was forced to meet at parties.

By the time they had eaten *rösti*, Bettina's voice had returned and Glenn hoped she would see the joke for what it was: a moment of foolishness. Certainly when they bid each other goodbye, it was with warmth and sincerity.

'Thank you for everything, Glenn,' she said as the taxi arrived to take her back to the airport that evening.

'You're very welcome,' he said, smiling down at her. They embraced for a moment, before Bettina pulled away and disappeared into the car. Glenn watched her, wondering as ever at the melancholy on her face. *Where did it come from*, he wondered?

However, Bettina's melancholy was to be the least of his problems that evening. When he checked his phone, he had a host of messages waiting for him, all from Eleanora. Concerned by the amount, he called her immediately.

'Baby?' Glenn said as soon as he heard the phone pick up on the other end of the line. 'It's Glenn, it's me. Has something happened?'

'Finally!' he heard his wife's angry screech. 'What time do you call this?'

'What?' he said, looking at his watch. 'It's seven p.m. here.'

'Exactly!' she cried. 'You said you would call me when you arrived. Call me stupid, but I'm pretty sure a flight to Zurich at seven a.m. does not take twelve hours from London Heathrow. What the hell have you been doing? What could possibly be more important than calling me to let me know you're safe?'

'Honey,' he said soothingly. 'Calm down. I'm sorry, OK. Things moved pretty fast here. I'm safe, everything is fine.'

But before he could say anything else, he heard a cry of anger. It was a wild, animalistic screech. Glenn yanked the phone away from his eardrum to avoid permanent damage.

'I am sick of your games, Glenn!' Eleanora shrieked. 'I am fed up with it all.'

'Games?' he muttered, utterly confused. 'What games? Fed up with what?'

'This travel,' she spat down the line. 'These women. It's enough now. Do you hear me? It's enough.'

'Baby, I...' Glenn started, but it was too late. The dial tone returned after a small, curt click. She had hung up on him.

Glenn sighed and his shoulders sank, then he looked at his watch again. It was already time to go to the airport. So much for a warm welcome awaiting him back in London, he thought to himself, groaning as he made his way to the station to catch a train to the airport.

CHAPTER TWENTY-FOUR

Making it up to Eleanora became Glenn's main priority on his return from Zurich. He knew what he needed to do with Herbert. He knew that he needed to keep Bettina informed. What he did not know was how to make his wife happy again. Since his return, the equilibrium and intimacy they had shared those past six months seemed to have evaporated with those missed phone calls. Eleanora started to spend long hours down with the tenants on the estate, tending to farming duties and the bureaucracy that came with Ronda Round Manor. When Glenn tried to catch up with her she avoided him, her eyes tired and her expression stern. The only time they spent in proximity with each other was in the bedroom, but every time Glenn reached out to touch her, Eleanora shivered and shrunk away. Glenn lost all faith in his ability to draw her close to him; before sleeping they both lay awake, no doubt pondering each other's unhappiness.

'I'll see you tonight,' Glenn called to her one morning as she disappeared through the door. The sun was barely rising but she was already heading out.

'Alright,' she called back.

As Eleanora was spending so much time on her responsibilities, Glenn too began to throw himself into his work once more. Early mornings and late nights at the office became the norm. That morning Glenn would have welcomed his wife's counsel, however. It was the morning he planned to put the call through to Farrand. He knew he would have to remain as nonchalant as possible to pull off his disguise.

When it came to it, though, the phone call with Farrand was as easy as Glenn had initially suspected it would be.

'Now, as you know, in order to raise funds for you I will need access to the charity accounting ledger,' he said, thankful Farrand was not in the room but thousands of miles away. If he was there, Glenn thought, Farrand would surely have seen through the cool, calm façade he heard on the phone. 'Could your fiduciary company give me permission to access that?'

'Sure,' said Farrand. 'You'll need to speak with Mr. Martinoli. I'll ask my secretary to put him in touch.'

'Great,' said Glenn. 'That's all I need for now.'

'Don't spend too long crunching numbers, Glenn,' Farrand laughed down the line. 'The sooner we have more money coming into the charity, the better. I don't want to keep the ladies waiting, if you know what I mean.'

Glenn gritted his teeth, clenching his jaw shut at the injustice of it all. How did Farrand think he was going to get away with it, he wondered?

'I'm working as fast as I can,' said Glenn, trying as hard as he could to keep the anger from his voice.

'Good man,' said Farrand, before hanging up.

Glenn did not have to wait long to hear news from Martinoli, the chief accountant of Farrand's fiduciary company.

'You need the accounts?' came the Italian's broken English. 'I send them by email?'

'That would be just fine,' said Glenn. *Easy peasy*, he smiled to himself. 'I'll also need an income statement. Will that be available to me too?'

'No problem,' said Martinoli. 'We are very modern. Give me ten minutes.'

As soon as the accounts arrived in his email inbox, Glenn printed them out. He hastened to the printer to scan through the streams of numbers and coloured boxes as they landed in his hands. On the surface, at first glance, nothing looked amiss, he thought. All looked fine. But Glenn knew instinctively that with a closer look, all would be revealed. He hastened upstairs to Operations, where he knew the accountants would be working. One look from them and he would know more.

Stepping out of the lift, Glenn scanned the floor for someone who did not look particularly busy. As his eyes passed over the desks, he caught sight of a familiar figure. He would recognise the curly, brown quiff anywhere.

'Mr. James?' he said gently, approaching from behind.

The man spun slowly around in his chair, putting down what looked like an enormous rectangular magnifying glass. The young man stared blankly at Glenn for a moment before pulling on a pair of thick spectacles. He looked well, Glenn thought, clean-shaven and far from the pale, sleeping figure he had last seen in a hospital bed.

'Ah, Mr. Tebbhurst!' he cried out, stumbling to his feet and thrusting a hand forward. 'It's great to see you! I've been meaning to come and visit you.'

'And I you,' said Glenn, marvelling at the man before him. 'Though I didn't think I'd be coming to visit you in the office. You've made quite the recovery, huh?'

'Yes, sir,' said Mr. James, nodding shyly. 'I took some time out to, well, process.'

'Of course,' Glenn nodded. 'Things didn't turn out how we expected them to.'

'No, sir,' said James. 'I had quite a shock back there.'

'It was not how it should have been,' Glenn said quietly, feeling his insides twist and turn uncomfortably.

'No, sir,' James shook his head. 'But it was my decision. I chose to take the risk. I am grateful to the DCF for giving me the chance.'

The words washed over Glenn like cool relief. But guilt lingered in his heart.

'If I could go back,' he said. 'If I could have convinced the board that there was another way, I would have. I want you to know that, Mr. James.'

'There wasn't another way, sir,' the young man shrugged, smiling sadly.

Glenn stood awkwardly for a moment, not knowing what to say. Yes, Mr. James had chosen to take the risk. But hadn't he and the other board members made that risk possible, he asked himself? Had there not been another way all along? The way of the ICB?

'You're back at work then,' he said, brushing his thoughts aside, keen to keep up a positive face for this courageous young man. 'Working hard?'

'Oh yes, sir, doing my best,' James grinned. 'I couldn't stay away for long. Especially when I started learning about the support tools in place for workplace rehabilitation.'

'Oh?' said Glenn, curious to hear those words on Mr. James' lips. The only other place he had heard them was in the context of the ICB.

'Yes,' he said, looking away and blushing slightly. 'It was my girlfriend, sir. Do you remember? You met her, at the hospital?'

'Of course,' said Glenn, remembering the pale, shaking woman he had seen watching her boyfriend sleep after the operation. She knew that when he woke up, she and the doctor and his parents would have to tell him that he was even blinder than before.

'She looked things up for me,' he said. 'She searched the internet, went to meetings, and found out all sorts of useful information. I was in bed, wondering where it had all gone wrong, and she was out and about finding a way for me to live again.'

'She sounds like quite a woman,' said Glenn, smiling at the thought, remembering another woman who dedicated her time to finding ways for the blind to learn to live again.

'She is, sir,' said Mr. James, and Glenn was surprised to see tears forming in the man's glazed eyes. 'She brought me back from a very dark place.'

'Good man,' said Glenn, clasping the man's shoulder for a moment, giving him time to let that emotional explosion of gratitude pass. When the last few tears were swept from James' cheeks, the young man looked down to the papers in Glenn's hands.

'What's that, sir?' he asked. 'What brings you up to Operations?'

'This?' said Glenn, looking down at the paper, momentarily forgetting the sickly reason he had come up Mr. James' department. 'Ah,' he remembered. 'A little bit of my own darkness I need someone to shed light on.'

'Can I help, sir?' the young man asked, taking the large magnifying glass from his desk. Glenn considered for a moment.

'I don't see why not,' he grinned. 'Thank you, Mr. James. I'd value your opinion.'

Glenn handed the balance sheets and income statement over to Mr. James, who sat down to scan through the multitude of figures. He looked through, leafing through the papers until he came across one number. He focused in with his magnifying glass, and then started working his way backwards through the papers. Glenn's heart leapt at the sight; he had found something.

'What is it?' he asked the young man.

'There's something not right,' he murmured, focusing in on different pages. 'There's a negative net worth here. The liabilities make up for more than the assets. If you count the liabilities outside the balance sheet the total liabilities are more than the assets and the company has a negative net worth.'

'That sounds bad,' said Glenn. Mr. James looked up at him.

'It is bad,' he said, a small frown forming on his forehead. 'More liabilities than assets is a ticking time bomb.'

'What can it mean?' Glenn asked, keen to hear the words he knew were coming; the words that would confirm Farrand's treachery.

'It's hard to say,' Mr. James shook his head. 'You need to speak with an auditor to find out more.'

'An expert eye,' Glenn nodded in agreement, scanning his mind for resident auditors at Diversified Charities. He would have to go to another floor. Turning back to the young man, Glenn smiled.

'Thanks, Mr. James,' he said.

'I don't know how useful I've been, sir,' James replied, an apologetic look on his face.

'You've been brilliant,' said Glenn, slapping the young man on the back in the way of thanks. 'And seeing you back here in the office has made my day.'

In fact, it had made his year, but Glenn did not want to scare Mr. James by telling him how deeply his ordeal had affected him. An amazing recovery, he thought to himself. Striding back to the lift, he marvelled at the wonders of the human spirit. Mr. James' girlfriend had proved that miraculous cures were not the answer; love and support worked their own kinds of miracles.

Arriving on the fifth floor of the Diversified Charities building, Glenn quickly found who he was looking for.

'John?' he called, knocking on the office door which declared its inhabitant with big, bold letters: JOHN SPINOLA, AUDITOR

'Come in!' came the cheerful voice of a man Glenn had not spoken to in a while. John Spinola sat behind his desk, dressed in a black suit and nursing an almost-empty cup of coffee. Glenn had known Spinola for many years, and worked closely with him whilst checking for fraud and money laundering schemes when the DCF was approached by new donors. Moreover, he counted Spinola as a friend.

'Glenn!' he cried. 'What a nice surprise! Oh, is Amelia there? Can you spot her? I thought I heard her tea trolley passing by and I could murder another coffee!'

Thrusting his head back through the office door to scan the corridor, Glenn was pleased to see that his colleague's hunch was correct.

'Amelia!' Glenn called to the middle-aged woman pushing her cart of condiments and hot beverages.

'Mr. Tebbhurst?' she called back, spotting him. 'You're on the wrong floor, love! Are you chasing me for my biscuits, now?'

'No,' laughed Glenn. 'Not at all. But Mr. Spinola here and I could do with a couple of coffees. Can you help a couple of thirsty gentlemen out?'

'You know I can, sweetheart,' she chuckled. 'I'll be over in a minute.'

When Amelia had served both men steaming cups of coffee, she disappeared once more, leaving a big smile on John Spinola's face.

'How do you do it?' he grinned at Glenn. 'You've always had a way with the ladies, you old toad!'

'I think it's my accent,' Glenn laughed. 'British gals go wild for it.'

'The constant American,' Spinola sighed admiringly. 'Well, I suppose we chaps can't compete with that.'

'Better to know your limits,' Glenn nodded in mock sincerity.

'You old dog!' Spinola guffawed, before asking: 'How's the wife? How is the lady of the manor herself?'

'She's fine,' said Glenn, knowing that only he could hear the lie in his answer. Eleanora was not fine and nor was he. He wondered if his wife would ever want to make love to him again. Just talking to him again would be a start, he thought. Like Eleanora, Spinola came from a rich family and had never had to worry about money.

'Good, good,' smiled Spinola. 'A fine woman, that one.'

'How is Hilary?' Glenn asked, looking over at the picture of a handsome woman and two chubby, dark-haired boys.

'Oh, she's well, she's well,' smiled the auditor. 'Wants more babies but I'm having none of it, no sir! Two's enough for a lifetime. I envy you your liberty, Glenn, you know that, don't you?'

Glenn laughed. He never really considered not having children as a liberty. Somehow it had just never happened, and he suspected for Eleanora it seemed like too much work. The two men sipped coffee and looked out over Spinola's fantastic view of the dome of St. Paul's cathedral.

'So what brings you up to me, Glenn?' Spinola asked, scanning Glenn's face for signs of what he was up to. 'It can't be all pleasure and no business. I know you!'

'It's an audit I'm looking for,' said Glenn. 'I'm coming to the best auditor I know.'

'An audit?' asked Spinola, pushing his spectacles from his nose up to his eyes and turning to his computer. 'What's the audit number? When was it sent over?'

'Actually, it's not a DCF audit,' said Glenn. 'It's something I'm reviewing externally.'

'Oh?' said Spinola, his eyebrows raising, his lips pouting. 'What's this all about, Glenn?'

'Look at this,' Glenn passed the auditor the balance sheet.

'The International Charity for the Blind, eh?' said Spinola, scanning the documents in front of him. 'Let's take a look, shall we?'

Glenn sat back in his chair and allowed his mind to wander as the auditor looked through the ICB accounts. After a short review, Spinola took off his glasses and looked at Glenn.

'What is this, Glenn?' he asked, eying his friend warily. 'This doesn't feel right.'

'You tell me,' said Glenn, matching Spinola's look with worry.

'I see an income of a couple of million euros here,' said Spinola, turning back to the documents, a frown creasing the folds of skin at his forehead. 'But zero minus profit. This charity is living off accounts payable and its debts.'

'As I feared,' Glenn said eventually. 'Can you tell me what the main outgoings are spent on?'

'Travel,' said Spinola, leafing through the sheets. 'Flights, petrol, cars, a lot of first class travel. In one month we have trips to Denmark, Nepal and Thailand.'

'What?' yelped Glenn. 'Are you sure?'

'Yes, it's right here,' said the auditor. 'Why are you so surprised? Would ICB delegates not be travelling to these countries? It's the *International* Charity of the Blind, no?'

'The ICB does not operate in *any* of those countries,' Glenn shook his head. 'First class travel, you say?'

'Every time,' nodded Spinola. 'There are also off-balance sheet transactions.'

'What the hell does that mean?' Glenn asked, feeling sick.

'It's money that comes in but does not appear in the accounts,' said Spinola. 'It goes out another way. It can be a guarantee for some other transaction. It's dodgy stuff, Glenn. Terribly dodgy.'

Shaking his head, Glenn started to tell Spinola about Kirschenbauer and all he had discovered in Zurich. He shared his fears about money laundering and the implications of this association with the Swiss tycoon.

'Kirschenbauer?' yelped Spinola. 'That devil?'

'The very same,' said Glenn. 'I think him and Farrand are as thick as thieves. Jeez. This is bad.'

'If funds are being diverted, yes,' said Spinola. 'Yes, yes, yes. This is bad. But these accounts in themselves are not enough to prove anything. Nor is Farrand's connection to Kirschenbauer.'

'What can I do then?' Glenn asked.

'You can hire a private detective,' Spinola shrugged.

'Are you being serious?' Glenn asked, searching his friend's face for signs of sarcasm.

'Deadly,' nodded Spinola. 'I know someone.'

'And what would this private detective do, exactly?' Glenn asked, wondering about the legality of such a mission.

'The best way to prove this man's guilt is to follow him and find out what he does with his life,' said Spinola. 'Look at this guy. Our friend Herbie visits bankers all over Europe. He goes to places where there are no offices, no work and no outreach for the charity! Why? Look at this: South Africa, Russia, Madagascar. Why does he go there? You need to know, Glenn.'

The weight of the auditor's words fell heavily on Glenn's shoulders. He knew there was only one way forward.

'You said you know someone?' Glenn said, letting out a deep sigh.

Spinola took a pen and began to scribble a name and number on a piece of paper. When he was done he pushed it towards Glenn.

'Dylan Marlowe,' Glenn read the name aloud.

'He's good,' nodded Spinola. 'He'll get you what you need, believe me.'

Glenn stood up to leave.

'You'll send me the full audit when it's done?' he asked. His friend nodded.

'I'll set my team to work,' he said. 'Give us a day or two, will you?'

'Thanks, John,' said Glenn. 'I owe you one, buddy.'

'One more thing,' Spinola called over as Glenn reached his office door.

'Just one?' Glenn grinned.

'Gather as much information as you can to help Marlowe,' said Spinola. 'These women, this Bettina you've told me about? They're all gold mines of information for us. To catch a fly, we need to build a big web.'

Glenn nodded, wondering what Bettina would think of this idea of hiring a private detective. As much as he trusted Spinola's good advice he wanted to check with his friend first, to see if this really was the only way forward.

'I'll ask her,' he said, and left.

When the final audit arrived some days later, the verdict was depressing. Glenn put a call through to Bettina straight away. When he reached her, she was flustered from gardening. The office in Frankfurt sounded like a beautiful place to be.

'I've been repotting flowers in the office,' she said, a tinkling laugh in her voice. 'Christina brought in some orchids. The place is looking lovely, Glenn. I think you'd like it.'

'Then I'm sorry to be the one calling with such bad news,' he sighed.

'Glenn?' she said. 'Glenn? What's happened? What have you found out?'

'It's Herbert,' said Glenn. 'He's ruining you.'

'What?' she said, lowering her voice. 'How bad is it?'

Glenn looked down at the ledger sheets in front of him and slowly explained how the audit had been done. How the results were accounting manipulations and how Farrand was borrowing money against the assets of the company.

'Listen, I'm not even looking at total assets,' said Glenn, running an anxious hand through his hair. 'I've been looking at your liabilities. Your cash, stocks and bonds are your ownership, but your liability, such as debts and the accounts payable, are the assets of some other people. He's borrowed money, a lot of it. This is worse than we thought.'

'What does that mean?' Bettina asked in a small voice.

'It means the ICB's net worth is negative,' he said.

'But what does that *mean*, Glenn?' she asked, unable to keep the frustration from her voice.

'It means you can go bankrupt at any time,' he said. 'And on top of this, Kirschenbauer is dealing with Farrand. That's a bad association for the charity right there.'

'Oh God, Glenn,' came Bettina's shaky voice. 'I so hoped the audit would prove that things were fine. I want this nightmare to be over. I want things to be OK.'

'They can be,' he said quickly, hearing the panic in her voice. 'I really believe they can be.'

'But how?' she asked. 'You said we could go bankrupt at any time!'

'I believe that even Herbert is not stupid enough to let that happen,' said Glenn. 'Think about it. If the ICB goes down, he will be exposed. What we need to do is pretend like we know nothing for just a little while longer. Can you do that for me, Bettina?'

'I don't know,' she said in a small voice. 'I feel so…'

'Betrayed?' Glenn asked. 'I bet you do. But you've gotta be strong, at least for now, at least for this next step.'

'What next step?' she asked.

Glenn launched into Spinola's suggestion of hiring a private detective. He mentioned Dylan Marlowe and the potential collaboration.

'What do you think?' he asked her when he had explained all.

'I'm not sure, Glenn,' she said, clearly hesitant. 'A private detective? That's so shady. We are better than that, surely?'

'Bettina, do you know what Farrand is doing?' Glenn demanded, suddenly filled with righteous anger. 'He is running his decadent lifestyle on your charity's proceeds! You guys are bankrupt! You're running a charity but your charity has no money. Who is benefiting from this? Where is it all going? How the hell can you work and build for the future? He subsidises rent for you in Frankfurt, I saw that in the balance sheet. He pays your salary. But where is the rest going? God, Bettina. This man is eating you alive.'

'I know, Glenn,' she said quickly. 'I know something is wrong. I've known it for a long time.'

'Then help me,' he said simply. 'Hell, Bettina. Help yourself. Help *me* help *you*.'

'Do you really think this is the only way?' she asked.

'It's the advice I've been given by a man who knows how these crooks work,' said Glenn. 'Yes, I trust him. Yes, I think this is the way forward.'

'And I trust you,' she said.

'Really?' asked Glenn, touched by her words. The passion searing through his veins softened for a moment as his heart filled with a warm, glowing feeling.

'Yes, I trust you,' she said once more and again the words ricocheted around Glenn's heart. 'I think it could work,' she said, seemingly convincing herself more with every passing second. 'Yes, it could be exactly what we need.'

'OK, well I'm going to do all of that for you then,' said Glenn, silently releasing a sigh of relief. 'I'm going to need a few things from you in return, though.'

'Like what?' she asked.

'Like your total secrecy,' he said. 'You cannot breathe a word of this to anyone else, Bettina. Not to Christina, not to your brother, not to your friends or parents. Certainly not to anyone in the ICB.'

'OK,' Bettina confirmed. 'What else?'

'I need you to prepare an internal audit,' he said.

'What?' she cried. 'But Glenn, I have no idea how an audit works. How can I do this?'

'Marlowe will explain everything,' Glenn said calmly. 'He will ask you to collect specific information for him. He will ask you questions, ask you to make us copies of travel documents, give us addresses Herbert has visited in Aachen, Zurich and any other cities he frequents. We need names and addresses of people he visits so we can also investigate them. We need emails. Everyone thinks emails are private, but they're not. We're going to need all the ammo we can get to bring him down, Bettina. Can you help us?'

'Absolutely,' came her defiant answer. 'I am ready, Glenn. I want to catch Herbert out. On all counts.'

As soon as he had this go ahead from Bettina, Glenn wasted no time in making contact with Marlowe. He was inspired by her strength in the face of disaster. Catching Farrand out 'on all counts' – or perhaps, on all accounts – would be his new mantra, Glenn decided. He agreed to meet Marlowe for the first time at a small café near the office after work hours, so Glenn could brief the detective on the situation. The whole arrangement made Glenn feel inexplicably nervous. There was something illicit, almost dangerous, about engaging the services of someone who would essentially spy on another person in order to bring about their downfall.

Marlowe, however, was a well-educated, intelligent man; there was nothing unusual about him. In fact, he was impeccably ordinary, no doubt an attribute that was an asset in his profession. He wore a brown leather jacket over a chequered shirt, and had a well-trimmed brown beard. He looked more like a kind university professor than a private detective.

'Indeed, people often expect Pierce Brosnan or another Bond-type,' the polite man laughed quietly when Glenn expressed his surprise. 'But I am the real deal, I assure you. I speak seven languages and uncover crooks and adulterers for a living.'

Marlowe listened carefully as Glenn explained the case to him, making a few notes in a notepad. When Glenn had described Farrand's profile, Marlowe gave a little smile.

'I know men like this, Mr. Tebbhurst,' he said. 'They are far too arrogant to make my job difficult. If Mr. Farrand spends as frequently and frivolously as you say, his fraud should be easy to document.'

'I can't tell you how much that reassures me, Mr. Marlowe,' Glenn nodded gratefully. 'And I hope I can count on your discretion?'

'Naturally,' said Marlowe, bowing his head slightly.

Glenn walked away from the meeting with his faith restored. Perhaps the ICB was not doomed after all, he thought. For Bettina's sake, and the sake of the other five women, he prayed this would be the case. Looking down at his watch, he saw how late it was and wished the tubes and trains carrying him home would move faster. He was relieved, even happy, and he wanted to share that happiness with Eleanora.

Arriving back at Ronda Round Manor, Glenn was surprised to find the house eerily quiet and empty. He searched the downstairs room for Eleanora, but found only her painted ancestors staring coldly down at him in their judgemental way. He climbed the stairs to their bedroom, only to find it empty. Thinking she was out somewhere, he began to head back downstairs, but as he did so, he noticed the light beneath the door in the grand guest bedroom. He walked over and pulled it open to find Eleanora tucked up in bed with a copy of *Horse and Hound*.

'There you are,' he said, smiling warmly at her. 'I was looking for you.'

His wife did not look up from her magazine. She seemed utterly engaged in the contents of the middle pages.

'Are you sleeping in here now?' he asked her, looking around at her clothes draped over the antique chairs, her slippers at the bottom of the bed. His heart sunk to see her so casually in another bed, wondering if that last thing they shared, their nights in bed together, had just fallen away.

Eleanora said nothing, continuing to read silently.

'Am I invisible now?' he asked her, keeping his tone light but unable to mask the hurt on his face. 'Have I turned into the ghost of Ronda Round Manor?'

His wife turned a page in her magazine.

'Honey,' he said gently, approaching the bed. 'Why are you in here? Why are you being like this? Won't you come back to our bed?'

Eleanora stopped reading for a moment and stared ahead.

'Why would I do that?' she asked coldly.

'Because I want you to,' he said, swallowing hard.

'Well, I don't want to,' she said, pulling the magazine closer to her face as if she could block her husband out behind those glossy pages.

'Because I love you then!' he cried out, almost angrily, losing his patience. 'Doesn't that count for anything round here?'

Eleanora lowered her magazine slowly, putting it down. Turning to face him, Glenn saw a sad look in her bright blue eyes. It was a look he had never seen before.

'Love is presence, Glenn,' she said, a small, hurt frown resting between her eyebrows. 'And you are not present.'

With that she set down her magazine, reached over and turned out the light. Darkness fell, separating them. Glenn had never felt so alone.

CHAPTER TWENTY-FIVE

Glenn felt the exhaustion of the previous week fall upon him: seeing Mr. James again, hiring the private detective Dylan Marlowe, fighting with Eleanora. He needed a break, and he knew exactly where he needed to go. He sat before the computer in his office and began to look for some flights to New York. He would leave the following Thursday evening, which would give him a long weekend back home with his parents. Before then, he wanted to make sure Marlowe was on track with his tailing of Herbert, and to put his affairs in order at the office.

Glenn had wondered if he should ask Eleanora before booking his trip, but a rebellious streak inspired by her rejection left him oddly uncaring. He booked the flights and would inform the office the next day, leaving the investigation in Marlowe's hands.

Such was his mood when he arrived home on Thursday evening to pick up his luggage for the flight. He searched the house for his wife, finding her in the stables, brushing the mane of her favourite horse. She looked up when he came in, her eyes full of a strange mixture of guilt and irritation.

'Sally needed brushing,' she said, avoiding Glenn's gaze. 'I'll be half an hour longer.'

'I just wanted to tell you I'm going away for the long weekend,' said Glenn. 'My parents have asked me to visit them over in Sutton Place.'

'When are you going?' she asked, her blue eyes looking up at him in surprise.

'Tonight,' he said, before looking at his watch. 'In five minutes, actually.'

Eleanora looked away, seemingly searching the straw around her for words. When she finally looked up at him, if was with defiance in her eyes.

'So *this* is your response to my feelings,' she said, nodding coldly.

'Excuse me?' said Glenn.

'Your response to everything I said,' she said. 'I tell you you're never here and you respond by leaving again. How intelligent of you, Glenn. Bravo.'

'What the hell,' he shook his head. 'Why are you saying this? You've barely spoken to me for a month. How exactly should I have read from that behaviour that you want me around?'

'Perhaps if you paid any attention to our marriage, you would read what's there and not what you want to read,' she said sternly.

'How does that work?'

'Well, you've simply twisted the situation to your advantage, haven't you? It's so easy for you, Glenn. It always has been. You see what you want in people. You see in my sadness an opportunity to run away.'

'But that's madness,' he wanted to say, but his wife would not hear it.

'Well, alright then,' she said curtly. 'Go.'

'What!' Glenn cried. 'Eleanora, stop this!'

'No,' she said coldly. 'I will not stand in your way. Don't you have a flight to catch?'

'Yes, but,' he began. But she cut him off.

'Then catch it.' Stooping down, she picked up the brush she had dropped in her anger and began to smooth down the horse's coat, hushing the beast. Even Sally had sensed the tension between the man and woman for she whinnied gently.

'Fine,' said Glenn, angry and finding nothing else to say. 'I'm going.'

Eleanora said nothing. She began to hum softly to her horse to calm her. For all she cared, Glenn might as well have been invisible. He left the stables in a fury.

Grabbing his bags, he threw them into the car and fled Ronda Round. He couldn't bear the sight of it any longer. He checked into his flight in a haze of anger and confusion, wishing the eight hours of flying ahead were already over. He just wanted to be at home with his parents, chatting and laughing and relaxing with people who cared about him.

To his surprise, a familiar figure was at the airport waiting for him in New York. She had written a large sign, which read: *Mommy's boy.*

'Mom, do you know what the time is?' he cried, looking from his mother's face down to his watch which had automatically updated to New York time.

'It's never too late for a mother to pick up her son,' Iris beamed at him. Glenn fell into his mother's arms, desperate for her warm hug. She too seemed desperate for she held him tight.

'Honey, you're home,' she murmured in his ear.

'Thanks, Mom,' he said, holding back the tears that threatened to choke him.

The drive over to Sutton Place was filled with Iris's babbling chatter about her life in New York and the latest on his father's adjustments. Glenn listened to all with a sense of deep comfort. He could not wait to see his father.

'Now, you boys will have to take care of yourselves tomorrow, OK?' she said.

'Do you have plans?' Glenn asked.

'It's a full-day Pilates workshop over in Central Park,' she said. 'I'm dead keen.'

'Go for it,' smiled Glenn. 'It'll be nice to spend some time with Dad. I want to chat with him and see how it's been.'

Glenn was already looking forward to tasting his father's cooking. He wondered if Bertie had learnt the same techniques he himself had learnt from Odile in Aachen. When they finally reached home, however, the silence of the night told them that Bertie had drifted off to sleep. Reunions would have to wait until the next morning, they decided, much to Glenn's relief. As much as he wanted to see his father, he also wanted to sleep.

Morning came in shafts of light creeping through the shutters. Looking down at his watch, Glenn saw that it would already be noon in London. Yawning, he lifted himself quietly to his feet and went to the kitchen to make some coffee.

'Son, is that you?' his father called to him from the stove, making Glenn start.

'It's me, Dad,' Glenn laughed, going to his father and pulling him into a bear hug. 'Man, what's this? You're up and cooking already?'

'You betcha, fella,' he said, holding Glenn by the shoulders at arm's length as he used to do when he could see. Glenn wondered what his father did now that his eyes could not gauge his son's health or happiness. He suspected Bertie simply imagined the man in front of him.

'Is Mom up?' Glenn asked, growing uncomfortable beneath his father's blank gaze.

'Are you kidding me?' his father whispered, releasing his son and turning back to the stove. 'D'you think I'd be allowed in the kitchen if she was? Hell no! Your Mama is sleeping, son. Let's leave her that way and make some pancakes.'

'Did you do all of this?' Glenn asked him, reaching over to take a strawberry. He was ravenous, popping the strawberry straight into his mouth.

'You bet I did!' chuckled his father. 'Batter's ready, stove's fired up, all I need now is my right-hand man beside me to bake us some of the good stuff.'

'I'm impressed. Where did you learn to do all this? Mom mentioned some lessons you took at a community centre?'

'That's right.' Bertie paused a moment and raised his hand gently over the electric hob to feel how hot it was. 'I'm a born again chef, son. I think I'm cooking better blind than I ever cooked with my eyes!'

'Why don't I be the judge of that, huh?' Glenn teased his father. 'You're talking a lot of talk there, Dad. Time to put your money where your mouth is. I wanna see you cook some pancakes.'

'Pancakes comin' up, big fella,' his father chuckled.

Glenn watched with great interest as Bertie felt for the frying pan on the stove. When he had located it, he turned slightly to pick up his bowl of batter.

'Hand me the ladle, won't you, son?' he asked Glenn. Glenn scoured the kitchen for a ladle and when he found one, he passed it gently to his father.

'There,' he said, taking Bertie's hand and putting the ladle into his grasp.

'Thanks,' said Bertie, taking the bowl of batter in his other hand. Moving over to the stove, he dipped the ladle into the batter and slowly drew it up and deposited thick dollops into the hot pan.

'How do you know where the pan is?' Glenn asked.

'With my hands of course,' Bertie chuckled. 'I feel the heat rising up and let the heat waves guide me. When the heat disappears, I know there's no pan below.'

The technique seemed to be working, for Bertie had now deposited three pancakes in the pan. He put the ladle carefully back into the bowl.

'What next?' Glenn grinned.

'Now we let our noses do the work,' he said. 'Without my eyes, I can't tell golden brown from burnt black. But with my nose, I can smell it! See for yourself, son. Close your eyes.'

Glenn did as his father commanded and closed his eyes.

'Now, there's a certain point where the smell goes from being a broad, pastry-like smell to a more sugary, sweet smell,' he said. 'That's when you know your sugar is starting to cook, beginning to caramelise, you know? That's when you wanna flip these babies over.'

'And how do you do that?' Glenn asked, wishing he could open his eyes to see the next stage.

'That, my boy, is an *art*,' he said. 'Pure and simple. I'm gonna take my spatula, here, from the work top. I had it ready before I even turned on the stove. Now, I'm gonna slowly reach for my pan handle. My griddle has a big handle here, extra big for me because of my disability. There, I've found it. I'm gonna hold real tight, now. I've got my pan handle in one hand and my spatula in the other, and I'm gonna reach down into my pan and feel for resistance. Ah yeah, I feel it! There it is. Once I've found my sticky base, I'm gonna dig in and get it on my spatula. Then, not thinking too much about it, I'm gonna flip it.'

Glenn watched his father go through every step he described down to the very last detail.

'Dad, this is amazing,' he said quietly. 'You're making pancakes. You're really making pancakes!'

'Whaddayathink I'm doing!' his father laughed. 'Jeez, and they tell *me* I'm blind.'

Glenn burst into laughter. Glenn had rarely seen his father cook in his lifetime. Bertie had made sandwiches, occasionally grilled meat on a barbecue, but he had never baked or prepared pancakes with such skill.

'This is really a first,' he told his father when the two of them sat down to eat. As they ate the deliciously baked pancakes, father and son exchanged stories of new technologies available to the blind.

'I've been taking classes,' said his father between slowly cutting up his pancakes. 'You know I don't like counselling, but your mother insisted. I saw someone, a nice lady, who told me life wasn't over. She put me on a rehabilitation program, and I'm telling you, son, this cooking class was just the start! Now they have me using special running machines to work out on. It listens to me! It's like a robot. I say "speed up" and it goes faster, I say "slow down" and it stops. Then there's all the e-something classes, which teach me to use smart tablets commanded by my voice. We can check emails, dictate messages and even call people using these little machines. They're extraordinary! I'm even taking a Braille class!'

'Wow, you could even go back to work,' Glenn grinned.

'Sure, I could, but why would I?' chucked Bertie. 'I'm a demon with my walking cane and I'm all signed up to Blind Power Walking! They take us through Central Park. Your mother even saw me once, from her yogi class.'

'Her Pilates class?' said Glenn, laughing at the thought of his mother spotting his father power walking through the park. 'My parents are more active than me!'

'Maybe,' laughed Bertie. 'This lady, this counsellor, she has me living my life again. I'm learning to be wholesome and happy once more. Like I used to be, minus the stress of work. She calls it "coming to terms with blindness" or something like that. Some technical term! I just call it being happy in the skin I'm in. I don't feel blind anymore. I feel like I'm just learning new ways to be me.'

'Wow, Dad, you seem super wised up,' Glenn nodded his head in admiration. 'It's great to hear you talking this way. You sound like a lot of the people I've met who have had the same story. Coming to terms with your blindness is the only way to live with it. It becomes part of who you are, as you say.'

'Well, I am blind, in case you haven't noticed. It makes sense for me to be wising up. You, though, you're an enigma. How come you know so much about all this stuff?'

'Well, in case you haven't noticed, my father is blind,' Glenn laughed.

'*Touché*,' grinned Bertie.

'Plus I've been learning so much through this ICB. The International Charity for the Blind? Remember me telling you about them?'

'Ah, your blind beauties?' chuckled his father.

'Right,' grinned Glenn. 'But they're so much more than that, Dad.'

Relishing the opportunity to share with his father all he had learnt and discovered about the six blind women he had met in Aachen, Glenn launched into a quick debrief of the past year. He had just finished describing Zu-Ting's factory in Hong Kong when his mother announced her arrival at the breakfast table.

'I thought I smelled pancakes!' Glenn heard Iris call cheerfully as she walked over to join them. She was already dressed in her sleek Pilates outfit, dragging a soft mat behind her. 'Honey, did you come all the way to New York to make us pancakes? What a hoot! You should have waited. I'd have done you my special. I know you like eggs with those.'

'Actually, I didn't make these,' Glenn grinned up at his mother, sitting up to kiss her on the cheek.

'Who did then?' she asked. Glenn glanced over at his father.

'She won't believe you, boy-oh,' his father chuckled, tucking into his second pancake. A mess of blueberries and crème fraiche lay scattered around his plate. He had not quite mastered toppings yet, Glenn noted.

'My, oh my, Bert!' she exclaimed, her face breaking into a grin. 'You're a miracle, do you know that?'

'Tell me something I don't know, honey,' Bertie said through a mouthful of pancake.

'Alright, fellas, well it looks like you're all set,' said Iris, ignoring her husband's attempt at machismo. 'I better get going. You'll take care of your father, Glenn?'

'Of course, Mom,' Glenn nodded, taking his mother's hand in his. 'Go. We'll be fine.'

'I need to have some talks with my son, honey,' Bertie nodded in agreement. 'We're all good here. Go and do your yuppie thing.'

Glenn waited for his mother to leave before quizzing his father on his choice of words.

'Talks, huh?' he asked. 'What are we gonna be talking about, Dad?'

'Oh boy,' laughed Bertie, letting out a low whistle. 'What talks are we *not* gonna have?'

Still puzzled by his father's words, Glenn agreed to get ready for a walk around Sutton Place.

'I'm becoming quite an ace with this white cane,' said his father. 'I gotta show you. Best part of all is that you get to hit anyone you don't like with it, no questions asked!'

'Dad!' Glenn laughed, imagining his father taking liberties with his ex-enemies on Wall Street.

'What? The ladies love it too,' he went on enthusiastically. 'You won't believe it, son. They fawn all over me as soon as they see my stick!'

'How does Mom feel about that?' Glenn asked in a slightly exasperated tone.

'Oh, you know your mother,' smiled Bertie. 'And more importantly, *she* knows *me*.'

How simple an explanation, Glenn thought for a moment. His parents knew each other and that was enough, in his father's eyes, to relieve all sins.

'So what's going on, son?' his father asked when they had walked for ten minutes beneath the bright June sun. Glenn was enjoying the humming bees and the gentle clacking sound of his father's white cane against the pavement and walls around them.

'Going on?' asked Glenn. 'What do you mean, Dad?'

'You know what I mean,' his father sighed. 'What's going on with you?'

'Things have been busy,' said Glenn, not knowing how much more to share. So much was going on, he thought to himself. Where exactly should he start?

'Busy is a gentle word for it!' chuckled his father. 'Your mother's always telling me you're somewhere new. New Orleans, Mexico City, Hong Kong, some place in Germany. You're everywhere.'

'Yeah, well,' he sighed. 'It's funny. I feel a bit like I'm nowhere.'

'Nowhere? What, you feel lost?'

'Something like that,' said Glenn, knowing he couldn't hide his unhappiness from his father. He explained the difficulties with Eleanora and expressed his guilt over all that had come to pass with Mr. James.

'Listen, son,' his father sighed. 'Don't be so hard on yourself. Take it from me. I know better than anyone that those lessons, those little steps I have taken lately to accept my condition were the last things on my mind when I lost my sight. I wanted the miracles. I wanted the operations, the transplants, the technological advances that would bring my eyes back! No one, I repeat, no one could have convinced me otherwise. I think your Mr. James was the same.'

Glenn said nothing for a while, remembering what Mr. James had said just weeks before: *It was my choice.*

'Maybe you're right,' said Glenn, feeling the heavy weight of guilt shifting slightly. 'Thanks, Dad.'

'You're very welcome, kiddo. Now, tell me. Your mother has some idea in her head that you're struggling with the lady of the manor. Is that true? Or is she just stirring up nonsense? It wouldn't be the first time!'

Glenn laughed. 'No, she has the right idea. Things are bad, Dad,' he said, shrugging his shoulders. 'I'm lost.'

'Do you love her?' his father asked him. Glenn was surprised by the question for a moment.

'Yeah,' he said quickly. 'Yeah, of course I love her.'

'Then what's stopping you from working it out?' his father asked him. 'Marriage ain't no picnic, son. Ask your mother.'

'I know,' said Glenn. 'I'm trying, really I am.'

'Is there someone else?' Bertie asked.

'What?' Glenn answered quickly, turning to his father. A small smile rose on Bertie's lips.

'Who is she?' he asked.

Glenn searched his brain for the right course of action, stumbling over the pros and cons of mentioning the name on his mind. Eventually, he knew he could not hide it from his father for long.

'Her name is Bettina,' said Glenn, and slowly he told his father the story of how they had met. He told Bertie all he had learnt about her in the interim between seeing her again. Her heroism, her courage in the face of travel and her disability. He discussed their recent trip to Switzerland and the scandal with Farrand, detailing the vulnerability of Bettina's position and his desire to do all he could to save her and the ICB from disaster.

'I love looking at her, you know? I love being around her. She makes me better somehow,' he said, shaking his head. 'But at the same time, she makes me worse.'

'Worse?' said Bertie. 'How?'

'I'm married,' said Glenn. 'I love my wife. I shouldn't think these things.'

'Is it not possible that you love both women?' Bertie asked his son.

Glenn said nothing, for there was nothing to say. Was he in love with both women at the same time?

'Listen, son,' said Bertie. 'Can an old timer like me give you some love advice?'

'Please!' laughed Glenn. 'Go ahead, Dad.'

'I say go for it, Glenn.'

'Go for what?'

'I know you, son,' sighed Bertie. 'I can tell that you're disillusioned with Eleanora. She's your wife, sure, but it seems clear to me that you want this Bettina lady. If you want her, you should go for it.'

'But,' Glenn stammered. 'But, Dad… I can't. No way, man. This is not the way you raised me.'

'Pah!' laughed Bertie. 'You really gonna play that one on me? Go for it, fella. Maybe you'll find you want this Bettina gal more than you want your wife.'

'But what if it's the other way around?' Glenn asked, his mind tossing and turning with possible outcomes. 'What if it's Eleanora I wanted all along? Then all I'd do is hurt Bettina and live the rest of my life feeling like a guilty schmuck.'

'My son? A guilty schmuck?' laughed Bertie. 'I don't think so somehow. I think you know what you need to do, my boy. Don't go against your instincts. All of my successes sprang from my instincts. Either way, you'll know.'

Father and son walked on until they grew tired and headed home. Bertie's words hung in Glenn's mind like a door that had been left ajar. As the weekend in New York passed pleasantly by, he wondered more and more how right, or wrong, his father might be.

CHAPTER TWENTY-SIX

The change of continent had not made his father's words go away, Glenn realised as he got up from yet another sleepless night. Nor had a whole summer. The balmy then hotter months of June, July and August had passed stuffily at Ronda Round Manor. Glenn could not bring his mind to a calm place, despite his best efforts. *Go for it*, were the instructions his father had given. *Go for it*.

'Listen, son,' he recalled his father saying as they said goodbye at the airport. 'Seems to me you've had enough of all this aristocracy in London. You're fed up, I can see that. Your mother can see it, too. Maybe leave the lady of the manor to her social life for a while, huh? *Pursue this Bettina! Go for it, son!*'

As he lay awake in his empty bed, Eleanora sleeping in another room, Glenn wondered if there wasn't some wisdom in Bertie's words. His wife had barely acknowledged his return. When he saw her he felt the usual stirring of desire in his heart and body. But that soon cooled when she ignored him or threw him an irritated glance. He had tried for months to make it up to Eleanora, to push his anger aside and make her warm to him once more, but all in vain. He had not travelled since that trip to New York, nor did he work overly long hours. Nothing, it seemed, could appease her.

Meanwhile, whether he liked it or not, he was more in touch with Bettina than ever. Over in Germany she was working hard collecting anything she thought could be used as evidence against Farrand. She was working so hard, Glenn thought, with the same diligence she applied to her work for the ICB. However, it soon became apparent that the energy she was putting into tracing Farrand's indiscretions was leaving her less than herself. Glenn heard as much from Marlowe, who was surprisingly intuitive.

'Do you check in with her often?' he asked Glenn one afternoon when they had met to share a few details of the investigation.

'Yes,' said Glenn, shuffling papers before slipping them back into his briefcase. 'Once a week or so. Why?'

'Well, it's just that last time I spoke to her on the phone she sounded stressed,' said Dylan, his intelligent eyes crinkling in concern. 'I know from experience that this whole process can be very hard on those who are asked to gather evidence.'

'How so?'

'Well, in most cases there are multiple emotional responses at work,' said Marlow, prodding his glasses further up his nose. 'There's guilt; fear of discovery; the burden of keeping silent – to name a few.'

'She's a strong woman,' said Glenn, considering all Marlowe had said. 'I don't think Bettina would have taken this on if she didn't think she could handle it.'

'I'm sure,' said Dylan, looking at Glenn in his shrewd, calculating way. 'But if she's sworn to secrecy, there's no one she can share this with, is there?'

'I'd never thought about it like that.' Glenn suddenly thought about how lonely Bettina must be feeling. He had been so wrapped up in his own dilemma with Eleanora that he had not given Bettina's burden enough thought. 'It's true,' he said. 'There's no one. Not her parents, not her colleagues. Nobody.'

'Perhaps,' Marlowe began tentatively. 'Perhaps you could fly over there and give her a hand?'

'With the investigation?' Glenn asked, surprised by the suggestion. 'Won't that look suspicious?'

'No more than a friend visiting a friend, surely?' said Marlowe. 'Ah, there's my bus! I'd best run. Think about it, OK? She's our ticket to framing this bastard. Remember that.'

Glenn nodded, raising his hand in goodbye as his private detective pelted after a bus. Slowly, as if to seal his dark thoughts, the skies opened and rain poured down on London. Staring up at the gloomy sky above the city, Glenn wondered if the weather was better where Bettina was. Taking out his phone, he decided to find out.

'*Hallo?*' came Bettina's voice on the other end.

'You're working late,' said Glenn, checking his watch. It was just past seven o'clock in the evening in London, so it was already past eight there in Germany.

'Glenn!' she said, and his heart jumped to hear a smile in her voice. Or was it relief? 'Yes, I've been working on something. You know how it is.'

Glenn knew that 'something' was the investigation. Bettina rarely spoke openly about Farrand in the office for fear of the phone lines being tapped or volunteers overhearing. He wondered if the ICB President was there with her now. He grew hot with anger just thinking about him.

'Do you always work this late?' he asked her.

'Not always,' she said. 'But often, yes. There is a lot at stake these days.'

'Indeed,' sighed Glenn. 'Well, listen. I was just calling to see how the weather was over there?'

'The weather?' laughed Bettina. 'I've been listening to the pattering of the rain for two days non-stop.'

'Oh dear,' laughed Glenn. 'I was hoping it might be a bit better than here.'

'When you're blind, the rain is more beautiful than a sunny day, Glenn.'

'Oh yes, of course,' Glenn replied, musing on this thought. He blinked and then fixed his mind on what he was about to say. 'I would like to *listen* to the rain myself then, if the forecast I looked at is right and it's meant to be a washout...'

'You're coming here? To visit?' Bettina asked, excitement breaking through her voice like lightning.

'Would that be OK?' he asked nervously. 'I've just been wondering how you're getting on. I'm sorry it's taken me so long to come over there. I know this can't be, well... I know this can't be easy for you.'

'It's a nightmare,' she said and Glenn heard the tension in her voice. 'People are asking for their budgets to be delivered but how can I tell them we're almost bankrupt? What's worse is that I know. I know everything. I know the money is spent on expensive cars, many of which I've been driven around in, paraded like a bird in a cage, like a *whore*...'

'You should never feel like that,' said Glenn. 'You should never have been treated like some object for men to stare at. Farrand has used you in a terrible...'

'Glenn, I can't talk now,' she said quickly, interrupting him. 'You know why.'

Glenn knew they had to be careful. If Farrand caught wind of what they were up to, their operation would fail before it could even begin. Neither knew what he was capable of; perhaps they were not the only ones hiring private detectives.

'But please know that I'd love to see you,' Bettina added with great warmth in her voice. 'Christina would too, she'll be so happy…'

'Let's not tell Christina, OK?' Glenn said, thinking fast. 'We really do have to keep this whole thing as secret as possible. Christina will wonder why I'm there and we won't be able to talk openly. I'm sorry, Bettina. As much as I'd love to see her, I think this is the only way.'

'I understand. I won't mention it, but she might find out. If she passes by the office, or someone sees us. I'm just afraid she'll be hurt if she knows you came over and we didn't tell her.'

'Then we'll have to get out of town. Will you be free this weekend?'

'I have no plans,' she said, before adding with what sounded like relief: 'Well, none I can't cancel!'

'Then wait for me at the ICB office on Saturday morning.'

'Where should we go?'

'Leave that to me,' said Glenn, grinning to himself as the rain fell around him. 'I have an idea.'

Glenn hurried home, keen to set his plan in motion. The thought of asking Eleanora's permission about travelling had not even crossed his mind but Glenn knew that he would have to tell her eventually. He had been back for months and she barely said hello once a day but manners were manners; he did not want to risk her wrath for leaving unannounced. Only this time, when she met Glenn's announcement with fury, he wasn't going to take it lying down.

'So what if I'm travelling again?' he said. 'It's for business. I've made a commitment to this cause. I have to see it through.'

'Do your commitments to *me* mean nothing then?' Eleanora demanded, her blue eyes flaring with anger.

'I've made commitments to the ICB too,' he said coolly. 'We have a joint venture and joint stakes in the outcomes of this travesty.'

'And we don't?' his wife cried. 'Do we not *both* have stakes in this marriage?'

'I've gotta get out of here,' Glenn muttered under his breath.

'What did you say?' she shrieked at him. 'Don't you whisper things about me before my very eyes.'

'Sorry,' he said firmly. 'But look, I have to...'

'Oh go on, get out then,' she spat, before turning on her heels. The door slammed in his face, leaving a ringing in his ears, and an angry Beaumont portrait swinging on its hanging nails. Glenn shook his head and left the room to pack his bags. He had an incredibly strong impulse to run away, to flee Eleanora and her mood swings, her unfair demands and her cold gaze. For once he decided to honour that impulse, and he boarded the plane to Frankfurt that Saturday morning with no regrets.

Sick of hearing about Farrand and his convertibles, Glenn decided to put his plan into place. As soon as he landed in Frankfurt he went straight to the car rental desk and hired a Mercedes SLC. He picked it up at the airport parking lot and felt a buzz like no other. Finally, he thought: a chance to show Bettina that riding in a sports car didn't have to be an awful experience. He remembered her words, how she had felt like one of Farrand's whores, and Glenn gritted his teeth. The day that man was brought to justice would truly be a happy day.

When Glenn arrived at the office, he pressed on the buzzer, announcing himself. Bettina came downstairs and as soon as she opened the door she threw herself into his arms.

'I'm so glad to see you,' she said, buried in his shoulder. Glenn inhaled the scent of her hair. When she drew back, he looked at her blonde locks pulled tightly back in a bun, away from her face which looked pinched and tired. Her pink cheeks looked thinner than before. She had lost weight, Glenn thought.

'Hello,' he smiled down at her. 'Bettina, you look tired.'

'Do I?' she raised a hand to her face, tracing the soft, grey skin around her eyes; she looked crestfallen. 'God, it's just been so... so...'

'Hard,' Glenn sighed deeply. 'I know. The secrecy, the duplicity, keeping up appearances… Come on, let me buy you a coffee.'

'Can anyone see us?' Bettina asked, her face fearful. Glenn glanced around and saw the street was almost empty.

'No one,' he said, and hooked his arm gently in hers. He led them to a coffee shop he had spotted near the office and they went inside. Only when they were settled did Bettina begin to talk in a weary voice.

'I didn't realise before just how bad this was,' she said, cupping her mug of coffee with two twitching hands. 'You told me it was bad. The auditor found things, I know. But somehow I couldn't imagine what Herbert had been doing. But now, now that I know, I feel so frustrated. Where is the money going? We've had so many applications from women who need our help over the years, and I, the fool, believed Herbert when he said they were receiving everything they needed. I believed him every time. I had no reason not to. But they're not getting their budgets, Glenn, and that's not consistent with the fundraising I have done. My own projects are being delayed and there's often no response from Aachen when I make enquiries. It's all becoming clear to me. We've been so stupid.'

Glenn listened carefully to all Bettina said. His heart grew heavier with every passing moment. To his horror, Bettina seemed to be blaming herself for Farrand's fraud.

'He's worse than I thought,' she said quietly.

'Worse?' said Glenn, noting the darkness in her voice. 'Does that imply he was already a source of difficulty for you?'

Bettina's face grew rigid for a moment and then she blushed. She began to wring her hands, like someone waiting for a judge to pass sentence.

'Bettina?' said Glenn, watching her with increasing concern. 'Is everything alright?'

Slowly, Bettina swallowed hard and let out a short, bitter sigh. She began to shake her head.

'Herbert is a bully,' she said eventually. 'He always has been. I was quite young when we met and I was impressed by his vision. I was… how can I say? *Charmed* by him.'

'He's a charming man,' said Glenn, feeling uncomfortable. He remembered when he had first seen that chiselled, handsome face on the campaign poster in Aachen. Had he not also been charmed by this man at first?

'No, I mean,' Bettina began, clearly embarrassed, 'I mean, when I was younger I had feelings for him, Glenn.'

Glenn felt a lump in his throat and his heart sink. Though his mouth had gone dry, he knew he needed to say something.

'Go on,' he urged her gently.

'I was young,' she said. 'No, I was stupid, I think. I always hoped… well, it's crazy to think this now. But, well, I always hoped he would choose me, you know? After every mission, I'd come back hoping he would say more than, "Well done, but you can do better next time." I came back from Mexico, Hong Kong, New Orleans, and every time I hoped he might have missed me. I hoped he might notice me, you know? He took me to parties, he hung me on his arm like a doll. I said nothing. I always thought that was his way of telling me he liked me. But then, of course, I always met his girlfriends. I was foolish.'

'You were young,' Glenn said firmly. 'There's a difference.'

'Maybe,' she shrugged. 'But I've always found it hard to refuse him. Even now, it makes me scared. I always do as he asks. Until recently. I realise now that it was my actions and my choices that made my career what it is, not him; I am not merely the benefactor of his grace and esteem. But he was very powerful back then, Glenn. He still is. He has this way of making one feel like one owes him something; like there is a debt that can never be fully repaid. I was scared sometimes. I never challenged him. Never. After all, he had given me all I ever wanted: a mission in life, a mission I was born to carry out.'

'You gave yourself that,' Glenn said quietly. 'You are a self-made woman, Bettina. And it's damn impressive.'

Bettina nodded proudly.

'Yes,' she said, her brow furrowing. 'But it's taken me some time to realise that.'

'And now?' Glenn asked, hoping that this crush, this youthful infatuation was over.

'Now? Now I'm lost,' she muttered. 'When people ask me if they can start new projects I want to tell them, yes. I want to say, yes, of course we can help, we are a charity. We are the ICB. But I don't believe we can anymore. I can't bring myself to lie to people.'

'Bettina,' Glenn said gently, taking her hand in his. 'You've had to shoulder this burden alone. You must feel overwhelmed, facing this betrayal without a soul to talk to. I'm sorry if I haven't been here.'

'I'm just so tired.' She shook her head. 'I feel *broken* by this.'

'I think you need a rest,' said Glenn, and without further ado, he clapped his hands together. 'So if you'll allow me to whisk you away, that's why I'm here. Can I escort you to our secret getaway vehicle?'

'Glenn?' she laughed. 'Secret getaway? What vehicle?'

'Well, I thought about what you told me on the phone,' said Glenn. 'About Herbert forcing you to drive around in those ridiculous cars, parading you around like an object. So I thought you might like to drive with *me* in a nice car. See how that feels. I gotta tell you, Bettina, I feel like a nine-year old all over again. I'm so excited!'

'Why? What kind of car is it?' Bettina asked.

'Come and see for yourself,' he grinned.

When they reached the car, Glenn led Bettina's hand down to feel the Mercedes signature metal symbol on the bonnet.

'Very nice, Glenn.'

'I just wanna show you that road trips can be fun,' he grinned. 'And comfortable. And, well, I just want to get to know you more. I hope you'd like to get to know me more too?'

'Oh Glenn,' Bettina smiled. 'That's so sweet. Of course I would. Where are we going?' she asked as he helped her into her seat. 'Wow, that *is* comfortable!'

'Leather seats. You won't believe this car. It's like something from an old movie. As for where we're going, that's up to you. The car is my side of the deal. The destination is yours.'

Bettina sat back in her seat, shaking her head and smiling. Glenn waited while she thought in silence about where she wanted to go. He watched her, enjoying the colour returning to her cheeks once more, relishing this chance to make her happy and bring her some rest.

'Well, I've always wanted to go to Europa Park,' she said at last, a small, girlish smile rising on her lips.

'Europa Park?' he laughed. 'The theme park?'

'Is that sad?' she asked, her smile fading.

'What? No!' cried Glenn. 'I'm just surprised, that's all. Why would that be sad?'

'I don't know,' she shrugged. 'Because I'm nearly thirty years old!'

'You're never too old for theme parks, and that's a fact,' Glenn chuckled. 'Let's find out how to get there, shall we?'

Taking out his sat-nav, Glenn searched the route for Europa Park. It was almost three hundred kilometres south, on a route that would take them back down along the French border, towards Switzerland. Spotting something on the map, Glenn gasped.

'What is it?' laughed Bettina.

'It's not far from the Black Forest!' Glenn laughed with excitement. 'I've always wanted to go there.'

'Why don't we travel there today then, and stay close to Europa Park so we can go there tomorrow?' Bettina suggested.

'That sounds like a plan to me,' Glenn nodded. 'Now, shall we start the journey with some breakfast?'

Reaching into the back seat, Glenn brought out a bag full of fresh croissants, fruits and freshly squeezed orange juice.

'Oh Glenn, you've thought of everything!' Bettina laughed. 'How lovely. A picnic breakfast.'

'Wait until you see the lunch hamper,' Glenn smiled, taking a long sip of orange juice.

'Glenn, I...' Bettina began, but before she could thank him for the tenth time that day, Glenn stopped her.

'Bettina,' he said, shaking his head affectionately. 'You do so much for other people. Let me do this for you, OK?'

Hesitating for a moment, she nodded, smiling a small, shy smile. They ate the buttery, fluffy pastries in silence before starting up the car and beginning their journey south. As they drove out of Frankfurt onto the autobahn, Glenn relished the lack of speed limits and Bettina began to chat to him, comfortable in the safe, enclosed space of the car. They talked about their work, their friends, their parents. Glenn enjoyed making her laugh with tales of his father's flirting and pancake baking. He told her about their visits to Ronda Round, and the clashes with Eleanora's parents.

'What a family you have,' she smiled. 'I can see why you're so warm.'

Almost three hours later they reached the Black Forest. The sun came out at just the right time to shine over the incredible autumn colours of the countryside around them. Bettina rolled down her window to feel the warmth on her face.

'Shall we put the top down?' Glenn asked her.

'The top?' she said.

'We're in a convertible,' he laughed. 'Didn't I tell you?'

Glenn pulled over and adjusted the convertible roof. It slid away, filling the car with fresh air. As he pulled away, Bettina rose up in her seat to feel the wind against her hair, her neck and her chest. To Glenn great's surprise, she stood up, letting the wind drive around her body, an insatiable force making her flowing, linen tunic wrap around each curve. She screamed with joy. Glenn watched her, barely able to keep his eyes on the road.

'It's heaven, Glenn!' she called out to the sky. 'Oh God. It's heaven!'

Glenn smiled as he drove into the Black Forest, taking in the dark patches of coniferous forest crinkling the hillsides and flattening out into valleys as Bettina laughed and chatted with him. This *was* some kind of heaven, he thought, grinning from ear to ear.

'It's beautiful here,' he breathed.

'Describe it to me,' said Bettina, settling back into her seat amid her cries of laughter.

'I'm no poet, OK?' Glenn warned her, suddenly shy.

'Glenn, you're writing these case studies about us all,' Bettina laughed. 'That gives me some faith in your ability with words.'

Taking a deep breath, Glenn took in the hills around him.

'Well, it's not black, that's for sure,' he started, laughing nervously. 'I don't know why they call it the Black Forest.'

'I had gathered that much already,' Bettina laughed too. 'Tell me, Glenn. Tell me what you see.'

So Glenn, swallowing his self-consciousness, began to talk about everything he saw. From the ancient castles they passed to the traditional wooden chalets on the tumbling, emerald slopes, he described everything as best he could. There were waterfalls and quaint villages along the way, all hard to describe due to their stunning beauty. But Glenn did all he could to share what he saw, regardless of the challenge. It was only when his voice grew hoarse and the sky grew heavy with dusk that he realised he had spoken for hours.

'Now the sun is starting to set in the west,' he said, bringing his monologue to a close. 'It's beautiful. All fiery oranges and pink over the silhouette of the trees. It's like the sun is giving up on the earth and the sky is releasing all these colours in angry protest.'

'That was perfect, Glenn,' said Bettina, sighing with satisfaction. Glenn looked over to see his companion lying back in her seat with her eyes closed, smiling.

'Did you like my running commentary?' he asked her.

'It was great. Like a movie.'

'You'd be the star if this was a movie,' Glenn laughed. 'Standing up in your seat and letting the wind whip your hair up like that! All you need is some sunglasses and you'd be a regular *Thelma and Louise*!'

'Says the man who is driving a sports car. I think *you're* the movie star here, Glenn. No?'

'So it's *Glenn and Bettina: The Black Forest*,' laughed Glenn. 'Sounds like a hit.'

'That sounds like a horror movie!' Bettina squealed. 'There would be an axe murderer in there for sure. I've seen enough American movies to know what happens in forests in Hollywood.'

'What does it feel like to see a movie?' Glenn asked, unable to stop himself. He was so curious. His father loved movies. Would he too be able to 'watch' them as a blind person, Glenn wondered?

'I don't know any different,' Bettina said, clearly pondering the question. 'I listen to the audio accompaniment and let my imagination do the seeing for me. It's like listening to a story. A great story, full of details and rich colours.'

'I'll have to try that sometime,' said Glenn.

'You'll have to,' Bettina said.

They drove slowly towards Europa Park, Bettina calling ahead to make a reservation at a hotel in the resort. Glenn smiled when he heard her speaking German. It made her sound extremely authoritative, he thought. When they finally reached the resort, Glenn parked up and carried their bags inside.

'Will that be a double or a twin room, sir?' the hotel receptionist asked in heavily accented German. Glenn's insides froze at the question. He looked over to Bettina to see if she had heard, and to his relief he saw that she was resting in an armchair across the lobby, out of earshot. He watched her for a moment, admiring her easy elegance as she sat, cross-legged, in her long, blue coat, the same bright colour of her eyes. Blue, he thought. *She always wears blue.*

'Sir?' the receptionist asked again, jolting Glenn out of his reverie. He looked back at the receptionist, wondering if his indecision was etched on his face. Looking down at his hand, he saw his wedding ring. The receptionist must have noticed it too.

'Two doubles,' said Glenn quickly. 'We'll be, uh, sleeping separately.'

'Very good, sir,' nodded the receptionist.

'I'll see you for dinner at seven, then?' said Glenn, after walking Bettina to her room.

'Sure, Glenn,' she grinned. 'See you at seven.'

Seven could not come sooner. Glenn felt younger than he had in years. Something about spending time with Bettina was invigorating and life-affirming. After those gloomy summer months stuffed up in Ronda Round Manor, the fresh air of Germany was like oxygen to his brain. The mixture of the sunshine, the green pastures of the Black Forest, and the excitement of arriving in Europa Park had left him buzzing. Lying down on his bed, Glenn looked over at the phone beneath the bed-side lamp. He knew he should call Eleanora to tell her he was safe. He knew he should, but he didn't want to. *Go for it*, his father had said. How could he really see how he felt around Bettina if he called through to Eleanora, he wondered? Deciding to throw caution to the wind, Glenn fell into a light snooze instead, his mind exhausted from the day's travel from London to Frankfurt and from Frankfurt to southern Germany. What an adventure, he grinned to himself.

The dinner that night passed by with delicious starters, exquisitely cooked German dishes and desserts that made both Glenn and Bettina's smiles double in size, if that was even possible. They both seemed deliriously happy.

'I'm not sure if I'll be able to walk after this,' laughed Bettina, taking a sip of her coffee and throwing her napkin down. 'I'm totally stuffed.'

'I was starving,' Glenn chuckled. 'It's amazing how talking makes me hungry.'

'Do you not talk much in England?' she asked.

'Not at home, no,' he said, thinking of those long, excruciatingly painful dinners at Ronda Round Manor. His pain must have shown for Bettina began to apologise.

'I'm sorry,' she said. 'I didn't mean to intrude.'

'It's no intrusion,' Glenn said, forcing a smile. 'I guess my wife and I just don't talk much these days.'

'Poor you,' said Bettina, forcing her own smile, and doing her best to change the subject. 'And I made you talk the whole way! You must be exhausted.'

'I should be,' said Glenn. 'But look at me, I'm so alive! There must be something in the water over here.'

'Something in the *food* maybe!' Bettina chuckled. 'The healing powers of *schnitzel*. Who'd have guessed it?'

Glenn paused a moment. Then, setting his jaw, he whispered, 'Or something in you.'

Bettina's laugh slowed down and petered into silence, though the smile never left her lips. She was still and quiet for a moment.

'It's strange,' she said.

'What is?'

'I think there must be something in you too, Glenn,' she said. 'Because I also feel alive. For the first time in a very long time.'

Before Glenn could ask a burning question, which was why *had* Bettina been unhappy for so long, the young woman stood up.

'I have to sleep now,' she smiled serenely. 'Otherwise I won't make it onto half of the rides tomorrow. I would never forgive myself if I came all the way to Europa Park and was too sleepy to catch a few rides.'

'You're right,' said Glenn, clearing his throat and shaking his head slightly. The sight of Bettina smiling so intensely had utterly enraptured him. He stood and walked with her back to the elevator, where they rode to their separate floors.

'Goodnight,' said Glenn, smiling warmly and holding out a hand.

'Goodnight,' said Bettina, squeezing his palm. She turned back, raising a hand. 'And Glenn?' she called.

'Don't,' he warned her, laughing softly.

'Just once,' she laughed. 'Please?'

'Just once then,' he grinned.

'Thank you,' she said. 'For this day. For everything.'

'You're welcome,' said Glenn, his heart glowing with a precious, beaming light. 'For everything.'

The lift closed, leaving him all alone. He was suddenly facing himself in the mirror. His jawline was stubbly and needed a shave; his shirt was loose and his jacket creased; his sandy hair was messy and his brown eyes looked tired. But hell, he thought. He looked happier than had looked in years.

CHAPTER TWENTY-SEVEN

'Are you ready?' Bettina asked him, smiling to give him courage. Glenn looked down into her calm, excited face. How was she so cool about this, he wondered?

'As ready as I'll ever be,' he said, swallowing hard.

'Alright then,' she grinned. 'Let's do it?'

Taking one step forward, Bettina pulled Glenn with her into a queue for one of the longest and scariest rollercoasters in Europe. Five loop-the-loops loomed out of the morning fog in Europa Park, goading Glenn from a distance.

'Glenn, are you shaking?' his friend asked, clearly suppressing a giggle.

'I'm cold,' he lied.

'No, really, why are you shaking so much?' she asked, patting his arm.

'Huh?' Glenn suddenly felt it too. He looked down to see the zip on his jacket buzzing. Realising even he could not be that nervous, he reached down into his pocket to see his phone vibrating. The screen flashed bright with messages:

You have 6 missed calls.

Glenn recognised the number immediately. It was the house phone at Ronda Round Manor. *Damn it*, he thought. Eleanora must be calling him.

'Sorry,' he said quickly to Bettina. 'I should take this.'

Stepping out of the queue, Glenn pressed the button to call back. He waited one dial tone before the call clicked into place. He dreaded whatever lay on the other side of that click.

'Too busy to answer your phone, are you?' came Eleanora's scathing tone, piercing through his ears, slicing away the peace of that morning. 'I've been calling you all morning. I called…'

'Six times, I know,' said Glenn coldly. His heart, softened in Bettina's presence, hardened now at the sound of his wife's accusations.

'Then why didn't you call back?' she demanded.

'Because I've been busy,' he snapped. But as soon as he had said the words, his heart flooded with guilt. Busy with Bettina, he thought.

'Busy with business or pleasure?' she cried.

'What do you think?' he cried back, swallowing hard. He was lying, he thought, feeling sweat rising at the back of his neck. He was lying to Eleanora for the first time in his life.

'Why can I hear so many people laughing, and what is that? Children crying?' his wife's angry voice tore down the line. 'Where are you?'

'I'm at a conference,' he lied. 'It's hectic. There's a lot of people.'

'Who with?' she demanded.

'An associate of the ICB,' he said. 'Who else? That's why I'm here, right?'

'Why can I hear music then?' she said angrily. Glenn glanced over at a loudly chiming merry-go-round spinning nearby.

'Look, we're just adapting to the situation,' he said quickly. 'And why all these questions? I sit in that damn palace all summer and you say nothing to me. I leave for one day and you're throwing all this crap my way? What do you want, Eleanora? Why are you calling me like this?'

'Can a wife not call her husband?' she answered, her voice weakening. 'I didn't hear from you yesterday. You always send something; you always leave a message... but there was nothing. I was worried about you.'

Glenn's chest heaved with a sickening pang of guilt. Had he not looked at the phone and callously decided to avoid the call? Had he not actively chosen to ignore her?

'I've been thinking,' she continued, her voice breaking into a sudden, sharp sob. 'I know things have been terrible. I know we've been living like strangers and we're missing each other. I'm not living in denial, darling. God knows, and I know, things have changed. But I want us to talk again, when you're back. I want us to talk like we used to.'

Glenn's mind reeled with confusion. He glanced back to the queue, where Bettina was standing patiently, waiting for him. He hoped she could not hear anything he was saying. He remembered what she had always told him about heightened senses and just prayed he was standing out of earshot. She looked so innocent, standing there, smiling faintly as she listened to the sounds of the park around her. Glenn forced his mind back to his wife, wracking his brains for the right response.

'Nora,' he said, his voice tight with emotion. 'I know, honey. I know what you're saying. I think we should... jeez, well... this isn't a good time. Can I call you back later?'

'Do you miss me?' she asked him, sniffing. The question stung him.

No, he thought, saying it aloud in his head. *No, I don't.* The pain it would cause was unimaginable.

'Of course, honey,' he said gently. 'Of course I do. I'm gonna call you real soon, OK?'

'Alright,' she sniffled. 'Speak to you later then. It was good to hear your voice.'

'You too, baby,' he said.

Eleanora hung up and Glenn let out a long, silent groan. For a moment, he wished he could just hand his phone to someone else. A man walked by with his small son, chattering innocently in German. Couldn't he just thrust the phone into the man's hand, Glenn wondered? Couldn't he just say, here, take my phone, take my marriage, you decide what to do with it? If only life were so simple. He turned instead and walked back to the queue, where Bettina was waiting.

'Everything OK?' she asked him, sensing, as ever, his presence before it was announced.

'Yes,' he lied. 'Everything's fine. It was just...'

'Your wife,' she finished his sentence for him.

'Yeah,' he nodded. Bettina looked strange for a moment. She neither looked happy, nor sad. If anything, she looked uncomfortable. She said nothing and together they joined the queue once more.

The rollercoaster was nothing compared to Eleanora's pleas and protestations but it had the desired effect of throwing Glenn utterly out of his comfort zone, and subsequently clearing his head. He followed Bettina onto many more rides, relishing the chance to lose himself in adrenaline.

'Whoa, now who's the nervous one!' Glenn laughed when they climbed off their sixth ride, suddenly feeling Bettina vibrate beside him. She started at the sensation and laughing, reached down into her blue coat pocket to pull out her phone.

'Glenn!' she cried with excitement. 'It's Dylan.'

'How do you know?' he asked, puzzled by her intuition. Glenn saw the name 'Dylan Marlowe' flashing on her screen, but how could Bettina know?

'I can tell from the vibrations,' she said. 'They're personalised for every caller.'

Wow, Glenn marvelled to himself as Bettina answered the phone. Technology was endlessly impressive. He listened as Bettina answered the call. She and Dylan spoke in German at first, until Bettina pulled the phone away from her ear and pressed a button.

'OK, Dylan, you're on speakerphone now,' she said, switching into English.

'Thanks, Bettina,' came Marlowe's voice on the line. 'Hi Glenn. I thought you two might be together.'

'What's up, Dylan?' Glenn asked, curious as to why their private detective would be calling them on a Sunday afternoon.

'I've got some news for you both,' he said. 'Are you free to talk?'

'Sure,' said Glenn, looking to Bettina for confirmation. She nodded. An anxious look had returned to her face and Glenn's heart sunk. The great work of the day before had disappeared, her newfound ease and happiness replaced by the same fear and stress he had seen on arrival.

'You probably haven't checked your emails yet, Glenn,' Marlowe began. 'But I've seen one that's been sent to you in Farrand's Sent Items.'

'Wow, you're really tracking him,' said Glenn, impressed and slightly unnerved by this man's ability to breach privacy.

'If I'm doing my job properly, there's nothing he's doing or saying that I'm not tracking, Glenn,' said Marlowe. 'But listen, this is important.

This email, it went out yesterday. It's an invitation to a fundraiser in Sydney next weekend. He's rented out a big beach house and is hosting a conference in the city. It's called "Asia Vision" and it's basically a bid to get big investments from the Asia Pacific region.'

'OK,' said Glenn slowly, wondering if he had missed something. 'What's suspicious about that?'

'I think we should go,' said Marlowe.

'But it's next weekend!' said Glenn. 'That's too short notice. I'm not sure if I can take time off and the flights will be super expensive.'

'I know,' said Marlowe. 'I think that's exactly what Farrand will be thinking too. He had this sent out to major donors and investors *months* ago, even up to a year ago. I think him inviting you at such short notice means he doesn't expect you to show up. Which makes me think he's got something to hide, or at least something he doesn't really want you to see. This invitation is playing the game of good partner, making token gestures, when in fact it's just a formality. He doesn't want you to really go, Glenn.'

'Dylan's right,' said Bettina, a frown growing on her forehead. 'Herbert told me about this almost a year ago. He was angry I wouldn't come, but I know what these things are like. Girls, drink and rich men. It's all about money.'

Glenn thought about what they were both saying for a moment.

'And you really think this late invitation means something?' said Glenn.

'I would bank on it,' said Marlowe. 'It's suspicious as hell. You're fundraising for his charity, Glenn. You should have had an advance invitation and a front row seat. But this guy knows you play by the rules. He knows you play straight. I think this could be an excellent opportunity to gather evidence.'

Glenn turned away from the call for a moment.

'What do you think, Bettina?' he asked her. 'Should we go?'

'You have to decide, Glenn,' she said. 'But I do agree with Marlowe. It's suspicious as hell.'

'Look, listen mate, we have to go,' said Marlowe. 'This is a big shot. Take it or leave it, but understand this: Farrand is a slippery fish. This fundraiser is where other slippery fish will go. It's a sort of slippery fish net, if you will. We would be wise to strike *now*.'

Glenn considered all Marlowe had said. He looked at Bettina, taking in the dark circles beneath her eyes. She was doing so much on her own to gather evidence to crush Farrand. Perhaps it was time for him to help in earnest too.

'I'll book flights,' said Glenn, deciding on the spot. 'Dylan, you'll come as my "assistant" or something. Come up with a convincing cover, OK?'

'That I can do,' he said. 'Just send me the details and I'll be at the airport.'

Marlowe hung up the phone, leaving the fun sounds of the theme park all around them a little duller to their ears. Glenn let out a deep sigh.

'Sydney, huh,' he laughed bitterly. 'So that's his next target.'

'I would imagine he's invited some very rich men to fill his pockets,' Bettina said bitterly.

'Asia is a huge bread basket for charities,' Glenn nodded. 'It's a smart move. Under different circumstances I'd be thrilled. This means big money for the ICB. I know this trickster is up to something. He'll have an agenda, that's for sure.'

'Well, there's one positive thing about your trip at least,' said Bettina.

'What's that?' Glenn asked, surprised that there could be anything positive in such an event. Bettina was beaming from ear to ear.

'Zu-Ting will be there,' she grinned.

* * * *

The thought of seeing Zu-Ting again was the only thing that Glenn looked forward to about their upcoming trip to Sydney. He told Eleanora when he returned from Frankfurt, weary from the drive up from Europa Park and his late flight back to London. She was incensed, and quite the opposite of Bettina's calm, cool composure in the face of change and upheaval.

'What a fool I was to think you actually might want to resolve the difficulties in our relationship,' she spat, shaking her head with rage. 'I reach out to you, I make myself vulnerable, and all you can do is throw it back in my face! I don't even know who you are anymore.'

'Throw it back in your face?' cried Glenn. 'How exactly am I doing that? I'm here, am I not? I came back?'

'Only to leave again straight away!' she exclaimed. 'For Australia, of all places! To the other side of the bloody world!'

'Do you really think I *want* this?' he demanded. 'Do you really think I *want* to sit on a flight for twenty-four hours of my life, to watch this schmuck take people's money and use it for himself? What do you take me for, baby?'

'I take you for a coward,' Eleanora said coldly, still shaking with anger.

'Of course you do,' Glenn shook his head, feeling hysterical. 'Why did I even begin to believe anything you said on the phone? All that nonsense about loving me and wanting to make changes…'

'I do!' she yelled. 'I do want that! But how can we when the first thing you say on return from a business trip is that, within two days, you'll be heading off on another?'

'I never said there would be no more travel,' said Glenn firmly, shaking with the injustice of her words. 'But honey, you've got to believe me. I don't *want* to go. I *have* to.'

Neither of them seemed to have anything more to say after that. Eleanora threw her hands into the air and left the room, leaving Glenn to head to his office and prepare for Sydney. Luckily the DCF at least had not had a problem with his request to travel. They had considered it a natural step to take in solidifying Glenn's proposed partnership with the ICB, offering even to cover his travel expenses. They agreed to let an external consultant travel with him too, not knowing that Dylan Marlowe was in fact a private detective.

When the time came to check in at Heathrow, Glenn spotted Marlowe buying two coffees at a stand in the Departures hall.

'G'day mate,' he grinned when he saw his employer heading over to him.

'Let's do this, shall we?' Glenn sighed, taking the coffee handed to him with a grimace.

'I think Farrand has sealed his fate with this invitation,' said Marlowe. 'Just you wait and see. I think we're in for quite the spectacle.'

The flight to Sydney connected in Dubai with a quick stop. Glenn tried to relax into the journey but his head was pounding with thoughts of Eleanora and Bettina. His wife's angry words tore through his mind and the sight of her indifferent shrug as he said goodbye left him feeling cold. Was that how they said goodbye now, he wondered? He compared it to the warm embrace Bettina had left him with that previous Sunday evening. She had gone with him all the way to the airport, saying goodbye before the security gates. To calm his mind, Glenn imagined her instead, watering her plants at the office in Frankfurt, her fine, round shoulders tucked warmly into a blue sweater. After all, he did not need to know if she too was thinking of him. She had said as much in an email:

Thinking of you this weekend, Glenn. Don't let him get away with this. Thanks again for everything.

Sydney was pleasantly hot, bright and buzzing in the full summer of the southern hemisphere. Arriving at the Harbour Hotel where the conference was being held, Glenn was unsurprised to see the ICB's logo plastered across large posters in the lobby, indicating which way guests should arrive. Herbert Farrand's face loomed larger than life above them too, that same chiselled, handsome visage Glenn had seen in Aachen staring out at him. The words *Asia Vision: Making the East See* were written boldly on the conference posters.

'OK, we've only got tickets for this evening's fundraiser,' said Marlowe, taking out a print-out of Glenn's invitation. 'That means we have the afternoon to sleep off this jetlag before we put our party faces on.'

'Thank God,' Glenn groaned, dreading the evening's activities.

'Come on, we've been upgraded to rooms on the ninth floor,' said Marlowe. 'With views of the Sydney Harbour Bridge, I believe.'

'What?' cried Glenn. 'No way, that's way too expensive.'

'A welcoming gift from Farrand,' shrugged Marlowe.

'He didn't do that for all the guests, did he?' Glenn asked, not even daring to imagine the cost of such a gesture, no doubt billed to the ICB.

'You do know who we're dealing with here, right?' said Marlowe, raising a quizzical eyebrow.

When he reached his room Glenn saw that Marlowe had been telling the truth. Sydney Harbour spread out magnificently before him. He could see yachts crossing the water and the wide arcs of the Sydney Opera House gleaming in the sun. Feeling guilty about the price-tag that came with such a view, Glenn immediately called through to Ronda Round to tell his wife he had arrived. When no answer came, he left a message, and immediately felt relief. A niggling feeling at the back of his heart bothered him though. His relief came from that fact that she had not been there to pick up, not because he had done the right thing.

When he descended to the lobby later that evening, Glenn was impressed to see how Marlowe had dressed up impeccably for the fundraiser. His tuxedo and smoothly combed blonde hair made him slip elegantly into the crowd of guests buzzing around reception, slowly moving towards the event. It was an international crowd, full of different languages, faces and accents, and overwhelmingly Asian.

'You scrub up well,' Glenn laughed, taking in the size of the man before him.

'You too,' Marlowe nodded approvingly. Glenn had packed his best tuxedo and tried his best to look comfortable in it. A few appreciative glances from women passing through the lobby assured him he had done a good job.

'Did you manage to get a few hours of sleep?' Glenn asked Marlowe.

'Nah, I was too eager to start working,' he replied, before lowering his voice. 'I've been checking out the guest list and chatting around. There are a lot of Chinese, Korean and Thai people here, and many of them were grateful for the visa opportunity.'

'Clever,' said Glenn, admiring Farrand's political tactics as he walked side by side with Marlowe into the event. Offering a free trip to Australia was an excellent way to loosen people's purse strings.

The evening event room spread out magnificently before them, decorated with gold and blue drapes, chandeliers, magnificent ice fountains and an array of banners announcing the theme. Champagne flutes clinked and twinkled all around them. It was an incredible display of wealth, Glenn thought.

'The most important thing tonight is not to arouse suspicion,' Marlowe said in a low voice to his companion, glancing around so no one would hear. Spotting a waiter, he beckoned him over.

'Champagne, sir?' the waiter offered his tray of flutes. Marlowe shook his head and whispered something in the waiter's ear. The man returned shortly with a glass of what looked like scotch. Marlowe thanked him and took a short sip.

'Apple juice,' he whispered to Glenn with a grin. 'People are far more likely to open up and say things if they think you'll have forgotten everything they said the next morning. You'll see me with plenty of these tonight. You should try it.'

'No need,' said Glenn. 'I don't drink.'

The speeches were announced by a fanfare of pipes. Glenn looked over and saw an array of around thirty musicians in the corner of the vast hall, all dressed in traditional Asian costumes. Farrand really had gone all out. Everywhere he looked, the rich and beautiful were milling around, including a stream of extremely attractive young women, dressed exquisitely and carrying white canes. Where had Farrand found such a group of beautiful blind women, he wondered? Marlowe had clearly made the same observation, for he turned to Glenn with incredulous eyes.

'Do you think they're really blind?' he asked Glenn in a low whisper.

'What?' Glenn yelped. 'He would never sink that low, would he?'

'Again,' Marlowe cocked his head to one side. 'You do know who we're dealing with here, don't you?'

But before Glenn could even begin to fathom that thought, a fanfare of music started up.

'Ladies and gentlemen, ladies and gentlemen!' a familiar voice cut through the room, ringing on the loudspeakers. Everyone turned to look at the small stage, where the ICB logo was flashing onto a large screen, followed by the slogan *Asia Vision: Make the East See*, and Farrand, standing elegantly there in his smart black tuxedo. To his great pleasure, Glenn saw Zu-Ting standing just behind him, dressed in a red silk dress, woven in a traditional Korean style. She looked stunning, Glenn thought.

'Alright, alright, thank you!' he heard Farrand calling above the din on a microphone. Glenn would recognise his heavily accented English anywhere. 'Please, everyone, take a moment to listen to your host,' he said, laughing lightly. 'I would like to raise a glass to you all for coming to join us today, from as far as Singapore to as close as the Sydney suburbs!'

The crowd clapped politely in approval.

'We have a true representation of Asia here tonight, my friends,' he said. 'We have delegates, donors and investors from China, Myanmar, Thailand, Japan, Singapore, Australia and New Zealand. Some of you have joined us in our conference today already, and others have only joined us now. To all I say welcome! Now, before we get down to the important business of eating and drinking and getting to know one another, I invite you all to listen to a small introduction to what we do at the ICB. Ladies and gentlemen, thank you for your time.'

Glenn watched as Farrand stepped back and passed the microphone to a young man he had never seen before. The man thanked Farrand and began to give an overview of the work the ICB did around the world. He spoke with a strong Australian accent and seemed very intelligent and capable. Glenn only wondered why Zu-Ting had not taken the microphone.

'Who's the suit?' Marlowe asked.

'I have no idea,' said Glenn. They listened as the man spoke passionately about the charity's vision.

'This is all false,' Marlowe muttered in Glenn's ear as the man offered the crowd grand statistics and summaries of spending.

'It doesn't add up,' Glenn nodded gravely.

'So, as the West have opened their eyes and hearts to living with blindness, winning the fight, so we invite the East to join us!' the man concluded. 'Tonight we seek to raise five million dollars, ladies and gentlemen. By the end of this evening, I hope we will have the means to fulfil our promise; to make the East see. Enjoy your night. Thank you.'

'A rousing speech,' said Marlowe, raising one sarcastic eyebrow. Glenn however, had stopped listening long ago. His only wish was to reach Zu-Ting and say hello to his friend. She looked vulnerable there, on the stage, so close to Farrand.

'I'm going to say hello to an old friend,' he told Marlowe.

'Right, well it's time for me to get on with this investigation then,' said Marlowe, taking a long sip of his apple juice and switching his facial expression to charm. 'Starting with these ladies.'

Glenn watched as his private detective headed off towards the line of beautiful women holding white canes in the distance. The crowds began to mingle and chatter as the speeches ended, and though he longed to reach Zu-Ting, Glenn found himself drawn into conversations. With every person he met, he saw how it was a conference of cowboys: the rich of Asia had descended to give a little money and make a lot more. Many people were networking and openly discussing deals and investments. Smartly dressed men gawked at the blind women who passed them, their blindness providing an open pass for the men to stare at every cleavage that passed by. They then laughed, and reached out in longing to the silk stretched tightly across a waist or buttocks. Glenn wondered if Farrand had asked the women to dress so scantily, but more importantly, he wondered why he had invited men like these to an event about blindness. They were despicable. Glenn could have sworn he saw one of the women disappearing with an elderly Chinese diplomat.

Unfortunately, Farrand found Glenn before he could find Zu-Ting. Hoping to avoid too much contact, Glenn kept a low profile, but the president was already doing the rounds. Sleek and smart in his tuxedo, the man was impressive as ever.

'Glenn!' he cried. 'Glenn, Glenn, *Glenn!* There you are! I'm so glad you could make it. I thought my invitation might have been too short notice, but I see you know where your interests lie! Good man. Welcome.'

'Thank you,' said Glenn, forcing a smile. 'Yes, I was lucky. I was due some leave and this seemed like the perfect opportunity to see what you're up to over here.'

'I trust your suite is comfortable?' he asked pointedly.

'Very,' said Glenn. 'Really, Herbert. You didn't need to do that.'

'Come now, are we not business partners now?' he laughed. 'I couldn't let you come all the way to Sydney without seeing the sights, could I?'

Glenn shivered at the thought of himself in partnership with Farrand. Here was the man Bettina had called a bully and who siphoned millions away from the charity she loved. Glenn only hoped his distaste was not etched across his face.

'We are both very comfortable, thank you,' he nodded in thanks.

'Yes,' nodded Farrand, his grey eyes sliding from Glenn to Marlowe, who was chatting away to a group of women in the distance. 'You have brought someone else with you this time. A friend perhaps?'

'My assistant, Dylan,' said Glenn. 'He's working as an external consultant with me these days. Come, I'll introduce you.'

Leading Farrand over to Marlowe and the three women he was speaking to, Glenn cleared his throat to announce their arrival.

'Glenn,' smiled Marlowe, turning around. 'May I introduce you to Suzy Nell, Kayleigh and Chantelle? I've just been listening to their tragic stories. Fascinating and terrible. Ladies, this is my boss, Glenn Tebbhurst. Senior fundraiser at the Diversified Charities Foundation in London.'

The women were incredibly beautiful, bejewelled and smiled enticingly at the new arrivals. Glenn bowed slightly, before remembering the women were blind. Two of them bowed back though. Glenn caught Marlowe's eye, a moment of shared suspicion. His private detective was convincing in his role. He was even smiling benignly at Farrand, pretending he did not know who he was.

'Nice to meet you,' Glenn said to the ladies, trying hard not to look at the three bosoms bursting from their dresses. 'Uh, Dylan, may I introduce you Mr. Herbert Farrand, President of the ICB, and the reason we are here tonight?'

'Ladies, please excuse me!' said Marlowe in his charming, exuberant way. The ladies giggled and turned towards another group of men, this time from the Thai embassy, staring at them, almost drooling.

Marlowe turned to Farrand with a broad smile, his youthful face glowing with curiosity. He thrust a hand forward.

'A pleasure to meet you, Mr. Farrand,' he said enthusiastically. 'May I congratulate you for this evening, and for your entourage? They are *stunning*. You have quite the team to manage, sir.'

'Yes, and every one of them has a sad story to tell,' said Farrand, hanging his head and sighing deeply. 'One can only admire them for the courage they have shown in coming here tonight.'

Clearing his throat so others around could her them, Farrand let out a deep, audible sigh.

'They are poor, innocent girls! They are here for our protection and help,' he said loudly, his face a mask of pity. 'The ICB is just happy to satisfy their needs.'

Glenn saw the businessmen around them eyeing the girls with a mixture of excitement and pity. Some went quickly to fawn over them with the Thai consulates.

'Who was the young man who gave the speech back there?' Glenn asked Farrand, looking around for the Australian speech maker.

'Who?' asked Farrand, still wearing his pitying frown.

'The kid who gave the speech,' said Glenn. 'He spoke very eloquently. Is he a new campaigner?'

'Oh, Malcolm?' said Farrand. He laughed and then leant down to Glenn's ear. 'Actually, Glenn, he came with the PR team who helped me set up this little soiree. They write speeches, that sort of thing. Hired help, if you know what I mean! Gives me more time to actually enjoy myself. Speaking of which, I could do with a drink. What's your poison?'

'Oh, I don't drink,' said Glenn, raising a hand in thanks.

'Suit yourself,' Farrand smiled falsely. 'Enjoy your evening, Glenn. You too, Mr. Marlowe.'

When the president had sauntered away into his crowd of admirers, Glenn turned to Marlowe.

'What have you found?' he said.

'There's something wrong with these girls,' Marlowe said in a low whisper. 'And I'm not talking about them being blind, because they're not.'

'I think you might be right,' Glenn sighed, watching one woman laugh seductively as a Singaporean tycoon tickled her arm nearby. For a moment Glenn thought of Bettina, and how she must have felt at events like these. Had she too had to endure the unwanted attentions of these rich, powerful investors? Had Farrand made her dress that way, and humiliated her all to fill his own pockets? He grew hot with anger at the thought. He remembered that Zu-Ting was somewhere in that room and felt a sudden, desperate urge to find and protect her.

Leaving Marlowe to probe further, Glenn set out to find his friend from Hong Kong. Zu-Ting was holding a fierce debate with five businessmen, three from China, one from Hong Kong, and another from Australia. It was abundantly clear to anyone watching that she was winning.

'Are you canvassing for votes?' Glenn said in a loud, clear voice, as he entered the small group. Zu-Ting's head ticked to one side when she heard him speak. A small smile rose to her lips.

'Glenn Tebbhurst,' she grinned. 'Bettina told me I might see you tonight.'

Excusing themselves from the crowd, the two friends found a quiet spot to catch up. What felt like hours passed as the two of them chattered about the past few months. Things had been busy over in Hong Kong, Glenn was happy to hear, with steady profits fuelling the factory. Zu-Ting's work at least would not be directly impacted by Farrand's fraud, he thought, though the factory would be considered an asset if liquidation took place. Glenn told her about his recent trips to Frankfurt and his difficulties with Eleanora.

'I don't have eyes, Glenn,' said Zu-Ting in her direct, matter-of-fact way. 'But even I can see that you two are different people.'

Just then, Farrand marched towards them.

'Ah, there you are!' he called out. His grey eyes were fixed on Glenn. 'I didn't expect to see you two canoodling in a corner!'

Glenn ignored the stupid comment, and wished Farrand would go away.

'Zu-Ting,' he turned to his employee. 'The Chinese minister needs, uh, *convincing* about the investment potential in his country. Could you go and chat to him? Soften him up a little? No politics, do you hear me? Just use your feminine charm. That always works best.'

'Noted,' said Zu-Ting coolly. 'Your wish is my command, Herbert. See you later, Glenn.'

Farrand seemed intent on putting her to work all night it seemed. Turning to the president, Glenn saw him watching Zu-Ting's departure too.

'Sorry, Glenn, but I couldn't have her cooped up with you all evening,' he said. 'She's here for a reason. For the ICB.'

'I understand,' said Glenn. 'We were just catching up. She's a great woman. I saw her factory in Hong Kong. It's impressive, what she's done over there.'

'A fine woman, that one, yes,' he said, eyeing her with a grimace. 'If only she kept her mouth shut sometimes. But that's women for you.'

Glenn bit his tongue as Farrand laughed at his own joke. The slick man held a glass of champagne in his hands and had a constant grin on his face. He was clearly drunker than earlier in the evening.

'Have you tried the champagne, Glenn?' he asked.

'I don't drink, thanks,' said Glenn, forcing a warm smile. 'I told you, earlier?'

'Go on,' laughed Farrand. '*Live* a little!'

'No, really,' said Glenn. 'I'm good, thanks.'

'Shame, it's an Australian grape,' said Farrand. 'Quite extraordinary. There's not much on this dusty little continent, but they do make good wine.'

'It's quite a party you've put on,' said Glenn, changing the subject quickly. He gazed around at the sea of people chatting, roaring with laughter and clinking glasses.

'You cannot imagine,' said Farrand, letting out a happy sigh. 'We have done well. Five-million-dollars-well to be exact.'

'You raised five million?' Glenn asked, half-surprised, half-impressed. Farrand started to laugh.

'Don't be so shocked, dear Glenn!' he chuckled. 'Do you know what the net worth of this room is right now? Billions, Glenn. *Billions.* We raised most of it from the Chinese and Thais, though we were surprised to receive twenty thousand dollars from the Burmese. I didn't see that coming. Poor nation, you know? Then there was a half a million from Japan alone and another half million from Australian organisations.'

'That's impressive, Herbert,' Glenn nodded, forgetting the man's fraud for a moment and admiring a great feat of fundraising. 'Well done.'

'Well, anything for the ICB!' he chuckled lightly. 'All sorts of expansion can get underway now. You can't imagine. We can redecorate the offices in Germany, expand our activities worldwide and build new outreach centres in new countries. We can break new ground.'

Glenn's admiration faded fast. He listened with increasing frustration as Farrand went on and on about the changes this new funding would usher into the ICB. He remembered a similar conversation after the conference in Aachen. Had not Farrand boasted then, to the six blind women, about the millions they had raised and all they could do? Glenn now knew where most of that money had gone and it made him feel sick. He tried to hold himself steady, to keep the rage from his face as Farrand spoke to him.

'Is everything alright?' he asked after a while.

'Yes,' Glenn stammered. 'It's just… it must be the jetlag.'

'Of course,' Farrand nodded. 'Well, listen, I need to keep moving. Too many people to thank and see, as always! But what are your plans tomorrow?'

'None so far,' said Glenn.

'We're having a beach party, down at Bondi Beach,' said Farrand. 'Come! It will just be close friends, and fundraisers like you and me. Enough of business. Let's get down to the pleasure, no?'

Farrand chuckled darkly and Glenn said nothing; he could think of nothing worse than a beach party with Farrand and his cronies. He simply nodded politely, a gesture his host interpreted as enthusiasm.

'Come at midday,' he said. 'We'll be down by the surf club. And Glenn, perhaps leave your weird friend at home, OK? This is an exclusive party.'

Glenn turned around to see what Farrand was looking at in such a distasteful way. He saw Marlowe nearby, charming the ladies and making them laugh. Glenn turned back to Farrand, whose jealousy was as clear as day.

'Alright,' Glenn forced a laugh.

'Good man,' Farrand clapped him on the shoulder. 'Until tomorrow then?'

Glenn nodded, counting down the seconds until Farrand walked away. When he did, Glenn let out a deep exhalation of pent-up anger. *The arrogance of the man!*

Meanwhile, the event was slowly winding to a close and the throngs of people were thinning out. Finding a quiet spot, he waited for Marlowe to finish talking to the ladies. When the private detective finally drifted over, he loosened his bowtie and sank into a chair.

'So?' said Glenn.

'So, those women think I'm a billionaire,' he said, laughing lightly. 'I made up a bit of a back story; I told them I come from old money. As soon as I made them think I could invest, they pulled out all the stops. One of the ladies, Vivian, was offering to help me raise money… in the bedroom! Whatever kind of operation Farrand is running here, it has no limits. These women were paid for and they're here to do a job.'

'Sick bastard,' Glenn muttered under his breath. He scanned the room for any sign of Zu-Ting, but she was nowhere to be seen. The jetlag was setting into his body now and he felt exhausted.

'Any leads on your side?' Marlowe asked him.

'Just one,' said Glenn. 'There's a beach party tomorrow. I'm invited, but you're not.'

'Should I be offended?' Marlowe gasped in mock outrage.

'You should be relieved,' Glenn groaned. 'But you should come. We can hide you somewhere, in the trees, under a parasol, something. I think you need to see it.'

'Now you're starting to think like a private investigator,' Marlowe smiled.

'I'm not sure if that's a compliment or an insult,' Glenn groaned.

'Me neither,' chuckled Marlowe, and they both set off to their rooms to sleep.

CHAPTER TWENTY-EIGHT

'How's my disguise?' Marlowe asked as he climbed into the passenger seat of the four-wheel drive Glenn had hired to venture out to Bondi Beach. Glenn looked over at the man's attire. Dylan Marlowe could not have looked more like a tourist if he tried. Wearing a bright yellow shirt adorned with palm trees, baggy swimming shorts, huge sunglasses and a sports cap, Marlowe looked far from the attractive consultant who had chatted endlessly with the beautiful blind women of the previous evening.

'Foolproof,' said Glenn, grinning before adding: 'And terrible.'

'Excellent,' smiled the young detective. 'Terrible enough not to recognise, I hope.'

The pair drove through Sydney, taking in the space and beauty of Australia's east coast city. They drove in silence. Glenn had slept badly and could not shake his discomfort from the night before. Seeing Farrand again had unearthed some dark, angry feelings in him, and Glenn longed to be as far away from him as possible. He resented missing the opportunity to spend more time with Zu-Ting. He only hoped she was at the beach party, or if not, had received his message about meeting that evening, before he flew back to London.

'What are your thoughts on last night?' he asked the detective as they drove, curious to hear the man's impression.

'There's a lot of bad stuff going on,' sighed Marlowe. 'I met those girls. I spoke with them and though I think a few of them might have been the real deal, might actually have been blind, the rest were faking it. I think they were phonies. I certainly don't think they gave me their real names. Who the hell is called Suzy-Nell?'

Glenn tried to put names to the heavily made-up faces in his memory. The flashiness of the whole evening was sickly and bright in his mind's eye. The women faded into the gross opulence of the evening's events, a heaving mass of madness.

'And, excuse my scepticism,' Marlowe went on. 'But isn't it just a little bit too convenient that *every single one* of the women the ICB assists in Australia is so bloody attractive? They were beauty queens!'

'I agree, but that's hardly a crime,' said Glenn. 'Aside from these observations, was there any real evidence of foul play? Could you actually prove they were in fact fully-sighted?'

'Probably,' said Marlowe. 'The way some of them talked, it was as though they had lived twenty years with sight. Is that a crime, though? To hire women and introduce them as blind? Probably not.'

'It is fraud though,' said Glenn. 'It's false advertisement. Farrand paraded them around for sympathy.'

'It's also a drop in the ocean compared to the real charges against this dog,' said Marlowe. 'See what you can discover today. I'll be nearby. I've brought my camera with me so I can capture anything important.'

'Observe from a distance,' Glenn warned him. 'I don't want to give this bastard any reason to be suspicious. It will look bad if he finds you.'

'I agree,' said Marlowe, nodding quickly. 'But look at me, seriously. I mean, I'm already in my swimsuit. To him I'll just look like another bather.'

'Just don't get thrown off the beach for snapping pictures of women in swimsuits,' said Glenn, laughing at the thought. 'That won't look good either. And watch out for sharks if you swim. Sydney Harbour is full of them.'

'I think you're more in danger of sharks than me, sir,' smiled Marlowe.

The white sands of Bondi Beach suddenly stretched out before them as the road reached the coast. The turquoise Pacific crashed into the shore and surfers could be seen testing the waves. It was marvellous to see the ocean, Glenn thought, after two long days. He only wished he was there under different circumstances. With a friend, perhaps. Or with Bettina.

'I'll drop you here,' he told Marlowe, finding a place to stop just a few hundred metres from the Bondi Beach parking lot. 'That way no one will see us together.'

'Good luck,' was all the private detective said as he pulled on his sunglasses and opened his door. The music from Farrand's beach party was audible even from a distance. As he drove on, Glenn listened to loud bass thumping across the sands.

When he turned the corner, he saw a live band playing rock and roll on a small stage, surrounded by people. Bouncers guarded the entrance to a small settlement of gazebos, DJ decks and an open bar. Glenn could not believe his eyes; Farrand had not been joking when he said he was throwing a beach party. Parking up, he followed the red carpet on a wooden path that had been laid out for guests above the burning sand. When he reached the entrance, marked by two women in bikinis serving champagne flutes, a thick-chested bouncer stepped forward.

'May I see your invitation, sir?' he said in a heavy Australian accent.

'Oh, I don't have one,' said Glenn, smiling calmly at the tall, imposing man.

'Then I can't let you in, sir,' said the bouncer.

Before he could even begin to think about explaining Farrand's introduction, someone called his name.

'Glenn?' came a woman's voice. Leaning around the wide bulk of the bouncer, Glenn spotted a woman he faintly recognised walking towards them. She had flowing red hair and a cute button-nose. Dressed in a loose shirt over a bright red bikini, she was strikingly attractive.

'Do you know this man?' the bouncer asked her.

'Yes, he's a friend of Herbert's,' she told the bouncer, pouting and giggling at him. 'Let him in, mate. He's on the guest list.'

The bouncer nodded and allowed Glenn to enter. The girl in the red bikini met him with a smile.

'Thanks,' he said, smiling back at her, wondering how she knew him. 'Have we met? You look familiar.'

'Last night,' she said. 'I looked a bit different for the event, but we definitely met. Is your friend with you?'

'Which friend?' said Glenn.

'The cute one, with the castle in Ireland?' she said.

'Oh, Dylan?' he said, laughing at his detective's illustrious cover. 'No, he couldn't make it unfortunately. Herbert didn't invite him.'

'That man,' the woman tutted, raising a knowing eyebrow. 'He doesn't like to share, if you know what I mean.'

Wondering what this could mean, Glenn frowned. He remembered Farrand looking over at Marlowe the night before when he spoke with three women: one blonde, one brunette, and one redhead.

'Hold on, I remember you,' said Glenn, speaking slowly, considering the implications of this recognition. 'You're Chantelle, right?'

'Right,' she laughed, rolling her eyes. 'Chantelle! Whatever you want, buddy. Can I get you a drink? I'm heading to the bar.'

'Sure, I'll come with you,' said Glenn, puzzled by the girl's answer. They walked into the small crowd of half-naked beachgoers, some Glenn recognised from the night before, others complete strangers. When they reached the bar, Glenn was surprised to see the girl he knew as Chantelle go behind it.

'What can I get you?' she said, turning to Glenn but flashing a smile at a small group of people waiting. 'I'll be with you in just a moment!' she called to them.

'Uh, just an orange juice,' said Glenn. 'Are you working here?'

'Only for a few more hours,' she said, glancing up at the clock then. 'I get off at six if you want to keep talking?'

The young woman he assumed was Chantelle held eye contact with him for a moment. Her intent was as clear as day. She winked and pouted her lips into a kiss before turning to her other customers. Glenn swallowed hard and turned around. If she was the girl from the night before, then Marlowe had been right. She was not blind. Moreover, she was working behind a bar, which meant she was employed to be there.

'Five mojitos over here!' Glenn heard a familiar voice call above the noisy crowd and din of the live band. 'These men are thirsty!'

Looking over, Glenn saw Herbert Farrand, dressed only in his swim shorts, entertaining a group of handsome young men. He looked like a god between them all, his muscles rippling down his chest, his blonde hair wet from a swim. A woman dressed only in a bikini, hung on one of his arms, and another, dressed in a long, black kimono – which was so thin it revealed that she was naked beneath it – rested on the other. Glenn recognised them both from the night before. The only difference was that now, instead of holding white canes and staring serenely ahead, they held cocktails and made salacious eye contact with anyone looking at them.

This is sick, Glenn thought, turning away from Farrand for fear of exposing his expression of disdain.

'One orange juice,' said the girl behind the bar, snapping Glenn out of his dark look. After smiling in thanks, he moved through the crowds, brushing past women in bikinis, waiters bearing trays of drinks, and the strange melange of slick business types and blonde, muscled surfer boys. He managed to reach an exit on the other side, leading out to a small, fenced-off terrace by the sea. There were relatively few people there, only the live band, so he sat down in the shade and listened to the heavy bass guitar's riff. Something about seeing those girls so shamelessly… seeing had sent Glenn into a stupor of shock.

'Geronimo!' came cries of joy as people ran by him. A few men were heading into the sea to swim, so Glenn stripped down to join them, hoping the wash of waves would take away his dark mood. He dived into the water and felt it crash over him. The feeling was cathartic. He thought of the sharks swimming nearby and remembered Marlowe's words about the party. His private detective had been right: it truly was a den of sharks.

Turning back to the shore, Glenn saw a familiar figure walking by the water's edge, leaning on the two women he now recognised as Suzy-Nell and Kayleigh, if indeed those were their real names. Unable to avoid an encounter any longer, Glenn swum slowly back to the beach, standing up as he reached the shallows to stretch. One of the girls saw him first, her eyes clearly drawn to his broad shoulders, dripping wet with seawater. She gave him a small wave. Glenn waved back. What else could he do, he asked himself? His task was to observe, not to judge.

'Glenn!' Farrand called over, looking around to see the source of Suzy Nell's interest. 'You made it!'

'How could I miss such a great party?' Glenn called back. He forced a smile, striding through the waves towards them.

'Girls, you remember Glenn?' said Farrand, turning to each of the women in return and squeezing them at the waist. They giggled.

'Of course,' said the girl called Kayleigh. 'Where's your friend?'

'What a party last night, huh?' said Farrand, ignoring the girl's question and slapping Glenn on the back. 'I'm still buzzing. Where's your drink, Glenn? Did Sara serve you?'

'Sara?' said Glenn.

'Yeah, she's behind the bar this afternoon,' said Farrand. 'The red-hot fox crushing mojitos?'

'Chantelle?' said Glenn. Farrand raised his eyebrows at the name, letting out a small laugh.

'Who's Chantelle?' he asked. 'Perhaps you had more fun than I gave you credit for last night, Glenn?'

Glenn tried to swallow his anger but it bubbled up inside him like lava. He could not hold it back.

'It's interesting,' he said, keeping his voice level. 'Sara, is it? She looks just like a girl I met last night called Chantelle, except of course that Chantelle was blind and this girl has clearly been seeing all her life.'

Farrand's smile faded. He said nothing for a moment, then let out a small, knowing laugh.

'You ladies seem to have made a remarkable recovery too?' Glenn continued, looking from the blonde woman to the brunette. 'I know the ICB does some incredible work, but this, well, this! It's nothing short of miraculous.'

The ladies looked from Glenn to Herbert, suddenly awkward. Their pouting smiles vanished.

'Ladies!' said Farrand, suddenly all smiles and charm. 'Can you leave us boys to discuss something for a moment?'

The women nodded, smiled and quickly disappeared, leaving Glenn alone with the ICB's president. Farrand took a deep breath and let out a long sigh. Glenn could not stop himself.

'Why did you do it?' he asked.

'Do what?' Farrand faced him with a smile, but his eyes were cold.

'These women can see perfectly,' he said. 'Sara, Chantelle, Suzy-Nell, Katie or Kayleigh – whatever they're all called. Why did you parade them around as blind women last night? It is a moral crime, a misrepresentation to the public, and a gross misconduct in the write up to the charity donors. That's my question, Herbert – if indeed *that* is your name. You're a crook!'

Herbert took a deep breath and set his jaw.

'They came with the PR agency,' he said sternly. 'Last night we made a lot of money, did we not? That is the important thing. Now, as to your interrogation – such as it is – if people thought the girls were blind, that is entirely subjective.'

'People didn't *think* that, Herbert,' Glenn said icily. 'You *told* them these women were blind. You sold them on pity stories.'

'And you're not doing the same?' Farrand asked, tipping his head to one side and smiling.

'Excuse me?'

'Come on,' Farrand drawled. 'All this nonsense about writing case studies. Let's be honest, you're a fantasist. You're a businessman like me, you want to bed them. I imagine you probably want them all at the same time…'

'You… Me…' Glenn said, his lip trembling. He was still digesting what he just said. 'We are not the same.'

'We are the same,' Farrand laughed. 'You visit these women, *my* women, *my* employees and team, in their countries around the world. And even if – and this is a big if – you *are* just writing up their stories, then you are selling pity stories, just like me.'

'*I* don't use girls for fundraising. *I* don't parade them around like meat to be sold.'

'Don't deny it, Glenn,' Farrand said softly, and he took a step forward and leaned in close. 'We understand one another, you and I. We know what makes people pay up.' Then he leant back and took a step back. 'Now,' he began to add, looking at his watch, 'you'll not indulge these fabrications anymore. The girls came with a PR package, yes, but you won't tell anyone, you understand? Anyway, it's all part of the event. There are plenty of agencies in Australia committed to making the most of an event. Yes, some of them are escort agencies. You've run these fundraising events before, Glenn. You know how it is.'

'No, I don't,' Glenn shook his head, his emotions rising. 'You are using lies for fundraising; you are using actresses to make money. You don't care about the blind community, you're just a pimp.'

'The blind community!' laughed Farrand. 'If you're that obsessed with the blind community, you'd be smart and think about the benefits my "pimping" brings to the blind community. Have you thought about that? I do a lot more than you, Glenn. I'm a much better fundraiser than you are. Even Bettina knows how important these events are. Has she never told you?'

'Told me what?' said Glenn, nervous to hear Bettina's name mentioned.

'She knows what men are like,' said Farrand, a small smile growing on his lips. 'She knows how to *please* them to get what she wants, if you know what I mean. Women have a function, and at these events it's to look beautiful and open their legs.'

'Who the hell do you think you are?' Glenn roared in outrage, advancing on Herbert, fists balled in rage.

Farrand let out a laugh of surprise. 'Oh really, Glenn – so primitive?' Then he threw a glance over his shoulder to where two large men the size of gorillas in black suits and wraparound sunglasses were approaching across the sand. 'I wouldn't if I were you,' he smiled. Then, staring at Glenn with his cold, grey eyes, appraising his every expression, he said, 'Tell me, Glenn. Does your wife know how personal your interest in these beautiful victims of the blind community has become?'

'That is none of your business,' Glenn said weakly, tempering his rage now at the sight of Herbert's musclebound security.

'You know, you're just like Bettina,' Farrand laughed. 'You have the same soft heart. She's always been like that, ever since I met her. She was always desperate for my approval, always wanting to do the right thing. She was like a little lap dog. And she would bounce right into the laps of anyone I chose. She wanted to hop in my lap most of all, I think...'

Glenn turned his eyes up – no longer rage-filled, but sad and pleading. He didn't want it to be true – it *couldn't* be true.

Herbert laughed. 'Oh, don't worry, Glenn. I didn't bother, not with her. I didn't want to damage the obsession she had for me, so I've left her lingering on. But I have been tempted, more than a few times. No, I just needed her to get on with her job: to look pretty and raise some damn money. With all due respect, that's why you're here too. If you care so much about Bettina and the blind community, as you say, you'd stop whining and start raising some money for me. Bettina, well, she has proven her worth. Oh yes, she's brought in a lot of money over the years. Men see her and want to satisfy her, but I don't think I need to tell you that, do I Glenn?'

All Glenn wanted in that moment was to grab Farrand by the collar with one hand and launch the knuckles of the other onto the end of his nose as hard as he could. He wanted to toss him on the sand, bloody and beaten, and take pleasure in declaring that he was going to go to prison for all of his misdemeanours. The words boiled up inside him and threatened to burst out, even if it meant taking a good hiding at the hands of the burly bodyguards looming a few feet away. But before he could say or do anything, a dull thump of footsteps made him spin around. It was Marlowe. He had come to a stop; his hands were on his knees and his chest was heaving from running towards he and Herbert.

'Glenn!' he said quickly, peering up and grimacing as he caught his breath. 'Glenn! Sorry, mate. I was swimming and I saw you. I just wanted to come and say hi. Oh, hello! It's Mr. Farrand, isn't it?'

Marlowe made a show of barely recognising Herbert before quickly looking into Glenn's eyes. Glenn saw warning there. He looked away, turning back to Farrand, who was eyeing the pair with indifference.

'Well, Glenn, it seems like you have found a friend to spend the afternoon with,' he said, a forced smile rising to his lips. 'You'll have no more need for our little party today. Ladies!'

Farrand called over to the women leaning against a table nearby and went to them. Spreading his hands across a cheek of each of their behinds, Farrand turned and led the girls away. He twisted his head back to Glenn to cry one last thing.

'Safe flight, Glenn! And you, Mr. Marlin.'

'It's Marlowe,' the detective called back, still recovering his breath. 'But thanks, Mr. Farrand! Looks like a great party!'

Farrand turned away, raising a disinterested hand in goodbye. Marlowe waited until he knew the president was out of earshot before turning to Glenn. He let out a huge sigh.

'You can't lose your cool like that,' he said quickly, his eyes suddenly fierce and angry. 'You almost blew it, Glenn. Jesus! How do you expect Farrand to trust you after an outburst like that? What were you talking about?'

'I don't care,' Glenn spat through gritted teeth. 'The way he talked about Bettina... the way he talks about all women! All I want to see is him go down.'

'Then you have to be careful,' Marlowe hissed, his youthful face full of exasperation. 'We are this close to nailing him to his own goddamn cross.'

'I want to see him pay for this!' Glenn whispered angrily.

'And I only want to act on *evidence*,' said Marlowe. 'Do not jeopardise this mission, Glenn. There's too much to lose. If Farrand catches one whiff of this, he'll disappear and the ICB will take the rap. They will go down in flames, Bettina too. Think of that, will you?'

Glenn forced himself to calm down, barely hearing what Marlowe was saying. All he could think about was Bettina and the words Farrand had used to describe her. How could she have put up with it for all those years?

'Alright,' he said quickly, glancing back up at the party to see if anyone had seen them. The coast was clear it seemed. Everyone was too busy drinking and dancing to care about a strained conversation between two colleagues on the beach.

'Let's go then,' said Marlowe. 'Come on. There's nothing left to see here.'

The two men walked in silence back to the car, then drove back to the hotel. Lost in his thoughts and anger, Glenn had almost forgotten his proposed meeting with Zu-Ting. When the receptionist passed him the message, he assumed it would be from Eleanora. It was not. Zu-Ting proposed a coffee together before her taxi to the airport. Reading her instructions, he looked at the clock. He was just in time to see her before she left. Leaving Marlowe to pack their things, he hurried to the lobby café, where Zu-Ting sat, surrounded by her suitcases. She was dressed in a fine travelling cloak and looked as beautiful as ever.

'I'm so sorry, I just saw your message,' said Glenn when he reached her.

'Glenn,' she smiled, recognising his voice. 'No worries. I knew you'd be off having fun with Herbert at the party. How can I compete with beaches, babes, and booze?'

'No, no, it wasn't like that,' Glenn said desperately. Did Zu-Ting really think Glenn was like Farrand, he wondered? The president's words rang in his ears. *We understand one another, you and I,* he had said. Glenn could not bear the comparison. Panic rose in his heart for he could not bear to be associated with Herbert Farrand, not after everything he knew and everything he had just heard.

'I know, Glenn, I'm just teasing you!' laughed Zu-Ting. 'Come and sit with me. I still have time.'

Relaxing slightly, Glenn joined her with a smile. The two of them sat and picked up their conversation from the night before, chatting away until the time came for Zu-Ting to leave.

'When will I see you again?' she asked.

'Probably sooner than you think,' said Glenn gravely, before thinking. 'Though I only wish it were under better circumstances.'

'Glenn?' she said, laughing slightly, clearly listening for signs of a joke. 'Are you coming to Hong Kong?'

'No,' he shook his head.

'Then why will we be meeting soon?' she asked.

Glenn hesitated for a moment, wishing he could tell her everything that had happened, wishing he could warn her of things to come. But he remembered Marlowe's words. *If Farrand catches one whiff of this, he'll disappear and the ICB will take the rap.* Instead, Glenn forced himself to sound jovial and light.

'You just never know in life,' he said. 'I hope I'll see you soon. That's what I meant.'

Zu-Ting was still and observant for a moment, frowning.

'Glenn, is everything alright?' she asked.

Glenn swallowed hard. His mind suddenly filled with images of the factory in Hong Kong closing down. So much was at stake. There was so much to lose.

'Yes,' he said, pushing the images from his mind. 'Everything is alright. At least, it will be.'

A taxi horn beeped outside the hotel.

'I have to go,' she said, her face still concerned. 'Will you keep in touch, Glenn?'

'Of course,' he said. They hugged and she left, squeezing his shoulder as she walked away.

Yes, Glenn thought to himself. Everything would be alright. It had to be. Farrand could not get away with this, he thought. As he walked uneasily towards his bedroom to pack up his things and head back to London, Glenn made a silent vow. He would bring Herbert Farrand down, no matter what it took. For Bettina, for Zu-Ting, and for the incredible women of the ICB, he would bring this criminal to justice.

CHAPTER TWENTY-NINE

Glenn knew that before he could face the final battle against Farrand, he would have to face a battle closer to home. The long plane ride back to London gave him the time and space to think clearly about Eleanora and all that had come to pass between them. Her angry calls still rang in his mind, as sharp and fresh as ever. His mind passed through the moments of intimacy they had shared in their lifetimes: the outline of her bare back arching against the Norwegian sky, holding her in his arms as they spun around the ballrooms of their youth, the strolls through the estate in spring, summer and autumn. When they were hot they burned with a passion like fire, he thought. But when they were cold, the pain ran as deep as frostbite. He shivered at the thought.

As he recalled those memories, of recent moments and days long gone, they felt so far from him and who he was, there on that plane. They came from a different life, he realised. It was a life that no longer felt like his own. His destiny, whatever that was, did not lie in his wife's arms any longer. It was time to face the music, he realised, stepping back onto English soil. He had played the part of the American husband in England for too long. The opportunity had come to reclaim himself from the Beaumont dynasty.

Ronda Round Manor loomed at him out of the darkness as he arrived that night, menacing in its majesty, as if the building itself already knew what he was coming to do. Glenn felt oppressed already, on top of his exhaustion, and wondered whether it might be wise to sleep before starting the conversation he desperately needed to have with his wife. Jetlag would not help him, he knew, but he also knew something else: he could not wait.

'Eleanora!' he called as he put down his bags. His voice echoed in the great entrance hall. 'Eleanora!' he called again, louder this time.

Footsteps approached and his wife appeared at the top of the stairs. She was dressed casually in an outfit of lilac and yellow, her hair tied back, showing the elegance of her long, fine neck. She looked beautiful, thought Glenn. His heart plummeted.

'You're back,' she said in a soft voice, clearly surprised by his shouting. 'You must be tired, shall I…'

'No, honey,' he said, swallowing hard. 'We need to talk.'

'Now?' she said, descending the stairs slowly.

'Now,' he nodded.

When they had both settled themselves onto the sofas in the drawing room, Glenn cleared his throat to speak. He wished the paintings staring down at him from the walls were not there. He felt awkward enough as it was; the additional Beaumont judgement did nothing for his confidence.

'I think we can both agree that things have not been easy between us lately,' he began, avoiding her eyes and searching for the right words. 'The travels, the calls, the difficult conversations. It's been awful. It's been…'

'Hell,' Eleanora nodded slowly. Glenn looked at her. She was looking at him with a cool fierceness in her eyes, like a lioness surveying her prey.

'Exactly,' he sighed, strangely relieved to hear her agree. 'So, I've been thinking.'

'Go on,' she said calmly.

'I've had some time to really search my heart,' he said. 'These long trips give me so much space to think. They give me a break from us, and a chance to look objectively at us. To question, too.'

'Me too,' Eleanora said coolly. 'Don't think I haven't been taking the opportunity to do the same.'

'Finally I think I've come to my conclusion,' he said at last, looking away from her.

'Finally?' she raised an eyebrow.

'Yes, finally, Eleanora,' he said firmly. 'And, finally, it's clear to me.'

'What is?' she asked impatiently.

'I am no longer in love with you,' he said quickly. The words rushed out of him, then hung in the air like barrage balloons, floating there in the room between them, threatening to bring destruction in their wake. The silence that followed only exaggerated their power.

'What?' his wife whispered, her blue eyes narrowing, her mouth slightly open in surprise.

'I don't love you anymore,' he said, looking up at her. He had to be brave. He wanted her to see the honesty in his face, to feel the truth in his confession.

'How can you say that?' she asked in a small voice. 'After all this time? After *everything* we've been through?'

'It's because of all of that,' Glenn said quietly. 'It's because of everything we've been through. So much pain, so many arguments, and no change. Just two people who want different things.'

'You're breaking my heart,' she whispered, visibly shaking, clasping her chest and swallowing hard. 'I can feel it. My heart is breaking.'

Glenn stared at his wife, blinking, trying to keep her sorrow from entering his own heart. But he could not. He knew he was saying what needed to be said. He knew he was the one saying no, giving up on their marriage, but somehow it was breaking his heart too. His wife gasped in front of him, tears rolling down her face.

'Oh baby,' he said, his voice breaking. 'I'm sorry. I'm so sorry.'

Standing up, he went to sit with her, taking her in his arms and holding her tight. She wept there, in his embrace. He hushed her and rocked her, telling her it would be alright. After what felt like an age, her sobbing slowed and became sniffles. She stopped shaking. She froze in his arms. Pulling away, she wiped the tears from her face and stared at him with cold eyes.

'How dare you?' she said slowly. 'How dare you end this? What right do you have?'

'What right?' he frowned, confused by her question.

'What right!' she screamed. The sound echoed around the room and shot through his ear drums. He leapt to his feet.

'Honey,' he said quickly. 'It's alright.'

'Don't tell me it's alright!' she screamed, her pale cheeks flushing red. 'It's not alright. You have ruined everything. You're a terrible man. You're a monster!'

Without warning, Glenn's wife threw herself at him, thumping his chest with her fists. She sobbed and screamed as she did so.

'Eleanora, honey!' he cried with desperation. 'Stop that!'

'I am not your honey!' she shrieked.

'Alright, Eleanora, then! Stop,' he said. 'Stop, please! Be calm.'

'Why are you doing this?' she wailed, sobbing and groaning in pain. 'Why?'

'Because I've outgrown you!' he cried. 'Look at this. Look at you! Look at the way you treat me! Look at me! Look at our life together. We have a few sexy trips abroad then spend a summer ignoring each other. How is that a life? How is that love?'

His wife fell to her knees, shaking her head and sobbing.

'Please,' she cried. 'Please, don't do this!'

Glenn was stunned. He had never seen his wife so out of control.

'Eleanora,' he pleaded, sliding down onto the floor to be with her. 'Baby, please. Listen to me. I want you to live life the way you wish to live it. I do. I want that for you.'

He took deep breaths as he tried to keep a steady voice. Meanwhile his wife sobbed quietly in his arms.

'I cannot fulfil your demands,' he said. 'We both know that. Whether that's being around more or being the man you want me to be. I've changed. I'm not the man you need, honey.'

'Glenn!' Eleanora sobbed, her face a mask of red and tears. 'Oh, Glenn! Who is she?'

'Who is who?' Glenn asked, his heart beating fast.

'Don't lie to me!' his wife cried out, like a wounded animal in pain. 'Who *is* she? Just tell me.'

'Eleanora, there's no one,' Glenn said, shaking his head and swallowing hard, praying his face did not betray him. His wife stared at him warily through her mess of blonde hair and tears. She watched him, her eyes narrowing until they widened once more. To his surprise, Eleanora began to chuckle lightly. She looked delirious, hysterical even.

'Oh God,' she spat, chuckling whilst shaking her head in disgust. 'Not one of those blind bitches?'

Glenn said nothing. Eleanora continued to laugh and sob all at once. It was a terrible sound. She pushed herself to her feet and, without another word, stumbled out of the room. Glenn remained on the floor, looking at his hands. They were shaking. The shame and guilt he felt was overwhelming. He listened as his wife climbed the stairs and heard a door close on the floor above. Then, like an axe, silence fell, condemning him to his thoughts and fears. Lying down on the carpet, he closed his eyes, exhaustion washing over his body.

* * * *

By the time Bettina came to London, one month later, Glenn had already moved out of Ronda Round Manor. He was renting a spacious apartment in Mayfair from a friend, happy to be out of Eleanora's way. Her anger had been hard and her retribution dangerous. Within two days of announcing his change in heart and mind, his wife had thrown all of his belongings, clothes and valuable possessions down the stairs. They lay waiting for him in a huge heap after work one evening. Eleanora herself, like a ghost, was nowhere to be seen, though Glenn suspected she was staying with her parents on the estate.

Life in London was an invigorating change for the new bachelor. His pain and distress at having ended the marriage was softened slightly by his newfound independence. He threw himself into the case against Farrand, happy to be able to work late whenever he wanted. He was so determined to bring the ICB president's criminal activity into the light that he barely left the office each night. Sonia encouraged him to slow down and take it easy, but Glenn would not hear of it. Working on the case kept him occupied and far from the dark thoughts about his failed marriage.

When the day came to meet Marlowe and Bettina together in London, to discuss the evidence and their next steps, Glenn felt nervous. He was excited but worried about seeing Bettina again. She was so sensitive, he was sure she would sense his pain and probe deeper. Glenn, however, was not ready to talk. He could not find the words. Not yet.

'So this is where you work,' she remarked when she entered the DCF offices in Cheapside that Monday morning. Glenn was, as ever, immediately impressed by Bettina's style. She wore a smart blue suit, cropped tightly at the waist and pale at the lapels. Blue, he smiled to himself. 'It's so great to finally see!' she laughed, spreading her arms to show she could feel the building all around her.

'You are most welcome, Bettina,' he grinned, taking her in his arms. 'I am so glad you've arrived safely.'

'Safely, yes! Quickly, no. London is always a joy to navigate,' she laughed. 'I'd forgotten just how hectic it was here.'

'How is Laura?' Glenn asked. He knew Bettina was staying with the ICB's representative in London over in her apartment in Bayswater. To preserve the secrecy of their mission, now at such a delicate stage, Glenn had asked Bettina not to tell Laura she was seeing him.

'She's well,' his friend smiled. 'She wants us all to meet up, but don't worry, she doesn't know I'm here today. She thinks I'm visiting an exhibition at the National Gallery.'

'Good cover,' grinned Glenn. 'Dylan would be proud of you.'

'I just can't wait for this all to be over,' she said, sighing and shaking her head. 'All this lying and secrecy. It's exhausting.'

'Soon,' Glenn promised her. 'Now, come on, let's get you a coffee before Dylan arrives.'

Leading Bettina by the arm, he took her to find Amelia the tea lady.

'A tea trolley!' cried Bettina. 'How charming! Wow, we really are in England.'

'Is it a cuppa for you, dear?' Amelia asked Bettina sweetly. 'Or a coffee perhaps?'

'Coffee would be just perfect, thank you, Amelia,' smiled Bettina.

When the tea trolley had departed for thirsty workers on other floors, Bettina let out a small sigh of pleasure.

'What a wonderful office you have here, Glenn,' she said. 'It's so wonderful. There is such an energy here. I can feel it! It's how I feel when I have all the girls in one room. It's how I felt at that conference in Aachen, actually.'

'That's great to hear,' smiled Glenn. 'We try our best to work as a team, like you guys.'

Marlowe arrived shortly after, dressed in a causal suit. It was hard to imagine that just a few weeks ago he had been running up to Glenn in swimming trunks, warning him not to spill their secrets to Farrand. That beach party in Sydney felt so long ago, thought Glenn, and yet simultaneously like yesterday. The breakup with Eleanora had cast everything into a weird time vortex.

The last person to join their meeting was John Spinola, the auditor, who entered a bit later, having chased Amelia across three floors for a second coffee.

'Alright, let's put all our cards on the table,' said Glenn, taking the lead as the trio sat down in his office. 'As you all know, we're here to share what we know and what we don't know. Let's start with the positives, I say. What do we know? What do we have?'

Bettina began first, sharing with the group all she had learnt over the past six months.

'When I really started looking into things, and paying attention, I realised just how much of Herbert's lifestyle must be funded with the money he's diverting,' said Bettina. 'There have been chalets in the Austrian Alps, long breaks away for business he could not report back on, and countless lifestyle choices that should have made me wonder.'

'Why didn't you?' Spinola asked. 'I'm curious. What has kept this damn guy free from suspicion for so long?'

'I thought he came from a wealthy background,' said Bettina, shrugging. 'I know he has family in Bavaria so I assumed he came from old money. We all did.'

'He does have some old world charm,' said Marlowe, cocking his head.

'That's one way of putting it,' Glenn sighed darkly.

'This man is becoming a legend,' said Spinola. 'He has built up a strong image to avoid suspicion, there's no doubt about that.'

'What do you have for us, John?' Glenn asked the auditor.

'Well,' Spinola sat back in his seat, letting out a long sigh. 'I have many transfer notes and emails from people sending over money, confirming their contributions to the ICB, but many times that money does not reach the accounts. It's not there. If we combine all of this missing money, we hit a figure of around two million euros.'

'Two million?' breathed Glenn. 'But how can two million euros just disappear?'

'I've looked everywhere,' said Spinola. 'There is no trace or credit of this money in the ICB account. The transfers must have been sent to third party companies, even though they were meant for the ICB.'

'Third party companies?' said Bettina. 'What does that mean?'

'A third party is accepting money on Herbert's behalf,' Glenn explained.

'Which means it's going straight into Herbert's pocket,' Spinola added.

'But what kind of company would accept a transfer like that?' Bettina asked, appalled.

'Welcome to the financial industry,' Spinola said with a bitter smile. 'There are hundreds of companies doing just that. Our friend Kirschenbauer in Zurich is an expert, like many of his Swiss compatriots. Funds are diverted, no questions asked. All suspicious income heading into Farrand's personal accounts, which Mr. Marlowe has kindly provided me with, is listed as coming from a third party. Theoretically, his fraud cannot be traced.'

'But still, we know he's diverting funds now,' said Glenn, nodding confidently at their progress. 'It's bad news for the ICB, but it's good news for us. Now we know he's doing it, we can bring him to justice. The next thing we need to know is how he's spending those diverted funds.'

'He's a lover of luxury,' shrugged Spinola. 'That should not be too hard to illustrate.'

Glenn however was now looking at his private detective, who sat patiently, waiting for his moment to speak.

'Dylan,' said Glenn, beaming at the man in front of him. 'I think it's time for you to tell us what you've found.'

Marlowe smiled before reaching down into his briefcase. Groaning slightly with the weight, he brought out an enormous pack of files.

'This, gentlemen, and lady,' he said, nodding to Bettina. 'Is your case against Farrand.'

Opening up the file like a dirty Pandora's box, Marlowe divulged all he had discovered. He told them how he had been following Farrand for six months now and could fully testify to the man's sleazy lifestyle. He shared their experience in Sydney with the false blindness of the women named Chantelle, Kayleigh and Suzy-Nell, drawing on Glenn to share more.

'He's using these women as pity puppets,' Glenn shook his head. 'They were escorts and bartenders paraded around like the blind women supported by the ICB.'

'But Zu-Ting was there,' said Bettina, a frown forming on her forehead. 'Didn't she notice anything? She's usually so outspoken?'

'Farrand was like a master puppeteer,' said Marlowe. 'She was passed from group to group, with barely a chance to talk to anyone.'

'It's true,' Glenn nodded. 'Even if she had wanted to chat to them, Farrand would not have allowed it. He even interrupted us speaking. As ever, everyone there was under his command. He made it clear they were working for *him*.'

'I know the feeling,' Bettina nodded sadly. Glenn wished they were alone so he could hug her and banish the dark thoughts he knew would be clouding her mind. Meanwhile, Marlowe continued to share all he had learnt with the group.

'In terms of where this money is going, I can pin down different transactions to different dates,' he said. 'Mr. Spinola and I have already found correlations between huge purchases in Farrand's private life, with notifications of funds deposited, but diverted, with the ICB. A generous donation from a wealthy American in support of the centre in New Orleans, for example, was mentioned in an email dated to the summer of last year. The funds never appeared in the account, but that same summer, Farrand purchased a villa in the Bahamas.'

'He had just come from there when he arrived that day in Frankfurt,' said Glenn, shaking his head. He recalled the president's unexpected arrival in the Porsche, one of his blonde bombshells in tow.

'I remember,' Bettina nodded. 'He was with a new girlfriend.'

'Which one?' groaned Marlowe. 'Some of the main expenditures come from Mr. Farrand keeping his many girlfriends happy,' he continued.

'In the past six months alone Farrand has rented seven apartments, one in Paris, one in Copenhagen, one in Berlin, one in Zurich, and three in Aachen, none of which he has ever stayed in longer than a week. Different women live in each apartment, and I have traced each of their names to private transfers and gifts made from Farrand's accounts.'

'Is that a crime though?' asked Spinola. 'The man is a damn cad, and a polygamist, that's clear. But will that stand up in court?'

'No, I guess not,' said Glenn. 'But if he is funding these affairs with ICB money, you're damn straight it's a crime.'

Marlowe nodded in agreement and continued. As he spoke, Glenn glanced over at Bettina, sensing the sensitivity of the subject. Her face was so still and undecipherable. He remembered what she had told him on their weekend together, about Farrand's promiscuity and her own crush on him. He could only imagine what it must have felt like to have had feelings for such a callous individual. He also knew now what Farrand really thought of Bettina: she had been a vessel, a fundraising tool for him to secure millions. He kept her around because she served a purpose and that purpose was to look beautiful. The thought made Glenn's stomach twist and turn uncomfortably.

'Glenn?' said Marlowe. 'Is everything alright?'

'Huh?' Glenn muttered, jerked out of his reverie. 'Yes, sorry, I was just thinking about Farrand.'

Looking over at Bettina, he saw a strange strain in her face. He knew she had been thinking about those dark days. With a strong, urgent stirring in his heart, he wished he could hold her.

'I was just asking you if you could share with Bettina and John what Mr. Farrand told you in Sydney,' said Marlowe.

'Which part?' sighed Glenn.

'His ideas for renovating the office in Aachen,' said Marlowe.

'He said he wanted to redecorate,' said Glenn, recalling the conversation. 'He mentioned putting the money to use to improve the work environment. Why do you ask? Is it important?'

'Very,' said Marlowe, flipping through his files. 'There are notes in the accounts for "office renovation purchases" made previously. We have them entered into the accounts on several occasions, for Aachen and Frankfurt. They are often in sums reaching thousands, if not tens of thousands, of euros.'

'But the office in Frankfurt hasn't been renovated for years,' said Bettina. 'Nor has the office in Aachen. I don't understand?'

'I think I do,' said Marlowe, his eyes bright with suspicion. 'We can trace that expenditure to purchases made in multiple locations, purchases for Persian carpets, silk drapes, artwork, crystal chandeliers, various antiquities, and more.'

'But why would the offices need those things?' Bettina asked.

'They wouldn't,' said Marlowe darkly. 'But Farrand would. I've been in the apartments he is renting for his mistresses. Many of the purchases I've just listed can be found there, including, most incredibly, this.'

Reaching into his file, Marlowe brought out a picture of a full-length oil painting hanging on a wall beside an ornate lamp. It was a portrait of Herbert Farrand, dressed in a traditional Bavarian suit.

'He had it painted for one of his lovers,' said Marlowe. 'Or perhaps just for himself.'

'He commissioned a painting?' yelped Spinola.

'How much did it cost?' Glenn asked, wondering why a man would commission a portrait of himself.

'One hundred thousand euros,' said Marlowe. 'The payment was made to an artist of some renown in southern Germany : one Fata Abedermann.'

'What does it look like?' Bettina asked, running her fingers over the picture, her face a mixture of shock and disgust.

'He looks like an absolute ponce!' Marlowe laughed.

'You're not missing out,' Glenn said, smiling bitterly. 'What an idiot. What *arrogance*.'

'This is beyond arrogance,' spat Spinola. 'This is fraud, clear as day.'

'You're right,' said Marlowe. 'And I believe we can prove it now.'

The private detective began to pull countless pictures from his files, from photographs of villas and apartments in St. Tropez, Gstaad, Davos, to the title deeds of condos in the Caribbean islands, to the purchase agreements for over twenty cars.

BEAUTY IN THE DARK

'This is nothing,' said Farrand, shaking his head. 'He's also charging legal fees and expenses to the ICB, none of which relate to the charity's work. It's crazy.'

'How can one man possibly use so many cars?' Spinola asked, scanning image after image of flashy sports car.

'Farrand is so good at what he does now, and so convinced he'll never be caught that he's holding nothing back,' said the detective. 'These purchases are nothing to him. He has become invincible. That is his weakness here.'

'Dylan's right,' said Glenn. 'He has not been clever about covering things up for a while. If it was just a few discreet diversions, he would never have been discovered. But this shows a man in full stride, taking advantage of the assumption that he will never be caught. He's exactly where we want him.'

'And he *wouldn't* have been discovered if you hadn't discovered him,' said Bettina quietly.

The three men looked over at her. Her face had turned very pale and a pained expression haunted her blind, unseeing eyes. Her brow was furrowed, thinking fast.

'What a fool I've been,' she whispered, swallowing audibly. 'I've known this man for over a decade. It took strangers to see what was in front of me the whole time.'

'Ms. Hartmann, this man is a criminal,' said Spinola incredulously. 'He is a master of deceit! Do you really think you could have spotted this alone? Please do not blame yourself. There is a reason why men such as myself and Mr. Marlowe here have professions. Why do you think auditors and private detectives are employed in these situations? To see what others cannot see.'

'I have worked with many clients in life, Bettina,' Marlowe nodded. 'It's incredible what people are capable of hiding, if they are so inclined to do so. Mr. Farrand is an exceptionally manipulative man, and I'm saying that from experience.'

'They're right, Bettina,' Glenn said gently. 'Farrand is a manipulator. I've seen that first-hand. You are such a trusting person. You believe in

BEAUTY IN THE DARK

every one, no matter who they are or where they have come from. How were you to know?'

Bettina nodded, but Glenn could see she was not convinced. He looked down at his watch and saw midday was approaching.

'Listen, I think we've covered enough for today,' he said. 'I also think we have enough evidence at our disposal now to call the others in.'

'The others?' said Spinola.

'The other people who have so much at stake if this case goes forward,' said Glenn.

'The board members?' asked Spinola.

'No,' Glenn shook his head. 'The five other women who make the ICB stand for what it stands for.'

'The others?' said Bettina, in a small, hopeful voice. 'You want to tell the others?'

'I think it's about time, don't you?' said Glenn. 'You've been handling this on your own for too long, Bettina. It's time the others knew what was going on. Whatever happens next, we have to decide together. We have to move forward in a way that's right for all of you.'

'But how?' asked Bettina.

'Let's fly everyone in,' he said decisively. 'I'll ask my secretary to arrange it all. Laura is here, you are, we just need to send word to the others. I'm going to need your help in convincing them to come.'

'When?' she said.

'There's no time like the present,' grinned Glenn. 'As soon as possible.'

'But Glenn, their work, the regional branches, I'm not sure…' Bettina began, but Glenn stopped her.

'There won't be regional branches to run if we don't resolve this now,' he said firmly. 'Hell, there won't be an ICB! We need to act, Bettina, and we need to act now, but we can't act alone.'

The young woman nodded her head, her mind clearly racing with thoughts.

'I can write to them,' she said. 'I can write to them this afternoon.'

'Call them,' said Glenn. 'This needs to be fast. We can start now by telling Laura together.'

'Yes,' Bettina nodded. 'Laura can help us.'

'Dylan, John, be ready, OK?' Glenn addressed both men. 'As soon as these ladies fly in, we will arrange a meeting to take this bastard down once and for all.'

'Aye, aye, captain!' cried Spinola.

'I'll be there,' Marlowe nodded.

'Meeting adjourned then!' grinned Glenn. 'To be convened with more of a gender balance in a few days' time.'

'Six women and three men doesn't seem more balanced to me, Glenn!' Spinola chuckled. 'But I'm not complaining. After all I've heard about this Farrand fraudster, there is nothing I'd enjoy more than seeing him taken down by Bettina's troop of wonder women.'

'We're all agreed on that then,' smiled Glenn. 'Thank you, lady and gentlemen. Until next time.'

Glenn stood up to walk Spinola to the door, but before he could offer a handshake in goodbye he saw concern on his old friend's face.

'Listen, old boy, I heard about Eleanora,' said the auditor. He was trying to speak quietly but his voice was not naturally discreet. Glenn wondered if Marlowe, or worse, Bettina, had heard.

'Thanks,' he said, swallowing hard. Glenn did not know what to say.

'How are you?' Spinola asked, his face pained with pity.

'Fine,' Glenn lied, forcing a smile. 'Everything is fine. It was for the best.'

'How is she?' Spinola enquired. 'How is the dear lady?'

'I don't know,' Glenn shook his head. 'We're, uh, not talking.'

'For the best, perhaps, old chap,' his friend nodded quickly. 'These storms are hard to weather. One is often best sticking to one's own helm and steering the course one sees fit to steer for oneself.'

Glenn nodded, not even attempting to decipher Spinola's cryptic nautical advice.

'Yes,' was all he could say. 'Yes, well, you're probably right!'

'Onwards and upwards, eh?' said the portly auditor. 'You'll make it through, old boy.'

With a small squeeze of Glenn's arm, Spinola left the office. Marlowe had packed up his files and made a swift exit too, muttering thanks to

Glenn, before leaving him alone with Bettina. Sitting back in her chair, Bettina was running her fingers across his big oak desk.

'Are you OK?' Glenn asked her quietly, pulling up a chair beside her. 'I know all of this can't be easy for you. This Farrand is a nasty piece of work.'

She shook her head, swallowing hard before the tears came.

'Oh no,' Glenn said, hushing her. 'Bettina, no. Don't let him get to you. Not now, not when we're so close.'

'I'm not crying because of him, Glenn,' she said, wiping the tears from her eyes.

'No?' he said gently. 'Good, that's good. He doesn't deserve your tears. You know that, don't you?'

She nodded, sighing deeply.

'Hey, do you know what I think we should do?' said Glenn, keen to inject some happiness into their day.

'What?' she said through sniffles.

'I think we should get out of this office and head down to see Laura in Whitehall,' he said. 'What do you think?'

'We're meeting for lunch anyway,' said Bettina. 'She'll be happy to see you, I'm sure!'

'Great,' he said. 'Let's get her on board. Farrand's secrets have stayed secret long enough.'

Leading her down the stairs and out of the office, Glenn took them to the edge of the Thames where they could walk arm in arm to their destination. London sprawled around them with all its business and elegance, and for the first time since his breakup with Eleanora, Glenn really saw the city again. He had forgotten how peaceful and enriching it was to walk along the river at lunch time. He had also forgotten how comfortable and at ease he felt around Bettina.

When they finally reached Laura, who was waiting for them in a café near Big Ben, Glenn wondered affectionately if the whole of London had heard her scream of joy at finding out he was there.

'Two of my favourite people in my favourite café!' she squealed, her long red hair flying around her face as she jigged with happiness. 'To what or whom do I owe this delightful surprise?'

Not knowing how or where to start, Glenn was comforted by a small hand slipping into his. He looked over at Bettina, who squeezed his palm encouragingly. *Go on*, she seemed to say, without saying anything at all. Glenn took a deep breath.

'We have something to tell you, Laura,' he said, and slowly, they began to share the secrets of that year so far.

CHAPTER THIRTY

With Laura on board, Glenn and Bettina made quick headway alerting the five other women to the need for an emergency meeting. Laura was shocked but quickly understood the need for a global conglomeration of minds. After work, in the evenings following their reunion, the three friends worked hard to arrange the travel of the four other women, ensuring that all relevant parties would be present to discuss Farrand's treachery.

'I've kept it vague, as you instructed,' said Laura, shaking her head as she sat in front of her laptop, preparing to dictate another email. 'Odile was asking what this was all about, so I told her she would find out more on arrival.'

'That's good,' said Bettina. 'At the moment, Farrand has no clue. If he finds out, we might be trying to find an invisible man.'

'We've come too far to let that happen,' Glenn shook his head darkly, taking a sip of camomile tea. He poured out cups for the others, enjoying using Laura's colourful tea set.

'Well, Zu-Ting and Elfrida have come without questions asked,' said Laura. 'I think they're just excited to be getting together again!'

'And Christina?' asked Glenn.

'I called her last night,' said Bettina. 'She sends blessings to you both. She'll be there on Friday.'

'And you told her to avoid contact with Farrand until then?' Glenn asked.

Bettina nodded, looking pensive for a moment. She turned to Laura.

'You did the same, right?' she asked. Laura nodded, letting out a deep sigh.

'They all know not to tell him about the meeting,' she said. 'It's incredible, isn't it?'

'What is?' Bettina asked.

'Who could have imagined Herbert would turn out to be such a crook?' she said.

'None of us,' sighed Bettina. 'I knew he was a womaniser, but this?'

'It's unbelievable,' Laura spat, a dark shadow passing across her face. 'The others are going to be so shocked.'

Glenn watched the two women conferring and felt the weight of the situation. He knew breaking the news to the other women would evoke great unhappiness and uncertainty in their lives. The dark shadows beneath Laura's usually bright, green eyes, were disheartening to see.

'Sonia has arranged their travel,' he said, forcing a smile and swiping through a flurry of travel confirmation emails on his smartphone. 'Everyone will be here by Friday. Bettina, there's only you left to consider.'

'Me?' Bettina answered, her brow puzzled into a frown.

'Yes, will Farrand suspect something with you being away for so long?' Glenn asked.

'No,' she shook her head, her blonde hair quivering as she did so. She let out a sharp, bitter laugh. 'He thinks I'm taking my annual one week holiday in Wurzburg.'

'What do you mean by one week?' said Laura, her girlish face confused.

'Herbert only lets me take one week,' Bettina said with a small, sad smile.

'What?' yelped Glenn. 'But that's illegal, surely?'

'He doesn't impose it on me,' she said quick. 'The law is very clear in Germany about vacation days. Oh no, Herbert simply lets me know he does not like me to take too much time off. Before all of this, I didn't mind. I thought he only wished for the growth of our charity. But now I know about his, well, his *dealings*...'

'You poor thing,' said Laura, her eyes now bright with anger. 'He has such a hold over you, doesn't he? If only we had known, Bettina. You should have said something.'

'I didn't know myself until recently,' Bettina said, a frown straining her smooth brow. 'I must have been under some kind of spell.'

Glenn bristled at the thought of everything Farrand had said about Bettina. He recognised the insecure way in which Bettina held her shoulders when she spoke about that period of infatuation. More and more, Glenn believed that it was less her infatuation, more Farrand's own manipulation. Sensing that this was a conversation Bettina needed to have alone with her friend, he bid both women goodbye. As he headed out into the London streets, Glenn was excited by the thought of seeing all six women in one room again. It had been so long since that conference in Aachen, and since then, he had visited all of them in their native communities. He remembered the hot, sticky air of Mexico, the chaotic humidity of Hong Kong, and the delicious flavours of New Orleans. More than anything, he remembered the inspiring stories of every one of the women he had visited. He only wished they were coming together again under better circumstances.

* * * *

A week later, when Friday came, Glenn woke before his alarm. Adrenaline pumped through his veins as he headed to the office early in order to prepare the board room. Some of his colleagues had been informed of the meeting, including his friends from the International Department, and arrived at nine a.m. to join him. Natasha and Tuni-Tung had begun the important work of negotiating the tea break with Amelia.

'Can you bring butter *croissants* and *pain au chocolats*?' Natasha asked the kind tea lady, scribbling down a list as she wrote.

'What? No, that's far too continental!' Tuni-Tung scolded her friend. 'Amelia, can we please have a Victoria sponge, fruit scones and biscuits?'

'Whatever you like, dears,' Amelia smiled serenely, nodding to them both.

'French pastries are the best in the world,' Natasha protested. 'These women have travelled thousands of miles to receive the worst news of their lives, and you want to offer them *English* food?'

Turning to Glenn, Natasha tried to bring him onside.

'Glenn, have you heard this?' she demanded. 'Tuni is suggesting *biscuits* for our guests!'

'They are coming to England, aren't they?' cried Tuni-Tung. 'We need to give them a proper British welcome!'

'In Russia, we would never dream of offering anything other than the finest Russian delights to guests,' protested Natasha, crossing her arms in defiance. 'It is to honour them.'

'I hate to break it to you, Natasha, but English food is not going to honour anyone,' Tuni-Tung shook her head with exasperation.

'I'm sure whatever you choose will be fine, ladies,' Glenn sighed. 'As Natasha said, these women are going to be in for a shock, so sweet tea should be on hand at least. Can you manage that, Amelia?'

'Tell you what, I'll bring up a selection of pastries and cakes,' the tea lady smiled kindly. 'How does that sound?'

'That sounds like a great compromise,' Glenn chuckled. 'My, my, Amelia. You are becoming quite the diplomat.'

The tea lady grinned and disappeared, leaving Glenn alone in the boardroom with his colleagues. He looked around at the wooden table, the empty chairs, and the upturned water glasses. Everything was ready. He turned to the women arranging the white board.

'Natasha, Tuni,' he said gently, going to them and taking their hands in his. 'Thanks for your support. It's great that you want to be part of this today.'

'Of course, Glenn,' Natasha said, smiling confidently. 'We have heard so much about these women. They sound so brave, and so fearless. They've become a part of your life, we can see that. If Diversified Charities can help, we want to see that happen. After everything that has happened recently...'

'With your wife...' Tuni-Tung added cautiously.

'Yes, with Eleanora,' said Natasha. 'Well, it's the least we can do.'

'You just need to get everyone through today,' Tuni-Tung nodded reassuringly. 'Then you'll know what the next step is for this charity, and for these women.'

'You're right,' Glenn nodded gravely. Deep discomfort set into his stomach. A part of him wished he could simply skip today, and fast forward to the next step, past prosecution and retribution: surely then, when all was said and done, the six blind women would be in a more secure place.

Grateful for the coffee Amelia had left them, Glenn settled into a chair and waited for his guests to arrive. He did not have to wait long for the first arrival. It was Sonia, who would be taking minutes for the meeting.

'Sir, I will go down to reception now to meet all the guests,' she said, slightly flustered as she walked through the door. 'They should be arriving in a few minutes.'

'Great. Thanks, Sonia,' said Glenn.

'Are you nervous, sir?' she asked.

'Is it that obvious?' he let out a small laugh of surprise.

'Yes, sir,' Sonia nodded with a smile.

'A little,' Glenn admitted.

'Don't be,' she said. 'You're a good man. You're doing a very good thing today.'

Glenn nodded his thanks and hurried his secretary to go down and welcome the women. Soon Dylan Marlowe arrived, followed by John Spinola.

'Ah, my right-hand men,' Glenn grinned in welcome, standing to shake their hands. 'Are you ready for this?'

'Ready to break six beautiful hearts?' Spinola groaned, his thin black hair plastered to his head. 'Not at all, old chap, not at all! But I'll be here with the facts and figures, don't you worry.'

'We have the evidence,' said Marlowe, his young face fixed and confident. 'They need to hear it. It's as simple as that, Glenn.'

Glenn knew Marlowe was right. Herbert Farrand had stolen from every single one of these women; he had robbed every single one of them of their futures. Ignorance would only be bliss for so long, thought Glenn. They needed to know. When he heard voices outside the door, Glenn stood up and buttoned up his suit. His nerves reached a crescendo until he saw their faces enter the room, one by one. Then his face broke into an enormous smile as Laura walked into the room, followed by Elfrida, Odile, Zu-Ting, Christina and last, but never least, Bettina.

'Welcome, welcome!' Glenn called to them, embracing them all as they filed in. For a moment the room was filled with a delightful chorus of six women joyfully calling: 'Glenn!' He welcomed them one by one, admiring their collective ability to dress for the occasion. Laura, with her tumbling auburn hair, was dressed in a smart green suit, which contrasted dramatically with Elfrida's bright red dress. The Mexican looked simply exquisite with her dark hair pulled back into a plait and her lips painted the same deep red as her dress and shoes. Out of the corner of his eye, Glenn saw both Marlowe and Spinola gazing in admiration. Neither men seemed to know where to look, for the room was suddenly full of beauty, in every direction.

Zu-Ting was already passionately introducing herself to the men, stunning Spinola to silence with her black silk dress. Traditional cherry blossom patterns flowered across her bosom. Odile wore a flowing patterned dress and a stylish belt, hugging her elegant figure. Christina wore a burgundy jumper over a light blue shirt and her dog collar, an autumnal combination which set off her rosy complexion. Bettina, as ever, wore her flowing linen robes, as blue as her eyes, and smiled as she shook Glenn's hand.

'So,' she said, squeezing his palm. 'We're all here.'

'So you are!' Glenn laughed. He looked around at the six blind women, wondering how he could have forgotten how uniquely beautiful every one of them was. For a brief, shimmering moment he forgot why they were all there, at the DCF, in London. Then it came back to him, like a dark snake creeping through his heart.

'We should probably get started,' he said to Bettina in a low voice. Bettina nodded, but held onto his hand a bit longer. As ever, she sensed something unsaid.

'Perhaps we could delay a little longer,' she said. 'At least until everyone's had a chance to be comfortable?'

Glenn nodded. How does she always know what I'm thinking, he asked himself? He knew Bettina felt his anxiety.

'Yes,' he said. 'That's a very good idea. Ladies! Please, make yourselves comfortable, there is tea and coffee in the corner. I believe there might even be English Victoria sponge to hand! My colleagues, Natasha and Tuni-Tung, are here to welcome you and make you feel at home.'

The clatter of plates and cups were music to Glenn's ears. The room suddenly filled with chatter as the six women mingled with Glenn's colleagues, Marlowe and Spinola. Glenn watched with a heavy heart as they shared a few brief moments of happiness before he broke the bad news. He watched as his colleagues happily met the women they had heard so much about. He listened to the meetings and introductions with interest, at once glad to be bringing the two worlds of the ICB and DCF together at last, and at the same time forlorn that it was for such a sorry occasion. When everyone had finished their second cup of coffee, and shared various travel tales, Glenn finally called the meeting to order.

'Thank you all for coming here today,' he said, as everyone settled back into their seats. 'I know many of you have left your work to come here. All of you have left your homes, your countries, and some of you have even left families behind. I think you can imagine, then, the gravity of the reason for which I have brought you here today.'

'What's going on, Glenn?' Zu-Ting asked suddenly. 'We saw each other only a month ago. You didn't mention anything then?'

'It's something to do with the ICB,' said Christina. 'It must be, else why would we all be here?'

'Christina's right,' said Glenn, raising his voice to assuage their worried guessing. 'The ICB is the reason I brought you all here today. Ladies, how can I say this? Your charity is in danger.'

'Danger?' said Odile, crying out. 'What kind of danger?'

'I'm going to tell you,' said Glenn. 'But to do so, I must ask for your patience.'

'Sorry,' Odile said quickly.

'No problem. I think I should first introduce you to the two men at my side,' said Glenn, indicating Spinola and Marlowe. 'The first is John Spinola, an auditor here at the DCF. The second is Dylan Marlowe. He is the private detective Bettina and I have been working with this past year.'

'Auditors and private detectives?' said Zu-Ting, her face a mask of confusion. 'Bettina, what is this?'

Glenn looked at Bettina. She was staring ahead, her face calm. She turned in Glenn's direction, as if asking his permission.

'Go on, Bettina,' he gently urged her. 'You can tell them.'

'Ladies, I have grave news,' she said. 'As Glenn said, there's no easy way to break this to you. Herbert, our president, the man we have known and trusted all these years, is a fraud.'

'A fraud?' breathed Christina.

'A fraud,' Bettina sighed. 'He has been stealing the ICB's money for years. I was alerted to this by Glenn. He found out when he was handed the accounts in order to start fundraising for us. He will tell you more.'

Glenn's heart sunk as the room filled with gasps.

'What?' whispered Odile.

'How?' muttered Christina.

'No way!' cried Zu-Ting.

'My God,' groaned Elfrida, before murmuring a small prayer in Spanish.

'It's true,' sighed Laura.

'How do Bettina and Laura already know about this?' Zu-Ting demanded.

'That's a good question,' said Glenn, wondering how to start telling his story. 'We've known this for a while now, but didn't want to tell any of you until we were absolutely sure, until we had a solid case against him. It would have been too much of a risk to share this information with you all earlier on. Even now, we must exercise the greatest caution: if Farrand gets wind of any of this, we risk exposure, and losing him.'

'We can't let him get away,' said Laura firmly. 'I found out about this only days ago. You are all here today to hear Glenn out. You need to hear the evidence for yourselves.'

'I've wanted to tell you,' said Bettina, a note of guilt in her voice. 'I couldn't even tell Christina, and we see each other so often.'

'Bettina, my child,' Christina said softly. 'Have you been carrying this burden all alone?'

'Glenn has helped,' she said. 'I owe... no, we *all* owe Glenn our deepest gratitude.'

'But how can this be?' Elfrida asked, her Spanish accent clipping through her words. 'Herbert is our President! Please don't tell me he's as corrupt as everyone else.'

'I'm afraid Farrand is not only corrupt like your Mexican politicians, Elfrida,' said Glenn. 'He's a crook, and he's arrogant enough to think no one will ever notice.'

'How long have you known?' Christina asked him.

'I first had doubts about Farrand after our meeting in Frankfurt,' Glenn began. 'He said he would contact me about fundraising, do you remember?'

'Yes,' Christina nodded.

'Well, when he eventually contacted me, he suggested I meet a man called Kirschenbauer in Switzerland,' said Glenn. 'Anyone who has spent ten minutes in the financial industry will hear alarm bells when they hear that name.'

'Kirschenbauer is one of the most notorious money launderers in Europe,' said Bettina.

'A wolf in sheep's clothing,' Natasha shook her head.

'A damnable villain,' spat Spinola.

'I therefore asked for the ICB accounts to be audited when the fiduciary handed them over,' Glenn continued. 'My friend, John, here will tell you what he found.'

Clearing his throat, Spinola opened up his laptop and began to share his findings with the group. He covered every incident of fraud, outlining the diversion of funds and how it looked on the accounting sheets.

'Because Farrand uses third parties to siphon off the funds, transfers to his own accounts cannot be traced,' sighed Spinola. 'That, ladies, is how the rich and great of this world fill their own pockets.'

'How long has he been doing this?' Christina asked in a small, wounded voice.

'For years now,' said Glenn.

'The sad fact is, your charity is being used for money laundering,' said Spinola, sitting down. 'And I'm really sorry to say to all of you that you have been used as instruments for fundraising, but to raise money for one man.'

'Herbert Farrand,' said Glenn. 'Though God only knows if that is his real name.'

'Could that be a lie too?' Elfrida asked.

'I'm going to let Mr. Marlowe share what he has found out,' said Glenn. 'Let's talk about what we do know before we talk about what we don't know. God knows we know enough now.'

Marlowe stood up, heaving his file of evidence onto the table. He shared with the women all he had discovered. When he had recounted his discoveries up until the fundraiser in Sydney, his conclusion was grave.

'Money came in from all over Asia,' he sighed. 'But it seems that a huge percentage of that five million dollars will be used for personal use. It has been credited outside the ICB, towards antiquities, cars, decorations and improvements to Farrand's own life, to the detriment of the blind people he professes to serve. The case against him is strong. We have to act now. You're in shock,' he said, looking into every one of their faces. 'I can see that.'

'You're damn right we're in shock!' Zu-Ting cried angrily.

'So talk to me. Let it out.'

'He has made fools of us!' she cried, her eyes bright with tears. 'He has taken away our lives, our dignity and our faith in what we do. He has taken away our honour!'

'*Bastardo!*' spat Elfrida.

'I thought today would be a moment of rejoicing,' said Christina. 'All I feel is God's punishment.'

'That man is the only one who will feel punishment,' Odile snapped. 'He will feel the weight of the law.'

'I think we're all angry,' said Laura firmly, speaking above the others. 'But I think we are all in agreement on something else too,' said Laura. 'We want justice.'

'He must be punished,' Elfrida nodded.

'Justice!' Zu-Ting cried. 'Something must be done.'

'Yes, there has been an outrageous theft,' Glenn said quickly. 'Farrand has turned a good, wholesome charity into a crooked foundation. He is using you all to raise money that has been used for the wrong purposes. I wanted to tell you what's going on, and now you know. I wanted to tell you, all of you, that you are the victims of a terrible crime. I feel a responsibility, having made the discovery, to you, the victims. Together I would like us to think about a way out of this mess. A way forward.'

'That is why Glenn has invited you all to be here today,' said Bettina. 'This is our task.'

'Yes,' said Glenn. 'I know also how heavy this news must be. But whatever happens, we must not act rashly.'

'Glenn, we need to act now,' said Marlowe, repeating the advice he had given earlier. 'The urgency is great.'

'But what can we do?' Zu-Ting cried out. 'We all have so much to lose. My factory will be closed down if the ICB stops funding it. What will I tell my workers?'

'My school!' cried Elfrida. 'What do I tell the children?'

'We've just started building a new health centre in Louisiana,' said Odile. 'Does that mean the ICB will no longer be operating in the United States? Will I lose my job? If I lose my job my husband will take custody of the kids. I'll never see them again.'

The room descended into chaos as the reality of this news set in. Every woman at that table had so much to lose. Odile began to cry and Bettina went to her.

'Shh, Odile, that will never happen,' she said gently. 'I will never let anyone take your children away.'

'How can this be?' Odile sobbed. 'We have lost everything, for what? Cars? Villas? Paintings?'

'One man's greed,' said Christina quietly.

'Glenn, what do we do?' Zu-Ting asked her friend, her face full of uncertainty.

'How can we bring Herbert down?' Odile asked through her tears. 'Tell us.'

'I can't tell you what to do,' said Glenn, shaking his head. 'I have ideas, that's all. You all need to walk away from this unscathed, away from the stigma of Herbert, and the shame of the ICB. How, is a different story, and perhaps a conversation for another day.'

'Another day?' said Zu-Ting. 'But Mr. Marlowe says we have to act now!'

'We do,' said Glenn. 'Our first move must be to get this guy out of your hair. We need to stop Herbert from using you as instruments for illegal gain.'

'And how do we do that?' Zu-Ting asked.

'By thinking long and hard about this,' said Glenn, standing up. 'I know this has been a big shock to you all today.'

'I feel so numb,' Zu-Ting shook her head. Shock was finally replacing anger.

'I know,' Glenn said gently. 'So wait until you are thinking straight again. I'm inviting you ladies to my place tomorrow for a breakfast, before you fly home. We don't have much time, as Mr. Marlowe has pointed out. Every day we waste we risk exposure, and worse, more funds being diverted into the wrong accounts. Yes, tomorrow we need to sort this. But I also know you all need time to digest this news. Go home now, think about what I've said. Talk to each other, and tomorrow, come to me with your ideas.'

The room was quiet, the weight of the meeting hanging heavy on every mind. Glenn was glad to hear Bettina clearing her throat.

'Glenn is right,' she said. 'Whatever we do next, we do together. We need to think about this. As you have all shown today, you all have so much to lose.'

Glenn's heart stirred to hear the woman he admired so much supporting him.

'Thank you, Bettina,' he said. 'Are we all agreed.'

The murmurs of approval came from every corner of the table, convincing Glenn that by tomorrow, they would have their way forward.

'Until tomorrow then,' he said, determined to bring an end to Farrand's tyranny.

The joyous sense of reunion Glenn had felt fill the room when the women had arrived had vanished as they left. The meeting left a sense of disaster in its wake, and the silence almost broke his heart. Glenn nodded his thanks to Sonia and his colleagues as they led the women out of the conference room, towards the lifts. He shook hands with Marlowe and Spinola, thanking them for their time, before sitting down once more and burying his face in his hands. The loneliness he felt there in that empty room was comparable to the emptiness he had felt when he had left Eleanora all those weeks ago. The memories threatened to return and haunt him, there, alone at that table, but to his pleasant surprise, they were interrupted.

'Glenn?' came a familiar voice. Looking up, Glenn spotted Bettina in the doorway.

'Yes, Bettina?' he said, unable to keep the sadness from his voice.

'You are the good guy in all of this,' she said. 'You know that, don't you?'

Glenn said nothing, for what could he say, he wondered?

'I'll see you tomorrow,' Bettina smiled.

With that, the beautiful young woman disappeared. If only he had an ounce of her faith and courage, Glenn thought, marvelling at the power of Bettina Hartmann. Then, with a crashing moment of clarity, after all those weeks of insecurity and guilt, he felt something shift inside him. Barely recognising the feeling, Glenn realised that he felt proud of himself. Perhaps he was the good guy, he thought; perhaps he was the man Bettina saw.

CHAPTER THIRTY-ONE

Preparing breakfast at home was a pleasant excuse to call his father, Glenn thought that night after the meeting with the women. He was inspired by the memory of Bertie's pancakes. His father was happy to help his son with a menu, especially when he heard it was for the six blind women.

'You sure know how to please the ladies. You've come to the right man. Let's start with batter, shall we?'

Glenn listened carefully to all his father had to say, taking notes as he described measurements of butter, flour, eggs and milk.

'It was always your little English princess doing the catering if I remember correctly. Tell me, is Eleanora too busy to help you feed the masses? I'd have thought she'd be offering them fresh eggs from the hens and milk from the cows!'

The question cut through Glenn's happiness like a knife. He cleared his throat.

'Dad, there's something I should tell you. Eleanora and I, well – you see, we've…' he hesitated. 'We've gone our separate ways.'

Silence hung on both ends of the line. 'I had to leave her,' Glenn went on, to himself as much as to his father. 'I've moved out, it's over. I'm staying in an apartment in Mayfair now.'

'You went for it?' his father said uneasily, though the subtle smile with which he said the words was clear in his voice. 'So, you actually went for it with the other lady? With Bettina?'

Silence again.

'I guess not then,' Bertie added. 'Look, if you love her, you have to tell her, you schmuck!'

'Not yet. I can't…'

'Well, it's only a matter of time,' said Bertie. 'When are you seeing her next?'

'Tomorrow morning, actually,' said Glenn, smiling.

'Well, you listen to me. You cook that woman the best damn pancakes of her life, d'you hear me? And I swear, son, she'll be sweet as candy after that. She'll be yours before noon.'

'That's some swell confidence. Tried and tested I'm sure. But anyway, as much as I *appreciate* your love advice, Dad, can we please talk toppings now? My dilemma is do I opt for blueberries, mascarpone, or honey?'

'Honey, son,' laughed his father. 'Sweet and golden. Like your Bettina.'

* * * *

Bettina arrived before everyone else that next morning. She looked beautiful, wrapped in a dress the same Pacific blue as her eyes.

'It's a peaceful place you have here,' she said a little awkwardly. 'And so large, I can feel the space of it.' Glenn watched as she held out her hands before her, fingers tapping gently at the atmosphere as if she was playing a piano.

'Make sure you feel comfortable, okay?' he called out to her as he checked the oven and swept excess flour into the dustbin. He was nervous, swallowing hard at the thought of Bettina relaxing on his sofa. When he joined her, he brought with him a steaming cafetiere of coffee.

'Here, try this,' he smiled, pouring a cup and passing it slowly to his guest. Bettina took it delicately in her hands and sipped at the cup.

'It's my father's blend,' Glenn said nervously, before she gave a reaction. 'He's also responsible for the feast we're about to tuck into.' Bettina smiled. 'He gave me some top tips on pancake making. I'm afraid this is going to be more of a New York breakfast than an English breakfast!' he added.

'Well, it sounds like your father's rehabilitation is really progressing. I wish he were here to share his secrets with us.'

'I assure you he feels the same,' chuckled Glenn, remembering his father's jealous groan when he heard of Glenn's meeting with the blind and beautiful women of Aachen.

'So, it's time for solutions,' Bettina sighed, taking another sip of her coffee. 'I thought I'd come over early to see how you're doing. You seemed sad yesterday. But you've done such a great thing this week,

Glenn. You've made every one of these women feel like they matter. If the ICB had gone down without this chance to put things right, the betrayal and loss would have been so much greater.'

'I hope you're right,' sighed Glenn. 'I just hate being the bearer of bad news.'

'Does anyone like that job?'

'I doubt it,' Glenn said. 'It's decision time now though. Whatever we decide today will shape the future of the ICB.'

Bettina swallowed hard. 'Yes, it's time.'

Glenn wished they had longer together before the others arrived, but the sound of the doorbell brought an end to their cosy chat. The sound of five women chattering away beyond the door warmed his ears, for the voices sounded bright and happy. Glenn had been worried that yesterday's meeting had left the women feeling forlorn and lost.

'Ladies, welcome,' Glenn beamed upon opening the door. Dressed as impeccably as the day before, the ladies swept in to kiss Glenn's cheek, one by one. Zu-Ting even pulled him into a tight bear hug.

'I'm sorry if I was a bit loud yesterday,' she said with a wry smile. 'I was just so damn angry. That man… he could have ruined us.'

'Could have,' said Glenn, nodding. 'Let's focus on the "could" in that sentence, OK?'

'OK,' smiled Zu-Ting.

'Now, help yourselves to coffee,' Glenn said after leading them through to the circular dining table. 'I've taken the liberty of attaching some Braille tags to what's on offer. There's toast, butter, maple syrup, all in the middle of the table in front of you. Just reach out your hand a half-metre or so and they are all lined up.'

For the first hour of their meeting, the ladies simply tucked into the breakfast Glenn had prepared, happy to be chatting and socialising around his large dining table. Glenn only wished they could stay like that for longer, but he knew there were lots of things to talk about. In that brief pause, however, he felt like they could have been back in the 'Day in the Dark' workshop, enjoying a meal together. The only difference was that Glenn could see. Before he could rectify that, with a blindfold or a scarf, Odile made an observation and Zu-Ting asked a question which caught Glenn quite off-guard.

'There's a great energy in this apartment, Glenn,' she said. 'I can feel the sun on my face! Do you live here alone?'

'Yes, is Mrs. Tebbhurst not joining us?' asked Zu-Ting. 'I would have thought she would be preparing English muffins with little Union Jacks imprinted on them.'

Glenn cleared his throat, unsure of how to answer the question. He heard Bettina offer everyone more pancakes in a loud voice.

'I'm sorry, is she not here?' Zu-Ting asked once more. 'Have I said something wrong?'

'No,' Glenn said quickly. 'No, that's alright. Mrs. Tebbhurst, uh, Eleanora, does not live here.'

That was enough for now, he thought. He did not want to waste time discussing his own personal sorrows when there was so much else they needed to talk about. He saw Bettina's face out of the corner of his eye; there was a strange expression there, a curious frown. More than ever, Glenn wished he had covered his eyes. He did not want to see her face as she worked out the truth. He knew he needed to tell her about Eleanora, and about how he felt, but he did not want to force that conversation. Not now, he thought; there was already too much change afoot.

Glenn was grateful to Zu-Ting for not pressing the issue and laughed as she recounted Eleanora's horror at the fish restaurant in Hong Kong. When she had finished her story, he took the opportunity to move the meeting forward.

'Since you're all leaving today, I want to discuss strategy,' he said, throwing down his napkin and sitting back in his chair. 'Cars will arrive in a couple of hours to take you all to the airport or back to your hotels. Thank you all for being here.'

'Where else would we be, Glenn?' Elfrida said warmly, reaching over and putting a hand on his hand. 'Thank *you* for helping us.'

'As I said yesterday, I discovered this fraud so I feel duty-bound to help you weather this storm,' he said. 'You've all had a night to sleep on this, so tell me: what have you been thinking?'

'Sleep!' laughed Zu-Ting. 'Are you kidding. I didn't sleep a wink.'

'I guess we're starting with you then, Zu-Ting,' Glenn smiled. 'Where better to start than with an aspiring politician?'

'Alright,' she said, sighing deeply. 'I didn't sleep. I couldn't. Everything I heard yesterday, all the lies and deceit, went deeper than I imagined possible. I've been abused all my life and that is a fact. I was treated like dirt by factory owners who did not know better, who had grown up poor, abused, enslaved, and simply did what their employers had done to them. I've worked hard, down to my bones, and in many terrible environments, but I thought that didn't matter anymore. I finally thought that I had found something different. I have worked so hard for this charity. I wanted to dedicate my life to the ICB. Now I feel like I've had a knife pushed into my heart.'

'Me too,' muttered Elfrida. 'It hurts so bad.'

'The terrible truth is that I suspected this guy!' Zu-Ting continued. 'I knew there was something wrong with him. It was like an instinct, but my eyes were not open. I could not see. I wish my eyes were open because in Hong Kong we can tell a crook by his eyes, by his ears, by the way he talks. But I thought, no, Herbert is a charity man, he is a good man beneath it all. Lies, lies, lies! He pulled the wool over our eyes, girls, and now we have to go after him!'

'Go after him?' said Bettina warily. 'What do you mean, Zu-Ting?'

'I think you know what I mean, Bettina,' she answered in a hard voice. 'I have friends in Hong Kong.'

'Violence?' laughed Bettina. 'You can't be serious?'

'They will muscle him about a bit,' said Zu-Ting. 'They can find him and teach him a lesson. It is the way we settle things in my country. What do you think, girls? Shall I make some calls?'

The room burst into laughter but Glenn could not tell how much of it was real and how much was nervous giggling.

'I must object,' came Christina's serious voice. Glenn looked over to see the young priest gazing serenely ahead. 'Charity means peace, welfare and the greater good. It does not mean violence. There is something called forgiveness, and I think we all need to think about that.'

'There is also something called the law,' said Glenn, hoping Christina was not serious in her suggestion of forgiving Farrand.

'Glenn's right,' said Bettina, an impatient tone in her voice. 'We are not vengeful. We are friends, bound together by fraud. We said yesterday that we are united in one thing: we all want to bring this man to justice. Violence is not an option, Zu-Ting, and, I'm sorry, Christina, neither is forgiveness. Surely there is another way?'

'I have an idea,' said Laura. 'Can I share it with you all?'

'Be our guest,' smiled Glenn.

'I think we should simply threaten Herbert with the law,' she began.

'Threaten him?' said Odile. 'Why not just *go* to the law?'

'Because the threat will allow us to actually gain some compensation for his crimes,' said Laura. 'He will know our grievances, and know that he faces prosecution followed by up to fifteen years in jail. He will know that he has broken the law and will never find work again. I suggest that we push him to the point where he sees how much he has to lose and then demand that he return the money he stole from us. We can ask him to pay in instalments!'

'Instalments?' exclaimed Elfrida. 'Do you mean to negotiate with him?'

'Exactly,' smiled Laura, her green eyes wild and sparkling. 'A crook like that will have money put away. He's so calculating. He will have hoarded it in accounts all over the world.'

'But where?' asked Odile. 'How can we know where?'

'Probably in Zurich, the Cayman Islands, Japan,' shrugged Laura. 'There are not so many places a man can deposit laundered money, right? He's a world traveller and he takes his money with him. We saw as much in the balance sheet. Spinola was clear on that fact. The point is, I don't think we should go to the prosecutors and face him in court. Then we risk everything: our livelihoods and the ICB. Let's just make him do normal, honest business for once with a schedule of reimbursements.'

'It's genius,' said Glenn, impressed by Laura's business mind. 'But do you really think Farrand would agree?'

'He would disappear,' Bettina shook her head. 'And we would not have a leg to stand on, to use this English expression. We could not go to the law for they would ask why we did not report him earlier. We would lose him.'

'We need to be paid back,' Laura said firmly. 'This is a solution to that.'

'Reimbursement will not be possible,' came Christina's steady, preaching voice. 'We are all looking in the wrong direction. You speak of justice, but do you not remember that God is the ultimate justice? More importantly, have you never heard of the forgiveness of Jesus Christ?'

Elfrida crossed herself, remembering her Catholic faith. Laura let out a small laugh and Bettina bowed her head in respect to her friend.

'Have you never heard of turning the other cheek? Of the tolerance of Christianity? Farrand is a Christian man. He has defrauded us. We should try to revive the ICB in an honest way, not with threats of incarceration. I can rely on Bettina to do that. Let us revive our charity in the spirit of goodwill!'

'And Farrand?' asked Laura. 'What should we do with him? Should we not crucify him?'

'I fear he is already lost,' said Christina. 'He has to leave, he must resign. That is certain. But after that, we should try to forgive his fraud, as charitable Christians, as human beings with good hearts.'

'I am *not* Christian,' said Zu-Ting angrily. 'This is madness, Christina.'

'Zu-Ting,' said Bettina sharply. 'This is a democratic and open discussion. All views must be heard and respected.'

'Then listen to mine and respect it!' cried the Korean, beautiful and fierce in her anger. 'You would let this toad walk away because Jesus died to forgive Christina's sins? No, I don't agree. I will never agree. Not in a million years!'

'Does anyone else want to share an idea?' Glenn asked the group, hoping to move away from Christina's call for clemency and diffuse the tension. Glenn looked around and saw Elfrida raise a hand.

'Yes, Elfrida, go ahead,' he smiled.

'If I were you, I would say nothing,' said the Mexican, waving her hand to dismiss the issue, and smiling mischievously. 'Let's say nothing, and I'll tell him I'm putting on a large fundraising event in Mexico. It will be elaborate, with crowds of rich people attending. Like this Sydney conference, but Mexican style! There are many extremely rich people in Mexico. In fact, some of the richest people in the world live there.'

'So we lure him to Mexico for a fundraiser,' said Glenn. 'Then what?'

'Then I speak to an ex-student of mine, Miguel,' said Elfrida. 'Miguel is one of the best matador fighters in Acapulco. He is one of the first blind fighters and people know him in my region. They call him a miracle.'

The group began to laugh as they saw where Elfrida was going with this idea.

'Then,' she smiled. 'I will ask Miguel to invite Herbert into the ring, and without warning, we will release the bull! He will be torn up like a piece of meat! It's a nice revenge, no?'

'How could he refuse an invitation into the ring!' laughed Zu-Ting, clapping her hands and whooping in support. 'It's a brilliant plan!'

'Yes, he will be trapped by his own greed,' said Elfrida. 'This man will not ask questions. If we mention money, he will come running, even if it's all the way to Mexico.'

The women laughed at the idea of Farrand dressed up like a matador, his Germanic cool already disturbed by the Latin passion of the event. Bettina laughed harder than anyone, clearly savouring this moment of joy in the midst of such uncertainty.

'Ladies,' Glenn said after a while, unable to share in their mirth. 'I must press you now to be serious. We are trying to develop a strategy here, not a spectacle.'

'Oh, but what a spectacle it would be!' chuckled Bettina, wiping tears of laughter from her eyes.

'Alright, folks, alright!' Odile called above the laughter. 'Let's be serious now. Glenn's right. We need a strategy. Now, tell me, have any of you heard of the racketeering act? Often known as the RICO act?'

'Yes,' nodded Glenn, recalling the law upheld in the United States. 'Go on.'

'Well, it's the law set down for fraud,' Odile went on. 'In 1970, The Racketeer Influenced and Corrupt Organizations Act came into law across the United States. Most folks call it a RICO, as I said. It requires jail sentences and the payment of penalties. Those penalties amount to three times the losses incurred by victims because of some kind of diversion of funds or fraud. Here we have a proven case of fraud, right?'

'We have a proven case of fraud,' Glenn nodded quickly, confirming what Odile was saying.

'Then we have jurisdiction possible in the States because of the office installed in New Orleans,' she continued. 'I'm a US citizen and as such can go to a contingency lawyer and file a RICO. Best part is, we only pay the lawyer if we succeed. It's a win win!'

'That's the best idea I've heard in ages,' said Glenn, shaking his head in disbelief. 'Odile, that's brilliant. Truly! What are we gonna get in Germany, or the UK? The maximum penalty we'd get is a jail sentence. Compensation will be off the cards. This is a great idea: Farrand will receive a penalty and the FBI will have a way to find out where his money is. We will get three times the money stolen.'

'Odile,' laughed Bettina. 'This is amazing. How did you know about this?'

'I read about it,' smiled Odile. 'When they are trying to bring down mafia members or a tycoon from Wall Street, they always talk about RICOs. I researched it last night and it's really possible: we could regain three times our losses.'

'Thanks you, Odile, for this amazing idea,' smiled Glenn. 'Now we're really talking about justice!'

'What a meeting,' laughed Bettina. 'What a team we have with all of you! We make a great sorority, including Glenn.'

'Happy to be a sister for a day,' Glenn grinned.

'Look at us,' Bettina beamed as she gazed ahead. 'We have a tough girl, a tolerant Christian, a secret lawyer, and a stand-up comedian!'

'You like comedy, huh?' smiled Elfrida. 'I have seen how people regulate accounts in Mexico. They use real revenge. There are two methods we understand: bullfights and spicy food!'

Everyone laughed once more, and Glenn marvelled at the group of women around him. Bettina was right: they were an incredible team.

'So, Glenn, what do you think?' Bettina asked him. 'You have heard from all of us now.'

'Actually, no, we haven't,' said Glenn. 'We haven't heard from you, Bettina.'

'It's true,' she laughed. 'But perhaps we have already heard enough? There are so many ideas on the table.'

'To quote *you*, Bettina, this is a democratic and open discussion,' laughed Zu-Ting. 'Come on, sister. Tell us what you think.'

Bettina smiled and conceded, thinking carefully for a moment.

'I've listened to all of your ideas,' she began. 'You have all made valid points. My feeling, though, is that we have to stay in the German jurisdiction. The ICB is based in Aachen, in Germany. We should bring Herbert to justice where we know we can pin him down.'

'Farrand is a slick customer,' Glenn sighed, nodding in agreement. 'He will try to wriggle out of every trap we set. We cannot face him with too many attempts and invitations or he will grow suspicious. We should corner him where we know he cannot escape. Is that what you think, Bettina?'

'I'm not a vengeful person,' said Bettina. 'You are wise, Glenn, and experienced in these matters. I follow your guidance, as I believe every one of us will.'

'We go for German jurisdiction then?' he said. Bettina nodded.

'I think it's best, despite all our other options,' she said determinedly. 'There is no other way: we have to go to the police with evidence.'

Bettina spoke with such passion that Glenn knew the decision was made. Just as she followed his guidance and experience, he followed her conviction.

'When?' he asked.

'The annual general meeting is in three weeks' time,' she said. 'Luckily, we know Herbert will be there. It is a safe bet.'

'We corner him at the AGM?' said Zu-Ting. 'I like it!'

'We will alert the police,' said Glenn. 'We can do it quietly, discreetly, so as not to attract negative press. Let's follow the meeting through to the end as if nothing has changed.'

'But how will we face him?' Laura demanded. 'How will we be able to sit in the same room as him, talk to him, listen to him? It will be impossible!'

'With grace,' sighed Christina. 'We must all find some grace to deal with this situation.'

'We will face him with the knowledge that he is going down for this,' hissed Elfrida. 'That will be our courage and our comfort.'

'I hope it will be enough,' swallowed Odile. 'I don't know if I can do it.'

'We can *all* do it,' said Bettina with such fierceness that Glenn felt the hairs on the back of his neck stand up. 'Believe me, my friends,' she went on. 'You are stronger than you think.'

'Bettina's right,' Glenn said quickly, supporting his friend. 'Does anyone have any objections to prosecuting in Germany? If so, speak now.'

The room was quiet. Glenn nodded, glad it was decided.

'Then we will strike in Aachen,' he said. 'Until then, I need you all to keep contact with Farrand to an absolute minimum. If it is necessary to speak with him to avoid suspicion, go ahead, but give him no reason to run away. We are so close now. This is the home run.'

'What will happen to us, Bettina?' Odile asked in a small voice. 'Will we lose our jobs?'

Bettina said nothing but Glenn saw the pain on her face.

'That remains to be seen, Odile,' she said gently. 'One step at a time, OK?'

Odile nodded. Glenn wanted to say something to reassure them all, but he knew nothing he could say could ease their fears. Indeed, uncertainty walked hand in hand with this move against Farrand. Looking up at the clock he saw that even if he wanted to share words of comfort, there was no time left. It was early afternoon and the cars would be arriving to take the women home.

'You guys have planes and trains to catch,' he said, clapping his hands together in a final way. 'Until we meet again in a few weeks, I wish you restful and peaceful days. Hang in there, OK?'

Saying goodbye to Zu-Ting, Elfrida, Odile and Christina was easier knowing he would see them again so soon, Glenn thought as he hugged them one by one. Laura and Bettina were going to walk home, so lingered as the others went out to catch their planes. Watching the women embrace one another gave Glenn courage: they were a sorority, as Bettina had said. They would get through this, no matter what happened next.

'Right, well I should head off,' said Laura brightly. 'Now this is all sorted, I need to pop in and see a friend. She lives just around the corner. See you later, Bets. Glenn, always a pleasure!'

Laura kissed Glenn on the cheek before setting off along his street, her white cane whooshing from side to side. With a jump of his heart, Glenn realised he and Bettina were alone once more.

'Are you not going too?' he asked in astonishment.

'Oh,' said Bettina quickly, blushing slightly. 'Sorry, did you want me to?'

'No!' Glenn said quickly, laughing nervously. 'No, not at all. I'm glad that you are… well, here.'

'You're glad I'm here,' she laughed. 'That's good to know. I'm glad to be here.'

Glenn searched the air around him for words to say for he was suddenly tongue-tied. He noticed the warmth from the sun beating down on the autumn pavement.

'It's beautiful out here,' he said. 'Would you like to go for a walk?'

'I'd love that,' said Bettina.

Glenn offered her his arm and they began to walk slowly through Mayfair. He enjoyed the gentle weight of her body against his and felt relieved that the day's meeting was over. Finally, they had a plan: finally, they would expose Farrand's fraud. A problem shared was truly a problem halved, Glenn thought.

'It's nice to wander,' he said, taking in the new avenues around him. 'I haven't really had much of a chance to explore since moving in.'

'How long has it been since you moved out?' Bettina asked him.

'A month,' he said, before realising what Bettina was asking him. He stopped in his tracks. 'Wait. How did you know I've moved out?'

'From the descriptions you gave me of your manor house in the country, I expected something a bit bigger,' Bettina smiled a small smile. 'This isn't where you usually live, is it?'

'Right,' Glenn laughed uneasily. 'Sure, that's true.'

'Glenn,' Bettina said softly, after a small pause. 'I heard Mr. Spinola after the meeting earlier this week. I heard what he said about your wife.'

'Yeah,' said Glenn, letting out a sigh. 'Yeah, that happened.'

'What happened?' she asked him and he felt the smallest squeeze on his arm. That light pressure and Bettina's gentle probing gave him the confidence to speak. He knew it was now or never. Without hesitating any longer, he told her everything, speaking for the first time about the separation from his wife. He told Bettina all, sparing her no detail of the heart, body or soul.

'And how do you feel now?' she asked him.

'I feel free,' he shrugged. 'Sometimes I feel guilty, but I know it was the right thing to do.'

'You're sure?' Bettina asked.

'It was time,' he said, shaking his head. 'I don't love her anymore.'

Like an avalanche rumbling in the distance, Glenn could feel an important moment approaching. Looking down at Bettina's beautiful face, at this caring, kind and expressive human being, he knew what he had to do. He knew what needed to be said and before he could stop himself, the words spilled from him.

'I can't pretend anymore, Bettina,' he said. 'I think you're amazing.'

'Glenn,' Bettina said quickly, her arm growing rigid against him. 'Don't say…'

'Oh, but I will, little lady!' he said, spinning around and grinning at her. His heart felt light and free. 'I've been thinking that since the moment we met. We have so much fun together. We listen to each other. And, correct me if I'm wrong, but I think we love each other.'

The words hung in the air between them like stars in the sky. Glenn felt their power and he knew Bettina did too.

'Glenn, I don't know,' said Bettina shaking her head. 'You were married… you *are* married. All this time we've been… oh God. What have I done?'

To his horror, Glenn watched as clouds of guilt descended on Bettina's face. Her smile had vanished and her blue eyes were staring ahead in that familiar, melancholic way.

'What have you done?' he asked, shaking his head. 'Bettina, you have shown me what love is. You have brought me back to myself.'

'What?' she whispered.

'You have done nothing wrong,' he said, taking her hands in his and holding them tight. 'I was in a bad marriage. What Eleanora and I had died a long time ago. We just didn't want to face it. We clung unhappily to one another to avoid the hurt and separation that we're feeling now. I walked away, but in truth, she left me a long time ago. She didn't trust me anymore.'

Bettina was quiet, listening as Glenn told her his truths. After a kilometre of walking this way, Glenn could not bear her silence any longer.

'Bettina, talk to me,' he urged her. 'How do you feel? Do I have this all wrong?'

'Tell me I didn't break up a marriage,' was all she said, after another long silence. 'Tell me, Glenn. Tell me the truth!'

'You broke nothing,' Glenn said firmly, taking a chance and wrapping his arms around her. 'But I do love you, Bettina, and God knows you'll break my heart if you don't tell me you feel the same.'

At first, she did nothing. She felt rigid in his arms. Then, like ice to his warm, beating sun, she began to soften. As if feeling him for the first time, Bettina raised her hand and placed the palm against Glenn's chest. She felt his heart beating its tremendous beat, then moved her fingers slowly upwards, to his collar, to his neck and up to his cheek. She traced the firm line of his jaw and the softness of his lips before moving around to the back of his neck. Gently, but with confidence, she pulled him down to kiss her. Their lips touched and Glenn sighed with pleasure.

'Oh Glenn,' she whispered in his ear, brushing her soft cheek against his. 'Kiss me again.'

Glenn kissed her once more but opened his eyes when he felt tears against his skin. They were cold and dripping steadily down Bettina's face.

'Tears?' he whispered, laughing slightly. 'Are those tears?'

'Yes,' she smiled, nodding. 'It has been so long since I felt this.'

'And what do you feel, Bettina Hartmann?' he whispered. 'Can I know at last?'

Bettina smiled and let out a small laugh through her tears. She took a deep breath.

'Love,' she said, though it was barely a whisper. 'I feel love.'

CHAPTER THIRTY-TWO

As the plane tore off the runway from Heathrow, Glenn glanced down at England with disinterested eyes. The previous few weeks had left him tired. Since kissing Bettina, his mind was fixed on Germany alone. The thought of his return that day filled him with a renewed sense of longing for the woman he could not stop thinking about. If only seeing Bettina again were the *only* reason for his flight that cold autumn morning, he thought.

Dylan Marlowe, buried studiously in a newspaper beside him, was a reminder of the delicate operation underway. They just had to make it through the next twelve hours without arousing suspicion. At this stage, all Glenn could do was hope that the six blind women could stave off suspicion and act normal around Farrand; he knew from experience that this was no easy feat.

'Relax,' said Marlowe, clearly sensing Glenn's nerves. 'The more anxious you are, the more Farrand will suspect us.'

'Marlowe's right!' squeaked Spinola, leaning forward in his chair from the row behind them. The auditor had offered to accompany Glenn for moral and factual support.

'You're sure he'll think it's normal that we're there at the AGM?' Glenn asked them both anxiously. 'He won't think it's suspicious that I've brought you two along?'

'Positive,' Marlowe nodded, turning his youthful blue eyes to Glenn. 'You're becoming a major fundraising partner for Farrand. It makes sense that the DCF would send representation.'

'I'm just afraid that after what happened in Sydney, he'll be defensive,' said Glenn, remembering their spat by the ocean. The ICB President had been scathing in his dismissal of both Glenn and Marlowe from the beach party.

'Do you really think a megalomaniac like Farrand is going to care about a little tiff you had at a beach party?' Marlowe raised one disbelieving eyebrow. 'To him you're just a big dollar sign. He has bigger fish to fry.'

'So do we,' Spinola said darkly.

'You're right,' Glenn nodded.

Plotting Farrand's downfall was not the only thing that made Glenn nervous on that flight, however. Though he trusted himself enough to conceal his feelings for Farrand, his feelings for Bettina were something else entirely. From the moment he had held her in his arms he had known something beautiful and terrible: they loved each other, but now what? What happened next? Though Eleanora was no longer a part of his life, his life was still in London at the DCF, and Bettina's life was in Germany. Moreover, he knew that Bettina was about to face one of the greatest challenges of her life. She would lose everything and have to start again. The weight of this crisis would be crushing.

Such worries puzzled Glenn as he debarked from the plane, silently following Spinola's briefcase and Marlowe's confident stride towards the luggage claim. As they drove into the city, Aachen spread out around them, speckled with autumn colours, just as it had been when Glenn had attended the 'Living With Blindness' workshop. His mind travelled back to those three incredible days in which he had met Bettina and the five other women. He had learnt so much since then, he thought, about blindness and about himself. Their taxi took them straight to a location pre-arranged by Marlowe, where a plain clothes police officer would be waiting for them.

'I've already briefed the police on the situation,' Marlowe informed them both, buttoning up his suit in preparation for the meeting. 'They have the evidence already. We just need to make a plan for this evening.'

'Farrand will be at the meeting until the end,' said Glenn. 'He has to be, as president.'

'In which case we should strike then,' said Marlowe. 'Before he has time to disappear.'

Arriving at a hotel in the city centre, Glenn felt an ominous feeling. A tall, blonde man with a closely shaved beard met them and shook each of their hands. He seemed to recognise Marlowe, reassuring Glenn that they had been in contact about the case prior to that day. The policeman showed them his badge.

'Robert Heinmann,' he introduced himself in heavily accented English. 'I will be accompanying you to make the arrest this evening.'

'Thank you for your assistance in this, Mr. Heinmann,' said Glenn. 'As you can probably imagine, this is a delicate situation. Mr. Farrand is a master at his chosen criminal vocation. We are sure he will run away at the first sight of trouble.'

'We need to catch him where we can,' Marlowe nodded.

'I have enough experience in this field to understand what you are telling me, Mr. Tebbhurst,' Mr. Heinmann nodded curtly. 'I will make the arrest quietly. Please arrange for Mr. Farrand to meet us in a room at the centre, away from any press, after the day's events. There I will read him his rights and take him away.'

'Good,' said Glenn, relieved to know Farrand would not be able to escape. 'Mr. Marlowe here will meet you towards the end of the day, at an arranged time. We will then find a suitable place to make the arrest.'

When the last few details had been arranged between Marlowe and the police officer, they said goodbye. Glenn, Spinola and their private detective headed to the ICB headquarters, where the AGM would soon be starting.

'Gosh, this is exciting!' Spinola chuckled. Glenn smiled at his friend, wondering if this was the most adventure the auditor had enjoyed in years.

As they drew closer to the ICB's office, Glenn braced himself for the meeting with Farrand, praying he would be able to keep his cool. As ever, Farrand was milking an opportunity for publicity. It looked like he had invited half the press of Germany to the AGM that day.

Wrapped in a thick fur coat, he stood outside, welcoming guests. Farrand had a cold smile fixed upon his handsome face. Zu-Ting stood beside him and Glenn was happy to see she looked quite relaxed. He had half-expected the fiery Korean to be eyeing her enemy from a distance, planning when to pounce, but she seemed serene as she shook hands with arriving guests. Glenn waited for the moment Farrand would set eyes on him, and when it came, he fixed a smile upon his face.

'Glenn!' the president called out. 'You made it! Excellent. That is truly *excellent*. And you have brought your trusty assistant along with you? Mr. Martins is it?'

'Mr. Marlowe,' the private detective corrected him with a polite bow of his head. 'Hello again, Mr. Farrand.'

'And this is?' Farrand gleamed at Spinola.

'Another associate from the DCF,' Glenn explained quickly. 'Mr. John Spinola is curious to hear about future projects.'

'Well, well!' laughed Farrand, slapping his palm into Spinola's outstretched hand before turning his smile back to Glenn. 'We are lucky to have such *diligent* fundraisers in our team. Welcome back to Aachen, Glenn. You remember Zu-Ting, of course?'

'Of course,' smiled Glenn, taking Zu-Ting's soft, outstretched hand in his.

'Glenn!' she said with a small laugh. He felt her squeeze his palm meaningfully. 'It's great to meet again. Are you missing the Australian sunshine?'

'You bet,' Glenn said with a chuckle, pretending the last time they had seen each other was in Sydney. 'Will I see you later?'

'You bet,' Zu-Ting grinned. 'Welcome back to Aachen, Glenn. And hello, gentlemen!'

Spinola swallowed hard, his eyes widening as he tried not to give himself away. Glenn remembered how taken he had been with Zu-Ting at the meeting in London.

'The other ladies are inside,' said Farrand, looking past Glenn to the line of guests waiting to be welcomed. 'I'm sure you'll be desperate to meet them again?'

'Indeed,' smiled Glenn, for once grateful for Farrand's blatant display of disinterest. 'It's been a long time.'

As soon as he had passed Farrand, Glenn let out a small, silent sigh of relief. He had made it past the first round and, so far it seemed, Farrand did not suspect a thing. Now all they had to do was get through the rest of the day. Searching the crowded entrance for signs of the other women, Glenn was astonished by the lavishness Farrand had displayed once more. A colourful feast of German pastries and cakes lay on display, presented by the same blind bakers Glenn had met at the 'Living With Blindness' conference. With a jolt in his stomach, Glenn remembered the models Farrand had hired and paraded around as blind women in Sydney. He wondered how many of those blind bakers were *actually* blind, and if they were, how they would feel if they knew how Farrand represented the ICB abroad. The thought sickened him. He felt trapped in Farrand's web once more, not knowing what was real and what was fabrication. Turning to Marlowe he saw the same look on his private detective's face.

'What do you think?' he asked Glenn. 'Another fraud?'

'I think I'm tired of counting,' Glenn said through gritted teeth. 'We have enough on him now. I fear if we keep digging we'll never stop.'

'We'll only find darkness anyway, old chap,' sighed Spinola.

'Have you seen the others?' Glenn asked them, scanning the room.

'There!' whispered Spinola, pointing at two women in the distance. Glenn was glad to spot Elfrida's long black plait beside Christina's blonde halo of hair. Walking quickly towards them, he knew Farrand was safely outside so he did not need to hide his true intentions.

'Ladies,' he said in a low voice, approaching them from behind. 'It's me, it's...'

'Glenn!' cried Christina.

'Yes,' he chuckled. 'You are so good at that!'

'Call it a sixth sense,' smiled Elfrida.

'Or God's will?' Christina suggested.

'Something like that. How are you both?' Glenn asked urgently.

'We're holding up alright,' sighed Elfrida. 'It's so hard to speak to Herbert knowing what he has done. I just want to set a huge, angry bull on him and watch him beg for mercy! I can see it in my mind's eye: the hooves, the roars of the crowd, his squealing as he runs away...'

'We have already discussed this,' Glenn smiled, whispering in a low voice. 'That option is off the cards, Elfrida. We have a plan, remember?'

'What is the plan?' Christina asked. 'He is here, we are here, but what next?'

'Mr. Marlowe is here with me,' said Glenn. 'And Mr. Spinola. We travelled together from London. Dylan has arranged for a plain clothes police officer to wait for Farrand after the conference. All I need you ladies to do is make sure Farrand goes where he is supposed to at the appointed time.'

'We can do that,' nodded Christina. 'I can arrange a place for us.'

'It's brilliant!' grinned Elfrida.

'Where is Bettina?' Glenn asked them.

'She's busy preparing for the conference,' said Christina. 'Shall I take you to her?'

'Yes, thanks,' said Glenn. Turning to Marlowe, he laid a hand on the private detective's shoulder. 'Dylan, go with Elfrida and find Odile, alright? She needs to know the plan. Zu-Ting should be told also. Take John with you.'

'Leave it with us,' said Elfrida.

'I think I'll follow her lead!' said Marlowe, grinning at the young woman's confidence, clearly impressed.

'Blimey!' grinned Spinola, still buzzing with excitement.

Glenn followed Christina through the crowds to where Bettina was discussing something in German with members of the press. He could not understand what she was saying, but noticed that she faltered in her words as he drew nearer.

'I'm sorry,' he heard her say. 'I believe there is someone here I should say hello to. Please excuse me.'

As Bettina walked slowly towards him, Glenn could barely look at her. She looked so beautiful, with her blonde hair tied up into a loose ponytail, wearing a flowing suit of navy and periwinkle blues. She was the image of grace.

'Glenn,' she said softly, her voice a little nervous. 'You're here. I'm so glad.'

'I am,' he said, wishing for a moment that he could take her in his arms and reassure her. Instead he took her hand in his. 'Are you ready?'

'I've *never* been more ready,' she said, though her shaking hands betrayed her confident words. 'We should be getting started soon. Tell me, what's the plan?'

Glenn leant in close and quickly explained everything to her: Marlowe, the police officer and the need to divert him to a room after the conference.

'Leave that to me,' she said. 'I will make sure he does not leave this building.'

'I will go and tell Zu-Ting,' said Christina. 'She needs to know.'

Grateful for a moment alone with Bettina, even though it was in the middle of the crowded conference room, Glenn leaned so close that his face brushed hers.

'I've missed you,' he whispered in her ear. He felt her round cheeks tickle his chin as they rose into a smile.

'I've missed you too,' she said, half-groaning. 'Oh Glenn, what have we started? Are we star-crossed lovers now? It's surely a recipe for disaster.'

'Or the chance of a lifetime,' he grinned. He would not share her pessimism, not now, not as he stood before her and experienced first-hand the incredible effect she had on him. 'When this is all over, when we have put Farrand away, I will come and find you. If you like, I will even kiss you again. Then let's see where disaster leads us too, shall we?'

'I should go,' said Bettina, smiling as she shook her head. 'Farrand can't see us like this.'

'I wouldn't worry about that, I think he already suspects,' said Glenn.

'What do you mean?' Bettina frowned.

'We had a bit of a squabble, he and I, in Sydney,' said Glenn.

'A squabble?' she laughed. 'About what?'

'About you,' he said, frowning as he recalled Farrand's ugly words.

'About me?' said Bettina. 'But what about me?'

'Farrand seemed to be under the impression that you were only worth as much as your beautiful smile,' said Glenn, gritting his teeth with anger. 'I simply informed him that this was not the case. I told him you were so much more. I think I might have called him a monster, or something like that. I would have thrown him to the ground if Marlowe hadn't arrived just in time to break it up.'

'You defended me?' said Bettina, a small, curious smile growing on her plump lips.

'Of course I did,' said Glenn, grinning at the thought.

'I always knew you were a knight in shining armour,' she laughed. 'Well, more like a banker's suit, but still: a knight to the rescue all the same.'

'At your service, my lady,' Glenn said, unable to suppress the huge smile on his face.

'I should go,' said Bettina with a sigh. Could they not just hold hands and flee the confrontation ahead, he thought; to a nearby park bursting full of autumn leaves, or better yet, the soft bed in Bettina's apartment?

'You should,' he said, pushing his thoughts aside and giving her hand a reassuring squeeze. 'Good luck.'

Bettina smiled at him in thanks and disappeared into the steadily growing crowd. Glenn backtracked, hoping to find Marlowe to receive an update, but the private detective was nowhere to be seen and the conference was already beginning. Herbert Farrand was already ascending to the stage, where a small podium had been set up before a sea of cameras. If one positive thing could be said about Farrand, Glenn thought, it was the publicity he drew to the ICB. It was impressive, despite the ulterior motives behind it.

'Ladies and gentlemen, welcome, welcome to our AGM!' he called out to the crowds through his microphone. Dressed in a Gucci suit, Farrand stood like a man on top of the world.

Sparing no exaggerations and lavishly detailing his successes, Farrand entertained the crowds with his chatter of millions and empty promises. Glenn grinned a conspiratorial grin; Farrand would never guess that the women closest to him in the ICB were about to betray him just as he had so soundly deceived them for so many years.

'One big announcement we would like to make to the press today is related to piloting a different model of fundraising,' Bettina began, pleasing the crowd with her warm, rich voice. 'As grateful as we are to our patrons, friends and investors for their contributions so far, we would like to try a different approach to raising funds. I don't want funds to come in as endowments only, though we of course welcome them. I would like to harness the great good of the general public by allowing them to contribute however little they can to our programmes. For this we will launch a whole public appeal for fundraising, and we will accept five dollars as happily as we will accept five hundred dollars.'

Bettina paused, bathing in a soft light that lit up her in the gloom.

'With the increasing prominence of the internet in daily life across the globe, we can now reach areas that were impossible to reach before. We can touch small communities, from those in the townships of South America to those in the mountains of Bali. We can finally reach further, with the support of these local communities. We will present our programmes and raise funds this way, worldwide, to work towards our goals of financial sustainability. This will take much effort but we are willing to make it happen.'

A round of applause burst out as Bettina finished her announcement. Only Farrand seemed less than impressed, frowning despite his constant, cool smile. He stepped forward for a moment, requesting the microphone from Bettina.

'She's brilliant, no?' cried Farrand, shouting into the microphone. 'A round of applause again for the beautiful Ms. Bettina Hartmann, ladies and gentlemen! And of course, let me re-emphasise one small point she made. Endowments are still welcome at the ICB, very welcome. I like the internet idea, but we also like big money.'

The crowd laughed at this, snapping pictures of Farrand as he spoke in full confidence.

'We are now embarking on big programs after all,' he continued. 'We've exceeded in raising millions in Australia, and now we have great prospects to do the same in Turkey, Indonesia, Brazil, Argentina, Mexico and Thailand! We may even go to the Arabian Gulf and raise money from the princes of oil over there! They are sat on fortunes of oil and mineral resources. The same can be said for South Africa. There is no place I will not go to for the ICB. No stone will be left unturned in our plight to raise money for the blind!'

The crowd clapped and applauded Farrand's passionate display.

'After all,' he went on, 'we have our six blind beauties to support in Hong Kong, Acapulco, New Orleans, London and, of course, here in Germany. You can meet them all here, today. My ladies! My brave and beautiful ladies! We will use the money we raise to renovate their offices, expand their projects and support them in fulfilling their great potential across the globe.'

Glenn searched the room for the faces of the women Farrand spoke about. They all stood together in a line, each one of their faces fixed with a pleasant smile. No one else in that room except Glenn and Marlowe could know what hid beneath those smiles. Glenn could only imagine how their insides writhed with every lie Farrand uttered. Odile alone looked close to tears.

When Farrand had finished his opening speech, the general press left the meeting, leaving the core members of the team along with any interested contributors. Bettina started to run through the more banal agenda of the AGM, working through the list over a couple of hours. When the meeting finally drew to a close, Bettina did her best to leave everyone with excitement in their veins by introducing future programmes and the discovery of new technologies.

'New technologies are being created every day,' she insisted passionately. 'We will endeavour to work with innovators, doctors and biomechanical engineers to push the limits of blind-assisted living. In a century where we have sent machines to Mars, can't we focus our energy on helping those down here on our own planet? I want to *invest* in these evolutionary technologies. So please, fundraisers, consultants, fellow blind here today, think about this when you tell others of the ICB. Think of our vision. Thank you.'

Bettina's final words had a great effect on those attending the meeting. They broke out into rapturous applause. Farrand was smiling at everyone, enjoying the happy applause. Bettina herself had a firm smile fixed on her face but Glenn immediately recognised the melancholy there. Only he and the five other blind women knew the true significance of her plea; Bettina was asking people to remember the ICB for what it was, not for the terrible fraud that would later emerge around Herbert Farrand.

Slowly, people began to leave the meeting, shaking hands with Farrand as they did so. Glenn kept a keen eye on the president, making sure he was always in sight. Luckily there were so many guests insisting on shaking Farrand's hand that it would be impossible for him to slip away. Glenn felt someone tap sharply on his shoulder. He turned to see Marlowe standing behind him.

'It's time,' he said quickly in a low voice. Glenn looked behind Marlowe and saw Robert Heinmann standing there, in plain clothes. No one would suspect he was a policeman.

'OK, take him to a room out back,' said Glenn. 'Take Spinola with you.'

'We'll be in the marketing office,' Marlowe nodded. 'Christina is leading us there. She'll come back for you. Tell Bettina and join us there, alright?'

Glenn nodded and turned back to Bettina. The crowds had considerably thinned and only a few guests remained to bid the president goodbye. Glenn walked over to Bettina and whispered the news in her ear.

'What a wonderful idea, Glenn!' she said loudly, taking Glenn by surprise. He looked over at Farrand, who had turned to Bettina with interest.

'What is?' the president called out curiously.

'Glenn has proposed a toast to a new year of the ICB in the marketing office,' said Bettina cheerfully. 'He's brought us champagne from London, Herbert!'

'Oh,' shrugged Farrand, clearly disinterested.

'Oh come now,' laughed Bettina. 'You have to celebrate with us. How often are we all here in one place together? The girls will be thrilled. Besides, there are a couple of things I need to talk to you about.'

'OK, sweetheart,' sighed Farrand, glancing down at his watch. 'Let's make it quick then? *Ja?*'

'I'll go and get glasses,' Glenn lied, impressed by Bettina's quick thinking.

'We'll be with you in a minute,' said Bettina. 'Odile, Elfrida and Zu-Ting can finish up here. Herbert and I will crack open the fizz!'

Glenn retreated to the marketing office, spying Christina at the entrance to the conference room, awaiting him. She led them both to the room where Marlowe, Spinola and Heinmann sat waiting for the criminal to arrive. Joining them, Glenn let out an uneasy sigh. His heart was beating fast. There was no turning back now: the trap was set.

CHAPTER THIRTY-THREE

Footsteps approached, signalling Farrand's arrival. Glenn swallowed hard and leant causally against a desk. Bettina entered first, acting cheerfully, chattering away to Herbert about the success of the meeting.

'You put it perfectly, Herbert,' she was saying. 'We still need the big investors, that's a fact.'

Farrand walked into the marketing office behind her, looking bored but clueless. Glenn was reassured: so far, the president did not suspect a thing. Farrand nodded arrogantly at Marlowe and Spinola, glancing curiously at Heinmann sat by their side. When he saw Glenn empty-handed he tutted and rolled his eyes, an impatient smile on his face.

'Come on, Glenn, I thought you were opening the champagne?' he said, eyeing the room with playful irritation. 'I don't have much time and I'm gasping! Where is it? Where's the damn fizz!'

Glenn said nothing. He simply walked over to the door to close it gently. Bettina stood behind Farrand, her face surprisingly calm.

'Don't tell me you've drunk it already, you cheeky fellow?' laughed Farrand.

'I don't drink, Herbert,' Glenn said coolly. 'I've told you that before.'

'What is this then?' Farrand said, laughing slightly when no one said anything. His eyes drifted back to the three men sat in front of him. 'Why are Martin and his friend here?'

'It's Marlowe,' the private detective corrected him for the second time that day.

'Right,' Farrand shook his head disinterestedly. 'Well, sorry, *Marlowe*. I thought this was a private party. That's all I'm saying.'

'You thought wrong,' said Glenn. Farrand spun around when he heard this. There was an icy tone in Glenn's voice. He could hide his disdain no longer.

'What's going on, Glenn?' he asked, his tone light, his eyes dancing with interest. 'Four men, six women, is that the gist? You dirty dog!'

Glenn refrained from grabbing the adventurer by the scruff of his neck and giving him a good slap. It wasn't so much the mention of anyone else but Bettina that kindled flames of fire in his stomach. *Justice will be served*, he told himself.

'No,' he shook his head. 'I think I'll let the ladies tell you.'

'Oh, the *ladies!*' Farrand nodded. 'I see. Well then, Bettina? Can you enlighten me?'

Bettina said nothing. She was waiting for the others to arrive.

'Bettina?' Farrand snapped impatiently.

When Bettina said nothing, Farrand turned back to Spinola, Marlowe and Heinmann. He looked from them to Glenn, then to Bettina.

'Who are these men?' he demanded. 'What's going on?'

'These are the men who have been helping us uncover a secret, Herbert,' Bettina said at last. 'You know Glenn, of course. He has been helping us in accounting this past year. Mr. Spinola is an auditor, and he has been casting his keen eye over the ICB accounts. They make for interesting reading.'

'What?' laughed Farrand. 'But that is ridiculous! An audit is serious business. I should have been made aware that an audit was taking place.'

'Serious business indeed. Why is that, I wonder?' asked Glenn, but before he could say more, the door burst open. Zu-Ting walked in, followed by Odile, Christina, Laura and Elfrida. They formed a sort of shield against the wall, closing the door behind them. Farrand gazed at them all, keeping his expression very neutral. After a moment he smiled.

'Ladies, forgive me,' he spluttered, suddenly he seemed very nervous, almost afraid. He reached down and picked up his coat as he did so, he muttered, 'I have just remembered, that... that...'

'Yes? Somewhere to be?' said Glenn.

Farrand's head whipped round to Glenn. 'Yes, actually, I have an appointment,' he sneered, his tongue flicking over his lips. 'Unlike you, I'm a very important man – I *have* places to be. Now, I am so sorry to leave in such a rush, but duty calls. You see, Glenn – mere employee – a *president's* work is never done.'

No one moved an inch, despite Farrand's clear attempt to make for the door. Glenn just smiled in the face of the German's jibes. They stood their ground, five beautiful women, each standing proudly, resolute.

'Oh, but we also have an appointment, Herbert,' said Laura. 'With you.'

'You *are* the appointment,' said Odile. 'We are here right now to discuss *you*.'

'Yes, it would be a great shame if the subject of our meeting was not actually present,' said Zu-Ting. 'Besides, I think it's important you hear all we have to say, Herbert.'

'About what?' he snapped, laughing once more in his baffled, dismissive – but increasingly nervous – way. 'As flattered as I am to be the subject of your thoughts and discussions, ladies, I really must insist. I have to go.'

'We really must insist that you stay,' said Elfrida, sidestepping to close a gap that Herbert was trying to slither through with his snake hips.

'You see, you have become a bit of a problem, Herbert,' she went on. 'It's bad news, I'm afraid.'

'What is?' he asked, looking at the women with defiance. He scanned their ranks, looking for a way through to the door.

'We are having some money problems,' said Laura. 'And we would like to talk to you about them.'

At this, Farrand's face paled considerably. Glenn could have sworn he saw one of the president's glacial blue eyes twitching slightly.

'Money problems?' he repeated, forcing his smile to return. 'You ladies know you have no need to worry about money. Did you not just attend the same AGM as me? We are richer than ever before! The ICB is booming.'

'*You* are richer than ever before,' Elfrida hissed at him.

'I think what Elfrida means to say is that an issue of misappropriation has come to light,' said Glenn, choosing his words carefully.

'Misappropriation of what?' scoffed Farrand, still searching for a way out.

'Of funds,' said Glenn. 'In recent months we have become aware of some foul play.'

'May I ask what any of this has to do with you, Tebbhurst?' Farrand said with more confidence this time. 'The last time I checked, you were neither accountant nor auditor at the ICB. Little birds also tell me that you are a failure in marriage. What was it? My women drawing your eye away from your loyal wife?'

Glenn was stunned. Eyes pinned wide, his mind screamed at him to launch his fists at the smug face of the German; they were twitching by his side, ready to be thrown. Taking a deep breath, he blinked gently and spent a moment composing himself – though his heart was thumping out of his chest.

'I've just tried to help these women out,' said Glenn. 'As a fundraiser for the ICB, it was my responsibility to check out how funds have been spent in the past. I think you should listen to what Bettina and your colleagues have to say, and to what Mr. Spinola has travelled all this way from London to share with you. John, will you do us the honour?'

Spinola hoisted himself up smoothly from his chair. He eyed Farrand warily, then he took a file out of his briefcase and opened to the first page, clearing his throat as he did so.

'This document here details, with evidence, the misappropriation of funds and accounting fraud committed by Mr. H. Farrand over the past six years,' he read aloud. A small squeak shot out of Herbert. 'Notifications of incoming funds,' he went on, 'retrieved by Mr. Marlowe have been unaccounted for on countless occasions, and correlations between Mr. Farrand's personal spending and missing amounts from the ICB's accounts have been established.'

'You!' seethed Farrand, eyes suddenly wild, pointing a finger at the smug-looking detective in the corner. Marlowe was sat back in his seat, feet on the table, hands behind his neck, enjoying all of this unfold. 'How dare you look at my personal accounts! Who gave you access to them? Who? What kind of prying rat are you? Why would you fabricate lies to incriminate me? You snivelling bastard.'

In that moment, muscles pulsing through his slim jacket, shoulders wide, Herbert was suddenly daunting.

'Mr. Marlowe is a private detective,' said Glenn, folding his arms across his chest. 'Bettina and I hired him when we found out you had dealings with a Mr. Kirschenbauer in Zurich.'

'Kirschenbauer?' laughed Farrand. 'What does he have to do with any of this? What has he said?'

'He has said nothing,' said Glenn. 'I think you're doing that for us.'

'He doesn't need to,' said Bettina. 'Your association with him was enough to rouse our suspicions. Kirschenbauer is a money launderer in eight digits. Why else would you know him?'

'Kirschenbauer is an acquaintance, nothing more,' Farrand said quickly with a weak chuckle, his eyes darting from Glenn to Spinola to the door. 'We've drunk wine together at a gallery opening one time. We barely spoke,' he said, backtracking.

'How can you lie like this?' Bettina demanded in a low, angry voice.

'Bettina,' Farrand snapped, staring at the woman who stood defiantly before him. 'Why have you involved yourself in such matters? And where is your loyalty? You have allowed yourself to be tricked by this American *Arschgeige*.'

A shot of laughter burst out of Christina, who couldn't help laugh at Herbert calling Glenn, literally, an 'arse-violin'.

'Private detectives! What next? This is a true Hollywood drama!' he added scornfully.

'How dare you say that?' Bettina demanded incredulously. 'You, who have robbed us blind! Literally, because you did so in the full assumption that we would never suspect you, that I would never see what you were up to!'

'That's rich, isn't it? Of course you wouldn't *see* what people were up to…'

The collected gasp sucked all the air out of the room.

Herbert's face was wash with the immediate regret he felt. Arms held out, he said, 'Come on! That was a joke. Bettina, look, you are mistaken, *mein Mausebär*. These men are lying! This is Tebbhurst's idea of a seduction! He simply wants to frame me to win you over. He has hired this monkey to make up lies, all to manipulate you and your ICB sisters! It's classic Hollywood!'

'I have been following you for six months, Mr. Farrand,' Marlowe spoke up, his young face etched with disdain. 'I can assure you that the only comparison to Hollywood to be made here is that of your lifestyle. You have used funds meant for the support of blind communities to buy villas, cars and apartments for you and your mistresses – your "*Mausebärs*". So yes, I have been collecting evidence, day by day, week by week, month by month. Portraits, sculptures, hot tubs, cruises, the list goes on.'

'Lies,' Farrand snapped. 'Creative lies. You're quite a comedian, aren't you, funny man?'

'Say what you like, Mr. Farrand,' shrugged Marlowe. 'It's all on the record. Try defending all of this in court. You've made some classic mistakes in covering your tracks.'

'So what?' sneered Farrand. 'You'll get nowhere with this. Do you really think the reports of a man who has breached my rights and privacy on multiple occasions will stand up in German court? You are grossly misinformed, boy. I am impressed though.'

Turning to Glenn, Farrand watched him appraisingly.

'You, Glenn, have put on quite a show. You have done very well,' he said, chuckling in a cool, unnerving way.

'Done what very well?' Glenn asked, disturbed by Farrand's sudden light humour.

'Fabricating these lies to get my six deputies on side,' said Farrand. 'What is your game, hmm? Are you trying to rob the ICB? Are you jealous of what I have built, of what I own, of a *true* fundraiser?'

With this, Farrand raised an eyebrow and looked purposefully at Bettina before looking back to Glenn. A small smile crossed his lips.

'Any man would be jealous,' he winked. 'I've seen the way you look at her.'

'How dare you!' cried Bettina, sensing that he was talking about her. 'After everything you have done, how can you talk about me like that?'

'Bettina, please, be quiet,' Farrand warned her. 'You're mixing yourself up in things you don't understand.'

'I think Ms. Hartmann understands everything perfectly,' said Spinola, standing up in an attempt at chivalry. 'You, sir, are a damn cad!'

'John, it's OK,' said Glenn gently, raising a hand to calm his friend. 'Bettina can take care of herself. It's Mr. Farrand here who needs to understand what's happening.'

'Is that so?' yelped Farrand. 'You come here, with your auditors and detectives, expecting me to believe this bullshit?'

'If you won't listen to me, listen to your colleagues,' said Glenn, flinging an arm towards the five women at the door. 'They know the truth. They have seen the evidence.'

Herbert glared at Glenn, his eyes fixed on his American nemesis. His agitation faded and a cool calm returned to his handsome face once more.

'This is quite enough,' he said, laughing lightly. 'I will not waste a second more of my life listening to your petty accusations. You have taken advantage of these six poor, beautiful creatures, from whom fate has stolen the all-seeing power of sight and perception. I will not let you blind them more than they already have been by life.'

To everyone's surprise, Odile, often demure and quiet, began to laugh. It started off as a small titter but soon turned into a roar of giggles. The sound set everyone on edge. She eventually wiped the tears from her eyes and let out a long sigh.

'Oh, Herbert,' she said, shaking her head and releasing one last laugh with a hiccup. 'You know I am the oldest here, of all your "six beautiful creatures".'

'The oldest, but by no means the least beautiful,' Herbert nodded sympathetically.

'I have seen enough of life to know its cruelties and its scars,' Odile went on. 'All the times you have visited the ICB centre in New Orleans, you have seen what I have built. You have seen how it has built me in return, allowing me to have a family once more. In return, I have dedicated so much to you. We all have. How could you be so selfish? You have ruined everything I have built, that *we* have built, and if I had my way you would pay us back every cent.'

'Odile, my dear, you are mistaken,' Farrand shook his head, smiling in a puzzled, bemused way. 'How can you have fallen for Glenn and these phonies?'

'Glenn and these "phonies" have been honest with us,' cried Laura, shaking with rage. 'Not *once* have we questioned where these millions of yours go. We simply do the work we feel privileged to be able to do. I remember when you last came to London. You tried to kiss me and I pulled away. I thought you were a gentleman, respectful of women, caring for the misfortunate in this life, but you're not. I've heard from Bettina what you've been like all these years. If you could do that to her, and to me, and all these poor women you have caged up in apartments across Europe, I have no doubt you are guilty of every crime Glenn has you pinned down for.'

'Laura!' breathed Farrand. 'How can you be so subjective at a time like this? You know my feelings for you were real, but surely you can be more level-headed than to wage false battle against me based on petty jealousy? You're worse than Glenn. I expected better from you!'

Reeling with anger, Glenn went to say something, but he was too late. Zu-Ting had already stepped forward.

'Herbert, you wretch!' she shrieked. 'Of all the dirty, raping, evil bastards I have put up with in my life, you are surely the worst. You have visited the factory in Hong Kong. You have seen what life was like for the women there who now have a second chance, you have jeopardised the comfort, safety and futures of thousands of people! Their families depend on them, and you know that.'

'I have always supported your factory girls, Zu-Ting,' Farrand protested. 'Their well-being is extremely important to me.'

'I know that all too well enough,' Zu-Ting spat bitterly. 'I didn't want to believe the rumours or hear the girls who whispered about it when they thought I was not listening. You and your sordid advances towards them! I heard it all, Herbert, but I turned the other cheek, wishfully thinking it was simply idle gossip. But now I know it all must be true. You groomed those girls for your own pleasure, every time you visited us.'

'Nonsense!' laughed Farrand. 'If they spent time with me it was because they wanted to! Dear Zu-Ting, for all your talk of equality and women's rights, you are very quick to judge the women you work with for their liberty of mind and body. Women *like* me and I like women. What more can I say?'

Zu-Ting threw herself at Farrand in a rage, but Glenn caught her just in time. He held her gently, but with force.

'Not now,' he whispered urgently in her ear. 'Not yet.'

Elfrida roared something in Spanish, a sentence of such ferocity it barely needed translation.

'We have a word for you in my country,' she said. 'But I will not invoke God's wrath by speaking it aloud here today. How do you think the children in my care will react when they learn that their school must close down, Herbert? Do you think they will be happy? No, they will go back to working on the streets, begging, propped up by their parents to earn a bit of money to put food on the table. You have reduced them to poverty and shame. Some of them might even die. This is on your conscience, and only God can save you. I pray that he leaves you to the Devil.'

'That is enough, Elfrida,' Christina said in a sage voice.

'Thank you, Christina,' said Farrand. 'I'm glad at least one of you can see sense.'

'Oh, I see sense,' said Christina. 'I have spent hours in conversation with the Lord about your behaviour and great deceits, Herbert. God is forgiving, but only to those who admit their sins and seek absolution. He does not listen to those who lie and deceive those around him.'

'Lies?' laughed Farrand. 'Oh Christina, not you too? My God, you're an intelligent woman! Surely you don't believe all of this?'

'Stop defending yourself!' Glenn heard himself shout from the depth of his lungs. The sound of his bellow silenced the room. 'Jeez, have you no shame? Just apologise or something!'

'I'm not apologising to anyone,' Farrand snarled. 'I have done *nothing* wrong.'

At this, Spinola dived into his own briefcase and drew out a balance sheet, annotated with examples of fraud. He thrust it beneath Farrand's nose.

'We have enough evidence to put you away for a very long time, old boy!' he said, his eyes narrow and sharp. 'You are a cheat, a dirty cad! Why do you deny it?'

'He will deny everything,' Marlowe shook his head in disgust.

'I will deny everything to *you*, you sneaking excuse of a man!' Farrand spat at Marlowe, a playful smile rising on his lips. 'Hanging around at my parties, spying on me! How exactly do you plan on putting me away?'

'I believe I can help there,' Heinmann spoke at last, standing up and pulling out his police badge and a piece of paper. 'I have a warrant for your arrest here, Herr. Farrand. You do not need to deny anything now. You will have your time in court to defend yourself.'

Heinmann began to read out Farrand's rights in German, taking a pair of handcuffs out of his pocket as he did so. Spotting the metal cuffs, Farrand's eyes darted across the room for the door. Finally, his cool calm dissolved. Without a word, he bolted for the door, crashing through the wall of women as he did so. With cries of panic and anger, the women turned on the man in their midst. Glenn, Marlowe, Spinola and the plain clothes policeman had already darted after him, but it seemed their help was unnecessary. Like a troop of trained policewomen, the six blind women coordinated among themselves with shouts and cries, taking Farrand down in a few swift motions. They pinned him to the ground.

'Put him to the carpet, ladies!' Bettina called above the fray.

'You think because we can't see, you can get away?' Zu-Ting demanded, thrusting a knee into Farrand's back. He cried out in pain. Heinmann knelt down beside the group and quickly cuffed Farrand's wrists together before calling for backup.

'He is secure,' the policeman nodded to the group, allowing them to stand up and extract themselves from pinning their president to the ground.

'It's over,' sighed Bettina, addressing the group, panting as she tried to recover her breath. She moved towards her colleagues and drew them all into a group hug. Glenn nodded to Heinemann. As they had requested, no policemen arrived to take Farrand away. The press could still be close by and Glenn did not want to draw any unnecessary publicity to this sad, embarrassing event. Farrand was taken to the nearest police station to be charged, leaving the women alone to comfort themselves. For a while no one spoke. They simply recovered from the shock of the evening's events.

'What now?' Odile asked at last, breaking the silence.

'Now we look to the future,' said Bettina. 'Whatever that might look like.'

'We need to look to our legal form as a charity,' said Laura. 'The ICB as it was can no longer raise funds. We will need to dissolve or risk exposure.'

'I can help with that,' said Glenn. 'I'll make available the DCF's best lawyers.'

'No,' said Bettina firmly. 'You have done enough, Glenn. You have helped us get rid of a tyrant. We can ask nothing more of you.'

'Bettina, I want to help,' he said urgently. 'The DCF wants to help.'

'I know, Glenn,' said Bettina, trembling as she spoke. 'But this is something we have to face, all six of us. You have helped us through our darkest hours. If our meeting in London showed me anything it's that among us six we have the skills and power to end what we all started together. We are so grateful to you, to John and Dylan too, but this part, this end, is something we have to work out on our own.'

'Bettina's right,' said Laura. 'We should end this together. The six of us.'

'God is with us,' said Christina. 'He sent you as a blessing, Glenn. He will not abandon us now.'

'Go home, Glenn,' said Zu-Ting, smiling sadly. 'Leave this mess and build better things with charities you already support. The DCF needs you.'

Glenn listened to all that was said and concluded, with a heavy heart, that for too long these women had dealt with a man who listened to nothing they said. He did not want to follow the pattern.

'If that's what you wish, I will respect that,' he said.

'It is,' Bettina said firmly.

'Then I guess we have a flight to catch,' said Glenn, turning to Spinola and Marlowe. Both men nodded in agreement.

'I'll walk you out,' said Bettina, putting her hand gently on Glenn's arm.

Wandering slowly through the now deserted Aachen office, Glenn was glad that Spinola and Marlowe had walked quickly ahead. He wanted nothing more than to hold Bettina in his arms, safe in the knowledge that this monstrous threat to her had been taken away. Herbert Farrand would bother her no more. They walked in silence, both reliving the adrenaline of those last moments.

'You were great back there,' Glenn said eventually, looking down at the beautiful woman beside him.

'So were you,' she said, nodding sadly.

'We make a great team, don't we?' Glenn smiled.

'Glenn,' Bettina said softly, stopping in her tracks. 'I am so grateful for everything you have done for us.'

'I told you, Bettina, I could not turn my back on you all,' he said. 'I discovered this mess. I'm just sorry this has come to pass.'

'I'm grateful also for everything you've done for me,' said Bettina. She raised a hand to feel the heart beating in his chest.

'Then let me stay,' said Glenn, gently taking her hands in his.

'I need time,' she shook her head, the familiar melancholy returning to her face. 'This has all happened so quickly. Everything is so uncertain. I don't know how to… I don't know if…'

'I understand,' said Glenn firmly. 'You need not say another word. Whenever you are ready, let me know, OK?'

She nodded and tears began to stream down her face.

'Hey,' he whispered with a smile, cupping her chin with his fingers. 'Don't let them see you cry. They need you now. Every one of them. You have to be strong for them.'

'I know,' she nodded quickly, wiping the tears away.

'Then be the woman I know you can be,' said Glenn, feeling his heart fill with pride. 'Be the woman I love.'

'Goodbye, Glenn,' she whispered.

'I'll be ready to say hello again, whenever you are,' Glenn whispered back.

Pulling her into one last passionate kiss, Glenn stood back and took in her beautiful face one last time. He studied her pretty frown and the roundness of her cheeks before letting her go. She turned away, walking quickly back to the room, where her responsibilities awaited her. Glenn walked slowly away from the chaos of that evening. Marlowe and Spinola stood by the entrance to the building, waiting for him. A taxi stood waiting to take them to the airport. It was time to go home, he thought, climbing into the seat beside his friends. How strange, then, that he felt like home was what he was leaving behind.

CHAPTER THIRTY-FOUR

That feeling of leaving something behind lingered as Glenn put down his suitcase in the hallway of his Mayfair home. If home was what he had hoped to return to, his apartment was less than convincing. The rooms felt empty and had done since the day the six blind women had visited for breakfast. Odile's warm smile, Zu-Ting's outspoken views, Laura's biting rhetoric, Christina's peaceful presence, Elfrida's fiery laughter and, of course, Bettina's gentle dreamy voice had left a vacuum that silence could not fill. Yet despite its flaws, his apartment was a peaceful space: Glenn certainly did not long for the wide halls of Ronda Round Manor and his wife's passive aggressive behaviour.

Some things were hard to escape, however. His wife's anger had found its way into his new life. Standing on the doormat, with a stream of letters and bills, stood a notification from the Beaumonts' solicitor. Eleanora had filed for divorce, deciding to, in her family solicitor's words, save him the trouble and pain of requesting it himself.

Leafing through the papers, Glenn read over the requests his wife had made with growing disdain. Glenn was not entitled to, nor should he request entitlement to, any properties on Ronda Round Manor Estate. He was requested to pay a large annual stipend for his wife's upkeep due to the fact that she had never worked. This he found laughable, considering that it had been Eleanora, not he, who had insisted on not working besides collecting rent from her tenants. Reading through the list of demands and regulations, Glenn felt the anxiety of those years of marriage return. The adrenaline rush and success of all that had happened in Aachen evaporated. But Glenn came to one important conclusion: whatever Eleanora requested, nothing could compare to the agonising loneliness of that period of his life. He would sign and accept all, he decided, then and there. He would not meet with her, nor suffer the humiliation of denying her requests.

The days following his signing of the papers were filled with conflicting emotions. It was the end of an era in his life, and he knew, over in Germany, Bettina too was facing the end of an era in her own life. Yet she had not called him. She did not need him yet, and he would respect her request for time. But the combined crises of the fall of Farrand and his divorce left Glenn feeling restless and uncomfortable in rainy, wintery London. He was distracted at work and longed for a change of scene. With the Christmas holidays approaching, there was only one place he knew he could go to for guaranteed comfort.

Arriving in New York, Glenn could not have been more grateful for his parents' welcome. The warmth of their Sutton Place home engulfed him and he felt a sense of home at last. Glenn unpacked his suitcase, taking out his winter clothes and books. His divorce papers were among them.

'They've come through, huh?' said Bertie when Glenn told his father about the divorce papers. Winter sun poured in through the windows, catching the lights on the Christmas tree. The room seemed to sparkle. Iris sat on the bed and read through the agreement.

'That woman wastes no time,' Iris tutted irritably. 'She could never wait for anything.'

'Perhaps it's better this way,' sighed Glenn. 'We needed to get this out of the way, one way or another. For once I am glad of Eleanora's impatience. Now that's over with I can focus on other things.'

'Other things, huh?' said Bertie with a knowing smile.

'Oh, leave your son alone, you old letch!' Iris scolded her husband playfully. Glenn was grateful for his mother's defence for he was not ready to talk about Bettina yet. He had other things to think about.

Glenn had arranged to spend the Christmas holidays in New York for a month. The real reason for his break away from London was to set to work on his case studies. The drama of Farrand's treachery had taken him far away from the writing process, leaving his precious notepad of stories untouched for almost one year. Glenn knew that in the vibrant, buzzing streets of New York, and the quiet comfort of his parents' home in Sutton Place, he could make real headway at last.

Hoping to find inspiration in the halls of the New York Public Library in Manhattan, Glenn headed over to Bryant Park one morning. His feet crunched through the December snow and his cheeks burned in the cold. It was a relief then to experience the warmth of those light, cosy halls inside the library. All around him, Glenn saw people studying volumes, enjoying moments of study, curiosity, happiness and discovery. When he sat down, however, the only book he longed to study was the little notebook in front of him: it was a treasure trove of experience and he was ready to start exploring.

Turning to the first page, Glenn began to re-read what he had written about Laura in that first interview:

> *Fiery and brave, this girl's story is incredible.*
> *Abandoned by mother. Adopted by farmers in Wales.*
> *Mistreatment, forced work. Bullying.*
> *Escape to London…*

Reading on through the interview with Laura, Glenn was amazed once more by her story. How could someone endure so much pain and yet emerge so strong and unscathed, he asked himself? As he wrote, he began to weave these questions into his narrative, using his enquiring external perspective to form Laura's character and place her at the heart of her story.

Working through the pages of his notebook, Glenn repeated this ritual every day for two weeks. Setting to work on the case studies took his mind far away from his divorce, and the buzzing city of New York took him far from that cold, hard day in Aachen. As he wrote he rediscovered just how instrumental Bettina had been in every one of the women's recoveries. She had given them hope where there had been none and now she had watched all that hope drain away with Farrand's squandered millions. She was a force of nature, and every word Glenn wrote about her made him feel the pain of not being near her all over again. He longed to take her in his arms and kiss her once more, but somehow savoured the distance too. To miss someone was a wild and new feeling for Glenn. To yearn for a woman's body with all his heart left him tingling with warm curiosity.

When Christmas Day arrived, Glenn was surprised to find his father and mother laughing over something in the kitchen. Wiping the sleep from his eyes, he saw that they were holding his manuscript.

'Hey,' he said, chuckling lightly. 'Where'd you get that? This is top-secret information.'

'Glenn, this is wonderful!' his mother beamed at him, taking off her reading glasses to marvel at her son. 'These stories, these women… this is a masterpiece!'

'I gotta hand it to you, Glenn,' smiled his father. 'You're a damn good writer. Your Mom's been reading me this all night long. It's like *A Christmas Carol*, but better.'

'Really?' Glenn laughed in surprise.

'Honey, it's beautiful,' Iris said softly, coming to her son and cupping his face gently in her hands. 'This is such a gentle, eloquent work about your meetings and adventures. The section on Hong Kong had your father in stitches!'

'Don't forget the cat-walking in London!' Bertie grinned.

'Then we were just so lost in the sorrows of your dear friend, Odile,' said Iris. 'I couldn't believe it. I just couldn't. She lost everything and then Bettina came…'

'Boy, this Bettina,' chuckled Bertie. 'Son, I know why you love her.'

Glenn blushed scarlet and looked away. He did not know what to say.

'You really like it?' he asked.

'The chapter about Elfrida was so painful and warm all at once,' sighed Iris. 'I could feel the hardness of Mexico but the beauty of the school, the hope those kiddies had. Oh shucks, honey! It was wonderful!'

'Son, we've been crying, laughing, remembering these past two crazy years all over again,' said Bertie, shaking his head, a proud smile fixed upon his face. 'You did it, fella! You wrote something that meant something to people like me.'

'People like you?' said Glenn.

'Folks who lost their sight,' his father said, his glazed eyes filling with tears. 'My boy, it's wonderful.'

'You guys have come so far,' said Glenn. 'I see it every time I come visit. You have adapted amazingly to this difficult situation. I'm so proud of you both.'

'We had to, honey,' said Iris, shrugging her narrow shoulders. 'Like the women in your book, we had no choice. So many people have helped us, and, luckily for us, we had a son in our corner through it all.'

'Your mother's right, fella,' Bertie nodded. 'Your optimism and faith has been there from the start. You're one hell of a man.'

Swallowing hard, Glenn could barely believe what he was hearing. Had he not gone to Aachen all those years ago, to the conference where he had met Bettina, Odile, Elfrida, Zu-Ting, Laura and Christina, to learn more for his father? Had a part of him not wanted to listen to their stories to know better how to help him? His journey, it seemed, had come full circle. For the rest of the holidays, Glenn picked over the manuscript with his parents, highlighting problem areas and asking their advice.

Working hard on his writing cast Bettina far from his mind. He still had not heard from her, not even Christmas wishes. Respecting her wishes, he did not contact her either. Over the New Year he made great progress, but he still felt the case studies were far from finished. His parents, however, had other ideas.

'You get this ready by next week,' said Bertie, raising a knowing finger. 'We're taking it to a friend of mine. He works in publishing. He'll set you up for the Pulitzer, baby!'

'Dad, this isn't a novel,' Glenn laughed at his father's words. 'This is a collection of stories to be used for fundraising purposes. These stories are personal and were told in strict confidence. I can't just share them around like that.'

'Other people need to feel what I feel!' Bertie protested. 'You could change lives with a book like this, Glenn! Tell him, Iris!'

'That is my intention, Dad, believe me,' said Glenn. 'But I can do that better by showing this to the board at the DCF. With this documentation I can show them what these women are capable of, what Bettina is capable of, in the hope that they will see what I see: great potential. Then these women can continue to work and change lives. They can move out of the shadow Farrand has cast over their charity.'

'Alright, alright! But look, what if I change the names?' said Bertie. 'Leave me a copy of this and let me write it up into something I can show Marty! Call it a father-son collaboration.'

'Who is Marty?' Glenn asked.

'Marty, my friend in marketing!' said Bertie with excitement. 'He works in some publishing house in the Bronx.'

'Are you offering to be my ghost writer, Dad?' Glenn laughed at his father's industriousness.

'Sure,' laughed Bertie. 'We'll split the profits! Better still, we'll give all the proceeds to your blind ladies!'

'Mom, can you talk him out of this madness?' Glenn turned to his mother for sanity.

'You know as well as I do that once your father has an idea in his head, there's no stopping him,' she sighed with a small smile. 'Best let him do his thing, Glenn. Maybe he'll make you proud. Besides, it will give him a chance to try out all his new machines.'

'I just dictate to them and they type!' Bertie cried in delight. 'Send me a digital copy, son, so my machines can read the script to me again. I can add in a few things for spice. We can cast Eleanora as a witch or something. She could be Kirschenbauer's evil mistress? How about that? They elope to Switzerland!'

'Dad!' Glenn scolded his father, though in truth he was just happy that Bertie could not see his smile.

'Come on, she screwed you over with that divorce!' Bertie chuckled, a wicked grin on his face.

Glenn left his father's proposal open-ended. There was nothing he could do if his father had an idea in his head, and besides, he was due to return to London for the start of the year. His manuscript was at last ready for presentation to the DCF board. He forwarded it over to them from New York and, saying a warm goodbye to his parents a few days later, set off for London, ready to see what the new year would bring.

To his surprise, Glenn did not have to wait long. When he arrived back to Mayfair, a message lay waiting for him on his answering machine.

'Glenn, we've read your script,' came Florence Valon's voice. 'Come and talk to us on Monday. We're really excited about this.'

Glenn's heart leapt and fell in quick succession as he heard the Secretary of the Board's message. It sounded extremely positive, a sure sign of engagement from his senior colleagues. But now Glenn would have to describe the difficult situation the ICB had found itself in. He wondered how sympathetic his senior colleagues would be to the tragedy of Farrand's fraud.

Glenn's return to the office was somewhat marred by this anticipation. He trudged through rainy London with a worried heart, sidestepping irritated commuters as he went.

'Welcome back, sir,' his secretary greeted him with her usual warmth.

'Hi Sonia, how were the holidays?' he smiled to her, hanging up his coat.

'Wonderful, sir,' said Sonia. 'How was New York?'

'Pretty wonderful too,' said Glenn, smiling. 'My parents are crazy, but what's new?'

'Indeed, sir. This came for you by the way,' said Sonia. 'It arrived before Christmas.'

The secretary had reached into a pile of post awaiting Glenn and pulled out a neatly typed envelope, postmarked Aachen. Thanking his secretary, and asking her to order him a coffee from Amelia, Glenn retreated into his office with the precious cargo. Sitting down, he slit open the envelope:

Dear Glenn,

Wishing you a very Happy Christmas, and a new year full of all you hope for. Though this past year has been so hard, I have enjoyed getting to know you. I look forward to seeing you in the new year.

Thanks again for everything,

With love,
Bettina

Glenn's heart leapt at the sight of her love, there in print. His hand jumped instinctively to the phone to call through to Germany. This was the sign he had been waiting for: the end of Bettina's silence. But before he could pick up the receiver, it started to ring.

'They are ready for you upstairs, Mr. Tebbhurst,' came Sonia's cheerful announcement. 'Ms. Valon and the others have prepared an agenda.'

'Right, thanks,' he said quickly, sobering himself for the meeting ahead. His call to Bettina would have to wait.

When Glenn arrived in the board room, the familiar set of faces were there to meet him. Florence Valon was already chatting away to Derek Scott, Nick Davis, and Chris Hodges. Four copies of his manuscript could be spotted between them, all heavily thumbed.

'Ah, Glenn!' cried Scott. 'Here's our Mark Twain!'

'Fantastic work, Glenn,' nodded Davis appreciatively.

'There was a real majesty to your writing, Glenn,' said Hodges, frowning pensively. 'A true craftsmanship.'

'Hello, Glenn, come in,' Florence smiled warmly. 'As you can probably tell, we have all read your manuscript.'

'Do I detect positive reviews?' Glenn grinned hopefully at the Secretary of the Board. She nodded with a broad smile on her face.

'We are very impressed with these case studies,' she said. 'This provides us with excellent material for donors. These women have suffered, recovered and contributed to communities across the globe, against the odds. After the unfortunate events of last year...'

'The tragedy,' Davis shook his head.

'Mr. James,' Glenn said quietly. The name still created a pang of guilt in his heart.

'Yes,' sighed Florence. 'I would even suggest we use his as a case study too. He has made a remarkable recovery.'

'That's a great idea,' said Glenn. 'I'll look into it.'

'Well then, we are fully ready to seek donor funding for the ICB, in partnership with the DCF,' the Secretary of the Board announced cheerfully.

'Yes, about that,' Glenn sighed and began to explain in a slow, heavy voice. There was no way to hide Farrand's foul play. Slowly, he recounted all that had come pass, sparing them no details.

'Aha, you forgot to include that unfortunate epilogue,' said Scott, raising an eyebrow. 'Such a shame. What a devil.'

'But what does it matter?' said Davis, leaning back in his seat. 'So we can't support the charity. Let's support these women.'

Glenn's heart leapt at Davis' words.

'What are their plans?' Florence asked Glenn.

'Their plans?'

'Yes,' she said, a puzzled expression forming on her brow. 'Surely these women are not going to give up, just like that?'

'They'll have to reform and create something new,' shrugged Scott. 'But that's easily done.'

'So you're telling me that if Bettina starts again, with a new charity, you'll fundraise for her projects?' Glenn asked, not daring to believe the words he had just spoken.

'Outreach of this quality is hard to find,' said Florence firmly. 'These women have exceptional profiles for fundraising. We can use their stories, the stories you have collected, to support them.'

'We could even publish this,' said Hodges, slapping his hand down on the manuscript. 'It's an excellent piece of writing.'

'I'm afraid someone else has already offered,' laughed Glenn, remembering his father's ideas. 'I can't believe I'm hearing this. Of all the outcomes I could have expected from this meeting today, this was only in my wildest dreams! I can't wait to tell Bettina.'

'That would be helpful at this stage,' said Florence with business-like snappiness. 'Why don't you find out about Ms. Hartmann's next steps?'

Glenn nodded, utterly speechless. As the board members began to discuss the stories in his manuscript at greater depth amongst themselves,

Glenn drifted into a daydream. He began to imagine Bettina's face as he told her the news. He saw the tears rolling down her cheeks and felt the warmth of her embrace as she threw her arms around him.

As soon as he could leave the meeting, Glenn raced down to Sonia's office with instructions to book him onto the next flight to Frankfurt.

'Today, sir?' she asked, astonished by his sudden reappearance. 'But you only just came back?'

'Today, Sonia!' Glenn urged her. 'Now, this afternoon, as quickly as possible! I'm going to the airport!'

Dashing back to his apartment, Glenn threw clothes into a suitcase and headed to Heathrow. Sonia had emailed him through his ticket, and with growing anticipation he waited for his flight to Frankfurt. Time passed painfully slowly until his flight was announced but then, as he boarded the flight, buckled up, and set off for Germany, it seemed to be running too quickly. Glenn suddenly panicked, his conscious mind catching up with him, bringing about a sudden realisation. He was going to see Bettina again.

CHAPTER THIRTY-FIVE

As soon as he landed, Glenn jumped into a taxi and headed straight for the ICB's Frankfurt office. The sounds, sights and smells of Frankfurt filled him with a thrill that neither New York nor London could compete with. Bettina was there and nothing, no landmark, culture or buildings could compete with the simple power she gave a place, Glenn thought. It wasn't until he reached the empty, sad building that he realised the ICB office would no longer be there.

Stepping out onto the street, Glenn saw how the big sign, which had once proudly announced the charity's name to the world, had been torn down. A German sign from what looked like an estate agent stood outside. Of course, Glenn thought, his heart sinking. Bettina would not be here anymore. Wandering along to the café they had shared a coffee in once before, Glenn dialled through to her. The phone rang for what felt like an eternity until eventually a familiar voice answered.

'Hallo, Bettina Hartmann?' she said in rapid German.

'Hi,' said Glenn, suddenly nervous at the sound of her name. 'It's me.'

'Glenn,' she said in surprise. 'I've been wondering when you were going to call. I haven't heard from you in a while.'

'I know, I'm sorry,' Glenn said quickly. 'I was in the States and I only picked up your card this morning. I wanted to call or write but I didn't know if you were ready. Like I said, I'll be ready whenever you are.'

'I understand,' she said gently. 'It's OK. Things were, well, complicated back there. That night was so tough. These weeks have been really hard. Everything's gone, Glenn. Everything.'

Glenn was sad to hear the familiar melancholy in Bettina's voice. He did not want to remind her of heavy moments.

'How are you?' he asked.

'That's a dangerous question,' she answered with a small, bitter laugh. 'Let's talk about you. How are you, Glenn? Are you back in London now?'

'No,' he said, grinning up at the grey January sky. 'I'm in Frankfurt. I thought you would be here at the office but, of course, the office doesn't exist anymore. Where are you?'

'You're in Germany?' she asked, her voice brightening. 'Oh Glenn! Well, I'm in Wurzburg of course! I have just spent the Christmas holidays with my parents. I'm at their house.'

'Ah,' said Glenn. 'I'm sorry to disturb you, truly. I needed to see you so I flew over this afternoon. I have something to tell you.'

'Disturb me?' laughed Bettina. 'Glenn, how could you ever think that? Can you catch a train? We are just one hour from Frankfurt.'

'I can,' smiled Glenn. 'But Bettina, are you sure? You're with your family.'

'Which is why I am asking you to come,' she said warmly. 'You are so welcome here. I want you to meet them. I will ask my brother to pick you up from the station. There is a train on the hour, every hour. Take the next one, OK?'

Glenn agreed to take the next train, hurrying across Frankfurt to catch it on time. As the train pulled out of the station, he listened happily to German people around him chatting to one another. A family with small children laughed together, enjoying the last few days of the holidays before school started once more. Glenn wondered what Bettina's family would be like. His previous experience of greeting families in a relationship setting was riddled with impending battle. Glenn thought of the Beaumonts and their condescending, haughty stares. Spending time with Eleanora's parents had never been fun. His nerves began to prickle as he anticipated arriving at the family home he had once seen in a photograph.

When he arrived in Wurzburg, Glenn was happy to spot Bettina stood waiting for him on the platform. A tall, blonde man stood next to her, sporting an uncanny likeness to his sister.

'Bettina!' Glenn called cheerfully as he approached the couple. 'Happy New Year!'

'Glenn!' she smiled slowly. 'I can't believe you're here. Please let me introduce you to my brother, Heiner.'

Heiner was a handsome young man with his sister's sparkling blue eyes. He looked kindly on the embracing couple.

'It is a pleasure to meet you at last,' he spoke in crisp, clear English. 'My sister has told me so much about you.'

'I've heard a few things about you too,' Glenn grinned, taking the strong handshake that was offered. 'You're a doctor, right?'

'Yes, we have lots to talk about,' Heiner smiled in welcome. 'Come on, it's cold. The car is just here. I'm driving.'

Glenn followed Bettina and her brother back to their small, red car, feeling surreally content in the this new, strange city. He sat back and enjoyed the small tour Heiner gave them, marvelling at the landmarks and quaint buildings.

'This is such an antiquarian city,' he smiled.

'Ja, Wurzburg celebrated its one thousandth and three hundredth birthday in 2004,' smiled Heiner.

'The university is one of the oldest in Germany,' said Bettina.

'That's where your parents work, right?' said Glenn.

'You have a good memory,' she grinned.

Glenn listened to everything the Hartmanns told him about their home city. He especially enjoyed all the stories Bettina shared of their adventures there as children. It seemed there was not a corner of Wurzburg that Heiner and Bettina had not made mischief in. They drove slowly out of the town towards the neighbouring countryside.

'Your house,' Glenn exclaimed as he saw the house from the photograph appear beside a small country road.

'Yes,' grinned Bettina. 'Do you recognise it?'

'I do,' said Glenn. He also recognised the woman who had just stepped out onto the doorstep. A woman with silver hair and the same round, rosy cheeks as her daughter stood waiting to welcome them. When Glenn stepped out to meet Bettina's mother, he was charmed by her heavy German accent.

'What a wonderful surprise, Glenn,' she said with a big smile. 'We have been so looking forward to meeting you one of these days. You have done so much for our daughter. Come in, come, my husband is cooking! My name is Marta.'

Glenn thanked Marta and walked into a house bursting full with charm and the smells of spiced fruit. Decorations from the holiday season were still twinkling and tinkling across the old wooden beams of the ceilings. Glenn listened with great interest as Bettina's mother told him how the house was converted from a farm, and since her and her husband's retirement from university, had become something of an ongoing renovation project for them.

Bettina's father stood chopping up vegetables for salad in the kitchen. The delicious, warming smell of freshly cooking pretzels filled the room. He was as tall as his son, and shared Bettina's fine, intelligent forehead. Striding forward, he welcomed Glenn with a firm handshake, inviting him to come and warm up by the kitchen stove.

'Tell me, Glenn, what do you know about Bavarian food?' Bettina's father, Fritz, asked his guest.

'I know I might be lucky enough to eat some *Weisswurst* tonight,' Glenn smiled, remembering the famous white sausage of southern Germany. To his surprise, the whole family burst out laughing.

'Oh, don't be hard on him!' Bettina chuckled. 'He is a foreigner.'

'We know that now,' smiled Marta.

'Huh?' yelped Glenn. 'Did I say something wrong?'

'There are rules we have about *Weisswurst*, Glenn,' Heiner explained gently. 'For example, we never eat this sausage after twelve p.m.'

'Why?' Glenn asked.

'It's a long-standing rule,' Bettina explained. 'The *Weisswurst* was first invented back in the 1800s, by Bavarians in Munich. In those days, refrigerators did not exist so any meat had to be eaten quickly. There was no way to preserve fresh sausage, so if it was not eaten quickly, people could get food poisoning. For this reason, they made a rule: no *Wurst* after midday!'

'That's fascinating,' grinned Glenn. 'Are there any other rules I should know about before I make a fool of myself again?'

'How could you have known?' Bettina groaned sympathetically.

'You should also never eat *Weisswurst* with potatoes or vegetables,' said Marta. 'Only with pretzels. A bread roll is also fine.'

'One must never eat *Weisswurst* with a knife and fork, only with your hands!' Heiner added. 'Dipped in delicious sweet mustard.'

'Well then, I'll look forward to trying that someday,' smiled Glenn. For hours, the family made Glenn feel at home in their house in the country. They ate a delicious dinner, forcing Glenn to taste every meat, dumpling, pretzel, cheese and special cake from the region, before collapsing into comfortable rounds of coffee. The sky had blackened into thick darkness beyond the window.

'I've made up a room for you,' Marta told Glenn as she served him another cup. 'You can stay with us for as long as you like.'

'Thank you, Marta, that's very kind,' smiled Glenn. He looked over to see Bettina blushing slightly, and remembered why he was there. 'In fact, I wonder if I can ask Bettina to take a small walk with me? I have some news to share with her.'

'Of course,' said Fritz, her father. 'Heiner and I need to tackle the dishes and Marta has some work to do on her new book. Thank God you are here to entertain our daughter!'

'Bettina, won't you take Glenn to see the stars?' said her mother. 'I am sure it will be so beautiful out in the snow. It is a clear night.'

'With pleasure,' Bettina smiled. 'I'll give Glenn a pair of Heiner's wellington boots.'

Glenn laughed as he pulled on the thick rubber boots and followed Bettina out into the cold, crisp night. The air was so quiet and clear there. Glenn felt the briskness alerting his senses after the long journey and the sleepy evening of eating and drinking.

'Your family are great,' Glenn said as they walked side by side along an old farm track. The snow crunched eagerly beneath their boots.

'They seem to like you too,' smiled Bettina. 'I'm sorry if my father asked too many questions. He's a psychologist. He is totally fascinated by the world and everyone in it.'

'He sounds like you,' Glenn chuckled. Slowly, he reached out to take her hand, gave it a quick squeeze and dropped it again. 'So, tell me. How are you?'

'Fine,' she said, nodding quickly.

'Bettina,' Glenn said gently. 'How are you, really? I saw the office in Frankfurt. Well, what used to be the office. You said everything was gone?'

'Dissolved,' sighed Bettina. 'The ICB has been dissolved. It doesn't exist anymore. We have ended the leases for all offices in an attempt to reduce expenses and pay off the charity's debts.'

'That can't have been easy,' said Glenn, feeling the struggle in her words.

'What else could we do?' Bettina shrugged, a dark cloud of anger washing over her face. 'I can't help but wonder if it was all worth it now...'

'If what was worth it?' asked Glenn.

'Getting Herbert arrested,' she said bitterly. 'We brought him to justice but at the expense of losing the charity. He took everything and now we've lost all that was left.'

'It was a tough call,' Glenn nodded. 'But now that call has been made, you can't look back, Bettina. You did the right thing.'

'Did I? Because I can't look forward either,' she whispered, tears suddenly brimming in her ears. 'Oh Glenn, I've tried to be strong. I've tried to keep it together for the others, for my parents, for Christina. But I'm not sure how to come to terms with this loss. Everything I've worked for has disappeared. It has vanished, like this snow on the ground will vanish in days to come. It was all for nothing.'

'That's simply not true,' Glenn shook his head. 'Listen, Bettina. Everything you have done up until this point has mattered. It has made a huge difference in so many people's lives. You don't have to stop. That's why I'm here today.'

'I don't understand,' she said, blinking away her tears.

Glenn stopped and turned to her, reaching out to take her hands in his.

'Do you remember the case studies I've been writing?' he asked her.

'About the six of us?' she asked, with a small hiccup.

'Exactly,' said Glenn. 'Since I left you in Aachen I've been working on them. I finished what I started and sent it to the board at the DCF. What's more, my father is trying to publish them in New York! I'm not so sure about that, but the board in London were so impressed by the stories you women had to tell. They have agreed to unconditionally sponsor any new charity project you set out to establish.'

'What?' breathed Bettina.

'They told me just this morning,' he laughed. 'I jumped on a plane as soon as I could!'

'But, Glenn, I don't have a charity to be sponsored,' she stammered.

'Not yet,' Glenn grinned.

'You mean...?' she began.

'Maybe it's time to build a new charity,' Glenn nodded. 'With you at the head, its president, CEO, founder, whatever you like.'

Glenn watched as a light returned to Bettina's eyes. The glow of hope moved across her face.

'A new ICB,' she whispered.

'A new charity for the blind,' Glenn nodded. 'Your charity. I've been sent here to ask if you could consider doing this. Do you think you could do this?'

'Of course I could!' she laughed. 'But Glenn, what? Why? How? How have you done this?'

'I've done nothing,' he laughed. 'All I did was tell your story. This is your story, Bettina. In every tale of misfortune those five other women told, you were the common denominator. You were the magic that bound their recoveries together, not the ICB.'

'But president?' she murmured, a frown revealing her racing mind. 'Glenn, I'll want to spend most of my time on the actual work and outreach of the charity. I won't be a traditional partner. You know that, don't you?'

She said this last part with such conviction that Glenn had to smile.

'I don't think you would *ever* be a traditional partner,' he chuckled. 'And that's totally fine.'

'You came all this way just to tell me this?' Bettina asked, raising a hand to his face.

'Not just this,' said Glenn. He swallowed hard and hoped for courage. 'Bettina, I came here to show you my loyalty too. My wife and I, well, we're going through a divorce.'

'Oh Glenn,' she sighed, shaking her head sadly. 'I'm so sorry.'

'Well, I'm not,' said Glenn firmly. 'I've waited my whole life to meet someone I can actually live with. Someone I can dream with. That was never her.'

'Well then, it's a new start for you,' Bettina said shyly. The strange melancholic look came over her face and Glenn wondered if she had even the slightest inkling of why he had travelled across Europe that day.

'I've signed the papers, now I'm free,' he said slowly. 'I wanted you to know that. I want you to know that I love you – that I offer myself to you. I give you my heart. It's yours.'

Bettina was silent for a moment. All around the quiet of the landscape seemed to wrap them in a cocoon. The stars above twinkled expressively, as if listening to their every word.

'I wish you could see the stars,' Glenn said, laughing as he shook his head. 'They're watching me and telling me I'll be a damn fool if I don't do what I gotta do now.'

Taking Bettina's hands in his, Glenn sunk to one knee.

'Bettina Hartmann,' he said, so loudly it would have echoed if there was anything around them. But there was only snow, freezing and soft beneath him. 'Jeez, it's cold!'

'Glenn! What are you doing?' Bettina gasped. 'Stand up, you'll freeze!'

'You'd never marry me if I stood there and just asked,' Glenn laughed. 'I'd lay down on the ground and die for you, Bettina. Don't you know that? Don't you know I love you to pieces?'

'Glenn,' she said, shaking her head, smiling but also frowning. 'Wait.'

'Will you marry me?' he asked her. 'I swear the stars will go out if you turn me down!'

Again, Bettina said nothing. Glenn waited, and slowly rose to his feet once more. He waited patiently for her to speak.

'You offer me your heart, Glenn,' she said softly, shaking her head. 'But your heart is wherever you are. Right now, I'm in Germany and you live in England. I think you already know my feelings towards you. I love you. I love you so much it hurts!'

'That's all I need to know,' Glenn whispered, drawing close and wiping tears that from her rosy cheeks.

'But I cannot be with someone in this way,' she said, swallowing hard. 'I cannot live my life in Germany, when the man I love is so far from me.'

'You wouldn't have to,' he said.

'What do you mean?' she asked.

'Would you reconsider if I was here with you in Germany?' Glenn asked, determined now to knock down any obstacles that stood between him and Bettina being together. He had come too far; he was too sure of how he felt. He would not leave her again without an answer. Glenn felt as if his life depended on it.

'But Glenn, your job,' she said. 'Your apartment in London. You have a life there.'

'I have half a life there,' he corrected her. 'The other half is with you. Tell me the word and I will be here, by your side.'

'I don't know if I can ask that,' Bettina shook her head unhappily. 'You've already done so much for me.'

'Let me worry about the logistics,' laughed Glenn. 'The truth is, Bettina, I have given a great number of years to the DCF. Ever since I started visiting your five other colleagues around the world, looking at their projects, hearing their stories of personal development, I have resented returning to that office in London. It feels more and more disconnected from the work we support across the world. Did you know I studied International Relations? That side of me is lost in an office in Cheapside. I've been thinking for a while now about consulting, on a freelance basis, and I can do that from anywhere. Why not Frankfurt, Berlin, or even Wurzburg?'

'But Glenn, are you sure?' she asked him. 'This is such a huge step—'

'The only thing I'm sure of right now is you, Bettina,' he interrupted, astounded by the clarity with which he could express his deepest feelings. He watched her as she shook her head slowly, fresh tears falling down her rosy cheeks. She began to laugh, a beautiful sound.

'I can't believe this is happening,' she said. 'In one day, you turn my life around. You give me back my dream, and you offer me your love. I don't know if I deserve it!'

Glenn smiled and pulled her towards him and kissed her passionately.

'Who does that sound like to me?' he asked, drawing away but keeping his hands wrapped around her cheeks. 'Who is the woman who gave these days to Odile, Elfrida, Laura, Zu-Ting, and Christina? How can you, of all people, not deserve happiness?'

Bettina, misty-eyed, buried her face in Glenn's coat as she sobbed uncontrollably. The emotion of the moment had carried her far away. Glenn hushed her, feeling his heart ache at the sounds of her distress. Slowly, her tears subsiding, Bettina wiped her cheeks. She shook her head and to Glenn's surprise, a small smile rose on her lips.

'You'll come to Germany?' she said in a small voice. 'You'll really come to Germany? Not just for visits, but to stay?'

'Well, I do have one condition,' he said, drawing her closer to him.

'What's that?' she asked.

'That you will let me love you, every inch of you, every second of every day,' he said, pulling her into his embrace. 'That when you're sad, you'll let me comfort you. You'll let me be your rock, your champion, your best friend. That when you're happy you'll smile at me and let me try to make you smile more and more with every passing day.'

Bettina let out something between a laugh and a choking cry. For a moment she said nothing, simply tracing the lines of Glenn's shoulders with her gloved fingers.

'If you move to Germany,' she said. 'And if everything you say about the DCF sponsoring my new charity is true, I'll consider anything.'

'Is that a yes?' he asked.

'Yes,' she laughed, swallowing hard. 'Yes is my answer.'

Kissing his fiancé, Glenn felt the earth move beneath him. He felt like a man reborn, enlightened and blessed with good fortune. As the darkness crept around them, Bettina led Glenn back to the house, where the others had already gone to bed. She led him upstairs, pausing at the guestroom only to pull the door shut. Glenn's body danced with excitement as she walked two doors further, to her room, and pulled him inside. Within seconds they had undressed each other and stood naked, shivering by the bed. Glenn's skin tingled to ecstasy as Bettina traced her fingers over every inch of him, pressing, pulling, teasing and probing the depths of his muscles. He too closed his eyes, tearing them away from the beautiful body in front of him to share in the sensuality of making love without sight. His hands reached out and felt flesh in a way he never had before. It was, without doubt, the most erotic experience of his life.

CHAPTER THIRTY-SIX

The sweeping landscape of the Alps bordering Germany and Austria stretched out before them as Glenn and Bettina drove south from Frankfurt. Glenn looked over to see Bettina sitting pensively as he described all he saw. That was their favourite travelling activity: Glenn describing the world around them as Bettina listened. Glenn could hardly believe it was now two years since their first road trip together, from Frankfurt to the Black Forest. He still found it difficult to believe he and Bettina were getting married. It had been one year now. He had never been happier.

Living in Germany with Bettina, as Glenn had promised he would, was a pleasure beyond anything he could have imagined. In a cottage just outside Frankfurt, the couple enjoyed the peace of the countryside as much as they enjoyed the proximity to the city. With Glenn's assistance, Bettina had set up her new charity in her beloved Frankfurt, far enough away from the former ICB building, but close enough to not confuse previous beneficiaries. After some deliberation, she came to a decision on a name.

'*Sight Plus*,' she had beamed at Glenn, taking his hand in hers and kissing it. 'What do you think?'

'It's perfect,' he said.

Both Glenn and Bettina had been surprised by how supportive the previous sponsors and beneficiaries of the ICB had been. The news of Herbert Farrand's trial had been published across Germany, attracting a lot of sympathy for the charity. The German justice system, to everyone's relief, had not been forgiving; Farrand's fraud had created a media storm around him, and he was to be made an example of. His trial concluded with a long jail sentence. The repercussions Bettina feared had been minimal, and the ICB, though forced to dissolve, gained support from Germans far and wide. Many were quick to support the young Ms. Hartmann and her

American fiancé in their endeavours to launch a new project with funds from the internationally respected Diversified Charities Foundation.

Glenn's withdrawal from the DCF office had been well-received by his colleagues in London. The board understood his need to be more hands-on with projects he fundraised for, and admitted that his talents and abilities were not used to their full potential in the office.

'Some men spend their whole lives aspiring to sit behind a desk like yours, you know,' Florence Valon sighed as she countersigned Glenn's new freelance consulting agreement. 'Are you sure you want to do this? There's no going back.'

'Positive,' Glenn grinned. 'The truth is, Florence, this job might be some man's dream, but it was never my dream. I'm wasted cooped up in here. Some men just need to spread their wings and do what they do. I won't disappoint you, I promise.'

'Alright, Tebbhurst,' Valon smiled exasperatedly. 'You take care now.'

Glenn's promise to Florence Valon and the DCF was to pursue different missions and projects on a freelance basis. One of those agreements would be to support Bettina in the early days of the Sight Plus Foundation by fundraising for her in Germany, on a project-by-project basis. Within a few months of leaving London, Glenn had secured funding for Odile, Elfrida, Laura, Christina and Zu-Ting's work overseas, allowing the five women to work once more in their respective communities. The loyalty of subscribers and donors to the former ICB had been remarkable, allowing Bettina to rally support for her new charity and quickly set up her Frankfurt office. With a full year having lapsed, Glenn was keen to see their five friends again and hear how their projects were going. How wonderful that all five would be waiting for them up in the mountains overhanging the Bavarian town of Garmisch-Partenkirchen, he thought.

'Are you nervous?' Bettina asked him, interpreting his pensive silence as fear of the events to come.

'Nervous?' he laughed. 'Of what?'

'Of getting married,' said Bettina.

Glenn looked over to see Bettina staring steadily ahead. It had been her idea to get married in the borders of Austria and Germany, in the small town she had skied in as a child. She was dressed up in blue woollen warmth and her blonde hair glowed slightly against the fading daylight beyond the window.

'Darling girl,' he said, raising a hand to softly brush her cheek. 'Marrying you is the best gift this life has given me. I could never be nervous about that.'

'Are you sure we shouldn't have invited your parents?' she asked.

'No,' Glenn laughed, shaking his head. 'It's a lot to ask of them, coming over from New York. Anyway, Dad is way too busy with his new "Glow in the Dark" project. Besides, I'd prefer it to just be us and our friends.'

'It will be lovely to just have the girls around,' Bettina smiled. 'Finally, a good reason to have a reunion!'

As their car wound deeper into the mountains, Glenn thought of the last time they had all been together – that had been when cornering Farrand in the marketing office. Glenn was glad now they could all meet again, and what better way than to celebrate the love between their new president and her chosen husband?

Arriving at the chalet, a few hundred metres down a private snowy track, Glenn stepped out of the car to gaze in awe at the surrounding landscape. Mountain faces and sloping hills of snow rose around them. Twinkling flakes were falling onto the roof and Glenn was glad to see the glow of a small wood-fire through the window that was already burning. A sharp spire in the distance showed that the church and town hall where they would marry the next day was, as Bettina promised, within walking distance.

'It looks like we'll have a white wedding,' he grinned at his fiancée, taking in the deep, soft snow all around.

When Glenn had carried all of their bags into the chalet, and set the kettle to boil on the stove, he found Bettina sitting down on the soft, sheepskin rug by the crackling log fire. Her face was highlighted by dancing flames of light. Slipping down beside her, he took her in his arms and began to stroke her gently.

'I can't believe we're here,' he said, smiling down at the woman he would soon call his wife.

'It's perfect,' said Bettina. 'The place has a great energy. It feels surreal to be here with you. Are you ready for take two?'

'Of marriage?' Glenn said, surprised by the question. Bettina nodded.

'You've done it once before,' she said. 'It didn't work out so well. I would understand if you had some reservations.'

'No,' Glenn shook his head. 'Deep down I think both Eleanora and I knew we were worlds apart. Our lives never really touched. With you, I can't wait to see what we can build together, between us, and in the wider world.'

Lost in their dreams of the future and the pleasure of the present, Glenn and Bettina cherished their last night together alone in the wilderness of the mountains.

Knowing that the only wedding guests, their five friends from London, Acapulco, Frankfurt, Hong Kong and New Orleans, would be arriving the next day, the couple collapsed into each other and made love by firelight.

The next morning, after a delicious breakfast prepared by the chalet girl, a young German woman called Anna, Glenn and Bettina prepared for their wedding. Snowflakes had left blankets of pristine white all around the wooden building, glittering in the sunshine like a million stars. Anna's father had risen early to dig a path down to the village for them, and Glenn watched his last few shovels as he waited nervously in his smart black suit for Laura to arrive and Bettina to come downstairs. Soon enough the young British woman could be seen stomping up the path towards the chalet. Glenn greeted her quickly before hurrying her upstairs to help Bettina with her dress.

'We'll catch up later,' he said. 'There's not much time!'

'Don't worry, Glenn!' Laura called back to him as she climbed the creaky, wooden steps, her red hair streaming behind her. 'Everyone is at the church, everything is prepared. We just need to get Bettina and you down there pronto!'

'I'm ready when you are,' Glenn called back. To his surprise, he did not have to wait long. Creaks on the stairs announced his bride's arrival, and when he saw her in her dress for the first time, Glenn's jaw dropped.

'Wow,' he breathed. He knew Bettina had heard him, for she let out a small, nervous giggle. She wore a pale blue dress, so pale it was almost white, and her bright blonde hair was twisted into perfect curls, tucked behind plaits. White jasmine flowers could be spotted at her breast, her wrists, and on the trails of her dress. A soft ermine shawl hugged her shoulders and her cheeks were rosy with excitement.

'Ready?' she asked him in a small voice as he took her hands in his.

'Oh yes,' he laughed.

Slowly they began to make their way down the snowy path towards the town, where they knew Christina would be preparing the church for a wedding. Glenn could not have hoped for a more picturesque setting for the start of their marriage. The mountains were welcome wedding guests, looming beautifully all around.

Sure enough, when they reached the central place where the church stood, coated in snow, three familiar faces could be seen awaiting them, all dressed in ski suits. Elfrida, dressed in a bright-red suit, stood next to Zu-Ting, who wore her classic Korean silk over black ski trousers. Odile held a small bouquet of flowers, as orange as the one-piece suit she wore, which she handed to Bettina when they arrived.

'Oh, what a beautiful bride!' she laughed as she ran her hands over Bettina's face, then the ermine at her neck, and the soft material of the blue on her arms.

'Glenn, Bettina!' Zu-Ting squealed, throwing her arms around them both. 'What a great day for humanity.'

'A match made in heaven,' Elfrida smiled, tears brimming her eyes as she took their hands in hers. 'Christina is waiting for you at the altar.'

Glenn was not religious, and nor was Bettina, but Christina had insisted on giving her friends a church wedding. They would register their union at the town hall afterwards. Stepping into the warm, low light, Glenn grinned as the bridal march began to play on an ancient organ. Their friends followed them in and served as the witnesses to their marriage, first in the church, and then with the registrar at the town hall. Bettina went through every step with a beautiful, quiet smile on her face, clearly absorbing every sensation the day offered.

Retiring to the chalet for a lunch of cold meats, cheeses and a delicious spread of German pastries, the happily married couple enjoyed the company of their closest friends as they ate their first meal as man and wife. Merry laughter and an abundance of hot, spiced wine flowed, filling their little wooden chalet with the quintessential delights of life: friendship, love and happiness.

'Oh dear, Christina has found the *Apfelwein*,' giggled Zu-Ting.

'What's that?' Glenn asked, noticing how Christina was swaying slightly and laughing louder than usual.

'It's a kind of cider they make in this region,' Bettina whispered in his ear. 'Christina goes wild for it!'

Glenn chuckled, looking around at the six women in the room. The fire crackled in the corner as they chatted to each other, reflecting on the day, the year, and, eventually the fall of Herbert Farrand.

'I'll never forget the way we took him down,' Elfrida said, smiling wickedly at the memory. 'He did not expect that, the foolish son of a...'

Elfrida's sentence trailed off into Spanish, and Glenn suspected the English translation would have been quite shocking.

'He can rot in jail for all I care,' Odile sighed bitterly. 'Good riddance, that's all I have to say.'

'Let's not waste this precious time together discussing Herbert,' said Glenn, raising his hands as if to stop Farrand's spirit from entering the room. 'I want to know what you've all been up to since Sight Plus gave you back your lives!'

The room burst into whoops and applause.

'Thank God for you, Bettina!' Christina called merrily from the top of her bottle, swallowing a small hiccup. 'If it wasn't for you, I wouldn't have been able to set up my orphanage in St. Gallen.'

'So it's all set up?' Glenn asked her. 'You've opened your doors?'

'Yes,' Christina nodded with a smile. 'We've been accepting blind children for six months now, orphans mostly, but some abandoned.'

'It's a wonderful place,' said Bettina, smiling at the memory. 'I visited in the spring.'

'We were able to put on our first mini opera this summer,' said Christina. 'Oh, Bettina! You would have loved it! The children love to sing, especially gospel. We developed a program with Zu-Ting, using smart tablets to help teach children the lyrics. We even have prayers and hymns on their smart phones!'

'Is this true?' Glenn asked, turning to Zu-Ting, who was tucking into a large piece of wedding cake.

'Mm-hmm,' she smiled. 'We've been busy over at the factory in Hong Kong. The funds we received from Bettina made it possible to invest in an innovation team. My girls are brilliant: they can make anything! We just needed the vision and an influx of new skills to bring our workshop into this new age of technology.'

'So you're developing tablets now?' Glenn asked her, unable to hide his surprise.

'They're just the tip of the iceberg!' Zu-Ting giggled. 'Our real secret, the one I'm truly proud of, is the new smartphone we've been developing. It is "blind-friendly" and I helped write the software. Here, I've brought you one as a wedding present.'

Reaching into her bag, Zu-Ting brought out what looked like a normal smart phone, except that the buttons were much larger than a regular model. The group filled the chalet with delighted whoops and sighs of awe as the phone revealed its genius. When they pushed every button, the phone announced its number, and a clever tool listened to their every command, responding with different application suggestions.

'Every App is tailor-made for people without sight,' Zu-Ting explained. 'The one I'm happiest with is our descriptive NowPic App. Let's try it together, shall we?'

Holding up the phone, Zu-Ting asked the phone to open the NowPic App. When the App was open, Glenn saw that it had connected to the phone's camera. Zu-Ting held it up and smiled.

'Let's take a picture of the newlyweds,' she said, slowly angling the camera towards Glenn and Bettina's direction.

Curious to know what would happen next, Glenn drew close to his wife and posed for a photo as the App commanded him to 'Smile.' A small camera clicking sound came and then the App began to speak in a slightly jolting but nevertheless clear tone. It began: *'She is smiling, wearing a blue dress, besides a fire and a smiling man. He has dark hair and is wearing a black suit. She wears white flowers in her hair. He wears a white flower in his breast pocket.'*

Glenn was stunned. The App had perfectly described them.

'That's amazing,' he breathed, shaking his head in disbelief. 'You developed this?'

'With some help, yes,' Zu-Ting laughed. 'It takes pictures, but in audio form. It explains the picture in colours, sounds, horizons, and descriptions. Any smartphone can use it, like any other App.'

'Thank you, dear friend, for this wonderful gift,' Bettina leant over and held her friend close. 'You never fail to amaze me.'

'It's nothing compared to what Laura is making,' Zu-Ting said. 'That's really something.'

'You're also developing software?' Glenn asked in amazement.

'Not quite,' grinned Laura. 'Alas, I do not have anything to show because we are still in the developmental stages. We're working towards the ICB's old vision of creating helpful technology for the blind, just like Zu-Ting. For about eight months now we have been in the early stages of developing a house-help robot for the blind, one that can read for the beneficiaries, collect post for them, even make tea or coffee. The aim is for the robot to perform general services like this, making life easier and people more efficient, especially if they are living alone.'

'And Sight Plus is sponsoring this?' Glenn asked.

'Yes, partially, but as you can imagine, it hasn't been hard to attract funding,' Laura smiled. 'Everyone's mad about robotics these days.'

The rest of the afternoon passed in happy chatter and a series of photo shoots using Zu-Ting's camera. Evening soon fell around the chalet and the firelight danced across the wooden walls, casting shadows of the seven friends in every direction. Glenn could not have been happier, and looking over at his new wife, he knew Bettina felt the same. When the night made them sleepy, the five women made their way to bed, leaving

Glenn and Bettina alone. Slowly, with sweet smiles, the couple headed up to their marriage bed, where they made love as snow fell outside.

The next day, Glenn woke early to prepare a picnic for the hike he had promised his friends. They had planned to collect snowshoes and take a trail which ran along the valley, up towards a beautiful view point. Sunlight glanced off the German mountains as dawn crept through the sky. Taking a deep breath, Glenn closed his eyes to savour the moment: he was married to Bettina. What a wonderful feeling to wake up to, he thought.

Soon the group was hiking, enjoying the fresh snowfall beneath their feet and the sun on their faces. As they walked, Glenn was finally able to hear how Elfrida was getting on since the creation of Sight Plus. She had been a bit quieter than the others, and it soon transpired that the freezing cold of the mountains had taken her far from her comfort zone of the blistering heat of Mexico.

'How are things at school?' Glenn asked her.

'Wonderful,' she said. 'They could not be better. With the new funding we can finally go ahead and build the high school.'

'But that's your dream!' Glenn cried. 'That's what you told me you wanted to do, when I first came to visit you in Acapulco.'

'I know,' Elfrida nodded with a smile.

'I didn't realise Bettina had raised enough for the expansion,' said Glenn, wondering where the money had come from.

'She didn't,' said Elfrida. 'The others all dedicated a portion of their funding for my school. They have shown me again that dreams really can come true. Not just for me, but for hundreds of students who will benefit from a further stage of education. I owe them all so much. We owe you so much too, Glenn.'

'If I can fundraise more and more funds for your school, I will,' Glenn grinned. 'I'm so proud of what you're achieving, Elfrida.'

Glenn could not believe what the women had achieved, though it was only when they were eating lunch, on a snowy bench on the mountainside, and Odile held a toast, that he realised just how far they had come.

'To Glenn and Bettina!' Odile called in her Louisiana accent. 'To their health and happiness!'

'To Glenn and Bettina!' the other women called.

'And may I say that I owe so much of who I am today to Bettina,' Odile went on. 'I would not be here if it wasn't for her.'

'Did you hear that, Bets?' said Laura. 'A New Orleans city councillor owes her success to you!'

'I'm honoured,' Bettina grinned.

'City councillor?' said Glenn. 'Is this true, Odile?'

'It is,' she nodded. 'After everything that happened with Herbert I saw how damaging criminals like him can be. I wanted to change things, not just for the blind but for everyone. I'm running anti-racism and anti-prejudice campaigns across the city. I learnt a lot about justice lately. I wanna put that into practice.'

'That's brilliant, Odile!' Glenn laughed.

'*She's* brilliant!' Zu-Ting cried.

'Let me know if you ever need anything, OK?' said Glenn, marvelling at his friend's progress. 'I may be based in Germany now, but I'm still an American. I have connections.'

'I know you do,' smiled Odile. 'One of them has already made himself known to me.'

'Really? Who?' asked Glenn, wondering who she spoke of.

'Your biggest fan,' said Odile. 'And he has an idea he would like all three of us to work on.'

* * * *

'I give you "Glow in the Dark!"' Glenn's father cried out to the crowd at the official opening of his blindness simulation workshop in New Orleans. A huge number of people had turned out for the opening, including countless children, and members of the city council invited by Odile. Glenn stood with Bettina and the others, Elfrida, Laura, and Christina, who had all come to help out.

'Now, all you little squirts, go have fun!' Bertie cried. As he cut the ribbon and children poured into the workshop, Glenn clapped louder than anyone. His mother clung to her husband's arm, smiling and waving at the crowd. Iris had never looked prouder to be Bertie's wife. Looking to Bettina by his side, Glenn was so glad he had found happiness that could match his parents' marriage.

Over the past few months since his wedding, Glenn had been working with Odile and his father to create an experience for children and families to come to and learn about blindness.

'Well done, Bertie!' Odile called to his father over the roar of the crowd. 'We did it!'

As city councillor, Odile had overseen the planning and advertisement for the event. Bertie had called her up to ask if she could help him, having found her details in the manuscript of case studies Glenn had shared with them. Her own children stood shyly by her side, tugging at their mother's skirt to ask if they too could go and join the fun.

'Go on then, my babies,' she laughed. 'Don't get lost. Ah, I hear the new group arriving. I should give these children a hand.'

Odile wandered over to a group of parents and their children. They were clearly not local for they did not understand much of what was being said. By the way they dressed, Glenn wondered if they spoke English at all.

'Welcome, welcome!' Odile called out to them. 'Where's Laura? Ah, Laura! Will you come and translate?'

To Glenn's surprise, Laura wandered over to the group and began to speak to them in Arabic. Odile smiled and left her to it, returning to Glenn.

'Isn't she wonderful?' she laughed. 'She's been taking Arabic lessons in London to help assist the children affected by the Syrian crisis arriving in the UK.'

'Are they Syrian refugees?' Glenn asked.

'They are,' said Odile. 'I invited them here to learn more about what we do here with Sight Plus. Sadly, we have lots of folk coming to the States from Syria. Poor babies. These families have children suffering from blindness caused by chemical bombing. Can you imagine?'

'That's terrible,' Glenn shook his head. 'I hope they can learn something today and take some coping skills away with them.'

'I hope so too,' said Odile. 'Good, I hear your father is talking to the press. I'd best go and help him out. Official duty calls!'

Glenn looked over to see his father already answering questions from the local journalists.

'The idea is to sensitise people to what blind folks go through on a daily basis,' Glenn heard Bertie say with great pride. 'It's for parents of blind children, and children of blind parents, sure, but it's also for the general public. This workshop is about adjusting psychologically to the changes blindness brings into families. We've developed a series of experiences for them. Go try them, them come talk to me! Get outta here and have fun!'

Taking him at his word, the journalists dispersed into the workshop with curious looks on their faces. Glenn followed them, wandering through the stalls and scientific experiments on show. Zu-Ting was holding a practical workshop with her new digital creations, and Laura was now trying her best to control a wayward robot. Children squealed as it chased them through the crowds. In classic teaching mode, Elfrida had masterfully commanded the attention of a group of little ones, leading them on a tour of the exhibition with blindfolds on.

'Remember to swish your cane from side to side to feel the edges of the path,' she called out to them.

Glenn laughed as he dodged a child swishing his cane rather erratically. A hand on his arm made him jump and he turned around to see his mother.

'Hey, Mom,' he grinned. 'Having fun?'

'Your father has done so well, honey,' she smiled. 'He's in his element! Who'd have thought he'd be doing this two years ago?'

'It looks like he's found a new lease of life,' Glenn smiled at his father answering questions in the distance.

'Me too!' chuckled Iris. 'I gotta run, I'm teaching Pilates for the blind in two minutes!'

'What?' laughed Glenn. But his mother had disappeared, leaving him shocked and then pleasantly surprised.

Volunteers were arranging leaflets and posters nearby, the impressive logo of Sight Plus glowing behind them where once the ICB's logo would have stood. Glenn felt a rush of pride flow through him as he thought of all Bettina had achieved in that past year. She had given hope back to the people she supported, and created something far more impressive than the ICB had ever been. Looking for her, he spotted his wife chatting to a small group of children about opening up their senses to the world around them. When they wandered off to their next activity, Glenn walked slowly over to join her.

'You're wonderful with kids,' he said, taking her in him arms and holding her tight.

'I like children,' she laughed. 'They don't judge. They only ask questions.'

'It makes you wonder, doesn't it?' he said, kissing her softly on the cheek.

'Wonder what?' she asked him.

'About having a family,' said Glenn.

'Does it?' she asked with a smile. But before Glenn could say any more, Bettina wandered off to find more children to talk to. It wasn't until later that evening, when the opening day of the workshop had ended, that Glenn discovered the meaning behind his wife's smile. Odile and Bertie joined culinary forces to create a fantastic dinner for them all, which was served, naturally, in the dark.

Toast after toast celebrated the success of the day.

'To Odile!' Bertie cried. 'The best city councillor in the States, and the best cook in the north Atlantic!'

'To Bertie!' Odile cried back, throwing an arm around her young son as he watched them all. 'The finest Yankee speaker I've ever heard, and a damn good cook too!'

'To Glenn and Bettina,' Elfrida cried. 'For making this possible with their never-tiring fundraising efforts!'

'To Zu-Ting for fixing my mad robot!' laughed Laura. 'I fear we'd all still be running around if she hadn't put him out of his misery.'

The group laughed at this.

'To all of you, for being here today, for sharing your time, energy and experience,' said Glenn, raising his glass high. 'And to my mother, for supporting Bertie during this challenging time.'

'To Glenn,' Iris said gently. 'For always finding the positive in the most negative situations.'

The toasts went on, and, as ever, the women were overwhelmed with happiness to be altogether again. The food appearing on the table was exceptionally delicious, a true testament to the chefs. When the succulent duck had given way to creamy tiramisu and sharp, rich expressos, Bettina tapped a spoon against her glass.

'I have an announcement to make,' she smiled.

'Uh oh, Glenn's in trouble,' Zu-Ting chuckled.

'Oh, we're having so much fun!' laughed Laura. 'Can't we keep official stuff for meetings, Bets?'

'This isn't official,' Bettina laughed, a small smile rising on her lips. 'I wanted to wait until we were all together again to share something with you.'

Reaching over, she squeezed his knee gently.

'Honey?' Glenn whispered.

'I'm pregnant,' Bettina told the table. 'Glenn and I, well, we're going to start a family.'

The table erupted into delighted applause and happy cries of congratulations, but all Glenn could feel was his heart bursting in his chest. He stared at his wife, who could not stop smiling.

'Is it true?' he whispered. Bettina nodded.

'Oh, Betty!' he cried. 'This is incredible!'

'If it's a girl, call her Iris, after your mother!' Bertie called over.

'And if it's a boy, for heaven's sake don't give it your father's name!' Iris added with a chuckle.

'I knew something was up,' Christina said, giving Bettina a congratulatory hug. 'You didn't want to drink *Apfelwein* with me today.'

'I think that *might* be more to do with the fact that no one else likes *Apfelwein* as much as you, Christina!' Zu-Ting laughed, also leaning in to give Bettina a kiss.

Glenn was overwhelmed with joy. He looked around at the faces at the table: his father, his mother, Odile, her children, Elfrida, Laura, and Zu-Ting.

'It looks like our Sight Plus family is growing,' he smiled, happiness overflowing inside of him.

'A child made by you two is surely a blessing to us all,' Christina grinned serenely. 'One more visionary for the world.'

As the group gravitated towards Bettina, laughing and praising her, Glenn felt a great moment of clarity dawn upon him. How strange, he thought, that a stroke of tragedy had brought so many wonderful things and people into his life. There was beauty beyond imagining in the darkness they had all faced together. Gazing around at his family, Glenn wondered if the darkness was in fact what he had needed to finally see the light.

BELLA BEESTON

Bella Beeston, educated in Chicago and San Francisco, has travelled widely and is a contributor to and editor of several publications in London and the Middle East. Bella lives with her children in Surrey, England.